CHAPTER 1

Light.
Too much light.
Alone.

Kharnek awoke to find himself slumped against the wall of a dark hallway. The basalt that composed structures in Zel Morakh chilled his back. His head throbbed. He lifted a hand to rub his face and winced when the stone shards stuck to his palm dug into the skin of his eyelids.

He attempted to stand, and his surroundings whirled. He recalled the events of the last shadowfall after the moon dipped beneath the horizon. His duties were completed with time to unwind before another restless sleep. Too many drafts of 'cano ale with his warrior brothers and then—

An ululating wail startled Kharnek into full alertness. Torchlight flickered into existence near the hallway's end to his left.

"Where is he?" a manic voice demanded. A woman's cry crescendoed from grief into rage. "Let go of me! You cannot protect him!"

The creak of polished leather armor and boots registered in Kharnek's trained ears. Three male silhouettes danced in the orange light, struggling to restrain the woman, who wore a spectral violet gown that wafted about her clawing arms. One of the men broke away to move toward Kharnek.

In an instant, he surrendered to the compulsion that lurked in the back of his mind, the voice that haunted him. The voice that was not his but had infected him like a disease.

Light.

Too much light.

Kharnek's hangover melted away. He slipped past the advancing man, moving so fast that his assailant appeared frozen in place, arms caught mid-swing with his step. When Kharnek walked in shadow, no living creature could see him or match his pace. He paused near the other two men and the woman; they resembled a violent still-life painting. To his surprise, he recognized the woman, Myal, the wife of one of his closest friends. Kharnek remembered this was her home and that just beyond her at the end of the hallway lay the dining hall. He flowed past Myal and abruptly halted at the dining hall's entrance.

Destruction personified had torn through the room. The twelve-foot-long table, hewn from a single slab of basalt, played host to the broken bodies of several warriors. Kharnek's friend and Captain of the City Guard lay among them. Hedek's face was locked by rigor mortis into an expression of horror.

Kharnek instinctively drew his sword. Blood reflected torch light on the cold metal. He dropped the weapon, its clatter echoing as he examined his hands; crimson stains smeared across the map of indentations.

"No. This is a dream."

The words tumbled from his mouth, half statement, half plea. Kharnek backed away, and his connection to his preternatural abilities broke. Behind him, the frantic struggle between Myal and the two guards resumed. She screeched and broke free of the men restraining her. In her right hand, a slender dagger appeared. A purple jewel set in its handle was filled with a familiar, swirling darkness.

Kharnek turned and opened his arms in welcome as her hand drove toward his chest. The blade pierced his flesh, but he felt no pain. He laughed as the shadow in the jewel joined the darkness inside him, and he unleashed its terrible power. A black miasma enveloped Myal and the guards.

When the darkness cleared, only ashes remained.

Kharnek fell to his knees, overcome with guilt. A soft swishing noise of fabric against stone heralded the approach of his masters. Anguish turned to anger as the priests encircled him. One of them held a flickering torch, revealing a malicious grin on the man's face as he spoke.

"Well done, son of Komor. Morakh's Shadow within you is powerful indeed. You will be a great asset in the war to come."

Kharnek's eyes flew open, darting in the death throes of his 'burn dream. Sweat

TRIALS
OF THE
INNERMOST

The Etherea Cycle, Book 1

Jonathan Fuller & Kristina Kelly

TRIALS OF THE INNERMOST. Copyright 2023 © Jonathan Fuller and Kristina Kelly. All rights reserved. No part of this book may be used or reproduced in any manner whatsoever without written permission except in the case of brief quotations embodied in critical articles and reviews. For more information visit www.hansenhousebooks.com.

Cover design by Elizabeth Jeannel

ISBN 978-1-956037-19-7 (hardcover)

ISBN 978-1-956037-20-3 (paperback)

ISBN 978-1-956037-11-1 (eBook)

Second Edition

Second Edition: May 2023

This eBook edition first published in 2023

Published by Hansen House

www.hansenhousebooks.com

HH
Hansen House

soaked the coarse red blanket wrapped around him. His muscled chest heaved as he took in the familiar confines of his bedchamber. He rolled out of bed and stood, the coolness of basalt under his bare feet dragging him further into reality.

The volcanic glow that perpetually limned the skyline of Zel Morakh painted the room in shades of red and orange through its sole, slit-like window. Though dim, it was enough for Kharnek to distinguish the geometric outlines of the black ceremonial tattoos that adorned his pale skin—the marks of a warrior of Komor. He brushed his chest just above his heart, his fingers tracing the raised skin of the scar where Myal had stabbed him. It was a visible reminder that his dreams were grounded in reality.

Kharnek moved to the window and gazed upon the muted sprawl of Zel Morakh, the capital city of Komor. Nestled in a large rift created by ancient tectonic shifts, the metropolis was shielded from the bitter cold of the tundra that comprised most of the realm's surface. Volcanic activity beneath the city kept its residents warm, their primary defense against the eternal darkness that shrouded the western hemisphere of Etherea. Neither of the moons were visible at this time, which the other realms called "night", but Komorese knew it as Morakh's Shadow. The stepped ziggurat of the Temple of Morakh dominated Kharnek's view from the Warrior's Wing. It was no accident that the military housing in Zel Morakh lay in the shadow of the residence of the Priesthood elite. Even though Komor's army was the largest in Etherea, its state religion—and its priests—were the realm's true rulers.

The sight of the Temple awakened a mixture of anger, remorse, fear, and anticipation. It was because of the Priesthood that he had these bad dreams and that his hands were soaked in blood. His prowess as a warrior and strange powers did not atone for his crimes, and at times he felt crushed by the weight of his guilt and the blood on his hands.

Light—

"No!"

He clenched his hands into fists and willed the darkness into the back of his mind. He did not need this distraction. Fear coiled in his gut. Though he had lived with his powers and the compulsions that came with them for nearly twenty epicycles, they had lately been more difficult to control, more insistent. Words and fragments of thoughts whispered in his mind, articulating a desire to sink into the darkness forever.

"Kharnek?"

The deep voice came from the bed behind him. He glanced at his timepiece and groaned. It was only an hour before moonrise when he would be expected to report for duty. Turning toward the speaker, he tried to banish the fatigue that tinged his words.

"What is it, Valin?"

"Are you coming back to bed?"

"I doubt it."

Valin grunted. Kharnek watched him roll out of bed and begin collecting his scattered garments.

"I'm going home, then. We have drills early at moonrise. Not that I need to tell you that. You are running them, right?"

"No. I will be attending a meeting with the Mahir and Captain Ahlet."

Valin snorted, shrugging on his gray shirt and shorts. Training garments, identical to Kharnek's own. Standard issue for members of the Brotherhood, Komor's military. "What do the priests want now? Didn't the Mahir just sanction more raids into Heathström and Sondrine, even though the Trials are about to start? So much for ceasing hostilities."

A wry grin lifted the corners of Kharnek's mouth. Valin referred to the Priesthood's orders to continue quietly exploring the defenses of Etherea's other realms. The sorties had never stopped even after the peace accords many epicycles ago. While Komor's neighbors might protest this violation of their sovereignty, they lacked the numbers to stop it. Were it not for the magic the other realms employed, the pretense of diplomacy would have long since collapsed, and Komor would have dominion over them, but if these latest raids proved successful, that time was much nearer than Komor's enemies expected.

"They did," Kharnek replied, "but Captain Ahlet mentioned some sort of special assignment. I suspect that I will be leaving the city for some time."

Valin cocked his head. "It must be serious if they're sending you. The City Guard barely ever leaves Zel Morakh, right?"

Kharnek shrugged. "You are correct. But my talents are wasted on protecting dignitaries from imagined threats from Sondrinel or one of the Heathström witches."

As Valin finished dressing, the soldier faced Kharnek. "This is a fact. Well, I hope I can see you before you leave."

He leaned in for a kiss, but Kharnek twisted his face away. Valin pulled back with a wounded expression.

"What's wrong?"

"Nothing is wrong," Kharnek answered, not making eye contact.

"Then why not—"

"Valin." The clipped reply was as much a warning as a plea. Kharnek felt the allure of the other man's company, but after the dream, it was intertwined with a deadly hunger. "This has to stop. You and me."

The words struck Valin with visible force, but to his credit, he did not reply immediately. Kharnek forged ahead into the silence. "I am probably going to be gone for a long time. It would not be fair to ask you to wait for me."

Valin's countenance transformed from hurt to anger. "So you just get to make that decision for me? For us?" He drew near Kharnek and placed his hands on the warrior's biceps. "*That* isn't fair. You know how I feel about you. And I think you feel the same."

Kharnek's resolve crumbled beneath Valin's steady gaze. At first, their trysts had been just that, ephemeral and fleeting. But after enough of them, time had drawn new boundaries for their relationship, and "friends" no longer made for an accurate descriptor. But guilt shadowed Kharnek throughout the process, borne of his awareness of the evil within him that he did not want anyone to see—or worse, be hurt by.

"Kharnek." Valin pressed his body against the warrior's, kindling heat in Kharnek's lower abdomen. "Please, give me a chance. Give *us* a chance." He kissed him with a passion that stole Kharnek's breath.

The warrior pulled away, despite every nerve ending screaming for him to do the opposite. "Valin, stop. I am not who you think I am."

His words seemed to have no effect on his lover, who closed the distance between them again.

Valin's eyes flashed as he looked up at Kharnek. "I don't have to know you to know I want you." Then he leaned in and kissed him again.

Against his better judgment, this time Kharnek met Valin's fire with his own and felt it course through him. A low moan escaped the other man's lips as Kharnek nipped the hollow at the base of his neck. Valin's hands slipped beneath Kharnek's shirt. His touch was hot on the warrior's skin, and Kharnek surrendered to his desire, to the never-ending hunger.

The shadow in him seized control. All the flames of his and Valin's connection were extinguished by an endless well of cold, ruthless need to devour.

"I told you to stop." Kharnek's words slithered through the air, the usual deep timbre of his voice replaced by an oily tone that oscillated in pitch.

Valin looked down at him from where he was held aloft by an invisible, viselike grip around his throat. A stifled scream strained the muscles in his neck when his gaze locked on the pitch-black that Kharnek knew had overtaken his eyes.

The man's life started a slow spiral into oblivion, its diminishment strengthening Kharnek's power. The sensation shocked him, and he became aware of the darkness pulling him deeper into its grip, fed by his cruelty. He clenched his hands into fists and cried out, breaking its hold.

Valin dropped to the floor in a heap. He staggered to his feet; his body wracked by violent coughs.

"You…are a monster!" He gasped.

"Valin—" Kharnek reached to steady the soldier, but Valin stumbled away from his touch, one hand raised in a warding gesture.

"Get away from me!"

Kharnek pulled back as if stung. "Valin, I am sorry, I did not mean to. I…I would never hurt you."

The other man's eyes were wide with fear as he opened the door and looked back at Kharnek. "Don't ever come near me again."

Valin fled down the corridor, his words echoing off the stone walls of the Warriors' Wing.

Gritting his teeth, Kharnek slammed the door to his bedchamber shut. Tears coursed their way down his cheeks. With a snarl, he wiped away the unbidden moisture and paced to the window, turning a baleful stare upon the Temple. He spent the rest of Morakh's Shadow staring out the window, wondering when he would wake up from this unending 'burn dream. He could add Valin to the lengthy list of failed relationships that his inner darkness had cost him. But beneath the sting of rejection lay a cold, unyielding truth: It was better this way. No one would be hurt except him.

A knock at the door interrupted his reverie. Kharnek grimaced and composed himself before striding across the room and flinging the portal open.

"What?" he bit out, then immediately snapped to attention and saluted. "Apologies, sir," he mumbled.

His superior, Captain Ahlet, regarded him with a bemused expression. "At ease, Guardsman. I should apologize for the hour of my visit. May I come in?"

Kharnek waved him in, silently thanking Morakh that the man was not a stickler for formality. The captain seated himself at the small desk that occupied the other half of Kharnek's chamber and motioned for the warrior to sit. He perched on the edge of his bed, keeping a tight rein on his piqued curiosity.

The captain addressed him. "I trust that all is well with your command?"

"Sir?"

"I encountered Specialist Saita on my way here. He seemed quite distraught."

"Ah." Kharnek lowered his gaze. "A disagreement regarding a personal matter. Nothing that will impede his or my performance."

Captain Ahlet's brows raised. "I trust that it will not. At any rate, that is not why I am here." Leaning forward with his elbows on his knees, Kharnek's superior regarded him steadily. "I wanted to tell you before we meet with the Mahir, so you have some time to prepare. You have been chosen to represent Komor in the Trials of the Innermost."

Kharnek was so taken aback that he nearly missed the officer's next words.

"Publicly, this is a great honor and a reflection of your distinguished service to Komor," the captain was saying, "but in truth, the Priesthood intends to use the Trials as an opportunity to further weaken our enemies. And you, Guardsman, will be their instrument."

A caustic retort rose unbidden to his lips, but he swallowed it quickly. Captain Ahlet had been his mentor since Kharnek's promotion to the City Guard from the regular ranks of the Brotherhood. Although the Priesthood's involvement rankled, his superior displayed confidence and trust in him by disclosing this information in advance. He would do as he was asked out of respect for the other man and his sense of duty.

"I know the Priesthood has been…unkind to you," the captain said quietly.

Kharnek looked up, his eyes widening.

The officer spread his hands, the gesture creasing the sleeves of his blood-red dress uniform. "I looked into your background when you were assigned to my command. Some of it is hidden from me, but I learned enough to understand what was done to you. They made you into a weapon and gave you little choice in the matter."

"They view all of the Brotherhood as their tools," Kharnek interjected, "I am not alone in that regard."

Captain Ahlet sighed. "Indeed not, but we both know you are a special case. Which is why you've been chosen as one of the two Truthseekers from Komor."

"Who is the other?"

A frown creased the other man's forehead as he leaned back in his chair. "A priest, I'm afraid. But I'm given to understand he's a political dissident, part of a growing faction within the Mahir who want peace with our neighbors."

Kharnek digested this news with equal parts disdain and confusion. No matter his political beliefs, he had no desire to spend months with a priest.

Sensing his puzzlement, the captain elaborated, "I suspect the other Mahir want him as far from Zel Morakh as possible. Without a figurehead, this movement will be easily quashed. We've seen this cycle repeat itself before with other groups that were eventually branded as 'heretical.'"

Kharnek nodded. He had taken part in punitive action against such groups, but that had been many epicycles ago and did not fully explain his involvement now. "So," he began slowly, "what is expected of me during the Trials?"

The captain sat up tall and looked Kharnek in the eye. "What I'm about to tell you remains strictly between us. The other Truthseeker must remain ignorant of your mission at all costs…even if it means silencing him. Permanently."

"I understand. What of the other four?" Kharnek referred to the pairs that would come from Heathström and Sondrine.

"If they discover or seek to interfere with your mission, eliminate them. Discreetly, of course, we can't afford a major diplomatic incident until all our preparations are finished. But, assuming they remain in the dark for the duration of the Trials, you will cooperate with them to complete the tasks set out for the six of you. The first one is simple: you and the priest must reach Waverling together. There will be a departure ceremony here before you leave."

Kharnek groaned inwardly. Going to Heathström's capital was an eastward trek across the frigid surface of Komor that would last at least ten cycles, and no doubt the priest would expect him to act as a caretaker the whole way. And then he would have to tolerate more foreigners for however long the Trials lasted. Months, most likely, if the historical precedent was anything to go on.

"Once you reach Waverling," the captain continued, interrupting Kharnek's musings, "your mission will truly begin."

As his superior officer began to outline the Priesthood's scheme and his part in it, the darkness in him writhed in anticipation.

"Light," he whispered. "Too much light."

Captain Ahlet paused. "What did you say?"

"Sorry, sir, just thinking aloud." Kharnek's hands, which he had unknowingly clenched, relaxed when the other man did not question the utterance any further, but a sense of foreboding stole over him like frost creeping across a windowpane.

Soon, the voice in his head hissed, *soon, we will be whole.*

CHAPTER 2

The old parchment crackled and released its earthy aroma as Zinvar unrolled it. He loved the smell. It permeated the Great Library of Mora, where he and many other newly-minted priests toiled. Zinvar smoothed the document on the surface of a table littered with other scrolls and took in its content. Neat lines of Komorese text were bunched around diagrams of peculiar geometric objects, unlike anything he had ever seen. In the flickering light of the torches that lit the library, the depictions seemed to change shape with each fresh examination. They unsettled and intrigued him. Pulling up the sleeves of his rust-colored robes, he prepared to elucidate their secrets.

"You're still here?"

Zinvar jumped and spun to find another priest behind him, a smirk on his face. "Sneaking up on people won't make you many friends, Lem," he admonished, wagging a finger.

The other priest laughed. "I couldn't resist. Just be glad it was me and not one of the Mahir."

Zinvar cast a wary glance to either side to make sure none of the senior members of the Priesthood were roaming the shelves nearby and allowed himself an answering grin. "That's true. I'm already hopelessly behind on the work that Ezreth gave me, never mind any additional tasks they'd foist upon me."

"At least you were assigned to someone prominent after your initiation," Lem grumbled. "Instead of some old crackpot obsessed with water clocks." He moved closer to the table and looked over Zinvar's shoulder. "What is all that, anyway?"

Zinvar obligingly moved out of the way and swept his arm to indicate the heap of knowledge. "It would seem that the Mahir—or Ezreth, at least—have renewed their interest in ancient artifacts found across Etherea. I've been instructed to identify any texts referencing such things and bring them to him for review."

"Sounds insufferably dull," Lem replied, peering down at the scroll Zinvar had opened. "Although these illustrations are odd. Do you really think there were other civilizations here before Komor?"

Zinvar lifted his shoulders in response. "The Mahir seem to think so. I'm just glad to see them focusing on something other than fighting the other realms."

That elicited a snort from Lem. "Their favorite pastime. I doubt that that's ceased to be a priority."

"You're probably right," Zinvar agreed, slouching.

Lem faced Zinvar and placed a hand on his shoulder. "Zin…we've been friends for a long time. You're twenty-six now, right?"

"Yes."

The other priest shook his head. "Hard to believe we were acolytes for so long. Six epicycles from joining to initiation. And now we've been full members of the Priesthood for almost an epicycle."

"The time has flown by," Zinvar nodded, wondering where Lem was going with this jaunt through the annals of memory.

"It has. And we've both changed, but you've been consistent in your, ah, values, let's say. Which I admire about you! But not everyone feels the same."

Zinvar frowned. "Speak plainly, Lem. You're circling what you want to say like a varg that's cornered its prey."

His friend sighed. "You're an advocate for peace among the realms. That's made you enemies among the Mahir."

"I'm aware that my views are unpopular with some," Zinvar said dryly.

Lem's eyes narrowed. "But that's just it. Your stance *is* popular with some priests. More than I think you realize."

"Isn't that a good thing?"

"Yes and no." Zinvar's friend gestured at the tomes surrounding them. "You earned this assignment because you were a model acolyte. That's also why your position on diplomacy was tolerated, but now that you're a real priest and people are actually listening to you…well, I'm afraid that that tolerance is about to run out."

Zinvar blinked, his mind whirling. His hand strayed toward the ebon wood of his staff leaning against the table. Whenever he felt lost, its comforting solidity would ground him.

"I'm not saying this to frighten you," Lem went on, "but if the more traditional Mahir consider you a threat to their way of life, you could be in danger. You've seen what they do to blasphemers. Like your brother."

The painful memory made Zinvar grimace. "Yes, I'm well aware." His shoulders drooped. "Thank you for the warning, my friend. I understand if you need to limit your association with me. You have Celya and the children to think of."

Lem smiled. "I would never abandon you like that. But maybe tone down the divisive rhetoric for a bit, eh?"

"I can't promise anything," Zinvar cautioned, "especially with the Trials coming up. It's a perfect opportunity to remind the Mahir that our world could be so different if we'd only embrace the hope that the Trials represent."

His friend chuckled. "You never did back down easily. Remember when that ekkarid came marching out of the sea into the dormitory, and you chased it away with nothing but a broom?"

"Eight legs are entirely too many." Zinvar shuddered. Despite their terrifying appearance, the huge crustaceans that inhabited the cold waters around the Isle of Mora and southwestern Komor were actually quite docile. Even so, he had no desire to drive one off again.

"On that, we can agree." Lem stretched his arms. "Well, it's getting late. I should get home. Celya will kill me if I miss dinner again."

Zinvar flashed a wicked grin. "Better her than the Mahir."

"Ha! You have a point there. Take care, Zin. I'm sure I'll see you soon."

The priest waved goodbye to his friend and returned his attention to the scroll. Or tried to. His mind kept revisiting his conversation with Lem like a ghost haunting the place of its death. If everything his friend said was true, he found himself in a precarious position. While Zinvar generally enjoyed good relations with his peers—especially those close to him in age—he knew he had few allies among the most devout Mahir due to his pacifist leanings. An exception was his mentor, Ezreth, who steadfastly ignored any of Zinvar's attempts to engage him on such topics but also did nothing to curb them. The older priest's familial wealth and political connections shielded him from any fallout created by having a rebellious youth among his staff. Even so, should the other Mahir move against Zinvar, he suspected that relying on Ezreth for support would be akin to leaning on a splintered rod. His usefulness as a scholar and researcher was what his mentor prized.

Not that I'm doing the best at that right now, he mused.

Resigning himself to being too distracted to make further progress this cycle, Zinvar gathered up the scrolls and books he deemed of interest to Ezreth and collected his staff, then set off for the Mahir's office, his footsteps echoing in the cavernous library, empty at this hour save for him. Exiting the library, Zinvar made his way down the central corridor that linked all the buildings in the Priesthood's complex on the Isle of Mora. The vaulted ceiling of the passageway played host to frescoes depicting moments of triumph from Komor's history. If those artworks were not enough to instill pedestrians with reverent awe, statues of prominent Mahir lined the sides of the corridor. Pride blossomed in Zinvar's chest. For all its flaws, Komorese civilization had produced great wonders.

At the corridor's midpoint, Zinvar paused. A huge statue of Morakh dominated the central space, stretching upward beneath a grand rotunda. This depiction of Komor's deity showed him in his most common form: a tall man shrouded in a heavy cloak. While outsiders might find the effigy rather bland in appearance, followers of Morakhism knew that this was an accurate representation of the mysteries that could only be known in the glory of absolute darkness, and Morakh, the lord of all shadows, offered up his secrets only to the faithful—or so the Mahir said. Privately, Zinvar had begun to doubt that Morakh was truly a god. The few canonical writings the Priesthood made available regarding Morakh's origins were clearly propaganda, with their fantastic stories of the deity shaping the land from his shadow and none-too-subtle encouragements to make offerings at Morakh's temple. Stranger still, none of the texts he had reviewed for Ezreth made mention of a divine entity of any kind. Writings from the dawn of Komorese civilization ought to speak of Morakh *somehow*, but the oldest reference he had found was a mere two hundred epicycles ago, roughly a decade before the Priesthood united Komor's disparate city-states beneath its banner.

Thoughts like this are going to get you into serious trouble. If they haven't already, Zinvar chastised himself. Shrugging off his doubts, he moved on exiting the corridor to enter the rectangular structure that housed dormitories on its lower levels for junior priests and acolytes. The upper floors contained the spacious apartments occupied by the Mahir. Zinvar hurried up the five flights of stairs to reach the top floor where Ezreth resided. Offering a silent prayer to Morakh— or anyone that might be listening—that his mentor would be too distracted to notice his tardiness, he approached the entrance to Ezreth's apartment. Firelight flickered at the door's edges, and muffled voices emanated beyond them. Zinvar frowned. It was unusual for Ezreth to entertain guests this close to middark when the moon's light completely vanished, and Komor's eternal darkness reached its zenith. Perhaps another assistant had returned late. Zinvar tapped lightly on the door. The quiet conversation stopped.

"That must be him. Come in, Zinvar," Ezreth's reedy voice invited.

The priest opened the door. "I apologize for the delay. My–" He stopped short when he recognized the man seated across from Ezreth in the apartment's front parlor. Zinvar quickly offered a deep bow, which prompted one of the scrolls gathered in his arms to drop to the floor. His face reddened, but he retained the presence of mind to greet his mentor's guest. "Please forgive the intrusion, your holiness."

"Think nothing of it," the other man replied. "Please, join us."

Zinvar collected the rogue scroll and straightened to find Natak, the high priest of Komor, smiling at him. "Thank you, Mahiratha," he said, this time remembering to add the formal honorific bestowed upon the Priesthood's leader. He hurriedly deposited his collection of research items in Ezreth's study, then returned to stand by his mentor's side. If the older man seemed perturbed, his wrinkled visage held no trace of it. By contrast, Natak's handsome features were still graced by a smile. It was hard to look away, even beneath the scrutiny of the high priest's intense blue eyes.

"Well, he's here." Ezreth gestured impatiently. "Shall we get on with it?"

The Mahiratha chuckled. "Still sour about losing your finest assistant? I suppose I can't fault you for that."

"It was bound to happen sooner or later."

Zinvar listened to the interaction with mounting concern. Was this what Lem had tried to warn him about? The shadows dancing on Natak's face suddenly took on a sinister quality.

"Be that as it may," the high priest responded, leaning forward, "you have my thanks. I know you understand my reasoning."

Ezreth nodded. "The boy will serve you well."

"Indeed." Natak's eyes glittered. "Zinvar, you have achieved much in your short time in our order. Your treatise on the effects of overharvesting in our underwater farms was nothing short of revolutionary."

"You honor me." Zinvar inclined his head in a show of respect.

"It is I who am honored to call you a priest of Morakh. That being said…" Natak paused, and Zinvar's heart pounded. "There are some," the high priest continued, his gaze never leaving Zinvar, "who say you are not faithful to the traditions that have brought order to chaos throughout our history. That you question the guiding principles of Morakhism."

Zinvar held his breath. It seemed like Natak's eyes bored through him into the secret corners of his mind, scouring their depths for the blasphemous thoughts he must already know lurked there.

The Mahiratha abruptly stood and moved within arm's reach of Zinvar. While he was on the upper end of average height, the high priest towered over him. Gazing upward into the other man's face, Zinvar was gripped by fear's chill claws.

Natak stared down at him for a long moment before speaking again. "I am not like those people. Survival requires adaptation. Such change is not possible if we are enslaved by tradition. So I do not find your views problematic or offensive. On the contrary, I think they are healthy and essential to our order's growth. Anyone who is threatened by them has proven themselves an enemy of progress."

"Precisely!" Ezreth spoke up. "You are wise beyond your years, Natak. I knew you were destined for greatness from the moment I met you as an acolyte. *You* were my finest assistant, Zinvar's excellence notwithstanding."

Zinvar's eyes widened. He did not realize that Natak and Ezreth had such a personal connection, but he was grateful for it since they seemed to share at least some of his progressive mindset.

"Thank you, Ezreth. You are discerning as ever in your choice of proteges." Natak smiled down at Zinvar. "My only question for you, child of Morakh, is this: Do you *believe*?"

Zinvar sensed layers of hidden meaning behind the high priest's words, some of which he could not hope to decipher. Doing his best to keep his expression a neutral mask, he confidently answered, "Yes, your holiness."

Natak's eyes gleamed. "Then I am certain of my decision. Zinvar, you will be one of Komor's representatives in the coming Trials. You had best start preparing. You will leave for Waverling in three cycles' time."

Zinvar felt naked without his staff.

The fact that he actually *was* naked at present did nothing to help. He hated this part of the ritual cleansing that took place prior to any ceremony overseen by the Priesthood of Morakh. The idea was to clear the body and spirit of all influences that could disrupt communion with Morakh's presence. Zinvar had ostensibly cleared his mind with several hours of meditation prior to the physical scrub-down of his body. Yet his thoughts wandered as freely as the sponges cleansing every inch of his pale skin.

He remembered a time like this, many cycles ago when the occasion was far less joyous than his imminent departure to Heathström. The ululating cries of the mournful crowds still rang in his ears as his mother and father were entombed in the Valley of Monodium among Komor's honored dead. They had been slain during Morakh's Shadow in their own home by an intruder while Zinvar was away for his initiation into the Priesthood. Zinvar still carried the ebon staff given him that day as faithfully as the memories of what had transpired. It was a tangible reminder of loss, pride, power, and guilt. He felt incomplete without it.

A shiver coursed up his spine. The stone preparation chamber sat high in the Temple of Morakh where little of the volcanic heat that permeated Zel Morakh reached. Zinvar resisted the urge to cross his arms in an attempt to conserve body heat.

The attendant straightened and bowed, signaling the end of the cleansing. Zinvar's staff and dull orange robes were returned to him. He dressed, attuning his ears to the roar of the crowd outside the Temple. Natak was whipping the city's residents into a frenzy of religious fervor. His resonant voice, aided by a sophisticated sound-channeling system integrated into the Temple's construction, rumbled Zinvar's insides.

The priest's stomach lurched as the floor of the chamber shuddered and rose toward the stone ceiling. He watched the ceiling retract as he ascended toward the orange glow that suffused Zel Morakh's sky. His head cleared the chamber's fully retracted roof, now revealed as the surface of the platform atop the Temple. Screams of adulation assaulted his ears in unrelenting waves.

The floor came to a halt with a grinding clank. Zinvar's heart swelled with pride as he surveyed the masses surrounding the Temple's base. Zel Morakh's entire populace thronged about the black ziggurat. He wished his parents could witness their son's exaltation.

"Behold Komor's chosen sons, who will carry Morakh's flame into the faithless twilight of our world!" Natak called, his arms outstretched to either side. The High Priest's robes, made of crystalline rift wyrm scales, shimmered beneath the cold light of the nascent moons.

Zinvar looked past Natak to see who would accompany him to the Trials of the Innermost. Only two ambassadors were chosen from each of Etherea's three regions and sent to the twilit center to participate with the goal of fostering the fragile peace that existed between shadowed Komor, gray Heathström, and sunlit Sondrine. It was an honor greater than most Priests of Morakh ever achieved, but, as the Mahiratha had said, Zinvar had proven himself as an apt student and accomplished orator, useful qualities for an emissary of peace.

His breath hitched when he met the cinnamon eyes of the man to Natak's left. Zinvar's traveling companion and fellow honoree towered over him and even Natak, his muscular frame clad in the scarlet leathers unique to the City Guard of Zel Morakh. The chest piece was formed around the pectorals beneath it, outlining the strength of the man's torso. A strange expression flickered across the warrior's chiseled face, but Zinvar had no time to analyze it as Natak motioned for them both to approach.

"As the twin moons rise, so shall Komor's might increase until all the realms bow before the servants of Morakh!"

Natak ordered Zinvar and the warrior to kneel facing one another on either side of him. He raised his arms skyward. Zinvar's eyes flicked upward, past the rooftops of the city and toward the firmament above, silvered with stars. The roar of Zel Morakh's populace dwindled into a gentle murmur as Natak invoked their deity's presence.

"Show your face, he who stands upon the twin moons, who may only be known in the purity of absolute darkness! Let your shadow fall upon us, that all may bear witness to your greatness! Morakh, ruler of all that is, make your blessing upon these two sons of Komor known!"

Natak's voice intensified with each phrase, the veins in his neck bulging.

Zinvar looked back at the warrior, and his blood turned to ice. The man's eyes were pitch-black. Then he blinked, and Zinvar found himself gazing into the same intense brown he had seen before. Maybe Natak had put too much incense in the braziers burning atop the Temple.

An intense violet light flared at the center of the platform, interrupting Zinvar's thoughts. At its core, the light faded to an incandescent white. Zinvar shielded his eyes as the light pulsed and a dark figure manifested at the center. Enrobed in swirling black, the manifestation resembled a man who towered fifteen feet into the air.

"Behold our fell lord!" Natak exclaimed, falling prostrate.

A resonant voice that seemed to come from inside Zinvar's mind emanated from the figure of Morakh, their god.

"These are my sons, Zinvar and Kharnek, with whom I am well pleased."

Zinvar shivered at the sound of the warrior's name. *Kharnek.* An ancient set of syllables that bespoke power and, in the ritual language of the Priesthood, a nameless terror that stalked the darkness of Morakh's Shadow. His companion for the Trials of the Innermost grew more intriguing with each revelation.

He dared to glance up at the apparition and its violet aura. Tendrils of light coiled like the corona of a star. Zinvar watched, entranced, as Morakh's image began to collapse in on itself, before vanishing in a burst of brilliance. The spectators at the base of the Temple, who had fallen silent at the sight of Morakh, lifted their faces.

Natak rose and called out, "Morakh himself has testified: These men are the chosen! Let none question the divine provenance of their journey!"

The Mahiratha motioned for Zinvar and the warrior—*Kharnek*—to stand.

"People of Zel Morakh, I give you your champions!"

Natak threw his hands up once more, and the crowds erupted into wild cheering. Again, Zinvar felt a surge of pride and could not prevent a burgeoning grin.

He glanced at Kharnek and was surprised to see the same stern countenance as before. Perhaps his military training at work. There would be time on the journey to Heathström to ascertain the nature of this enigmatic warrior. For now, Zinvar basked in the adulation of the people of his home city and the knowledge that his parents would have been proud.

Hours later, once the crowds had dissipated and returned to their homes, the priest and the warrior met with Natak in his study within the Temple. The High Priest sat at his massive desk, contemplating a scroll spread across it. They knelt before the Mahiratha until he motioned for them to stand.

"You will leave for Waverling at the next moonrise. We will furnish you with basic supplies and tokens that identify you as Truthseekers, but it is up to you to find your way. Unlike the last pair, I trust that this first Trial will prove no match for your formidable talents."

Natak's tone made it clear that this was a command, not a supposition. Publicly, the previous Truthseekers Natak referred to had died with honor, but the whispers within the Priesthood told a tale of Sondrinel sabotage. Rising from his seat, Natak pulled a rope that dangled from the study's ceiling. Four acolytes entered in pairs. Each duo carried a large black cube between them. Zinvar regarded the objects with curiosity.

"These devices enable instant communication, regardless of distance," Natak explained. "They will be transported to Waverling by ship, where they will await your arrival. You will present the devices as gifts to Heathström and Sondrine during the portion of the opening ceremony reserved for the demonstration of your skills as Truthseekers—along with an announcement that formal trade between those realms and Komor will commence immediately."

Shock rippled through Zinvar. He glanced at the warrior next to him, who seemed unfazed. He must have already known about this.

"This will no doubt come as a great surprise to the other realms, as it has to you, Zinvar." Natak sounded amused as he continued, "But consider it a reward for your excellent service to the Priesthood. You have been an outspoken advocate for peace, and we have listened. Now I charge you with delivering your message of harmony to the rest of Etherea."

The weight of responsibility settled upon Zinvar's shoulders. Finally, everything he had worked for—often at odds with his peers—was coming to fruition. With the leader of the Priesthood's endorsement, no less!

Zinvar bowed to his superior. "I will not fail you, Mahiratha."

"Indeed not. I have the utmost confidence in you and in your companion. He will be the strength behind your words. Now, go and ready yourselves for the journey. The acolytes will summon you near shadowfall to provide your supplies and teach you about the communication devices."

The priest and warrior bowed at Natak's dismissal and exited the study. When they reached the Temple's exterior, Zinvar stopped Kharnek.

"We haven't had a chance to speak. I wanted to formally introduce myself."

Zinvar's cheeks heated beneath the handsome warrior's intense scrutiny. Awkwardly, he thrust out his hand.

"I'm Zinvar. Well, you know that. But I'm looking forward to starting the Trials and getting to know you better."

Kharnek tilted his head and slowly reached out to clasp Zinvar's forearm in the traditional Komorese greeting between equals. The strength in his grip took Zinvar's breath away.

"I am Kharnek, as you also know."

The warrior pulled him closer until their faces were inches apart. Dark brown eyes stared into Zinvar's own, and he knew he could lose himself in their depths.

"Make no mistake, priest—I am here to keep you alive and for no other purpose. So please, do not make my task more difficult than it already is."

Kharnek released his hold on Zinvar and walked away toward the section of Zel Morakh reserved for the Brotherhood. Red marks stood out on Zinvar's pale skin where the warrior's hand had clasped his arm. He rubbed at them, confused by Kharnek's hostile attitude and by how much he enjoyed the lingering warmth from his touch.

CHAPTER 3

Relentless heat scoured the broken plain north of Axiom, transforming the distant horizon into a wavering mirage. Although the terrain appeared flat between Kalis and that distant point, he knew it held countless hidden ravines and crevices. The undulating landscape traced the paths of rivers that once flowed across the desert, and navigating its contours was a perilous undertaking, even for someone trained to anticipate and overcome the wasteland's challenges, as Kalis was.

Mostly. As a Prioriate, he was well on his way to becoming a Sentinel, one of his homeland's guardians and warriors.

A familiar voice intruded upon his thoughts, "Do you ever wonder how it got to be this way?"

Kalis looked to his right as she joined him at the crest of a huge dune. The dry wind snatched at the other Sondrinel's robes and hurled sand and grit at her headscarf, yet she and her reptilian mount did not balk. Her short cerulean hair, like his own, was covered by the tough but breathable fabric.

"It was the Great Calamity. Everyone knows that Arinna," Kalis replied.

The other half of the scouting pair gripped her solendrake's reins in one hand while motioning with the other at the expanse. "Yes, but what caused that catastrophe? And why did it turn half of Etherea into this?"

"Hmm." Kalis wiped the sweat from his brow. "The Astronomers Guild says our world stopped rotating. That's why it's always light here but dark in Komor with Heathström in the middle."

Although her face was covered, Arinna's stiff body language conveyed disapproval. "Lucky them. They say that people in Waverling even get around the city by boat. Imagine having so much water that you can use it as a road. No wonder they've grown soft."

Kalis had read about the capital city of Heathström and its canal system, so different from the subterranean metropolis that was Axiom. His thoughts flitted back to home. Tomorrow was his best friend's graduation from Pedium. She would then join him at the Priorium for Sentinel training. They might even be assigned to patrols together, like the one he was on now, an idea that filled him with excitement.

Next to him, Arinna's solendrake hissed and tasted the air with its forked, violet tongue. The creature shifted its padded feet, and its club-tipped tail curved upward in a defensive posture. Arinna looked at Kalis and used hand signals to indicate that she would investigate while he flanked her. Her solendrake lurched into motion and sped silently down the dune's northern face. Kalis tracked its movements for a little while, then the beige and brown of the creature's scales and Arinna's robes melted into their surroundings. Spurring his mount on, he followed at an angle that would keep him close enough to help but far enough apart that he and Arinna could not be attacked simultaneously. Whatever her solendrake had detected would likely prove unfriendly.

The bottom of the dune was adjacent to a rock formation that thrust upward from the sand like a grasping hand. It offered the only cover for miles making it a likely hiding place for their quarry. Kalis reined in his mount's headlong plunge a short distance from the outcropping and waited. The soughing of the wind was the only noise that disturbed his vigil. A few moments later, motion caught his eye. Arinna and her solendrake crept along the jagged edge of the rock formation's base making for a shadowed gap in the stone wall. He held his breath as they disappeared into it. A long minute passed, then another. Kalis's pulse quickened, realizing they had not agreed on how long he should wait until coming after her. That would not make his Sentinel instructors happy. Inwardly cursing himself for the error of omission, he mentally recited one of their maxims to calm his frantic thoughts: *Do not let yourself be consumed by the chaos of thought. Only through serenity can you discern the path ahead. Breathe in the air, breathe out your fears, and in the stillness that remains, you will find certainty.*

A flash of blue light winked at Kalis from where he last saw Arinna. He relaxed his grip on the saddle horn. Blue meant all clear. He snapped the reins and followed Arinna's path between the rocks. It took a while for his eyes to adjust to the sudden dimness. Arinna had dismounted and was examining something on the ground. Kalis hopped off his solendrake and took in the space at the heart of the rock formation. It was big enough to hold at least ten Sondrinel with their mounts and was significantly cooler inside. Turning his attention back to Arinna, he crouched next to her.

She pointed at a glistening lump. "Wyrm sign. Only a few hours old."

Kalis looked at her in alarm. "Do you think they'll be back?"

"No." Arinna shook her head and stood up, lips pursed. "At least, I don't think so. We only found tracks from three wyrms, which implies a scouting party. They wouldn't be looking for a fight."

"I hope not." Kalis shuddered. "I've never seen a rift wyrm and would prefer to keep it that way."

His companion snorted. "As would I. But it's a bold move for Komor to send scouts this deep into Sondrine. They're up to something."

"Whatever it is, it can't be good, you know?" Kalis rose and faced Arinna. "Did they find the supply cache?"

"No." Arinna motioned toward the back of the space. "I checked. Even if they did, they wouldn't be able to use the diminishing crystals."

Kalis nodded. His training included learning how to find Sentinel supply caches with weapons, rations, and extra clothing, such as this formation, throughout Sondrine. The supplies were stored in crystals that could only be accessed by life force wielders, which made them useless to Komorese intruders.

"We should get back to the rendezvous point and let Sentinel Mysere know what we found," Kalis said. "He'll want confirmation that his suspicions about Komorese activity in the area were correct."

The duo left the rock formation and started back toward the location just north of Axiom, where they would rejoin the other Prioriates on patrol, all of whom were supervised by a veteran Sentinel. There was no better way to learn than by being in the field. Kalis enjoyed this form of instruction much more than the classroom setting where his mother taught. But both were part of the military academy's rigorous requirements, and he had to meet them to continue his family's legacy of service to their realm. So far, he was doing well, today's potentially costly slip-up notwithstanding. Kalis was somewhat mollified by the fact that Arinna, who was more experienced, had made the same mistake. He resolved to take the lead the next time he found himself in a similar situation.

Kalis and Arinna took a few hours to reach the cave where Sentinel Mysere awaited them. By the time they arrived, most of the other patrols had already checked in. Arinna took their solendrakes to be fed and given water, while Kalis reported their discovery to Mysere. Despite his weathered appearance, Mysere remained as spry and vigorous as ever. Many overconfident Prioriates were given a taste of humility in the training ring by his uncanny ability to predict his opponent's moves.

"You and Prioriate Arinna have done well," the old Sentinel praised, "even if you are late. I expected you over an hour ago."

Kalis's face grew hot, but he made no reply, knowing it was useless to argue.

Mysere scratched the faded cerulean of his short beard. "Even so, you made it back safely, which is more than I expected from most. So emboldened by the recklessness of youth is this new group. It will be a wonder if I can keep them alive." The Sentinel's eyes narrowed. "Speaking of which, how many riders did you say?"

"We found evidence of three, sir."

The other man grunted. "Same as the others."

Others? Kalis desperately wanted to ask for clarification, but Mysere was just as well known for his lack of forthcomingness as his fighting abilities.

"Your peers tracked two other such groups. The increased Komorese presence poses a greater risk than you are expected to face in training. You and the other Prioriates are to return to Axiom immediately."

Kalis slumped. When he first learned that they were hunting Komorese scouts, he feared this outcome. An olive-skinned hand squeezed his shoulder. He looked up at Sentinel Mysere, eyes wide.

"Don't take this as a reflection upon your abilities, Kalis. You are one of the finest Prioriates I have ever trained. If it were up to me, you'd be staying out here."

Kalis straightened with pride. Meeting the Sentinel's gaze squarely, he dared to ask, "What do you think the Komorese are doing?"

Mysere's face darkened, and he withdrew his hand. "I have my suspicions, but I would like to be proven wrong in this instance." The Sentinel waved in dismissal. "You have your orders. Leave as soon as your solendrakes are rested."

Snapping a quick salute, Kalis spun on his heel and went deeper into the cave searching for Arinna. His eyes traced the rippling layers of sediment that formed the cave's walls. Keeper's beard dotted the striated surface in brown and yellow clumps. The scraggly plant sprouted from niches where trace amounts of moisture had collected. An underground spring, like the ones used by Axiom, lay at the rear of the cavern. Kalis passed several other Prioriates on his way there, exchanging brief farewells as they saddled their mounts and departed for the

Sondrinel capital. When he reached the spring, he found Arinna conversing with another Prioriate.

"Mark my words; this is a prelude to war," the other trainee was saying. Kalis recognized the tall, slender woman as Bria. She waved as he approached. "Good to see you, Kalis."

"And you." Kalis crossed his arms over his chest. "What's this about war?"

Arinna frowned. "It's just hearsay."

"From a Councilor," Bria shot back, hand on her hip. "Unless you doubt my source?"

She referred to her mother, who represented the Eminents Guild in Sondrine's governing Council. Kalis had heard rumors that her mother's connections allowed Bria to join the Sentinels, but regardless, she was a more than capable fighter—and reliably had access to secret information.

"I didn't mean it like that," Arinna grumbled. "I'm just saying that no one really knows for sure what Komor's motives are."

A shrill laugh burst from Bria. "If we can be certain of anything, it's that Komor thinks they should rule over all of Etherea."

Seeing the wounded look on Arinna's face, Kalis jumped in. "True, but the one thing that has stopped them so far is our command of the life force. Nothing has changed on that front, which makes this sudden aggression even more peculiar."

Bria tilted her head. "Nothing has changed...that we know of."

Kalis and Arinna raised their eyebrows at each other. "What do you mean by that?" Kalis asked.

Their fellow Prioriate leaned in close and whispered. "You absolutely cannot tell anyone that you heard this from me, but rumor has it Komor has some kind of new weapon."

Arinna looked skeptical. "What kind of weapon?"

"Shh!" Bria glanced to either side. "They say Komor has a weapon powerful enough to match the life force."

Kalis blinked twice as he considered this possibility. "If that's true, then we've lost our only advantage over them. Their armies are huge in comparison with ours. Even if we combined our forces with Heathström's, we'd still be outnumbered."

"But Komor doesn't use the life force," Arinna pointed out, "they think it's some form of sorcery."

Bria's eyes flashed. "Exactly. So what did they find? What could be more powerful than the life force?"

An ominous silence descended on the group, broken only by the gurgle of the spring. Kalis was a fighter, not a scholar. His knowledge of the life force was limited to techniques that assisted in combat or survival, but he knew his people employed the essence of all living things for myriad uses, from healing to communication. It seemed impossible for anything to match such power, let alone exceed it.

Arinna was the first to speak. "I don't think such a thing exists. Sondrine was founded by the most powerful life force user there ever was. Nothing has ever come close to matching her strength—which is also our strength. If Komor wants to test themselves against Kadaan's legacy, let them come."

Bria shrugged. "An admirable sentiment. I just hope you're right. Well, see you back at Axiom."

Kalis and Arinna said goodbye and began preparing their solendrakes for departure. They exchanged a few words. Kalis assumed she was as lost in her own thoughts as him. He had always imagined a lifetime among the Sentinels culminating in an honorable retirement, at which point he would be free to spend time with the family he planned to start. Now that he was twenty-one sidereals old, it would not be long before his parents arranged his betrothal to a woman from another Sentinel family and that part of his dreams became reality. But that dream seemed unlikely now. It was expected that Sentinels would engage in the occasional skirmish with bandits or raiders from Komor—who selectively ignored the peace established by the Waverling Accords—but war was another prospect entirely, one that could overshadow all his hopes for the future. He heaved a sigh and braced himself for a long ride back to Axiom.

A soft plop from a stone plunging into water let Kalis know he had found Lyna. He descended the steps, hewn from solid rock, that led down to one of the underground pools that fed Axiom's water supply. The sound of his footsteps made her turn. Lyna's face lit up. Looking at her was almost like looking in a mirror, with her vibrant blue eyes and slender, patrician features. She would probably come close to his six feet once she stopped growing.

"You're home early."

Kalis joined her where she was perched on the ledge, feet dangling over the pool. "Yes, I am, little sister. Your powers of observation never fail to astonish."

That earned him a jab to the ribs, but it was tempered by a smile. Lyna tucked her long hair behind her ears and looked directly at Kalis, her eyes the same pale blue as his own. "Your sarcasm aside, I'm glad you're home."

Kalis threw an arm around his sibling and squeezed her. "Me too."

They sat in silence for a long while, enjoying each other's presence and the serenity of the pool. Lanterns glowed around its circumference, each containing a crystal infused with the life force. Natural diversity in the crystals resulted in a spectacular array of colors. The pool's clear water reflected shades of turquoise, ruby, gold, and azure. Kalis could sit here for hours with Lyna in the tranquil oasis, far enough removed from the bustling center of the cavern that housed the city that they would remain undisturbed for some time. No one came to draw water from the pools—it had been many hundreds of sidereals since Axiom's residents needed to do that—so only those looking for a moment of peace ventured here.

A school of tiny lambent cavefish swam near the place where Lyna dropped the rock, their sensitive whiskers twitching as they investigated the disturbance. Although there were warnings about feeding them, Lyna always secreted some breadcrumbs to toss their way. She produced some from her pockets now and sprinkled them into the water. The flurry of activity that ensued made her giggle as the fish devoured the morsels. They lingered for a few moments once the food was gone, their slender bodies twitching this way and that, before giving up and retreating to a dark corner of the pool.

Kalis's sister sighed and clasped her hands together. "I wish we could do this as often as we used to."

The wistful note in her voice was like a dagger to Kalis's heart. "I know," he murmured, giving her another gentle squeeze. "I do too. Whatever they may tell you, growing up isn't fun."

"I know that, silly. Being an adult is boring. All you do is work and pretend to be nice to people you don't like."

Kalis guffawed, the noise reverberating from the stone around him and his sister. He shook his head. "Lyna, you are too smart to be only thirteen, you know?" Withdrawing his arm from around her, he plucked a loose rock from the ground and tossed it. The projectile skipped across the pool's surface, leaving concentric ripples in its wake until it finally vanished beneath the water.

"We're a lot like those rocks, aren't we?" Lyna crossed her legs beneath her and idly traced circles on the ground with a finger. "We skip through life, making a splash here and there, until one day we just...disappear."

The frank description of mortality sent Kalis's mood spiraling downward. He did not want that day to come too quickly, but he also knew that there was hope even in those final hours. "The disappearance isn't the end, though," he countered, "The rock remains beneath the surface; we just can't see it. People are the same. When our physical bodies die, we rise and become part of the life force. Death is the gateway to another form of existence, as Kadaan showed us by being the first to rise."

"But how do we know that?"

Kalis frowned. "That's what we've been taught for countless centenary revolutions. The Keepers were entrusted with preserving Kadaan's truths and all our other knowledge—they wouldn't mislead us."

"Not intentionally." Lyna looked up at the cavern ceiling, so high above them that shadows swallowed parts of it. "But no one has any proof. For as obsessed as Sondrine is with accumulating knowledge, we take an awful lot on faith."

"We have the visions of the Occulum," Kalis argued, which prompted an eye roll from his sister.

"Which are just as much of a mystery." Lyna abruptly stood. "But enough of that. I barely get to see you now that you're a big, bad Sentinel, and I don't want to spend the time fighting."

Kalis scrambled to his feet. "Same here. But I'm a Prioriate, not a Sentinel."

"Whatever." Lyna smoothed out a wrinkle in her robes, which were white, tinged with pink at the edges, as was currently fashionable. "Let's get home. Vari is probably driving mother crazy. And we need to pick out your outfit for tomorrow's ceremony." Linking her arm with Kalis's, she pulled him up the stairs.

"It's just a graduation ceremony," he protested, "nothing we need to get too carried away with."

Lyna tossed her hair back. "Right, so Idrilia won't care at all if you show up covered in dust like you just got back from patrol."

"So long as I'm there, that's what matters."

A healthy dose of skepticism was written all over Lyna's features. "Well, your heart is in the right place, even if you are totally clueless."

"About what?"

His sister fell silent. They entered one of the outer districts of Axiom, a terraced ridge dedicated to agriculture. Long rows of leafy green plants were attended by members of the Rusthâllers guild, distinguished by their brown pants and yellow shirts. Essential as they were to the city's functioning, their guild still lacked the political influence of the Sentinels or Keepers, who represented the core tenets of Sondrinel society: the preservation of knowledge and military strength. Kalis knew he was fortunate to have been born into a family that belonged to one of the preeminent guilds, but he did not feel in any way superior to his fellow Sondrinel.

Turning his attention back to Lyna, Kalis nudged her with his elbow. "So, what did you mean about me being clueless?"

"Well," she drew out the vowel, "you're old enough now that mother and father will be looking for a suitable pairing for you. Someone from an influential family."

Kalis tilted his head. "Yes…I know. But—"

Lyna interrupted him before he could finish his objection. "And you happen to be close to someone whose family has ties to the Sentinels *and* the Keepers…"

It suddenly dawned on Kalis who she was talking about, and he stopped in his tracks. Lyna stumbled as her arm, still entwined with his own, arrested her motion. He caught her, and they continued walking, a thousand potential replies cluttering his lips. None of them seemed adequate. They eventually reached the outer edge of the residential district where they lived. It was dusk, and the Star of Axiom's light began to dim above the city. The stalactites above them retreated into shadow while light-sensitive crystals flared to life on the streets' edges. Kalis counted the pavers underfoot in a vain effort to impose order upon his wandering thoughts. When that failed, he turned his attention to the white pillars and their elaborate capitals that supported the entrances to the larger homes in the area. The symmetry and balance inherent to Axiom's dominant architectural style, called Cradelian, usually inspired peace and pride in Kalis, but at this moment, the stone felt cold and distant in its imperious regard.

Lyna ventured into the silence, "I figured the idea would come as a shock even though it really shouldn't. Idrilia has all the qualities that mother and father would want. And seeing as she's twenty and still available, I'm certain her parents have declined some other suitors in favor of waiting for her best friend."

"But we're just friends," Kalis blurted out. "I've never even thought about 'Dril that way."

Lyna shrugged. "It might be time to start."

CHAPTER 4

Idrilia looked up at the nearby structure of Priorium stretching to the cavern city's ceiling. She imagined Wen soundlessly soaring to the brown rock, her tawny feathers hiding her in Axiom's carved-out cityscape almost as well as a solendrake's camouflage. She hoped Wen was eating her favorite many-legged anthropods. Nestled between Priorium and Pedium, the line of youths in wrapped fighting robes, ranging from desert hues to brighter schemes from neck to knee, slowly shifted forward. Some carried weapons, visible with the shifting fabric where it split from hip to waist, like Idrilia. Unlike the solid orange in front of her, Idrilia's robe was gradient blue, starting white and moving into the darkest blue at the bottom.

Students who followed other disciplines had gone first to cluster together into their corresponding guilds, as practiced the day before. Those on the path of defending Axiom were reserved for last. To distract herself from how long this procession was taking, Idrilia examined the military academy's tiers, from the lower walled fortification to the alternating pattern of diamond, cylindrical, and hexagonal shapes, all steadily growing smaller as they rose.

"I can't believe we're almost Pedium graduates," Klaara said behind her.

"I can. Ten years is a long time," Idrilia quickly flashed a wry grin over her shoulder, "to figure out we both belong in the Sentinel Guild."

"We're natural-born warriors."

Idrilia didn't have to face Klaara to see the tilt of her head or how she brushed imaginary dust off her squared shoulders. Idrilia knew that lively tone in her voice and the playful expressions that went with it.

"More like bred," Idrilia grumbled. "Don't forget our families' affiliations."

"I'm only half-bred, remember?" Klaara poked Idrilia near her hip.

Fighting a laugh and squirming to the side, Idrilia dropped her elbow between them. "How could I? Your father bakes the sweetest bread of all of the Merchants Guild."

"He had to find something useful to do after his injury."

The line of students took a step forward.

Idrilia had been too young to remember the collapse of the new expansion in the residential section. Klaara's father had been there, and he instinctively caught a pillar of stone before it fell on members of the Artisans Guild. The action saved the builders but wrecked his back beyond the skills of the Healers Guild. While he appeared to be able to complete all normal tasks, his mobility was limited, and he couldn't lift more than a sack of flour. As a result, he couldn't ride a solendrake, let alone fight. The Council of Sondrine found he had been a much better baker than patrol guardian all along. It wasn't often the leaders of Pedium placed a graduate in the wrong guild. Idrilia wondered if it happened more often than they admitted.

"Have you heard from Priorium yet on your application?"

"Not yet. You?" Idrilia asked.

"Not a thing."

"I have." A new voice chimed in behind Klaara, dripping with bravado. "I start training as soon as we return from the Ettrascan Islands."

Idrilia rolled her eyes. "Didn't ask you, Jerrod," she called without turning.

"They must be considering who to assign where." Klaara offered. "I'm the obvious choice for learning how to guard the Steps of Light as a novi given how long I can stand in place without complaining. But you, you're so good at everything they're probably locked in debates on where to focus your talents or if to promote you to vigilem outright and let you tell everyone the right strategies to follow."

Idrilia snorted. "Your stationary talents are debatable."

She was glad Klaara was being flippant about the whole thing. It helped Idrilia not focus on why a no-talent flatterer like Jerrod was already accepted, but both Klaara and herself were not. She couldn't help but wonder if there was a connection between their encounter with the Komorese raider one sidereal ago and the delay.

"In all seriousness," Klaara continued, her voice quieting, "I wouldn't be here without you."

Idrilia's stomach flipped. "Nonsense. How many times have we had to call our sparring a draw? Your abilities got you here."

Klaara's hand rested on Idrilia's shoulder. "You know what I mean."

Heartbeat quickening, Idrilia faced Klaara. The few inches Klaara had on her made Idrilia tilt her chin up to meet her gaze. Both her choppy chin-length hair and her eyes were the palest blue shade of cerulean in the city, almost like the silver of daggers.

"You saved my life. I know I don't remember it, being unconscious and all," Klaara winked, "but if you hadn't acted so quickly with your fire crystal, I'd be dead, not the Komorese."

Averting her eyes, Idrilia swallowed. Images of that day burst into her mind though she tried to close them away. It had been Pedium's penultimate evaluation for those in line for Priorium. A Master Sentinel had been assigned to observe the students, but Idrilia had convinced Klaara that they could scout ahead unsupervised. They had quickly put an hour's travel between themselves and their instructor. Though they had no communication crystals, Idrilia had known they could protect themselves, and Axiom hadn't seen Komorese activity in the south for a long time. Then a figure materialized from the depths of the nearest fissure, grabbed Klaara, and disappeared into the rift. Idrilia had charged to the edge and spurred her solendrake over the precipice to descend the sheer rock in bounding leaps, anchored by its sticky toe pads. She had hurled a fire crystal at the fleeing rift wyrm's back legs, inadvertently dislodging Klaara. Battling panic, Idrilia had followed up by tossing a protective crystal at Klaara, surrounding her in a translucent shield that formed to the shape of her body. The assailant and his mount had tumbled to the crevasse floor, but Klaara landed safely nearby, the shattered absorption layer from the crystal smeared across the rock and sand. That was the story Idrilia had told. The real version she feared violated the Waverling Accords and their prohibition against retaliation.

Everything within her wanted to tell Klaara. Tell her the whole story that she hid from everyone. Guilt at keeping it from Klaara tightened in her throat.

"I couldn't lose you," Idrilia said softly.

"Thank you. My friend and savior."

Friend. The word froze Idrilia's muscles despite Klaara's smile, rekindling a recurring thought—was she content with being friends? Anything else wouldn't even be possible with the Sondrine edicts. Idrilia thought of her grandmother and how she challenged Idrilia to think beyond the confines of the rules and grasp what she wanted. *What do I want?* She touched the two green droplet jewels of her grandmother's circlet on her forehead, wishing her grandmother was in the waiting crowd. She blinked back tears.

"Idrilia?"

"Hmm?" Her eyes followed where Klaara pointed.

The line had moved several paces forward. Their group was next.

"I'll see you at the final rites. And then…Priorium!" Klaara's raised her fist.

Idrilia nodded, tugging her tunic sleeves over her leather scale-like gauntlets, and stepped around the corner of Pedium, quickening her steps. Ahead, groups of students clustered into their identified guilds. Each guild was arranged on a convex curve and headed by one of the thirteen corresponding council representatives. Those seeking to become Prioriates, including Klaara and Idrilia, filed into precise rows in front of Pedium's columns. Like a smaller version of Axiom's gates, Pedium's entrance had stone-hewn pillars the height of the school's single story, though the building's exterior lacked the bas-reliefs seen at the Steps of Light.

Falling into place, facing the crowd, Idrilia searched for her family. She sighed. At least they promised to have a special celebration after the final rites. Her father was always receiving important and confidential Sentinel messages that had to be acted on immediately. She understood, but she didn't have to approve. Other families would visit with their graduates briefly following the ceremony. Maybe she could practice cavern signals with Wen before she set off for the week-long combination of lessons and celebration.

Idrilia reached for Wen on her shoulder, finding empty air before her mind caught up with the habit. Without the light weight of the othwit, usually ever-present even when not training, Idrilia felt like a warrior stepping out into the desert with boots and headscarf missing. But the taloned bird was with the Familiars Guild getting her official collar. Idrilia understood why Wen wasn't a part of the graduation since Pedium students didn't train a combat companion before they got to Priorium. Still, she wished she could stroke Wen's feathers and hear her gentle hoot.

Idrilia's eyes fell on the dais centered between the student groups. High Keeper Veloran climbed to stand waist high above everyone, which put her pouches and tubes containing writing implements and crystals at eye level. Her sleeves were ornamented on the edges with a chevron pattern similar to the shape of her circlet over each eyebrow. The graduates all around her lifted their heads to watch the Council mediator and head preserver of the knowledge of the great Evocus library speak. Even after two sidereals Idrilia still couldn't get used to not seeing her grandmother in the role. First, her departure due to the progressing illness, and then a year later...Idrilia tore her eyes away to search for familiar faces.

"Another sidereal, another group of learners ready to carry on our founder's wishes." Keeper Veloran's voice carried across the plaza between buildings.

That was their cue. In unison, Idrilia and the Pedium graduates recited the original five edicts of Axiom. "Safeguard our history, Pursue knowledge, Pass on tradition, Participate in society, Protect against loss of numbers."

Idrilia cringed at the last edict as the High Keeper began announcing which students would be joining which guild. When she got to the Sentinels Guild, Idrilia quieted her mind's concerns about arranged marriages within guilds and why that particular amendment to the edicts had been necessary.

"The Sentinel guild has seen a larger than usual aptitude for its military academy this class. As such, applications are still under review for the most ideal candidates for instruction from the available Master Sentinels. Regardless, Axiom is fortunate to have so many willing to protect our gates. Announcements should be ready next week."

Idrilia's excitement dropped like a stone in her boots. She glanced around at the others—there weren't that many more than usual. The High Keeper's explanation didn't make sense, especially since Jerrod was already accepted, but with a final message of congratulations, her fellow students began to break away from their groups.

"If everyone will stay for just a moment," the High Keeper raised her arms with her voice over the disbursing crowd. "Normally, this is the end; however, there is an additional announcement the Council would like to share, given how many families are here with us. The Trials of the Innermost are quickly approaching. Although we seek truth every single day we live," High Keeper Veloran declared, the crowd mumbling affirmations, "the Council of Sondrine is proud to send two of our most promising young warriors, in compliance with the Waverling Accords, as our Truthseekers. Their families will add yet another entry to their lengthy and, until now, separate histories as documented in the Vitaetum. Kalis Vaktare, who became a Prioriate last year, and Idrilia Volundar, who graduated today. Please, come join me."

Idrilia's jaw dropped as clapping crescendoed in the plaza, and she froze. Taking a deep breath, she elbowed her way through the gathered spectators and climbed onto the dais. Kalis joined her a moment later, signaling a quick gesture of greeting with an accompanying lopsided grin. Idrilia mouthed, "*hi*". Idrilia still wasn't used to his close-cropped hair since entering Priorium. She missed his wavy blue strands that threatened to hide his ears entirely.

The High Keeper alternated between turning to address the crowd and the new Truthseekers. "Idrilia has not only proven herself to be the top of her class at hand-to-hand combat and dual-wielding weapons, but she has also trained a familiar, which—for those not in the Sentinel Guild—is typically only done in Priorium. Even so, not all accomplish this. Lastly, as many of you may already know, last sidereal, she saved her classmate from a Komorese raider—something no other student has accomplished unaided." Idrilia winced at the praise, and the Keeper paused. As the clapping diminished, Veloran held a hand toward Kalis. "Kalis, though he has only been a Prioriate for a year, has mastered many of the advanced life force combat techniques not taught until the final sidereals of training. These crystals are the most difficult to initiate and control. While I cannot give explicit details at this time, Kalis has shown over and over his attention to detail and leadership on patrols." The High Keeper rotated toward them both. "The Council has granted you both solendrake mounts and camelids to carry supplies, but it is up to you two to pick your path and reach our twilit neighbor and their capital, Waverling. This is your first trial. When you complete that task, you will join the other realms' Truthseekers for the opening ceremony where you will demonstrate the same skills for which you were chosen." She pivoted so that the two friends were at her back. "Idrilia and Kalis will leave next week. Until then, you have time to congratulate them and their families. Let us celebrate all of the accomplishments seen here today."

The crowd began to move off as Keeper Veloran addressed Idrilia.

"You can continue to the final rites and the Ettrascan islands as planned. It will give you time to mentally prepare for the task rather than rushing into things. The Council has confidence in your abilities, but some caution you to think on how your actions will represent Sondrine."

Idrilia stiffened. She'd heard that lecture before. Insinuating she was rash. Well, the Council of Sondrine rarely made a decision in one meeting. They could use a bit of rashness. But did they suspect…

"And Kalis," the High Keeper set her gaze on him, "your Prioriate education will continue but here in the city. The Council does not want you caught on patrol when the time to leave arrives. I encourage you to prepare for the upcoming task in your free time."

A resonating tone chimed through the cavern like a ship's bell. Idrilia searched Keeper Veloran's face for reactions, finding only a twitch of her eyebrow. The toll was reserved for guild meetings, though one wasn't scheduled for today. Perhaps the information her father had mentioned warranted a secundarium.

"Again, congratulations, you two. But my presence is required by the Council. You will need these," she removed two square slabs of crystal and handed them to each Seeker. Each was etched internally with tiny dots that formed the image of a floating Kadaan. "It proves that you are a Truthseeker. We created new ones since the previous ones vanished with the last Seekers, but it is the same design." Nodding at them, the High Keeper left the platform, likely heading for the Council building.

Kalis cleared his throat. "Standing up here feels a bit exposed. Should we…"

The pair headed for the crystal garden near Priorium. Technically, it was shared with Pedium, but the sculptures crafted by the Kristallgares Guild were prominently Sentinels. Their progress was laborious, however, as people they had never met moved into their path and offered their best wishes and advice. Idrilia's favorite was an older woman who suggested leaving all their crystals behind since this was a peace-keeping venture. Idrilia fought an eye roll. As if she would be within arm's reach of someone from Komor without access to the life force.

When they reached the garden, a few others and their families sat on benches or clustered around the crystal statues.

"I didn't know you were back in the city," Idrilia said as they meandered on the garden path.

"Just returned today. But it made it so I could see you. Uh, graduate." Kalis scratched the back of his head. "Where's your family?"

Idrilia groaned. "A runner came to the house early. Sentinel Mysere summoned father to review some activity north of the city."

"And your sisters?" Kalis moved closer.

She shrugged. "Mother must have some Sentinel duties and kept them. Fey can easily dart in a crowd."

"That's a nice way to say Aluan doesn't want to watch her." Kalis elbowed Idrilia's arm. "You alright?"

Idrila opened her mouth, closed it, and then shrugged. "With them missing it? Yeah, they have important duties. It's fine. They promised to celebrate later."

Kalis nodded. "Well, I'm glad I was able to be here. I wonder if what I found on patrol is what summoned your father."

"Komorese?" Idrilia whispered, leaning forward.

He tilted his head, looking at her from the corner of his eye. "I can't say, you know."

She huffed and spun away, chin high, as something struck her elbow and fell softly at her feet.

"So, uh, are you ready to have fun at the final rites?"

Idrilia glanced at the ground, then Kalis. "Exercises in the desert with people who have scarcely been out in the heat for more than a few hours? That is not my definition of fun."

"They'll certainly be thankful for that sea breeze. It went well with my group last year. Very few passed out." A grin grew on his face.

A small pebble bounced off of her shoulder, and Idrilia stiffened. Kalis raised an eyebrow. As Idrilia pivoted to face the source, another pebble struck her cheek.

"Alright, make peace with me, or I'll make pieces of you." Idrilia crossed her arms as a figure in a nuala fighting robe stepped out from behind a sculpture. "Klaara!"

She grinned. "That's an interesting version of a Sondrinel request for identification."

Idrilia shrugged. "It needed a new ending anyway. What were you doing hiding back there?"

"You thought I'd just go home after hearing you're a Truthseeker? Hey, Kalis." She nodded once in his direction. "This is definitely why you haven't heard from Priorium about entrance. You'll be gone most of the first sidereal."

The duration of the Trials always varied based on the actual tasks assigned to the six Seekers, but generally, the participants were sent to all three realms, which required travel time. Time that put her at least half a sidereal behind Klaara and the rest of her graduating class. She'd go from being one of the best to needing to catch up. Idrilia's jaw clenched. Priorium might even hold her back to join the next set of initiates.

"We should celebrate you two!" Klaara added.

"We could go to the Portly Pectully. Fill our stomachs with pastries until we're sick." Kalis laughed.

Klaara strode past him, drawing nearer to Idrilia. "I hear everyone entering Priorium does something daring before Sentinel training starts."

Eyebrows shooting up, Idrilia rounded on Kalis. "Is that true?"

Her friend crossed his arms. "I certainly didn't jeopardize my entrance by seeking an unwise stunt."

"That'll be a yes, it is," laughed Idrilia, smacking his shoulder. "Let's do it! Ideas?" The council thought she was rash, so why not.

"We could," Klaara pursed her lips, squinting toward Evocus, "rearrange some of the Keepers' record books."

"Too much effort." Idrilia tapped her foot against the pebbles, eliciting a rhythmic crunch. "There has been one rumor I've wanted to investigate."

"This better not be what I think it is." Kalis frowned. "It is, isn't it?"

Idrilia grinned.

"No, no, no, this is a terrible idea."

Idrilia caught Klaara's eye. "I trust you." She smiled, and Idrilia's heart quickened. "Lead on."

"I can't believe I let you drag me here," Kalis grumbled behind her.

Idrilia heaved her body over a boulder, climbing higher on the pile of rocks at the back of the abandoned residential district.

"You're just as curious but won't admit it."

"You could always go do some Prioriate stuff," Klaara offered.

"And leave you two to cause mayhem? I think not."

When it had originally happened, the Frids Guild moved rubble from the incident to pile it in front of an already existing heap. The smoother cuts of the rocks had the same light tan as had been used in building Evocus, the first large structure of Axiom, which told her the pile was from the city's earlier days. She was glad she didn't get assigned to a guild that dealt with social responsibilities, like waste, all the time. It seemed uninspiring. Idrilia surveyed the amount of unused rock, red-hued and striated with cream and brown, laying there at least ten sidereals after the incident. *Looks like the Frids don't accomplish anything, anyway.*

She checked over her shoulder. Kalis kept glancing back toward the row of carved living spaces, and Klaara stood with her hands behind her back. Both looked like guards with their nuala robes cinched around their waists, long sleeves and pants covering their olive skin. They just needed headscarves, and Idrilia could imagine they were on patrol investigating Komorese activity.

Behind them, twenty leaps of a solendrake away, stood the empty residential district. The half-crafted structure would have housed families in divided units, most designed to fit four. But when the incident that injured Klaara's father occurred, the Frids Guild declared this area too unstable to withstand any additional stone shaping.

This far from the city center, homes blocked Idrilia's view of the steps to the lower districts and the ledge looking down onto the central buildings. As a result, the landscape looked tight and so close to the outer edge of the cavern it felt like a cave trapping them. Suppressing a shudder, Idrilia returned to her climbing.

"What are you looking for?" Kalis called.

Idrilia grabbed a handful of rock dust gathering on the top of the nearest stone and faced the wall of various-sized boulders, their striations in cream and orange hues dancing in a mixed pattern like the blocks of a child's stacking game. She raised her fist and released a tiny stream of dust that scattered away from the flow.

Hair flipping as she whirled around, she flashed her biggest smile. "Air! This could be it."

"How do we get in?" Klaara asked.

Idrilia was already moving back down the rocks toward her two companions. When she reached them, she flipped a red crystal into her hand. She focused her thoughts like a beam of light—narrow and compressed—and used the crystal like turning the key to a locked box, opening the path to the life force as she shook the crystal, then launched it at the upper pile of rocks.

"Get down!" Kalis shouted, flattening himself against the stone floor.

Idrilia ducked, covering her head with her arms. A deadened explosion sounded, then pebbles rained down, pelting against the fabric of their robes.

Idrilia chuckled at the irony of rain inside their desert fortress. She peeked over the boulder.

"I knew grandmother was right," Idrilia bounced on the balls of her feet.

"Do you think it is one of the original tunnels Kadaan used?" Klaara asked.

Idrilia shrugged. Dust swirled in the air like miniature othwits in front of a dark opening wide enough to allow all three to walk shoulder to shoulder. Grandmother Elsuota had only written her theory of tunnels to the surface but had not investigated. That was something more for the Delvers Guild, but since Idrilia wasn't part of any guild...

"One way to find out." Climbing back up the pile toward the new opening, Idrilia motioned for her friends to follow.

"Those crystals aren't expendable, you know." Kalis grunted as he heaved himself over a large rock. "Besides, someone still could have heard that."

"Then we better move fast, huh?" Klaara offered, quickening her pace.

Reaching the new opening, all three activated light crystals, allowing them to float above their heads and bathe the area in silver-white. The opening stretched beyond the reach of their light, and, without further comment, they entered the tunnel, following the dust-covered tube as it bent and twisted at intervals while gradually inclining. The tunnel appeared natural, the stone edges rough rather than sculpted by stone carvers or blasted by fire crystals. Quiet but for their footfalls.

"Do you think water once ran through here?" Idrilia asked after they had traveled in silence for some time. Her echo made her jump.

"It's possible," Kalis replied. "Could be one of the ways our underground lake originally formed."

"What did your grandmother say about it?" Klaara asked.

"Her theory," Idrilia leaned forward to look past Kalis as they walked, "was that Kadaan found what would eventually be Axiom from above the Leske Chasm rather than exploring the old riverbed. Since we think our forebearers lived above before the Great Calamity, it would have been easier to transport people and supplies down into the cavern through such a tunnel."

"Instead of lowering it down the cliff face into the crevasse. Would have been a good plan," Kalis added.

"Hey, speaking of plans. How are you two going to get to Waverling? I can't believe the High Keeper said you had to come back here after being in the islands. You could just take a boat over to Heathström from there."

Idrilia shrugged. "I think part of the trial's test is us working together."

"Not like we haven't worked together before. This will be easy."

Idrilia snorted and looked at Kalis. "Probably take the Leske Road to the south pass. What do you think?"

"That would be best, you know. So that we can keep our camelids and solendrakes."

"Then it's settled. But I don't want to do any more planning until after the final rites. I need to focus on impressing the Master Sentinels." *If I do great training the others tomorrow, maybe they'll put in a good word for me with Priorium.* "Besides, you're the planner, Kalis, not me."

"Don't I know it," he mumbled.

"Too much time thinking leaves too little time for doing. Come on, pick up the pace." Idrilia pressed forward ahead of the other two.

Before long, the passageway began to narrow, and they shifted to walk single file. Her nuala robe clung to her skin in places where sweat had begun to bead. Cool air filled the tunnel for most of the journey, like in the city itself, but now the air felt like standing beneath the shade of a rock overhang in the desert. As she started to hunch over to avoid bumping her head on the stone ceiling, light from one of their crystals glinted off something at the base of the wall.

Idrilia crouched, picking up a silver rectangle with rounded corners. The back of the object pricked her finger, and she dropped it. It clinked against the stone, and light from the crystals above traced etched symbols on its surface. As Idrilia reached for it again, a green light shot out, and she pulled her hand back to her chest.

A figure no taller than her index finger formed—a glowing woman with braided hair spun around to face Idrilia. She reached out a hand, then vanished.

"Did you see that?" Idrilia looked over her shoulder.

Kalis pointed. "The flat metal thing?"

"No, what came out of it."

"I couldn't see anything with this walking rule book in my way."

Grunting, Klaara slid past Kalis, pushing him close to the wall.

Idrilia picked up the object as she stood and handed it to Klaara. Her friend flipped it over, but nothing happened.

"Is this some sort of writing?"

"It seems deliberate, but I don't recognize the markings." Idrilia shrugged.

Klaara looked further down the tunnel, eyes widening. "I think we've found the surface," she grinned, handing the rectangle back.

Idrilia held her breath as Klaara's arm brushed against the fabric across her breasts as she pressed past. Klaara hunched over, then began to crawl toward faint light.

"Let me see." Kalis peered over her shoulder.

"Here." Idrilia handed the metal to him, her eyes not leaving Klaara's crawling form.

"Makes me think of the plates on the shelves in Evocus."

Frowning, Idrilia shifted her eyes away from Klaara. "Huh?"

"You know, at the ends of the rows, telling us the topics and authors."

"Oh. Yeah, maybe."

"Idrilia!"

Klaara's hushed summons through the opening sent a cold wave through her veins. She scrambled forward, striking her head on the ceiling as she dropped to the ground. Knees bumping on the hard surface, Idrilia thought about the goggled eyes of the Komorese raiders, of rift wyrms ready to claw flesh and men who'd take Klaara. *Not again.* She moved as quickly as she could down the narrow tunnel toward the growing light.

Her breath came quicker as she tumbled out of the hole into the brilliant blaze of the sun. She withdrew her daggers from her hips, raising a leather gauntlet to her eyes and stepping forward to give Kalis space to exit.

His hand touched her lightly between her shoulder blades. "At your back."

Idrilia blinked away tears, squinting against the sun. "What's going on?"

"Vargs." Klaara's voice came from ahead and to Idrilia's right. "They're preoccupied at the moment."

Breathing out, Idrilia's shoulders released. She dug into a bag on her side and pulled out orange fabric. She wrapped it deftly around her head and into her nuala robe so that a slit at her eyes was the only opening. She glanced to her left and saw Kalis do the same with his yellow headscarf.

Ahead, creatures the color of sunlit sand prowled low to the ground, fangs bared in tapering snouts as a pack of three surrounded a torav nest. Their prey's smaller bodies amassed into a clump of cream-and-brown fur, twitching noses and dark eyes flitting between the vargs. Idrilia tried to count the oversized ears that rose from their heads, but their tails kept getting in the way.

"It's odd they are so close to the city," Idrilia said quietly.

"Should we just go back?" Kalis asked.

The vargs' ears perked up. One swung toward them and raised its barbed tail. Its eyes lacked an iris; where there would have been brown, there was black, like its pupils, making its eyes seem like hollow pits.

"Well, that's new." Kalis drew his curved blade.

In unison, the three vargs left the torav nest, their former targets disappearing into their den beneath the sand.

"So's that." Klaara moved closer to Kalis and Idrilia. "Since when do they care more about us than a torav snack?"

Idrilia reached into her crystal bag, feeling for the right shape. "Basja," she cursed, "I only have training crystals left. What about you?"

"Same. Kalis?"

He shrugged and looked sheepish. "Don't be mad, but..."

"You didn't bring any?" Idrilia's voice rose in volume and pitch.

"Nothing offensive. I hardly expected to get attacked at a graduation ceremony."

Idrilia wished she had Wen with her. The othwit could swoop down and distract the creatures. Maybe that's all she and her friends needed.

"Klaara and I will protect your retreat. Our swords have a longer reach. Get back to the tunnel, and we'll follow," Kalis directed. The Prioriate settled into a defensive posture as the vargs advanced toward them.

Idrilia's nostrils flared. There was no way she'd leave Kalis and Klaara. She planted her legs in a wider stance. She grabbed a crystal and launched it as soon as the lead varg was near enough. The shimmering object hit the creature squarely on its chest, knocking it onto its back. Idrilia smirked. Training crystals though they may be, they still packed a punch thanks to concentrated life-force energy. The moment of triumph dissipated as the varg scrambled onto its feet, snarling and slavering. Its pack members had slowed when it was struck but now moved into flanking positions.

"Nice throw, but I think you just made it mad."

"Not helping, Klaara," Idrilia said through gritted teeth. She only had a couple of crystals left. They could not make it back to the tunnel in time to avoid engaging the vargs, and a fighting retreat into a confined space seemed unwise. Her mind raced as she pondered alternatives, but hope slipped away with each step the pack took toward them.

The lead varg froze. Its legs began to twitch, and it retched violently. The sound made Idrilia's stomach turn. After a few seconds of dry heaving, the canid spewed forth the contents of its gut in a bilious stream.

"Gross!" Klaara squealed, pinching her nose with one hand while brandishing her sword with the other. "What in Kadaan's name is wrong with this thing?"

Kalis pointed frantically. "I don't know, but I think that did something!"

The normal color of the varg's eyes was restored, and instead of menacing, it now just looked...scared. Throwing its head back, the varg unleashed a piercing howl, echoed by the rest of the pack. Then they all fled, hastening toward the deep desert where their normal hunting grounds awaited. To either side of Idrilia, Kalis and Klaara lowered their blades.

"What...just happened?" Kalis asked.

Idrilia and Klaara looked at each other and shrugged. "I've never seen anything like that," Idrilia replied. "Maybe it was sick?"

Klaara tilted her head. "That was unlike any sickness I've ever heard of. Desert vargs are hardy creatures. If they came down with something, it could threaten our domestic animals."

Grimacing, Kalis waved at the pool of vomit. "I suppose that means we should collect a sample for the Healers Guild to study."

"Be my guest."

Kalis stuck his tongue out at Idrilia and moved toward the yellow and brown mess. Idrilia turned to Klaara. "Well, I think this little adventure qualifies as sufficiently daring, don't you?"

The other woman laughed, and the sound was sweet to Idrilia's ears. "Yes, I'd say so. This certainly beats any story I've heard from other graduates."

Idrilia returned her smile and wondered, not for the first time, how severely her family would react to the idea of her matching herself with one of her best friends. It was uncommon for two women to pair, thanks to the reproductive stipulations of the edicts. Idrilia couldn't think of one in her lifetime. But unprecedented actions were kind of her thing. And if she got a say, instead of her parents deciding the connection, maybe her pairing would feel less like an exchange of goods in the Ettrascan market.

"Hey!" Kalis called to them from where he was hunched over the varg vomit. "This thing coughed up a crystal!"

The other two Sondrinel pivoted as a unit. "A crystal?" Klaara asked, her voice pitched high enough to rival Wen's battle screech.

"Yes! Come look."

Idrilia's nose wrinkled as she drew closer and got a whiff of the undigested remnants of the varg's last meal. Peering around Kalis's shoulder, she spotted the glimmer of a small, faceted crystal. It was unlike any crystal she had ever seen, deep purple in hue. Moving closer, she realized that it was really more of a shard. Its jagged edges would have made it difficult to swallow.

Klaara spoke the question in everyone's minds. "Now, why do you suppose it would have eaten that?"

Her curiosity overcame her squeamishness, and Idrilia plucked the crystal from the pool, wiping its facets off on the ground. Upon closer examination, she saw that the purple color was shot through with traces of black that appeared to swirl within the shard. The longer she looked at it, the more she felt like sand was under her robes.

"We should get this to Axiom." She shoved the disconcerting object into her pocket. "And I don't want to be out here anymore."

Kalis shook his head. "I second that. Let's go."

He led the way back to the tunnel, Klaara and Idrilia in tow. Idrilia's fingers unwittingly made their way to her pocket and closed around the shard. Faint whispers clawed at the edge of her hearing. Unnerved, she let go and pushed past her friends to enter the tunnel first, eager to get home and rid herself of the strange object.

CHAPTER 5

To the lowlanders, the jeroti might have passed undetected in the tall brome, the steps of his large, soft paws indistinguishable from the susurrus wind through the plants' yielding spike tips.

But Vayriel was a Highblood. A Watcher of the mountains. She knew the voice with which the slopes whispered. The gentle tickle under her skin of the blue-winged birds' swooping presence at the tree line behind her paled in comparison to the thrum, like a heartbeat, pulsing along an invisible thread that stretched to her core from the white-furred creature stalking her.

Crouched on a boulder, Vayriel leaned on her spear. Its tip was a rose-tinted, diamond-shaped crystal. The jeroti's body, six feet from nose to haunches, slinked low to the ground. Twin tails hung limply behind him in his slow march; Vayriel could tell he was not poised to attack. Yet.

From beneath her fur-lined hood, she stole a glance across the misty valley between ridges. Underneath the haze, the familiar dull green, the same color as the gems tied to her spear, the ever-twilit land of Heathström gazed back like a young-one peeking from behind their mother's sheltering arm. Nestled between the ever-dark land of Komor in the west and the ever-bright land of Sondrine in the east, Vayriel's people named the land that gave them life and comfort Skyveil. Further down the mountain, where the slope leveled, rested a silent lake and through a patch of forest beyond was Beechmarsh, the nearest village of the lowlanders. True to their name, they did not often venture into the heights of the Agermath Range. But while Vayriel was unlikely to encounter a lowlander, the voice of the mountain reminded her she was not alone.

Vayriel felt the tug against her bond in the life force grow stronger. Pushing against her spear, she rose from her perch, still facing the overlook and the clinging mist that hovered over the valley. Her left hand gripped her weapon tighter.

From his hiding place, the white creature flattened his triangular gray ears and let a quiet huff escape his jaws. Vayriel grinned at the sound and braced herself. The vibrations of emerging movement flowed through their connection to touch her chest, heralding the creature's attack.

Dropping her left foot behind her, Vayriel pivoted to face away from the overlook. She focused on her life-force energy, guiding it from her fingers and toes to her center, where it gathered in a concentrated ball within her chest.

The four-legged creature broke out of hiding and leaped into the air, a long, graceful pounce that seemed to move slower than reality. His mouth was closed, but his cyan eyes were bright.

Vayriel dropped to the ground. She released her constricted energy, and felt it move out from her core to her extremities and beyond, enveloping her in a bubble that shimmered nigh undetectable in a pale rose hue. Vayriel *pushed* the protective sphere away from her as the jeroti landed atop it, vaulting her attacker over her head.

Rolling to the left, she kept one hand on the rock while the other spun her spear behind her back to rest, quivering, where her hood fell between her shoulder blades. She slowly raised her head, strands of peach hair falling across her face with the cool mountain breeze. She focused on the creature's face, his eyes now narrowed. Then she laughed, the sound echoing across the landscape. The jeroti fell to his side, rolling over to reveal his gray underbelly.

"We need to work on your sneaking abilities, my life-friend."

Vayriel crawled the short distance to sit with the jeroti. His feet faced the sky, the claws of each retracted within paw pads as large as her fist.

"It was easier to connect to the life force today with you, Orgar." She smiled as she stroked his belly. "I felt the vibrations of the Mother-of-All's creation, like a story sung loudly, and I connected with them—with her. She told me when you were to strike at me."

Orgar sighed, his whole body rising and lowering dramatically.

Vayriel nodded, a feather of disappointment passing over her. "You would rather be able to surprise me, I know."

Orgar opened one eye lazily, batting a front paw at her nose. She brushed it away, blocking further soft taps with her free hand.

Leaning on Orgar's gray belly, Vayriel cradled his conical face, studying him as she always did, checking for injuries and committing each feature to memory so that she would not forget a single one like she had forgotten what her parents had looked like.

Orgar bared his teeth, revealing his top fangs as she tickled the side of his face. He nipped lightly at Vayriel's fingertips, and she snapped her hand out of reach. Orgar huffed and repositioned himself to lay his heavy head in her lap. He looked upward expectantly until Vayriel began to stroke the space between his ears.

Her eyes gradually focused on the sky and the moon, marking the position of the Daughter's Journey across Skyveil to check the time.

Low on the horizon. It was still early. They still had time before the other Watchers expected Vayriel and Orgar to join them this Daughter's rise. Absently, she flicked the crystal adornments beneath the tip of her dark spear, each crafted like a wilting petal.

"We move the alusarean herd to fresh brome to graze today. It will likely take until tomorrow to find a bountiful location. They have eaten much surrounding us."

Orgar grunted, shifting to nuzzle against Vayriel's side.

"I will miss Mo'mo and Mo'fa, too, but the herd needs our protection," Vayriel countered, thinking of the wisdom-lined faces of her mother's mother and father.

Her thoughts strayed to the expanding grazing areas. Would her coil move from the current site of their collapsible dwellings? So safe had they been that it was almost easy for Vayriel to forget that the spiral arrangement of dwellings she called home would move again. And it must for the health of the mountain and for her people's protection. "Even though we have not seen a trägen for a while, the great-claws could come to feast on the alusarean at any time."

The jeroti gave a short growl. They had spent at least a month without any such excitement.

"You are not bored. You will feel differently when we are practicing our skills with the others. Come." Vayriel patted his muscled shoulder and shifted out from beneath his weight. "We can practice our stealth as we approach the other Watchers. I promise to try to avoid squashing a pile of sticks and startling one of the herd into a fearful rampage this time."

Vayriel and Orgar walked side by side, the tall grass parting silently as they meandered through the greenery. Vayriel rested her hand on Orgar's neck, and they moved into a patch of trees, going higher into the mountains. She felt light as a cloud at the prospect of the new tasks waiting for them this day.

As they crept through the forest Vayriel's mind wandered, thinking about how high the tallest peak was and if it pierced the veil of the sky. She had just decided to ask Mo'mo, who had named their people after that height and the body's life-giving fluid, when Orgar's nose dropped to the ground, sniffing intently. The warm breath of recognition brushed Vayriel, and she knew that the herd was close.

True to her promise, Vayriel watched each placement of her canvased feet. She saw the potential misstep before Orgar's tails began to twitch from side to side and halted.

"There are many paths to where one is going. Focus too much on one, and you miss what the other has to offer."

Vayriel looked up to see the leader of their coil, familiar lines of wisdom tracing her face. The woman was dressed like her, though her dark hair was braided and pulled in front of her right shoulder, and alusarean fur adorned her hood on the outside as well as the inside. Her eyes were brown, while Vayriel's were lavender. But it was her staff, the end bearing a crystal light-holder, that set her apart. No one else carried such an implement. It glowed a soft yellow in the shade of the forest.

"Path-Shaper. I did not know you were joining the Watchers today."

Memories bubbled up unbidden of the Path-Shaper, intent eyes watching her train in the way of the spear as a young-one under the care of a seasoned Watcher. How well her Path-Shaper had seen and directed Vayriel on the right path for her own journey. She breathed easily, comforted by the woman's presence and resonating voice.

"It is always a pleasure to see our warriors guarding and watching out for our coil." She glanced above at the low ball of light shining inert down on them. "Such a reflection of the Watcher's own task to keep his vigilant gaze upon us. But you are right; I am not here for the other Watchers. I have very special news to share. But let us first join the others—they should hear it, too."

Raising an eyebrow, Vayriel nodded, and together the three of them stepped into a clearing. Her two fellow Watchers stood on either side of the herd, their clothing nearly identical to Vayriel's. Bran's had swirls of climbing vines that reminded Vayriel of the vegetation that would often cling to the windward side of gray-bark trees. Both he and Sapa had matching half cloaks with fur only on the inside of the hood. Sapa's neck was wrapped twice by the orange and maroon tail fur of her ratufa life-friend, and Vayriel could just see the rodent nibbling on a nut between her purple paws inside Sapa's hood.

Vayriel passed her eyes over the alusarean heard, perfunctorily counting their numbers as she surveyed the animals.

All seemed well and accounted for. The massive creatures stood eight to ten feet in height, their matted fur dangling from their chests to their knees. One nearest the forest edge looked up, a mouthful of broken stems applying a green mustache to its bearded face. It glanced behind itself, its horns twisted in a lateral spiral, glinting from the middle spike in the sunlight. Vayriel smiled, thinking how the horns looked like lowlander earmuffs.

Her smile faded into pressed lips, and she shifted her spear to her non-dominant hand as she noticed a third Watcher. Counting Vayriel, that made four present in the glade. Usually, three guarded the alusarean, after the trio of celestial young-ones born of the Mother-of-All.

Vayriel bent her head toward her Path-Shaper, a question pressed between her pursed lips.

As if reading her mind, the woman answered her unspoken question. "Anish is here to take your place in the path-finding for the herd. But do not be worried. Your new task is of even greater importance than the safety of one Highblood coil. It has been many journeys of the Daughter since a Highblood was sent, but the time has come. You, Vayriel born of Motesh and Kerru, have been chosen to represent us all in the Trials of the Innermost."

The Watchers whooped, their arms raised to the sky. Vayriel hadn't noticed them draw closer as the Path-Shaper spoke. They approached now as Vayriel's stomach fluttered and pressed their hands on her shoulders, muttering words of encouragement. But her mind raced while Orgar lay protectively over her feet, sensing through their bond some of her discomfort. She knew of the Trials, but that was something the lowlanders did. Fighting to keep her expression neutral, Vayriel recalled how wars long ago between Komor, Sondrine, and Heathström had prompted the tradition. But the Highbloods had not been a part of that war. What did being a participant now imply?

"It is a great honor, but I am sure you have questions." The Path-Shaper motioned with her staff at the alusarean, which continued munching as if nothing had changed.

"The Coil is preparing for your Sending, and your mother's parents are waiting to give you their blessing."

The coil Watchers waved to her as Vayriel and Orgar quickly recovered and joined the older woman, Vayriel belatedly nodding farewell at those staying with the herd.

"We will talk of peace and sharing of knowledge at your Sending. But there is another task for which I want you to be prepared. A task that is a closely guarded prediction from those who can see the lines of the past and the future."

The Path-Shaper spoke of the Daughter's Eyes, the storytellers and story-keepers who could access memories throughout time in great visions. Those like her mo'fa. Had he seen this vision?

"There is something much larger than the harmony between realms at stake. It moves unseen between the folds of the world. You, my young-one, will find the light to vanquish this awakened darkness."

The statement hung like a pectully between them, the tiny bird whose wings moved in a blur of motion just before its poison-laden tail uncoiled and lashed out to strike. Vayriel clenched her staff and let her free hand fall between Orgar's ears, gripping his fur. He did not protest at the ferocity of her hold but kept his side against her leg as they listened to the Path-Shaper relate the prophecy.

It took an hour to reach the tip of the coil. Before they reached the first dwellings beyond the treeline, Orgar sniffed the air, and Vayriel felt his recognition and anticipation through their bond. The familiar smoky-sweet scent of conifer boughs mixed with vegetables and meat comforted Vayriel's heightened nerves. Swirls of gray floated lazily out of the openings at the top of the alusarean-skin cones, remnants of recently extinguished flame. These dwellings began the curl of the Highblood arrangement.

A shrill whistle from one of the nearest dwellings cut through the silence of the trio, and a boom of distant drums answered the call.

"Your people wait to celebrate with you," the Path-Shaper said softly.

Vayriel nodded, her heart beating faster than the drums, concentrating on propelling herself into the unknown.

On their trek through the forest, the Path-Shaper spoke about the prophecy but had reserved information about the Trials for the Sending. As she had explained, the whole coil would be present to hear an explanation of why a Highblood will be going, and the Path-Shaper wanted to save the words for the right time. The two Highbloods slipped into an easy silence, aware of the forest sounds of rustling leaves and scurrying creature-sons and daughters for the rest of the journey. Vayriel had no memory of a Sending. The last Highblood to participate in the trials did so shortly before her birth, and she did not recall anyone from the coil being chosen to leave for a similar journey. Instead, Vayriel had asked her coil's leader what to expect. What the Path-Shaper had tried to prepare her for lay before her.

Every dwelling appeared empty, though some had their door flaps tied shut so she could not see inside. They could have cut across the meadow to the center of their coil, but instead, they followed the natural path, grass and flowers worn flat by footsteps, eventually swirling into the heart of the coil. And the drums grew louder with each stride.

Rounding the last Highblood home, Vayriel's breath caught in her throat. Normally the gathering area had any number of wandering Highbloods; the elders like Mo'mo would huddle around the central fire pit to discuss coil affairs with the Path-Shaper, while young-ones kicked wooden balls to each other, Watchers and jeroti listened to stories told by a Daughter's Eye. Never had she seen the gathering area so full. Even with the Path-Shaper's warning, it gave Vayriel pause.

The drums stopped beating. Every member of the coil twisted toward her. Orgar bumped against her leg as the pair stopped. The men mostly had their hair braided, while the women and young-ones wore their long locks in a variety of styles. The majority wore a style of alusarean clothing consistent across all coils, though Vayriel's coil embossed representations of plants and creatures into their leather; fur-lined cloaks fell to the mid-back, a secondary pant layer hung to their ankles and laced up their sides; belts and ankles with fur like the gloves the people furthest from the fire wore, although some were just a spear length away.

Vayriel wished she could summon her protective sphere and vanish from their stares, but the Mother-of-All's life force did not work like that. So many eyes observed her. She would have rather been chasing Orgar and the creature-sons and -daughters between dense trees. A chorus of ululations erupted into the east wind.

Their Path-Shaper pressed a hand to her shoulder, then went forward, the crowd parting to allow her passage to a three-tiered tower erected next to the central blazing fire. The woman climbed a ladder laid against the lashed wood frame and ascended to the top platform. Vayriel beamed as her gaze fell on two familiar figures standing at the base: Mo'mo and Mo'fa. They motioned for her to come closer, and as Vayriel led Orgar between the crowd, the Path-Shaper began to speak.

"Etherea needs healing," the Path-Shaper called out. "The lowlanders no longer listen to the Mother-of-All, no longer hear the message of her creature-daughters and -sons. Hatred of one another fills their hearts again, and the Highblood coils fear their peaceful efforts are like a mist trying to make the desert bloom. Though we think we are removed from the concerns of the lowlanders, we are all a part of the Mother's creation. And we are not so far removed from the actions of the lowlanders. We have seen this when the lowlanders depict our life-friends as dangerous beasts in their art. We have seen this when they avoid us or will not trade with us in their settlements. We have seen this when brothers from Komor steal the crystals under our protection and murder our Watchers to reach them."

Vayriel flinched, glancing at Mo'mo and Mo'fa for their reaction. Whether the words conjured memories of Vayriel's parents, she could not see, but the crowd murmured in agreement.

"Our ancestors wanted to protect Etherea and guard the Mother's creation against those who would do her harm. We rotate our grazing fields to allow new growth to return. For each red-bark we cut down, we plant two more. We teach our young-ones the stories of our ancestors so that our knowledge is not lost. But we can do more." The Path-Shaper swept her staff through the air, gesturing over the crowd. "It is true that our coils do not fight amongst themselves as the realms of the lowlanders do. The wars of their past are not our wars. But their future is our future. We must share our knowledge so that all of Etherea may grow in peace."

Many in the crowd hooted in agreement. Orgar wagged his tails, thumping them against Vayriel's thighs. Did all of the coils' Path-Shapers agree with the decision? Vayriel could think of several that would be unlikely to want to help lowlanders. She could hardly blame them, given they suffered the worst long ago when the lowlanders tried to tear down sections of forest, attacked Highblood settlements, or slayed life-friends out of fear.

Vayriel blinked, drawing herself back to cast her full attention on her Path-Shaper as the woman tilted her head down and, with her staff, gestured to Vayriel.

"Daughter of Motesh and Kerru, strongest of our Watchers, you will bring them once again the wisdom of the Highbloods. Each realm sends a pair of Truthseekers together to Waverling as their first trial. They must navigate treacherous land and the treacherous hearts of their companions. But you, Vayriel, Watcher of the mountains, you know these lands and the way through Beechmarsh. Which is why your trial begins there. Traveling to Waverling is but an easy task for one who can use the life force and the Mother-of-All's guidance. It is not so far away. No, you must find your counterpart on your own on your way to the capital city. Go to Beechmarsh, you who hears the jeroti, who grows the young-roots, who protects the coil. You must plant the young-root of healing in the hearts of the companions you find. We pray it thrives as quickly and easily in them as it has in you. May you walk the true path."

Light erupted from the crystal wedge on her staff like thousands of yellow shafts through the air as the crowd finished the statement. "May you see the true light."

The drums began to beat again, joined by wooden flutes and other instruments as the Path-Shaper descended the ladder. Gentle hands pressed against Vayriel's shoulders, and she saw her mother's parents at the start of a chain. Highblood after Highblood linked their bodies, hands to shoulders, like a vine that wove out from her and beyond her vision. The weight of what was being asked of her sat on her chest as if Orgar had rolled on top of her. Yet, pride spread its wings within her, ready to soar above the treetops.

Light-weavers climbed the tower, taking a position on each of the tiers, and began moving their staffs to paint the air around them as if turning the life force into tangible brush strokes that formed temporary pictures. The crowd began to disconnect from each other as the Path-Shaper stopped in front of Vayriel.

"I hope you participate in the festivities before you begin your journey. The other two realms have likely already set out, but it will take them longer to reach their destination. Also, you will be expected to demonstrate your abilities at the opening ceremony. Which you choose to display is up to you."

"I understand. Thank you, Path-Shaper."

The woman bowed her dark head to Vayriel.

"But…I do not fully understand. Why was I chosen and not another?"

A knowing gleam flashed in her oblique eyes. "Among other things, your skillfulness in growing plants nearly matches our elders. You and Orgar were important in saving the alusarean herd two months prior from that trägen. And while it seems natural to you that you've been bonded with Orgar since you were a very small young-one, you must also notice how few Highblood have been chosen by a jeroti to be life-friends. The Mother-of-All honors you with her gifts."

Vayriel averted her gaze, and the Path-Shaper moved off.

"The elders agreed in your selection," Mo'mo added, "though for fairness I did not participate. Use this journey to expand those gifts." Mo'mo rotated Vayriel to face her. A smile spread across her face, making her narrow eyes cheerful slits. "We are so proud of you Vayriel."

Returning her expression, Vayriel wrapped her arms around her mo'mo and mo'fa, bringing them into a huddled embrace. Mo'fa placed a hand on Vayriel's head and spoke a prayer to the Watcher to protect their daughter's daughter on her journey, while Mo'mo called on the Mother-of-All to guide her feet.

They pulled apart and Mo'fa gestured for them to walk through the gathering area. A group of Highbloods dressed as talon-wings danced across their paths, their arms adorned with the approximation of feathers and wearing masks with tufted ears and short beaks.

Vayriel looked to the side where Mo'fa walked. "Did you have the vision?"

Mo'fa silenced her with a gesture that said *not here*. The four of them weaved their way to a smaller, side fire where a table, almost like a merchant stall from Beechmarsh, stood with steaming meats. Vayriel silently thanked the creature-sons and -daughters for their giving.

"A Sending is a great event," Mo'fa said as if sensing Vayriel's reservations and took a stick with what looked like smoked fish. "And it does not happen often. In preparation, all of the coil were asked to bring something to share with you. Some had recently hunted for new clothing and…" He gestured to the Highbloods roasting food around the fire.

Vayriel nodded once. "Waste not."

"They had a few hours to prepare before the Path-Shaper went to retrieve you," added Mo'mo. "Partake in what you want. There are no expectations of you."

Eyeing the available selection, Vayriel took a stick for herself and five others for Orgar. Seeing an empty log nearby, she sat down and tossed strips to Orgar's snapping jaws. Her mother's parents sat on either side of her. More instruments had joined the music, and voices had begun to sing. Families danced hand-in-hand around the central fire.

"And yes," Mo'fa tilted his head closer, "I saw the vision. But I do not have more to share. Not that I do not want to, I just did not see anything else."

"I understand why we must partake in these Trials." Vayriel paused, eyes fixed on a distant bird winging its way across the twilight sky. "I know that the Mother guides my steps, but this task seems immense. I hope I am enough."

"You will be," Mo'mo said, squeezing her shoulders. "Trust in the Mother's path for you."

Mo'fa placed a wooden box with a jeroti engraved in its lid into Vayriel's hands. "Here, we have gifts to aid your journey."

Vayriel licked her fingers before opening the carved top, finding dried meat inside.

"Snacks," he said with a grin, "in case you get hungry and forget how to find food."

She laughed as Mo'mo passed her a small bag made of alusarean skin.

"For your herbs, to protect them from moisture."

Vayriel's heart felt like it would overflow. The entire coil was here to celebrate her Sending, and her mo'mo and mo'fa were presenting her parting gifts. Suddenly everything seemed too real. A tear formed in the downward corner of her eye. Orgar nuzzled up into Vayriel's armpit. Her long sleeves protected her from being tickled by his soft fur.

"I will miss you," she whispered.

"We will see each other on the path soon," Mo'mo said wrapping a curl of Vayriel's peach hair around her finger.

"Besides, you will have Orgar," Mo'fa added, winking. "The two of you spend most of your time alone together. It will not be much different if your path is here or there."

Mo'mo gave Mo'fa a side glance. "Perhaps she spends too much time alone. She does not see a potential life-mate when he stands right in front of her."

Vayriel sighed. This was not the first time she had heard such a speech. Mo'mo raised her chin in the direction of the dancers. A Watcher—Bealorin, Vayriel thought was his name—looked at her from where he stood near the larger fire. He waved in greeting, a small motion before turning his back to her. They'd said a handful of words to one another during their Watcher duties.

"I am happy with Orgar," Vayriel stated.

"Yes, but there are other relationships worth pursuing. Distance can make the bond stronger, as your father and mother learned. Perhaps when you return you will find yourself drawn to one of these."

Looking at her jeroti companion, Vayriel stopped herself from shaking her head. How could she explain that she knew the rocks of the river better than she knew most around her age? She knew when it was better to stay quiet.

Eventually, Mo'mo and Mo'fa left her to explore the Sending on her own. Before they left, they presented her with the shape of a paw, glazed and smooth, made from pieces of stones and shells of many colors. It had a white spiral accenting the pad shape, reminiscent of the shape of Highblood coils. A token, they said, given to all Highbloods who participate in the Trials, to prove she was their representative when she reached Waverling, or any time her validity needed to be proven.

The Daughter's position in the sky had moved beyond the halfway point. They placed kisses on each of her eyelids and she to theirs before they retired to their dwelling. Orgar left her briefly to return to the forest for jeroti self-care. Vayriel wandered, watching the dancers whose garments were a range of creature-sons and -daughters of the mountain. She stopped to listen to a Daughter's Eye tell the story of how Highbloods came to be to a group of young-ones. Despite her reservations, she took part in a giant rope tugging contest, her side victoriously pulling the other to the ground.

She sampled cooked fruit and fruit dried into tangy chips, roasted vegetables glazed in sticky nectar, and bread dipped in spicy herbs until she could eat no more. The sounds of laughter drew her to the edge of the heart of the coil. A small group of Highbloods not much younger than Vayriel watched one of the elders accelerate a vandling's progress from worm to its final winged form, flitting out of his hands in search of a flower.

Then the fire twirlers appeared. Orgar had rejoined her, and together they watched the long lengths of rope swing around the performers arms and necks, her jeroti companion whining in sympathy as the flames seemed to dance over their bodies.

The Daughter began to set on the horizon and as each Highblood tired, they returned to their home; first, the parents tugging young-ones by the hand. What would her parents think of her? She hoped they would be proud. She found she was grasping her upper arm where the three circles of her mother's armband fit snugly against her skin, and she relaxed to stroke Orgar's fur.

The pair decided to slip away from the now much thinner crowd. Vayriel crawled under the fur on her sleeping mat, her back against Orgar's prone form, and attempted to rest in her family's dwelling. But her mind kept wandering to the tasks before her and the Highblood prophecy. Of light vanquishing darkness. Nerves gripped her muscles until she quietly slipped out with Orgar, spear in hand, and headed back where the clearing merged with the forest and, eventually, the downward slope of the mountain.

Before stepping into the trees, Vayriel took one last look at the coil and the smoke trails in the sky.

"I am glad that you will be with me, my friend," she whispered to Orgar. "The Path-Shaper and the elders believe in me, or they would not have chosen me. I will not fail. Come, Orgar. Lingering will only make it harder. To Beechmarsh."

CHAPTER 6

"Excuse me!" The prop master bustled past Kilahym, a large log cradled in her arms that bumped him in the back as he peered out from the wings of the stage.

"Quite alright." Kilahym pulled his head back behind the curtain. He imagined himself blending with the darkness in his black tunic and pants.

Only a few students sat in the chairs of the practice theater in the Bard Academy. Not unexpected, given that most had headed to the student quarters at moonset. *The name really should be changed*, thought Kilahym. The Bard Academy of Waverling had evolved since its founding, producing actors, like the ones bustling around him now, and other specialties, such as troubadours, who focused on love, like his friend Ansgar. *What was that rogue up to these days?* Kilahym had lost count of how many small towns he'd visited since their last outing.

The director called from the back of the room, "Opening scene, go!"

Or was it technically the front, since it was the entrance? Kilahym shook his head and fixed his eyes on the curtain.

It opened with the clinking of metal from above, and three actors entered, the ends of their gray cloaks rustling on the deep brown wood of the stage.

As the women meandered across the boards, mimicking travel, the narrator's disembodied voice boomed from off stage. Kilahym thought he would make a fine baritone were he to switch his Academy concentration.

"Before our great city of Waverling was built, so it was that three pious women came upon Laphrim, the Grey Lady Herself, upon a hill."

A lantern ignited, illuminating a section of a thin white curtain further back on the stage. It gave the woman standing behind it the appearance of being shrouded in fog. The ethereal atmosphere was furthered by her being obscured by a gray cloak.

"There were those who doubted her existence," continued the narrator, "but the followers of Laphrim had never disbelieved. Their faithfulness was rewarded that day. But as quickly as she appeared, she vanished from their sight."

The lantern extinguished, dissolving the curtain from perception. The three women hurried to the place where the light had been. One got too close and bumped her hood against the fabric. Kilahym reached out a hand, as if he could help from where he stood in the wings, but the woman took a small step back. He nodded—it was a good save, unlikely to be seen from the audience.

"From that day they called themselves her Spectres, for the Grey Lady moves unseen across Heathström. And, like Her, they would spirit themselves where they were needed without drawing notice. The women saw Her footprints in the soft hillside, and commanded the power She grants Her faithful—"

Multiple lanterns flashed as someone shook a sheet of metal that rumbled.

"—they preserved Her footprints in stone. This would be the future home of Waverling's Shrine of Laphrim."

The women shuffled off stage opposite Kilahym, and the curtain closed, scraping against the rod. He moved toward the crease that opened to the audience.

"Well, what did you think?"

Kilahym rounded to the director's voice. *How long had he been standing there?* "Er, well, Kyran, not bad. Not bad at all." He motioned with both hands above his head. "Certainly an enthusiastic use of theatrics."

The shorter man's eyebrows raised. "But?"

"Well…" Kilahym scratched the sculpted hair around his mouth. "While visually interesting, it sounded like a volume of history from the archives at Axiom."

"Ouch."

"The whole scene depends on the delivery of the prose by narration. Your reader has a fine voice—would he be interested in performing a duet?"

Kyran's eyebrows furrowed.

"No? Anywho, a play depends on the interactions between the actors and the interaction they have with the audience. Our job, as Academy graduates, is to entertain the people as well as pass on historical accounts, though oft embellished. I dare say that the entertainment piece holds the greatest weight.

Otherwise, they'd just read a tome. Your narrator just read the first page to them."

Crossing his arms, Kyran's mouth opened.

Raising a finger, Kilahym spoke again. "I think you've got a solid start here on your composition, especially with the visuals. They'll certainly bestow a degree on you, and you'll have nary a problem leading your own troupe. But for a selection to perform on the Day of Laphrim, the holiest celebration of the Order of Spectres, well, you'll have to get a bit more creative. You've got several lunations." Kilahym slapped Kyran's shoulder with his palm. "You can do it."

The man sighed. "Any suggestions?"

Kilahym's eyes shifted as he thought, and his stomach growled, reminding him he hadn't eaten since breakfast. "Try to make the Spectres less…boring. Alright, see you around."

As Kilahym retreated backstage, the entrance doors clanked. Murmurs from the small audience susurrated like the wind on the other side of the curtain. Curiosity got the better of him, and Kalihym stuck his head out of the folds of fabric at the side of the stage. Two figures, their faces obscured in the wide hoods of their gray cloaks, glided down the main aisle. Kyran had already moved to center stage and pushed his way through the curtain's gap.

"Can I help you, Spectres?"

The one on the right spoke. "Is the bard Kilahym here?"

"Er, umm, yes, here. Right here," Kilahym babbled, pushing through the curtain. "I didn't really mean boring boring." He laughed, a hand straying to the ocarina hanging from his neck, as if his music could shield him.

The woman responded in a voice as icy as the peaks of the Agermath Range. "The Magister wishes to see you."

"Oh! Well. Why?"

"You'll find out when you get there. Your audiences may wait for you, but we will not." The Spectres withdrew toward the entrance.

Kilahym turned to Kyran, splaying his hands. "Uh, sorry but…"

"The Magister awaits," finished Kyran.

Nodding, Kilahym jumped from the stage and began to follow the Spectres.

"What's it like," Kyran called after him, "being an accredited bard?"

Kilahym thought of the last year, his dulcimer and pack his sole companions as he meandered across the meadows and valleys of Heathström, and spun around, a wide grin spreading across his face as he walked backwards. "Complimentary food and lodging anywhere I go, freedom to compose anything my heart desires, and an audience I can enchant with strings and wind? It's everything I ever wanted."

He debated admitting that his performances were mostly the same five songs everywhere he went when the backs of his legs hit something hard and he toppled backward into a seat. Apparently he'd been walking crooked. Kilahym unfolded himself from the chair, stood up and straightened his tunic. He tucked the green ocarina back under his shirt, tightening the strings of fabric at his sternum, and retied his light-brown hair into a short bundle at the base of his neck.

"Right," he muttered, jogging to close the gap between him and his escort.

As the Spectres pushed the doors of the theater open, one of them whispered something his mother would say, "If he's capable of anything but poetry, I'm a jeroti pup."

Kilahym and the Spectres left the wood and stone of the Bard Academy behind them. He looked over his shoulder and admired its multiple levels with decorative windows, pointed arches, and curved supports along the structure, which, though stunning, paled in comparison with the building he walked toward. Kilahym wracked his brain for what misstep he could have possibly taken to bring the attention of the religious order to his activities or what tenet of the Order of Laphrim he'd crossed. He was just a bard. Granted, he hadn't entered a Shrine of Laphrim in lunations, but how could they even know that?

Kilahym adjusted the pack on his back and swallowed a metaphorical egg as he looked down the avenue that led east from the Academy to the Shrine of Laphrim. The sanctuary never ceased to amaze him. He latched on to the mental diversion it offered. It was ever-changing from the Spectres' sculpting like a vandling still with antennae and filum spines on its soft length that had yet to metamorphose into its beautiful, winged adult form. Kilahym doubted the Spectres would ever find the perfection they were seeking. However, the mental image of a larval vandling gave him an idea for a new shape for an ocarina.

The two Spectres escorting him were the worst companions for conversation with their stiff silence. When he attempted to ask questions, they simply advised him to wait until they reached the Magisterium. To calm his nerves at being summoned by the governing body of Heathström, Kilahym focused on the structure of the Shrine as more became visible, trying to convert the images into a song.

He failed to find more than an ominous chord reverberating through his soul at the sight of the towers that rose higher than any other building in Waverling. *Spikes and spears, ripping through the fabric of the world with righteous vengeance.* He suppressed a shudder. The meeting wouldn't be that bad, would it? But he could hear his mother's shrill voice as if she walked beside him.

"Serves you right for leaving us," she'd say, hands on hips. *"Leave it to you to mess up so bad the whole religious order is after you. Don't look to me for sympathy. You got yourself in this disaster. Can't even remember what you did. Disgraceful."*

Kilahym took a steading breath. He hadn't seen his parents for many synodies, yet his mother continued to poke her head where it didn't belong. He tried to focus on the present.

They passed gondolas navigating the city's canals on either side of the street as they walked to the crystalline tower. It housed the religious leaders and served as the largest shrine for the followers of Laphrim. Long ago, the Magisterium had intertwined with the Order of Laphrim, and they mixed with the Grey Lady's blessed servants, the Spectres, until they became one liquid. Religion and government in one. The Magister led them both.

Sweat gathered in places where sweat had no business being, and Kilahym swallowed hard again as they approached the entrance. The front resembled vertically arrayed flower petals, concave layered ovals in groups of three. Each section rose wider and taller than the one before it. The protean construct reigned over the canal that encircled it. Gondolas bobbed in the waters before the Shrine, dispensing the Grey Lady's worshipers into the building's main entrance.

A male page held the ornate door open for him and his Spectre guides, and Kilahym walked through the filigree depictions of the Grey Lady blessing Her followers with light and into the Shrine.

"This way." One of the Spectres motioned to the right, stopping Kilahym before he walked into the central part of the Shrine.

The trio entered a small door obscured behind a beam. On either side of him, the Spectres simultaneously weaved their hands in front of themselves as if they were turning a wheel. The floor jolted beneath his boots, and he experienced momentary weightlessness. He looked out of the corner of his eyes at one Spectre and then the other and decided to hold as still as possible. A few moments passed before another jolt vibrated the floor, and the Spectres opened the door again.

Kilahym's jaw dropped. Before him was a wide rotunda. The dome above flaunted symmetrical patterns of color dancing on the surface. Where walls should have been, there were translucent crystal panes. He could see the three great concentric rings of the canal below, the hub of the wheel-shaped city. A smile spread across his face as his heartbeat drummed a song of elation against his chest. They were at the top of one of the spires.

"How did we get up here so quickly?" he asked.

One of the Specters rotated, only her mouth and nose visible beneath her hood. "Only with the Spectres' magic, by the grace of the Grey Lady, can anyone use that lifting chamber. Once here, the rooms of the Magisterium and Spectres can be accessed through the stairs over there." She paused, pointing to the left. "Do not attempt to use the lifting chamber without a Spectre's magic. We have locked it in place, but tampering with the mechanisms could have…unfortunate consequences."

Kilahym gulped. "Noted. So, I'll just be off down the stairs then?"

Receiving only a nod, Kilahym started down the stairs. He reached a small landing and the single door within was labeled with a glimmering plaque.

"The Magisterium Oratory," he read aloud. "Well, that sounds official. Guess I'll give it a try."

His heart accelerating its tempo, he pushed the door. It opened into a room with panes like the one he had just left. A polished mosaic floor boasted a design of three interlacing circles that mimicked the patterns of flower petals, like the Shrine's exterior, while tiles flowed around the main design. In an arc around the room stood a handful of Spectres, the familiar gray cloaks dropping hoods like beaks over their eyes. They stood unmoving behind a woman in the center of the room clothed in an off-white robe.

The Magister swiveled to face him. He recognized her from her dress, which he had seen before from a distance. A large collar arched behind her head—a toothless maw opened to the widest point before it clamped down on its meal.

"Ah, Kilahym, at last. Do come in. You no doubt know why you have been summoned here." Her deep voice held as little expression as her face.

Kilahym wrung his hands. He most certainly did not. His mind raced as he searched for what he had done to incur the religious and government leaders' reprimand.

There was that time he played the wrong Hymn of the Fallen for a funeral, and coincidentally the candles nearest him fell over and blackened the pew seat before someone doused the flame. But that was almost a synody ago, and the candles were not his fault. The song on dulcimer, unfortunately, was meant more for a tavern gambol than a somber affair.

"We have had others watch your performances for some time," she continued. "However, we had to see for ourselves."

He opened his mouth then closed it again as another memory surged. Surely she wasn't referring to the last Day of Laphrim celebration in his hometown. The ratufas knocked over the carts of fruit in the middle of his ocarina solo for the Laphrim play, scattering pineberries. It wasn't his fault the principal Spectre in attendance had slipped on them.

Kilahym fiddled with the triangular stone of shadowed verdant around his neck. The polished surface of the ocarina and six holes beneath his fingers were like a breeze across his worries.

"In addition, the song you composed has gained our interest. Many tales have been told, many songs sung, of the Grey Lady and the Order of Laphrim. However, the ballads fail to capture the Spectres' devotion and service to the religion and Her followers. If it is satisfactory to those here, we will add it to the official approved canticles. Play it for us."

"Play it?" His chest constricted. "Oh, uh, of course."

Fumbling behind his back, he withdrew his dulcimer from his bag and began the song. His voice cracked with tension when he tried for the first high note in a verse. Then the familiar embrace of the music captured him, and he surrendered to it. Motes of light sparkled in the chamber's air in varying size and color. The Spectres gasped. The twinkling array persisted while Kilahym finished his song, then slowly faded with the last notes.

The Magister leaned forward, a toothless smile upon her face. "So the rumors are true. A male with magical talent."

"That he cannot control," another Spectre put in.

The leader of Heathström waved away this concern. "It is enough that he has it at all. Sending him to the Trials will silence our critics." The Magister's eyes gleamed. "Congratulations, Kilahym. You are the second Truthseeker to represent our realm."

Kilahym looked around the room. Awash in a sea of robes with no eyes to lock onto, he focused on the Magister but a Spectre to his side spoke, "You'll stay here in the pillars. We won't have time for a full Spectre's initiation but enough so that you'll know how to behave as a Truthseeker representing us."

Kilahym mouthed the words "Spectre's initiation."

"When the Trials are completed, we can discuss the possibility of adding you to the Order," the Magister added.

"Did you say magic?" He scratched the back of his head, jumping with the scratch of his dulcimer's wood.

He quickly put it back in his bag.

"You haven't noticed things happening around you that are odd?" one of the other Spectres asked. "Just now. With the lights."

He thought about the candles and the pineberry. "Now that you mention it…perhaps a few coincidences have seemed oddly tied to me. But I thought people like me, I mean men, were not given the blessing."

"They aren't," the first Spectre ground out.

"How did you do it?" yet another interjected. "Is your instrument laced with crystal?"

"Uh, no, just stone and wood. I mean the ocarina is stone, the dulcimer is wood. Separately. Not together."

The Magister drew near, placing her hands on Kilahym's shoulders. "This is an extraordinary gift you've been given, Kilahym. We will learn how you are able to use the Grey Lady's blessings without our tutelage." She pivoted Kilahym's body to face back toward the door.

His eyebrows raised; two more Spectres had entered the room.

"For now," the Magister nudged Kilahym toward the door, "settle into the room we have provided for you. In two days' time, your first Trial will begin. You must locate the other Heathström participant and come back here in time for the Etherea Assemblage celebration, where you will display your magical, musical talent. Preferably without destroying anything."

Kilahym's heart beat like the blur of pectully wings, unasked questions pressed between his lips.

"And Kilahym—" At the Magister's voice he rotated to face her. An object released from her hands soaring in an arc. He caught it, pressing the object between his palms. "We know who you are, but the other realms do not. You'll show them this token if your identity as our representative is ever questioned."

"Can't let someone else take my place!" Kilahym laughed, then cleared his throat when the room stayed silent. He inspected the object: a porous gray stone embossed with a pair of footprints—the symbol of the Grey Lady.

The Spectres by the door ushered him back up the staircase,

"You're a jeroti pup," whispered one of the robed figures while elbowing their colleague.

A grin spread across Kilahym's face and the beat of an unsung song lightened his steps. Magic and a Truthseeker. Ansgar would be extremely jealous.

CHAPTER 7

Black.
Still black.
A hint of a shape. An outline?
Black.

Kharnek opened his eyes and sighed.

"Everything all right?"

"Yes."

Kharnek avoided Zinvar's gaze. He would have to be more discreet about his attempts to penetrate the darkness that swirled in his mind.

"You seem troubled." The priest's green eyes displayed earnest concern.

"I am eager to leave this place," he admitted.

Kharnek rose from his cross-legged position and secured his sword and scabbard. Pale moonlight lined the edge of the cliff walls above him with silver. Even if it was the fastest way to the twilit realm of Heathström, Kharnek disliked traveling through the canyons and underground passages that riddled the surface of his homeland. Concealment meant confinement, and many dangers stalked the moonless dark of Morakh's Shadow. But his companion was not prepared for prolonged exposure to the cold on Komor's barren tundra. The Priesthood rarely ventured from their enclaves within Komor's cities, and Zinvar's lack of appropriate clothing showed it.

"We have Morakh's blessing," Zinvar said. "He will safeguard our travels, and we will complete this first Trial in His time." He wrapped his thin robe tighter around him. In the depths of the canyon, the chill penetrated to the bone.

"You misunderstand." Kharnek scanned the shadows around their camp, on the lookout for threats. "I fear nothing, but you would be wise to exercise caution."

"A bold statement, even for a Guardsman."

"It is the truth. You are trained to elicit knowledge from dusty tomes not defend against the perils of our world."

Zinvar picked up his staff, fiddling with the wooden length. "I can't argue with that. But, without fear, how do you stave off recklessness?"

"Fearlessness and recklessness are not the same."

"To fear is to be human," the priest countered, jabbing a rock at his feet with his staff and smiling when it caromed off another stone. Kharnek found the somewhat childish display rather endearing.

"A warrior must be both more and less than human," he tossed back.

"What does that mean?"

Kharnek sighed. How could he explain that? This was the most he had spoken to someone outside the Brotherhood in epicycles. But Zinvar seemed uncowed by Kharnek's brusqueness, which, the warrior grudgingly admitted to himself, was impressive. There was also an undeniable allure about him, created by the combination of his lean good looks and sharp intellect, and so he felt compelled to be forthcoming with the priest more often than not.

"More than human because he must master his thoughts and feelings to achieve clarity of purpose and to focus on his objective without the intrusion of emotions," Kharnek elaborated, "less because once in battle, his primal instincts keep him alive. He becomes something animal, acting on intuition and knowing without knowing where to place his feet next, where and when the next blow will arrive."

"That's a neat little paradox."

"It is balance."

Zinvar seemed to have no retort for that.

Kharnek settled himself on a nearby boulder. He felt the bite of the cool stone even through his thick leather pants.

"There is a simplicity to your point of view that is appealing. The Priesthood sometimes complicates things needlessly." Zinvar sounded distant.

"A bold statement…from one of its own."

Zinvar shrugged in response. "I've always been at odds with some of the Priesthood's ways. Apparently that's what got me here."

"The Mahiratha said you are an advocate for peace.."

"Not just peace," Zinvar corrected, "but change. I've spent epicycles trying to get the Priesthood to allow women into the Order and stop the persecution of religious minorities like the Arakhists."

Kharnek said nothing, but his estimation of the priest rose. It took courage to defy the Priesthood so openly.

"These communication devices change everything," the younger Komorese man continued, excitement in his voice. "Not only will we have access to the other realms, they will have a window into Komor. And that open window will cast light upon all the problems the Priesthood tries to avoid."

"You really think that those cubes are for that purpose?"

"I do."

The naiveté of Zinvar's response made Kharnek laugh out loud.

"What's so funny? You obviously seem to know something I don't."

A perceptive comment but the warrior did not rise to the bait. Instead, he drew from his own experience to respond. "I know that people who say they want peace and change beget more violence. It is the way of such things, just as rivers of lava carve their path of destruction to the sea. They do not ask for it, but they enact it even so."

An uncomfortable silence descended in the wake of his reply. The priest set his staff down and crossed his arms, apparently disinterested in further conversation.

"I'm going to check on the mounts," Kharnek said eventually. Zinvar ignored the statement and huddled deeper into his cloak, leaving the Guardsman feeling disappointed.

For what felt like the hundredth time, Kharnek wished his companion were a fellow warrior. He understood steel and the clash of man against man, but he despised the arcane practices of the Priests of Morakh. His hate grew each time a red-garbed acolyte shuffled by him in the streets of Zel Morakh, seeking donations for coffers already overflowing with wealth. Kharnek felt the phantom sting of the Mahir's whips from when he was a boy training to be a soldier on the Isle of Mora. And then they discovered his abilities. He went from just another trainee to the subject of twisted experiments. They forced him to kill, probing the limits of his alien strength with each subsequent tragedy. Kharnek became the weapon with which Komor would finally crush the rest of Etherea.

This priest, though, claimed to want something different. And though Kharnek hated to admit it, there was an air of innocence, a purity, about Zinvar, that made him believe. Its appeal was powerful, especially when the light flashed in the other man's dazzling green eyes as he spoke, words full of earnest intent.

Shaking his head to clear the distracting image, Kharnek stepped away from their temporary campsite. A short walk brought him around the boulder the site abutted and into view of their sleeping mounts. He approached with caution. It was unwise to startle a rift wyrm.

The warrior stopped a sword's length away, arms crossed over his form-fitting chest piece, and admired the pair. The wyrms were ten feet in length and five feet tall when they stood. The claws that tipped their four legs and their mouths full of fangs could rend flesh and armor in equal measure. Their large luminous violet eyes caught even the smallest motion in the darkness. Yet the wyrms' most distinctive characteristic was also their least noticeable: crystalline scales that reflected their surroundings so perfectly prey was known to walk straight into the creatures' mouths. These two had come from the depths of a volcanic rift near Zel Gorragkh; the northernmost city in Komor was renowned for breeding the finest mounts.

Only the best for Komor's representatives in the Trials of the Innermost, Kharnek thought. One of the wyrms hissed and shifted in its slumber. Its claws scratched a trio of thin gouges into the rock of the canyon floor.

Kharnek headed back toward the campsite. Zinvar was tolerable, for a priest, but his curiosity about Kharnek would become problematic if he probed too deeply into the warrior's motives for being in the Trials. Thankfully, they were only a cycle's journey from the boundary between Komor and Heathström. Then another few cycles from Waverling itself, where their next Trial would be revealed—after yet another ceremony. The thought made him groan.

The soft swish of displaced gravel was the only warning he had before a clawed, lupine gray form catapulted out of the darkness on his right. Finely honed reflexes kicked in. The warrior's sword flashed out of its scabbard to plunge into the chest of the leaping varg. He watched with satisfaction as the dull red light faded from its eyes.

Kharnek slid the obsidian blade out of its victim. The varg collapsed to the ground in a tangle of four lifeless limbs. He knew he had seconds at most before the rest of the pack descended on him—the beasts never traveled alone.

Kharnek thought briefly of Zinvar before the darkness inside him, fed by bloodlust, consumed him.

Time slowed to a crawl as Kharnek's heightened senses picked out the positions of the rest of the pack. The scarlet glow of their gazes betrayed them. He counted ten pairs of eyes, three of which were frozen in mid-leap toward him. A predatory smile crept across his face as he walked calmly between the suspended animals, his blade dispatching them with swift stabs to their hearts.

Too easy.

Kharnek slowed his pace to match that of the vargs. The three he killed dropped to the canyon floor with wet thumps. The rest of the pack circled him, their caution renewed by the loss of their brethren. Seven against one. The vargs still believed they held the advantage, and they tightened the circumference of their slow stalking.

Kharnek lowered his sword, glistening with blood, in a clear invitation for the creatures to attack. The pack sprang into motion. In response, the darkness within him welled up and out, stretching its lethal touch toward the animals. The hungry tendrils stole the life force from each varg they contacted. The vargs' lifeless husks collapsed to the ground. Kharnek shuddered as he fought to reign in his power. Strengthened by the life force that it stole, it threatened to sublimate his will entirely to its own.

The Whole. We will be whole!

Unleashing a primal roar, Kharnek focused the rampant force on the varg corpses. A wave of dark energy surged outward and consumed the bodies, leaving only ashes in its wake. Its strength spent, Kharnek finally succeeded in banishing the darkness to a distant corner of his mind just in time to see Zinvar race around the boulder that defined their campsite and skid to a surprised halt, surveying the carnage with awe and fear.

"Brother?"

Zinvar used a greeting borrowed from the City Guard in Zel Morakh. Kharnek gritted his teeth willing the priest to just leave him alone.

"Brother?" The other man repeated. He placed his hand on Kharnek's shoulder.

What happened next was driven by instinct and epicycles of anger. Kharnek found himself pressing Zinvar against the boulder, the lethal edge of the warrior's blade caressing his throat like a lover's breath. Zinvar gasped as he looked into Kharnek's eyes, which he knew had turned pitch-black.

"I am not your brother," Kharnek snarled.

The priest raised his hands in a gesture of submission. "Alright! I'm sorry, I just wanted to make sure you were safe."

Kharnek held him there a moment longer. Then, as his wrath subsided, a sense of guilt and shame replaced it. Kharnek withdrew his sword and released Zinvar, who staggered back warily. "No, I should be apologizing to you," the warrior mumbled, "You meant no harm. I just…I need to be alone."

Refusing to look the priest in the eye, Kharnek stalked away into the shadows.

CHAPTER 8

Gray suffused the blackness of Komor's eternal shadow ahead of Zinvar. Stars in their familiar patterns were washed out as he and Kharnek approached the western border of Heathström. The air had warmed from frigid to tolerable, prompting Zinvar to drop the hood on his heavy outer cloak.

The bleak landscape of a barren tundra greeted his emergence from the subterranean passage he and Kharnek had taken from the site of the varg ambush. For all their ferocity, vargs did not care for enclosed spaces. Neither did Zinvar. He had had several close calls with spiked stalactites in the caves, and sported a crimson scratch where one had scraped his forehead before he could redirect his rift wyrm.

"Mind the ceiling, priest," Kharnek had warned belatedly. Zinvar swore a sardonic grin had crossed the warrior's face before he turned away.

Kharnek's ambivalence toward the Priesthood had translated into several passive-aggressive jabs, which Zinvar ignored. He understood that his order's iron grip on Komorese society earned it as much enmity as reverence. Particularly from the Brotherhood, which outwardly paid homage to Morakh but resented the meddling of priests in its affairs.

"How much further?" Zinvar queried his companion.

Kharnek raised a gauntleted hand. "See that tower?"

Zinvar directed his gaze toward it. The tower stabbed into the lightening sky like an accusatory finger. He guessed it was about ten klicks away.

"That marks the eastern boundary of Komor. Once we reach it, another three cycles will bring us to Waverling."

"Thank Morakh. Riding these wyrms is murder on your legs," Zinvar quipped. The warrior remained silent. Zinvar rolled his eyes at his companion's steadfast composure. Beneath the stony exterior, some humanity must still exist.

"Have you ever been outside of Komor?" he ventured after a few moments.

"Yes." Kharnek's brief response was punctuated by a loud crunch as his wyrm snapped up a concealed tundrat. Zinvar shuddered at the speed with which the monster gulped down its impromptu meal. He had never liked tundrats, with their beady blue eyes and long yellow incisors, but that was a cruel fate even for vermin.

"Where did you go?"

"I am surprised you do not know. The only time a warrior goes outside of Komor is at the behest of the Priesthood."

"Acolytes are only told what they need to know. I only recently attained full priest status," Zinvar replied.

"I see. You must have done very well to have impressed the High Priest so quickly."

Zinvar straightened in the saddle. Kharnek appeared only an epicycle or two older, but the gulf between the warrior and the priest was composed of hundreds of epicycles' worth of political maneuvering and scheming. Who was Zinvar to think he could bridge the gap? Unexpected compliments like that gave him hope.

Hours wandered past in a dull fashion as he and Kharnek progressed toward Heathström. Clumps of malignant green scragweed poked out of the ground. The spiked plant was the only vegetation that could survive in the perpetual darkness of Komor's surface, but it lacked any nutritional value. Zinvar's mount avoided the weed, but snapped up tundrats startled by its passage. After witnessing several gruesome devourings, he consciously guided the wyrm away from the rodents. The wyrm hissed each time Zinvar tugged it away from its prey. He hoped its patience would last until he could rid himself of the fearsome creature.

"Why we decided to use these Everburned monsters as mounts, I'll never understand," Zinvar complained. "My arms are tired just from trying to keep it from jumping down a hole."

Kharnek's gaze remained fixed ahead. "We will rest when we reach the tower. It is only a few hours away."

Looking toward the horizon, Zinvar saw that the tower's shape had resolved from a vague outline into a crenellated spire. A memory stirred queasily in his mind at the sight of the crumbled battlements.

"That tower—" he began.

"It is the Tower of Nerekesh."

Zinvar suppressed a shudder. He remembered the older acolytes telling ghost stories in the dormitories on Mora. The legend of Nerekesh stood prominent among them.

"There are tales of that tower—exaggerated, I'm certain, but nonetheless unsettling. Is it the only shelter we can take?"

Kharnek twisted around and smirked. "What is the matter, priest? Afraid of the dark?"

"Is there reason to be?" Zinvar countered.

"It was the site of a tragedy. Nothing more or less."

"So you know what actually took place there?"

Kharnek turned away and did not respond. His silence stretched to an uncomfortable interval. Words bubbled in Zinvar's mind, but his warrior companion answered before he could speak.

"Not firsthand. It is not a tale that the Brotherhood is fond of repeating."

"Why is that?"

"It is an uncomfortable reminder that in battle, every soldier balances on a knife's edge between bloodlust and madness. Those who succumb to madness…it is unfortunate."

Kharnek fell silent. Zinvar waited a moment and then decided to press his luck. It was rare for the warrior to be so forthcoming.

"Have you been there before?"

"No," Kharnek replied, quick as a whip crack.

"I see. Then what did happen there?"

"Tell me what you know, priest, and I will tell you if what you have heard is a fanciful fabrication, as I suspect it is."

"What I was told is that Nerekesh, then the Captain of the Border Guard, was at the tower with a complement of soldiers under his command. They were attacked by raiders from Sondrine, who came in overwhelming numbers. Nerekesh prayed to Morakh for deliverance, and his prayer was heard. Morakh granted him strength beyond mortal men, and he slew all the invaders."

Kharnek snorted at that, but Zinvar continued undeterred.

"It was a mighty victory, and because of it Nerekesh became arrogant. He claimed that it was his own prowess that wrought the defeat of the Sondrinel. Our dread lord would not suffer this slight to his power and struck Nerekesh with a deadly madness. The captain murdered all his men before taking his own life. To this cycle, Morakh's curse lingers in the tower, which is why it remains abandoned. Or so I have heard," Zinvar appended.

"As is the case with many legends, what you have heard is a half-truth."

Kharnek jerked the reins of his wyrm, which had drifted uncomfortably close to the edge of a deep crack in the tundra's surface. Zinvar felt relieved that the creatures' noncompliance was not solely his problem.

"Nerekesh did indeed kill all the men under his command in the tower and himself," Kharnek continued, "but there were no invaders and no divine intervention. The reason for Nerekesh's descent into madness remains unknown."

"Then why does the tower remain abandoned?"

"After the slaughter at the tower, the Border Guard continued to use it, but there were many unexplained…incidents. Men were found dead with no visible cause; others claimed to see fallen comrades walk during Morakh's Shadow. Even the most battle-hardened began to draw their blades at the sound of whispers in the dark. The effectiveness of the guard was so diminished by these events that the decision was made to withdraw from the tower. Ever since, the garrison at Zel Gorragkh has kept watch over the eastern border."

Zinvar shuddered. "And you want us to take shelter there until moonrise?"

"Legends are just that, priest."

"My name is Zinvar, you know."

"It is not for me, a lowly warrior, to address a servant of Morakh so informally." Kharnek's voice dripped with sarcasm.

"You must be much more than that to be chosen as a Truthseeker."

"I am a soldier, here to keep you alive. That is all…Zinvar."

A thrill of joy arose in his chest when Kharnek used his name. Zinvar knew there was more to the man than he was letting on but decided to let the matter be.

"We will reach the tower before shadowfall," Kharnek went on. "Until then, it is best that we remain silent. The borderlands harbor rogues and, as you have seen, the occasional varg pack."

Instead of responding, Zinvar dug his feet into the sides of his mount. The wyrm increased its pace with a hiss. Overhead, the moon's gleam faded into the gray that signaled Heathström's growing proximity.

CHAPTER 9

"'Dril!'" Her father's voice boomed cheerfully as she strolled into the living area. The familiar brightly colored pillows strewn across the stone furniture strengthened Idrilia like the house's own support stones. The past few days had felt like a desert whirlwind: her basic education completed with her Pedium graduation and the surprise announcement that she was a Truthseeker, followed by the final curriculum rites. Her entire life was on the verge of change. It was nice to see something that remained.

Cern's muscled frame climbed the three steps out of the oratum, their home's sunken square sitting area. He spread his arms wide, encompassing his daughter in a tight hug. She melted into his comforting strength as her othwit winged from her shoulder, perching on the stone banister of the house's upper level, and preened her tawny chest. The scent of parchment clung to the long sleeves of the tunic under Cern's fighting robe, which meant he had spent another day poring over maps and battle plans with his fellow vilicus of the Sentinels. His rank, second from the top, gave him leadership over several corps of novi guarding the gates of Axiom and escorting merchant caravans; Idrilia wondered if his latest consult was related to what had kept him from attending her graduation.

"Your gift finally arrived from Ettrascus." He clasped her shoulders as if reading her. "Storms off the coast made the shipment cross the whole length of Sondrine by caravan instead. But just in time after all."

From his hip bag he removed a rectangle on a cord. "I hope it helps you stay in sync with our Star of Axiom, even when your journey takes you to the far places of Etherea."

"A Komor timepiece?" Raising an eyebrow, Idrilia took the object.

Her father held up a warding hand. "The simplicity of their design makes them more practical than our crystal-driven orreries."

Idrilia wanted to protest. Using technology from people who continued to ignore the Waverling Accords seemed senseless. But many in Axiom, including the Sentinels, used them. Idrilia suppressed her urge to make a disgusted face. Having just returned, she did not want to start an argument with her father. She never knew how those would end. Instead, she studied the timepiece; the phases of the moon along the bottom moved to align with a mark indicating the real position of the moon in the sky.

"'Drilia!" The voice of her youngest sister, Felune, broke joyfully into Idrilia's thoughts from the next room, and the rest of her quickly followed.

At seven sidereals of age, Felune reached nearly to Idrilia's shoulder. She had Idrilia's aquiline nose, the same nose as their father, and the same cerulean tint of eyes and hair. Everyone thought she would grow to be as tall as her sister.

Felune folded her arms around Idrilia's waist, face pressing into her hip bags, hugging her as best as her short arms could. "I missed you, sis."

"I missed you, too, Fey." Idrilia dropped one arm to stroke her sister's back through her waist-length blue curls. As her father stepped away, Idrilia saw a figure leaning against the cream wall where the arched opening led to other rooms.

"Say hello to your sister, Lu," their father prompted.

Idrilia wrinkled her nose at her other sister's scowl. When Aluan remained motionless, Idrilia stuck out her tongue and crossed her eyes.

"Fine," Aluan laughed, pushing away from the wall and uncrossing her arms, "but I'm still mad at you for not telling me yourself." She flipped her darker blue hair behind her left shoulder as she approached.

"Come on, Lu," Idrilia said, tightening her hair tie high on her head. "It's not my fault you skipped my graduation." She tried not to let bitterness creep into her voice. It was their parents who chose not to come, and Lu would have needed to follow their instructions. "And then we all left for the east desert. It's a little hard to send word to my sister during training exercises for the final rites."

Idrilia embraced Aluan, the middle sister, whose height only came to her nose. Technically if she hadn't gone exploring she could have seen Lu…but that didn't cross her mind before leading her two best friends through forgotten tunnels.

"You could have found a way. You always find a way. Being a Truthseeker is *the* news to eclipse all news."

Idrilia mentally winced. Normally Idrilia's decisiveness served her well, but she hadn't considered how her sister would feel. Idrilia moved to poke the ticklish spot near her sister's ribs, but Aluan was too fast, twisting her arm to block her.

"Nice try," she grinned, stepping away.

"Ooh, been training, have you?"

"Only enough to pass the Pedium finals. I can't wait to make my guild choice."

"That's, what, seven sidereals away still?"

Aluan shrugged.

"Still not thinking Sentinel?"

"Nope."

Idrilia dropped her voice. "Dad won't be happy about that."

"Protecting Sondrine is our duty and honor," they both whispered, heads close, laughing.

"Just…don't have any regrets, Lu," Idrilia added, her tone serious as she tugged on the small rings on the edge of her right ear. Priorium had been her goal for so long. Now that she was so close to attaining it, had she made the right choice?

"Come here, come here!" Felune tugged on Idrilia's hand. "I want to show you something."

Smiling, Idrilia followed her youngest sibling into the next room.

Like the rest of the house, it was carved out of and into the canyon stone of Axiom. The shelving on the walls that displayed her mother's scented oil collection; the reading alcove by the quarter round window, overlooking the crystal garden plaza—they were all part of the house itself.

Felune led her to a stone table, the surface polished and the pattern a swirl of black and amethyst. On the table, where they ate so many meals together, sat a small bird cage.

"Look what I got."

Idrilia looked at the wide yellow eyes gazing from the small gray and brown ball of puff, its wings so tightly tucked it gave the impression that it was just a ball with a beak and eyes placed in jest.

"Is that an othwit?" Idrilia asked, as if she didn't know exactly what those downy soft feathers would feel like.

"Mmhmm. Mum said I could get one, just like you. But it's just a baby."

"Then you'll be able to train him right."

"It's a her. Her name is Lessa."

"Oh, my apologies, Lessa. Well, there's no sense in getting an othwit someone else has trained." Idrilia winked at her sister.

"I know! I can train her like you did Wen."

"I think Wen would like to see Lessa, don't you?" Idrilia whistled three short bursts, much to Felune's delight.

Aluan ducked in time to allow the tawny bird to pass through the archway. "You and that bird," she grumbled, smiling and shaking her head as she joined her sisters.

Wen settled onto Idrilia's outstretched arm, talons gripping gently as she had been trained. Her head twisted in small jerks as she studied the smaller creature in the cage. One day the othwitling's ears would be as long as Wen's, and her tail feathers would cascade like ribbons rather than the short fuzz she had now.

Felune clapped her hands. "I think she likes Lessa!"

"I think she does too." The new voice came from behind them, soft and gentle, preceded by the fragrance of redbark like the timber used to build the ships of Ettra.

"Mother! Where were you hiding?" With one arm holding Wen away, Idrilia greeted Eranth with half an embrace, breathing in her mother's favorite scent, an oil from the Ettrascan market her mother said conjured visions of a pure, flowing stream. The only *stream* Idrilia had been to was where the dry Leske river met the southern ocean, and the water seeped back inland, creating the delta there. But she thought that place reeked of rotting solendrake eggs. No, to Idrilia, Eranth smelled like wood on a boat wet from the sea as it traveled between the southern islands, with just a hint of sweet pastries.

"I was so glad to hear you made it to the islands. Your father's recent patrol showed signs of Sunscorned activity. And not even a day's ride from your final rites."

"Mother…" Idrilia caught herself before she rolled her eyes. "The entire graduation class was there with the instructors. Besides, you know I can take care of myself."

"I do, dear. But as your mother, I will always worry." She patted the side of Idrilia's face then adjusted the front wrap of her daughter's fighting robes and tugged on the cinched belt, even though Idrilia knew the gradient blue fabric from neck to knee was already in place. "I want to hear about your final days in Pedium, but visit with your sisters first. The others should be here soon. It is almost midluminance, and I know this little one will want all the time she can get."

Eranth smiled at her daughters, but Idrilia frowned.

"What others?" When her mother had promised a celebration for her graduation, she hadn't mentioned it being a larger gathering.

"Your grandparents. And Kalis's family, of course."

Idrilia nodded as her mother left the room. It wasn't unusual to have the Vaktares over for dinner. The families had been close for many sidereals. And now she and Kalis were charged with representing Sondrine in the peace-fostering Trials of the Innermost. Might as well celebrate both events at once.

"What will Heathstorm be like?" Felune interrupted Idrilia's contemplation.

"Heath*ström*, silly." Aluan elbowed their younger sister.

"How will you get there?" Felune continued, unfazed. Before Idrilia could mount a reply, her sister peppered her with more questions. "Do you know who your companions will be? What if you have to sleep next to a snoring Komorese?"

"I'll wake him with a bath…of raining pebbles!" Idrilia replied, pretending to launch a crystal and mimicking a boulder exploding, complete with exaggerated sound effects.

Aluan laughed and Felune shrieked with joy. Releasing compressed energy in a violent fashion had the most satisfying outcomes.

The three sisters retreated to their sleeping quarters. Reclining on a layer of pillows on the floor, careful not to get her dusty boots all over the fabric, Idrilia summarized the events following her graduation. Like all other classes before her, the graduates progressed north along the Leske Road. The dry riverbed now served as a means for passage throughout Sondrine. They traveled east for the final curriculum rites before being transported to the Ettrascan Islands.

"It's like a final lesson," Idrilia explained. "To make sure we all know basic survival, even though we aren't all going into Sentinel training."

"'Passing on tradition,'" Felune quoted slowly.

"That's right. Look at you, memorizing your edicts!" Idrilia tapped her on the nose.

"So what did everyone do?"

"Your big sister got to lead several training drills in hand-to-hand combat." She dusted imaginary sand from her hands.

"Dril drills!" Fey laughed.

"Clever." Idrilia winked at Fey, then smacked her other sister's knee. "Aluan, you should have seen the apprentices to the Enumeration Guild. They were so busy calculating the angles of every move in their head that they spent most of their time in the dust. Anyway, then we made our way to the eastern coast and boarded a boat for the smallest island."

"That's the southernmost island of the archipelago, right?" Aluan asked.

"Yep. And it has thick jungle undergrowth, and the air is so heavy it feels like you're breathing water. No wonder no one lives there. But, in the end, everyone had a great time celebrating on the beach. They brought in this amazing triple-tiered trägenberry cake from the market in Ettrascus. So sweet and tangy."

"Yummy!" Fey clapped her hands.

"Sounds delicious!" Aluan said. "Did Klaara enjoy it?"

"The cake? She thought her father made better of course. Thankfully the baker was not present."

Her sister laughed. "No, I mean the island. Did you two go swimming?"

"She did," Idrilia paused, thinking of Klaara, her hair wind and salt tossed into messy waves along her back. She glanced at her sister and felt her cheeks flush. "I, uh, had Wen drop shells on her."

"You're terrible," Aluan punctuated her declaration with a pillow to Idrilia's face.

The discussion then changed to the Trials, as Fey had had enough of the *boring* island. Idrilia explained what her sisters had missed during the graduation announcement. All too soon, their mother returned.

"Aluan, would you keep Felune occupied here?"

"But—" Felune protested.

With a stern look, Eranth quieted her daughter.

"I'll see you both soon," Idrilia assured them, ruffling Felune's hair before following her mother toward the garden plaza.

Idrilia entered the grounds with her parents. Like other residential sectors across the city, Idrilia's family shared the crystal garden with neighboring families, cultivating the prismatic shapes as a meditative task in pursuit of the Rising. Today, however, only the Vaktares and Volundars were present. Across from Idrilia stood Kalis and his family. Her two remaining grandparents, one each from her father's and mother's sides, stood conversing with Kalis's grandparents.

As Kalis caught her eye, he left his parents' side, and Idrilia did the same.

What's this about? Kalis motioned the words to her in a quick succession of Sentinel hand signals.

I don't know, Idrilia signaled back, then dropped her hands. Every one of their family members was proficient in the non-verbal language—they wouldn't be hiding anything if one of them were to look their way.

The friends launched into a familiar series of elbow touches, hand claps, and boot clicks—a remnant from their childhood greetings. The pair laughed.

"Congratulations, again, Truthseeker," Kalis said at last. "It's finally becoming real."

"The same to you. This gathering is a bit out of the light, though. I didn't know they were going to make such an occasion out of it. What are we doing in the garden anyway?"

"They probably just wanted to make it special, you know." Kalis scratched the back of his head. Idrilia still wasn't used to his close-cropped hair since entering Priorum. She missed his wavy blue strands that threatened to hide his ears entirely.

"You're probably right. Thanks for coming to my graduation last week, by the way."

"As it turns out, it was good practice for the Trials…learning to cope with extreme boredom."

Idrilia skewered him with a look.

Kalis winked. "As was our…excursion. I hear they sent that goo to Keepers' Rest for testing. It must be rather volatile. What did you tell your parents?"

Idrilia shrugged. "That we were outside Axiom when we found the vargs."

"Hmm."

"What?" She crossed her arms. "It's the truth."

"The truth with holes in it." He paused but Idrilia made no comment. He didn't know the level of shouting her father was capable of. In public, Cern was most charismatic. "Anyway, how was the island?"

"Not bad. I saw one of the new ships being built as we sailed back. It looks bigger than the others. A suggestion from the High Sentinel?" She leaned in.

"Could be—"

"But you're not at liberty to discuss. Yeah, yeah. Well, something you *can* discuss is our first Trial. I still think we should leave first thing tomorrow. What do you think?"

"Sounds good to me. Still taking the Leske Road?"

"Yep. And how many crystals are you bringing?"

Kalis tapped his lip thoughtfully. "Probably just the standard set Sentinels take on patrol. A handful of the one-time-use, exploding-on-impact, only-use-if-you-have-to-because-they-are-in-short-supply ones."

Idrilia snickered.

"A light crystal," Kalis added, then paused. Something passed over his features that Idrilia couldn't read as his brow knitted ever so slightly. "And some others. I'll just have to put some thought into it. Besides, we have our combat training. What about you?"

"Probably the same. Though I won't have as many exploding ones. You know how they like to only give reusable ones to us Pedium students. Or the training ones—no real power to do any damage. Really, no one outside of the Sentinel guild would ever survive a Komor raider encounter. 'Stand still Komorese, let me shine this light at you and give you a soft fall from your mount.'" Kalis grinned and Idrilia laughed before adding, "Maybe I can convince my father to let me have some of his. Think one of our trials will send us into the Heathström caverns to harvest more of the rarer ones to bring back?"

Before Kalis could reply, the voice of Idrilia's mother called out. "Kalis, Idrilia—if you would join us over here, please."

The families sat on benches nearby; so many of them, like Kalis and Idrilia, wearing the traditional billowing pants of the Sentinels that they looked like a row of flags at the Ettrascan markets trying to lure in patrons. Seeing her grandfather alone was still painful. Idrilia wondered if she would ever get used to the idea of her grandmother, Elsuota, not being there. Grieving the loss of a loved one took time—a duration unique to each individual, the Healers' Guild had told her last sidereal. But that didn't help the emptiness in her chest every time she thought of her.

"Congratulations, Kalis!" Idrilia's father began as the two friends approached. "I can't think of anyone more worthy—other than our 'Dril, of course."

"Cern, we feel the same about Idrilia," Kalis's father replied.

"You all know that I'm not one for prolific speaking. I'll leave that to the Keepers." Cern's jest was met with laughter, but Idrilia bristled. It felt like a jab at her deceased grandmother. The Keepers were considered the most educated, spending as much time as they did in the repository of knowledge, Evocus, and writing all of the city's records. Some members of the military did not seem to value it, despite one of their edicts dictating knowledge be held in the left hand.

Cern cleared his throat before continuing. "Idrilia, Kalis, I am very happy to let you both know that our families have decided you will be matched for marriage."

Idrilia blinked. Her stomach churned, making her wish she had not snacked earlier. She barely heard what came next over the sound of her heartbeat in her ears. *A betrothal?*

"We cannot express enough the joy we feel at joining our two families," said Leiria, Kalis's mother. She was an instructor at Pedium, and most of Idrilia's interactions with her had been in passing as a student. Leiria led another division of Prioriate hopefuls, like Idrilia, who had been identified to apply for entry into Priorium. Which reminded her that her application still had not yet received a response. *Had Klaara received hers?* That thought, combined with the news from her parents, made her head spin.

"I agree," added Kalis's father, Noval. "With such military prowess in our two families, we will be a driving force for maintaining the potential in the Sentinel Guild for future generations."

Noval held the rank of vigilem, the highest within the Sentinels. If all went well, Idrilia's father would soon attain the same title, an elevation from his current rank of vilicus. Noval would be instrumental in making that possibility become a reality. He and Leiria were kind, and Idrilia could find no fault with them as people, but she had no desire to call them family. Or anyone, for that matter. Hadn't she made that clear to her parents already?

"I know some frown on the traditions we follow, but it is our obligation. Since Kadaan's Rising, we preserve our knowledge and skills through family lines."

Idrilia wondered bitterly if her paternal grandmother's words were directed at her. Everyone knew the basis of the arrangements; she didn't need a history lesson. Idrilia clenched her teeth at the thought of the edict from the Council, an archaic remnant issued so many generations ago.

Protect against loss of numbers. The Keepers said the first rules, including the population edict of the then new city of Axiom, were inked by Kadaan herself, Sondrine's first leader. That edict was eventually expanded to encourage marriage within guilds, to preserve aptitude for certain skills. Or some solendrake basja like that.

Idrilia raised her eyebrows as Kalis joined the prattling. "If I might say, I feel very lucky that you have chosen my best friend. You could have paired me with another family, and I am grateful that you did not."

"Chosen? There is no *choice*," Idrilia interjected, her voice low.

Kalis seemed taken aback. "What do you mean?"

"Grandmother always said we should have a choice. Sondrinel are free to choose their vocation, so why are we not free to choose this?"

"It is more complicated than that, as you know," Cern chided. "We've talked through this before. Elsuota was an idealist, not a realist. What do the Master Sentinels do throughout your entire time in Pedium?"

Idrilia narrowed her eyes at her father's belittling question. Again, he painted the memory of her cherished family member in a pale light. "They watch and assess our progress," she grated.

"And they find the aptitude you naturally gravitate toward. The last few sidereals test if the path they recommend is right for you. In your case, the path to Priorium. This choice you hold so dear is whether to follow what your elders have determined to be most appropriate or to ignore them."

Idrilia held her breath, feeling heat rise in her face and fighting to restrain the shaking that crept toward her extremities. The coolness of her grandmother's circlet on her forehead felt like the only part of her that wasn't about to explode.

"This is very similar to that." Eranth's soft voice broke through her daughter's heated thoughts. "Our pairings create the greatest potential for our pursuit of knowledge."

"You make it sound like you are breeding prized solendrakes." Idrilia's tone was caustic. She unclasped her hands only to ball them in fists.

"Dril…"

Kalis's use of the nickname was the match that ignited the blaze.

"The only thing that seems to matter to you is getting the right offspring," Idrilia spat. "I am more than just a breeder."

"Of course you are!" Kalis protested.

"For all of our *advances*, our *knowledge*, our pursuit of *enlightenment*, we are backwards in this."

"You're out of line," Cern cautioned.

"No, you are!" Idrilia pulled away as her father reached to touch her shoulder. "I told you before, I don't want this!"

"Idrilia." Cern's tone was harsh. She cringed and took one step back, fearing the wrath she had surely provoked. His next statement turned her sight red. "It's not about what you want. This is the way things are."

"Then change it!"

"You *will* accept this truth known by all Sondrinel. You *will* sit down as a part of this family to discuss the arrangement of your wedding day *logically*. And you *will* apologize to Kalis and his family."

Idrilia laughed, a hysterical guffaw.

"Maybe that's it. Maybe I'm not a part of this family anymore. I'm twenty sidereals old, for Kadaan's sake. If you deny me basic choices in my life, *my life*, then…then I *choose* to leave it."

Idrilia spun, her gathered hair flipping in her parents' faces, and raced out of the crystal plaza. She blinked ferociously at her burning eyes. She could no longer suppress the quivering of her muscles as voices yelled and pleaded for her return. But she did not stop, breaking into a run as she whistled for Wen. Her othwit dove after her as she charged around a stone corner.

Idrilia raced into her home, signaling for Wen to wait for her outside. She ascended the stairs to her room two at a time. It only took a few minutes to throw everything she needed into a bag. Her training had instilled in her the importance of always being ready for a rapid departure. And she had been ready for the Trials ever since she was named one of Sondrine's Truthseekers.

She took one last look around the surroundings she had called home for so long. The walls felt closer together now, the ceiling oppressively near. Idrilia's resolve strengthened. She was meant for more than what any marriage of convenience could offer.

Her father's voice bellowed from outside, calling for her. Idrilia fled downstairs, out the door and into the street, never looking back at her home.

A faint echoing of hooves against stone reached her ears again. She stiffened.

Facing away from the source of the sound, Idrilia continued to squeeze the rag in her hand. Water dripped down her back and under the soaked fabric of her nuala robe, Sondrine's sleeveless fighting and travel wrap. She imagined the droplets traveling down her heated skin and disappearing as they were absorbed along her spine instead of guessing who or what trailed her.

Cooled enough to continue, Idrilia looped the damp cloth around the wide belt she wore, above one of two side-slits in the robe. She closed the water sack and returned it to its place with the other supplies, making sure the packs were securely hanging from her camelid. Unlike the solendrake she was riding, the camelid had a slender neck and four long, gaunt legs supported by cloven hooves. Lengthy lashes protected its bulbous eyes. Everything about the camelid's beige body was long.

She paused to regard the beasts. One of burden, one for travel—in her brisk exit from the city, Idrilia had grabbed her set of Axiom's gifts to each of its chosen Trials participants and immediately left. Teeth clenched so tight she could have bit through riftwyrm scales, she passed through the sky-hued life force barrier, down the stone steps, past the columns, and on to the crevasse rode. She ignored the Sentinel guards calling warnings, never glancing back.

She frowned beneath her headscarf. Sentinels. Priorium. Hadn't she shown them how capable she was during the final rites? The same doubt that had plagued her at her graduation reared its spiked head. *Do they know?*

No. No one knew what had really happened with the raider from Komor a sidereal ago. Still, her heart beat quicker at the thought of the truth becoming known. There wasn't just one raider…

She sighed, pushing away images of blood and broken goggles. She patted the side of the camelid and focused on the fact that she had been chosen as a Truthseeker. If only Grandmother Elsuota could see her now.

Idrilia reached her ungloved hand, still wet, to her forehead, where the orange scarf hid her grandmother's golden circlet. The double teardrop, inset with emerald-colored stones, was stuck to the sweaty skin of her brow. Idrilia wondered what her grandmother's advice would be regarding her forced betrothal, as she had challenged the other Keepers and the Council to think beyond their long-held beliefs. Idrilia's stomach sank to her knees at her failed attempt to do the same with her family.

Sure, Idrilia conceded to herself, her and Kalis's families had a long history of representing the two most highly respected guilds in Axiom. But that didn't mean they had to join the two families for forced propagation. She shuddered. Idrilia wanted to scream every Sondrinel obscenity she could think of and let it reverberate off the canyon walls. She wanted to spar with a wooden training post until her forearms bruised. Anything to excise her pain. She grumbled as loudly as she dared, feeling the frustration build in her chest without release. *Betrothed.* More like *betrayed.* By her family. By Kalis. By expectations of her family.

Squinting, Idrilia looked above. Her eyes followed the cliff faces of the gorge, the stone lined with random patterns of sediment in shades of tan and cream, up to where they finally touched the pale blue sky. Though not wide, the canyon was deep; the fine-grained floor of dirt and salt offered a partially shaded escape from the overhead sun. The sides touched by the light became intensely reflective surfaces. Idrilia blinked, unable to stare through the slit in her scarf any longer. She did not spy Wen above but knew the bird would return to her shoulder should a threat emerge. The animals had rested enough. It was time to move on.

A few steps to her left, Idrilia's stone-colored solendrake, its body speckled tan and cream like the gorge walls, lay motionless. The shaded rock floor must have felt cool to its softer underbelly.

Slipping her glove and wrist guard back on as she walked, Idrilia flung her leg over the creature and sat in the saddle. With a quick tug at each boot, she tightened the leather binding around her feet. Wrapping the lead around the horn of the saddle, she secured the tawny camelid to her mount.

She grasped the reins, tugged up once and clicked her tongue against her cheek. The creature heaved its body from the ground and stretched its neck, twisting its horned head from side to side. Idrilia squeezed her legs against the creature's sides twice, feeling the interlocking scales give slightly. They moved forward, the solendrake's club-like tail dragging behind them. The camelid, tethered on their right side, began to keep pace.

Her pursuer, whether friend or foe, stayed out of eyesight but not out of earshot. They were careless with their sounds. She spent another two hours establishing a pattern, daring them to take advantage of her methodic stop lengths. They did not. She felt the growing tension in her shoulders anticipating a foe. If the follower was Kalis, he should have approached her by now. Though she didn't particularly feel like seeing him at the moment.

Although the walls of the canyon bent and arched on occasion, nothing had presented itself as an opportune location to lay an ambush. Until now.

Ahead, the path was dotted with large rocks and a few boulders, dislodged from several outcroppings of the canyon wall above. Cracks appeared in the stone enclosure. Idrilia surmised that this portion of the Leske Road had suffered a quake, though how many sidereals or tens of sidereals ago, she was unable to gauge.

Idrilia shifted in her saddle, looking at the path behind. She and her two beasts were almost in the middle of a bend, dust kicked up in their wake. A few more patient minutes and the previous, straight section would disappear behind them. She would have to move quickly to make the most of the little time she had bought.

Loosening the leather straps, she freed her soft, calf-high brown boots from the stirrups.

Almost there.

She glanced over her shoulder and watched the final feet of the curve disappear.

Idrilia leaped from the saddle and whistled, barely louder than a hiss, a quick descending glissando. The solendrake jerked its head into a tilt, then faded from view, blending in with the surrounding stone and sand. Idrilia made a quick motion with her right arm: fingers extended together, moving at her elbow from her hip to her head.

The air shimmered and passed in front of her like a floating mirage as the creature jumped toward the wall. Though she could no longer see it, she knew the solendrake had landed on her right. Its toes, covered with tiny bristles, enabled it to cling to the surface. Pebbles dislodged and quietly tumbled down the rock face dislodged by its otherwise silent movements. Idrilia's trained eye could see the outline of the solendrake as it climbed higher, the shimmer faint but still present.

Grabbing the reins of her pack beast, she led the floppy-eared creature to the nearest crack in the stone wall. With the sacks piled on its back and dangling from its sides, the camelid appeared wider than it was; it was not going to fit inside the crack.

Idrilia lowered her chin to her chest as she thought. She dropped the reins and opened one of the packs. From it she withdrew a translucent pentagonal prism the length of her palm and clasped it between her two gloved hands. Bringing her hands to her lips, hidden beneath the scarf, she focused her thoughts on the object. Then she tossed the activated crystal into the crack in the rock and watched.

The air began to swirl within the small cave, tighter and faster, until the image was obscured by a gray haze. Slowly, the crack seemed to lengthen, the expanding cloud seeping out in an illusion of the space it occupied. Idrilia alternated between watching and glancing back for her pursuer as the haze turned darker, forming a shape of its own.

"This is taking too long," she whispered, stepping away from the cloud toward the boulder behind her, making sure to keep empty space between herself and the camelid. She did not want to get sucked into the crystal's depths with it. The creature huffed, its slitted nostrils flaring, and raked a front hoof on the ground.

"Shhhh," Idrilia soothed, lifting a hand before her chest, gloved palm out. "It will only be temporary, I promise." The camelid's tail wiggled slightly, the bundle of hair at its end tickling the backs of its knees.

The cloud grew, stretching a thick tendril down to wrap the camelid's feet in a fog blanket. Soon, the mass had expanded to encapsulate and obscure the creature entirely.

Finally the fog receded, its progress still sluggish like a slow inhale. As the last tendrils of fog entered the crack in the stone, Idrilia approached. She watched the remnants swirl into a single gray stalk, then diminish into the crystal with the camelid inside.

Idrilia plucked the crystal from the alcove and turned toward the largest boulder near her.

"You'll be safe here," she whispered, placing the now camelid-hued crystal in a pocket of the shirt beneath her outer robe.

Then she made herself ready.

CHAPTER 10

Kalis's chest constricted again as he saw the distant dots of Idrilia and her creatures, obscured by the heat haze of a near mirage, disappear behind a bend in the road. If a soul could be pulled in two directions, by duty and friendship, Kalis thought this is what it would feel like. He increased his pace slightly, hoping to close the gap between them.

"You holding up?" he asked his solendrake, leaning forward in his leather saddle to pat the side of its speckled tan neck with a gloved hand. He sighed. "I don't think I am. It would be worse above, you know," he added, tilting his head back to look at the high canyon walls through the slit in his light-yellow headscarf. "At least we have a bit of shade down here."

How different Heathström must look, with the sun always on the horizon instead of overhead. If all went well, they would soon see it for the first time—the burning sphere appearing to move across the sky as they traveled away from it.

He tried not to let his mind wander, an absent resolve in the wastes was a recipe for disaster, but he couldn't ignore the swirling emotions that seemed to only be held in by the fabric wrapped around his head. Though they hadn't talked much about the particular edict, Kalis thought they both understood that one day they'd each be betrothed to someone. Kalis's heart leaped at the thought of being betrothed to Idrilia and a smile spread across his face. Childhood friend. Sparring partner. He couldn't have asked for a better pairing. Some arranged marriages were between people who had never met. He was lucky to be marrying her.

But as he recalled her words, and the flash of betrayal across her face as she stood defiantly against their families, Kalis felt the stab of an ice crystal's explosion in his stomach. He'd missed something, horribly. As he thought about it, Idrilia had often avoided any conversation about the propagation edict by quickly changing topics. He'd always thought it was just what everyone felt at their age about it: awkward.

"Apparently," Kalis muttered to his mount, "I didn't pay half as much attention as I thought I did."

Kalis inspected his camelid, checking its gait and mannerisms. All his supplies were in place, and the animal's ears were in a rest position, rectangular and floppy; the creature was well-suited for long, dry travels. Kalis nodded to himself and spurred the solendrake into a marginally quicker lumber, its toe pads silent on the sand-dusted road as it pulled the camelid along.

Trying to distract himself from thoughts that made him want to continually blow puffs of frustration, Kalis recalled some of the words the High Keeper had announced to all of Axiom, "Their families will add yet another entry to their lengthy and, until now, separate histories as documented in the Vitaetum."

Although their families weren't really separate anymore. Kalis shook his head. It was no use. His thoughts were tugged back to the betrothal, and the spark of excitement for the first trial snuffed like a fire crystal hidden in a tight fist. He wished Idrilia would stop so that they could travel together as planned. And talk about all of this. Kalis knew there were reasons behind the edicts, and it was their duty to carry out the founders' wishes. It felt logical to protect their numbers and their history since so much was lost in the Calamity. Preparing to never be caught in that situation again just made sense. Regardless of how an individual felt. But there was that tug again on the other half of his heart— someone he cared about didn't like it.

Kalis blinked. He'd reached the curve where he last saw Idrilia.

It was empty.

Only boulders and rock fragments littered the canyon floor. Pulling back on the reins, Kalis slowed the solendrake to a halt before a rock taller than himself. A flash of silvery light appeared near the rock's side. A quick ascending whistle followed.

He reached for the curved sword at his hip. At the same time, a figure leaped in front of his stationary steed. He hesitated at the familiarity: clothed much like himself in a slitted robe, though gradient-blue instead of beige.

Shifting out of camouflage, a solendrake appeared behind the figure as she brandished two slightly curved daggers. "Make peace with me!" she demanded.

Any of Kalis's doubts about her identity washed away with her clear, unwavering voice. He should have known she would do something like this.

"Idrilia!"

Her daggers bobbed twice indecisively before she finally lowered them to her sides.

"Kalis? I could have killed you. Stalking me like a Komorese. Why didn't you signal?" She clicked the daggers into their sheaths.

Kalis smiled beneath his headscarf, glad she could not see his expression. She knew the Priorium Edicts better than most in his class. *In the left hand, knowledge; in the right hand, combat.* Fighting should not be an automatic, compulsive response.

"Why did you leave without me?" Kalis countered as he dismounted and closed the short gap between them. He suspected now what the answer would be, but he also knew where assumption had recently got him. He could see Idrilia's eyes now, within the folds of fabric: a piercingly bright shade of blue, lighter than his own. He imagined they were the color of a frozen lake though he'd never seen one.

Idrilia crossed her arms over her chest and shifted her weight to one leg. "You say that as if you slept through our family get-together."

"Well, I..." He paused, choosing his words, "I thought that we'd still travel to Waverling together, you know, as we said we would before—"

"I'm quite able to travel alone when I choose. As are you." She presented her back to him and approached her now visible solendrake.

Kalis raised his eyebrows. He knew when he was being told to find a pile of solendrake basja to bathe in. Sometimes it was better to go around the torav's nest than risk a venomous bite by pushing the subject.

"Where is your camelid?" he asked instead, leaning to one side to get a better view of the road ahead.

"I diminished him."

"What? Why?" Kalis watched as Idrilia stroked the neck of her mount, just behind its horns.

"I didn't want a spy from Komor to have my supplies. I thought, since they can't use the crystals, he would not be used for their purposes. *Your* purposes, as it turns out."

Kalis scratched the back of his head. "Couldn't be helped, you know. Not like there's a secret tunnel I could have taken under you instead. But that was good thinking with your camelid!"

"And the more I practice a connection with the crystals, the closer I get to the Rising."

The Rising. Kalis nodded. He admired Idrilia's devotion to every Sondrinel's ultimate goal.

"Well, you're here now," Idrilia continued. She faced him, one hand reaching into her front pocket, the other holding the reins. "Are you ready to keep going? We have a lot of ground to cover."

"Can we travel together now?"

Kalis heard her sigh. "It would be ridiculous to split up now," she said, moving to mount her solendrake again. Kalis turned to do the same.

"Did you bid your family farewell before you left?" Kalis inquired, his mind drifting to his own siblings. Vari, his eleven-sidereal-old brother, had shown disinterest and scowled as Kalis tried to embrace him. Difficult as always. Kalis had felt a twinge of guilt as he hugged his sister, Lyna. He felt an indescribable sadness at leaving her. He would sorely miss her company and guidance.

"I…," Idrilia hesitated. "I didn't."

"What? Not at all?" Kalis guided his mount to her side, letting his camelid drop behind them by loosening the cord. Their beasts lumbered along, kicking up dust and pebbles.

"No." Idrilia dropped her head. "Aluan is really going to be unhappy with me this time. I was just too angry and grabbed my things as quick as I could. I hope Felune isn't upset."

"She's sensitive, but she's also smart. She'll understand, you know."

"Maybe." Idrilia sighed. "Maybe I can write to them when we get to Waverling."

Kalis thought about all the times he and his siblings had seen Idrilia with her sisters in their shared crystal garden. Felune was always at her side, learning from and doing the things her older sister enjoyed. Aluan laughing and playing with them both. If they were anything like Kalis and his siblings behind closed doors, there were typical sibling scuffles, but he could tell the sisters meant the world to each other. He wondered if Idrilia could feel the same about him with time.

"—but I'm not sure. How far do you think it is?"

"Hmm, what?" Kalis looked at Idrilia, immediately sorry for his lapse in attention as her blue eyes narrowed.

"The southwest passage? I'm guessing you heard none of that." She looked forward.

"I'm sorry. Can you repeat it?"

"The slope that will lead up and out of this ravine. I was just wondering how many days ahead you thought it was."

"You don't think we should see if a ship is available on the coast?"

"Absolutely not. Stick to our original plan. If a ship isn't there, we'll have to backtrack. If one is, it has to travel all the way down to Ettra. And who knows if it will have space for all four of our creatures. The path west is best. So how far?"

"Hard to say—maybe two days? I put my map in my pack." Kalis motioned toward the lanky animal behind him. "The canyon doesn't have very many branches. It should be pretty easy to see it, you know?"

"Hmm," Idrilia murmured. "I should release my camelid before he gets diminishing sickness."

She fished the camelid's crystal from her pocket and tossed it a short distance away. They paused to watch the peach-colored fog escape and form into her camelid, keeping away from the expanding cloud lest they interrupt the process.

"Hopefully I won't have a reason to do that again for the rest of the journey." Idrilia retrieved the crystal, now devoid of color, as she and Kalis eased their solendrakes into a comfortable gait.

Kalis reached into his front pocket. The sight of her returning her crystal to safekeeping reminded him of the small rectangular prism he'd stowed away. He held out his hand to Idrilia with it resting in the palm of his glove.

"What's this?" she asked, not removing her hands from the reins, but turning her head to look.

"It's a Sentinel communication crystal. I wanted you to have one."

Idrilia shook her head. "I don't understand. Why would Priorium give me this? Beyond the animals, they weren't supposed to aid us in this first trial. Besides, these are for Sentinels."

"They didn't, exactly. I—I took it."

"Kalis?" Her voice rose higher as if mimicking quizzical eyebrows.

"I wanted us to be able to use the same method of contact. Like Sentinels do when traveling outside of the city. What if we need to communicate from a distance but speaking would be unwise? Or we can't see each other's hand signals? If we are within range, we can use the crystals to share information."

He showed her the back of his other gloved hand. A small pocket from wrist to knuckles bulged with the shape of a similar prism contained within.

"Since you don't have a pair of these, you'll need to hold the crystal to make the connection. This pouch keeps the crystal in contact with my skin so that communication can be instant, without having to find and touch the stone." He lifted the bottom edge of the pocket just enough to show Idrilia where the crystal slid in.

"My father spoke of these," Idrilia said, plucking the transparent crystal from Kalis's palm. "Aren't they rare? That's why not everyone in Priorium gets them."

"That's right." Kalis nodded, glad she had accepted the offering. "There's a limited supply, enough for each Sentinel assigned to patrol. When that runs low, we have to trade with Heathström for more. Sometimes it's not easy."

Idrilia sighed. "I hope they don't know you took this. I hate that you've put yourself at risk for reprimand. I didn't ask you to steal for me." She laid her hand on his upper arm for a moment.

At her touch Kalis felt a tingling through him like a breeze. "It was a choice I'd gladly make again. We are both excellent warriors, but as we've been taught all our lives, relying on only one asset is folly. Two of us, leaving Sondrine for the first time, with no Master Sentinels, on a long journey—I thought it was a prudent decision."

"Ah, but you did think they'd stop you. Otherwise, you wouldn't have smuggled it out."

Kalis suppressed a laugh. She was right. It was that uncertainty that had fueled his action. Maybe the Sentinels would have given it to him. Then again, maybe not. He couldn't have risked that. For Idrilia, he would do most anything.

Her voice cut through his thoughts. "How close do we have to be for them to work?"

"Most lose contact after about half a klick. There are some who can use it over longer distances, but that is rare."

"If I remember what my father said, you *think* at it to use it?"

"It will take some practice, you know, but that's essentially it. You can send images and feelings, mostly. The more skilled can send words, or even sentences. I am mostly the former."

"Well, at least I can signal you if I don't learn this right away. We've done that before, many times."

"Even when we weren't supposed to." He winked. "Practice using the crystal, and you'll get it, I'm sure."

"And let you hear all of my thoughts? I think not." Idrilia's voice had taken on the teasing tone, precise vowels and articulation, he knew well. She might have been serious about hiding her thoughts, but she wasn't opposed to learning the skill. He admired her pursuit of knowledge, never shying away from something new.

"Unless you practice, I won't get anything from you. Which might be the case anyway as I'm sure it's mostly empty space up there."

She responded with a single bleat-like laugh. Kalis was glad he had broken through the wall of her crossness. He wished he could see her accompanying smile, and the way she wore her hair high, revealing jewel-studded bands along her ears' edges. He knew her every feature so well.

"I'll practice. Just not right now." Idrilia dropped the crystal in her front pocket.

"Fair enough. There's so much to see in the rocks and boulders, such diversity in the sand and dust. Look at those cream-and-tan striations. I think I see some dark-brown specks just there."

A low grumble issued from Idrilia. Keeping his attention on the bends in the path, Kalis suppressed a laugh, thankful that his headscarf hid his large grin.

CHAPTER 11

Laughter and voices mixed with the clanks and bumps of cutlery filled the inn. Kilahym more firmly strummed on his dulcimer, accompanying his clear tenor voice as he sang *The Lay of Agermath the Great*. It was doubtful that anyone recognized the obscure tune with its many stanzas dedicated to the man for whom Etherea's largest mountain range was named. Kilahym was merely the tapestry on the wall accenting the town's end-of-day merriment.

He was comfortable with that. He'd come to Beechmarsh in search of his fellow trail participant; if his fellow Seeker wasn't in the northernmost town, he'd work his way south until he found them. This inn seemed as good a place as any to start his search. It also afforded free lodging and fulfilled his wish to avoid returning to his parents' home at the edge of town. Hopefully he'd be in and out before they even knew he was here. It had been several years since he last attempted a homecoming and that experience wasn't any less disagreeable than the ones before. Sometimes he amazed himself at how easily he tricked himself into believing things had changed. They never did.

Kilahym bowed his head over his hourglass shaped instrument and watched his fingers pluck the music between verses from the six strings, letting the music fill him better than a plate of food ever could. His gaze traced the vine carvings and the sound holes in the reddish wood, then moved up the fretboard painted with a bird between each fret. As the music rose, he shifted his eyes back to the people who filled the tables and ate their meals, and he began to sing the next stanza.

His fingers slipped, creating a dissonance as his eyes caught on the back of the room. The nearest tables frowned in his direction before returning to their bowls.

A woman stood near the door; her peach-toned hair parted on the side, wavy like the ripples made from dropping a pebble into a pond.

He *knew* her.

Not just because he recognized her as a Highblood from the downturned corners of her eyes, the distinct cut of her leather clothing, and the cloak she wore over it. But his memory filled in details that weren't visible; like the three silver bands she wore on her upper left arm. His chest filled to bursting. It had to be her.

His song ended and a few patrons clapped, but, for the most part, the inn's activities carried on without pause. Ignoring his need to observe the patrons for signs of a Truthseeker, the bard set aside his instrument. He announced a brief break, tightened his hair, and straightened his black tunic as he navigated the rowdy crowd until he reached the wall.

The woman hadn't made it much further into the establishment than when he had first noticed her. Her striking lavender eyes, previously surveying a few tables, focused on him as he approached.

"May you walk the true path," he greeted her. He bent his head slightly in respect, trying to remember how the other bards had greeted Highbloods all those years ago.

She stared, unmoving, and for a moment Kilahym thought he had misremembered that the Highbloods spoke the language of trade, the language of Heathström. He noted that they were the same height, though he felt shorter somehow.

She bowed her head and spoke in a strong voice. "And may you see the true light."

Kilahym placed a hand over his heart, blowing out a puff of air. His memory wasn't as faulty as his mother always said it was. "It isn't often that a Highblood visits the Moon's Quiver." He motioned to the large room. "What brings you here?"

"I come to Beechmarsh from time to time during the Daughter's hours," she replied. "But, as you say, it is not often to this gathering place."

"Er, Daughter's hours?" He scratched behind his ear. "Is that a new festival? I know I haven't been here in a while but…"

"It is the hours everyone is awake while the Daughter, the moon," she pointed above as if the sky was there and not the rafters of the inn, "can still be seen." She glanced past Kilahym. "I must continue my search. Excuse me."

She took a step forward.

"We've met before," he blurted, holding up a hand. "Not officially—we never exchanged names."

He searched for a hint of recognition, the expression she showed him while cupping seeds in the forest. Kilahym dared to hope she remembered him as clearly as he did her, the memory of their childhood interaction already a bubbling joy like a river within him. Her eyes never left his, but whatever she was thinking did not show.

"It was many synodies ago, when we were much younger." He closed his eyes, calling up images from his memory for every detail he could assemble: the cold, crisp air of the mountain; the wonder and awe of hearing music and stories from Highbloods for the first time; the crackling fire whose light reflected off nearby crystals; the sounds of the Highbloods' animal companions.

He opened his eyes. "A small group of us had come to your village, to trade stories and music. You were the only one near my age, and you had a small jeroti at your feet."

"They are called coils."

At the sound of her contralto voice, Kilahym's focus returned to the woman. "My apologies. I thought we had the same name for the mountain animal."

She smiled for the first time, the action softening her features and releasing his previous worry. "Our *village*, as you called it, is a coil. Named for the shape it takes," the woman explained, making circular motions with her finger—small at first, then wider, "and how, like a coil, we can collapse it quickly, move it, and spring it open again in a new location. Whether the coil is the tail of a pectully, or the shell of a mollusk, each coil is similar." She paused. "And I am sorry, but I do not remember your face."

Kilahym's heart dropped. "Er, uh, that's alright. Perhaps it was someone else. Yes, quite possibly you just look like her. Not to imply that you don't have unique qualities. I mean, not to imply I think you look the same." He cleared his throat. "You were saying the coils are similar?"

"There are some differences, but now does not seem to be an appropriate time."

"Oh, I would be most interested to learn more. But you're right," Kilahym added, jostling to the side as a patron squeezed past, "perhaps another time."

He looked over his shoulder, his eyes narrowing as he glared at the back of the male figure continuing his way through the crowded space between tables.

"I would be pleased to share with you more about our people if we meet again."

He nodded in agreement, returning her smile, only to shake his head as the words finally registered. "You—you aren't staying at all?" His eyes widened.

"I leave at Daughter's rise for Waverling."

"Well, that leaves plenty of time, then, after you find what you seek." Kilahym gestured to the inn.

A stranger intruded on their conversation. "You should go now, Highblood. Your kind isn't welcome here."

"Well, that's rather rude!" Kilahym's brows shot up.

A man taller than either of them tapped Vayriel on the shoulder. She pivoted to face him.

The man's scowl didn't leave her. "We don't need your unnatural magic corrupting our minds. Grey Lady protect us."

The woman lifted her chin. "The world is strengthened by unity. The Mother's gifts are for all to use for hope not fear."

"What are you accusing me of, Highblood?"

"Woah, woah." Kilahym splayed his hands, taking a step forward as the man did. "My friend, why don't you have yourself another thirst-quencher, my compliments. Danlem!" He cupped his hand next to his mouth, turning toward the bar, and shouted, "Give my drink quota to this fine example of the locals."

The man hesitated, and Kilahym added, "You really have made your position clear, and I compliment your ability to identify yourself so quickly to us. Go on, mind-altering indulgences await you," the bard nudged the man, "as does the day after that you deserve."

The accoster stumbled forward, and before his sarcastic tone could register, Kilahym focused on the Highblood. Patrons whispered behind their hands and glanced their way. He gestured back toward the door, and the pair shuffled past the newest arrivals looking for an open table.

"Some people. Did you say you're headed to Waverling? I'm traveling there myself."

"I was told to find my companion for the Trials of the Innermost on the road to Waverling. Are you the one?"

Kilahym tilted his head to the side. "How fortuitous this would be, were it true—nay, you must jest!"

Her mouth opened then closed. "I would not lie."

"Then our first quest is half complete! Greetings, my fellow Truthseeker." He bowed low, bumping glasses over on the table behind him.

Those nearest hushed their conversation; as if a curtain had been pulled back, Kilahym became aware of how many people were around them. Staring. If nothing else about the evening had sparked their interest, the patrons had heard that last exchange. The bards and traveling troupes kept the denizens of Heathström mildly entertained, but the Trials would give the towns new gossip for many lunations. And in Beechmarsh, where precious little happened, nothing was as exciting as that—except maybe for the Day of Laphrim, with its poles weaved with ribbons by the celebrators and the market full of special treats like candied berries, all in honor of the goddess also known as the Grey Lady.

He'd prefer the news of two Truthseekers being in town not spread until *after* they had left Beechmarsh. Adoring admirers was one thing, but inquisitive locals who might recognize him and report back to his parents…

He reached for the Highblood's wrist to guide her out of the inn so they could talk, but stopped short when he saw her withdraw, evading his grasp. He drew back his hand and rubbed the reddish stubble on his chin.

"I—umm…sorry, I hope I didn't overstep. May we step outside to chat?"

She nodded once and headed toward the door. Kilahym studied the hood resting on her back as he followed. The black-and-white fur—alusarean, he thought, given that the Highbloods were known to care for their herds—not only lined the edges but covered the entire inside, no doubt very warm in the mountains of the Agermath Range.

As Kilahym closed the door behind them, the sweet scent of thatch replaced the heavy aroma of baked bread and sloshed alcohol on the tables of the Moon's Quiver. A chill breeze seeped into the fabric of his clothing, robbing it of the warmth of the tavern's fire. He began to wish he'd gone back for his things. Near where he had been playing his dulcimer lay his hooded cloak. Plain and gray as it was, it would have kept him warm. The Finishing Winds were beginning to blow out of the north, named for how they swiftly swept through the valleys during the final moments before moonset, as everyone finished their tasks before retiring to sleep.

The Highblood retrieved her spear, hidden from view behind barrels stacked on the side of the building. Their backs to the sun, they followed the path that led out of the village. The shadows were long, as they ever were, and the clouds thin. Patches of sky clear enough to show the sun on the horizon cast a yellowish glow.

Kilahym lengthened his stride until he walked shoulder-to-shoulder with his new companion.

"Here."

At her voice, Kilahym saw the item in her proffered hand; a paw print pressed into shells.

"Oh, yes." He fumbled in his pocket before mimicking her gesture, the Gray Lady's footprints cradled in his palm. "Well then, there's our proof of one another."

Kilahym glanced over his shoulder, confirming neither inquisitive townsfolk nor the man from earlier followed. Instead, he saw red-roofed houses, swathed in thatch dried from the surrounding fields, dotted the meandering line of the village, broken up by various trade buildings and changes in elevation. Kilahym's gaze followed the line to the last structure—a Sanctuary of Laphrim, where the moonset service would have just ended—and then traveled up to focus on the mountains and waterfall behind. Out of the corner of his eye, Kilahym noticed how the Highblood used her spear more like an ornamental accent than a necessity for walking.

"Thank you…for stepping in," she broke the quiet, which was accented only by the distant thunder of the Agermath Falls plummeting over rocks and boulders. "When I visit, I do not often encounter the hostility my people say the lowlanders have for us. But occasionally—"

"—occasionally the uneducated rear their varg heads. I'd blame the ignorance on how little your people are discussed, but that is no excuse. Say no more of it." He clapped his hands together. "We're Truthseekers! And we've found each other, which means all we have left is to get to Waverling. And since I know Heathström like the soles of my shoes, we shouldn't disappear into the Fens in the far south or whatever actually happened to the last set of Truthseekers. Probably. I'm not worried. Are you?"

"Worried about the last Truthseekers?" She raised a single brow.

"Disappearing. Poof. Never to be seen again. Judging by your expression, the news did not reach the mountains."

"I am not aware of this tale."

"They left Waverling and never reached the site of their first trial. All three realms searched, but no one found any trace of them. Well, no matter. We'll be fine, I'm sure. Not far to Waverling from here. But where are my manners? My name is Kilahym. Friends call me Hymn."

"I am called Vayriel." Her eyes cast down at their feet. "It is unfortunate that your friends do not use your true name."

"It is a nickname I approve of. No harm done. It is nice to meet you, Vayriel. You have a lovely name. I think it would flow nicely in a ballad." At her quizzical glance he explained, "I'm a bard. That's what I do. I tell tales and sing songs and make up new ones when the fancy strikes." He mimicked a few steps of a jig as they walked.

"Is this why you were chosen for the Trials of the Innermost, your ability to 'tell tales'?"

Kilahym's smile faded. "Mostly, but it had more to do with what sometimes happens when I am engaged in my tale-telling."

"I do not understand."

Kilahym began to relate the story of his selection as a Truthseeker, but then paused.

"Here, let me show you."

Taking his ocarina in hand from where it dangled around his neck, he blew into the instrument and moved his fingers across the holes in various combinations, playing the melody he wrote for the Spectres. The stone emitted an airy, flute-like sound that he weaved into a slow yet rhythmic succession of notes. He began to retreat, his feet moving backwards in small steps, until Vayriel stopped walking. He circled her slowly, facing her as he revolved around her stationary figure.

Vayriel's lavender eyes widened as the tip of her spear began to glow, the crystal emitting diffuse scarlet light from within, and Kilahym stopped his music. He gently laid his instrument against his chest, noting the faint warmth of the stone against his skin as it slid beneath his black shirt. The Highblood's spear tip returned to its normal appearance.

"Your expression is almost as confused as the Magister's was that day."

"I have never seen a lowlander use the life force before. Though I know the Mother's blessing is there for all."

Kilahym returned to Vayriel's side, and they continued their stroll.

"The Spectres call that magic," he continued. "But they were apparently just as surprised. No, *shocked* is a better word. I was just as shocked to find out that whatever little trick I performed was forbidden outside of the Spectre Order. I'm not clear on which peeved them the most—that I wasn't a regular Shrine attendee or that the Grey Lady must have blessed me."

"What *trick* did you perform?"

"That." He pointed to the top of the spear, its light now fading.

"And that is forbidden? The man from the resting place said something similar. Do others like yourself not also have the ability to…use magic, like your Spectres?"

"In Heathström, magic is a gift from the Grey Lady Herself, so they say. If you are a devout member within the Shrines, she may bless you with the talent. The Spectres will then take you to train secretly. Using magic untrained isn't allowed. I spent two days under their wings. But now that I think of it, I spent more time answering their questions than learning how to use my gift. I can't really control it." Kilahym shrugged.

Vayriel seemed to stare ahead, lost in thought. They passed through the gate and began to walk the dirt path, which ran parallel with the forest that grew over the foothills into the mountains. Before them, the path stayed on solid ground, out of the marshy barrier, as it arched around Lake Gamin and wound south toward Waverling. Beechmarsh sat at the base of the mountains near the lake but not on its shores. He hoped the traveling would be as uneventful as he had suggested, but then it wouldn't be much of a trial if something didn't challenge them.

"Well, regardless, I have magic, though it appears to be minimal. A two-lined poem, if you will. Which, as a man, makes sense, I suppose."

"Lowlander women, then, lead your coils and protect them with magic?"

"That would be a succinct but apt way to look at it. I learned more about how our society functions at the Bard Academy than I ever would have he—uh, I mean, at my rough-spun hometown. Though they'd never admit it publicly, the Spectres believe men…cannot use magic. There's certainly discord between genders in our lovely capital, no doubt due to this topic. Though, I've read several *very* old tales that say otherwise. Agermath the Great—the subject of the song I was singing earlier—he seemed to have some sort of magic. Well, anyway. That's that. And here I am."

Tilting his head back, Kilahym focused on the location of the moon, a kinetic counterpoint to the motionless sun, its faint shape visible in the twilight sky. He sighed. It was near moonset.

"We should probably get back. I still need to finish my performance if I'm to expect lodging—'tis only fair. I'm staying at the Moon's Quiver. I can speak to the innkeeper for you. Get you a room—maybe even for free!" He beamed. "Being a bard does have some perks."

"That is kind of you," Vayriel said, shaking her head, "but I will sleep where

I always do." She motioned toward the forest.

"Oh! Of course. Well, um, I'll meet you at the gate then, tomorrow? At moonrise?"

"I will meet you then Kilahym." She bowed her head slightly. "Until then, may you walk the true path," she said, raising her head and fixing her eyes on his.

"And, er, may you see the true light." Kilahym returned Vayriel's smile.

He watched her cross the tall meadow until she was halfway between the path and the first line of trees. He'd completely forgotten to ask her what skill had granted her the title of Truthseeker. Mumbling criticism at his lack of polite inquiries, he started toward Beechmarsh when movement caught his eye— something contrasted against the green.

He stopped. Turning to look again, he caught a glimpse of a whitish shape near the underbrush before it retreated and was hidden once more.

CHAPTER 12

Kilahym's ocarina twittered in a way that Vayriel thought was much like birdsong. The sound seemed faint as it attempted to spread out into the vaulty canopy of the forest. He and Vayriel followed the Agermath River as it meandered south, cresting and descending the landscape in and out of the forest that, like the river and mountain range, was also named for the historical figure.

Using the river as a natural guide would lead them to their destination in just over three days' time as the waters eventually passed through the capital city. Though she tried not to dwell on it, her thoughts continued to turn toward home. Even the river. Out of sight, it added a humming backdrop to his music, reminding her of the droning instrument carved of bone that her people used to accompany somber melodies. Vayriel wondered how many drops from the streams of the mountains found their way to travel beside her like invisible companions.

The bard dropped his instrument to his chest and opened his journal, scribbling something into the pages. It wasn't the first time she had watched him do this since leaving the Beechmarsh meadow, tapping his writing implement to his lips. While she enjoyed the silence of the Mother-of-All's creation and Kilahym's music, a fluttering vandling in her stomach told her she needed to get to know her traveling companion. Sharing knowledge and healing the broken places of the world would not be accomplished by inner thoughts.

"What marks do you make in your book?" she asked at last, her voice quieter than she intended.

Kilahym looked up as if searching for the interruption, his brown and gold honeycomb eyes finally settling on Vayriel. A smile spread across his lips, and he snapped the book shut.

"Ah, yes. At the present, I was notating that little composition." He slid the pencil into the tie of his hair.

"And before?"

"Some notes on our journey. Never know when a tiny detail might spark a magnificent flame. Metaphorically, of course."

Or a memory. After their encounter in the inn, Vayriel thought about what the bard had said. She remembered a group of lowlanders visiting ten Journeys of the Daughter prior, but she could not place Kilahym's face. Something about his eyes, how they looked like a bee's home, the corners without any tilt, seemed almost familiar. She studied him now, as she often studied Orgar, committing his features to memory.

His life-friend might be a pawilo if they matched with people of similar looks. Orgar disliked the slinky creatures, who teased him from the underbrush with their playful, whiskery faces. She had not encountered a Highblood who had a pawilo life-friend. So far, her own life-friend seemed cautious but not overly concerned about the bard's presence. This gave her confidence.

"What did the Spectres teach you about using the life force?" she asked, settling on a topic she knew well.

"Each city's Shrine of Laphrim has a crystal sculpture that…enhances their magical capabilities. They are able to perform impressive feats before the Grey Lady's followers. Though, I'm only supposed to use magic under the supervision of another Spectre. Guess I failed that rule already." He laughed. "They do not want my abilities to result in messes for them to clean up or putting an ordinary citizen in peril. Until I can control it."

"And did they teach you how to control it?"

Kilahym shrugged. "Not really. Rules and history, which normally I do appreciate history, and then as I may have mentioned before there was a lot of just watching me try to," he waved his hands in the air, "magic…things."

Vayriel took a deep breath, focusing on relaxing muscles that had tightened. Using the life force was natural to her people, almost like breathing. But everyone needed training and practice.

Orgar nuzzled her thigh as she pushed a branch out of the way.

"I will help you."

"Really?" His eyebrows shot up. "Highbloods can do that?"

Overhead, light from the Watcher filtered through the dark green leaves in soft beams. She pointed above. "There are many paths the light can take. So are there many paths a Highblood can walk. Some fear repeating the past—that sharing knowledge with those outside of the coil gives them ways to take advantage, to betray us. I do not think that you are one of those."

Kilahym stopped, clasping his hands together. "Absolutely not. Whatever you teach me, I promise to use only for good."

Vayriel motioned for Kilahym to continue walking, and together they moved through the thinning trees. More undergrowth was present here, and she suspected they'd reach an opening soon—a good place to practice.

"What do you know of how the life force works?" she asked.

"Uh, just what the Spectres tell, 'Blessings of Laphrim to the faithful' and all that."

She shook her head. "Though I have never heard of a lowlander bonding with a creature-son or -daughter as a life-friend, the ability to use the life force is born to all. Everything that is alive is part of the life force and has an energy that can be felt or used. It is through training and practice that each individual's skills are sharpened like a spear. How do you connect to that energy?"

Kilahym stumbled over a root. "Right now, other than being somewhat tied to my music, I'm not entirely sure."

Vayriel nodded, thinking of the occurrences he had shared. "And it seems that half of the time it surges as something visual. At least for now. We can start with that connection."

"It's odd, don't you think? Most of what I do as a bard is auditory, yet none of my magic is as such. Is that normal?"

"I am a Watcher. What you might name a warrior, a fighter. Yet I heal and make things grow." As she spoke, Vayriel focused on a small tendril of energy, coaxing a shin-high blade of grass to grow taller between the bard's feet. "My Path-Shaper teaches that everyone can use all of the Mother's gifts, but some forms are easier for each of us. We naturally focus and perfect those abilities. She helps us find what that path is. We can start with what has been natural for you."

Kilahym glanced down as the tall stalk she grew opened its yellow flowers in a puff of pollen. The bard sneezed, scattering more into a thin cloud.

"Well that's a neat trick," Kilahym said, wiping his nose on his sleeve.

Vayriel hid a smile behind her free hand. "We will stop here. Sit. And listen."

"Shouldn't we keep moving to the city? I'd hate for us to be late on account of teaching me the ways of the Highbloods."

Vayriel sat, laying her spear across her crossed legs. Orgar disappeared into the tree line. "Orgar is in need of something to eat. And it is good to pause for rest and reflection even when moving toward a goal."

The bard looked once toward the horizon, then sat his pack and instrument beside him on the grass. Vayriel removed her gift from Mo'fa from her bag and munched on a dried scale-glider strip as she watched Kilahym. Her thoughts focused on what she had said to him. If the Path-Shaper expected her to defeat a dark presence, surely she would need to master more of the Mother's gifts. Could she defeat it with vines and redbark trees? Her stomach sank. She did not know anything about this darkness, so how could she know how to defeat it?

Kilahym sat with his eyes closed for several moments.

"I'm not sure what I'm doing."

"The Mother-of-All speaks. She speaks with the wind of the mountain and the whisper of the trees. To connect to the Mother-of-All, you must listen for her voice."

"Right. Got it. I'm a very good listener. In fact, I think I once received a good listening distinction from an educator at the academy when—"

Vayriel tapped her ear.

"Ah, yes, I will listen." Then he whispered, "What am I listening for?"

"For you it may sound like your music. Maybe far in the distance. Focus and bring it closer."

The bard nodded and closed his eyes again. Vayriel watched him while she focused on the energy around her. Reaching out with her energy, she lightly grazed the nearby insects and birds before detecting what she thought was Kilahym, tentatively touching the life force like a young-one, weak as it was. And with it she could almost see a purple aura around the bard and…her own eyes gazing across a fire? "Ugh, it's no use. I'm not getting anything." Kilahym sighed.

Vayriel blinked. The image vanished before her. She kept her face from showing the confusion she felt. Whatever she had felt was unlike anything she'd ever felt from other Highbloods. She swallowed, forcing herself to focus on helping Kilahym.

"When you find a new instrument, do you know how to play it immediately?"

"No. And I know where you are going with this. But an instrument is physically there. Whatever I do with my finger placement or embouchure has a direct and immediate response, which I can then tweak and perfect over countless hours of practicing."

"It is the same with the way to the true path. It is a long journey in search of the true light. Where do your words and notes come from? For the songs and poems you create. How do you find the right ones?"

Kilahym's brow furrowed. "I—don't know if I can fully explain. At times it's as if the notes play themselves, which sounds ludicrous now that I've spoken it aloud."

"The true path is to seek the true light. You feel that path, just as you feel the music. Focus on your path. This is a journey of understanding yourself. A journey that can take a lifetime, but with each step you come closer. Understand where your music comes from, and make your life force create that music."

"The path and the light…your Highblood greeting is starting to make more sense now."

"Play and see what happens."

Nodding, Kilahym picked up his dulcimer. As he plucked a few strings, Vayriel felt Orgar returning. He curled up next to her as Kilahym played a melody she did not recognize.

"Take what you are feeling and push it out before you. See it become real."

For a moment, Vayriel wondered if she was just unable to teach another how to connect to the life force. Then faintly an image formed like the light-painters. Two young-ones beneath a tree. It hovered then disappeared.

Kilahym panted. "I forgot to breathe. Remind me to breathe next time."

"You created something! Very good. Who were they?"

"Oh, erm, it was just a memory. I see Orgar is back. Should we continue?"

Vayriel nodded, pushing up with her spear. "Keep practicing, though. You will grow stronger."

Kilahym beamed. "Thank you, m'lady. For the lesson. And the vote of confidence."

Traversing the meadow, Kilahym attempted again but stopped when a dozen bees circled above Orgar's head like a crown. They reached the next forest before Kilahym tried again. He played a fast tune on his ocarina, and almost immediately, Vayriel noticed a creature-daughter come closer as if pulled into the music. A squeaky ratufa shadowed and mimicked Orgar like the jeroti were its father, bouncing in front of him and pining for his attention. One of Orgar's paws was the size of the creature's purple body and beige tail combined. Eventually tiring of the antics, the jeroti deftly scooped up the creature with a front paw and tossed it at Kilahym. The ratufa scrambled up and around the bard's torso, its lengthy tail wrapping around him like a rope of fur, reminding her of Sapa's life-friend, until it perched atop Kilahym's head and chittered angrily at Orgar. Despite her efforts to stifle her amusement, Vayriel laughed.

"The bard has become the comic." Kilahym swatted at the ratufa's tail. "Go ahead. Laughter is good for the soul." Eventually, Kilahym untangled the creature, and it scurried back into the trees.

"Now, you've learned a bit about me on our journey." Kilahym brushed his palms against his sides. "Might I learn a bit about you?"

Vayriel tilted her head. "What would you wish to know?"

"Everything! Er, anything rather. I know, let's play a game my friend taught me. He uses it to find out if someone would be interested in, well, if he would be interested to..." He cleared his throat. "That is to say you can learn a lot rather quickly. Just answer the question as quickly and succinctly as you can, and then I'll do the same. Do you have siblings?"

Vayriel hesitated. What kind of questions would the bard ask of her, and would she feel comfortable enough telling a stranger? This, at least, was innocuous to start. "I do not."

"Neither do I! What is your favorite color?"

"The green that lives between the mountain slopes and the snowy peaks."

"That is rather specific. I like bright colors, especially if they are together. The names of your parents?"

Vayriel made her face like a stone before she responded. "My mother was Motesh and my father Kerru."

"My father is Firran and my mother—Grey Lady's unbesmeared hems! You said *was*. My condolences. And my sincerest of apologies for carrying on this silly game without proper acknowledgement." Kilahym stopped and placed a hand on her shoulder.

Vayriel swallowed, glancing at his hand. Something about the look of concern in his eyes knotted her stomach, but not unpleasantly. "There is nothing to apologize for. It was before the Mother-of-All began to paint memories within me. It is the memories of my mother's parents, and a keepsake, that I carry with me."

"Would you share the story with me?"

Vayriel nodded. "Raiders came for the crystals that grow in the caverns my people guard. Many Highbloods returned to the spirit-world then—and continue to do so, for the raiders still come."

"Raiders from Komor?"

Vayriel glanced down at her jeroti and patted his head. "Yes. We think a similar band took Orgar's family as well. Highbloods have always protected the Mother's treasure, only harvesting the crystals in a way that allows more to grow and replace the ones taken . But the thieves ripped them from their roots, and nothing would grow in the scars left behind. It was such a raiding party that my parents faced. When Mo'mo and Mo'fa began to worry that my parents had been gone so long, they left me with a friend. They found their daughter and her life-mate slaughtered at the mouth of a cave."

"That…that is terrible!" Kilahym ran his hand over the scruff on his chin. "I can see why some of the coils would be opposed to outsiders." The bard paused, and Vayriel took the opportunity to start moving again.

"Our coil relocated near other crystal caverns."

"If I'm putting this tale together right, that would mean you live with your grandparents?"

"That is correct." Vayriel missed them already but tried to focus on the present.

"And the keepsake. Oh!" He snapped his fingers. "That must be the brace—umm, armlet?—that you wear."

Vayriel glanced down at her left arm. The band was still obscured by the lacings of her jacket. "How did you…it is the only possession I have from them. My mother used to wear it. I have worn it since."

"Surely not," he countered. "A child's arm would be too small to wear it where you do now."

"It has always been the right size, and I have always worn it here." She clasped her upper arm over the bands.

Her thoughts shifted toward the vision of the Daughter's Eyes. Those who could access those visions had seen a Highblood woman wearing her silver armlet. To their knowledge, no other Highblood had one like it except for her mother. She had found it in the crystal cavern, the same one she would later return to the spirit world in. The woman in the vision could not be her, but her daughter. Vayriel clenched her teeth almost as hard as she gripped her spear while the bard continued through her thoughts.

"That reminds me of a legend from the woods near Beechmarsh. A cruel weaver of spells kept a dremeniad, a tree spirit, imprisoned with an enchanted cuff that changed in size as he aged. That particular tale ends with the dremeniad reversing the spell to shrink the cuff, losing his foot but gaining his freedom. But…you aren't really interested in that."

"It's not that—" But she couldn't tell him. What was the darkness? *Who* was the darkness?

"Say no more." Kilahym waved his hands. "I brought up a painful memory and followed with a morbid tale. Let us continue our question game. Have you ever licked the bark of a tree?"

Vayriel's eyes widened. She turned her head slowly to regard him. "No?"

Kilahym bleated like a newborn alusarean, grinning ear to ear. She scrunched her nose, a smile tugging at the corner of her mouth. Kilahym danced ahead of her, and she shook her head at his back as Orgar yipped. The bard had made a jest. It would take a while for her to get used to his manner.

Then there was a flash of light. Vayriel's body lifted from the forest floor as her arms flailed around in the encompassing white, trying to grab anything to steady herself. As she landed hard on her back, she remembered to use the energy around her. She heard nothing—neither the sound of tree leaves rubbing, nor Orgar's unmistakable footfalls. Panic settled on her limbs like the weight of ten jeroti. But as she reached out to gather strength from Orgar, a new energy crossed her path, and she couldn't help but grab on to it. It was like a spear on a steep climb or a step on a ladder. And she pulled herself up out of the white.

Vayriel gasped, the hollow feeling in her chest burning cold as her lungs filled after their sudden emptying in her fall. Using the new energy, she mended the bones at the base of her spine. She pushed up on her elbows, raising her head and shoulders from the ground. Orgar stood guard over her, his back arched, his two tails horizontally extended. Beyond him stood Kilahym. The bard's hands waved in front of his chest, and his mouth moved soundlessly, yet Vayriel heard the tinkling of bells from far away. And she felt concerned for herself, but it wasn't her own feelings. It was…

She looked up and a strand of purple light quivered in the air between Kilahym and herself. Vayriel blinked. The thread vanished. Slowly words became clear, as if drawing closer.

"Nice jeroti. Good jeroti. Just want to see if she's okay," Kilahym said in a rush. "Not going to hurt her. Look, I'm smiling. Does someone who smiles hurt people? I guess they do. Bad example. You've got big, pointy teeth. I have musical instruments. You, sir, have the advantage."

"Orgar, life-friend, we are safe." Vayriel raised a hand to stroke his fur.

Orgar bent his head to sniff her hand briefly before swiveling his head back forward. Questions raced in Vayriel's mind about what she had felt with Kilahym. How easy it had been to draw on his energy. Only the most skilled Highbloods attempted such a dangerous connection. It was easy to draw too much from another. And then the emotion she'd felt…she had detected another's moods before through the life force, but this was different. It was as if Kilahym's mind was inside of hers for a moment. Feeling like she'd taken what she didn't have permission for, she couldn't meet his eyes.

That's when she noticed why Orgar had not sat down. Peeking out from behind gray-bark trees were two lowlander young-ones with eyes wide.

"What happened?" Vayriel asked, watching the boy and the girl.

"You stepped on a pyreflower," Kilahym explained. "Beautiful colors. Lovely explosion. Not so nice for you. Any injuries?"

Vayriel examined her body as she repositioned herself to sit cross-legged. She suspected her tailbone would be bruised though she had mended her insides. Now that her senses were clearing, she could sense that Orgar had not been affected.

"I am…uninjured. What are pyreflowers?"

"Have you never seen a pyreflower?" the girl asked, taking a step out from the tree.

"Aine, no," the boy whispered.

Kilahym whirled around. "Well, hello there! Are you from a nearby village?"

"Yes, just on the other side of the river. We came looking for farrow. Jydin was stung by a pectully when we were playing on the rocks," Aine answered then met Vayriel's eyes, "Are you a Highblood?"

"I am." She studied the two young-ones. The boy still cowered behind the tree, and Vayriel wondered what stories had been told to him to fear her.

"Do you not have pyreflowers?" Aine asked.

"I don't think they grow in the mountains," Kilahym jumped in, "as, if I recall, they appear in *Silverman and Sörsen's Practical Guide to Flora South of the Agermath Range*—ridiculously long title if you ask me, and dull, but the drawings are magnificent. Anyway, I should have warned you," he said to Vayriel, "and I apologize for that. Though, you did make for a picturesque example of their intensity." He laughed as he sat down, then added quickly, "But I'm glad that you are all right."

Vayriel nodded. The dangers outside of the mountains might come in hidden forms not unlike those of her home. She was a young-one in this new place.

"Pyreflowers are rare but not unknown," Kilahym was saying. "How does that definition go? The Silverman and Sörsen's guide in the library of the Bard Academy said something like—"

He cleared his throat, adjusting his posture and tone. Vayriel hid a growing smile behind her hand.

"Characterized by their blooms, pyreflowers are recognizable as they look like the explosions they make. A bloom typically has two colors: an outer and inner. The colors vary and are made from small tubular filaments. The closest flora relative is bushy to the touch, furry even, but pyreflower blooms feel like noodles."

Vayriel laughed once, loudly, then recovered. She was not sure if he was once again teasing her. "Noodles?"

"Well, not exactly. I can't remember what the book said. But *I* think they feel like noodles."

Aine giggled. "They do!"

"And the explosion?" Vayriel prompted, stroking Orgar's side.

"Yes! As I understand it, beneath the blooms are two sacs." Kilahym used his hands to accentuate. "If the sacs break, two unique ichors mix and the flower bursts into sparks. Weeping willows of color dance in the sky and fade as they slowly return to the ground. They are often used in celebration. A bit dangerous to harvest, but when done right, the pyreflower can be preserved for later use. There's a tale of a disgruntled lover and a bouquet I could relay that is—"

"You're funny." Aine laughed. She had moved closer to them as Kilahym spoke and stood only a few steps away.

"Uh, thank you?" The bard scratched his head.

"Is that a jeroti?" The girl pointed at Orgar to her brother's apparent dismay; he gestured and whispered pleas for her to come back.

"Indeed. His name is Orgar. Are you not afraid?"

"My mother says that they are dangerous, but I don't believe her. Can I touch him?"

"Orgar?" Vayriel watched her life-friend's tails wag, and he lowered his head. "He says that you can."

As the girl rubbed between his ears, Vayriel opened her bag. She withdrew white flowers with pink-orange centers.

"Pectully stings can kill a jeroti. I always carry some farrow with me." Vayriel extended the newest shoot she'd picked in the meadow on the way here. "Do you know how to make it into a paste to relieve his itching and swelling?"

Aine hopped once and took the stem. "Too well. My grandmother leaves out fruit for them, and my brother gets in their way." She gestured toward her brother, who was shaking his head with red cheeks, then looked back at Vayriel. "Thank you, lady."

Vayriel bowed her head. "May you walk the true path."

This young-one had knowledge of the creature-sons and -daughters or at least did not fear them. And she knew how to use the Mother's gifts. This lowlander was not so different from herself.

As the girl returned to her brother, Vayriel asked, "Why do you not believe your mother?"

Aine shrugged, guiding the boy back the way they had come. "She's never seen one, so how would she know? Besides, if Highbloods live with them, how could they be that dangerous to people?"

Vayriel's heart swelled as the young-ones departed, and she picked up the direction toward Waverling again. Perhaps there was hope to mend the distrust between Highbloods and lowlanders. Perhaps she could bring healing to Etherea after all.

CHAPTER 13

Kharnek lied.

Not an abnormal behavior, but this instance of deceit troubled him. If he was honest with himself, the source of his discomfiture rode next to him. Kharnek did not know why lying to the priest bothered him. Zinvar belonged, after all, to a religious order that Kharnek despised with every fiber of his being. Yet the young priest had proved nothing but congenial on the trip thus far, even in the face of Kharnek's thinly veiled hostility. And, truth be told, he was not like any other Priest of Morakh the warrior had ever encountered. Zinvar's skepticism about his own religion surprised and intrigued Kharnek though he did his best not to show it.

For the first time since they had begun their journey together, Kharnek permitted himself to study his companion at length—surreptitiously, of course. Zinvar's lean but taut frame and pale skin were standard for a Komorese. The vine-like tattoos that coiled up the side of his neck and presumably elsewhere defied the Priesthood's standards of keeping their outward appearance plain. He stood shorter than Kharnek though not by as much as the warrior had first thought. There was nothing remarkable about Zinvar's appearance, but Kharnek judged him to be attractive by most standards. His intelligence and amiable nature certainly had something to do with that.

Perhaps that was also why Kharnek had felt the pinprick of guilt in his heart when he'd lied to his companion about the Tower of Nerekesh. Kharnek had indeed been there, once, and as the monolith drew nearer, the memories loomed in his consciousness. He remembered the strange compulsion that had grown in his mind to ascend the stairs to the chamber where Nerekesh had slashed his own throat. The darkness inside him uncoiling into his limbs, attempting to assert its will and guide his steps toward something it knew, something strangely familiar…

Kharnek quashed the recollection. He and Zinvar would spend only a few hours at the tower, to rest themselves and their mounts, and then arrive in Waverling within the next few shadowfalls. Kharnek could control the power within him for at least that long.

The moon had dwindled to a silver crescent by the time they reached the Tower of Nerekesh. Its pallid light limned the edifice's crumbling battlements. Kharnek reconnoitered the area while Zinvar tended to the mounts. He smirked at the way the priest shuddered when asked to feed the wyrms.

"All clear," Kharnek announced upon his return to the campsite. They were ensconced in the remains of a stable that crouched against the fortress's circular outer wall: a twenty-foot-high barrier that stood in proud defiance of the ravages of time and neglect. Like the tower it guarded, it was made of black stone. The stable itself was less well-preserved. Half of its eastern wall lay on the ground, open to the wide inner courtyard with the Tower at its center. Even this close to more temperate Heathström, the wind sheared like wyrm claws through flesh. Kharnek judged it safe to build a small fire for warmth, as the outer wall would mostly conceal its light from prying eyes. Zinvar had inquired about lodging within the Tower or the keep at its base, which Kharnek flatly denied.

"Can I ask you something?"

Zinvar's mellifluous voice interrupted Kharnek's survey of their encampment. The priest managed to sound like a public speaker even in normal conversation. No wonder he had been chosen for the Trials. The warrior elected to let his icy demeanor thaw a bit further. He and Zinvar would be expected to work and live together for the duration of the Trials, however long that might be, and a small part of him was beginning to enjoy the other man's company.

Kharnek regarded his fellow Seeker. "You're quite inquisitive for a priest."

Zinvar's face fell. "Oh. Sorry, I don't mean to be obnoxious. I'll leave you alone."

"No, wait." Kharnek sighed. Even his attempts to be sociable came across as brusque. "What I meant is—I have not met a priest who was curious about the opinions of others. Most servants of Morakh take little interest in any interpretation of facts save their own."

"Ah. You say that as though you do not count yourself among Morakh's faithful."

Kharnek paused before responding. In Zel Morakh, apostasy merited death at the end of a priest's sacrificial knife—or the sword of a Guardsman.

"As part of the Brotherhood, I serve Komor and its citizens first and foremost."

Zinvar's eyebrow arched. Perhaps he sensed how uncomfortably Kharnek had settled upon his choice of words.

"Some in the Priesthood would call that blasphemy. Putting anything before Morakh that is." He knelt next to the fire. Its flames twisted in his eyes as he looked up to meet Kharnek's gaze. "I, however, take a more liberal stance than many of my peers. As you have noticed."

Something about the way the priest stared and the tone of his voice sent a shiver down Kharnek's spine. Not an unpleasant chill. More of a warm tingle. Few things could crack his composure, but Zinvar did it with a few words and a look.

"I should check on the mounts," He muttered. Kharnek turned away, noticing a flash of disappointment in the priest's gaze as he did. The warrior stepped through a hole in a support wall, careful to avoid the splintered ends of rotted timbers that protruded into the opening. Alone now, he took deep, slow breaths to calm himself. Kharnek glanced at the rift wyrms, tethered to a stone column in two of the stable's long disused stalls. His mount had opened a wary eye at his entrance, but it descended back into slumber. The other's tail twisted in its sleep, in the throes of a hunting dream.

Kharnek felt the darkness within him slither into his mind, lured by the creature's violent subconscious. Then the tendril of malevolence snapped taut, like a drawn bowstring. Kharnek's perception flew into the upper levels of the Tower of Nerekesh, where a familiar evil lingered.

Cold.

Black.

WHOLE.

The last word resounded in Kharnek's mind with the force of a thunderclap. He staggered back against the cold stone of the stable wall. Abstract black-and-white patterns burst across his vision. They pressed into his thoughts, an insistent message that he could not interpret.

"Stop!" Kharnek shouted.

With his mind, he *pushed* the madness away. He heard a loud crash. The images vanished and, with them, the voices in his head. His vision cleared in time for him to see Zinvar leap through the hole in the wall beside him, brandishing his staff in an offensive posture. The priest rushed to Kharnek's side.

"Are you all right?" Zinvar gestured to his left. "And what happened to the wall?"

Kharnek blinked at the question. "The wall?"

A pile of stone and shattered beams was all that remained of the far wall of the stable. Two very angry and very awake rift wyrms hissed and scratched at their chains. Kharnek lurched away from the remaining wall. He swayed for a moment, a dizzying feeling settling over him. Zinvar grasped his upper arm to steady him. In an eye blink, Kharnek had twisted out of the priest's grip.

Zinvar flinched back and held up his hands. "Sorry! I was just trying to help."

"Instinct. Do not let it trouble you." Kharnek briefly clasped the priest's upper arm. "I appreciate your concern."

"Oh. Of course. And the wall?"

"Time must have finally claimed it. The tower is old, and has not seen any upkeep for many epicycles now." Kharnek knew it sounded implausible even as he said it, but Zinvar possessed the good grace to not question the explanation.

"Guess we'd better move the wyrms, then."

The priest reluctantly advanced toward the riled creatures, but Kharnek clapped a gauntleted hand on his shoulder. "It would be unwise to approach them in this state. Leave them."

"In the cold? Won't that bother them? They are creatures born of fire after all."

Kharnek shook his head. "They carry that fire within them. It would take more than the wind to snuff it out."

"I was hoping you would say that."

Tangible relief permeated Zinvar's body language, eliciting the ghost of a smile on Kharnek's face.

The companions moved back into the larger room where their small blaze awaited. Zinvar took a seat upon an overturned feed pail, his robe bunched about his feet. Kharnek leaned against the opposite wall, positioned where he could see into the wyrms' enclosure and the entrance to the stable.

"Have you ever seen a fully grown rift wyrm?" he asked, crossing his arms.

Zinvar cocked his head. "No. It is said that they guard the tombs of the faithful in the Valley of Monodium. At least, that is part of the Priesthood's folklore. Why, have you?"

"Yes. I doubt the Priesthood cares, but the City Guard loses more men trying to contain those beasts than in any skirmishes with the Sondrinel."

"Really?" Zinvar laid his staff down and hugged his knees to his chest. "That's the first I've heard of that. What do they look like? I was given to understand that it's rare for a wyrm to reach adulthood."

"The Priesthood encourages that perception, as does the Brotherhood. And our containment efforts are successful. That is why the trade routes around Zel Morakh are relatively safe. Every once in a while, though, one is wily enough to evade our patrols and lay waste to a caravan. The wyrms change form again when they reach adulthood and attain their greatest destructive powers."

"Again? I thought they were born looking like that." Zinvar turned his head toward the stalls.

"No. They have no limbs to begin with. They begin their lives swimming in the fiery rivers beneath Zel Gorragkh. Their arms and legs develop over time, and then they crawl onto land. That physical form, like our mounts, is what most Komorese identify as a rift wyrm. Have you noticed the scarred nubs on their shoulders?"

Zinvar nodded.

"Those are where wings would have been. We clip them when the wyrms are young, which stunts their growth. Wild wyrms, however, can gain the ability to fly and to exhale flame. As the wyrm ages, its control over the latter improves. Those are the deadliest of all."

Kharnek stopped, amused by the priest's slack-jawed expression.

"You're not serious," Zinvar said. "The arakh are a myth."

"Look."

The warrior stripped off his left gauntlet and the leather bracer beneath it. He held out his forearm for Zinvar to examine. The priest got up for a closer look, and gasped when he saw the swath of ruined skin.

"That was the price I paid for underestimating an arakh."

"That must have hurt."

Kharnek felt Zinvar's light touch upon the scarred flesh, the sensation palpable despite his deadened nerves. Their eyes locked for a moment, and he saw genuine compassion soften the priest's countenance. It had been a long time since anyone had looked at him with anything besides fear or loathing. The joy and relief that arose within him in response shocked him. It must have translated into his expression, and Zinvar swiftly withdrew his hand and moved back.

"F-Forgive me," the priest stammered.

"There is nothing to forgive." Kharnek began to strap his black leather back on. "Just pray that we do not suffer the misfortune of encountering one of these creatures."

"Now, that's a prayer I would be happy to see answered."

Kharnek's answering smile was mirthless. "As you should be, priest."

"Are you ever going to call me by my name? Or am I doomed to just be 'priest'?" Zinvar asked, plopping back onto his pail.

"Sorry. Zinvar. Is that the question you wanted to ask me?"

Zinvar blinked. "What?"

"Earlier, you said you wanted to ask me a question. Before the wall collapsed."

"Oh." A look of discomfort stole across the priest's face. "I'm not sure that it's a good time to ask it."

It was Kharnek's turn to be confused. "We have no pressing demands, though we should rest soon. We still have two or three cycles to go before we reach Heathström."

"That's not what I meant." Zinvar squirmed beneath the warrior's scrutiny. "It concerns a personal matter. One that may mean little to you."

"Ask."

"It's…about my parents." The priest looked up at Kharnek, a mixture of anger and sorrow on his face. "They were killed—murdered—when I was younger. The investigation never got anywhere. My father was part of the City Guard, so I thought that perhaps you'd know something or be able to ask."

Zinvar stopped, averting his gaze.

"I'm sorry. It's very presumptuous of me to ask that when we barely know each other. It's just been so frustrating, all these epicycles of not knowing what happened, and it seems like no one cares but me."

Kharnek frowned. "The formal investigation never found anything?"

"No. Which makes no sense. My parents were in their home with friends. It had to be someone who knew them."

"The archivist's office in the Warriors' Wing has all the records of formal investigations performed by the City Guard. Have you registered an inquiry there?"

"Many times." Zinvar's words were tinged with bitterness. "They won't reopen the investigation without definitive evidence."

"I see." Kharnek chose his next words carefully. "I make no guarantees as to what may be found, but upon our return to Zel Morakh, I will speak with the archivist. He will not refuse a request from me."

The priest's jaw dropped. "You will? I mean, thank you!" Tears sparkled at the corners of his eyes. "I didn't expect anything, with us just barely knowing each other."

"It is an injustice, and I would see it made right. I cannot undo what was done, but perhaps I can uncover the perpetrator. He will pay for his actions," Kharnek vowed. He was uncomfortable with the show of emotion from his companion. It stirred empathetic responses in him. Feelings he'd been determined to bury since the fiasco with Valin.

The warrior looked away from Zinvar's grateful eyes. "Who was your father? I will need his name."

"Oh, of course. His name is Hedek."

Hedek.

The name had fallen upon Kharnek's ears like a death knell. Even now, as he circled the tower courtyard on his patrol, the shock refused to dissipate. He was glad that Zinvar had not disputed him taking the first watch. Kharnek needed the time to collect himself.

But even the bracing cold of Morakh's Shadow did not clear his mind. The warrior looked up at the sky, the blackness pinpricked by stars. Their brightness unsettled a deeper part of him: the darkness within. It longed for the dark voids between the stars and, above all, to become whole again, whatever that meant. Kharnek could not understand this alien force or the strange compulsions it foisted upon him. Even the powers he wielded in its grip were like leaning on a splintered rod. He performed great feats, but he also committed atrocities. Evil deeds.

Like the slaughter of Zinvar's parents.

Somewhere beyond the walls of Nerekesh's ill-fated tower, a stone pectully whistled. The dull gray bird sang for a mate—prospective or lost, Kharnek could not tell. Its forlorn sound reminded him of another voice that whispered in the shadows.

It had a name, Kharnek now knew. It had spoken to him when he had slain the varg pack.

We are the Penumbra.

Kharnek shuddered at the recollection. And in that moment, with his mental defenses shaken, the Penumbra seized him. At the same time, the pectully screamed as a hungry tundrat's jaws closed around its throat.

The Penumbra laughed at the way the warrior's consciousness hammered against the mental walls surrounding it. He was strong and difficult to control. Separated from the Whole, this fragment of the Penumbra was barely powerful enough to subsume a trained soldier. But lately Kharnek's resistance was diminished by distraction. The newcomer, the priest, had unwittingly given the Penumbra the opening it needed. Emotion. Ever the downfall of sentient beings.

As it crossed the courtyard and entered the central keep at the base of the Tower of Nerekesh, the Penumbra's anticipation of rejoining the Whole grew. Incomplete for so long. But now so close. The Penumbra moved through the great hall until it reached the spiral staircase that led to the Tower's peak. With each step upward, the echo of itself that it sensed ahead intensified. Its puppet body stumbled onto the landing at the top of the spiral staircase. The Penumbra could feel its hold on Kharnek growing tenuous. It had to act quickly.

A small vestibule opened into the chamber at the tower's pinnacle, where Nerekesh's madness first began. The Penumbra looked around with its stolen eyes until it spotted a dagger, still clutched in Nerekesh's skeletal grip. A thought ripped the weapon from the corpse's hand, shattering bone into powder, and it flew across the room into the Penumbra's waiting grasp. Black smoke swirled within the crystal set in the dagger's handle, awakened by the presence of another part of itself.

The Penumbra's cold sense of triumph twisted Kharnek's face into a demented grin. Reunited with more of the Whole, its power would grow, enabling it to find the last remaining fragments scattered around Etherea by its nemesis—

Brilliant white light pierced the darkness of the tower. Luminous needles stabbed into the Penumbra. It shrieked in fury and pain. Kharnek's body collapsed to the floor, the dagger falling from his grasp.

The light resolved itself into a human shape at the chamber's center.

"You," the Penumbra hissed, as its host body writhed.

In response, the figure raised its arm, palm outstretched. A fierce radiance flooded the entirety of the chamber. The Penumbra screamed. Relinquishing its hold on the warrior, it retreated deep within his subconscious mind, defeated.

For now.

CHAPTER 14

Lightning ripped through a violet sky behind two alabaster mountaintops. Between the peaks stretched the battlements of a mighty fortress. Chunks of the thick walls were torn out by invisible hands and hurtled upward toward a rippling distortion in the storm clouds. They vanished into its nebulous black depths, and the distortion grew larger with each piece it consumed. The mountains themselves trembled. With a thunderous crack, the leftmost peak shuddered free of its foundations. It rose, with half the fortress dangling from it, toward the hungry maw in the sky. A thousand voices cried out in terror as a burst of white light engulfed the scene—

Zinvar woke from the dream with the brilliant afterimage still seared into his retinas. He shook his head and vowed never to touch the ekhroot travel rations again. Did they have the same effect on Kharnek?

Speaking of which…where is he?

Zinvar propped himself up on an elbow. The fire burned low, and the silver hint of moonrise colored the sky. It was long past the hour that Kharnek should have woken him to take the second watch.

Rolling to his feet, Zinvar warily surveyed the stable, empty save for the wyrms. He took up his staff and entered the courtyard. His alarm increased when he did not sight his warrior companion. The priest's eyes were drawn to the Tower next. The edifice speared into the darkness, like a questing finger, with no sign of movement at any of the narrow windows cut into its cylindrical surface.

Then he noticed, on the ground before him, a pair of footprints that shimmered pale azure. Beyond them lay a trail of luminous steps that led straight to the yawning entrance of the tower itself.

Zinvar blinked, certain that he was still dreaming, yet the footprints persisted. A vague sense of dread stole over him as he reluctantly followed the shining trail. He passed through the shadowed arch at the tower's entrance and into a vaulted hall, its walls bleeding with tattered crimson tapestries. The marks led Zinvar through the hall to a spiral staircase at its end, which he climbed. Chambers branched off of landings along the staircase, laden with shards of broken furniture and decayed skeletons. Chills shivered up and down Zinvar's spine.

The priest crested the final flight of stairs and reached the tower's pinnacle chamber. He was greeted by the sight of Kharnek's form sprawled across the center of the floor. Zinvar started to rush to his companion's side, but came to an abrupt halt when he realized that another figure was already crouched next to the warrior.

He took a hesitant step forward, and called out, "Who's there?"

The figure did not respond. Zinvar moved closer.

It was a woman. She was not dressed like a Komorese. Her garments were a dull gray, like the moonlit sky, close-fitting in a way that allowed freedom of motion. She wore black boots, similar in design to the warriors of Komor, and her auburn hair was pulled back in a braid that dangled to the small of her back. Zinvar froze when she looked up from Kharnek's limp body to meet his gaze with her own. Her large gray eyes captured sparks of moonlight that danced about her irises. Zinvar was struck by the feeling that he knew her.

"Who are you?"

"A friend," the woman answered. Her voice was rich and warm. She shifted her attention back to Kharnek. "This one will need your help in the days to come."

"My help? What do you mean?" Zinvar came to kneel beside Kharnek, and the woman rose to her feet. It seemed to the priest that an azure haze shimmered around her form.

"A darkness threatens this world, as it once did long ago." The woman stepped back into the shaft of moonlight that speared into the chamber. "Learn to use your sight so that you may help him see."

"My sight? Help him see what?"

Zinvar's eyes flicked down to Kharnek for a moment. When he looked up, the woman had vanished.

He vaulted to the window and scanned the tower courtyard, but there was no sign of her. His concern for Kharnek drew him back. The priest crouched next to him, searching for visible signs of injury. He found none. He placed his hand on the warrior's neck and felt a strong pulse. Zinvar was surprised by the softness of the tattooed skin.

Kharnek's eyes popped open, his back arching as he gulped air in loud gasps. Zinvar fell backward and cried out. His staff clattered on the stone floor as Kharnek sat halfway upright.

"What happened? Where am I?" Kharnek pushed the words out between shuddering breaths.

Zinvar rolled to his knees and edged next to the warrior, hands extended with palms up. "We're in the Tower of Nerekesh. Well, at the top of it. I have no idea how you got here."

"The Tower of..." Kharnek trailed off as he took in his surroundings.

"Nerekesh. We stopped to rest here for this cycle's end. On the way to Waverling."

"I...remember standing watch. But how did I get here?"

Zinvar shrugged. "I was hoping you could tell me. I woke up and you were gone, and then I found you here. And there was..." He paused, uncertain of how much to reveal. "I'm just glad you're not hurt."

"It would appear not." Kharnek twisted his neck and stretched his limbs, testing their responses. He moved to stand and winced. "However, I wound up on the floor—not gently, it would seem."

Zinvar sighed. His companion's sense of humor chose strange times to manifest. "Do you need help?"

"No." Kharnek's answer came sharp and quick, like the thrust of a blade. The warrior rose to his feet, and Zinvar stood with him. "Though I do believe it is time for you to stand watch."

"Right you are," Zinvar agreed. He stooped to collect his staff. When he lifted the ebon pole, its shaft dislodged another object that clanked against the floor.

The priest retrieved it from the shadows. A dagger with an amethyst-studded pommel. He examined the sharp blade, admiring the elegant scrollwork on the hilt. Zinvar thought he detected a flicker of motion within the gemstone's faceted depths, but dismissed it as a trick of the light. He had already seen enough peculiar things for one journey.

"Find something?" Kharnek asked, halfway through the chamber's exit.

"An old dagger. Though it looks to be in good condition."

The warrior cocked his head. "You have no other weapons. Keep it. It may prove useful in the Trials."

Zinvar regarded the dagger with apprehension. "It isn't cursed, is it? Coming from this tower?"

"Even an ill-fated blade may be repurposed by the right hands."

"How very philosophical." Zinvar secreted the weapon within the folds of his cloak and followed the warrior down the stairs.

CHAPTER 15

The Leske Road varied little. Idrilia and Kalis passed boulders of fluctuating sizes and placement while the sand and pebbles beneath them crunched in a hypnotic drone. The dry smell of soil, long devoid of nutrients, filtered through Idrilia's scarf, which kept her nose free from the irritating dust. She and Kalis were pierced by the sun if they strayed from the intermittent shadow on the sides of the dried riverbed.

It was a prison, blistering and arid, guarded on two sides by impenetrable walls. Although the rock face could be climbed by the solendrake, riding one on a vertical ascent was risky. The leather saddles were not built to support their backs from a potential backward slide, and the attached foot straps only secured their legs from excessive bouncing.

Idrilia's thoughts drifted to why she was here, making the ten-day journey to the land between light and darkness. Meeting Sondrine's enemies and allies in Waverling, Heathström's capital. Marrying Kalis when they returned home.

No. She shook her head to clear her thoughts. *Don't think of that now.*

She latched on to a memory of another journey; traversing the salt flats of Lake Stelwin with Klaara. White and coarse like dead coral, the surface preserved remnants of life in sedimentary form. *Preservation of life.* Priorium's edict drew forth another image: A face from Komor beneath the stranger's headscarf, his neck twisted at an odd angle. Staring into his eyes, cold and empty. Dead.

The sound of Kalis's voice brought her out of her trance. "Ouch."

Idrilia turned to see Kalis rub the top of his skull with a gloved hand. Spikes of his blue cropped hair escaped his displaced headscarf.

"You alright?" Idrilia asked.

"Something hit my head. Ouch! " Kalis rubbed his right shoulder this time.

This time it couldn't be Klaara trying to get their attention. Turning to squint above the line where the rock wall ended, Idrilia searched for Wen. The brown and gold othwit had flown on her own for some time now. Perhaps she was dropping things on them for entertainment. But Idrilia did not see her in the bright, empty sky.

What she did see caught her breath.

Idrilia lowered her head slowly and restrained herself from turning to look at Kalis. Instead, she focused on behaving normally, glancing ahead then back at her reins, surveying the rocky outcrops, and fiddling with her hip bag.

Her fingers found the shape she was looking for: the smuggled prism Kalis had given her. She removed a glove to grasp the crystal tightly in her hand. She focused her thoughts into one feeling: *danger*.

Kalis snapped his head toward her. Releasing the crystal, she pulled her glove back on while making a circle shape with her thumb and index finger. She tapped her other wrist twice.

Enemy.

Kalis brought his hands together, still on the reins in front of him, and his fingers touched.

Explain.

Midway up the right rock face.

How many?

There were two of them: creatures much like solendrakes but with crystalline scales that reflected the bright sunlight. Their long claws dug into the sedimentary surfaces. With each movement, their scales blinked in a random pattern. Rift wyrms. Astride them were men clad head to toe in black. They must have dislodged the stones that had hit Kalis.

Two. Mounted.

Plus one behind, Kalis signed back.

Idrilia chastised herself for having missed the follower. She listened closely, but only heard the wind whooshing through the canyon's bends. Perhaps the third enemy was on foot…

She needed her crystals, but reaching for the bag again might signal to their pursuers that they had been detected. She debated internally until Kalis signaled again.

Fight or flee?

Picturing the map Kalis had brought, Idrilia estimated where the next side passage would be. If they avoided confrontation until they were closer, they might be able to use the tight crevice to their advantage.

She conveyed her decision by moving her hand down to hover over her knee, palm flat.

Steady.

Their enemies were still too far away for crystals to be effective. Idrilia watched from the corners of her eyes for movement, waiting for an opportune moment. She felt their eyes on her, staring into the back of her tunic. A drop of sweat dripped down her spine and she shivered.

There. Sunlight glinted on crystalline scales as the riders began to descend. From behind a fallen boulder the third Komorese emerged from concealment on foot as she had suspected.

Fight or flee? She signed the question back to Kalis.

He made a fist in each hand and crossed his arms at the wrist over his chest. *Fight.*

At your signal.

Kalis loosed a shrill battle cry and pivoted his solendrake. Idrilia mirrored his movements, jerking the reins left. She felt the stiffness of her mount's torso turning beneath her as it raised its tail defensively. The appendage was like a stone cudgel, poised nearly perpendicular, ready to strike.

While the man on foot stayed back, the riders, now on the canyon floor opposite the Sondrinel, approached side by side on their rift wyrms. The Komorese mounts were like monsters from a lightless dream. Black lenses shielded their eyes from the sun, like those worn by their masters. Idrilia felt a grudging admiration for their cleverness—bringing nocturnal creatures into Sondrine's constant light should have put them at a disadvantage.

The voice of Idrilia's instructor filled her head: *Stay out of reach of the claws, or they will split you open.* A stark contrast to her mount's sticky pads for feet. What the solendrake lacked in offense, though, it made up for in defense. Spikes along its head and interlocking scales provided some protection, and its tail would bludgeon anything that came too close. Still, Idrilia had to keep its soft underbelly away from the wyrms.

She activated a crystal and tossed it at the feet of her camelid, distancing herself from the diminishing fog as it encompassed the long-necked quadruped.

She trusted that it would soon vanish into the relative safety of the crystal's confines.

Reaching into her hip bag, noticing Kalis do the same beside her, Idrilia withdrew several smooth, rounded crystals. She cupped them in her right hand and wiggled her fingers, twirling them in her palm, her scale-like gauntlet reflected in their facets as they clinked against each other. She felt a momentary hitch in her movements as she debated using the crystals now, but the need for action triumphed. These were Komorese raiders—they would have no such hesitation. She would just need to be accurate with her throws so as to not needlessly expend crystals.

Dropping the reins from her right hand, Idrilia grasped one crystal. She cocked her elbow and flipped her arm and wrist forward in one smooth motion. The crystal flew from her leathered grasp. It grew to the size of two fists as it approached its target, blazing orange and yellow with destructive energy.

The fireball struck the left rider in the chest as Idrilia positioned her arm for another throw. She winced at her aim, as she'd only meant it as a warning— the Waverling Accords were clear: no killing, an accident or necessary for self-defense, and technically they hadn't attacked. Something she'd like to avoid. But the Komorese let the fire from the crystal dance across his torso and spread out from the impact point. He hadn't protected himself and hadn't tried to put out the flames. Idrilia faltered, releasing another crystal higher than she wanted. Her target ducked, and the fireball flashed overhead.

"It's not working!" Kalis called out beside her. "I—I don't understand."

Idrilia dropped her throwing hand to the reins. Her first target's cloak was burned away, revealing a black and metallic layer.

All three enemies continued their advance.

Flee! Kalis signaled.

She shook her head.

"We retreat to fight again," he countered, as if reading her mind without the communication crystal. "Aim at the legs of their mounts. We can outrun them if they are on foot."

Idrilia nodded and, using the remaining crystals in her left hand, propelled fireballs at the attackers' formation. The second connected with a rift wyrm's chest.

The ammunition she had grabbed exhausted, Idrilia tugged her solendrake to follow Kalis, who grabbed the tether of his camelid as they passed. Its hooved feet begin to clip-clop in a gallop along with the padded thump of the solendrakes' movements.

Idrilia directed her solendrake's head to where her camelid's crystal lay. At the pressing of her heels, it flicked its long pink tongue out and rolled it, with the crystal inside, back into its mouth.

The scratch of claws on stone caught her ear. Idrilia looked over her shoulder and saw the rift wyrms climbing each side of the canyon, attempting to flank the Sondrinel. That left the man on foot behind them, who had summoned a third wyrm to his side. He mounted it and took off in pursuit.

Kalis veered right, avoiding a boulder Idrilia noticed belatedly. She urged her mount to climb the rock instead, using its adhesive toe pads to pull its weight up and over.

It clambered down a few strides behind Kalis. Idrilia reached into her hip bag and withdrew another spherical crystal. She shook it, then released it as she tossed it underhanded behind her. The sound of an explosion reverberated through the canyon. Idrilia twisted to see the fragments of the boulder she had just crossed raining down on the third Komorese. Focusing on Kalis's back, she urged her mount faster.

"There's a crack ahead. Let's go in there!" he yelled.

"That's crazy! We'll be trapped!"

She willed her eyes to see further ahead, but Kalis's body blocked the side of the ravine.

"Just trust me!"

Idrilia pushed her knee into her solendrake's stiff side and adjusted its position to better see around Kalis. To their right, less than half a klick ahead, was an opening she had seen on Kalis's map earlier.

Claws glinted in the corner of her vision. A rift wyrm landed near Kalis then leaped again, grabbing the haunches of Kalis's camelid. The creature shrieked as its back legs buckled, collapsing in spurts of blood that tainted its orange skin.

Idrilia guided her mount to the left, moving further away from the injured beast. Kalis jerked back, still tethered to the camelid. Its cries echoed in the canyon as it thrashed about, attempting unsuccessfully to work its back legs. Kalis's solendrake began to turn, pulled toward the doomed creature, but he deftly released the knot on the saddle's horn, and the solendrake snapped forward like a bent tree branch suddenly released.

It had to be done—their lives depended on it, she rationalized—but still, Idrilia felt her heart pull toward the creature they were leaving to die. Then a new cry echoed from above, joining the camelid's death throes. Idrilia whistled a response. A staccato screech trickled down to her ears in a waterfall of sound. A smile tugged at the corner of Idrilia's mouth, quickly disappearing as a rift wyrm landed in front of her. Dust exploded in a thin plume.

Her solendrake halted. Idrilia tumbled over its head, narrowly missing the top spikes, and somersaulted. She landed nimbly on her feet, one hand braced against the ground.

She snapped her head up to face her enemy. Reaching for the daggers sheathed on her belt, Idrilia rocked back into a fighting stance. She stared at her robed reflection in the dark lenses over the rift wyrm's eyes. An idea formed and she snapped her wrist forward twice next to her ear.

Idrilia heard the screech again, and her view was filled with Wen's umber wings spread wide. The othwit's claws clamped around the eye-shaped lenses. With powerful strokes, she lifted skyward, breaking the leather strap and ripping the rift wyrm's protective covering from its eyes. Blue specks dotted the blackness around its slit pupils.

As it backpedaled, the creature arched its neck and shook its head from side to side. Its mouth opened and issued a hissing shriek. It raised its front legs to swipe at empty air, blindly reaching for Wen. The othwit was already out of range, safe in the heights from which she had swooped.

Idrilia used the distraction to mount her solendrake at a run. She heard Kalis's voice and urged the beast toward where he stood at the tunnel's opening. She mentally checked off the locations of the three Komorese warriors: one with Kalis's camelid, one with the blinded mount—where was the third?

Her answer came in the form of a rift wyrm, which landed between her and the tunnel opening. Idrilia used a combination of signals with her legs and the reins to force her mount to keep its speed. The solendrake lowered its head as Idrilia pulled her feet into the saddle and grasped the saddle horn with both hands.

The Komorese faced his assailant as Idrilia launched her body, using the solendrake's momentum, and plowed into the rider in a tangle of arms and legs. They tumbled to the ground, Idrilia's arms locked around the man.

Her grip slipped as the enemy's elbow connected with her jaw, but she maintained her hold.

"Lightspawn," the raider hissed from beneath his head covering.

Idrilia heard the *thwump* of her solendrake's tail beating like a club against the rift wyrm's hard scales.

"You dare to touch me?" The Komorese squirmed beneath her grasp. "I will make you long for a swift end."

Idrilia shuddered. The words were similar to promises made by another raider. But instead of at her friend, these were aimed at her. She clamped her teeth, her eyes narrowing.

"Enough," she snarled and launched her left arm at his face.

Her fingers found their target. Mirroring what Wen had done, she yanked. His head moved toward her, and then the goggles came free.

The Komorese snapped his hands up to cover his eyes, dislodging Idrilia's other arm. She pushed him away and rose to her feet. Fire exploded behind her. She whirled to see the third pursuer—apparently having survived her attack—closing in on her location. She was close enough. She could make it.

Idrilia whistled to her mount, signaling it to hide. The solendrake's skin began to alter in hue to match the desert landscape as it scurried away from the battle.

"Let's go!"

She pumped her arms and legs, sprinting toward the crack. The tail end of her headscarf unwound and snapped behind her. Kalis moved out of the way as Idrilia whizzed past.

She heard a crash behind her.

The tunnel went dark.

CHAPTER 16

"Kalis?" Idrilia's voice sounded close.

"I'm all right."

"What happened?"

He blinked as if to clear the darkness. "I collapsed the entrance."

A faint light appeared at waist height a few strides ahead. It grew brighter as it floated several feet above Idrilia, bathing her in a silver-white glow. Her head was uncovered, the orange scarf dangling over each shoulder to her thighs. She ran a finger along her ear and seemed satisfied that all her adornments were present.

He felt his heartbeat in his ears at her silence. Kalis cradled a crystal in cupped hands, then tossed it upward. It ascended above his head, illuminating him and the surrounding area like a beacon.

Idrilia approached, crossing her arms over her chest as she stopped in front of him.

"Did you check that my solendrake had made it in first?"

"No. I wanted to—" His explanation that they could share one mount to make it to Waverling was cut off as the air escaped his chest in a huff.

Idrilia whistled, the ascending glissando echoing in the chamber. The creature appeared near the rubble, its skin reverting to normal pigmentation.

"What about Wen? Did she make it in?"

Kalis paused.

"No. I—"

Idrilia's arms had come up in a flash, her palms striking his shoulders.

"You left her? In the hands of our enemy?" Her light blue eyes were narrowed, her voice heavy, and she moved closer. She pushed him again. Her light frame belied her strength. "Wen is out there, and those—those *monsters* could have her! They will kill her, Kalis. Kill. Her."

Kalis raised his arms, batting away her next onslaught. His mind raced, but he knew that look in her eyes. She would not let him explain everything he'd debated before choosing his actions. "You've trained Wen well. She'll stay safe and return to Axiom if she can't rejoin. I had to save us. I had to save *you*."

"I didn't need saving." Idrilia's lips pursed, her eyes narrowing even more. She struck lower, but Kalis blocked her attacks from reaching his chest. She went for his hip, and he grabbed her wrist. Their bodies bent, their faces inches from one another.

Kalis stared down into her fierce eyes. "You agreed we'd escape to the tunnel."

A sound like a growl issued from Idrilia's throat, and she ripped her arm free. "I told you it was crazy."

Kalis took a step back. "What else were we to do? This was the best option with the highest chance of survival. You must see the reason—"

Then Idrilia was on him again, her hands looking for openings as her feet deftly kicked out. Kalis parried with both arms and legs, their exchange like a rigid dance in the pale light. Their movements were quick, succinct, echoing their previous training sessions.

"Don't tell me what to do," Idrilia growled between clenched teeth.

Kalis switched from pure defense and looked for opportunities. He aimed for her collarbone, but she ducked and carried her motion through, connecting two palms to his stomach.

He bent over, the air knocked from his lungs, but used his falling shoulders to conceal his next attack. He launched his hands forward like the claws of a rift wyrm, latching on to Idrilia's nuala robe, pulling hard. She staggered momentarily, and Kalis pulled himself closer, using the leverage to stand. He wrapped his arms around her torso, holding them both in place. His heartbeat quickened at their closeness, her lips parting so near his.

"Release me, or I *will* hurt you," she whispered harshly.

Kalis broke his hold and took a step back, his arms out to his sides with palms facing Idrilia.

"Wen is a smart bird. She might continue on to Heathström."

"Oh, right. I forgot you had secret conversations in othwit language and told her our travel itinerary."

Kalis winced. "Don't be like this."

"Like what? Perturbed that my friend might be killed by our enemy? Angry that the last gift my grandmother ever gave me is shut out of my reach?"

Kalis blinked as he searched for a way to break through the walls of her anger. Maybe if he explained some of his reasoning...

"Dril, we can—"

"Don't call me that!" She cut his idea short. Idrilia took a step forward, fists clenched at her sides. Her face was laced with malice Kalis wasn't prepared for.

"What?" It was his turn to frown. She'd never asked him not to before. "Your family calls you that," he offered weakly.

"You aren't family!"

Her pronouncement resonated throughout the chamber. *But I will be*, he wanted to say but hesitated, afraid that she might run away again in response to their betrothal. His stomach churned with what he wanted to ask next, what he feared he already knew.

He took a deep breath. "You're more upset about that idea, aren't you? Marrying me." Idrilia glared at him but retreated a step and lowered her hands. "I'm going to get the solendrakes and start checking out the tunnel. Your foolhardy heroics may have sealed us into a place with no exit," she muttered bitterly as she moved toward the rubble.

Her last statement made Kalis clench his teeth, his body stiffening, and he didn't like the feeling. He didn't like when she insulted his character, as if he didn't study the map already, and she knew it.

"My 'heroics' were the best way to assure our survival. You think that I acted on an impulse? No, that's you, *Idrilia*." He mentally clapped a hand over his mouth.

"And you know *my* actions are more than impulses." Her hands were on her hips, and if Kalis didn't know better, he would have thought she was reaching for her daggers.

Kalis sighed, rubbing a hand across his forehead. "Sometimes I can't help but mirror your emotions." Kalis softened his voice. "You could have retreated here as planned. Instead, you tried to single-handedly take out the riders while I was left vulnerable in the entrance. When a patrol leaves the city, they must trust each member to act in the best interests of the group."

"I don't need a lecture from teacher Kalis," Idrilia hissed, turning her back to him.

"What about a friend?"

"And I don't need a *friend* telling me about duty and what must be done or is supposed to be."

"That's not what I—" he took a tentative step toward her.

She didn't even look at him, merely walked toward the solendrakes. He watched her retrieve her mount and lead it past him, never flicking her sky-blue eyes his way.

They traveled in silence for several hours, their light crystals floating above them and following their steps along the mostly straight tunnel. Idrilia paused once to release her camelid from its diminished state. Although the tunnel was wide enough for both travelers and mounts to walk side by side, Idrilia pushed ahead of Kalis.

He attempted to initiate conversation several times but was left with the echo of his own voice. Instead, he spoke to his solendrake and made up responses in an imitation of what he thought it would sound like if it could speak. When he tired of that, he began thinking of the Trials of the Innermost. What would the two Seekers from Heathström be like? Would the representatives from Komor really work with them, or would there be conflict from the start? Would they perish in this tunnel, just a lost memory like the Seekers before them?

Then he saw it. At first Kalis mistook the shadow as a larger section of rock offset from the left wall. Then light slowly began to bathe it. As they drew closer, the form resolved into a shape unlike anything he had seen before. Its geometric lines rebelled against the surrounding rock in stark contrast to the Sondrinel method of integrating the environment.

In the left third of the tunnel, a beam that resembled polished onyx traversed the passage at a diagonal. Its length crossed from left to right, protruding from the low ceiling, then plunging into the rock floor. The beam's surface looked wet, although no images were reflected in the shiny material. Instead, it seemed to absorb the light from the crystals.

Kalis studied it as they drew closer. Idrilia slowed down enough that they were nearly side by side. Five smaller but similarly shaped beams met in the upper middle of the main projection, intersecting at different angles and in varying lengths.

"Don't touch it," Idrilia commanded.

Kalis halted his outstretched hand inches from the burnished surface. "What do you think it is?"

Idrilia was on the other side, studying the rectangular sections where they met in a geometric cluster.

"I don't know what to make of it. Best to be safe, though."

"Do you think it could be from Komor? Maybe that's why they were in this section of the Leske Road."

"That's an idea." Idrilia sat back on her heels, studying where the primary shaft entered the floor. "One that raises many questions."

She was talking to him again and that gave him hope that their conversation could progress back to what was troubling her.

"This could be the same metal their armor was made from," he offered.

Idrilia stood and tilted her head. "You saw it, too?"

Kalis nodded. "Our attacks were effective on their clothing, just…."

"Not on whatever was beneath them," she agreed, her eyes unfocused as they gazed at the ceiling.

"Some sort of armor, I'm guessing, as a shield against our attacks."

"I've never seen anything like it. It was like the fire was absorbed." She paused, shaking her head. "No, I don't know if that's true. What I do know is that the Komorese were unharmed by our crystals. That is…most concerning."

"We have to tell the Sentinels. Sondrine needs to know that our enemy may have a new asset."

"All the epicycles we've had 'magic' and they have not. They may have just neutralized our only advantage."

"Why do we keep finding these mysteries?"

"We're destined for greatness." She winked.

His stomach flipped. They lapsed into silence, contemplating the revelation and the object before them.

Idrilia's voice broke the muted air, her normal tone sounding hushed. "I'm…sorry about your camelid."

A grimace tugged at the corner of Kalis's mouth. "It was a good beast. We'll be alright, you know. We'll share the supplies, ration them to make them last. That's…it's what I wanted to tell you earlier. I knew you still had your camelid safe with your supplies."

"What about sending word to Axiom?"

"We can do that once we get to Waverling."

Idrilia nodded once, and then motioned toward the strange structure. "Whether this is of Komor or not, I think we should leave it. For now."

"I agree." Kalis tapped the side of his face absently, then returned his gaze to Idrilia. "I had an idea about Wen before I closed us in," he began, watching her face closely for signs of anger. Finding none, he continued, "Did the Familiars Guild fit her with a collar?"

"Yes. During my graduation."

"The included crystal allows you to see through her eyes."

"I didn't even check for something inside the band. That's the same thing they'd do for a Sentinel training a familiar?"

"Yeah. They must have made her ready for Priorium at the time. Saves another trip to Evocus, you know?"

A rueful smile tugged at the corner of her mouth. "Does it use the same communication crystal you gave me?"

"Same basic principle, but since othwits can't focus their thoughts like we can, you have to be focused on receiving them."

"Why didn't you tell me this earlier?"

"Well, I tried but…" Kalis chose his words carefully, "we weren't communicating well." He cleared his throat. "That, and I couldn't test it, so I didn't want to upset you further at that moment."

"Why couldn't you test it?" She tilted her head.

"Sentinels train with their familiar. They establish a unique bond that enables them to be attuned to the creature. It's more difficult than learning to channel your thoughts to others through the crystal. And takes even more practice."

Idrilia scratched the side of her face. "I wonder why they never mention that in Pedium."

"I think it might be so people don't get their hopes up, you know? Not everyone can have a familiar with a communication crystal."

"That makes sense. Thanks, Kalis."

Kalis flinched as Idrilia threw her arms around his neck, breathing a sigh of relief when he realized she wasn't aiming a punch at his head. Before he could return the gesture she stepped back.

"I'll start practicing immediately." Idrilia squeezed her hand around her communication crystal. "I don't want Wen to fly home without me. Ready to move on?"

Kalis paused, sand writhers squirmed in his stomach. The conversation was going well so far. He imagined trying to talk about their betrothal, but of her possible reactions, he only saw it going poorly no matter how he brought it up.

"Yeah, let's go." He smiled instead. Leading his solendrake to the far wall, he avoided touching the beam and moved past.

As the onyx fixture faded into darkness behind them, Kalis thought how similarly inscrutable Idrilia could be.

CHAPTER 17

They spent the moonrest of their third day camped in the Agermath Forest; his back sorely missed the luxuries of a town's inn, but Kilahym at least was able to sing several ballads to his Highblood companion before attempting rest. After a breakfast of roasted sporestalks and berries, foraged by Vayriel, and slightly stale bread from Kilahym's pack, they left the last line of the forest and followed a road that mirrored the river's flow. Waverling's clerestory roofs were beginning to dot the horizon amid other architectural shapes as Kilahym explained that this was the largest city in Heathström.

The dirt road led to a bridge that stretched across the Agermath River. Multiple arches that vanished into the rushing water supported the flagstones of the bridge. On the far side, two towers guarded the entrance to the city.

"Welcome to Waverling," Kilahym announced, stepping onto the first gray stones of the bridge, "where the river winds to and fro, and the occupants meander by leg and boat."

Vayriel raised an eyebrow.

"The city is built with roads and canals," he elaborated. "The main thoroughfare is a road, due to the high traffic—it leads to the Shrine of Laphrim. Other areas you can"— he made a rowing motion, pausing until he'd mimed a few strokes—"your way around."

"Should we find an inn inside to ask where we find the…" She paused as if dredging the name from her memory.

"I know where the Etherea Assemblage is. I studied to be a bard here at the Academy for many years. I'll show you."

A brilliant burst of red and orange lit the sky beyond the nearest buildings. A boom followed, vibrating her insides. Orgar flattened his triangular ears to his skull and sniffed the air. Vayriel's hand dropped to the jeroti's neck, her fingers disappearing into his white fur.

"Spectacular!" Kilahym exclaimed as green-and-gold, then blue-and-lavender bursts exploded in quick succession. They tilted their heads back to watch, halting their progress with a third of the bridge left to cross.

"Invisible brushes paint the Watcher's canvas. Pyreflowers?" Vayriel asked.

"Aren't they beautiful? I bet they saw us and set them off as a welcome."

"I feel sorry for the people," she commiserated. Her spear-free hand rubbed the small of her back as reflections of the red-and-yellow burst drifted down slowly in her eyes.

The bard laughed. "No one is being injured. They have a launch mechanism that lets them do it from a distance. Hard to explain, but they are safe."

At the entrance, as always, Kilahym was reminded of the gate of Beechmarsh, how it was an open circle, giving the false impression of acceptance, but this gate barred anyone from walking straight through. The center of Waverling's gate was made of dark metal, and near each of the two watchtowers stood an unmoving gray-cloaked individual, face obscured by a hood.

The one on the right spoke first, her voice resonant with a hint of youthfulness. "We who follow the Grey Lady's footsteps greet you. Whether you are a citizen or visitor, Her grace be with you."

"We are visitors. May her grace be with us all." Kilahym used one of many relevant refrains for a follower of Laphrim.

"Travelers. State your name and your purpose for approaching the gate of Waverling," the left woman said, her voice husky but friendly.

"Let me just step into character." Kilahym moved pronouncedly with one foot and planted the other beside it. "See what I did there? I'm"—he took a single long stride again—"*stepping* into character." When no one responded he cleared his throat and continued. "Tough crowd. We are the reason for the pyreflower display, honored Spectres. It was a magnificent one, too. I haven't seen one like it in synodies. Kilahym and Vayriel, Trials participants, though you already know that." He bowed, dropping his foot behind the other in a flourished bow.

"You are mistaken." If the rightmost guard's voice sounded like she was frowning. "The Magister and her handmaiden have returned from their journey to Ettrascus."

Kilahym felt his face flush. "So…not for us, then?"

"I'm afraid not," said the Spectre on the left, "though we do recognize your names. Vayriel, Highblood of the Agermath Range, and Kilahym, bard of Beechmarsh. You were chosen to represent Heathström in the Trials of the Innermost. Vayriel, please present your token for entry. I already know Kilahym."

"You do?" Kilahym asked as Vayriel reached into her pack, pulling out the paw-shaped token he'd seen before. She held it in the palm of her hand for the Spectres to see.

"Yes, I escorted you from your meeting with the Magister a couple weeks ago."

"Ah yes," he smacked his forehead, "I should have recognized the pacing of your sentence delivery. I don't think I got your name?" He hoped his sarcasm was hidden within his joking tone. He wondered if this Spectre was the one who'd insinuated he was incapable of magic or the one who'd reminded her that she was a jeroti pup for thinking so.

"Tara."

"Leave your beast at the stables," the other woman added shortly beneath the beak of her hood. "The first left road when you enter," Tara chimed in. "Then follow the main road to Laphrim's Sanctuary. The Etherea Assemblage can't be missed beside it."

"I know where it is," Kilahym said. "I'll make sure she gets there."

"Orgar should come to the Assemblage with me."

"That would be unwise."

"Ifen," Tara whispered through her teeth. Then to Vayriel, "It will be fed and taken care of while you are in the city. You don't need to worry. But its kind cannot be permitted among us."

"He is a part of me. Where I go, he goes."

"It will be returned to you when you leave the city," Tara replied.

"I think you'd better do what they say," Kilahym whispered beside her. Ifen was stepping backward, closer to the gate. Kilahym got a bad feeling about that. She moved like an actor stepping backstage to grab a prop.

"Please," Tara said, "it is for the safety of all. There are many more people within the city for the ceremony, and the streets are crowded. The other Truthseekers will be asked to leave their beasts at the stable as well."

"Orgar is not a beast like a barb-tailed varg. We have bonded in a way that is more than a friend or family. He is as much a part of me as my hand is. He—"

In the gulf of her hesitation, Vayriel and Orgar were surrounded in a pale, rose-colored bubble just before a white spark bounced harmlessly off the barrier and ricocheted to the right watchtower. It morphed into a net around the stone structure as it made contact. Had they meant to capture Orgar? A low growl issued from his throat.

"Blasphemy," Ifen hissed. "She's not a follower of Laphrim."

"Hush, Ifen," said the older woman. Then, to Vayriel: "I apologize—she is new to the Spectres. Please, lower your shield. We mean you no harm."

Vayriel's eyes flicked from one to the other. She reminded Kilahym of his father when he was indecisive about something that caused him strain.

Kilahym placed a hand on his waist and tilted his body as if he were acting as the lead in a play. "Could it be that the Magister has made an exception for Vayriel and her friend? Perhaps we should clarify with the Magister. I can vouch that the jeroti has been nothing but civil on our journey so far. Vayriel, as you can see, has magic and could control him if things were to get out of hand."

"I—I suppose that would be acceptable," said Tara.

Moments of silence passed where neither Spectre moved.

"They can communicate telepathically," Kilahym whispered to Vayriel, anticipating she'd have questions. "When I was training with the Spectres, they said that because the Shrine is here it's the only place they can do it."

Finally, Tara addressed Vayriel. "The Magister says you can proceed but to make your way to the Assemblage directly. I hope you understand that this is highly unusual. We have a duty, and we treat everyone the same. I am truly sorry that your first trip to our great city has started on a sour note. Ifen, please open the gate."

Ifen turned her back to them and raised both arms. The dark metal displayed glowing symbols; several grew brighter and then floated closer to Ifen in a gray mist. Reaching up, the Spectre touched the apparitions and rotated them with her hands. They looked like gears spinning against each other.

With a series of clanks, the circular entry began to open, and the symbols vanished. The gate broke into five pieces. One by one, the pie-sliced fragments disappeared into the arched supports. Kilahym wondered if he would ever be taught to open the gate.

Together the trio stepped inside.

"You *have* to teach me how to make bubbles!" Kilahym exclaimed as the gate irised shut behind them. "I mean, a shield or what have you."

Vayriel knelt beside the jeroti, scratching behind his ears, but did not reply.

"Well, anyway, you certainly made an impression on the Spectres. Ifen certainly has a dislike for jeroti it would seem.

"Many fear that which they do not know."

"That's certainly true. Hey, what do you think about them communicating telepathically?"

"Highbloods do something similar; a person's thoughts are sacred, but we…sometimes sense the moods of others. Like how I knew Orgar would be attacked. I felt the hostility rise like a warning of danger. But they do not need a crystal to access the life force."

"I'm also not certain they have to wave their hands like they're conducting a chamber choir. Seems a bit showy and that's coming from me!"

"It could help them focus the energy."

"Mayhaps. But what do I know from a few rehearsals of life force wielding? Well, we should head to our destination as we promised."

"Why did they call you a bard of Beechmarsh?" She asked. "We both set out from the town, but they did not label me the same."

"Well, er, because I was born there." Kilahym shrugged.

"You do not live there anymore?"

"No. My family does. As a bard, I wander. The inns of our realm are my home."

"Why did you not stay with your family?"

Though he could not see her expression, Kilahym heard the confusion in her voice.

"It's—complicated." Shoving his hands in his pockets, he surveyed the broad thoroughfare.

Near the entrance there wasn't a lot of foot traffic, but the noise of the city was a steady murmur. The nearest shop was within a stone's throw from the gate. Memorabilia for the Trials hung in the window; bags with the map of Etherea painted on, handkerchiefs embroidered with the abbreviation TOTI in rainbow colors. Kilahym glanced left, where the extensive stables stood a block away, bumping up against the western bank of the Agermath River like a thirsty animal on the city's cobbled streets.

"I'm afraid we'll only see the shopping district as we follow the center street. But if there's time after we reach the Assemblage, perhaps I can show you around. If you want," he added hastily.

Vayriel stood. "I would like that very much. The canals you spoke of especially."

"Then see them you shall."

Glad to avoid more talk of his past, Kilahym motioned forward to the southern hub of the wheel-shaped city and the Shrine of Laphrim. He took the opportunity to educate his Highblood friend on the history of the edifice, how it was formed and continued to be constructed, and a brief explanation of the government. He recited a few lines from a ballad about the Grey Lady and Her footprints as they walked. If Kyran was still working on his play for the Day of Laphrim, Kilahym thought it would make for an excellent excuse to visit the Bard Academy while they were here.

"Have the Spectres ever come to your coil for the elusive shaping crystals?"

Vayriel shook her head. "Not to my knowledge."

"Hmm. Well, they grow only in Heathström, so they must get them from somewhere. And then they add to and take away from the Shrine, seeking perfection. Eternally it would seem." Kilahym's gaze traveled over the packed figures ahead, rushing between stores like insects, to rest on the crystalline towers which rose higher than any other building.

"As is with us."

Kilahym lost his step. He peered behind his shoes, studying the stones of the street as if they were the source of his misstep.

"What do you mean?" he asked, turning to her again.

A shopkeeper behind her swept stray twigs and leaves away from the shelves of rolls glistening with honey. She looked up, met Kilahym's eye, then disappeared into the shop with the slam of the door.

"We are all seeking our true path in life. We learn. We grow. We are shaped by all that is around us. It is an eternal endeavor to find the true light."

"Ah, spoken like a poet of life."

"My path…is a difficult one. I must find the ultimate light if I am to…" Her voice trailed off.

"If you are to what?"

"It is nothing. The city is very busy."

Temporary canvas-topped stalls were set up in front of the permanent store buildings, causing the walkway to be further clogged. The sounds of voices haggling and merchants vying for attention grew louder as Vayriel, Orgar, and Kilahym reached the edge where the shopping district truly began, which was marked with a string of maroon pennants, draped across the street from the second story of opposing buildings, each patterned with simple line art; a pot, a shirt, a pair of boots.

Several shoppers glanced their way, a few backing into displays while others tried to move further into the crowd. People started to part like a river around a log, and the seekers found the path much wider.

"Well that's nice of them to let us through," Kilahym observed.

"I believe they are trying to get away from me and Orgar."

Then he noticed it. Fear in some eyes, rage in others, a woman clutching a baby close to her breast. *Unfortunate.*

By this time, they'd reached a crossroads and a plaza with a grassy median ornamented with trees and bushes. With no stalls here, only a few shoppers wandered between the storefronts on either side.

"Hymn? Hymn! Over here!" A man in a long brown jacket and violet-plumed hat stood across the median with a bundle in his hand, waving fervently.

A smile slowly spread across Kilahym's lips. "Ansgar? You scoundrel! What are you doing in the city?" He crossed the soft grass between them. Just seeing the middle-aged bard brought waves of nostalgia and joy. "How many synodies has it been? Two? Three?"

"I believe only two. No matter where I go, you find a way to follow my coat tails like a tundrat looking for crumbs."

"In your dreams, Ansgar." The shop's aromas tickled Kilahym's nose as he drew close: spices and incense and wax.

The Bard Academy graduates clasped each other's forearms, and both spoke at once. Ansgar's bellowing overshadowed Kilahym's.

"You first," Kilahym conceded.

"Naturally. But who is that woman you left all alone?" He took a step forward.

Kilahym grabbed his friend's arm. He knew that tone. He'd heard it at the start of many flirtatious exchanges with patrons in the local pubs. "She's with me. Er, traveling. A Highblood. Her name is Vayriel."

"That explains the menacing but lovable furry creature at her side. Hullo there, bright-eyes!" He called, waving his arms. "Yes, you! Do come and join us!"

Vayriel and Orgar approached the shop, *Scentsations,* the hand-painted sign above the door read. *Clever pun,* Kilahym thought.

"Keep that thing away from my birds!" an old woman manning the next shop over shrieked.

"I think it's more likely to eat you than those miniature fluff balls," Ansgar countered.

The woman huffed, grabbing several hanging cages twittering with puffs of feathers within and vanished inside her shop.

"Vayriel, this is my friend—"

"Bright eyes and a protector of the mountains?"

"How did you—" Kilahym began.

"Typically a spear means fighting prowess," Ansgar's tenor voice cut in. "It's rather apparent, Hymn." Then, with a wink, to Vayriel, "You also have *striking* arm muscles. I'm Ansgar Farheart."

Ansgar took off his hat, revealing bright red hair, and laid it across his chest as Kilahym sputtered then choked in a fit of coughing. Vayriel slapped the bard's back.

"That's not his last name," Kilahym gasped between coughs.

"Would you like to go into the shop?" The troubadour thumbed over his shoulder. "There's a particular scent combination of moon blossoms and lady's breath that I think would suit you. It has a most…delectably intoxicating fragrance."

Kilahym cleared his throat. "What *are* you doing here, Ansgar?"

"Thank you for the offer but Orgar would not fit, and I do not want to leave him alone. Kilahym, I think we will rest under the trees until you are ready to proceed."

Kilahym watched Vayriel cross the road then pointed at his friend. "You didn't answer my question."

"Why am I here? I've decided to finally train others, the younger versions of ourselves, in the fine art of troubadouring."

"You? Teach? Ha! That will be the day. Why are you really here?"

"Thou believeth me not? Thou wound me." Ansgar clutched his chest in mock anguish, then sighed. "Fine. You know me too well. I'm here for the celebration. Tails of the Inner-host, or whatever they call it."

"Ansgar," Kilahym said, drawing out his friend's name questioningly.

"No good?"

"You could do better."

"Long-lost love?"

"No."

"Dying cousin?"

Kilahym only shook his head, to which the taller bard laughed heartily.

"I've got a new scheme as a procurer of fine waxen creations—"

"The truth at last."

"—which I'll explain. I'd like your opinion. Step inside?"

"For just a moment. I really must be going. Unlike you, I *am* here for the Trials."

"Is that so?"

Kilahym followed Ansgar into the dimly lit shop.

"Yes. I'm actually a participant." Kilahym relayed a summary from his choosing until now.

"Imagine that. Our little Hymn, a Truthseeker," Ansgar said jovially. He wrapped an arm around Kilahym's shoulder. "And here your mother thought you wouldn't amount to anything."

Twice in one day, Kilahym's thoughts had been pulled toward his mother and father. The life he had left. The life he didn't want. He brushed the older man's arm away, turning to look at a shelf of wax melts. "Let's not bring family into this, alright? Tell me about your scheme."

Leading the way through the haphazard maze of shelves, Ansgar informed his friend of his plans as he picked up a few items for purchase. Apparently, Ansgar was in the middle of a complex arrangement. He sold items he didn't have and delivered others' merchandise as his own, for a fee, while pocketing the surplus.

"What do you think?" Ansgar pressed.

"I think you'll be lucky not to get run out of the city even if this does succeed."

"Help me, and I'll split the profits. You won't have to lie up in beds infested with who-knows-what those tavern people carry. You could buy your own place."

"Ansgar," Kilahym clapped a hand to his friend's shoulder, "I appreciate the offer. But I am happy with my way of life. I really am."

The troubadour slowly moved a pointed finger toward Kilahym's forehead. "I never could get inside that enigmatic head of yours."

Batting his friend's hand aside, the bard laughed. "And that probably kept me out of the trouble you always seem to be in."

"Fair enough."

"Look, I should head back. But do think about coming to the celebration. It would be nice knowing I had a supporter among the crowd."

"Only if I get a peek at this newfound musical magic of yours you just told me about. You're being a little ostentatious with the whole 'improve your craft' dictum, aren't you? Adding Spectre magic to your performances is akin to cheating. Wish I had thought of it," he added with a wink.

Satisfied that Ansgar would consider attending, Kilahym stepped toward the door.

"Before you go, I have one more proposition."

"This ought to be good." Kilahym crossed his arms over his chest.

Ansgar surveyed the shop. Apparently satisfied he lowered his head closer and dropped his voice. "I'm part of, let's call it a network of knowledge sharing, completely removed from any of the political powers in control. They span all of Etherea. And pay well. In the Trials you could provide knowledge no one else has, and I could sell it to them. We'd split the profit, sixty–forty."

Kilahym frowned, "I don't know—"

"Alright, fifty–fifty."

"No, that's not what I mean." Kilahym sighed. "In the spirit of the trials, I don't think," he paused and whispered the next word, "*spying* on my fellow Truthseekers embodies the collaborative efforts they want us to make."

Ansgar straightened. "Very well, but if you change your mind…" He handed Kilahym a silver rectangle, almost flat, with rounded corners. "Squeeze this until a bell sound rings from it," Ansgar demonstrated, a tone ringing softly, "and I'll know. If not, you can add it to your collection of obscure instruments. Go ahead, tap it."

Kilahym hesitated, then took the object. He tapped a short pattern on it with his index finger, and it emitted a soft sound like a drum but laced with several inharmonic undertones. He'd never heard anything like it. Unsure what to say, Kilahym mock-saluted his friend and retreated to the door.

Still puzzling over the exchange. *What in Etherea could anyone want to know about the Trials before the official updates?* He exited into what the Spectres dubbed the "Shroud of the Lady"; a constant soft light made the prismatic Shrine cast rainbows across the city. He found himself mesmerized by the spectral display.

As Kilahym walked back to the other side of the street, his stomach lurched as he focused on the tree. He spun left and right, his heart pumping faster.

Vayriel and Orgar were nowhere to be seen.

CHAPTER 18

Moving beneath a thin tree in the thoroughfare's median, Vayriel signaled for the jeroti to sit on the light green sod. She knelt beside him, dropping an arm around his furry shoulder as she surveyed the crowd. The people were more varied here than Beechmarsh. Skin tones and hair colors she had never seen, and the assortment of apparel grabbed her attention.

"This place—it is so large. That building is as tall as the ancient redbarks. It is like a mountain."

Orgar licked her cheek in response, and she looked into his cyan eyes.

"I know. We will be alright." She hugged her friend, glad for his familiar comfort in this strange place.

Orgar's ears perked up, the triangular points rotating backward; a low whine issued from his throat. Vayriel felt his emotion like a wave of energy, raw and powerful. She fought to push past his feelings and open herself to the Mother-of-All, to sense what he was sensing. But Waverling was full of noises and clouded her concentration.

Orgar tilted his head back, fang-like incisors bared, as a short howl issued from his quivering lips. Vayriel felt as if several jeroti were surrounding her, then Orgar bolted. She shouted his name, but he did not stop. Vayriel looked back at the store, but Kilahym was still inside. She grabbed her spear and raced across the grass after her life-friend.

He entered an opening between the buildings as someone swung a basket at him. It missed, and Vayriel swatted it out of their hands with her spear as she followed. The jeroti darted around a corner, and Vayriel skidded to the side, brushing the wall to avoid crashing into a man in a simple gray robe. After several turns, the buildings and the spacing between them changed. Clothing hung from string that stretched between the facades. Perpendicular to the cobbled walkway flowed a clear stream, its waters appearing motionless within the fabricated sides.

Orgar paused on a bridge ahead of her that arched over the canal's calm waters to another street. The comforting scent of loam and moisture tickled her nose from the water tinted like Orgar's eyes.

"What are we doing, life-friend?" she asked as she climbed the bridge. "Kilahym will not know where we have gone."

Vayriel looked around, taking in the sights and the smaller crowd walking this part of the city. Her grin faded as she followed the sound of wheels grinding against the stones. Carts full of creature-sons and -daughters in crates were being transported further into the city. Vayriel felt Orgar's frustration just before she saw it: a cage with a jeroti within. Light sparkled on her pair of crystalline horns.

"Maristen's Magical Creatures!" A man with a large, pointed hat called out from the front of the convoy. "At the eighth hour past midmoon in front of the Bard Academy! Admission only fifteen laphtas."

"Why are they in cages?" If Vayriel had fur it would be bristling. She gripped her spear tightly and gently touched the life force energies of the captives. There was some calm familiarity but also novel confusion and fear. A young girl walked by, tugging on her mother's arm. "Can we see the animal show, mommy?"

Vayriel and Orgar descended the bridge behind the mother and daughter, slipping into the procession. The girl looked with wide eyes into the carts as they passed. Vayriel walked quickly to catch up with the front carts, noting they were tied to each other with yellowing twine.

"These creatures should be returned to their homes," Vayriel said when she was close to the man.

Without turning, he waved a hand over his shoulder. "Be gone, protestor. I have a permit from the Magisterium."

Vayriel looked into the cages nearest her. At least six different kinds of birds were hunched in too-small spaces.

"What are you doing with them?"

"Come to the show and find out!" He raised his voice, turning his head as if to address the people along the street as well. "Maristen commands many beasts to amaze you with song and daring feats."

"That is not their nature. You should let them go."

"You're one to talk," he spun around. "You own a jeroti."

"A Highblood's relationship with a jeroti is a mutual bonding. We are a part of each other's spirit. I do not *own* him."

"Whatever you say." The man shifted toward his carts.

Orgar stepped in front of him and growled, his lips pulled back from his fangs.

The man held up his hands, grimacing. "Look, take it up with the Magister. What I'm doing is perfectly legal."

Vayriel motioned with her hand, and Orgar retreated next to her. Some pedestrians had stopped and were staring, leaning heads together in whispers. Though she felt grief in her chest, Vayriel and Orgar began to walk back the way they had come. Vayriel was alone in a strange place, and she did not want to fail her first trial. She needed to get to the Assemblage, but she vowed to discuss this with the Magister as soon as she saw her. Vayriel touched the rope where some green remained as they walked. Orgar paused at the female jeroti's cage, and the two creatures pressed their noses together through the bars.

"I am sorry, my friend," Vayriel said once they climbed the bridge again, both of them watching the last carts pass out of view around a curve in the street. "We will do more when we have friends with us. Two against a whole city is not very wise."

Vayriel stroked Orgar's head as she gazed across the canal. From the northern end of the stream, a gray-blue water-glider appeared. Its glossy surface held a hint of green as well. The more Vayriel stared, the more the color shifted. A man dressed in dark pants and long sleeves stood inside the craft, using a pole to propel it. Vayriel recalled Kilahym's impression of such a movement.

As the vessel drew nearer, she saw the man was at its back end. It curved higher at the front, carved into the shape of an enrobed woman with her hands over her eyes. Inside nested a pair of deep-purple cushioned benches that faced one another. A woman in white sat in the one positioned toward Vayriel. Her large collar arched up and around the back of her head.

"Ah, Vayriel!" the woman called with a curt wave as the man paused the vessel before the bridge. Her voice was as deep as the Agermath River. "There you are. I heard you caused quite the stir at our gates."

From Kilahym's description, Vayriel was fairly certain who this woman was.

"Magister?" she asked, receiving a cut nod in return. "Thank you for allowing Orgar to enter the city. I am sorry for the trouble I caused."

"No trouble. You gave one of our newest Spectres a much-needed test.

Things have a way of working out in the end." The Magister smiled, a stark contrast to her monotonous manner of speaking. "You also passed your own trial at the gate. Well done. However, you are quite far from the Assemblage."

"We were just returning to our route. We must rejoin our companion." Vayriel glanced behind her and the alley they had come from, looking for any sign of Kilahym.

"I'm sure Kilahym will meet you at the Assemblage. I am on my way there now. Join me."

"Join you? In your water-glider?"

The Magister laughed. "Yes. Look there." She pointed behind Vayriel. "If you climb down those steps, our boat will swing near and you can step inside."

Vayriel spotted the gray steps, disappearing into water.

"What about Orgar?"

"He can come as well. Our craft supports more weight than you would think."

The Magister couldn't know that Orgar weighed almost twenty stones, but Vayriel would do as she suggested. She and the jeroti knew how to swim and hoped the boat's occupants did as well. She suppressed a growing grin at the thought of them all floundering in the canal.

Signaling to Orgar, Vayriel pointed to the steps. He moved none too quickly. His tails were low, and she thought he deliberately avoided looking at her.

As promised, the boat eased up next to the steps. Orgar double-pumped his paw before climbing onto the empty velvet chair. The boat rocked but stayed afloat. Orgar twisted around as he clambered onto the flat part at the front. Vayriel followed him, using her spear to keep her balance. She sat opposite the Magister, and the vessel resumed its languid voyage.

"I had meant to find you when we reached our destination." Vayriel balanced her spear on her knees, its dangling green jewels casting sparkles on the boat floor.

The Magister raised her eyebrows. "Oh?"

"It is about that man, Maristen. He has confined several creature-sons and -daughters, and they must be returned to their homes." Vayriel's voice cracked, and she took a deep breath to steady herself.

"The animals are not harmed. Do not fret. We make sure that they are not mistreated as part of the show."

"But—"

"Once the Trials Celebration is finished, the visitors of the city will be seeking entertainment. Maristen will earn most of his wages for the synody over the next few days, and the visitors will have a reason to continue to spend money in our city. It is good for commerce, you see. But on to Trials business."

Orgar huffed behind Vayriel, his breath passing over her ear. She swiveled to see that her companion had laid his head down behind hers. He looked as defeated as she felt. Maybe Kilahym would have an idea on how to assist since Maristen was setting up in front of the Bard Academy. From their travels, Kilahym had treated Orgar, as well as other creatures, with respect. She felt confident he would understand.

The Magister continued. "Your jeroti will have a place to sleep, eat, and his other business. Our pages will bring food and…clean up as needed. I understand that the bond your people have with the jeroti is unique. You must forgive the Spectres at the gate. A magnificent creature like Orgar can be rather unsettling. But seeing as you have brought him along, I've arranged for these modifications to your suite within the assemblage."

Vayriel brightened, "Thank you." The Magister recognized the nature of the jeroti, at least. Mo'fa always said that respect was half of understanding, and understanding was half of knowledge. Maybe there was hope in changing her mind after the ceremony.

"We want you to feel and look your best. We have provided a spacious tub for bathing, and the pages will quickly clean your clothing," the Magister's eyes traced Vayriel from foot to head, "should you desire."

The Agermath River had allowed them to freshen up themselves and their clothing along the journey, and she had changed clothes regularly. It was not that much different than what she would have done at her coil, but she did not want to seem rude, so she nodded.

Looking around, Vayriel committed as much of the new city to memory as she could. The way the buildings rose out of the water, their bases green with water-loving plants, and how they changed as one moved from southeast to southwest by way of an intersecting waterway. How some boats bobbed where they were moored while others left the canal by a connecting water road to traverse other parts of the city. The Shrine of Laphrim peeking over the rooftops.

"What do you think of our city so far?"

Vayriel turned to face the woman. Out of the corner of her eye, she caught Orgar dipping a white paw into the water, parting it like a jeroti herding alusarean. Vayriel could see more boats join the canal behind the woman's large collar, like a flock of birds floating in the current.

"It is all very new," she replied. "I am absorbing the experience."

In truth, it was exciting and daunting. There were too many people. Just as Mo'mo had warned, there were many who did not seem to understand Highbloods and their life-friends. The canal was comforting, like the streams of her home. But Vayriel could not convey those mixed emotions.

The Magister leaned forward to pat Vayriel's knee. "It has been at least twenty synodies since we had a Highblood Truthseeker. How much did your coil tell you of the events to come?"

"Only a little," Vayriel said. She did not wish to betray her ignorance or that most of her information concerned her task from the vision.

The leader of Heathström sat tall and squared her shoulders. In this pose, the woman's high collar gave her the appearance of a hood-necked serpent. "Many things have changed since then. The shadow of war looms over Etherea once again. In the past, the Trials proved we could all exist in peace. Now...ah, forgive me, I should not trouble you with my doubts. Let us remember that it only takes one great person to change the world! Why, think of Agermath, the first Seeker from Heathström! She safely led the other Seekers through the perilous fens to the south, across the scorched desert of Sondrine, and into the volcanic wasteland of Komor."

"I thought that Agermath was a man." Vayriel recalled Kilahym's tune from the Moon's Quiver.

"Oh, no," the leader admonished. "Someone so great could never be *male*."

Vayriel fought to keep her face impassive. It seemed that the Order of Laphrim's opinion of men went further than the topic of magic. She wondered if Kilahym knew. She gripped the loose cloth of her pants, praying to the Mother that Kilahym was not running around the city looking for her. If only the Spectres had trained him more maybe he would have known how to communicate telepathically with the Magister.

"Maristen, what are you doing?" the Magister called out.

"The carts' wheels are tied together! When I find the little scamp that did this—"

"Just get the street passable. Now."

Vayriel hid her smile behind her hand, then ducked behind the Magister's collar. The vines had grown and wrapped themselves around the wheels of every cart, pulling them into a tangled clump.

The Magister sighed. "What were we saying?"

"About the first Truthseekers," Vayriel prompted.

"Yes, they returned with treasures from their circumnavigation of our world, but the greatest treasure of all was their unity. They left as individuals but returned as friends and companions. I do hope that these Trials will be more like that."

"Recent ones have not gone so well?" Vayriel guessed.

"Indeed not." The Magister sighed and lowered her eyes. "I am sure your people heard of the catastrophe that happened last time. The entire group of Seekers just vanished on their way from Waverling to their first Trial. Terrible, really, such promising young people…"

"What happened to them?"

"To this day, we do not know," the Magister confessed with a shrug. Her face was clouded, but the expression lingered only a moment before a bright smile dispelled it. "But please, do not concern yourself with that debacle." Reaching out a slender arm, she patted Vayriel on the knee again. "You, my dear, are *special*. You have *talent*. And it will keep you safe on your journey."

"You are speaking of my connection to the life force."

"But of course! It is well known among the Spectres that you are a most powerful wielder of the Lady's gifts. We have watched your exploits with your coil with great interest."

While Vayriel found this troubling, she strove to put up a neutral front. "I did not realize that I, or my people, were of such import to the Order of Laphrim."

The Magister smirked. "Oh, indeed you are. You and all of the peoples the Seekers represent. In the past, we sought out the finest orators, teachers, politicians—all those we considered to have already taken the first steps on the path to being true ambassadors for our world. But this is a new era, one where strength is valued over tact, power over diplomacy. And so, you and the other Seekers for these Trials represent that paradigm shift. Not only must you be the leaders for our world, you must also possess the gifts to enforce your position of authority."

"I see," replied Vayriel.

At face value, she could not deny the soundness of the Magister's logic. And yet it stoked fires of unease deep within her. She had come here as a representative of the hope for peace among the realms, but the Magister painted a very different picture. Orgar whined, sensing her internal conflict.

"It seems your jeroti does not care to travel by boat."

Vayriel smiled and stroked the soft fur on Orgar's head. "He does prefer the warmth of the Mother's hands beneath him, but I believe he senses my…excitement for the coming Trials."

Satisfaction gleamed in the Magister's eyes. "I am delighted to hear that! Exactly the right attitude to have going into them. It is my most ardent desire that you maintain that feeling when you meet the other Seekers. Wonderful people, really."

"When will we be meeting them?"

"You and Kilahym are the first to arrive. We expect the Truthseekers from Sondrine and Komor to arrive shortly. If not, well, they'll miss the ceremony and fail the first trial. But our informants report they are on track. You will meet your fellow Seekers and demonstrate why you were chosen. As is tradition, I will explain to the crowd, and you, the history of the Trials of the Innermost, along with its significance."

Their boat was maneuvered to another canal, and Vayriel saw the magnificent Shrine. A crowd of people gathered on the lawn in front of it. She wondered if they were going in to see the preserved footsteps.

A contented sigh escaped the Magister. "The pride of Waverling, our Grey Lady's shrine."

Vayriel nodded. They were passing under the bridge that connected the city center to the shrine. It was like an island of green surrounded by the canals. Voices merged into a pleasant hum.

Orgar shifted behind her. She heard his claws scratch the boat's surface as he pushed himself to a seated position.

"Vayriel!"

She heard her name called several times to her right. Taking her eyes from the towers, she turned. There was Kilahym, running toward them on a small walkway parallel to the boat.

"Oh, by our Lady's grace!" The bard sounded a little winded as he eased into a fast walk. "Where did you go?"

"Orgar ran further into the city. I did not have time to find you first."

"Understandable. I'm just glad that you both are alright." He grinned and then addressed the Magister. "And blessings of the Lady to you, Magister."

"It is good to see you again, Kilahym," the Magister replied. The Highblood smiled and listened to Orgar's tails thumping against the bow. Kilahym's presence brought a welcoming warmth to Vayriel, and she felt like the city grew a little smaller around her.

Kilahym bowed his head slightly. "You honor us with your charitable escort. Are you taking Vayriel to the Assemblage?"

"I am. I'd ask you to join us, but we've run out of room."

It was Kilahym's turn to smile. "I can see that. I'll meet you inside, Vayriel?"

"We will see you there," Vayriel confirmed. "I am sorry that I worried you."

Kilahym waved his hand dismissively as he slowed to a leisurely walk. The boat pulled ahead, leaving him looking on. Vayriel watched him, feeling as if a part of her was tugged by his growing distance and wishing that she'd somehow created room for him.

"The Truthseekers from the other two realms have journeyed in pairs as well, though they did not have to seek out one another," the Magister explained. "Hopefully they will arrive before the rain does." She raised her chin to the sky.

Not sure what to say, Vayriel twisted in her seat to look where they were going. Orgar mimicked her movements and watched the new sights come closer. The Magister acted as a guide, commenting on features and history while Vayriel nodded politely. Turning left again, the boat (a *gondola*, Vayriel learned) floated toward the Assemblage. Her attention turned toward the building before them and the roar that grew louder as they approached.

"—where the realms in Etherea assemble," the Magister said, completing a thought that Vayriel only half caught. "Each realm is represented in the design."

Although smaller than the Shrine, the Assemblage was just as incredible. A central rotunda anchored three wings, each modeled after the architecture of one of Etherea's realms. The designs were unfamiliar. The eastern portion sported rectangular balconies that shrank as they grew closer to the roof. Columns topped with domes accented the corners. Inside the surface of the entrance were engraved images depicting places and events Vayriel did not recognize.

The gondola drew nearer to the Assemblage, and Vayriel saw the source of the roaring. Like the clustered residences at the Shrine of Laphrim, a tower stretched the height of the building and tapered to a rounded point at the top. The light from the sun on the horizon lit the feature with a golden glow. Water crashed down from the stepped heights, cascading into a narrow waterfall that met the canal in a splash of white. Her jaw dropped as she noticed the carved head at the top where the water began. It was a jeroti, its mouth wide as water tumbled from its fanged maw.

Halfway down the building, a female figure reached out, her carved hands bearing a bowl. The waterfall pooled there before streaming down the sculpture's lower half. Vayriel stared in awe at the representation of the Mother-of-All, though she guessed the Magister would say she was Laphrim. The rivulets moved in a repeating pattern, creating the illusion of fabric rippling in the wind as they captured the distant sunlight.

They were close enough now that Vayriel felt droplets of the waterfall's spray touch her face. The crash of the water filled her ears. Her mouth agape, she faced the Magister—they were going to plunge into the waterfall's base. The Magister gestured toward the torrent as if she were pushing a curtain aside.

Vayriel faced forward and watched the water part, revealing a tunnel beneath the building. They glided through and passed into the bowels of the Assemblage.

The waterfall collapsed into place behind them.

The sound of rushing water echoed in the passage. It grew darker the further the boat glided from the entrance. No longer able to see where they were going, Vayriel faced her fellow passenger. The Magister's outline sharpened in the fading light. Then, where there had been nothing but blackness, tiny specks of violet appeared, glowing faintly. The light from the star-moss intensified, revealing the shape of the arched ceiling. Vayriel had seen this before, in different colors, in caves of the mountains.

The gurgle of the waterfall faded as their gondolier positioned their boat between two similar vessels. Steps led up to a wide ledge.

The Magister motioned for Vayriel to disembark. "We will enter the Hall of Trials from here."

Vayriel collected her spear and bags and climbed the steps, followed closely by Orgar. She paused on the ledge while the Magister spoke into the gondolier's ear, the man leaning forward as she rose. He nodded and watched her step onto the ledge.

"Up here is the door. Follow me."

Overhead, the amethystine glow lit the way, and Vayriel followed the Magister easily. She dropped her hand behind her, checking for Orgar, and was rewarded with the roughness of his tongue on her palm.

The door was unremarkable. Vayriel watched it swing silently inward at the Magister's behest. Yellow light emanated from the spiral stairway behind the aperture. Vayriel angled her spear awkwardly to navigate the turns. Before long, they reached another plain door; its only feature was a crystalline knob.

Leading the way, the Magister once again pushed the door open, holding it to allow the Highblood and jeroti to pass. The chamber beyond was spacious, and Vayriel couldn't help craning her neck to stare at the ribbed vaulting.

"It's empty now, but it will be decorated and full of people for the ceremony. All six of you will be on the stage there to your right. Heathström's main entrance is to your left. Now, if you'll excuse me, I have a meeting in the Oratory."

Vayriel scanned the length of the room. Its polished floors reflected the ornamentation of the ceiling and walls. Channels that resembled empty riverbeds radiated from a depression at the center. Twin statues of Spectres, bowls in their hands like the Mother-of-All's image on the exterior, guarded the ends of the stage.

A loud click sounded behind her; Vayriel jumped and spun. The Magister was gone. Examining the wall, Vayriel noted painted scenes uninterrupted by the crack or knob of a door.

She and Orgar were on their own again, this time in the unexplored alcoves of the Assemblage instead of the mountainous wilderness or the foreign city. The silence was deafening.

"Come—" Vayriel paused, startled as her voice echoed in the large chamber. She continued in a whisper. "Come, Orgar. We must find Kilahym."

CHAPTER 19

"There's no reason to get all in a huff about it." Kharnek watched as Zinvar leaned forward. "You've only been expecting us for, oh, I don't know, three epicycles?"

"Your sharp tongue will not help you, Komorese spy. Neither will your hulking companion succeed in intimidating us."

In Kharnek's peripheral vision, Zinvar threw up his hands. They had not expected to be stymied by an overly zealous Spectre at Waverling's western gate.

The priest crossed his arms. "We provided you with our tokens. What more do you want? And, as you can see, we left our mounts tethered far outside the city, as your Magister dictated."

"Perhaps we should try my way now," Kharnek interjected. He reached for his sword. The Spectre shifted into a defensive posture, white sparks of magic dancing about her fingertips.

The gate behind her whirled open, preempting the altercation. Kharnek grudgingly admired how it silently split apart. Zel Morakh's mighty gates were far larger and more imposing, but their opening mechanism ground and clanked and relied on an elaborate array of chains and pulleys. This could only be the work of the witches' arcane practices.

The opened gate revealed another Spectre, clad in the ubiquitous gray robes of the religious order, but her face was uncovered.

"My lords Zinvar and Kharnek of Komor, my apologies for this most unfortunate misunderstanding." The new Spectre stepped through the opening and bowed, her raven hair spilling over her shoulders. A thin silver circlet glinted atop the mound of curls.

"And you might be?" Zinvar asked drily.

"Ilya, handmaiden of the Magister. And this," Ilya glared at the combative Spectre, "is Ifen. I beg your forgiveness for her suspicion."

"Suspicion well deserved!" Ifen protested. "The shadow of Komor has long haunted the followers of our Lady."

"Enough!" Ilya commanded and balled her hand into a fist. Ifen fell to her knees. A gray mist swirled up from the ground and wrapped around her, obscuring Ifen from view. When it cleared, the Spectre was gone and every muscle in Kharnek's body was tense. He realized and forced them to relax, but his eyes never left the handmaiden.

Ilya sighed and shook her head. "My apologies again for this scene. Many of our people are too quick to judge, which is not the way of the Grey Lady."

"I am certain it was just a misunderstanding, as you said," Zinvar offered.

A warm smile creased Ilya's broad face. "Thank you for your graciousness. And my congratulations on completing your first task of the Trials! I hope that your journey here was smooth."

"It was," Kharnek cut in. The priest seemed to take his cue and did not elaborate.

"Wonderful. Now, if you will please follow me, I will show you the way to the Assemblage."

Kharnek and Zinvar followed the handmaiden through the gate, which sealed itself behind them. As they walked down Waverling's western thoroughfare, Kharnek squinted at the pointed rooftops of the city, so different from his home's geometric architecture. He saw no other Komorese among the city's varied citizens but marveled at their diversity. Women with faces and hair darker than a moonless sky hawked textiles and pottery from behind canopied stalls. Ettrascans sporting rich tans, far from their island home, haggled over the price of fishing nets. The sailors mingled with olive-skinned Sondrinel casting discerning eyes over reams of blue fabric. The latter gave the Seekers a wider berth than the rest, which was fine with him. Even here, at the heart of the realms' efforts to promote peace, old grudges lived on.

"What became of the guard?" Kharnek asked, a few steps behind Zinvar. His head swiveled about as he scanned the crowds, ever vigilant.

"I sent her to my order for reeducation. But do not worry," Ilya added quickly over her shoulder, "no harm shall befall her.

Though her wrist may cramp from writing the Catechism of Understanding a thousand times."

Zinvar laughed but stifled his mirth when Kharnek scowled at him.

They arrived at a bridge that spanned one of the city's many waterways. Ilya veered to the right to walk along the canal's edge until she reached a stairway that descended into the water. An empty gondola bobbed at its foot. She motioned for them to board it.

"Our ways must part for now. This vessel will take you to the Assemblage, where one of my sisters awaits you, as do the other envoys. I shall rejoin you at the welcome ceremony." The handmaiden stepped back. The same gray fog that had taken Ifen away enveloped Ilya, and she vanished.

"Maybe I'm missing something, but doesn't a gondola need a gondolier?" Zinvar raised an eyebrow at the waiting craft.

"It is doubtless enchanted, as is everything in this 'burned place." Kharnek shouldered past Zinvar into the boat. The priest hesitated a moment before joining him. Once he had seated himself near the prow, the gondola sped into the center of the canal, propelled by invisible hands. Kharnek could not help but be impressed by the way it nimbly dodged other vessels.

"You really don't like it here, do you?"

"Ever the perceptive one, priest." Kharnek winked. "But I also have appearances to maintain."

Zinvar snorted and then turned bright red as Kharnek favored him with a slight smile. A twinge of satisfaction at his companion's reaction made him consider just how much his feelings toward Zinvar had changed since their journey began. In only two cyclads, his loathing stemming from Zinvar's association with the Priesthood had all but vanished. In its place was…Kharnek was not sure what to call it yet. Despite his vow to not get close to another man, he couldn't help but let Zinvar in. The swish of the gondola's quiet glide through the canal mirrored the rush of his flustered thoughts. It seemed that the vessel circumnavigated the city's perimeter. Kharnek saw an enormous structure in the distance that rose over the surrounding rooftops.

"The Shrine of Laphrim," he muttered.

"Center of the Spectres' power." Zinvar gazed upon the crystal spires with wide eyes. "I didn't realize how large it was. Did you know that it amplifies their magic throughout the city? Something about the crystal material creates a locus of magical energy. Or so I've read."

"Which makes this city a dangerous place for us. Don't let the witches' pleasant demeanor fool you. They hate us for who we are." The warrior spat the last word. Zinvar blinked in apparent dismay at his vehemence, and Kharnek inwardly chastised himself. He remained silent as the gondola veered northeast into the canal that ringed the Assemblage.

"I won't discount our history of conflict and the mistrust it has sewn between our realms. But I hope you can see how the Mahiratha's trade agreement could be of great benefit to Komor," Zinvar said. "If we can persuade Heathström to serve as the intermediary for trade between Sondrine and Komor, our people will have access to much-needed food and medical supplies. And imagine what we could do with this magic."

Kharnek scoffed. "The Priesthood would never allow magic wielders into Komor, as you well know. Such thoughts are blasphemous. Never mind the military implications. But the rest, I suppose, would be of use," he hastily added.

"You make a fair point. I'm not suggesting that all of this will happen during these Trials, or even during the next cyclad. But the Priesthood has begun to see the benefit of greater cooperation with the other realms. That is, after all, part of why they selected me to represent Komor. To show that we can be open-minded. That we can shed our violent, insular past."

"Ever the political idealist!" Kharnek winked again, but Zinvar winced. He reached out to lightly touch Zinvar's knee. "I did not mean—"

"It's alright; I've been called that before."

"I want to believe in the future you describe, Zinvar. You are, without a doubt, capable of inspiring others to greatness. But I have seen too much bloodshed and lost too many brothers while fighting on behalf of a Priesthood that, for a long time, has espoused the opposite of what it claims to want now. All of that makes it difficult to think this overture of peace could be authentic. And I would hate to see you disappointed if it turns out not to be."

Which it most certainly will, he added to himself. To his surprise, he meant what he said, his orders notwithstanding. Komor's future would be as bloody as its past if nothing changed. But he was only one man, and he would not betray his mission. All he could do was try to soften the fall for his fellow Seeker when it inevitably came.

Zinvar looked at him with mirror-bright eyes, and Kharnek sank into their pale green depths. He had never noticed the flecks of gold that dotted the circumference of the priest's irises. They glinted in the light reflected from the water. A sudden urge to kiss Zinvar's full lips overcame him, which he quickly suppressed. Kharnek twisted away to hide his face, certain that it would betray his thoughts. The Shrine of Laphrim speared into the eastern sky before him, its crystalline surfaces gleaming.

Zinvar cried out, and Kharnek whirled. The priest had his hands pressed to his face as if shielding it from something. "Zinvar? What happened?"

"The Shrine…it's *burning*."

Glancing at the structure, the warrior shook his head. "It is intact. What are you seeing?"

Zinvar stood and slowly lowered his hands. "The Shrine…no, the whole city is filled with light. It's like the Everburn. And there's someone at the center of it, a woman. She's–"

Staggering under an invisible onslaught, the priest lost his balance and toppled into the canal.

"Wyrmscales!" Kharnek cursed as Zinvar keeled over and plunged into the canal. The priest's robes curled about him like a frost-bitten bloom before they vanished from sight.

Kharnek reached inward for the dark power that would allow him to fish the priest out with a thought. He paused. Too many potential witnesses. Instead, the warrior stripped off his cloak and weapons belt, tugged off his boots, and dove into the canal.

The cold of the mountain-sourced waters stole his breath, but epicycles of training upon the frozen surface of Komor had given him a resistance to low temperatures. He silently thanked his warrior instructors for the repeated dives into the frigid depths around Zel Morakh, where he had learned to fight the ekkarid—spined, eight-legged creatures that would tower over men on land—that haunted the city's underwater farms.

Kharnek scoured the murk and spotted Zinvar's limp form below. With a few powerful strokes, he reached the priest and arrested his descent toward the bottom of the canal. The warrior kicked upward and broke the surface with Zinvar in his arms.

The gondola waited at the exact spot where Kharnek had exited it. He swam over and heaved the unconscious Zinvar into the boat, where he landed with a wet thud. The warrior pulled himself in, and the craft instantly resumed its voyage.

Kharnek began to assess Zinvar's condition. The priest's pallid skin seemed even lighter than usual. His breaths were shallow and tinged by the gurgle of inhaled water. Kharnek quickly laid his companion on the floor of the gondola and stripped Zinvar down to his undergarments, wrapping him in the dry outer cloak the warrior had shed earlier. He noted that Zinvar's tattoos coiled, vine-like, around his entire body in a fashion similar to his own harder-edged designs. Shivers wracked the younger man, eliciting a pang of sympathy from the warrior. He was struck by the impulse to gather Zinvar up in his arms and enfold him in a protective embrace.

Rejecting the notion, he refastened his weapons belt and settled in for the remainder of their voyage, keeping a close eye on the priest and willing their boat to quicken its pace.

As they drew nearer, the southern face of the Etherea Assemblage resolved itself into an echo of Komorese architecture. The tiered ziggurat resembled a scaled-down version of the Temple of Morakh, which made Kharnek think of when he and Zinvar first met. Its exterior lacked any windows or light-giving portals. Besides a smattering of gear-like projections that alluded to Komor's prowess with mechanical timepieces, there was no ornamentation. The gondola sped toward the structure's base, where an iron portcullis plunged into the canal's rushing waters. Flanking the entrance were twin statues of rift wyrms, twisted around obsidian braziers filled with burning coals. The portcullis lifted at the gondola's approach. To Kharnek, the cacophony of chains and pulleys heaving its mass upward sounded just like the opening of Zel Morakh's gates.

Inside the tunnel beyond, the Komorese plunged into merciful darkness, interrupted at intervals by torches set into the walls. At the passage's end, the gondola stopped next to a platform, where a woman dressed in Spectre garb stood. Unlike Ilya, this woman's face remained shrouded by her hood.

"Welcome, Kharnek." Her voice was soft, like the touch of a feather. "And Zinvar—oh! Is your companion well?"

"He fell into the canal." Kharnek gathered up the priest in his arms, their belongings thrown over his shoulders, and stepped onto the platform. He towered over the slight Spectre. "Take us where I may attend to him. He needs to be kept warm."

"Of course. Please follow me."

The woman led Kharnek up a staircase toward the arched entrance of a great hall. Statues of Komor's mightiest priests rose into shadow on each side of the hall's length, their shapes illuminated by round bronze braziers at their bases. The Spectre stopped near the hall's end, which was dominated by a flame-decorated sculpture of an arakh. The skin of Kharnek's left forearm crawled as he studied the representation of the rare creature, surprised to see it outside of

Komor. The witches knew more about his people than he had suspected.

"The passage to the statue's left will take you up to your quarters. I will send for a healer to help your companion."

The Spectre bowed and scurried off, leaving Kharnek to find his way. He walked past the fiery arakh and through another arched opening and found himself at the base of a cylindrical shaft that stretched upward to the top of the Assemblage. Kharnek scanned the shaft walls and found the etched symbol he sought: a rift wyrm. He pressed the stone tile that bore the wyrm's image. The entire floor of the shaft juddered into motion.

The platform's slow rise seemed interminable to Kharnek, but at last, it ground to a halt at the top of the shaft level with a short hall that ended in two doors. Kharnek chose the left one, made of wood so dark it was almost black. The door sported a gilt inlay modeled after rows of wyrm scales.

Behind it sprawled a well-appointed sitting room graced by a crackling fire, which Kharnek bypassed on his way to the bedchamber beyond. He laid Zinvar on the bed, covered in plush ebony cushions, and discarded the priest's staff, robes, and satchel. Behind him, he detected the sound of the platform descending, no doubt to bring up the healer the Spectre had summoned. Kharnek ascertained that Zinvar's condition remained stable, and then took his own travel pack into the other set of chambers across the hall. They too offered lavish furnishings that would suit a noble's tastes. Kharnek felt out of place among the excess on display, but it *was* comfortable.

He returned to Zinvar's quarters and closed the door behind him. He spread the priest's damp robes near the sitting room's fireplace, keeping half an eye on his companion. No sooner had he finished then a knock came at the door. Opening it, he was greeted by a healer dressed in deep blue robes. The man, who had wrinkled, tanned skin and long white, faintly cerulean hair, met his gaze.

"Sondrinel!" Kharnek hissed. His right hand found the hilt of his sword in a blur. "What are you doing here?"

The man spread his hands revealing that he was unarmed. "The Spectres sent for me, warrior of Komor. They said a healer was needed."

"A healer not a sorcerer," Kharnek spat. "Your wiles would see all my people dead."

"There are those among the Sondrinel who do indeed feel that way. But you are mistaken if you think I am one of them. Whatever my personal feelings about Komor, my mandate as a healer is to safeguard life in all its forms. Please, let me attend to your companion. You may watch to ensure that I do him no harm."

The healer stood in place, uncowed. Kharnek glared at him, torn between hatred of Komor's longstanding enemy and concern for Zinvar. At last he stepped aside so the healer could enter.

"Be quick, Sondrinel," he grated, "and if I so much as suspect any ill intent on your part, you will find yourself gutted by my blade."

"Of that I am certain," the healer responded wryly and crossed the chamber threshold.

He entered the room where Zinvar lay and knelt by the priest's side. Kharnek lurked behind him like a thundercloud waiting to burst.

"I am called Evanel," the healer said. He withdrew a clear crystal from his robes. "As you can see, I have plied my craft for many sidereals—epicycles, in your vernacular."

Kharnek growled in response. The Sondrinel was undeterred.

"You did well to keep your companion warm. It will make my work that much easier." Evanel held the diamond-shaped crystal over Zinvar's forehead and hummed softly. A faint white light stole over Zinvar's form. He coughed, and Kharnek tensed, but he remained in place as a sphere of water emerged from the other Komorese's mouth. The healer swatted it away to a wet demise upon the floor. Kharnek watched the priest's chest begin to rise and fall in its normal cadence. The soft glow from the crystal sparkled, then burst into a dazzling array of colors that danced about the chamber. Evanel withdrew his hand, and the radiance vanished.

"Well, well—that was unexpected," the healer muttered.

Kharnek strode forward menacingly. "What have you done, sorcerer?"

"Your companion is well; you need not fear for him." The healer stood and faced Kharnek. "Moreover, he is awakening to a great gift, one rarely seen outside of Sondrine—and never before in Komor, to the extent of my knowledge."

"What do you mean?"

"Your friend is one of the Occulum," Evanel said simply. Kharnek's brow furrowed deeper as he continued, "A seer of sorts. He can perceive other wielders of the life force, as well as glimpses of the past. And perhaps what is yet to come, though that is an unverified claim."

"'Other wielders'? You imply that he himself is one? Impossible. Komor does not practice your perverse use of magic."

"As we have heard. Those who study the life force believe that Komor has lost the ability entirely due to that aversion. Be that as it may, I have walked beneath the sun long enough to know what it looks like when an Occulum begins to discover his abilities. It is good that you are here, surrounded by others accustomed to using the life force. Even if it is couched in superstition as with the Spectres." Evanel's eyes rolled a bit. Then he strode toward the door with a puzzled Kharnek in tow.

"What am I to do? Komor will not condone this…ability. It is blasphemy." Kharnek had seen people executed for engaging in "witchcraft." If the Priesthood found out…

Evanel sighed.

"Your companion's awakening would have been difficult in ideal circumstances, never mind during such a strenuous time as the Trials." The healer looked Kharnek in the eye. "The Occulum are few in number, and even in Sondrine there are those who fear their power. If his abilities disturb you, you must not show it. He will be confused and frightened by his new perceptions and beset by visions he will not comprehend. Has he ever spoken to you about strange dreams?"

"No, but we have not known each other long."

"I see. Then the best advice I can offer is to care for him as you already have."

"He will be safe in my hands," Kharnek replied.

Evanel smiled, and his features lit up in a way that belied his age. The expression infuriated Kharnek. "As you say, warrior of Komor. I take my leave. Please send for me if your companion's condition requires further attention."

"I can assure you that will not happen," Kharnek grumbled as Evanel exited the chamber. He closed the door swiftly, glad to see the perceptive Sondrinel gone.

The sound of movement behind him made him whirl around. Zinvar stood at the other side of the sitting room, Kharnek's cloak wrapped around him.

"Who was that?" the priest asked.

"No one of importance." Kharnek unclenched his jaw and moved closer, bending over to examine Zinvar. "Are you well?"

"I feel fine. Although," Zinvar's eyebrow arched, "I am a little curious as to how I wound up mostly naked, but for your cloak."

Kharnek failed to suppress the heat that rose to his cheeks. "You must not remember falling into the canal."

"Actually, I do, vaguely. There was this peculiar light, and then the city was on fire—and then I woke up here. Speaking of which, where is here?" Zinvar looked around the chamber curiously.

"We are in the Etherea Assemblage." Kharnek motioned at the walls. "These are our quarters. The healer the Spectres sent said you suffered from exhaustion. Likely from the journey here."

"Really?" Zinvar frowned. "I don't remember feeling tired."

"Neither do you remember how we got here."

"Point taken."

Kharnek turned to leave, eager to abandon the conversation.

"Kharnek?"

The warrior stopped.

"Thank you. For saving me." The priest's voice was soft. Kharnek felt Zinvar's hand clasp his own and squeeze it. The contact triggered a surge of delight followed by worry. He was letting himself feel things he should not, for his own good and Zinvar's. He gently extricated his hand and looked back at the other Seeker.

"Think nothing of it. And Zinvar?"

"Yes?"

"You should get some rest. You will need your strength for the ceremony next cycle. I am going to find the acolytes and make sure the cubes arrived safely."

His friend smiled. "Thanks."

Kharnek returned the expression, then left the room, his thoughts lingering on how pleased he was to have Zinvar's gratitude.

CHAPTER 20

"But did you have to challenge them now? They probably thought you were being rude, you know."

Idrilia shrugged her shoulders as she and Kalis secured their solendrakes and remaining camelid in the Waverling stables. The stalls smelled of excrement and wet hay. Dampness clung to Idrilia's nuala robe. Her headscarf draped loosely, covering only the top of her head.

"I wasn't trying to be," she replied. "I simply was trying to inform them that Sondrine has no lady in the clouds, so their explanation isn't plausible."

The sounds of splashing rain were muted in here, and though the stables had an unpleasant smell, Idrilia held no desire to step back into the wetness that had suddenly arrived just as they did. If she believed in omens, it might have been one. But there was no sign of any mounts from Komor inside the stable. She felt her mental preparations for a confrontation fall away.

"You and I know that. Axiom knows that," Kalis said from a nearby stall, where he was removing the last of their supplies from the camelid. "But I don't think the eve of the Trials is the best time to correct our hosts on their deity."

Idrilia yanked the final strap loose, and the saddle came free from her solendrake. "Ever full of advice," she muttered, carrying the saddle to where the other gear lay.

"What did you say?" Kalis asked.

"Nothing."

"Seeing their gate in person though was fascinating! Why do you think so many in our academia have different theories?"

"What do you mean?" *Crystals must have at least one point of contact in order for a human to have influence over, or use of, life force energy,* Idrilia mentally quoted, memorized from the tomes on crystal usage she studied in Pedium

"Well, the Spectres themselves say they can use 'magic' anywhere if they've been blessed. But some of our scholars say the Spectres aren't honest and carry crystals hidden in their robes, and others say the landscape has so many more crystals than our deserts that the life force is just more accessible. Hey, do you think anyone in Heathström can throw fireballs like us?"

"How should I know?" Upon seeing the Spectres not use crystals, perhaps Sondrinel scholars misunderstood the nature of the life force itself. And if they were incorrect about the basics, what did that mean for things like the Rising? "Besides," she broke out of her thought to address his question, "they're supposed to remain neutral because of the accords. It's unlikely they'd try even if they could." A discussion for another time, perhaps, but they needed to keep on task. "How much do you think we should take into the city?"

"You won't need much." The stable master, a middle-aged man with rounded features, came around the corner from where he'd been tending to the locals' steeds. He wore trousers with a front flap over the chest held up by straps to keep the filth of the stable off of his clothing underneath, Idrilia surmised. "They will feed you and give you a place to stay. Your things will be safe here."

Idrilia glanced at Kalis, trying to see a response in his face. The rest of his body was hidden behind the stall walls, and she couldn't get a good read. "I'll take my personal bag, then, and leave the supplies."

"And your othwit? You'd best leave her here too. I hear one of the representatives brought a jeroti. I have a nice rookery in the back where she'll be comfortable. It's been awhile since I've had one of the coastal birds to take care of."

Idrilia stiffened. After the events on the Leske Road, she wasn't about to let Wen out of her sight again, though it had been exhilarating to communicate images with her. It was through Wen's eyes that they were able to get their bearings in the foothills of Heathström's mountains. She held a palm full of insects up to her shoulder, and her othwit eagerly snapped up the treat in her beak. Idrilia preferred the othwit where she was, or at least within whistling distance.

"What is a jeroti?" she asked the stable master. "Is it a predator to birds?"

"It's like a giant varg but with two furry tails. Sharp fangs and claws are just the same. A hunter from the mountains. Everything but the trägen is its prey."

"And the guards let such a creature into the city?"

"They had to. The woman who controls it put a spell on the Spectres."

It was all Idrilia could do to keep from rolling her eyes. She was sure the stable master meant well, but he didn't seem to understand how the life force worked. Idrilia used her back to hide her motions and signaled to Kalis, who had finally exited the stall.

Do you believe this?

Could be true.

His grin betrayed his teasing. Idrilia scrunched up her nose before turning back to the stable master. "I appreciate your concern, but I want to keep Wen with me. For the time being."

"Suit yourself. But don't say nobody warned you." He shrugged and returned to the other beasts.

Idrilia shook her head at his retreating back, then a thought occurred to her. "Excuse me. If we needed to send a message out of the city, how would we do that?"

"You'll need a Runner. Their office is at about the same spot as our stable, on the opposite side." He pointed back the way they had come.

"Thank you." Idrilia reached for her pack and swung it over her free shoulder. "Ready?" she asked Kalis.

"I can send the message. You head to the Assemblage."

"What? No, I'm going with you. I want to warn the Sentinels just as much as you do. Besides, it'll be strange if I show up without you."

It took fifteen minutes of splashing through the cobbled streets to reach the building the stable master had indicated. Idrilia began to think that this realm would keep her cloth and leather forever soaked. Past her knees, the blue of her fighting robe looked darker than ever.

They passed few citizens of Waverling, but the ones they did held transparent bubbles on sticks above their heads. Idrilia watched enviously as the droplets rolled off and away from their bodies. She had an idea of how to replicate the effect, but Kalis wouldn't like it.

Overlooking the edge of the outermost canal was the Runners' office. A sign hung from the roof on a metal rod, swinging gently in the breeze. *Send and Receive*, it read in the language of Heathström, the language of trade. The words were outlined with gold-colored metal shaped into a pair of feet.

"Looks like the place." Kalis opened the door, the tinkle of a bell sounding from inside.

Idrilia followed him in, glad to be out of the rain again. She removed her headscarf completely and wrapped it around her waist.

"Good day to ya. Ah, Sondrinel. Welcome," said a man who came out of a back room. He had a broad smile beneath his wide nose, and his tan skin was not unlike their own. His eyes were different than any Idrilia had seen in Axiom. They were small in comparison to the rest of his features, with a slight lift in the corner. Though he had an accent, he spoke the shared language of trade. On her shoulder, Wen spread her wings and quivered, spraying droplets on the shelves and the articles stored there.

"Sorry," Idrilia apologized, looking at a stack of parchment, the top piece splattered noticeably.

"Never ya worry. It'll dry out alright. What can I do for ya? Here for a package? Want to send a letter home?"

Kalis approached the counter. "The latter. We'd like to send a message to Axiom."

"That I can do." The man stooped and resurfaced with a large book, which he dropped heavily on the countertop. He flipped it open to near the middle and plucked a quill from its inkwell. "I will need the names of the sender and receiver and the destination."

Idrilia joined Kalis at the counter and watched the man scribble in his book. "Kalis Vaktare."

"And Idrilia Volundar," she added quickly, then in response to Kalis' quizzical glance, clarified, "It should come from both of us."

"And the receiver and destination?"

Kalis looked at her out of the corner of his eye. "Does it matter who we send it to?"

"I think the High Keeper is best," she answered, thinking of the duties her grandmother had performed while she was still alive. The High Keeper would document the message, then contact others as needed. "Address it to High Keeper Veloran, Evocus, Axiom," she said to the shopkeeper.

"Enchanted or original?"

Kalis leaned forward, peering at the book. "I don't understand the question."

The shopkeeper glanced up from his messy scrawls in the same trade. "We can make it so that the recipient is the only person who can read the letter or use standard ink."

Barely moving her arms, Idrilia made a signal below the level of the countertop.

Protect?

Yes.

"Enchanted," Idrilia confirmed.

"Very good." The man left his book and retreated into the back room, returning with a vial of iridescent ink and a sheet of parchment.

"Here ya go. If ya need more sheets, it'll cost extra—just let me know. I'll be over here."

Idrilia and Kalis exchanged a look. His blue eyes expressed the worry she felt. They hadn't brought any currency—Sondrine functioned mostly via the barter system.

"How much should we say?"

"Here, let me. We make reports on our practice missions in Priorium. Facts, mostly, and observations, you know."

Idrilia nodded. She trusted Kalis as the more experienced one in this area. She watched as he wrote, dipping the quill in the ink, the words vanishing each time he started a new line. He summarized their encounter with the three raiders and the geometric object in the tunnel, then put the quill down beside the parchment as the last line faded.

"Anything else?"

"Brief but complete. I have no suggestions."

"All done, then?" The shopkeeper approached, glancing from Kalis to Idrilia. The bell above the door chimed as it opened again. "I'll be with you in just a moment," he called over their shoulders to the newcomer. "A copper, please."

"We—we don't carry any money," Idrilia said, wondering if there was a way to pay him back later.

"Ah. Of course. Something to trade, then?"

"We didn't bring anything tradable either, I'm afraid," Kalis joined in. Idrilia felt like a fool, coming to this foreign city without thinking of the different means of commerce. Of course, the merchants traded often with Heathström through Ettra—the largest island in the Ettrascan archipelago—but those routes and customs were well established and only used for that type of exchange.

"Nonsense—ya've got a fine piece of tradable merchandise there." The shopkeeper pointed to Idrilia's forehead. She reached up reflexively and felt the two cool teardrop jewels beneath her hand.

"This isn't for sale." Her voice tempered. She could never, would never, sell her grandmother's circlet.

The shopkeeper held up his hands and nodded. "Fair enough. I think the green complements your blue hair and eyes nicely, anyway."

Idrilia felt her cheeks flush. She shrugged at Kalis. "We will have to figure something out. Would you keep the letter until we come back with payment?"

"Of course, of course. Now, if you don't mind, I need to check in the deliveries of this Runner."

Idrilia took a step back and briefly examined the person the shopkeeper had indicated. The Runner was young, no older than she or Kalis. He wore a satchel diagonally over his shoulder, various parchment and tubes sticking out of it. Raindrops clung to his short flaxen hair.

Remembering the weather, Idrilia sighed and scratched Wen's chest feathers. "You'd think after the heat and the dryness of Sondrine, I'd be happy for cloudbursts."

The earthy scent of the wet street once again filled her nose as she and Kalis exited the Runners' office. The door swung shut behind them. Its cheerful bell sounded remorseful after their failure.

"The green does accent your eyes, you know," Kalis whispered as they stepped into the street.

Idrilia's face burned. She was glad he was behind her and couldn't see her bewildered expression.

"You know, we could try to trade something we brought with us."

"What, like our ration bars?" Idrilia rolled her eyes as Kalis joined her.

"Those delectable treats? Why would I ever want to get rid of those?" Kalis raised an eyebrow.

Idrilia made a gagging face, and her friend grinned. He stopped beneath a shop's overhang and began rummaging through his bags. The rain dripped from the canvas but provided some shelter. She sighed and opened her bags.

"Oh! Oh! Come back!" the Runner called from the threshold of the office. Idrilia stopped her movement so quickly that Kalis stumbled into her. "I have a delivery for you."

Shrugging at one another, the two Sondrinel returned inside and followed the young man to the counter. A tube, no wider than two thumbs and sealed on both ends, was in the smiling shopkeeper's hands.

"Addressed to both of you. I just need one of you to sign here." He indicated another entry he had made in the large book.

Kalis signed while Idrilia took the item and broke one of the end seals, peeling off the wax. A rolled letter toppled into her other hand as she tipped up the cylinder. Setting it on the counter, she unrolled the parchment and read its contents.

> Idrilia and Kalis. We hope your journey was uneventful and that you are comfortable in our neighbors' care. The Occulum had a collective vision about an unknown enemy we will soon face and petitioned for a communication to be sent to you. The Council agrees that vigilance is the appropriate course of action until more is known about this ripple in the life force. Trust in yourselves and protect one another.

> -High Keeper Veloran

Idrilia handed the parchment to Kalis and approached the shopkeeper. "We have payment now, if you will trade." Idrilia held out a flat silver piece.

Kalis looked up, eyes widening. "You didn't give that to the Keepers?"

Idrilia shushed him, pressing down on the rectangle, careful to not prick her fingers on the protrusion underneath. The same brief image of a woman floated out of the surface.

The shopkeeper leaned forward. "I think I know someone who would buy this. I'll take it." The man placed a handful of coins on the counter. "This is payment for your item. I'll have your letter out with the next Runner today."

Thanking him, they left, taking the letter from the High Keeper and their new coins with them.

Out of the Runners' office again, the pair walked side by side back to the main thoroughfare "Strange message, you know," Kalis said. "What does it mean?"

"I'm not sure. What do you know of the Occulum?"

"They aren't able to use the crystals directly like we can, but they can sort of see the life force that the crystals channel. They see patterns in what surrounds them. And at times, they see echoes of what has come before."

They reached the main crossroad and began following the wide avenue toward the tall shrine. A girl darted in front of them, holding one of the shields Idrilia had noticed before, and crossed the grassy divider before disappearing down a side street.

"I can't believe you didn't give that to the Keepers."

"I gave them that strange shard but I forgot it was in my bag until I was home. And I was not about to explain to my father, first, that I had forgotten to hand it over and, second, where I got it. I had to get to the final rites. And then forgot about it."

"Again."

She stuck her tongue out. "I couldn't get it to do anything else so I doubt it has much of a purpose. Don't worry so much. Your face will have permanent lines. You know what else I'm not going to worry about?"

"Hmm?"

Idrilia held out her hand, showing Kalis a pebble-sized crystal tinted blue. The rain stopped splashing on every part of her body. The corner of her mouth lifted.

"We shouldn't use them for this, you know."

"Fine. I'll let the rain back in."

"No, no. I won't tell." Kalis brought his own crystal out and shook it gently. He released it to hover in front of them, where it glowed a pale red. Idrilia felt a gentle heat bathe the exposed skin of her hands and face and saw Kalis grin. Maybe they would be dry by the time they reached the Etherea Assemblage. Admiration for Kalis warmed her insides; she hadn't yet mastered the level of control it took to be gentle with a fire crystal. Though, truth be told, she enjoyed their explosions more, though her method consumed the crystal.

They turned to follow a side street. It narrowed toward a smaller canal that linked the outermost waterway with the inner passages. Idrilia and Kalis paused at a bridge where a gondola waited for them, just as the gatekeepers had advised, down a set of steps. The vessel would arc around Waverling's perimeter until it brought them to the Assemblage.

"I think I've had enough of water for today," Idrilia said. "Mind if we walk the rest of the journey?"

Kalis agreed, and they traversed the remaining distance to the Assemblage, crossing through the city center and continuing south by way of an arched bridge. The Spectres had indicated to enter through the eastern doorway, and by doing so, Idrilia and Kalis were able to admire the north side of the building, the clever way the architects had integrated features from Heathström.

The east side, Sondrine's, reminded Idrilia a bit of the gates of Axiom in the way the columns were constructed though without the immense canyon walls of the long-dead Leske River. Overhead was a tympanum set into the pediment.

The story carved into the triangular recess was familiar to the Sondrinel. The image looked to be one but was segmented from left to right to show different events in Sondrine's history; it started with the building of Axiom and moved to the discovery of crystals, the Rising of Kadaan, and the founding of Evocus and Priorium.

Keepers were represented by figures holding books, and the Sentinels carried curved swords. Kadaan's Rising was depicted more spiritually. Her likeness was the central image, surrounded by light rays, her arms outstretched to the sky. The last image showed the many guilds gathered around a table, led by a Keeper with a bejeweled forehead. The Council of Sondrine. Idrilia identified scientists, masons, and merchants in the array by the tools the stone figures held. Lining the outer edge were solendrakes, camelids, and the various creatures and vegetation of the deserts of Sondrine.

Pocketing their crystals, the pair paused on the quinary steps and glanced at each other. They nodded. This was it. Idrilia's stomach fluttered as they climbed the steps and pushed the double doors inward.

A long hallway with a polished tile floor led to another set of doors. The floor, golden-hued, was marked diagonally with a crosshatched pattern. At even intervals along either side of the hallway stood statues of Keepers and Sentinels, men and women, and they *moved*. While their upper bodies appeared animated, their legs were rooted in place by pedestals.

Idrilia slowed her pace and marveled. She found herself staring at the ceiling. Painted in brilliant colors, it depicted the scenes from the tympanum outside but in greater detail and with more characters, and the scenery moved like the statues. She watched Sentinels practicing defensive postures, Keepers writing or flipping through pages of books, and the Council silently arguing and gesticulating at one another.

Kalis commented on the artistry and effort that must have gone into creating this part of the Assemblage with such attention devoted to the details of Sondrinel culture. Idrilia agreed, and for a while the two childhood friends wandered the hall, admiring the craftsmanship. One of the Keepers reminded Idrilia of her grandmother, and she was filled with both comfort and loss.

Their reverie was broken when the inner doors clicked open. A raven-haired woman introduced herself as Ilya, the handmaiden of the Magister. She was to take them to their rooms where they would prepare for the ceremony to celebrate the Truthseekers' completing their first trial and announce their next. This was different from the previous Trials of the Innermost, Ilya explained, as usually the first task was announced at the ceremony.

"The other Seekers have already arrived and I'm sure they're practicing for tomorrow," the handmaiden said with a beatific smile. "I'd recommend doing the same, but please get some rest, too."

Idrilia and Kalis exchanged glances. They had been rehearsing the demonstration of their talents ever since learning of their selection as Truthseekers. It would not do to have one of the other realms outshine them. Idrilia felt confident that their display would capture the imagination of the audience and prove Sondrine's superiority among the Trials participants.

They followed the gray-robed woman deeper into the Assemblage. Idrilia knew that she and Kalis were ready to face whatever trials awaited them next. *Afterall*, she thought, *what could be more difficult than fighting off a band of crystal-resistant Komor raiders?*

CHAPTER 21

Two center statues, representations of Spectres, held bowls near their faces. Water poured from their fingertips and cascaded to their feet near the stage at the far end of the Hall of Trials. The crowd watched from their seats.

From where he sat near the room's center, Kalis estimated there were two thousand attendees, mostly citizens of Heathström or Waverling and dignitaries from the other realms. The modest contingent of his fellow Sondrinel was easy to spot with their characteristic olive skin setting them apart from the mixture of other tones. Kalis sat casually, one of the crowd idly interested in the surroundings, but he felt his insides protest. He was second-guessing having let Idrilia convince him to perform this contrivance.

The water that spilled from the basins grew into a stream, wrapping around the outside of the statues' square bases, trickling lower and lower until it spiraled into foot-width recesses in the floor. Like tiny canals, they lined the front row of spectators. The streams then branched to the left and right of the first row and moved out of sight. Water surged along the sides of the hall toward the back of the chamber, separating the audience from the walls. Kalis watched the water stream pass the outside of his row as it continued the length of the auditorium.

This was a new experience for Kalis. Although Axiom was fortunate to have an underground lake to sustain the population, they did not squander the liquid in displays such as this. Still, the exhibition possessed a tranquil, almost beautiful quality, accompanied by faint trickling. Some of the Watchers whispered. Their voices added a wind-like murmur to the room. Kalis kept his hands near his concealed shortsword, a habit of his training exacerbated by the surprise attack outside of Axiom.

Water shifted to Kalis's left, shimmering in his peripheral vision. He watched as it filled the depressions lining the main aisle. The water now came from the front as well. The streams met near the center of the room, creating a circular canal before becoming a pool.

Kalis flinched as the pool burst up, forming a faintly blue oval. From within the thin apparition stepped a woman clad in white. Several gasps issued from the assembly. A man followed her, dressed in black and brown, with sculpted facial hair.

Another woman appeared through the watery portal. Kalis noticed her peach hair first, a color he had never seen before. The woman carried a staff—no, a spear—and held herself like a warrior, expressionless. Kalis couldn't help but think she could pose as a Sentinel, and none would question her, if it weren't for the shape of her eyes. He guessed that she and her companion were slightly older than himself and Idrilia.

Another figure stepped through, and Kalis stiffened; there were only supposed to be two participants from Heathström. Kalis examined the white creature, noting similarities to a varg, but it lacked a barbed tail and instead had thick fur that looked soft to the touch.

The woman who had first emerged from the watery portal began to speak.

"On behalf of the Magisterium, I am honored as your Magister to lead this ceremony. Welcome, friends, visitors on this fifth day of Uma Vek. Young and old. Children of Laphrim, Sondrinel, Komorese. We gather another synody in the spirit of peace and camaraderie to celebrate the best and brightest of our realms. In their hands they hold the future of our people and a lasting peace."

She began to walk from the central pool toward the stage at the far end of the hall. Her powerful voice echoed in the chamber, and she commanded the pauses in a way that kept the listeners hanging on every word.

"Etherea has a troubled past. A past that should shame us and drive us to never make the same mistakes again. It is a long journey, to mend these wounds and change our future for the better. As our Grey Lady's tenets dictate: *Therefore, let there be beauty and strength, power and compassion, honor and humility. Seek knowledge through the giving and receiving of wisdom in the pursuit of harmony lifelong. For unless a person keeps this faith whole and entire, she will be lost forever.*"

Kalis noted how the words were similar to Sentinel edicts in their use of balanced opposites. The Magister reached the stage and mounted its steps, while the other three waited near the stairs.

"Every three synodies, two representatives from each realm are chosen for what they have done, what sets them apart from others, what makes them deserving of the honor to participate in the Trials of the Innermost. All have successfully completed their dangerous first task by arriving here on their own. Please join me in welcoming Heathström's Truthseekers! Kilahym, bard of Beechmarsh—"

The man who had exited the portal took the stage, a broad smile on his face. He bowed to the crowd with one arm across his stomach and the other behind his back. Kilahym waved his hand comically to the side, pointed a foot forward and then the other as if starting a dance. The audience laughed and cheered.

"—Vayriel, Highblood of the Agermath Range, and her jeroti companion, Orgar."

Kalis found the Highblood's expression hard to read; her thin brows and wide-set eyes revealed little. The cheering continued as she moved, with spear in hand, to stand next to Kilahym. The jeroti sat on its haunches at her left and looked up at her.

An explosion reverberated through the room. Heat washed over Kalis, and he jumped, as did those around him. While he'd been focused on the stage, a creature had appeared to his left in the darkened passage that led to the Hall of Trials. It was a giant rift wyrm, larger than any he had ever seen, blocking the opening with its bulk. It moved forward and extended its vast wings. Kalis gripped the hilt of his weapon, but then relaxed. It wasn't real.

Its mouth open wide, the beast let forth another belch of fire, singing the air over the heads of those closest to it and the Komorese wing of the Assemblage. Kalis shuddered, thinking what destruction this creature could wreak on all the people of Etherea, not just Sondrine, with its fire and flight were it to exist. Ordinary rift wyrms, thankfully, were bound to the rocks like solendrakes.

The Magister gestured over the heads of the audience. "I present the Seekers from Komor. Zinvar, Priest of Zel Morakh—"

The wyrm's mouth stayed open, the throat engulfed with churning fire. Through the flames, Kalis caught his first glimpse of the Komorese: a pale man with facial tattoos dressed in a long rust-colored robe. The priest waved his free hand in a dramatic flourish, and a giant of a man in crimson leathers appeared in the writhing interplay of light and shadow beside him.

The sacrifices of war burdened the newcomer's pale face with deep lines, leading Kalis to assume that the Komorese were the oldest members of their travel group. Like Vayriel, he held his posture inflexibly.

The Magister threw her arm up in a dramatic flourish. "Kharnek, warrior of Zel Morakh."

Kalis fought back the mistrust that threatened to surface as the Komorese duo moved to the left side of the stage. As Heathström's leader had said, this was a cooperative effort, and he would give nothing but his best for Sondrine.

The water portal began to hiss, where it still floated at the center of the room. Kalis saw droplets break from the form, hover, then begin to travel in bands no wider than a finger toward the stage.

Kalis didn't need to look to know that Idrilia was there, holding her blue crystal as the droplets converged and disappeared into her palm like magic, stealing it away from Heathström. Kalis heard gasps again, and the people nearest him pointed. He heard the Magister announce Idrilia's name.

Holding his own pale red crystal in a fist, Kalis stood, overlooked by everyone until he held out his hand. The still-burning fire from Komor flickered and bent, then mimicked the water. The fire converged in long red strings as it disappeared into the crystal in Kalis's palm.

Stepping out of the row, Kalis approached the stage, the filaments of flame following where the crystal went. The water portal's smooth surface wavered and disintegrated, its remains dotting the space above the audience as Idrilia summoned the last droplets to her crystal.

He felt all eyes turn to him, watching as he stole the fire from Komor. The spectators grew louder until they erupted in deafening applause. Kalis's crystal consumed the final length of flame when he was a few steps from the stage. He heard the Magister announce his name, but it sounded muted now over the adulation of the audience. He caught Idrilia's eyes where she stood on the right side of the stage. She beamed. It had gone as they planned, well, as Idrilia had planned. His reservations had faded now that it was done, and the crowd's reception exhilarated him. Maybe it had been the right choice after all.

"These six individuals will be tested as they pursue tasks set to them by the leaders of each realm," the Magister continued, raising her hands to quell the noise. "They will face dangers that test their greatest strengths and their greatest weaknesses. By doing so, they will uncover who they are beneath this exterior.

They must rely on one another and work together, otherwise they will fail. They will share the histories, knowledge, and customs of their realms, and, by doing so, gain an understanding of each other as a people. They will share this experience with all who cross their paths in the synodies to come, imparting that understanding. And it is our hope that they will create friendships that know no distances. These are the Trials of the Innermost."

The crowd cheered again.

"Now, Truthseekers, the time has come to prove yourselves, to let all Etherea know why you were chosen to be here." The Magister's garments swirled about her as she stepped back and motioned the bard and Highblood forward. "Let the demonstrations begin!"

CHAPTER 22

Nervous jitters afflicted Zinvar's extremities. He was thankful for the voluminous ceremonial robes that concealed his anxiety from the audience. Notably absent were any other Komorese.

Zinvar readied himself as his and Kharnek's turn to display their talents drew nearer. The bard from Heathström finished playing a delicate tune reminiscent of birdsong on an unfamiliar instrument. The rows nearest the front murmured gruffly as they wrung out their wet clothing. Zinvar assumed the impromptu shower inflicted upon the front row had been the bard's doing. It had appeared that he created the image of a creature with an oversized tail from the water held in the hands of the statues. It rose, then shook its tail, only to disintegrate across the audience. Tucking the instrument inside his shirt, the man bowed and retreated to the back of the stage. If his reddened cheeks were an indication, the ending had not been his goal.

Next was his counterpart from the Highblood coils. The woman produced a seedling from her simple garments and cradled it in her palms. She cupped her hands and whispered an indecipherable chant. From between her curled fingers, a thin green stem emerged, limned with pale pink light. The audience gasped when the stem produced a bud that unfurled into a crimson bloom the size of Zinvar's fist. He recognized it as a blood lily, renowned for its color and medicinal qualities. The tea made from its six delicate petals could cure most ailments. Applause rolled in waves throughout the hall.

"Beautiful, absolutely beautiful!" The Magister moved to center stage from her place behind the Highblood and bard. Her voice echoed throughout the hall without any visible strain; she must be using magic to amplify the sound.

"As you can see, Heathström remains a hub of culture for all of Etherea. Our Lady has blessed us with these two talented youths, whom we have chosen to represent our realm in the Trials of the Innermost!" The Magister stepped aside and extended an arm toward the pair. "Thank you, Kilahym and Vayriel!"

The crowd's applause was cut short by the Magister's introduction of the Sondrinel. The young woman—Idrilia, the Magister said—looked distinctly unimpressed by Heathström's showing. Her taller male companion, Kalis, displayed polite interest. With their matching blue hair and long, fine-boned physiognomy, they looked exactly how Sondrinel were described in Komorese texts. They even wore the same style of robes, cinched around their waists.

Triggered by an unseen signal, the Sondrinel launched into a flurry of acrobatic tumbles, each designed to achieve a better position from which to assault one another. Their lean bodies twisted in graceful arcs as arms and legs lashed out and were met with counterstrikes too quick for Zinvar to follow. Idrilia's gradient-blue robe whirled about her with each strike, a vivid contrast to the beige of her companion's. His fighting style appeared less aggressive and more measured. The jewels on Idrilia's forehead and ears caught the light, creating twinkling accents to her movement. The priest risked a sidelong glance at Kharnek, who was observing the mock battle with intense scrutiny. Zinvar snapped his gaze back when several spectators gasped.

For the moment, the male Sondrinel appeared to have achieved the advantage, as the woman backed away from a series of vicious kicks. Idrilia struggled to defend against Kalis's longer reach. She twisted away from an attempted hold and whistled.

A small golden creature hurtled down from the ceiling. It circled the fight for a moment, then dove in and beat the male Sondrinel's head with its wings. In that instant, Idrilia struck. Circling behind her beleaguered foe, she wrapped one arm around his neck below his chin, and slid her other beneath his to firmly clasp her wrist. Kalis raised his hands in surrender, and Idrilia released him to cheers from the spellbound crowd.

Once again, the Magister stepped forth.

"Most impressive, Prioriates of Sondrine! I do hope that I never find myself at your mercy." She smirked, and the audience laughed in response. Her flowing, high-collared white gown spun in slow motion as she turned to indicate Zinvar and Kharnek. "And now, for our final presentation. Please direct your attention to our guests from Komor."

A hush fell over the great hall. Zinvar felt a cold chill in his bones and took note of the scowls on many faces in the crowd. He moved closer to the edge of the stage. Not for the first time did he long for the warmth of the fire the Sondrinel's crystal had stolen.

"People of Etherea," Zinvar began, his voice raised to its most imperious volume. "For many epicycles the moon has sailed the dark sea beyond our realms since the Trials of the Innermost commenced. Throughout each passing, Komor has remained in shadow, a land of mystery. Many of you know of us only through the timepieces that you wear"—Zinvar raised his wrist—"made by our skilled craftsmen. Today, that will change." The priest spread his arms and raised his staff up in his right hand. "Today, Komor will fully open its borders to trade with Heathström…and Sondrine."

The revelation elicited looks of shock from the two Sondrinel, and an outburst of muttering among the spectators in the hall.

"As a token of our goodwill," Zinvar went on, quieting the murmurs, "we have brought gifts for our neighbors."

Two pairs of acolytes emerged, one from either side of the stage. They bore both of the High Priest's cubes, placing one at the feet of the Sondrinel, and the other before the Magister. Kharnek moved to stand beside Zinvar and produced from his weapons belt two carved obsidian objects that glinted in the light. The priest took the objects and held them aloft.

Clearing his throat, Zinvar addressed the expectant audience. "These keys, in conjunction with the devices you see before you, will allow instantaneous communication between the three realms of Etherea. An identical device is already in place in Zel Morakh and only awaits the activation of these two."

Zinvar approached the Sondrinel, who reluctantly accepted their key. Then he moved to center stage, where the second cube stood in front of the Magister. He displayed the key to her.

"Magister, it is my honor to present you with this key. With your kind permission, I will demonstrate how this device works."

The leader of Heathström hesitated, and then she bowed her head in acceptance. "Please do. I am most intrigued."

Zinvar nodded and inserted the key into a six-sided receptacle on the cube's top until it was flush with the surface. Orange light shot out from the key and traced the lines of the inlaid patterns. Shouts of surprise echoed throughout the hall, and even the Magister took a step back when an image of Zel Morakh manifested in the air above the cube. Zinvar recognized it as the top of the

Temple.

The High Priest stepped into view, clad in shimmering wyrmskin robes.

"Magister." His baritone voice resonated throughout the great hall. "I am Natak, High Priest of Zel Morakh. I see that my gift has reached your fair city."

"Indeed, it has." The Magister recovered quickly from her shock and smiled graciously, though it did not reach her eyes. "Thank you for your...unexpected generosity, a sentiment that I am sure is echoed by the ambassadors from Sondrine."

Natak inclined his head. "May it be so, by the will of Morakh. It is the hope of my people that this gift will enable greater cooperation between our realms and foster the mutual understanding that we presently lack."

"I am certain that the Lady would want it to be so," she replied. Zinvar noticed the emphasis the Magister placed upon "the Lady."

"As do we all. This will be remembered as the dawn of a new age in Etherea. I extend my personal gratitude to Zinvar and Kharnek for fulfilling this most crucial of endeavors. The strength of Morakh goes with you into your trials."

The warrior and priest bowed, and Natak's image flickered out of existence.

Timid applause spilled forth from the corners of the hall, a sound that swelled into a roar when the Magister removed the key from the cube and clasped Zinvar's hands in her own. She released him and walked to the front of the stage.

"This is certainly an unexpected turn of events to conclude our ceremony but a welcome one indeed! My thanks to all the Truthseekers for their participation and, to all those in attendance, let the remainder of this day be a time of celebration. And now..." The Magister raised her arms toward the audience. "Let the Trials of the Innermost proceed!"

The responding roar of approval faded as Zinvar drifted into introspection. He wished his family were here to see this, his finest moment. At last, there would be peace in Etherea. As the Magister conjured a curtain of gray fog to spirit herself and the Seekers away, a single tear coursed down his cheek.

Zinvar watched Kharnek slam his fist against the wall of his quarters. An ebony vase studded with rubies clattered in its alcove.

"I doubt that our hosts would look kindly upon us breaking the décor," Zinvar observed from the settee where he lounged. His fellow Seeker had seemed particularly agitated ever since the ceremony ended a few minutes ago.

"Since when do we care what they think? Nevermind the wyrmfodder Sondrinel."

Zinvar's brow creased. "You've known about this since before we left Zel Morakh, and we've talked about it many times in a more civil fashion. I don't know why you're so angry now."

"I assumed that our offer would be rejected. The witches will always do what best serves their own interests. It is unwise to trust them. This notion of cooperation is a fantasy."

Kharnek collapsed onto a golden armchair with black silk cushions and scowled. Heaving a sigh, Zinvar put down the book he was reading and looked the warrior in the eye. "That sort of attitude will most certainly doom our efforts to failure."

Kharnek's reply was cut off by a knock at the door. Zinvar hurried away to answer it, opening the door to reveal Ilya.

"Pardon the interruption," the handmaiden began, "but the Magister has summoned all the Trials participants. She will discuss the arrangements for the next part of your journey."

"We should go now?" Zinvar queried.

"Yes. I was sent to bring you to her."

Kharnek waved his hand in dismissal. "Go ahead, priest. These matters are your specialty."

"You are invited as well, my lord Kharnek." Ilya dipped her head.

"An invitation I must decline. My companion will brief me upon his return."

"The Magister is expecting you to attend," Ilya insisted, her voice hardening.

"I'm sure it will be brief…" Zinvar trailed off as Kharnek skewered him with a menacing glare. Taking the unspoken cue, he shrugged. "I apologize, but I'm sure the Magister will understand that he is indisposed at the moment. I will relay her instructions upon my return."

"Very well." Ilya's eyes narrowed. "It is disheartening to see such inflexibility at the dawn of a new era of mutual cooperation."

The sullen mask of Kharnek's face betrayed no reaction to her jibe. Zinvar shook his head, then gathered his staff and followed the handmaiden to the platform that would carry them downward. Once they stood side by side, Ilya depressed the rift wyrm tile and they began their descent. The cacophony of the lift mechanisms grinding made him wince. He wondered if the Spectres would be willing to share their impressive gate technology—or magic, rather—but then Kharnek's words about allowing such a thing into Komor returned to him. Perhaps the warrior was right to question the Priesthood's motives. Or maybe he knew something that Zinvar didn't.

Ilya interrupted his ruminations. "You are troubled by your companion's behavior."

Glancing at the dark-haired woman, Zinvar nodded slightly. "'Disappointed' might be a better term."

"It is only natural that change comes more easily to some than others. In time, he may see things as you do."

Zinvar did not miss the emphasis she placed on 'may.' "In fairness to him, he's only had a couple cyclads—pardon me, weeks—to get used to the idea. For all his outward contrariness, I've seen the desire for a better future take root in him. I am confident that he will embrace that future, in time."

An inscrutable expression flickered across Ilya's face. "A generous attitude. I hope he proves worthy of it."

So do I. The platform ground to a halt, and the pair began to make their way through the Komorese wing of the Assemblage. There was no sign of anyone else in the dim, echoing halls. "Is it always this empty?" he asked.

"The Assemblage? Oh, no." Ilya pointed toward the central hub they were approaching. "The wings are reserved for Truthseekers or important dignitaries, but each of the realms maintains an embassy in the Grand Atrium. There is also a museum with memorabilia from previous Trials. As such, it is busier there, as well as in the other two wings. Komor's wing is far less utilized, though perhaps that is going to change."

True to Ilya's word, once they passed beneath the arched entrance to the Grand Atrium they found themselves amid a throng of people. Zinvar tilted his head back and gaped at the domed ceiling. The left half was polished black tiles with inset crystals that glittered like stars. The right half gleamed in pure gold, while between the two sides a narrow band of smokey gray crystal bisected the dome's center. Zinvar was so distracted by the representation of Etherea's sky that he bumped into someone in front of him.

"Oh my, I am so sorry. Excuse me–" He cut off his apology when he recognized the female Seeker from Sondrine. She glared at him.

"Watch where you're going, *arslen*."

"Idrilia!" Ilya cut in smoothly, appearing between them as if summoned. "You must be on your way to see the Magister as well. Permit me to escort you."

It looked like that was the last thing Idrilia wanted based on her furrowed brow, but she nodded and fell in step with Zinvar and Ilya.

"I assume Kalis will also be joining?" the handmaiden asked lightly.

"He went ahead of me. For him, being on time is late."

Zinvar snickered, which earned him another look of disdain from the Sondrinel Seeker.

"An admirable way of living," Ilya replied. "I wish more of our junior Spectres adhered to it."

"Speaking of timeliness, where's your counterpart? Too scared of us to join in?" Idrilia sneered.

The priest bowed his head. "He had other matters to attend to."

"Right. And I'm a camelid calf." Idrilia spun on her heel. "Let's get on with it, shall we?"

The newly-formed trio exited the Grand Atrium and entered Heathström's wing. This section of the Assemblage mirrored the architecture of Waverling and the Shrine of Laphrim. Columns of smooth marbled stone flanked a long hall that culminated in a dazzling crystal sculpture. As they drew nearer, Zinvar recognized it as a miniature replica of Heathström's capital city. Water trickled through the spaces where canals delineated the metropolis's inner and outer districts. The detail and craftsmanship far surpassed anything he had seen in Komor, save perhaps for the most elaborate of timepieces.

"That is quite stunning," Zinvar gushed.

Ilya's face lit up. "Isn't it lovely? It was made by the same artisans who shape the Lady's Shrine."

"It reminds me of the Star of Axiom," Idrilia put in.

"What's that?" Zinvar asked, genuinely curious.

Idrilia eyed him warily but indulged his question. "It is a large crystal that is suspended over Axiom. We use its brightness to mark the passage of days."

"Ah, that's quite a clever way to account for being underground. I'm surprised that I never found mention of it in my readings on Sondrine."

Idrilia opened her mouth, but a commotion from one of the chambers that dotted the sides of the hall drew Zinvar's attention. A group of five men boiled out of the space, their faces red with anger. One of them jabbed a finger at Ilya.

"Mark my words, there will be a reckoning for this, Spectre! You cannot hide behind your magic forever!"

Several gray-clad women emerged from the same room and interposed themselves between the speaker and the Magister's handmaiden. The man spat on the floor, then led the others toward the Grand Atrium, followed closely by the Spectres.

Zinvar watched them go. "What was that all about?"

"A disagreement, nothing more," Ilya answered quickly.

"It seemed like more than that," Idrilia observed, hands on her hips, "and I couldn't help but notice that they were all men."

Her comment sparked a connection for Zinvar. "There are no male Spectres. Is that what they're unhappy about?"

A variety of emotions flickered across Ilya's features before they settled into an impassive mask. "In a manner of speaking."

It seemed like she did not want to elaborate, but Zinvar was not ready to drop the subject. "In my readings on Heathström, it was mentioned that men here are prohibited from using magic. I can see how that might produce some unrest."

The handmaiden sighed. "It is not prohibited, only…strongly discouraged. True followers of the Grey Lady understand that Her greatest blessings are meant for those most like Her. Men lack the wisdom to properly manage the gift of magic."

"As much as I want to agree, there are men who use the life force responsibly in Sondrine," Idrilia countered. "Do you not employ one of our male healers? Seems a bit contradictory."

"We are humble enough to acknowledge that, on rare occasions, the Lady's power manifests strongly in those who have not yet come to know Her truth. Eventually, all paths lead to Her. You should speak with Kilahym, one of our Seekers, about his recent blessing. I'm sure he'd be delighted to tell you more." Ilya gestured toward the end of the hall. "Come now, the Magister awaits."

The handmaiden turned away from them and started walking. Zinvar and Idrilia exchanged puzzled glances, then hurried after her.

A set of wide double doors opened into a small amphitheater. Ilya waved them forward. Making his way down the central aisle, Zinvar chose a seat a couple rows behind the Seekers from Heathström, across from where Idrilia joined her companion. The carved stone bench felt cold even through his robes. Behind him, the double doors closed with a dull boom. He jumped, then regathered his composure as the Magister emerged from a concealed doorway on the skene's right side. The pristine white of her high-collared raiment reminded Zinvar of Natak. Despite their differences, the two leaders also shared a penchant for drama. He watched her stern gaze pass over the gathered Seekers, pausing for a moment when it settled on Zinvar. It moved on and he exhaled, thankful that she did not single out Kharnek's absence.

"Many hundreds of synodies ago, Laphrim, the Grey Lady, ushered our people out of the darkness of the Great Calamity and into a new era," the Magister intoned. "Though our history has been marred by conflict since then, your presence here demonstrates that our faith in Her teachings is not misplaced. You, the Truthseekers, represent our hope for a better future. Bear this in mind as you set out to complete the rest of your trials. Your actions will be synonymous with the people you stand for, your example one to be followed by the generations to come."

Zinvar glanced at Idrilia and caught her eye roll. He suppressed a snort while he surveyed the other Seekers. The other Sondrinel listened to the Magister with rapt attention. Kilahym, the bard, squirmed in place, appearing to find the stone bench as uncomfortable as Zinvar did. Next to him, the Highblood sat straight and tall, her gaze fixed ahead. Of all those present, she was the most enigmatic. Her people were notoriously insular, which made her selection as a Seeker something of a mystery, her impressive display of magic notwithstanding.

As he studied her, a vertiginous sensation overcame him. The voice of the woman from the tower seemed to reach him as if from a distance: *"She will conquer the darkness. You must help her fulfill her destiny."*

The strange feeling and voice disappeared as quickly as they manifested. Zinvar blinked and shook his head, drawing a curious look from Idrilia. Ignoring his discomfiture, he refocused on the Magister.

"Your next trial will take place in the Fens," the politician was saying. "You are to recover an artifact that is of great importance to the people there. Upon your arrival in their village, you will receive further instructions."

"What about supplies?" the male Sondrinel asked.

The Magister motioned toward Ilya, who had remained at the back of the room. "My handmaiden will see to that. You will receive enough provisions to sustain you throughout the next trial. From there, it is up to you to obtain additional resources. We will provide you with a stipend to assist in this. Use it wisely."

That news came as a relief to Zinvar. The meager stores he and Kharnek were given when they left Zel Morakh were nearly depleted. They had a small amount of local currency for each of the realms, but that would not have lasted long.

"And after the Fens?" Idrilia asked.

The Magister shook her head. "I am unable to share any details about the trials you will face beyond that. Each task was selected by the leadership of the realms within which they take place and vetted by the Order of Laphrim for level of risk. But I can tell you this: Your journey will take you across all three realms. You must be prepared to face the unique challenges each one will present."

A Spectre appeared from the same place the Magister had and whispered something in her ear. Heathström's leader nodded slightly, and the messenger departed. She addressed the group once more. "I apologize, but an urgent matter has arisen that requires my personal attention. If you have any other questions, please direct them to Ilya."

Hushed chatter broke out between the Sondrinel Seekers as the Magister left. The Highblood stood and Kilahym jumped up to follow her into the central aisle. Rising from his own seat, Zinvar intercepted them on their way towards the exit.

"Hello! I don't believe we've properly met. I'm Zinvar, representing Komor. Although you probably already know that," he added in a rush.

The Highblood smiled. "I am Vayriel. It is good to meet you, Zinvar."

"And I'm Kilahym!" the bard exclaimed. He thrust his hand toward the priest in greeting. When Zinvar clasped it, a vision of the Shrine of Laphrim filled his mind. Light consumed the structure like he had seen before his plunge into the canal, but this time Zinvar stood at the heart of the inferno with the Seekers from Heathström. And someone else was there, wreathed in shadow…

"I say, you're looking rather pale, even for a Komorese. No offense."

"None taken," Zinvar replied to Kilahym, withdrawing his hand. "I'm just feeling a bit off. Probably nerves."

The bard shook his head sympathetically. "Understandable. It isn't every day you're told to set forth on great adventures."

"Indeed. Well, it was a pleasure making your acquaintance. I'm sure we'll get to know each other quite well in the cycles to come. Now if you'll excuse me." Zinvar bowed and scurried away. He could feel the weight of the other Seekers' curious stares on his back and heard them murmuring to each other, but their words were swallowed by the cacophony of his own thoughts.

CHAPTER 23

Kharnek watched the door close behind Zinvar, the receding sound of his footsteps accompanied by the swish of Ilya's robes against the basalt floor. He waited until he heard the grind of the stone platform descending, then sprang out of his slouched position. Although he felt guilty that his tirade had confused the priest and likely cost him some goodwill, he finally had the opportunity he needed.

From his travel pack he retrieved an ebony breastplate that gleamed in the flickering torchlight. He strapped it on over his black leather top, then fastened on a hooded cloak that hid his weapons belt and the armor. The cloak was made of wyrmskin and possessed the same reflective camouflage qualities. Kharnek stepped out into the hall and became nearly invisible, the cloak melding with its surroundings.

He was glad he had thought to bring the garment. Before the incident at the Tower of Nerekesh, he would have wrapped himself in living shadow and moved with peerless stealth. Now, when he reached for the darkness, he found…nothing. And what troubled him most was that he craved what he had lost, despite its insatiable appetite for fell deeds.

Kharnek turned away from the shaft where the platform had descended moments before and faced the wall at the end of the passage that led to his and Zinvar's quarters. Twin sconces on the wall flanked an engraved representation of a rift wyrm. Kharnek pressed on the gem that twinkled at the center of the wyrm's eye, and the engraved section of the wall swung away to reveal a stairwell. The warrior smirked. Unlike the other wings of the Assemblage, Komor had designed and built their own rather than entrusting its construction to the witches. And the Komorese builders and artisans had incorporated more than mere aesthetic touches.

Kharnek stepped down into the stairwell and the hidden door swung shut behind him. Overhead, milky white sibilstones dotted the ceiling. The stones shed a dim light reminiscent of walking beneath the waxing moon. He followed the stairwell as it spiraled down into the depths of the Assemblage, well below street level. It terminated at the edge of a circular opening. Lines of reflected light rippled on the walls of the stairwell.

Kharnek dropped through the opening and landed with a splash in a long tunnel; it extended away to either side as far as he could see. In the distance, searching fingers of sunlight pierced the shadows, dancing on the surface of a thin layer of water. They found their way into the tunnels through portals at street level. Reaching up, Kharnek could just brush the curved ceiling with the tips of his fingers. He stretched his arms to either side, testing the space available. His palms found the walls with little effort. Not much room to maneuver should he attract unwanted attention.

He strode forward, careful to mitigate the splashing sound his footsteps made. Many epicycles ago, in the first conflict between the realms, Komor had discovered and scouted this network of tunnels, determining that it was primarily used for maintenance of the city's canals. Now it would provide a means of covert entry into Waverling for Komor's invasion force.

The warrior thought of Zinvar and how the priest would react when he learned that his vaunted diplomatic overture was a ruse. After the healer's visit and the revelation of Zinvar's latent powers, Kharnek wondered how long he could keep his secret. Komor could not afford to have its intentions for the other realms become public knowledge. If Zinvar threatened to compromise that information, Kharnek would have no choice but to take action—but he felt uncertain of what he would do in that situation. His duty to Komor should supersede all else. But "Komor" to him was the Brotherhood not the hated Priesthood that had given him his current mission. Talking to Zinvar about their shared qualms related to the Priesthood only reinforced this reality, and it was the most he had opened up to anyone in epicycles. He found himself questioning his orders…and whether he could lose the person who was making him do so.

A sharp *plunk* in the distance brought Kharnek to a halt. The sound disrupted the soft drips of water leaking through the ceiling. He edged forward until he reached a point where the tunnel intersected with another and slowly peered around the corner. The passage lay empty, with no sign of whatever had disturbed the quiet. Kharnek prepared to venture onward until the faintest of whispers tickled his ears.

The tunnels were not so abandoned after all.

The warrior moved toward the susurration, which resolved into multiple voices. As their words became audible, an arched wooden door set into the tunnel wall came into view, inset with a barred grille. Kharnek stopped in the shadows across from it, ensuring his camouflaging cloak covered him, and observed a half-moon of five figures, two of whom were clad in the gray robes of the Order of Laphrim. One of the other three people—who were all males, he realized—spoke with anger evident in his words.

"The Magister's acceptance of this obvious falsehood only shows how weak she is—how weak *all* of Heathström is."

"And what would you have done differently, were you in her position?" asked the female Spectre on the left. "Rejecting the gift would only have brought down Komor's wrath sooner, something we can ill afford."

"Something we will never be able to afford if we continue on the course the Magister has set us upon, Jehana," another male said. "Her pacifist ways will doom us all to be broken beneath Komor's iron rule."

"The Magister cannot do anything else," the woman at the center interjected. Kharnek started as he recognized her: Ifen, the quarrelsome guard at the city gate. "If Heathström were to show any indication of favoring the Sondrinel, it would incite open conflict," Ifen continued, "and our survival is predicated upon abiding by the Waverling Accords, which dictate that our realm remains strictly neutral."

"Meanwhile, Komor has built a military force greater than Sondrine's and the Spectres' combined might," the first speaker interrupted, his words laced with sarcasm.

"Yes, Falsten, which is why we must all accept the inevitable fact that Komor will soon invade the rest of Etherea. And they will succeed in conquering it." Ifen's reply brought a silence to the room, as if all the air had been drawn out of it.

"What can we do in the face of such an onslaught?" The other woman sounded faint.

"We can take action, Jehana," Ifen said. "Action to ensure the continuation of our society. Action that will earn us the scorn of our contemporaries, but that our people will thank us for in the future."

"What exactly are you proposing?" the second male to speak queried.

"That we offer the surrender of Waverling to Komor when the time of their invasion comes." Ifen raised her hands to stop the immediate protests from her compatriots. "With the condition that we be allowed to self-govern so as to preserve our way of life."

"How could we ever be certain that Komor would abide by such an agreement?" Falsten asked.

"With Waverling removed from the conflict, the rest of Heathström will fall quickly. Komor will have a clear path to taking Sondrine. Also, it is no secret that Komor holds no love for the Highbloods and has long lusted after the crystal deposits they protect. Without the aid of the Spectres or the Sondrinel, the Highbloods are too few in number to resist Komor. They will be slaughtered."

Ifen's last statement lingered in the air.

"We must move quickly, then, if we are correct in our interpretation of Komor's actions," Jehana said at last.

"I have already contacted the Priesthood of Komor with a little help from their gift and my mother's idealism." Ifen grinned slyly.

The third man joined the conversation. "Ilya suspects nothing?"

"No. My little charade at the gate has her convinced that I am, if anything, overly zealous. She would never dream that I would be involved in a plot against her dear Magister."

"And so we have become enemies of the state," Jehana said. "This is a dangerous path, my love."

"We are revolutionaries, Jehana, harbingers of a change that has been forestalled for far too long. You can see the hunger on the faces of our companions. They chafe beneath the Order's female dominance."

"We continue to be led by a woman," Falsten added wryly.

"We are all equals here, Falsten. What I first conceived of will not be brought to fruition without the help of everyone present. I can trust in your commitment to our cause, can I not?"

The man inclined his head in agreement.

"Good. Then come, let us leave and begin our work. There is much to be set in motion."

Ifen rose, and the group followed her lead. Kharnek hastily retreated the way he came. He narrowly made it to the tunnel intersection and around the corner before the door creaked open and the conspirators filed out. When Falsten emerged, he stopped and looked directly down the tunnel toward Kharnek's place of concealment.

"What is it, Falsten?" Jehana asked as she emerged from the chamber behind him.

Falsten continued to stare for a moment before shaking his head in dismissal. "Nothing. I thought I detected someone nearby, but it was nothing. This is what happens when an Occulum gets old." The two Spectres chuckled, then shuffled off into the shadows.

Kharnek remained at his vantage point for a moment, pondering what he had overheard. He needed to reach his superiors in Zel Morakh and report this development. First, though, he had to complete his current objective.

After a few hours and a wrong turn, Kharnek found himself in a tunnel that ended in an archway guarded by thick vertical bars. Beyond it the warrior heard the rush of surging water. This was where the canals converged back into the flow of the Agermath River and exited beneath Waverling's southeastern wall. With the bars removed, an outside force could penetrate the city's defenses unseen.

Kharnek drew his sword, the black blade glistening wetly in the light reflected off the tunnel walls. He slashed across the bars twice, once on the upper and once on the lower portions. The sword cleaved through the metal with ease, the thick material offering no resistance to the unique Komorese weapon.

He stepped back, satisfied with his handiwork. A casual observer would not see the fine lines cut into the bars, which could now be lifted out of the way. Kharnek sheathed his sword and began the journey back to the Assemblage.

"I was beginning to wonder when you'd be back."

Kharnek suppressed the urge to reach for his blade when he opened the door to his quarters, pausing at the sight of Zinvar with his arms crossed over his chest, his staff leaning against the settee behind him. Kharnek entered the sitting room, glad that he had removed the camouflage cloak before entering. That would have raised even more uncomfortable questions than his disappearance.

"I had hoped to return before you. I went to the street market to acquire a few necessities for our journey."

"Is that so? Did you find what you were looking for?" Zinvar arched an eyebrow in open skepticism.

"I did."

Zinvar stared at Kharnek, who cursed himself inwardly for not coming up with a better alibi in advance.

An uncomfortable silence descended between them. Kharnek, in a rare moment of discomfiture, broke it first.

"What did you learn at your little gathering?"

"We leave the next cycle, at moonrise for us. Our next trial will take place in a region called the Fens."

"Which is what, exactly?"

"I'm given to understand that it's a huge area of swampland in southern Heathström. It's a little over four cycles' distance from here."

Kharnek grunted. "How pleasant. What about the trial itself?"

"We're retrieving some kind of artifact. More specifics to come when we get there."

"I see. Thank you for going to the meeting without me. I am sorry I could not join, but as you saw, I was not in the right frame of mind."

"You're welcome," Zinvar muttered.

"Was there anything else?"

"We were also given some additional supplies and local currency."

"Convenient." Kharnek unbuckled his weapons belt and laid it on the armchair to his left.

"Yes, especially since most of Etherea will not accept our money. The muura apparently holds little value outside of Komor. Here."

Zinvar plucked an orange canvas bag from the settee next to him, and withdrew another of the same size from within its depths. He tossed the bag at Kharnek's feet, where it landed with a dull clink.

"The Magister gave these to all the participants. Your funds are inside. The bag itself is enchanted in some fashion, because it can hold all of our traveling supplies."

Kharnek kicked the bag away. "We will not make use of their witchcraft solely for convenience's sake."

"I suggest that *we* do. Your absence at the gathering already caused enough of a stir. Rejecting the Magister's gift would only further damage our already tenuous standing." A hint of impatience tinged Zinvar's reply. "Nice armor, by the way. Were you expecting trouble while you were out shopping?"

"I am exercising a measure of caution, and you would do well to do the same. Despite our newfound friendliness with the witches and the Sondrinel, they do not view us in a kind light."

"Parading about their cities dressed for war certainly does nothing to dispel their preconceptions," Zinvar shot back. The priest sighed and sank down onto the settee. "I don't know why I bother. Nothing I say will make you think or act differently."

"On the contrary," Kharnek objected. "No one has ever made me think more critically about what Komor stands for…what *I* stand for." He chose his next words carefully. "There will be things I say or do throughout the Trials that seem to undermine your goal of peace. I want you to know that they do not necessarily represent my own views. I am only doing what I am expected to do: my duty."

Zinvar stared at him, unblinking, then lowered his head. "I don't think I fully understand. I doubt anyone but another soldier could. But…from the outside looking in, it seems like you're justifying actions you don't agree with by calling them 'your duty.'"

The observation landed as heavily as a physical blow. Zinvar was right. He had given voice to something that Kharnek had always known subconsciously but never dared to confront directly. Now that the truth had been dragged into the light, he realized how ugly it really was. He sat down next to Zinvar, head in his hands.

"Your words strike at the core of me. I feel their rightness, but if I acknowledge that, then I feel lost." He straightened to look at Zinvar and saw that the priest was already watching him. "I do not know any other way."

Zinvar's lips curved in a small smile. "Then let's learn another way. Together."

"Alright. I cannot promise anything, but I will try." Kharnek shifted, and the motion brought his leg into contact with Zinvar's. The air between them suddenly crackled with tension. Kharnek's knee tingled where it was pressed against the other man's thigh. He realized how close together they were and that he was holding his breath. A slight flush had dusted Zinvar's cheeks with pink. They had never talked about past romantic liaisons, so Kharnek did not know for certain where Zinvar's interests lay, but he had caught the priest staring at him enough times to suspect that the attraction was mutual.

Zinvar abruptly stood. "I should, um, get some rest before we leave," he stammered. "See you at moonrise!" The priest collected his staff and orange bag and swept out of the room. He let the door swing shut behind him, and the decorative vase jumped in its place again.

Kharnek, stunned by the sudden departure, wondered if he had misread the situation. Time would tell—he had enough to worry about without muddying the waters of their friendship. He stripped off his leather garments and headed for his bedchamber.

The knock on the door came so softly that at first, Kharnek wondered what had woken him. Then it came again, a timid rap that brought him into full awareness. He rose from his bed, crossed into the sitting room, and slowly cracked the door open.

Zinvar stood on the other side, a blanket wrapped around his thin frame.

"Sorry to bother you, but—I couldn't sleep."

"Oh." Kharnek waited, uncertain what he should say.

"Would you mind if I came in?" The priest's eyes darted to the ruined skin of his companion's forearm. "I just need to talk."

Kharnek shrugged and pulled the door open. Zinvar seemed taken aback by the sight of the warrior clad in nothing but gray shorts. A faint flush reached his pale cheeks as he stepped inside, shuffling to stand by the fire in the sitting room.

"Thank you. I was having the strangest dream. It was so vivid, like reliving a memory."

"A dream about what?" Kharnek asked, moving next to the priest. The healer's warning echoed in his thoughts: *"He will be confused and frightened by his new perceptions and beset by visions he will not comprehend ..."*

"You wouldn't believe me if I told you."

Kharnek grunted. "Try me. I have seen much you would disbelieve."

Zinvar was quiet for a moment before responding. "I saw a city full of strange creatures being torn apart by darkness. They cried out for help. Then a terrible silence fell." The priest shuddered. "It felt so real."

"It was not." Kharnek gently placed a hand on Zinvar's back. "It was only a dream."

"I know, but...I'm sorry, I shouldn't be so shaken up."

Kharnek was reminded of the way he felt after his own dreams and let empathy soften his words.

"I, too, have had such dreams. They are difficult to forget."

"Yes…they are. I have never felt anything like it, except right before I fell in the canal." The priest's shoulders slumped. "None of this makes any sense."

Kharnek pondered this revelation. "The feelings will pass. Your fears about the Trials are likely the culprit."

"You're probably right." Zinvar looked up at the warrior, his eyes full and mirror-bright.

The vulnerability in them kindled something in Kharnek that burned like the flames beside them.

The warrior motioned to the settee. "Would you like to sit down?"

"If you don't mind."

Kharnek guided him to the sofa then, mindful of their earlier interaction, returned to stand by the fire. The flickering light brought the geometric tattoos on his torso to life. Across from him, the vine tattoos on Zinvar's neck writhed in their own parody of motion kindled by the flames. The priest shifted in place, and the blanket fell open, revealing the angular planes of his lean upper body that were also covered in coiling inked designs. Kharnek swallowed. It was hard not to stare.

"I'm sorry about earlier."

Kharnek frowned. "What do you mean?"

"For leaving so suddenly." Zinvar crossed his legs beneath him and huddled in his blanket.

"Ah. No apology necessary. I hope that I did not do something to make you uncomfortable."

Zinvar gazed up at him. "Not at all. Quite the opposite in fact."

The warrior's pulse quickened. "I am relieved to hear that."

"It's just that it's been a long time since…" Zinvar broke off and looked away. Kharnek thought the pounding of his heart could be heard in Zel Morakh.

"Since?" he prompted.

"Since I've been interested in someone," Zinvar finished, eyes fixed on the fire. "There's not much romance in the life of a priest. I've sort of forgotten how to act. Then again, these *are* unusual circumstances."

The naked admission elicited a host of responses in Kharnek. Joy and the thrill of discovering this shared possibility. Desire stoked by the knowledge that the man he wanted wanted him too. And fear. Cold, numbing fear that he was already making the same mistake he swore not to barely a cyclad ago. "Unusual circumstances" had certainly played a part in bringing him to this moment so quickly. He had not expected to face it so soon.

Kharnek set aside the tangle of emotions and focused on the present. It would not be fair to Zinvar to not respond. "I think that this merits a longer conversation. Is it alright if we talk more over the next few cycles?"

"Of course."

An awkward silence ensued. Dozens of half-formed thoughts met an untimely demise at the gates of Kharnek's mouth. He wanted to say more, but he was caught between the conflicting urge to allow whatever was happening between him and Zinvar to unfold and the desire to protect the priest from his inner darkness. How could he explain that? Never mind the issue of Zinvar's parents' deaths at his hands.

"Well, it's late. I should go," Zinvar said. "We both need our rest."

The sorrowful note in the priest's voice wrenched at Kharnek's heart. He strode over and crouched in front of the settee.

"Stay. You will sleep better here," Kharnek insisted.

"Are…are you sure you don't mind?"

"I am sure. Sleep well, Zinvar." He rose halfway and softly kissed Zinvar's forehead, then stood and returned to his bedchamber. The warmth of the priest's skin on his lips lingered long into his own dreams.

CHAPTER 24

"Are you *sure* we're going the right way?"

"Yes, Kilahym, I'm sure. I know how to read a map," Idrilia replied over her shoulder. She smacked the back of her neck, killing whatever was stinging her skin.

Ever since they reached the Fens and received the instructions the Magister had promised, she had begun to think the real trial was tolerating everyone else. At least the Komorese mostly kept to themselves, which was fine with her. The bard, on the other hand, seemed determined to open his mouth with every footfall along the narrow, overgrown path they were following. Knobs like giants' knees poked out of the green film that covered the swamp water further into the Fens. The tightly packed trees and constant hum of unseen crawlies reminded her of the island her Pedium class visited after graduation minus the thigh-deep quagmire, though Klaara wouldn't be swimming in these waters. A smile tugged at the corner of her mouth; Klaara would toss stones from the path into the water to see if anything lived beneath the grimy surface.

"Idrilia and I learned land navigation at a young age," Kalis asserted from his place just behind her. "She's quite capable of leading us to the ruins."

"And we're doing what when we get there?" Kilahym asked.

Idrilia grinned, brushing another hanging strip of moss out of her face as Kalis huffed. "You would know the answer to that if you hadn't been too busy cataloging fungi while you were supposed to be listening."

Kilahym put his hand to his heart. "Have you any idea how rare Hoblett's spotted mushroom is? To think I should find one in the wild, not besmirched by cooking spices! Though they are rather delicious, truth be told."

Kalis groaned. "Can someone else please fill him in?"

Idrilia swatted a buzz by her ear. "We find the ancient ruins using the map the mayor gave to us. There, we are to recover the artifact that was stolen from Peatwick village."

"A village built on stilts!" the bard exclaimed. "What a sight that was. Each house like a long-legged bird wading through the tides, seeking its meal."

"They live in harmony with the Mother's creation," Vayriel stated. "The design of their dwellings is both practical and respectful of the creature-sons and -daughters with which they share this land."

"Not to mention it keeps them from getting wet," Idrilia tossed back, pulling her boot with a squelch out of a patch of muck.

"The same unfortunately cannot be said about us," Kilahym moaned, plucking at his soiled pant legs. "Why would anyone keep something valuable out here?"

Kharnek snorted. "For once, I agree with you."

"The villagers call the object 'the Prophet,'" Zinvar spoke up. "It is sacred to them." Idrilia glanced back at where he and Kharnek brought up the rear of their single-file line. The edges of the priest's robes were brown with dampness and crusted in mud, much like her boots. Humidity beaded his forehead with sweat. He looked miserable, but to his credit, he had voiced no complaints. Neither had Kharnek, the priest's hulking shadow that Idrilia reluctantly agreed to let take the rearguard position. At least he appeared capable should anything deadly emerge from the gloom between the tall, knotted tree trunks. The path wended its way through the swamp, which covered a sizable part of southern Heathström. Why anyone would choose to live here was beyond Idrilia, although the mayor had claimed that the villagers preferred their simplistic lifestyle over the bustle of Waverling.

Kilahym cleared his throat, drawing Idrilia's attention. "Not to cast aspersions on the goodly mayor's intentions, but if the Prophet was stolen, then how did she know where it was?"

"This mushroom of yours had better turn out to be useful to us for more than a snack." Idrilia rolled her eyes. "On their deathbed, the thief *told* the village where it was to taunt them. The villagers believe the ruins are sacred and won't go near them."

"How cruel!" the bard exclaimed. "But then why wait until now to have it retrieved? Surely they could have hired someone."

"They did. They never returned," Zinvar answered. As if to punctuate his words, a creature unleashed a high, keening cry from somewhere in the bog's depths. Idrilia reflexively halted and reached for her daggers. In her peripheral vision, she saw Kharnek's hand stray to his sword. The Highblood, in the middle of their group, closed her eyes, and her forehead wrinkled in concentration. Her jeroti companion whined and leaned into her leg.

"I do not believe we are in immediate danger," Vayriel announced to the group. "But it is difficult to distinguish one creature-son from another in this place. It is so full of life."

Kharnek snorted. "How reassuring."

Though she would never admit it, Idrilia privately agreed with his comment. She held up the map and compared the lines scrawled onto the yellowed parchment to their immediate surroundings. Thus far, the mayor's guidance had proven accurate, but it had clearly been some time since the map was drawn. Vines and tree roots coiled over the dirt path. In places, the trail had succumbed to erosion and sunk into the scum-laden water. Idrilia had managed to lead them around these obstacles, but they all had scratches and insect bites to show for it.

The wet squish of his footsteps signaled Kalis's approach. "What a miserable place," he said as he came up beside her, "Makes me nostalgic for the desert."

Idrilia swatted away a flying bug that wanted to perch on her nose. "You're telling me. At least we're close to the ruins. The sooner we get there and find the Prophet, the sooner we can leave this infernal mire."

"Do you think people will look at us differently when we get back?"

Although she knew what Kalis meant, Idrilia's mind went straight to their betrothal. She had done her best to avoid the topic while they were in Waverling, but eventually, she would have to address it. Having Kalis around day in and day out was a constant reminder of that. Even though it wasn't his fault, being around him was…uncomfortable. And she knew that distancing herself as she had was hurtful to him. But each time Idrilia thought about removing a stone from the wall she had built to protect herself, Kalis's presence felt like mortar that refused to let go. The internal conflict left her exhausted and anxious.

"'Dril? Are you alright?"

Blinking away the tears that threatened to spill over, Idrilia strode ahead, chin lifted. "I'm fine. Let's keep moving."

Time passed as slowly as their progress through the Fens. The weight of the other Seekers' expectations pressed Idrilia ever onward. When at last she spied a stone pillar emerging from the sea of brown and green, she released the tension that hunched her shoulders.

"There," she pointed, "that's the entrance marker. We've found the ruins."

"Well done, Idrilia," the Highblood praised her with a smile that made Idrilia's heart flutter.

The Seekers advanced past the marker and through the remnants of an archway decorated with orange flowering vines. More pillars, their upper halves surrendered to decay, flanked the path until it reached a wide, clear area that Idrilia guessed to be an outer courtyard. Broken flagstones peeked through a carpet of moss and lichen. Thin geometric lines were etched into the fragments that reminded her of the patterns on the communication cubes. She frowned.

Kalis's hand landed on her shoulder. "Something wrong?"

Idrilia shook her head and shrugged off his touch. "No, I was thinking that there's something familiar about this place."

"How so?"

"I can't really explain it." Idrilia surveyed the ancient courtyard. Gnarled trees draped in hanging moss lined its perimeter where the other Seekers had wandered. Above their branches loomed a tiered structure, each level varying in shape like the Evocus. She spotted a gap between the twisted trunks. "There. That must be the way inside."

Kalis dipped his head. "Lead on, then."

"Over here!" Idrilia shouted. Without waiting to see if everyone else followed, she made for the opening in the natural barrier. The wan illumination from the twilight sky could not penetrate the darkness beyond it. Idrilia produced a light crystal and focused her thoughts, infusing it with the life force until it glowed a dull yellow.

"That's a neat trick."

She spun to find Zinvar and Kharnek behind her. Beyond them, Kalis herded Kilahym and Vayriel toward her position. "I suppose you don't see it often in Komor," she responded to Zinvar.

"Never," Kharnek spat.

"Your loss." Idrilia smirked, then entered the dark passageway. The trees soon gave way to gray stone like she saw in the outer courtyard. It arced over her head close enough to touch if she stood on her toes. Kharnek would have to crouch to walk through, a thought which brought her no small measure of satisfaction.

She emerged into a vast hall, its ceiling so high that her crystal's radiance could not reach. Shafts of dim sunlight pierced the gloom through cracks in the stone, highlighting specks of floating debris. For a moment, she thought of a similar adventure with Kalis and Klaara. A need to know what lay further in this tunnel filled her chest to bursting as Idrilia shuffled forward. She felt something snap beneath her foot and stopped. Lowering her crystal toward the floor, Idrilia revealed a carpet of bones littering the ground. She gulped. The macabre sprawl extended as far as her light reached. She heard the other Seekers' footsteps approaching the end of the passage and called out, "Watch your step!"

Kharnek was the first to emerge, his broad shoulders scraping the sides of the opening. "What are you talking…oh." He stopped short as a rib crunched underfoot. If the sight disturbed him, Idrilia saw no indication of it on his square-jawed face. Zinvar popped out from behind him, lips flattened as he took in the grim scene.

"What happened here?" The priest's gaze darted about. "The designs in the stone, the tiered architectural style, the pointed arches…these ruins are pre-Calamity…"

"…but these deaths were not," Kharnek finished. The Komorese drew his sword. Its blade gleamed black; the length difficult to gauge. Idrilia stared at the weapon and noted its similarity to the raiders' armor in the canyons. Could it be the same material? If so, then Kharnek was even more dangerous than she originally thought. She would have to keep a very close eye on him during the Trials.

"Well that is certainly a revolting sight," Kilahym observed as he, Vayriel, and the jeroti joined the group, followed closely by Kalis. "I suppose that answers the question of what became of all the others who ventured here."

"But not how. We must be cautious," Idrilia advised. Her eyes widened when Kharnek nodded in agreement.

Kilahym wrung his hands. "These ruins are vast. How will we find the Prophet? I know it's part of the challenge, but we don't even know what it looks like."

"The mayor said we would know it upon seeing it." Vayriel patted Orgar's head. "And my life-friend can search for us. He will cover ground more quickly than we can."

Kalis's head bobbed. "That's a good idea. Just have him be careful. We don't know if what killed all these people is still here, you know?"

"We are always connected. I will sense if he is in danger."

The jeroti sprinted off. Idrilia watched his twin white tails disappear into the shadows and felt a pang of longing for her own "life-friend." The mayor had advised against bringing Wen along for the trial, claiming that "local fauna would find her quite appetizing." Against her better judgment, Idrilia had agreed. She hoped the mayor was taking good care of the othwit back in the village.

"Let's explore this area while Orgar searches elsewhere," Zinvar proposed, which met the group's approval.

The Seekers stayed close together as they set out into the hall, guided by Idrilia's crystal. Quietude prevailed in the ruins, disturbed only by the faint cackles and cawing of birds that penetrated their exterior and the Seekers' motion. As they perambulated the hall, Idrilia began to grasp its general shape. This tier of the structure formed a long rectangle, the shorter sides facing east and west. At the east end was an exit with stairs that led down, which she presumed was where the jeroti had gone.

"What do you think this place was?" she asked the others.

"The architecture reminds me of Evocus," Kalis stated, "but I don't see anything that makes me think this is a repository of knowledge."

"Nary a piece of furniture to be seen," Kilahym added.

"That could be the work of looters," Zinvar commented. "There have been plenty of epicycles for them to take whatever used to be here."

"Or die trying." Idrilia's words brought a halt to the conversation. The group traversed the southern wall in silence until Vayriel gasped. Idrilia whirled left and right but saw no obvious threat. "What is it?"

The Highblood pointed. "On the wall, it is…the story of my people." She raised her spear and the tip shone as bright as a full moon. Its pink-tinged light drowned out the amber of Idrilia's crystal and illuminated a swath of the wall covered in images. Depending on where Vayriel's light shone on the stone-absorbed paint, the images seemed to move.

"If I'd known you could do that, I wouldn't have bothered with the crystal." Idrilia extinguished her meager beacon. "What is it you're seeing here?"

"Unless I'm mistaken, it's an origin story," Zinvar offered. "I've read many of the realms' accounts of how they began."

Idrilia saw Vayriel's brows knit. "You are correct," the peach-haired woman replied, "These pictures tell the story of how the Highbloods believe the world—

how we—came into existence. But I do not know what it is doing here. We have called Skyveil home for many hundreds of journeys of the Daughter."

The priest waved his staff in a circle. "We—the Priesthood, that is—have uncovered a lot of evidence that suggests before the Calamity, there was only one civilization. The realms we know today didn't exist until after that. This could be a relic from that time."

"But what is the story? Will you tell us?" Kilahym stuck out his lower lip and Idrilia laughed, imagining the same expression on Felune when she wanted something.

"I, too, would like to hear the tale." Idrilia smiled at Vayriel, and the woman bowed her head.

"It would be my honor. By knowing the history of my people, I hope that you will join us in the sacred cycle of life. May you walk the truth path and see the true light."

As the Highblood launched into her story, Idrilia sidled over to Kalis. "Keep an eye out for trouble during our history lesson," she murmured. He nodded and rotated to put the wall at his back, mirroring the stance Kharnek had taken, although the warrior had sheathed his blade. Satisfied that they would not be ambushed, Idrilia focused her attention on Vayriel.

"In the beginning, the land of our people was empty." The Highblood placed her fingers on a dark gray circle etched into the stone. "The sky spirits painted the darkness with dots of light, but they were unhappy. The spirits had not yet lived and yearned to be born into the creature-world. So, the Mother-of-All pulled the spirits from the sky and created bodies for them to roam the land."

Vayriel gestured to a depiction of human-like figures beneath a field of stars. "Thus, were the first inhabitants of Etherea created. And the sky-spirits rejoiced to have their deepest longing satisfied, but they soon learned that their physical bodies were but temporary vessels for their celestial essence. They felt pain, grew old, and eventually died. Yet that was not the end of their journey. The sky spirits returned to the spirit-world when their bodies failed, having lived a life in the creature-world." The Highblood motioned at the Seekers. "So it is with each of us. We are all beings of light who exist only for a time in this world. That time is a gift from the Mother, as is our eventual return to her side."

"It's like the Rising," Idrilia murmured.

Kalis tilted his head, then raised and lowered his chin. "Maybe there is some credence to what Zinvar said."

Idrilia shrugged and followed Vayriel as she led them further down the wall to where three spheres clustered together, presiding over a mountain range.

"Then the Mother-of-All called her two sons and her daughter to her side and told them to watch over the creature-sons and creature-daughters as their own, sending new sky spirits in, and taking care of the spirits whose time in the creature-world was over." Vayriel took another step down the wall, her fingertips never leaving its surface. "First-son took the form of a golden othwit and watched by light. The daughter took the form of a silver-winged vandling, just after it escapes its gossamer cocoon. Second-son chose the form of a varg and, with his sister, watched by darkness."

Tilting her head back, Idrilia noted the three forms that the other Seeker had described. She enjoyed the richness of Vayriel's voice and watching how the other woman used her free hand to emphasize certain words. For the moment, it outweighed her impatience to get on with their trial.

"But second-son was not happy sharing the darkness with his sister," the Highblood explained. "And he tried to persuade her to go to the light with first-son, but he was unable to convince her to leave her duty to the spirits in the shadow." Vayriel's face darkened. "One day, second-son came to the daughter while she was tending the sky spirits. 'Come,' he said, 'I have something to show you.' And he led her to where the light and dark met. Unused to the light, her eyes were blinded, and second-son ripped her silver wings from her body with his claws."

Vayriel mimicked the action, the lines in her forehead deepening while the light from her staff imparted motion to the wings on the wall. Idrilia felt a momentary pang of sympathy for the fictitious daughter's plight. In some ways, it reminded of her own. The betrothal was second-son, coming to strip her of her freedom.

"Returning to the creature-world," Vayriel continued, "the Mother-of-All cried for her lost daughter, and her tears created the rivers and lakes and oceans. Seeing his sister floating wingless, first-son was filled with so much anger that he shone like the light itself."

Idrilia and the other Seekers followed Vayriel further down the wall.

"First-son attacked his brother," Vayriel said, laying her hand on a section of the wall devoted to a golden othwit, its claws outstretched toward a leaping varg's open jaws. "Their struggle shook the land. Mountains crumbled and rose. The creature-sons and creature-daughters fled the destruction. So fierce was the battle that the curtain between the creature-world and spirit-world was torn, and the sky spirits became lost in the spirit-world. First-son used the last of his strength to cast his brother from the edge of the creature-world into a place that was neither the sky nor the land."

The Great Calamity. The parallels between the Highblood's story and what Sondrine espoused as historical truth were undeniable.

"But the battle left first-son terribly injured. First-son could no longer move. His broken wings curled around his body, and he formed a ball where he was at the sky's edge. First-son has stayed at the edge of the creature-world, unable to move, guarding against his brother with his light. We call him the Watcher." Vayriel pointed skyward. "You know him as our sun. When the Mother-of-All looked at her fallen child and at the destruction caused by second-son's treachery, she was filled with sorrow. To protect the creature-world from another such betrayal, the Mother-of-All placed a shell around second-son and caused him to fall into an eternal slumber. He is hidden from our sight in Skyveil…what you know as Heathström. We call him the Sleeper." She walked to a depiction of Etherea and its two moons and pointed at the smaller of them. "He is only visible in the south."

"That's the main one we see in Zel Morakh," Zinvar noted.

"As you say. For her daughter," Vayriel slid her finger over to the larger moon, "the Mother-of-All made a blanket which reflects some of the light from the Watcher and casts light in the darkness she always guarded. We call her by her true name, the Daughter."

Idrilia squinted at the picture. "What about the torn veil? I don't see anything about it being fixed."

Vayriel raised her spear and walked to the end of the wall, the Seekers in tow, to where a line of figures streamed after a white creature that reminded Idrilia of Orgar. "The living are not meant to dwell with the spirits. The Mother-of-All led the sky spirits in their bodies to the jeroti, and the jeroti offered protection and guidance through the spirit-world. Together they found their way back to the creature-world, to the land of Skyveil, where they became the Highbloods. With our safety assured, the Mother-of-All restored the curtain and vowed to never step away from her creation again. She is everything in our land. Her skirt is the valleys and hills, her hands are the mountains as she holds our land like a bowl. She wears the shine of the spirits in her hair, which sparkles above us—where the light from the Watcher is faintest. And she guards against the Sleeper. For if he were ever to awaken, a fate worse than the Great Calamity would befall the realms."

Zinvar, who had begun to lean closer as the story neared its conclusion, flinched and drew back. The reaction made Idrilia tilt her head, but she dismissed it as inconsequential. "An interesting legend," she spoke, "thank you for sharing it with us."

The corners of Vayriel's mouth curved downward. "It is the truth," she said. "All stories begin with truth. Though it is not your own story, that does not make it less truthful."

"And a beautiful story it is," Kilahym jumped in. The bard placed his hand on Vayriel's forearm, which triggered a flicker of jealousy in Idrilia. What would the Highblood's skin feel like under her hand were she to offer comfort instead? Then again, it might not be welcomed, since she seemed to have offended the other Seeker.

"Fascinating as this was, we have a trial to complete. Have you heard anything from your animal?" Kharnek inquired, interrupting Idrilia's thoughts.

"Orgar has been searching the lower level," Vayriel answered, "but so far it is empty. He…" the woman's violet eyes flared. "He has found something."

Kalis sprang into motion. "Well, what are we waiting for? Let's go check it out!"

The Seekers hurried to the north end of the hall and took the stairs down. When they reached the bottom, Vayriel's spear-light revealed a low-ceilinged chamber that stretched only part of the length of the upstairs. A pair of cyan dots reflecting the pink glow revealed Orgar's location at the room's other end. The jeroti yipped and bounced in place.

"He must have found the Prophet!" Idrilia crowed. "We'll have this trial over in no time." As she moved toward Orgar, a clanking sound made her pause and look up. A contraption unfolded from the ceiling, round with a long cylinder sticking out of it. The device rotated and spun until the cylinder pointed directly at her. Orange light flared at its tip, and a smell like the aftermath of a lightning strike made Idrilia's hair stand on end. Her training kicked in and she dove to her right. A bolt of energy sizzled through the space she vacated. It struck the floor, and the rock exploded into molten fragments. Idrilia scrambled for the entrance to the chamber as the object whirred and spun, following her movements. It whined in preparation to unleash another blast, and she heard Kalis cry out. With a burst of speed, Idrilia leaped forward, turning her momentum into a somersault that brought her to the foot of the stairs. Melted rock splattered the stone behind her.

"Fall back!" she roared.

The Seekers sprinted back up the stairs. As they reached the top, Orgar streaked by them, seemingly untouched by the lethal assault. They did not stop running until they were back by the passageway that led them into the hall. Idrilia signaled for the group to halt, grateful that Kalis thought to flag down Kilahym and Zinvar, who completely missed her intention and probably would have run all the way back to the village.

"What…in the Lady's name…was that?" the bard gasped.

"I don't know. Some kind of trap or defense mechanism? I've never heard of anything like it." Kalis's eyes met Idrilia's. "Have you?"

"No." She bit her bottom lip as she considered this new obstacle. "I'm amazed it would still be functioning after all this time."

"There are some similarities to Komorese technology," Zinvar noted, "we have mechanical devices capable of the same movements. But we've never developed weapons like that." The priest glanced at Kharnek. "At least, not that I know of."

"Whatever it is, it did not target the animal," Kharnek pointed out. Orgar, who had taken up his usual position next to Vayriel, growled at the Komorese.

"I do not think my life-friend wishes to test its generosity. But it does seem to recognize the difference between creature-sons and people." Vayriel looked at Idrilia. "There is nothing in my experience that explains this. You have led us this far. What would you have us do?"

All eyes turned to Idrilia. The invisible pressure that was the mantle of leadership constricted her chest, but she closed her eyes and breathed as she had learned in Pedium, the faint scent of balsam and peat reaching her; nothing as pungent as the southern delta in Sondrine. Once she had control of her respiration, her head cleared, and she began to rifle through her assessment of the group and their abilities. A solution formed, clear and bright in her mind. It was unconventional, but then, so was she. Her grandmother would be proud.

Idrilia opened her eyes and grinned at the expectant group. "I have an idea."

CHAPTER 25

Sweat slickened Kilahym's palms, his hands trembling the ocarina into an unnaturally fervent vibrato. He pressed it hard against his lips, praying he would not drop it. So much of Idrilia's plan hinged on him being able to do something he had never done before, had never even considered attempting. When she outlined it, the responses had ranged from incredulous to shocked.

"By the warts on the Lady's toes! I've only ever created accidents with my magic, nothing like what you're describing!" Kilahym had protested.

"That's precisely my point." Idrilia had motioned toward the subterranean level. "We need a distraction. We need chaos. We need *you*."

His thoughts returned to the present and he looked over his shoulder at Vayriel, who waved at him from the top of the stairs to the underground chamber. She and Orgar stood there with most of the other Seekers.

"You can do this, Kilahym," she affirmed. "Listen for the Mother's voice. She will guide you. Picture that which you want to be and make it so."

Next to him at the foot of the stairs, Kharnek drew his sword and spun it in a rapid flourish. He had volunteered as the "runner" in Idrilia's scheme. "Look at how he trembles. I will say it again: I do not need his help to secure our objective."

Idrilia placed her hands on her hips. "Just stick to the plan we all agreed upon."

"That *some* of us agreed upon," Kharnek muttered.

Kilahym took a deep breath and faced the warrior. "I will do my best. Now, let's raise the curtain on this show before I succumb to stage fright."

The Komorese snorted but settled into a ready stance, leaning his weight forward on the balls of his feet, blade angled forward at the opening to the chamber. Kilahym inhaled and lifted the ocarina to his mouth. A picture formed in his mind of what he wanted to happen. Releasing his breath in a measured stream, he began to play. Though it would have been easier to slip into the familiarity of an existing tune, his instincts told him that this feat would require a new composition. Kilahym closed his eyes and surrendered himself to the music, allowing intuition to guide his choice of each note. A lilting melody formed. It swept upward on major chords punctuated by staccato dips. The song took shape, and with it, a sense of *rightness* that Kilahym felt when he knew that what he was creating was good. Better than good—it was magnificent. If only he were back in Waverling, playing for an audience of hundreds. This would be his finest performance yet, one not even his mother could criticize.

A gasp interrupted his reverie. His eyes flew open and his instrument nearly slipped from his fingers. Before him and Kharnek, a host of mirror images of themselves had manifested, each one perfect in its mimicry of one of their appearances.

"Keep playing," Kharnek growled, then he sprinted through the entrance.

Kilahym frantically resumed his song, the tempo quickening in time with his pounding heart. The replicas followed the warrior and began to wander aimlessly about the chamber. As before, mechanical sounds preceded the appearance of what Vayriel had dubbed the fire-spitter, which descended and began to swivel back and forth. It spat its lethal flame and Kilahym cringed, but the bolt passed through one of the apparitions and struck the floor.

A familiar blue-haired figure appeared in his peripheral vision. "It's working!" Idrilia reported to the others. "It can't differentiate between the illusions and the real thing!"

As if in response, the machine upped its rate of fire. The chamber transformed into an inferno of orange energy. Kilahym's concentration faltered. Where before there were dozens of false Seekers, now there were only a handful. The flashes of light from the fire spitter's attacks made it impossible to discern Kharnek's whereabouts. He hoped that the warrior survived the assault.

A flurry of energy ricocheted off of something unseen to Kilahym's right. He squinted, and through the bursts of light could just make out Kharnek's form running towards him. The fire-spitter had found its target, and it directed blast after blast toward the warrior. Kilahym's brows shot up as Kharnek intercepted each attack with his sword and the energy caromed off the polished surface. Out of the corner of his eye, Idrilia's jaw dropped. The speed and precision with which the other man moved could only be described as preternatural.

"Thank goodness he's on our side," he joked.

Idrilia grabbed his shoulder and pointed at the ocarina in his hands. "Kilahym! He's not out yet!"

"Whoops!" Replacing the instrument to his lips, the bard blew furiously into the ocarina. Whatever inspiration he had found was gone, and the illusions dissipated one by one, leaving Kharnek as the room's sole occupant. Kilahym dropped the ocarina to dangle against his chest. He placed his knuckles under his chin and squeezed his elbows together, mentally willing the warrior to make it the rest of the way unharmed.

"What is happening?" Vayriel shouted.

"The magic stopped working, but Kharnek's almost back," Idrilia replied. The Sondrinel shifted her weight from one foot to the other. "Come on, just a little bit further…"

Kharnek continued his impressive dance toward them, dodging some attacks and deflecting others. The closer he got to them, the more Kilahym felt the heat from the fire-spitter and smelled the charred leather from near misses. He grabbed onto Idrilia's arm. "Oh, this is so hard to watch!"

"Make a hole!" Kharnek yelled as he leaped toward them. Kilahym barely had time to process the instruction before Idrilia yanked him towards her. He lost his balance, and they crashed onto the steps in a tangle of limbs as Kharnek crossed the threshold in a blur of black and crimson. The whir and whine of the fire-spitter faded; the ensuing quiet filled with the hiss of cooling stone. Kilahym felt Idrilia's palm against his sternum.

"Kilahym, please get off of me," came her muffled plea.

The bard obliged and sprang to his feet, one hand extended to the Sondrinel. She eyed the proffered appendage and slowly took it. Kilahym hauled her up, his hand sore from the strength of her grip.

"Thanks," Idrilia said tersely. She swiveled and addressed Kharnek. "Did you get it?"

The warrior, sprawled out on the stairs and panting, held up a black orb the size of Kilahym's fist. "I hope this is it. If not, someone else can run that gauntlet."

"How on Etherea did you manage that, anyway? I've never seen a sword that can deflect energy," Idrilia asked. Kharnek did not respond; the Sondrinel's lip curled, but she said no more.

Zinvar and the other Seekers arrived at the bottom of the stairs.

The priest laid a hand on Kharnek's shoulder. "That was amazing. But more importantly, are you alright?"

"I am fine. A little singed, but the player's illusions bought me the time I needed." Kharnek stood up and nodded at Kilahym. "Well done."

The unexpected praise made Kilahym's heart leap. He swept into a low bow, his right arm flung behind him. "It was nothing, my good sir. Purveyor of magical mirages and mysteries I dub…well, myself." Kilahym straightened and wiggled his fingers in the direction of the Prophet. "Whatever secrets this orb holds, they will not remain hidden from me!"

Zinvar laughed while Kalis shook his head. "I don't know about the rest of you, but I've had enough of this place," the Sondrinel said. "If we're certain that that's the Prophet, let's get out of here."

All the Seekers exchanged uncertain glances. Kharnek sighed heavily. "Please tell me I did not just risk my life for a waste of time."

"Aside from bones, we haven't seen anything else here that's out of the ordinary. That must be it," Idrilia asserted.

Kilahym cocked his head as he considered Idrilia's words. "You know, not to jinx us, but all of the bones were upstairs…while the deadly contraption was down here. How do you suppose that came to be?"

"There could have been another fire-spitter," Vayriel offered, "but as with all material things, time consumed it."

"There's a cheery thought. Well, should we put it to a vote?" Zinvar waved his staff to encompass the group. "That seems like the fairest way to proceed."

"Works for me." Kilahym shrugged. "Any objections?"

Vayriel, Kharnek, and Kalis assented.

"Very well then, on the count of three, all in favor of returning to Peatwick village, raise your hands," Zinvar directed. "One…two…three."

Everyone's hands shot up.

"Well, I guess it's unanimous then." Kilahym waved to the stairs. "Shall we?"

The trip back to the village proved uneventful, although Kilahym wondered if he would ever get the balsam and brine smell of the Fens out of his tunic. A hot bath sounded wonderful, but he doubted that numbered among the amenities of Peatwick. The Seekers were gathered in the mayor's home awaiting her arrival.

Their return had come sooner than expected, according to the mayor's wife, who sent word for her spouse to come back early from a "bump and baggling" excursion.

"Baggling?" Kilahym asked, his mind already concocting a new ballad centered on this hitherto unknown activity.

"Oh, I forget that you city folk probably don't baggle," the woman answered, "but it's such a good sport and helps out the village. You see, the swamp around here is infested with baglets, gas-filled critters that like to drift into fires and blow themselves right up. Which takes care of 'em but sometimes also starts a bigger fire. My sister lost her house that way."

"You don't say. But where does the bump part come in?"

The mayor's wife clapped her hands, the long sleeves of her homespun dress fluttering. "Ah, that's the best part you see. Baglets are harmless so long as you keep 'em away from fire. So, every once in a while, we go hunting 'em with these big nets and move 'em somewhere they won't bother the village. But to get 'em in the nets, you gotta bump 'em!" She punched the air with her fist. "They're hardy things, so you needn't hold back. I was a pretty good bumper back in my day. Anyways, that's bump and baggling. You ought to try it afore you leave."

From the horrified expression on Idrilia's face, it was clear that she had no interest in trying such an activity, although the othwit perched on her shoulder twittered and danced in place. Kilahym had steered the conversation to safer waters, grateful when Vayriel jumped in and asked about other wildlife in the region. That left him free to contemplate what happened in the ruins, which had occupied his thoughts since they arrived in Peatwick at midmoon. It was nearly moonset now, and the mayor had yet to arrive.

Kilahym watched Zinvar get up from where he sat by Kharnek and make his way over. The priest motioned at the wooden floor. "Mind if I join you?"

"Not at all." Kilahym patted the wide boards. "Deep ruminations are best shared with company."

"What deep thoughts are you thinking?" Zinvar asked as he settled into a cross-legged position.

"Magical ones! I jest, though only in part," Kilahym admitted. "The illusions I made back in that ghastly ruin...never have I done such a thing. It made me feel, well, many things. Powerful. Special. Like perhaps I really do belong here among such illustrious company."

The other Seeker cocked his head. "You would not have been chosen as a Truthseeker if you were not capable of greatness."

"Greatness. Now there's a word rife with complexity." Kilahym scratched his beard. "Some would say we are born to it, others that it belongs to those upon whom the Lady bestows her blessings. My mother would say it's reserved for those far above my station."

Zinvar nodded. "And what do you say?"

He shrugged. "I say...those are all possible. I also think greatness can be achieved through hard work. But it is far beyond me, a humble bard, to know the answer to such a mystery."

The Komorese man smiled. "Whatever measure you use, I think it's undeniable that greatness is in your future, Kilahym. What you did in the ruins is only the beginning."

Kilahym ducked his head to hide that he blushed. He started to reply, then paused when he heard the sound of heavy footsteps. The door to the mayor's home flew open, and the town leader ran in, her curly brown hair streaming behind her.

"Melde, bar the windows! They're coming!"

A flurry of activity ensued. The mayor's wife hurried to each of the openings in the house's circular perimeter and pulled a pair of wooden shutters closed. She then hefted two large wooden planks into position across the windows, where they notched into metal hooks. The interior of the house was plunged into darkness, save for the flicker of candles set into sconces on the walls.

"What's going on?" Kalis asked, eyes tracking Melde's movements.

The mayor, who was busy putting similar protective measures in place at the door, grunted. "Olentos! A whole flock of 'em!"

Kalis frowned.

"Oh-what?"

Kilahym's hair stood on end. "Oh. Oh dear. Olentos were mentioned in the foreword of *Dartleby's Guide to Deadly Birds*. By his heir, who penned the introduction shortly after Dartleby's devourment by a flock of olentos."

"Carnivorous birds?" Kharnek folded his arms across his broad chest. "That hardly seems worth all this trouble."

"These are no ordinary birds. Olentos are half the size of a man with teeth as long as your fingers. And when they sing," Melde shuddered, "it's like the screams of the dying."

"But don't worry," the mayor said, "this house has weathered many an olento attack. You'll be safe. But we're going to have to tie you all up."

"You *what?*" Idrilia shot to her feet. "Absolutely not. How would that help, anyway?"

Kilahym waved to get the Sondrinel's attention. "It actually makes sense. Olentos are mildly telepathic. They attack their prey's mind and convince it to give itself up to them."

"Aye, the lad speaks the truth of it," Melde affirmed. "Hriga and I have heard the olentos' song enough to resist it, but none of you would be so fortunate. The bindings are for your own good."

"This is their home. We would do well to trust their wisdom," Vayriel agreed, her hand resting atop Orgar's head. "But how will we protect my life-friend?"

A high, keening shriek pierced Kilahym's ears. He clapped his hands to them, but the sound continued unabated. Idrilia fell to her knees, her othwit squawking and hopping madly on her shoulder. Vayriel clung to her spear, and Orgar's lips peeled back in a snarl as he faced the door. A pressure formed in Kilahym's head, so intense that he feared it would explode unless he went outside; he *needed* to go outside. Only semi-aware of his movements, he struggled to his feet and took a hesitant step toward the door. He could hear the olentos scratching and clawing at the barrier, eager to rend his flesh if he would just come out.

Hriga came and stood between Kilahym and the door, hands on his shoulders. She mouthed words, but all he could hear was the insistent voice of the flock. Someone bumped into him from behind. Glancing over his shoulder, he saw a dazed Kalis attempting to escape Melde's grasp. At the back of the room, Zinvar had hidden his face in Kharnek's chest, the warrior's arms wrapped around him like a mother othwit's wings. Kilahym struggled against the mayor's strength, but the woman remained rooted in place. The door beckoned to him. Beyond it lay release from all his troubles. He clenched his jaw and twisted out of Hriga's grip. Three paces and his fingers brushed the tarnished metal doorknob, but it refused to turn. He snarled and gripped it with both hands, twisting with all his might.

"Enough!" Kharnek bellowed, his voice louder even than the olento chorus. The screeching ceased.

The pressure behind Kilahym's forehead vanished, as did the compulsion to leave the mayor's house. An eerie quietness followed, like the pause that seemed to last forever when an actor forgot their line. Kilahym looked at Kharnek and while the flickering candlelight made it hard to see, there was something off about the warrior's eyes. He blinked and squinted, but whatever oddity he thought was there was gone.

"Well I'll be...I've never known olentos to give up on a hunt," Melde commented, her hands knit together tightly.

"Neither have I," her wife agreed, "unless there was something even more dangerous than them around. Could be a yulmandr around."

"We haven't seen one of those in these parts for at least twenty synodies," Melde argued. Then her thin shoulders dropped. "Whatever it was, I'm just glad those things are gone."

"You've got that right." Hriga took her wife in her arms and held the shorter woman's head on her chest.

Kilahym's gaze slid to Kharnek. The other man's face remained blank as a page awaiting words to be scribed upon it. Between his display at the ruins and now this, Kilahym wondered what secrets the warrior kept from them. Or maybe he was imagining a connection where there was none. The Fens were full of strange and mysterious creatures after all.

Pulling away from Hriga, the mayor's wife swept the room with her gaze. "Sorry for the ruckus. But I'm sure Truthseekers like yourselves are used to this sort of thing."

"Speaking of which," Idrilia produced the metallic orb, "we found your Prophet."

Hriga took the object and cradled it in her calloused hands. "And so you did," she murmured. "You have done our village a great service. The Prophet guides us with its wisdom. Our people suffered in its absence."

Kalis cleared his throat. "If I may ask, can you tell us more about it? What it tells you, what it is?"

"It may be simpler if I show you." The mayor depressed a circular indentation on the orb. Yellow-orange dots flared above an upward-curved line in the same hue and blinked rapidly. The display reminded Kilahym of a child waking from sleep. With nary a sound, the Prophet rose from the mayor's palms and hovered a few inches above them, spinning on its vertical axis to regard everyone present with its simulacrum face. When it spoke, Kilahym started and Orgar yipped, his tails drooping.

ICON connection established. Download initiated. Please wait, the orb announced. Its voice, though cheerful, sounded tinny.

"What is it doing?" Vayriel whispered in Kilahym's ear.

He spread his hands. "I don't know. More importantly, how is an inanimate object talking?"

Download complete.

A spherical projection fluoresced outward from the Prophet, swelling until it encompassed the mayor and Melde. They stepped back as the transparent image's growth halted and points of light began to appear around it, some blinking green and others red.

Alert: Data incomplete. Portions of the network are damaged or corrupted. Please effect repairs immediately to improve data quality. The Prophet's "mouth" moved as it spoke, its diction clipped and precise. Kilahym could not place its accent, but he noticed odd inflections on certain syllables compared with how natives of Heathström spoke. It most resembled the Sondrinel's speech patterns.

"It always starts with that warning," the mayor explained, "ever since we found it."

Zinvar motioned toward the Prophet with his staff. "Do you know what it means?"

Hriga's broad shoulders lifted in a shrug. "No. But it hasn't stopped it from being dead accurate with its other predictions."

"Other predictions?" Idrilia asked, her head tilted to the side. "The way this shows information reminds me of something I found in Sondrine…"

Current weather patterns indicate that planting conditions in this region are favorable for the next three months, the Prophet said, *after which, projections fall below the minimum acceptable level of accuracy. There is an 89% probability of heavy rainfall tomorrow due to unexpected temperature variations in the lower atmosphere 246 miles southeast of this location.*

The projection of Etherea zoomed in on a highlighted area off Etherea's southern coast, midway between the Fens and the island nation of Ettra.

This region has been identified as a frequent source of anomalous weather patterns. Should they continue unabated, there is a 97% probability that the local climate may experience further deterioration. It is recommended that contingency measures be implemented immediately.

"Well, that doesn't sound good," Kalis commented.

Analysis complete. Entering standby mode. The projection collapsed in on itself before disappearing as the Prophet sank the floor. It smiled and closed its eyes. Their orange light faded into the smooth dark gray of its surface.

The mayor and Melde dropped to their knees, palms upturned and outstretched toward the silent orb. "We thank the Prophet for its guidance," they said in unison, "its wisdom is our blessing and our strength."

Hriga rose and retrieved the Prophet, then faced the Seekers. "Thank you again for your part in returning the Prophet to us. As you can see, its words are invaluable to the livelihood of our village. It has guided us for many synodies in the planting and harvesting of crops, and helped us prepare for the worst of storms."

"That's quite remarkable. It was an honor to hear the Prophet speak," Zinvar said. "Perhaps, in the future, all the realms may benefit from its knowledge."

The mayor and her wife exchanged glances. "Perhaps so," Hriga agreed, "but for now, allow us to congratulate you on the completion of this trial."

Kilahym stood and stretched, his neck popping as he rolled it. "Thank you, your honorable grace. I assume this means we must now venture to another, hitherto undisclosed, location?"

Hriga addressed Vayriel. "Does he always talk like that?"

The Highblood grinned at Kilahym. "Yes, his ornate speech is a part of his livelihood, I think."

"Ah, well then," the mayor reached out and patted her on the shoulder, "you're a brave soul to partner with such a man. May the Lady bless your union."

Kilahym's mouth dropped open and Vayriel turned the same shade of pink as the crystal tip of her spear. "We, ah, well, you see, we aren't..." he tried to correct the mayor, but Hriga had already moved on to another topic.

"Your next trial will take place at Mount Hoestra, in Sondrine," she was saying. "You'll be met there by a representative from Sondrine who will explain the task itself. Don't ask me, I'm not privy to those details."

Kalis stroked his chin. "We'll need to outfit the others for crossing Sondrine. There are Sentinel caches along the roads that we can use."

The mayor cleared her throat. "I'm not supposed to advise you on what to do, but if I were you, I'd go by sea rather than land."

"Why's that?" Idrilia inquired.

"There've been rumors of people going missing on the southern roads in Sondrine," Melde answered, "and sightings of riders, clad all in black." The mayor's wife shook her head. "Dark tidings, to be sure. I wouldn't go east on foot unless you're forced to."

"You can charter a ship in Ferrimoore," Hriga added. "It's only a three days' journey from here. My cousin works at the docks. I'll give you his name, and he'll make sure you find an upstanding captain." Kilahym saw Idrilia and Kalis's eyes meet, their expressions grim. Whatever significance they found in the villagers' warning was lost on him.

"That seems like our best course of action," Kalis assented, "we could stop in Ettra to get any other supplies we may need. The selection there will be far better than anything we'd find in the caches."

The Sondrinel began to question Hriga on the best way to reach Ferrimoore, but Kilahym's attention drifted from their conversation to Vayriel, who had fallen silent since the mayor mistook the nature of their relationship. Her violet eyes were fixed on the mayor, but their glassy appearance betrayed her lack of focus. He wondered what she was thinking. Kilahym brushed his nose and crouched next to Orgar and scratched behind the jeroti's ears. The canine's tongue lolled and his tails twitched in approval.

"You want to know a secret, Orgar?"

The jeroti peered back at him. Kilahym patted its side. "Sometimes, I think I understand you better than people."

Orgar licked Kilahym's face and nuzzled his hand. Kilahym smiled. "I'm glad you're here." He stood up and brushed dust off his pants. "Alright, let's go save someone else's village."

CHAPTER 26

The boat lurched again to the right, and Vayriel slid, knocking her shoulder into the cabin wall. She winced and pushed herself upright as the boat shifted back into place, creaking like the boughs of wind-blown trees.

"If I could see the movements, I would be prepared," she bemoaned to Orgar. Her first trip on a water-glider was testing her resolve more than any trial so far. At least the chartering of the ship had proven straightforward. Hriga's cousin had connected them with a captain who often sailed the perilous route between Ferrimoore and Ettra. A day into their journey, they now navigated what the captain called the storm wall, a natural barrier formed of multiple powerful cyclones. Ever since entering it, the ship felt like a toy batted about by a jeroti's paws.

Vayriel pressed the back of her hand to her brow, as if to push the dim ache away before it could grow. Her stomach felt queasy, and she glanced over to see if her life-friend fared better. Orgar's ears pressed back against his head as he peered at her from the corners of his eyes.

"I know. I should be able to feel it coming," she sighed heavily. "But it is so tight in here. There is barely room to breathe. So little space—I cannot focus."

Vayriel's stomach jumped into her chest, accompanied by a giddy feeling as she was lifted into the air. She flew backward and crashed onto her bed, thrown by the plunging of the ship.

"I cannot stay in here." Stumbling to the door, Vayriel pushed it open into the hallway, fighting the urge to heave. A faint whine issued behind her. "I will be back soon. Stay here."

Fighting her way upward on unsteady feet, Vayriel climbed the stairway and opened the latch to the deck. Rain blew in thick waves, darkening the red timbers to black. Though the sun was nearly overhead, it was hidden by thick, gray clouds shaped like beasts of the mountains.

Raindrops pelted Vayriel's face and hair as she looked around, taking in the activity of the crew. The additional weight of her coat and pants helped steady her balance, and she moved toward the main mast. She suppressed a shiver as a gust of wind howled by her.

No longer a bright-plumed creature sailing from its nest, the water-glider seemed injured, struggling to get to its feet and escape its attacker. The wind-catchers were still full, the largest in the middle with the smallest in the back. They looked like the Watcher's wings, spread as if the curved hull was his body.

Muffled voices carried through the storm from the crew, though Vayriel could not make out their meaning. Suddenly the voices grew silent, replaced by a loud spattering. Her hair whipped heavily behind her as she turned to see water spray up in a shower and spill over the railing.

The ship dipped to the left. Vayriel grabbed the mainmast and steadied herself by leaning the opposite direction.

"Just keep our heading!" she heard someone shout above the storm. She looked where the captain had shown them how the rudder controlled the ship. Several crew members attended the mechanisms there.

"We're close to breaking through!"

Vayriel stayed where she was, rocking in tandem with the movements of the water-glider and watching the crew deftly manage each part of the vessel.

She lost track of time, unsure exactly when the clouds began to part, but soon the rain was no more than a drizzle. She returned to the bow. Across the choppy waves, a shape loomed in the distance.

It was not Ettra.

On the ship's deck, chaos reigned. Piles of fallen rigging were strewn about, mingled with splintered shafts of wood. Sailors called to one another for help. Above the din, the captain's voice, hoarse from shouting, commanded Vayriel's attention.

"Prepare to dock! All hands, prepare for docking!"

While the crew hurried to follow the captain's commands, Vayriel gazed back over the railing. Curtains of angry gray clouds enshrouded a circle of open water, the center of which their vessel now occupied. It shared the space with a colossal black tower that rose from the waves. Multifaceted and angular but without geometric regularity, the monolith's design resembled nothing she had ever seen in Etherea. Its surface swallowed the light that reached it, making it difficult to ascertain details from afar. As their ship drew nearer, a queasiness stole over her that had nothing to do with the ocean's swell.

"This object unsettles you."

The familiar voice came from beside her. She turned and nodded at Zinvar, who clung to the railing with a white-knuckled grip. A faint yellow pallor tinged his thin face, suggesting that he, too, struggled with the ship's unpredictable movements.

"Do your Highblood senses tell you anything about it?" he asked.

Vayriel inhaled and drew the life force into her, then sent it questing out toward the enigmatic object. To her surprise, she found a presence that displayed awareness of her touch. A sense of immeasurable patience and age washed over her. If the mountains of Skyveil could speak, this would be their voice. She shuddered and withdrew, then shook her head. "It is unlike any creature-daughter or -son I have ever encountered."

"Creature... You mean it's alive?" The priest's eyes widened. Two nearby sailors, their arms laden with coils of damp rope, paused in their work, fear etched on their faces.

"Back to work, you lazy scalawags!"

The captain's barked order set the crew back to their task but with a hint of hesitation. Doffing his hat, he waved at Vayriel.

"Young mistress, would you kindly descend and meet me in my quarters?" The captain pointed at Zinvar. "You too, young master, and on your way fetch the Sondrinel."

A few minutes later, all the Seekers were gathered in the captain's cabin. Despite his calm demeanor, Vayriel sensed that their circumstances had rattled the man.

"Thank you, all, for joining me. I thought it best to have this conversation in private, away from the prying ears of my superstitious crew."

The captain paused to look out the window at the black object to which they drew nearer.

"Needless to say, we find ourselves far off course. I have navigated the storm wall countless times, and never have I seen this place. We are undoubtedly in the eye of the storm, but what *that* is"—he motioned at the window—"is as far beyond me as the two moons."

"And yet we are preparing to dock with it."

The challenge in Kharnek's words did not escape Vayriel's notice or the captain's.

"If you have a better plan, feel free to suggest it."

Kharnek gave the captain an icy glare, but said nothing more.

"Docking with the structure will give us time to implement repairs without the risk of being pulled back into the storm. Once repairs are complete, we can continue our voyage."

"You're calling it a structure, but is it?" Zinvar queried. His eyes shifted to Vayriel.

She sighed heavily. "I do not know how to explain what I sense. I feel life but unlike any I have ever known. It has been here for a very long time."

"While I appreciate that you have insight beyond our regular senses that does not change our present circumstances." The captain stepped away from the group. "We will dock with the structure soon. Please return to your cabins and remain there until further notice."

"Well, this is a fine mess we're in," Idrilia groused.

Vayriel felt her frustration as if it radiated heat. Next to Vayriel, Kilahym raised his hand. "If I may, it could be worse. At least we still draw breath!"

The bard shrank from Idrilia's withering look. The Seekers, except for Kharnek, had gathered in the cargo area of the ship's hold to discuss their present circumstances.

"There was no way to know this would happen, you know?" Kalis put in. "And sailing to Ettra would have been much faster like we all agreed."

"*Would have* doesn't matter now, does it?" the daggeress shot back.

Kalis raised his hands in front of his chest. "I was just being objective. I don't know why you're so combative right now."

"Oh, I don't know," Idrilia glared at him, "maybe it has something to do with the fact that I haven't had a moment's peace since we boarded this ship because you won't leave me alone."

The other Sondrinel's face clouded. "You used to enjoy my company. You're being unfair to me because of a choice that I didn't make and a situation that isn't my fault."

That cryptic reply started a squabble between Kalis and Idrilia. Vayriel's mind drifted. The mystery of the monolith exerted an intangible pull upon her, like a memory half-forgotten. It was at once familiar and foreboding.

"I need some fresh air," Zinvar abruptly blurted, before he hurried away. Vayriel watched his rapid departure with curiosity. Did the creature-son also call to him? There were moments when, in his presence, she detected pulses of life-force energy. Erratic and varying in strength, they reminded her of Kilahym, who was just learning to commune with the Mother-of-All. She knew Komor forbade its people from using the life force, so Zinvar might not understand when the Mother spoke to him. Sadness welled in her at the thought of an entire realm cut off from Her voice.

A gentle nudge to her elbow interrupted her contemplation. Kilahym mimicked a person walking with his fingers, then pointed toward the door. She nodded, and they left, their departure unregistered by the arguing Sondrinel. They hurried out of the hold, bursting onto the deck in a flurry. Immediately the monolith drew Vayriel's eyes, looming over the ship, which was now anchored by its side. The duo scurried up the short flight of stairs to the upper deck at the stern for a closer look.

"You were told to remain in your cabin."

Vayriel and Kilahym halted, turning to regard the captain with guilty expressions. The seafarer stood at the bottom of the stairs; arms crossed over his chest.

"We came to check on our friend," she responded. "He went this way moments ago. I think he is feeling unwell."

"And you wanted another gander at that, I'd wager," the captain replied, tipping his chin toward the monolith. He chuckled. "Well, can't say as I blame you. Just don't linger too long."

With a shrug, the captain walked away. Vayriel rushed to where Zinvar leaned over the railing, Kilahym in tow. Barely a stone's throw away, the surface of the monolith tempted her with its mysterious black depths. The absolute darkness struck her as impenetrable, unknowable.

"Well hello, Zinny!"

The priest started at Kilahym's voice behind him. He turned and greeted the bard and Vayriel.

"Sorry, didn't mean to startle thee. The lady Vayriel and I wished to ensure your well-being. And"—Kilahym lowered his voice—"to escape yet another argument betwixt our Sondrinel companions."

"I don't blame you. That's what drove me up here as well." Zinvar smiled, but in the life force Vayriel sensed the anxiety that nibbled at him.

She decided to take a risk. "I think it is more than that, friend Zinvar. You asked me before if this creature-son bothered me. I believe you, too, feel its strangeness."

The priest swiveled his head to the immensity behind him, and he exhaled deeply. "I guess there's no harm in telling you. Yes, I do feel something. It's like how you know when someone is watching you, even though you can't see them. Just please, don't say anything to Kharnek. I don't know how he would react."

"Worry not!" Kilahym clapped the other man's back. "Your secret is safe with us! And Orgar, he is a master of the fine art of secret-keeping."

Zinvar laughed. "I appreciate that. Speaking of which, where is Orgar?"

"Resting," Vayriel answered. "He has not taken well to travel by water-glider."

"Water-glider? Oh, the ship, you mean. Well, in that regard I can relate."

"Bedraggled and waterlogged is what we all shall be by the time we reach Ettra," Kilahym exclaimed, wringing his hands.

"If we even do."

As if in response to Zinvar's doleful remark, a low thrum emanated from the monolith. The ship quivered from its resonance. A strange smell, like the smoke from a candle just snuffed, filled Vayriel's nostrils as chains of pale green lightning chased themselves around the top of the structure.

Abruptly, the deck lurched violently beneath the Seekers' feet, sending them tumbling toward the railing. Vayriel grabbed at it. Rough splinters tore at her fingers, but her hands found no purchase. The Highblood soared off the ship and crashed into the roiling sea.

Its chill took her breath away. Flailing her arms, she tried to orient herself toward the surface, but there was no light to be found. Darkness ate away at the edges of her vision as Vayriel thrashed about. Her heavy clothes clung to her skin and hampered her movements.

When at last she ran out of breath, her final thought was that she wished she could have said goodbye to Mo'mo and Mo'fa.

Vayriel awoke to the sound of someone coughing. A dull ache suffused her body. Gingerly, she propped herself up on her elbows. Water gurgled somewhere nearby, but she could see little. A circle of dim light hovered far above her, its wan glow revealing only its circumference. The coughing sound that woke her resumed, wet and spluttering with regurgitated water.

"Hello? Is someone there?"

A gasp and more hacking responded to her question.

"Dear me, I must have swallowed the entirety of the sea."

"Kilahym!"

"Vayriel! Is that you?" the bard exclaimed. "Thank the Lady for your presence in this vile pit. I wish we found ourselves in better circumstances, to be sure, but even so—"

"Kilahym, hush!"

A squelching sound had reached the Highblood's attentive ears. The bard fell silent, and she discerned movement nearby: the creeping tread of a predator. Vayriel focused and drew the life force into herself. With its power she could see with the Mother's eyes, her sight now penetrating the curtain of darkness to reveal the thing that stalked them.

It was roughly the size of Orgar, but moved on twelve spine-covered tentacles. An ovoid central body played host to several glittering eyes of varying shapes and sizes and a wide mouth ringed with sharp teeth.

"Kilahym, when I say 'now,' cover your eyes," Vayriel whispered.

"With my hands? Or perhaps my arm would be more suitable—"

"Now!"

The Highblood gathered tendrils of life force energy in her palms, forming a ball of white-hot light and tossing it into the air. When the orb reached the apex of its trajectory, she spun away, closed her eyes, and clapped her hands together. The orb exploded into a radiant nova.

A shriek issued from the monster, accompanied by a yelp from Kilahym. It fled into the shadows in a frenzy of whipping tentacles. Vayriel waited until she could no longer hear the sound of its retreat before dispelling the light.

"Vayriel? Are you there? I can't see. Apparently, I was too slow in heeding your proffered directions."

"I am here. Be still, I will come to you."

Moving through the darkness with her life-force-enhanced sight, Vayriel discovered Kilahym and, to her delight, her spear. She retrieved the latter before gently placing her hand on the bard's shoulder.

"I am here. Are you injured?"

He shook his head. "No, by the grace of Laphrim, this mortal vessel is intact. But what of you? What was all that about with the light?"

"A creature-son was hunting us. We should not linger here—it may return with its hunger."

Vayriel helped the bard to his feet, and channeled life-force energy into the crystal at the tip of her spear. Its soft pink glow illuminated the cave-like space in which they found themselves. At its edges, myriad openings yawned, but there was no sign of a way to reach its top.

"Now, where do you suppose we are?"

"Within the creature-son next to the ship. When we were thrown off, we must have fallen into it."

"Ah, yes," Kilahym mused, stroking his goatee, "I begin to recall. Oh! And what of Zinvar? He was tossed overboard with us."

"Let us search for him and hope that the Mother showed him the same mercy as us."

The duo examined the entirety of the chamber, but there was no sign of the priest. Vayriel cast her senses outward, straining to detect him in the life force, but it was like trying to find an alusarean calf in a herd. Dozens of creature-sons and -daughters filled the bowels of their titanic host, some like the tentacled hunter, and others unknown to her. Stranger still, entire swathes of the greater creature-son felt empty and lifeless, while others teemed with activity.

"Mayhap the priest went down one of those tunnels?" Kilahym ventured, breaking her reverie. Although every instinct screamed not to enter the gaping corridors, the Highblood could not in good conscience leave without investigating.

"If so, he has gone beyond my ability to detect him. We will have to be careful not to lose our way."

The bard shuddered. "Woe to us indeed if we are lost here—this place shivers my timbers worse than any locale to which I have sallied forth."

With that grim pronouncement, the duo set off down the nearest tunnel. Their progress was slow. The tunnel's surface, like the exterior of the creature-son, reflected no light, making it hard to find secure footing. Kilahym failed to heed Vayriel's warnings not to skip along the passage and slipped and fell several times, much to his chagrin. Fortunately, the ground was soft and squishy, as if they truly were in the bowels of a colossal monster. The echoing susurration of running water chased them everywhere. It masked the sound of the tentacle-walkers that lingered in their wake, but Vayriel detected their presence. None dared to approach—her light blast had succeeded in dissuading them from doing so. For now.

Although it must have been mere minutes, it seemed like hours of trudging through the eerie darkness before the tunnel deposited the Seekers into a large, cylindrical chamber. Here, the walls were festooned with lines of pale green light, reminiscent of the lightning they had witnessed at the monolith's top just before their fall. Instead of coruscating at random, though, the light in this chamber followed grooves in the wall to a central point in the ceiling, before arrowing down into a luminous egg-shaped object about Orgar's size.

"Now what in the name of Agermath's false eyelashes is that?"

Vayriel cast a quizzical glance at her companion, who waved dismissively at the air.

"Never mind, a story for another time. But my inquiry stands: what is this strange sight we behold?"

"I do not know," she answered honestly, "but we should not get distracted from our search for Zinvar."

"I suppose you're right. But it couldn't hurt to get just a teensy bit closer, could it?"

Before Vayriel could reply, the bard darted toward the glowing object. When he was close enough to reach out and touch it, a sharp series of trills emitted from its center. The chittering reminded her of an enraged ratufa, but Kilahym clapped his hands in delight.

"Why, I'd know that series of arpeggios anywhere!"

Vayriel cocked her head as the bard proceeded to whistle several notes back at the object and moved a bit closer to examine it. Veins pulsed just beneath its outermost layer, and she could not help but picture the beating heart of a creature-son or -daughter. Warmth radiated from it, a welcome relief from the cool dampness of the tunnel.

At the end of Kilahym's musical reply, the heart twittered back with cheerful notes and glowed brighter, before releasing a blast of off-key noises. Vayriel winced. The cacophony seemed not to bother the other Seeker, who muttered to himself, "A minor key? No, that's not what should have been next. It should be major, of course, but which one, which one?"

"You understand what this creature-son is saying?" Vayriel asked, intrigued by the exchange.

"Understand, nay, but it speaks a language of music and in that I thought myself fluent. Alas, it seems that our discourse may have run its course, for there is an unwanted harmony within it." Seeing her puzzled expression, the bard continued, "At first I thought its vocalizations to be the verses of a song, but the ending is all wrong. A jumble of flats and sharps and nonsense. What it *should* have been is this."

Kilahym whistled a bright-sounding scale that rose and fell, ending in a warm tremolo. For a moment, all was silent.

"Did you offend it?" Vayriel whispered.

"My dear Highblood, never have my dulcet tones offended any gentle being. Except for—"

A thunderous blast from the creature-son's heart cut off the reply. Streaks of green light spiraled away from the heart into parts unknown, and the chamber began to tremble. From the corridors branching off it, Vayriel detected the sound of water. No longer a gentle whisper, it roared with the ferocity of a trägen's battle cry. And it was getting closer.

Vayriel stretched out with the life force, and her eyes widened. The chamber where they stood was near the top of a creature-son whose true size she could now detect. Its ten mighty legs extended down to the ocean floor. The monolith above the surface was merely a fraction of its mass. For a moment, she felt its consciousness brush against hers. Vayriel flinched at the alien contact, but there was no malice in it. Instead, it seemed relieved to have fulfilled its purpose, and now only sought to disappear beneath the waves to live in peace.

She severed the connection. Already, foamy water surged around their ankles. Grabbing Kilahym's arm, she dashed toward the nearest exit.

"Vayriel? What's going on?"

"The creature-son is submerging."

"Submerging?" the bard yelped.

"Yes. You awakened him from his sleep. Come, we must hurry!"

The duo splashed through the tunnel at a frantic pace, the glow from Vayriel's spear lighting the way. They reached an intersection, and nearly collided with Zinvar on his way out of the leftmost passage.

"Zinny! You're alive!"

"Not for long if we don't get out of here!" The priest pointed behind him. "And that way is full of water."

"Then we will take the other."

Vayriel plunged into the right-hand tunnel, Kilahym and Zinvar in tow. Straining with all her might, she tried to sense where the passage ended. They were close, but the water reached their knees now, impeding their progress.

"Not much further," she encouraged.

"I hope not," Zinvar gasped, "or my lungs will give out before the water has a chance to drown me."

Despite their situation, Vayriel could not help but smile at the priest's macabre humor. She felt that there would be no issue bridging the cultural gap with him—unlike his companion. Not that any of that would matter if they did not escape now.

They barreled around a corner and found themselves at the bottom of a newly formed waterfall. Seawater plunged from an opening high above, through which Vayriel could just make out the sky. She reached out and probed the edge. It yielded beneath her touch, but the sheer vertical slope and cascading water would make climbing out perilous.

"I take it that's our way out?" Zinvar shouted over the roar of water.

"Yes, but I do not think we can climb. And it is too late to seek out another passage."

"How close are we to complete submersion?"

Vayriel closed her eyes and concentrated. "Perhaps a minute."

The Komorese's face fell as the import of her statement sank in. "So, even if we could climb, there isn't enough time to reach the top."

"Unless," Kilahym mused, "we could somehow let the water take us to the top. Vayriel, can your shield keep the water out?"

"I…think so. Yes, it is possible. But…"

She broke off and looked away.

"But what?" the bard asked gently.

"I would need more than my own strength. And to draw on the life force of another is very dangerous. Only the strongest of my people dare attempt it."

"What choice do we have?" Zinvar broke in, his hands spread in supplication.

"Aye, Zinny is right. A maybe death is better than a certain one."

Vayriel nodded grimly. "Alright. Stand as close to me as you can."

The other Seekers huddled next to her. She breathed deeply and drew the life force into her. Slowly, she released it into a protective sphere around them.

Water crowded around the shield's edge, but none penetrated it. A sigh of relief escaped her, but the most difficult test was yet to come.

"Together, now," she commanded.

With shuffling steps, they edged beneath the waterfall. The downpour hammered against the pale pink barrier, but still it held. Beyond the shield's circumference, the water climbed to chest height.

"Ready yourselves. The creature-son is about to submerge. I will need your help soon."

Zinvar nodded, looking paler than usual, while Kilahym wrung his hands like wet cloths. Closing her eyes again, Vayriel reached out with tendrils of life force energy. A curtain of foamy water collided with the top of the barrier as she established a connection with the bard. The sphere lurched as it was driven down, then lifted by the churning currents. Kilahym lost his footing and tumbled into the barrier, the jolt severing Vayriel's connection.

Reflexively, she latched onto the glowing core of Zinvar's presence in the life force to bolster the shield and gasped at the depths of power she found. The priest did not seem to be aware of it, but he was a conduit of incredible life force energy. As it surged into her, Vayriel felt her awareness expand to encompass the creature-son, then the sea, and then all of Etherea. The world appeared to her as a luminous beacon, a nexus of the life force teeming with creature-sons and -daughters. A thin strand of glimmering energy, its origin the monolith, trailed away from Etherea to disappear in the void between other points of light. Vayriel followed the thread to its terminus and discovered that the life force was still present, only dimmed.

Curiosity took hold, and the Highblood focused on the faint signs of life. Images from other minds flooded her own: a world lost to darkness, a desperate flight, and finally, the discovery of a new home. Now, in slumber they waited for their creature-son to complete the reshaping of this new home. Etherea.

"Vayriel?"

Zinvar's plaintive voice broke the trance, and Vayriel's surroundings rushed back in. It all seemed so small, now, compared with the vastness of what existed beyond this corner of the Mother's creation. She struggled to rein in her thoughts.

"I'm sorry, but I don't think I have much left…"

With a start, she realized that Zinvar's presence in the life force had dwindled to a mere spark. He slumped against her shield's edge with his hands pressed to his forehead.

A warm hand grasped Vayriel's shoulder.

"Take from me instead."

Kilahym smiled despite the nausea she could sense mounting in him. They were careening off the walls of the passage as the water thrust them ever upward. Vayriel relinquished her connection to Zinvar, and almost fell when a tide of fatigue rushed in. Quickly, she reached out to Kilahym, and sighed in relief as new strength flooded her limbs.

"What in Morakh's name is that?"

Vayriel and Kilahym looked down at Zinvar's exclamation. They were now clear of the passage. Beneath them, the titanic creature-son moved ponderously toward deeper water. A low, rumbling groan issued from it, vibrating the Seekers and their protection.

The bard made a dramatic flourish with his hand. "That, I do believe, is the thing within whose innards we were traipsing about for the last few hours."

An awed hush descended upon the group. It held as they slowly drifted to the surface, until finally, they burst through to bob atop the waves. Much to their astonishment, the sky was clear and sunny. Angry gray clouds still lingered in the distance, but they were no longer gathered into obstinate walls. If not for the welcome sight of their ship nearby, Vayriel could have mistaken this for any other part of the ocean.

"It's…gone. The storm wall," Zinvar clarified.

"You don't suppose that thing was causing it?" Kilahym ventured.

The Seekers looked at one another.

"Whatever the case, help is on the way." Zinvar pointed at the lifeboat that was being rowed toward them.

Once they were all safely aboard and heading back to the ship, Vayriel could no longer stave off the exhaustion from her efforts. Sleep stole over her. Her dreams carried her to places far beyond Etherea, places she had never been but somehow knew.

CHAPTER 27

The familiar cliffs of Ettra loomed off the port side; the same cliffs upon which Idrilia had stood, feeling the mist hit her face as she looked over the steep drop with her grandmother. The boat stayed far from the edge, unimpeded by the rolling waves, which crashed and sprayed droplets that created that mist at the cliff's tops.

Like every other vessel that made the journey, the ship approached the city of Ettrascus by following the island's curve and turning to the south. The currents were weaker here, making for a peaceful tide on the cove's shore.

"How many times have you been here?" Kalis asked, swinging his pack onto his shoulder. "Definitely more than me."

Idrilia faced him. Behind him stretched an unfamiliar clear blue sky where there once would have been thick, ominous clouds in the ship's wake.

"At least five times with my grandparents, a couple times with my family."

"Then I nominate you for our guide." Kalis gave a crooked grin.

"Good. I think we will depend on both of you for most of our time spent in Sondrine."

Idrilia recognized the newcomer behind her as Zinvar. His ready acceptance of her leadership in the last trial now forced her to admit that, despite her preconceptions, not all Komorese were intractable, violent brutes. His companion on the other hand...

"It will be more advantageous if we split up and complete our tasks in small groups."

The Sondrinel spun to confront the heavy voice dripping with disdain. Tinted lenses stared back at her, the same as those worn by the riders from Komor she and Kalis had fought. And by the one who had attacked Klaara.

Her stomach knotted at the memory. Stepping backward, Idrilia dropped her leg in a defensive stance. Only as a familiar sneer crossed the man's face did she realize that he was Kharnek. She barely stopped her arms from snapping up into a combat stance.

"What…are you wearing?" she asked Zinvar instead, tilting her head to the side as she studied him. Instead of lenses, he wore something similar to a Sondrinel headscarf, but his was tied only around his eyes.

"This?" He touched the black fabric where the wide band crossed his temple. "It's to protect my eyes, much like the warriors' eye coverings. But as with many things, the Priesthood takes a slightly different approach."

"How does it work?" Kalis prompted.

"The fabric filters the bright sun," he said, pointing above, "I see everything much…dimmer through it."

Idrilia leaned closer, peering at the fabric and noticing that she could still see the outline of his eyes. "The Sunscorned use something like this."

"The who?"

"Outcasts in the north of Sondrine," Idrilia clarified. "Rogues whose actions or ideas are so contrary to Axiom's edicts that they cannot be permitted to stay in the city. Not even Quorum, the guild of misfits, would take them in." She averted her eyes to the shore. Would the Council think her actions, her true actions, in saving Klaara were enough to exile her? While the records of noteworthy events in each citizen's life were documented in the Vitaetum texts, Idrilia had never looked up any Sunscorned while she was in Evocus. She didn't know what actions those people took that resulted in an existence in the unforgiving desert; she only knew what children said to one another to scare them.

"But unlike you," Kalis added, "they're used to the sunlight. You'll want to protect the rest of your exposed skin, you know, now that we are in the land of light."

"We will keep to the shadows," Kharnek replied gruffly. He moved to an unoccupied area of the ship.

The priest shrugged. "We will make sure we have adequate clothing for the journey."

"There's a pleasant breeze here that you will not have on the mainland,"

Idrilia added. "It makes the sun's heat more enjoyable. It might end up helping you get accustomed to our climate."

"Thank you." Zinvar nodded. "If you'll excuse me." He headed in the same direction as his companion.

The tan-and-cream landscape, itself brilliant beneath the sunlight, was outshone by the reflection off the cerulean-domed buildings of Ettrascus. Idrilia was excited in spite of herself to see the white-walled city. Strong memories of the trade port persisted in her: its bleached stone stairs and walkways seemingly carved from the island itself. Until her eyes began to water from the brightness, she would keep her head uncovered as they walked the streets and buildings, soaking in the warm sun on her olive skin.

"Do you think we will ever move past this open hostility?" Kalis's question interrupted her thoughts.

"Do you really want to?"

He appeared to ponder her question. "I mean, it might sound optimistic, but I would like our future to be one of peace, not conflict."

"Better do as I say, then."

Idrilia smirked as Kalis made a face at her, before turning to observe their approach to Ettra.

Surrounded by large fragments of rock like giant beige teeth rising from the azure depths, the cove came into view. The ship entered at the widest entrance with the deepest waters. In doing so, it faced the shore and the clear emerald water that faded into the multileveled white-and-blue buildings.

Sunbeams struck the city, setting it ablaze with light. Vayriel squinted and raised a hand to shield her eyes. Idrilia opened hers just enough to watch the smaller pleasure vessels bob in the shallower water and the dots of Ettrascans splashing in the cove.

"We'll dock here on the left," the captain announced, coming up behind the group of six, "where the water is deepest. While you get your supplies, we'll offload our cargo and transfer yours."

"Transfer?" Zinvar asked. "I thought you were taking us as close to our next trial as possible?"

"I'm afraid I won't be able to do that. We received a message from the harbormaster via othwit. A hurricane has formed to the east and it's between us and your destination. The storms out there don't dissipate for weeks, so you'll be better served by going on foot. But don't worry." He shook his head. "We will refund you for the unused portion of your fare, and we've hired a ferry to take you over to the mainland."

Zinvar glanced back at Idrilia, who shook her head. "He's right about the hurricanes. It's a setback, but at least Kalis and I know the way through the Sondrine."

And we'll be near Axiom in case we need to stop a Komorese scheme.

"Oh, I do hope there are no creatures between here and the mountain like that sea monster!" Kilahym wailed.

Kilahym launched into yet another retelling of their adventure within the monolith. Though she knew the bard embellished, the disappearance of the storm wall meant there had to be some fragment of veracity nestled within his tale. To her, it seemed likely that the storm beast was yet another monstrosity created by Komor rather than belonging to creatures from far beyond Etherea, as Vayriel had indicated. Perhaps gaining access to the mysterious communication cube would reveal the truth.

She signaled Kalis. *If you have an opening before they unload the cube…*

Idrilia improvised a modification to the hand combination for *block* or *rock* but dropped her hands quickly as the shape they made looked uncomfortably like a heart.

I'll investigate, Kalis signaled back.

Good.

The group moved closer to the disembarkation ramp as the ship maneuvered to dock. Idrilia whistled. From the white sails, Wen stretched and floated down to land on the Sondrinel's outstretched forearm, gripping her talons into the blue cloth as she climbed to perch on Idrilia's shoulder.

"So, what's the plan?" Kilahym rubbed his hands together, looking from face to face.

"I think we should focus on what we know and help get those items for the others," Kalis replied.

"Right," said Idrilia. "Kalis and I will point out items to help you through Sondrine. The market will have items suitable for all three realms, so we can walk together and browse the many vendors while we are at it."

Kilahym bounced in place. "A shopping spree funded by other people's resources? I can scarcely wait to begin!"

Idrilia rolled her eyes. "Only get what we need. The main thing will be proper attire for all of you for traversing the desert since this wasn't our original plan."

"This we already know," Kharnek interjected with a sneer. "What of the other trials? Do our self-proclaimed leaders have any suggestions for those?"

Idrilia caught the scowl Zinvar threw his companion's way. "I think we all understand that Idrilia and Kalis are the experts on their homeland, so we'll adhere to their guidance in this instance," the priest said. "But we should prepare for what comes after. Do you have any suggestions?"

"We know the other Trials will likely occur in each realm, and we could even come back to Heathström. We just don't know what they will involve. Prepare the best we can for this one, you know? We'll need coats for the mountains. They might block precipitation from falling beyond their peaks, but on their slopes, you can quickly forget that below is a desert," Kalis replied.

Vayriel raised her chin. "We will also need sustenance for ourselves and our creature-friends."

"Maybe we could get the more sundry provisions," Zinvar offered, motioning to the silent figure next to him. Kharnek shrugged.

"That should work. The food and medicinal items are at the back of the market. But if you want to explore the city first, that's fine too." Idrilia flicked her eyes at Kalis as she spoke, wondering if he thought she was too obviously sending the Komorese elsewhere.

"What method of transportation will we use to cross the expanse?" Zinvar asked.

"With our new bags, we'd only need to worry about carrying the water supply. I think one more camelid should do. Then a solendrake for each of us," Idrilia outlined.

Kharnek huffed.

Idrilia crossed her arms over her chest and scowled at the stoic warrior. "You have a problem with that?"

"Only that they are inefficient and slow."

"I didn't realize we had a time constraint," she countered.

"Really, they are the best for this landscape," Kalis jumped in. "They are hardy and, like the camelid, they don't need much water. They can run as well as walk on almost any terrain, including steep walls."

Kharnek drilled the Prioriate with a skeptical stare but made no reply.

Once the ship docked, the group traversed the long boardwalk and entered the city. White stone buildings with rectangular windows lined the narrow streets as they followed a gradual incline further into Ettrascus. The stone path was well suited to the many vendors' individual carts, hauled by nomyni, the short-haired, smaller cousins of the mountain alusarean.

Zinvar and his surly companion veered off toward the customs buildings, briefly explaining that they needed to make arrangements for the newly opened trade between their realm and the rest of Etherea. That left the rest of the group to follow the train of merchants up to the market. Idrilia saw the observatory in the distance, the highest point on the island. The great lidless eye of a telescope peeked out from its domed cerulean roof, indicating that the facility was in use.

The market was a series of stalls and freestanding tables in a large quadrangle, the more permanent vendors covered with sail-like awnings. Tight aisles were created by the displays, forcing them to walk single file at times.

Using some of the funds from the Magister, Idrilia made several purchases and instructed that the goods she obtained be delivered to their ship. One Sondrinel vendor made the connection that Kalis and Idrilia were the Truthseekers from Sondrine.

"Congratulations to the both of you. Word only reached us but a day ago that Axiom sent a betrothed couple to the Trials. Quite the way to start the rest of your lives!" the man laughed.

"Yes, I suppose it is."

"And the storm wall is gone! Kadaan truly smiles upon us." The vendor waved farewell to them. "May your journey be swift and untroubled!"

Idrilia schooled her features to remain impassive as she left the stall. Their parents must have made the announcement public—the union of two of the most powerful families in Axiom could not be kept secret for long, after all. Although she had known it would happen, she would have preferred that this reminder of the inevitable not be a common topic on their journey. Thankfully, the market's visitors were more preoccupied with the storm wall's disappearance, which she overheard numerous sellers and customers discussing.

She and Kalis surveyed the variety of goods, which ranged from ornamental clothing to large timepieces. He seemed to be always at her heels, ready to jump in with his opinion or inquire as to what she was looking at. She sighed heavily as he commented on a garment he thought would suit her.

Idrilia maneuvered around another shopper, attempting to put some distance between herself and Kalis. She moved to another table, then another vendor, until, lost in thought, she bumped into someone.

"I'm sorry." Planning to skirt around the person she had jostled, Idrilia nearly stumbled when she at last met the other party's eyes.

"This place is crowded." Vayriel squinted in the bright sun, and a small, forgiving smile graced her lips. The Highblood's crescent eyes moved up Idrilia's face to settle on her forehead. "What does your jewel represent?"

Idrilia reflexively touched her circlet, wondering if the green jewels sparkled in the sunlight. "This was my grandmother's. My, uh, father's mother," she amended, attempting to follow Vayriel's nomenclature, and explained Elsuota's role as High Keeper. "They allowed her to keep this emblem of her station when she…stepped down."

"It was then gifted to you by her?" Vayriel's brows rose.

"She…left it to me. She died about a sidereal ago. An illness our healers could not cure took her." Idrilia fought back tears as her voice threatened to break.

"This is all I have of my parents." Vayriel pointed to the silver bands on her bare upper arm. Idrilia thought her face had softened.

"How did they die, if you don't mind me asking?" Idrilia asked, relieved to draw the focus away from her own memories.

Vayriel explained, and Idrilia bit the inside of her lip, battling tears of rage. A commonality, although she took no satisfaction in finding this connection. *Arslen. Monsters.*

"I'm so sorry, Vayriel." Blinking, Idrilia pushed back heated thoughts, though anger still gripped her heart. "What about your father's family— your…fa'fa and fa'ma? Did they go with them?"

"No. They live in a coil far away from mine."

"Oh. Do you see them often?"

Idrilia studied the Highblood as she approached another table, her face hidden, running a hand over a collection of wooden boxes. Was she hiding her reaction?

"I do not," Vayriel answered at length. "There is a disagreement between their coil and mine that prevents me from doing so."

"A disagreement? About what?"

"Lowlanders."

The Highblood's eyes rose to meet Idrilia's.

"In my coil, lowlanders are welcomed, even encouraged to visit. In my fa'fa and fa'ma's coil, though, lowlanders are reviled. It saddens me that such hate exists among my people, but I understand the reasons behind it."

"Sort of like how I feel about Komor."

"Yes." Vayriel nodded. "Perhaps we will be the ones to finally change that."

"Doubtful, but I appreciate your optimism," Idrilia grunted. Vayriel went back to examining the wooden trinkets. Despite their differences, the Sondrinel realized that she and the mountain-dweller were similarly burdened by the values of their societies. If only they could break free of those chains without being ostracized for it.

"Oh! A moment, please," the Highblood touched Idrilia's elbow. "There is something I wish to acquire."

Idrilia followed Vayriel to another merchant's stall, where the Highblood purchased a glass vial full of shimmering blue liquid.

"What is that?"

A guilty expression stole across the Highblood's face. "Something for a friend," she answered evasively, stowing the vial in her bag. "He will need it later."

The cryptic behavior left Idrilia puzzled, but she did not probe any further. Her thoughts returned to Vayriel's comments about division among her people, and a wild thought occurred to her.

"Come with me," Idrilia whispered, elbowing Vayriel gently.

The Highblood glanced over to where Kilahym stood. Idrilia followed her gaze a fair distance across the market to see the bard engaging a female vendor in animated dialogue over a large glass shape that tapered at one end. It emitted a musical hum with several unique tones as the woman ran her hand over certain parts.

Idrilia led her new comrade away through several aisles with Orgar in tow. She glanced behind to confirm the others were not following.

They were halfway to the edge of the market when Vayriel hesitated. "Are we not waiting for Kilahym and—"

"They can get the rest of the supplies. I want to show you something."

"Will they not wonder where we have gone?"

"We won't be gone long."

With a reluctant glance over her shoulder, Vayriel followed Idrilia out of the market and back into the narrow streets.

"Are you doing this to escape Kalis?"

Perceptive woman. Idrilia sighed. "Yes and no. It's complicated."

"But you are to become life-mates?"

"You heard that? I bet everyone knows now…but there's more to life than getting married or not, you know?" She laughed, a bitter snicker. "I sound like him."

"You do not find him a suitable life-mate?" Vayriel's head tilted marginally. Idrilia wonder if the Highblood could see thoughts like they were etched into her face.

"I like him. We're friends—have been since childhood. But…it wasn't my choice. This whole thing was arranged by our parents sidereals ago. What right do they have?" Idrilia's cheeks grew hot like flames. "If marriage is to be a part of my life, then it will be because I want it to be so. Not because someone else chose for me."

"It is unfortunate that you do not get to choose your life-mate as we do—so long as they are not a lowlander, that is. But do you not wish to be with him because of who he is or because the choice was not your own?"

The sounds of the market had been replaced with the faint roar of the sea below them. From this vantage point Idrilia saw the barrier islands, formerly obscured by the storm wall, as faint blue-gray outlines. They had reached Ettra's summit.

"I…don't know. He's—we're…it's just not what I want. Not like this." *What do I want?* She shook her head. Romance from novels would only distract her from the Trials.

"I understand. My mo'mo has been asking me to seek out a companion. She says that I have not interacted enough with people of the coils. And the time will come when it is too late. But I am happy with Orgar. I do not understand why she is not happy with that." Vayriel shook her head.

"It isn't her decision. Our choices and actions, not when or who we marry—*those* define us."

Idrilia felt a growing respect for Vayriel. The way she articulated her thoughts reminded her of Klaara, direct but well-considered. Only time would tell if this newfound commonality would deepen their friendship. Idrilia realized that she might be open to more than that with Vayriel, the complication of her betrothal notwithstanding, but it sounded like that interest would not be reciprocated, for her or anyone else.

The Highblood seemed satisfied with Idrilia's response for the moment and did not push the topic further. Idrilia returned the courtesy.

They walked in silence past several buildings, until they found themselves at the foot of a staircase that curled up the side of a tall cylindrical structure.

"Come on. Let me show you the moon."

CHAPTER 28

"It would be unwise for you to back out of our deal now."

"I can't do it. What you're asking me to do…it's unconscionable."

"That is why I asked you in the first place. Your unconscionable reputation preceded you."

Kharnek's voice was laden with menace as he advanced upon the Ettrascan harbormaster, who backed away with wide eyes. The man quickly bumped up against the back wall of his office.

"A bribe here and there to keep the sails unfurled is one thing, but what you want is high treason! If I were ever caught—"

"Which will not be a concern once Komor assumes control of Ettra."

"If you succeed." The harbormaster wrung his white hat furiously in his hands.

"With the information on Ettra's navy—which you are about to furnish— our victory is certain."

"Yes, but—"

"There is no room for discussion, Master Tivoli." Kharnek slammed a palm onto the wall beside the harbormaster's head. The man jumped and cowered before him. "And trust me, you do not want to see what happens when I am forced to…*renegotiate* an agreement. Now, hand over the charts."

"I can't…I just can't," Master Tivoli said, his voice shaking like his trembling fingers. "I'm sorry."

Kharnek sighed. Before the harbormaster could blink or protest, the warrior buried a dagger in his heart.

Master Tivoli's eyes bulged, his mouth gaping in disbelief. He crumpled to the floor without a sound. A thin rivulet of blood began to trace the seams between the wooden planks beneath his body.

Kharnek dragged the corpse through the storeroom behind the harbormaster's office through swathes of netting and tackle. The storeroom opened onto a platform that overlooked the harbor. It sat high on the side of the island's cliffed coast. Kharnek rolled Master Tivoli's body off the edge of the platform and watched it sail down into a watery embrace. The waves around the corpse exploded into a frothed frenzy, churned by the coils of hungry tide writhers. They would dispose of the evidence.

The warrior used a bucket of seawater to rinse away the bloodstains on the office floor. Before he left, he paused and withdrew the dagger he had used from his weapons belt. The dark violet gem set into its hilt glinted as Kharnek examined the blade. Confusion surged in his thoughts. He did not remember asking Zinvar for this dagger. Yet it already felt like a natural extension of Kharnek's hand and will. It was rare for him to sense such a connection without the familiarity of time and use. He marveled at the dagger's balance and craftsmanship for another moment before replacing it in his belt.

On his way back to the ship, Kharnek skirted the edge of the market to avoid his fellow Seekers. He did not need their scrutiny interfering with his work, especially not that of the all-too-inquisitive Sondrinel. Kharnek had made his sole purchase right after leaving Zinvar at the customs office, saying he would catch up with him later. The priest had regarded him with curiosity but let him leave without any questions asked.

Kharnek took out the item he had bought to inspect it. He unwrapped the square of red cloth that protected the small glass vial and held it up to examine its contents. Dark-blue liquid swirled like the currents of the sea.

The elixir enhanced the innate abilities of an Occulum when ingested or so the frightened vendor had told Kharnek. The customs officer had found his request for a merchant specializing in such things strange but possessed the wisdom not to question the warrior. Now that he had the substance, Kharnek's desire to atone for his role in the loss of Zinvar's parents warred with his qualms about what the priest would see when he looked into the past. If he knew the truth—but perhaps he deserved to know. Kharnek could not let his own feelings toward the priest interfere with his pledge to bring about justice.

He arrived at the lower docks where the vessel that had brought them to the island was moored. He could make out the triangular sails of an Ettrascan warship on the horizon, silhouetted against the clear sky beyond them. The warrior scanned the docks for prying eyes and ascertained that the coast was clear.

He crossed the wooden pier and boarded the vessel. The creak and groan of timber accompanied him into the hold where the cube that awaited its new Sondrinel owners lay. Kharnek approached the device and withdrew the key Zinvar had given him. Unlike the keys presented to the Sondrinel and the Magister, which would only activate their specific cubes, this one was universal.

Kharnek inserted the key into the cube's upper surface. The device hummed and light spread out through its facets. An image of Zel Morakh wavered into existence above the cube, its towers and ziggurats stretching toward the rock walls surrounding the metropolis. A priest appeared, along with the Captain of the City Guard. Square-jawed with broad shoulders that filled out his scarlet jacket, the officer sported two angled black bars over his heart as rank insignia. Kharnek saluted, raising his right hand in a fist to his forehead while placing the other at the small of his back.

"It is good to hear from you at last, Guardsman," Captain Ahlet began, raising his left fist in return. Both men dropped their arms at the completion of the ritual. "I take it you and the young priest reached Waverling without difficulty?"

"Yes, sir. We have arrived at Ettra—and somehow, the hapless oafs from Heathström managed to bring down the storm wall on the way."

"The storm wall is gone?"

"Yes, sir. We encountered a sea creature during our voyage, which the Highblood claims was causing the storm. It disappeared at the same time the tempest was dispelled, so there does seem to be a correlation."

"Fascinating," the captain mused. "Some creation of the Sondrinel, perhaps? A biological weapon?"

"If so, it was unlike any suncursed weapon I have encountered, sir."

"Do you have any theories of your own?"

Kharnek hesitated a moment before replying. "The Highblood believes that this creature was trying to reshape Etherea, at the behest of its masters—from another world."

A frown creased the captain's forehead. "Do you agree with that assessment?"

"Though it pains me to say so, yes. Just before the creature disappeared, I—saw something. The Shadow of Morakh within me recognized the monster as an old foe and attempted to lash out. I was able to control it, but for a moment, I was connected to the creature. Within its memories was the destruction of its home by Morakh's wrath. And that home was most certainly not Etherea."

Silence reigned in the wake of Kharnek's final statement. The captain and priest exchanged looks and seemed to reach an unspoken understanding.

"A most disturbing account, which will merit further investigation—after our conquest of Etherea is complete. And the removal of the storm wall, however it was accomplished, is a boon for our plans."

"I understand, sir. The storm wall's disappearance has captured the island's attention such that it may distract them from our movements."

"What of the harbormaster?" the priest's gravelly voice intruded. The raised hood of his rust-colored robes obscured his features, but Kharnek guessed that this was a Mahir, one of the High Priest's advisors. He looked toward his commanding officer for assurance to continue. The captain nodded his assent.

"I am afraid the harbormaster has reneged on our deal."

"Most unfortunate. Master Tivoli was quite receptive to our initial terms," the priest mused.

Kharnek shook his head. "His conscience caught up with his greed. Do we have a contingency in place, servant of Morakh?"

"We do. Captain Ahlet has been successful in positioning one of our spies as the immediate successor to the harbormaster. In many ways, we have gained an advantage as a result of this development. Morakh is with us."

"Indeed," the captain agreed. "Guardsman Kharnek, how have the others reacted to the communication devices? And the prospect of open trade? The Magister had little choice but to accept our offer. Her response was not particularly insightful."

"The Sondrinel are suspicious of our motives, sir."

"That comes as no great surprise," the priest muttered.

Kharnek glanced at the cowled man before continuing. "Nevertheless, they have accepted the gift, if only to maintain an outward semblance of diplomacy. I am using their device to contact you now. The Seekers from Sondrine will transport it to Axiom."

"Excellent. Then all is proceeding according to plan." Captain Ahlet smiled in satisfaction.

"Yes, sir. There is, however, an unexpected development concerning the Order of Laphrim."

"The witches?" the priest hissed. "Always meddling in our affairs. Morakh's retribution for their actions will be second only to the fate suffered by the 'burned Sondrinel.'"

"Servant of Morakh, has the Priesthood received any communication from a Spectre named Ifen?"

The priest ruminated. "Yes, son of Komor. What do you know of this witch?"

"She is the leader of a faction of conspirators who seek to supplant the Magister. Malcontents, for the most part, but they are aware of our impending invasion. Their intent, should they succeed in their coup, is to surrender the city of Waverling in exchange for the right to self-govern."

Kharnek stifled a smirk when the captain laughed in response.

"They cannot be serious," his superior scoffed.

"They are quite serious, sir."

"How amusing. It would be fortuitous if they should succeed. We could cross Heathström unimpeded. Yet you say that they are small in number?"

"The leadership group I observed was, sir. They alluded to having additional support from men within the city who resent being ruled by women."

"Ah. Their cause may have found resonance there. I will task our spies with discovering the scope and nature of this rebel faction."

"There is no need, Captain," the Mahir interrupted. "The Priesthood will handle the matter."

The captain balked. "Surely the servants of Morakh do not intend to accept the offer?"

"To your point, Captain, it would be most beneficial should they succeed. It is a simple matter to maintain the pretense of honoring the bargain until such time as our foes are vanquished. If this group fails, am I correct in understanding that you can offer us a military solution to the problem?"

"Yes, of course. Guardsman, were you successful in locating a weakness in the city's defenses?"

"Yes, sir. As our intelligence indicated, there is an entrance beneath Waverling's southern wall where the river exits the city. I have removed all obstacles to our forces."

"Then there is no need for concern, Captain," the Mahir said. "The end result will be the same with or without the cooperation of the witches. I shall apprise the other Mahir of this new information."

The priest exited from view.

"A pleasure, as always," Captain Ahlet grumbled. "Guardsman, your orders are unchanged. Proceed according to the initial mission briefing."

"Yes, sir." Kharnek took a deep breath. "Sir, once the cube enters Axiom, I will be unable to report for some time."

"We anticipated this. The Brotherhood has every confidence that you can succeed. With your unique abilities, I suspect that you do not require our guidance anyway."

"Thank you, sir."

"Be wary of the Sondrinel. Their nest is a dangerous place. Ahlet out."

The captain saluted. Kharnek returned the gesture, and Captain Ahlet stepped out of view.

The warrior pressed down on the key, which popped out of its socket into his hand. Zel Morakh vanished, and the dimness of the hold flooded in. Kharnek blinked as his eyes adjusted to the displacement. *Unique abilities.* He wondered if the captain would hold the same opinion of his prowess if he knew that those abilities were gone.

Kharnek's fears dissolved at the sound of footsteps on the deck above him. He melted into the shadows of the hold as a figure descended the stairs.

CHAPTER 29

Vayriel approached a rounded building with a domed top, what Idrilia had called an *observatory*, which had a raised band over its middle. A rectangular building connected to its side stretched half the height of the observatory. Like the rest of the buildings in Ettrascus, its surface was white, while its domed top was a deep azure. Vayriel missed the colors of Heathström, how each tool or article of clothing made by the Highbloods celebrated nature. Even the lowlanders painted nature's hues in their buildings and art. At least Ettrascus's market was full of color, festooned with tapestries hung from display racks and piles of fabric.

This point in the city appeared to be the highest. Vayriel could see almost every edge of the island. She thought the shades of green and blue around the coast beautiful, yet different from the colors of Lake Gamin and the streams of the Agermath mountains.

Climbing the few steps, Idrilia pulled the single door open and stepped over the threshold, holding it for Vayriel. Inside, she blinked, trying to clear the invisible curtain that fell over her eyes. The pressure that had been building behind her forehead, like hands squeezing her temples, lessened. She relaxed her face, now aware that she had been squinting. She would likely need to start wearing her snow-eyes if the feeling persisted.

"We'd like to use the telescope for a few minutes, if it is available."

As Vayriel's vision adjusted, she saw Idrilia standing in front of a small desk. A petite woman, her lips ornamented with a silvery paste, sat behind it, fingers folded and elbows on the pale wood.

"Purpose?"

"Knowledge," Idrilia said, her voice rising in pitch. "Do people typically waste your time by swinging on it or climbing out the window?" She placed a hand on her hip.

"You'd be surprised."

"I think I would." Idrilia glanced over her shoulder at Vayriel and crossed her eyes. Vayriel covered her mouth to hide a grin. For a moment, Idrilia had reminded her of Kilahym, though he probably would have made the expression where the red-haired woman could see.

"Research or personal?" The woman tapped her nails against the desk in the rhythm of rainfall.

Vayriel surveyed the room as Idrilia handled the formalities, adding their names to the registry book. To their left, a staircase wrapped around the observatory's circumference. Behind the desk and to their right, a door led into the rest of the structure.

A movement below Vayriel drew her attention. Orgar's twin tails undulated, his hindquarters raised as his chin rested on the polished stone floor. His ears pointed up and twitched.

Chuffing, Vayriel knelt, balancing with her spear. "What do you see, my friend?" she whispered, then traced Orgar's line of sight. Beneath the desk a small creature curled against the woman's leg. Its long mouth yawned, creating a pink triangle. From the top of its head rose two outsized loopy ears. Its single bushy tail wrapped around its master's leg, the appendage matching the short cream-and-brown fur of its body.

"We'll see more of those." Idrilia now leaned down as well, her hands on her knees. "Torav. They live in Sondrine's deserts. This one has been domesticated. Don't worry, its venom has been removed. Come on, we can go up now."

The thought of altering a creature's natural essence bothered Vayriel, but she moved to follow her companion.

"Orgar," she prompted the unmoving jeroti, "come."

When her life-friend lingered, Vayriel nudged his hindquarters with the butt of her spear. Orgar turned his head languidly.

"Come."

The staircase followed the curvature of the building until it opened onto a landing that extended the full width of the dome. The ceiling was nearly as tall as the stairs they had climbed.

A segmented bronze tube stood in the center of the domed chamber, angled from the floor near Idrilia toward the opposite side of the dome. Vayriel recognized it as a far-seer, the largest she had ever seen. The lower segments tapered in width to a handbreadth, atop which the small cylinder of the eyepiece rested. Gold knobs and levers studded the bottom of the device.

"I want to show you what the southern moon looks like. And you'll see that there's no reason to fear it." Idrilia threw a lever on the wall, and a section as wide as the far-seer drew back. A wedge of light grew into a long arc as the panel retracted beyond the roof directly overhead.

Vayriel felt the pressure behind her eyes growing again. She squinted in the light and frowned at Idrilia. "As I told you before, the Highbloods see the Sleeper as a great betrayer, and yet you ask me to look on his face?" She took a step closer to the blue-haired woman, gripping her spear with both hands.

"You keep saying 'the Highbloods'—but is that how you feel, too? I've looked at the moon many times. Nothing bad has come from it. I want to show you this, so that you can be free of your fear."

Vayriel faltered. She defined herself by her devotion to her people's teachings. Why would she want to think differently? It was readily apparent that Idrilia discounted her perspective after all. When Vayriel had explained her vision about the storm creature-son aboard the ship, the Sondrinel had expressed disbelief, a reaction that lingered in the Highblood's mind. However, she wanted to learn and share new experiences gleaned from the Trials with her coil when she returned. Was this not a new experience? Just as she learned from the creature-sons and -daughters, perhaps there was something Idrilia could teach her as well.

"And we can look at the north moon, too. The Daughter? You will see they look much the same."

Nearly laughing—the Daughter and the Sleeper *the same*?—Vayriel saw the pleading expression on Idrilia's face. Just as Kilahym shared stories, this new companion wanted to share knowledge with Vayriel. A part of her wanted to know, to look on the face of the Sleeper and know that he would never hurt them again. She stood straighter and nodded.

"I will look on them."

Idrilia rotated a handle connected to a gear. By interacting with another gear, the support platform rotated in tandem with the observatory's dome.

"This is a very large far-seer," Vayriel commented, examining the cylindrical tube.

"Far-seer? That's a clever name to give a telescope."

"Is that not what they help us do?"

"It is. Water-glider, far-seer—you certainly have a straightforward manner of naming."

"When too many words are used, the meaning can easily be as lost as a leaf in a river."

Idrilia stopped her efforts. Above, the moon came into view, faint in the brilliant Ettrascan sky.

"There." Moving to the eyepiece, Idrilia made a few small adjustments with knobs before stepping back and motioning toward it. "All yours."

Vayriel took a deep breath and, with a final stroke of Orgar's head, she approached the far-seer. She closed one of her lavender eyes and let her other adjust, pressing it against the far-seer's eyepiece.

At first the viewfinder was clouded, a muddy brown sphere spilling to the edges. As her eye adjusted, the image sharpened, and Vayriel noted three distinct colors. Most of the surface was a deep orange, but with patches of light and dark blue and green: some in narrow bands, running like veins across the surface, others in broad splotches. Vayriel's attention was drawn toward the upper left where a light flashed.

The Sleeper's eye was open.

Vayriel cried out, batting the eyepiece with her arm as she moved to put distance between herself and the far-seer.

"What is it? What's wrong?"

"The Sleeper. He is awake." Her heart pounded and a sickness filled her stomach. She gripped her spear tightly.

"What? Don't be silly." Idrilia pushed past the Highblood and peered through the eyepiece. "Where was it?"

"To the left and up. His eye glinted beneath the Watcher's rays."

The silver eye of the Sleeper, an ellipse narrowing at its corner, made him appear to be scrutinizing her. Vayriel shivered. Mo'fa would know what the sign meant. More than ever, she wished her mother's parents were with her now. No one here could guide her as they could.

"Excuse me, I couldn't help but overhear…"

Vayriel and Idrilia were approached by a Sondrinel woman with aquiline features. "My name is Elina. I am one of the researchers here," she explained, "you were looking at Etherea's second moon, were you not? And you noticed a shiny patch?"

"Yes," Idrilia answered. "My friend here is concerned that it signifies some kind of impending doom."

The researcher smiled. "A reasonable interpretation given the mythos surrounding Second-Son."

"You know our stories?" Vayriel's eyebrows raised. "And of the Sleeper?"

"Indeed, I do. The Highblood myths are documented in Axiom, though perhaps not broadly read."

Vayriel's excitement dimmed at hearing the term "myths." "It seems that everyone outside of Skyveil considers the Sleeper to not be a threat."

Elina tapped her chin. "I don't mean to imply that he isn't. Most origin stories are rooted in facts that have been embellished. The Sleeper probably was real and an enemy of your people. But there's likely a scientific explanation for what you are seeing."

"What's that?" Idrilia asked.

"We have many theories, but they all center on an artificial construct of some kind. If you really focus on the shiny area, you can begin to discern shapes that are too regular to be natural. The sunlight is reflected on them, suggesting a metallic material." The other Sondrinel held her hands far apart, palms facing each other. "Whatever it is, it's quite large. At least a few kilometers in length."

Idrilia peered into the far-seer one again. "So, what could it be?"

"We can only speculate." The researcher pointed to the ceiling. "The remnants of an ancient civilization? The wreckage of a vessel that could cross the gulf between worlds? Whatever the case, it's an enticing mystery that we will someday unravel."

"Fascinating." Idrilia pulled away from the eyepiece and motioned for Vayriel to come close. She shook her head and stood motionless. Orgar pawed at the loose cloth of her pants.

"I promise. It's not an eye," Elina encouraged.

Though Vayriel felt reservation, she saw no reason why Idrilia or the researcher would deceive her. For the sake of her coil, and all coils, Vayriel knew she needed to confirm what she had seen. Stepping forward, the Highblood held her breath and looked again.

She saw a dark line leading to where the glint had been moments before. Vayriel released her breath. Idrilia was right; no eye peered at her this time. The "regular shapes" the Sondrinel had mentioned must be the dark gouge that resembled a spear's shaft. She stared a moment longer, waiting for the blink of light. The shape did not morph into an eye.

Vayriel pulled away. "I did not see the light again."

"So, no eye?" Idrilia queried.

"No. I thought—" Vayriel paused.

Idrilia regarded her sympathetically. "It's alright. Fears can cause you to see things, or do things, you otherwise wouldn't."

"Well said," Elina complimented, "I have intruded upon your time enough. I will take my leave."

"Thank you for helping us," Vayriel replied. "Will you be here still if we have other questions?"

"I was actually on my way out when I ran into you. I'm afraid I, and the other staff here, have been recalled to Axiom."

Idrilia frowned. "Recalled? Why?"

The researcher's face fell. "We weren't given many details. The Council feels it's no longer safe for us here." Elina lowered her voice. "I've heard the rumors from the sailors. Komor's fleet is amassing off the coast of Heathström."

"An invasion force." Idrilia's eyes narrowed. "That must be it."

"I cannot say for certain, but I don't know what else it could be. Please, be safe wherever your journey takes you next." Elina bowed her head and departed.

Vayriel ran her fingers through Orgar's fur while she considered Elina's words. "Why would Komor want to invade Ettra?"

"Many reasons, but foremost among them is that it would give them control over the southern trade routes. Sondrine relies on imported goods that all come through Ettra," Idrilia explained, her brow furrowed. "This would also make an excellent staging point for an invasion of Sondrine itself."

"I see. Such an action would go against the spirit of the Trials."

"Yes, but I don't think Komor cares about that. All the more reason for us to stop at Axiom on our way to the next trial." Idrilia whirled back to the far-seer, moving to the wheel again. "Anyway, we'll worry about that later. As promised, let me show you the northern moon."

As before, Idrilia positioned the room and apparatus before inviting her companion to observe. Vayriel studied the differences between the Sleeper and the Daughter. Instead of orange, the primary color of the Daughter was purple. It had similar patches and vein-like patterns of blue, but the green was scarce. She tried to find the outline of a wing, but the shape eluded her. Vayriel could see the similarities, though she held to the thought that the two were different. The lavender hues calmed her, and she felt her sickness recede.

"Fairly similar, right?" Idrilia's voice came from behind.

Vayriel pulled away from the captivating sight. "In some ways," she conceded. "Thank you for sharing. I will in turn share with my coil."

"No more fear?"

Vayriel felt both confusion and relief, yet a lingering unease also filled her. It wasn't fear—she resented the implication. It was a wariness of a possible future. Fear was debilitating. It was the result of being without the basic tools and training to solve the unexpected. It was hopelessness. What Vayriel felt was the need to prepare, to be ready for the role the Mother had destined her to take in the events to come. She knew what she saw, yet she knew it was also not there. The Sleeper did not look like the stories but that did not make the stories untrue. Though she may have expected to see the varg and the winged vandling, seeing the spherical bodies did not change her beliefs.

"Where there is fear, there is defeat," Vayriel decided to explain. "I am empowered to face my future."

Idrilia nodded, then returned to the lever on the wall, triggering the movements to seal the dome once more.

"Let's go back to the market. The others may be wondering where we are. And we need to buy you a headscarf," she added.

"Why?"

Idrilia pantomimed wrapping something around her face. "It will help with the light's intensity and protect you from blowing sand. You won't have to squint to see."

"Oh." Vayriel dipped her head. "Yes, I think that would be helpful. I use an eye covering when the Watcher's rays are bright against the snow. The light there reflects off everything."

They started back the way they came, Wen alighting on Idrilia's shoulder when they returned outside. Vayriel's mind remained in the observatory. Despite her confident statement to her fellow Seeker, Vayriel felt less certain about her future than ever before. She was so distracted that she collided with Kilahym when she rounded the next corner.

"Goodness me! I can now say I've literally run into someone." Kilahym clasped her forearm. "Are you alright, m'lady?"

His touch felt gentle and comforting, like when Orgar leaned against her. She blushed. "Yes, I am fine. I apologize, I was not paying attention."

Zinvar appeared behind Kilahym, his arms laden with packages. "You know, Kilahym, we do have magic bags that can hold all of these. I don't see why I needed to—oh, hello there!"

"What are you two doing here?" Idrilia folded her arms. "You were supposed to be buying supplies."

"Which we did, and then we came looking for you!" Kilahym answered smoothly. He winked at Vayriel before thrusting a finger toward the Sondrinel. "And we've caught you! Sneaking off to do...well, what *were* you doing?"

"Never mind that," Idrilia growled. "Did you get every...wait, where's Kharnek?"

"I think he went to the market. He's probably back on the ship by now. Where's Kalis?" Zinvar responded.

Vayriel watched a thundercloud settle in Idrilia's expression. "He's probably there, too," the Sondrinel stated, marching in the direction of the docks. "We should get back."

Kilahym waved his hands. "But we haven't made it to the restaurant district! Or seen the playhouse! The Ettrascan companies put on some marvelously intricate shows!"

"Back to the ship. *Now*," Idrilia tossed back.

Vayriel met Kilahym's eyes, and she briefly sensed the frustration behind them through the life force. She mustered her inner calm and let it well outward. To her surprise, she felt its effect upon him, like water dowsing a flame.

"I suppose we had better do as she says," he agreed.

Vayriel nodded and followed after Idrilia, Zinvar and Kilahym in tow. Her cheeks were flushed and she felt...something that she did not know how to put into words. Never before had she touched or influenced another person's essence so easily through her connection to the Mother-of-All. *What did that mean?* She pondered it the whole way back to the ship.

CHAPTER 30

Kalis returned to a mostly empty ship. With everyone preoccupied in the market, the opportunity he and Idrilia had discussed presented itself. Although, he had not expected to end up alone because of 'Dril obviously ditching him. He was beginning to think that the wall she had erected between them would never come down.

Despite his calm gait, a tightness gripped his stomach. This plan made sense—still, doubling back and leaving the others, who would undoubtedly notice his absence, felt nefarious. If they asked questions, what would he tell them?

He descended the stairway to the hold, dark and silent but for the faint sound of water lapping. The support beams, amply spaced, glowed a faint green-blue from rope-like bioluminescent vines wrapped around their top halves. The glow did little more than outline the vertical structures.

Squeezing his fist to channel his thoughts, Kalis brightened the space around him with a crystal. He held it rather than tossing it above to float as he and Idrilia had done before. He would only be here a few moments. With the dim illumination, Kalis inspected the hold. The camelids and larger cargo had been removed, leaving the Seekers' items among the sacks, barrels, and smaller crates.

Then he saw it, nestled between two similarly sized containers. The light from his crystal caught the slightly raised designs on the cube's facets, casting shadows of the geometric contours on the glossy surfaces. The material reminded him of the protective layer the Komorese riders in Sondrine had worn.

Kalis reached into a pouch on the outside of his fighting robe and withdrew the hexagonal key. His fingers brushed the other item in there: a gift for Idrilia he had purchased in the market. He hoped to get her alone before their journey resumed.

Twirling the key between his fingers, Kalis searched for the recess that would activate the cube. He dropped his pack and crouched in front of the enigmatic object, noticing a faint orange glow on its surface. Several smaller lines formed muted squares, brightening and pulsing as his hands grew nearer.

Kalis yelped in pain, releasing his crystal to remove the glove on his right hand. The growing heat had intensified to a burn.

He quickly removed the source: his aunt's ring, which he planned to give to Idrilia. Words written in fire writhed along the obsidian band in a script he did not recognize. Kalis had never seen the orange lettering before.

A hiss issued from the cube. His eyes darted to the device's surface. A small section crept open like a miniature door. Leaning forward, he saw a tray revealed, smooth but for a circular depression in the middle that matched the size of his ring.

Curiosity overcame his trepidation. Kalis placed the band in the tray, withdrawing his hand as lights raced on the surface of the cube, tracing rectilinear shapes. New lines connected the squares together and symbols appeared above the device. The translucent orange glyphs scrolled upward until they vanished near the roof of the hold. Recognition teased the edge of Kalis's thoughts, but he could not interpret the barrage of information.

He snatched the ring from the crevice and glanced behind him. Nothing was there. When he turned to face the cube again, the symbols had faded, and the device was as it had been before, a glossy black. He released a breath he didn't know he'd been holding and inhaled. A flurry of questions raced through his mind.

He wanted to discuss what he had seen with Idrilia. This was not simply a communication device. They would be wise to warn the leaders of Sondrine before they delivered the cube.

For the moment, his ring had returned to normal. Kalis stood, slipped the band back on and pulled the leather glove back onto his right hand.

"Do they not teach children in Sondrine not to meddle in the affairs of their betters?"

Kalis spun on his heels. Kharnek stood next to a support beam, his face bathed eerily in greenish light. Kalis debated how to answer, unsure how long the warrior had stood there or what he might have seen.

"Kharnek. I didn't hear you come in."

"You would not."

"Possibly. Was this not a gift to Sondrine?"

Kharnek answered with silence.

"Keep your secrets, then. While you can." Kalis bent at his knees and hefted the cube, surprised to find it was much lighter than he had anticipated.

In an eyeblink, a dark blade was at his throat.

"Apparently Sondrinel children are not taught to listen, either." Kharnek's words oozed malevolence.

Flicking his eyes to the Komorese, Kalis debated the best course of action.

"Unless you want to start a war now by slaying a Truthseeker, I suggest you let me pass. Who did you think would deliver this to Axiom's leaders?"

The warrior held the Prioriate's stare for a few elongated heartbeats, then lowered the sleek weapon.

Kalis moved past Kharnek, toward the ladder and the light. Mid-climb, he paused near the landing to glance back.

"You know, you'd do well to follow your companion's example. At least with hidden hostility, we'd be less likely to suspect you were up to something."

Kalis thought he heard the swish of a sword parting the air as he emerged onto the deck.

"He did *what?*" Idrilia's strained whisper reached Kalis with barely contained fury. Under the pretense of viewing the captain's maps of the coastline, the two Sondrinel had slipped away from the others, who oversaw the transfer of their remaining belongings to the ferry.

"And I swear, it was made of the same material we encountered on the Leske Road," Kalis whispered back, a hand idly touching his throat.

"Just as I suspected." Idrilia shot up from the chair of the captain's desk. "If he wants to see childish behavior, I'll—"

"Shh, no. It's fine, really. We can't expect sidereals of conflict to be forgotten in a single day, you know."

"Don't shush me." She frowned. "We should expect some civility. We're in this charade together."

"Now's not the time."

"If he taunts me or raises a weapon at me, it *will* be the time."

Kalis stared at the parchment on the desktop. "We need to figure out what to do."

"Not take the cube within the gates of Axiom, that's for sure."

Kalis's head snapped up to look at Idrilia, now perched at the edge of the captain's desk. "You think it's that dangerous?"

"Kalis. You just told me that some hitherto unseen sequence of symbols was triggered by a family heirloom, and Khar-pain-in-my-neck clearly doesn't like the idea of us taking a closer look at his toy. What about that says *safe* to you?"

"What if that's what he wanted? For us to doubt him and the gift—therefore not delivering it, resulting in an insult that would give Komor an excuse to close relations that were barely opened? Then the blame would fall on Sondrine."

"I think you grant the Komorese far more intellectual capacity than they've previously displayed," Idrilia retorted. "Besides, their fleet is preparing to invade Ettra. This cube has to be connected to their overall plan."

Kalis blinked. "Where did you hear that?"

"Apparently it's common knowledge here. Axiom has begun to recall Sondrinel from the island."

"I didn't know that." Kalis pressed his fingertips to his temples. "But there's nothing we can do about that. Let's get in range of the gate and use the communication crystals. The Council can advise what to do."

"That's if the High Keeper can call an ad hoc forum of the representatives in time. *And* if they can get to a majority decision quickly—which never happens."

"Some decisions should not be made hastily," Kalis countered.

Idrilia groaned. "Some decisions should. Fine. Let's do it your way. At least there will be some warning." She rose to leave.

"Wait."

Idrilia turned from the door, her face unreadable.

Feeling slightly shaky, Kalis continued. "Dril, I—" His hand found the tissue-wrapped gift he had cradled in the hold. "I know we haven't had much time to talk about us, about our betrothal…"

She spun away from him, her bundle of long cerulean hair swaying behind her. "I don't want to talk about it. I'm going to check on Wen."

Before Kalis could reply, she left the room.

A heaviness weighed on him and he turned his eyes again to the nautical charts, withdrawing his empty hand from his waist pouch. He sighed, remorse filling his thoughts, disappointed in not telling her what he wanted to. If only Lyna were here. She would know what to do.

Kalis shook his head. He did not need homesickness compounding his heartache.

Kalis stood upon the upper deck of the ferry as the Sondrine coast and Leske delta came into view. They had left the storm clouds behind them, and the sky over the thin line of Sondrine's shore was a pale blue. The heat from the sun was sweltering, but the breeze of the ocean dampened the intensity.

Kalis noted that Idrilia, Kharnek, and the jeroti remained on the lower deck in the shade, keeping to themselves. Kilahym had engaged Zinvar, most likely in a tale; Kalis heard the faint sounds of his ocarina. Vayriel stood at the bow looking toward their destination. He moved to stand beside her.

"What has so captured your attention?"

The Highblood did not take her eyes off the terrain ahead. "This land, your home…it is so different from my own. So barren and devoid of the touch of the Mother. I hope that Orgar and I will find the strength we need for this journey."

"It's not all desert, you know. There is green in Sondrine. Some of it is just ahead." Kalis pointed to the delta. "Then some along the Cliffs of Odium on the eastern coast, and again where the ocean seeps back into the old Leske River at the Reef of Pillars—Sondrine's northernmost point."

"The cliff name sounds…ominous."

Kalis laughed. "Cliffs of Odium. I suppose it does. I'll have to tell Kilahym some of our stories."

"What are they?"

"Well, they aren't the most pleasant, you know. Heartbroken lovers ending their lives. Things like that."

"With none of the Mother-of-All's soft grass for your feet or leafy trees for comforting shade, I can see how despair could consume someone."

Kalis laughed again. "It's not that bad. You'll see. We'll pass through the Proja Forest, a wood of petrified trees. They used to frighten me as a child. I did not understand what could make stumps out of trunks, even when my mother explained how the Great Calamity changed our realm."

He told her of the vast ridged and pocked salt flat that had once been Lake Stelwin and of the crystallized bones of creatures claimed by the shifting mud during the Great Calamity.

"That does not sound inviting," Vayriel said.

She was right. He laughed at himself. For someone who had never been to

Sondrine, these ancient sites would hold little value.

"You know, your home—the Agermath Range—is the one thing that truly connects all of our realms. Its upper arm stretches across the landscape beyond Axiom."

Vayriel's gaze remained transfixed on the northern horizon. Thinking her lost in thought, Kalis regarded the water, noting a few pink monodelphs poking their metal-tone nose horns out of the waters as they swam next to the vessel.

"All the realms share one fate. But can they embrace that?"

Vayriel's soft voice drew his attention. "What's that?"

He could almost see the effort she made to pull her focus to him. "Mount Hoestra is part of the range, yes?"

"That's right."

"Have you been there before? What is it like?"

Kalis beamed. "Once, when I was very young. My family sponsored the construction of the scientific research outpost there. It's quite fascinating what all they get up to."

They conversed about Kalis's impressions of the mountain until the mouth of the river became visible and the others joined them on the deck. The two Sondrinel demonstrated to everyone how to wrap their headscarves, and Kalis mingled with most, carefully avoiding contact with Kharnek and warily watching Idrilia. Privacy was no longer an option for the conversation he wanted to have with her. He'd have to try to open dialogue again when she was less hostile, and hopefully he could get her away from the others then.

The ferryman steered the craft into the dull green eastern bank, lined with roots that arched well above the water level, and toward the series of stone docks used for the many supply exchanges from the islands of Ettra. Kalis's nose wrinkled at the salty, sulfuric smell that wafted from the marshland. Unloading the solendrakes and water packs for the group, the crew then turned the ship around and headed back to the archipelago.

After strapping two camelids with water sacks, the group mounted the solendrakes. Kalis, after several minutes of persuasion with Idrilia, convinced Vayriel not to walk the entire distance. Orgar sauntered beside her like a white shadow. Kalis glanced behind him and saw a tiny red triangle in the offing, the helpful captain and his crew now departing Ettra and far out of reach, the pleasant islands becoming a memory.

CHAPTER 31

Distant yips and chitters echoed once again through the labyrinth of stone columns. The haunting sound of a torav pack trailing their movements gave hints of life to scattered bones. The thought of dying without a fight, like these long-dead creatures captured by the Calamity, haunted Kharnek more than the sounds could.

"Trees, now stone statues, outstretch to the sun in a graveyard of their kind. Ghastly."

Near Kharnek's side, Kilahym had started a string of dialogue with Zinvar. The two men had grown closer over the first half of the ten-cycle trip to the Sondrinel capitol. For Zinvar's sake, Kharnek was glad to see the burgeoning friendship develop.

"I have never seen the like," the priest commented. "Though it could be the Valley of Monodium, where the lava flows to spill over the resting dead and harden in basalt shapes rather than the tombs we use."

Kilahym stroked his chin. "How perfectly…unsettling."

"What a blow that would be," Zinvar mused. "Instead of memorials for the elite, those vying for status in Komorese society would all meet the same end."

"There will always be a hierarchy of power, as long as the Priesthood is in charge," Kharnek put in.

"I don't disagree with you. There needs to be sweeping change in our society to lessen the disconnects."

"What would you change about Komor, if you had the power?" Kharnek asked.

Zinvar's face lit up, which pleased Kharnek. "A lot of things, actually. I'd start by—"

The Whole. We will be whole.

The warrior blinked. Zinvar's mouth moved, but Kharnek did not hear his words. Kharnek looked from Zinvar to Kilahym, but neither appeared to have heard the statement. He stiffened.

"Kharnek?" Zinvar's forehead wrinkled. "Are you alright?"

"Just a headache. Excuse me," he mumbled, leaning back in the saddle and signaling for his solendrake to slow down. In comparison with rift wyrms, the club-tailed creature felt sluggish responding to his commands, but it was surprisingly intelligent and agile. He would remember their strengths and weaknesses to report back to the Brotherhood.

From behind the entourage, Kharnek evaluated the barren vista. The petrified trees cast thin shadows on the sand and debris; smaller particles from rocks and pulverized tree trunks dotted the hardened landscape. Otherwise, the Proja Forest was a desiccated void. A bright, hot, empty expanse, similar to how the Priesthood described the Everburn that awaited the unfaithful.

Kalis led the group while Idrilia flanked them on the right to watch for potential confrontations. It was true that Komorese raiding parties had infiltrated Sondrine's outskirts, but such a raid was unlikely to occur to the Truthseekers themselves. His presence guaranteed that they would be left alone.

Kharnek hissed as pain seared through his skull. The lenses of his goggles darkened, and he could no longer see. He tore them off but saw only shapes. His traveling companions and their mounts were mirages of bright white. Small light tendrils from their bodies wormed toward an inviting splash of darkness near the horizon.

Kharnek became the darkness. He floated high above an unfamiliar world. On its surface, dots and clusters of light pulsated. He craved their energy and reached out. Light tendrils swam into the darkness within him, and he felt his strength grow until the lights below were no more. He breathed in, and the world below imploded and vanished.

Beyond the space it previously occupied, there was another world with more dots of light, just out of his reach. He hungered to consume it, and he knew its name: Etherea.

Restore the Whole.

"Is that a tent?"

With Kalis's question, the vision ceased, and Kharnek's eyes were flooded with sunlight once more. He surveyed the others' reactions, but none of them had noticed his distractedness. He replaced his goggles and focused where Kalis pointed at the horizon.

"More importantly," Kilahym added, "are those *bones*?"

The ribcage of a creature the size of a full-grown arakh was draped with fabric fragments flicking in the hot, dry breeze. Several weapons were tied to the fabric ends, and a spear stood propped against the base of the deceased creature's spine. At the back of the structure, a tent, much like the ones the Seekers had purchased in Ettrascus, was pitched.

"It might be a Sunscorned camp," Idrilia moved closer to Kalis. "We should proceed with caution."

"This far south? I thought they only lived north of the city."

"There are also human remains." Zinvar waved his staff at what, at first glance, appeared to be a pile of torn rags. Now that he examined them more closely, Kharnek caught glimpses of bleached white between the shreds of fluttering fabric.

"They've been picked or scoured clean. Which means they've been here a while." Kalis swiveled his head. "So, we can rule out those raiders that the mayor told us about."

"There is only one here," Kharnek said, moving his mount near Zinvar. "And they are not what they seem."

The priest turned to him. "How do you—?"

Kharnek squeezed the side of his solendrake and moved in front of the group, cutting off Zinvar's question.

From the entrance to the tent emerged a figure dressed much like Kalis and Idrilia and with their hair color, though her garment ends were tattered. Two vargs sat beside her. Their tails appeared to be made of smoke. Kharnek stared, convinced the intense sun was creating mirages.

"Stay away! Stay AWAY! I'll kill you all!" she screamed, her voice carrying further than Kharnek would have thought possible.

"Don't have to tell me twice. Left or right, my esteemed associates? Whoa there, Salander—" Kilahym's mount began to veer left.

"Make peace with me!" Idrilia called back.

"I've been alone here for so long. The other five…it is too late."

In the blink of an eye the woman appeared before them, traversing the distance instantaneously.

Kalis and Idrilia commanded their solendrakes to veer to either side of her, leaving the robed figure directly in front of Kharnek.

"Witch."

He leaped from the saddle, drawing his obsidian blade, and landed facing her. From within her robes she withdrew two short staves, one tipped with a long crystal that swirled with dark mist. A headscarf covered all but her snarling mouth and black eyes.

Then he felt it. Cold seeped into his every blood vessel, and he was alive with power again, his body merely a container for the Penumbra's deadly energy.

Kharnek felt time slow. The Sondrinel's mounts froze in the middle of bringing their club-like tails to bear. Idrilia's othwit held a downward stroke of its wings inches from its mistress's shoulder. Kharnek stepped through shadow to appear behind the assailant and swung his sword at her neck. But she had already rotated, meeting his move with the hand that held the crystal-topped stave.

Again, Kharnek tried the same shadow step. Yet again, she met his move with a parry. And again. And again.

"Impossible," he muttered.

"You are we," she whispered in return.

Kharnek took a step back, breathing heavily as he considered her. The move should have worked. But she was just as fast.

The woman somersaulted backward as time sped up. Solendrake tails *swack*ed the empty space she had vacated.

"By the Lady, she's fast—"

"This way, please, Kilahym," Vayriel urged, no doubt attempting to lead the bard to safety. Briefly, Kharnek felt drawn to do the same for Zinvar, but the thought quickly faded. An insistent tugging at the corner of his mind vied for his attention.

Meanwhile, the two vargs charged, one to each Sondrinel, loping across the distance, unlike their human companion. Kharnek heard Vayriel command Orgar to strike the vargs. Kalis and Idrilia withdrew crystals as their mounts swung their bludgeoning tails and missed.

Idrilia shook her fist, then flung a fireball that caught one varg on its side. It slid across pebbles, kicking up dust. Orgar pounced at the creature's exposed belly, claws extended. Kalis gestured, the motion like ripping an invisible blanket from his mount's back, and conjured a stalagmite of dry clay and rock. It speared the other varg, injuring but not incapacitating it.

Vayriel appeared near the human foe, her spear creating distance between them as the tip pointed at the woman's chest. "Fight the shadow within you, and see that we are not enemies!" the Highblood beseeched.

Her position made it impossible for Kharnek to swing his blade. "You are in the way," he breathed, the pitch of his voice oscillating. Then he *pushed* with his mind. Vayriel flew up and back as if she had crushed a pyreflower, landing near a dismounting Kalis. Through his Penumbra-enhanced senses, Kharnek noticed a tendril of gleaming energy that stretched between the Highblood and the bard as the latter rushed to Vayriel's side.

He flicked his eyes forward. Lightning whipped from the assailant's hand as it arced toward him. He lifted his hands, and the fulgurations ricocheted off his blade and back at his opponent.

She dropped her hands to her sides and *absorbed* the light, a malicious smile creasing her lips.

The darkness inside Kharnek rose, detecting an echo of itself that intensified as he turned himself over to its power. Unlike other times he had let the Penumbra assume control, the outside world vanished. The void he found himself in was shot through by fractals of dark gray and colors that Kharnek did not have names to describe. Their patterns twitched and shifted in a restless dance, but no sound accompanied their movement. He attempted to move forward and became aware of a thin, transparent barrier between him and the chaos. It did not yield to his touch; the texture was similar to glass. Kharnek looked down and immediately wished he had not. Like the barrier, his hands and body were transparent and below them yawned an abyss. His head swam from vertigo. He closed his eyes and pressed his hands to them, willing himself to break free of the Penumbra's hold.

"So, you, too, are its prisoner."

Kharnek instinctively reached for his sword as he opened his eyes and spun around, but his hand came up empty. Before him stood a Sondrinel woman, her blue hair pulled into tight braids that encircled a central bun. She spread her hands to show that she was unarmed.

"I had hoped that I was the only one ensnared by the Penumbra, but as soon as I felt your presence, I knew it had taken someone else."

"Who are you? What is this place?" Kharnek grated.

"I am Adjira. A Truthseeker like you, not so long ago." She looked at a place behind him. "The Penumbra sensed itself within you as you approached. It was distracted enough that for a moment I broke free. I used the last of my strength to create this refuge. I cannot maintain it for long, but we are safe while it holds."

Kharnek lowered his hands and straightened. "We are inside the Penumbra, then?"

"In a manner of speaking. This place exists only within our minds, which are themselves hostages of the Penumbra."

The warrior struggled to grasp the concept. "How are you able to do this?"

Adjira interlaced her fingers in front of her. "I was once a healer, specializing in ailments of the mind. It was a simple matter to link our consciousnesses through the life force."

"Magic," Kharnek muttered, "of course." He motioned at the churning darkness beyond Adjira's barrier. "Why help me? You could have used that opportunity to save yourself."

Her translucent shoulders drooped. "I'm too weak to fully drive the Penumbra from me. But you...you are strong. It *wants* to join with you. It's forcing us to fight in the hopes that you will triumph and take my piece of the whole."

The patterns around them thrashed violently at Adjira's words. Her figure wavered in and out of focus, then stabilized.

"We don't have much time left."

Kharnek, despite the epicycles of loathing conditioned into him, empathized with Adjira's plight. This could very well be the fate that awaited him if he did not find some way to rid himself of the Penumbra. "Is there no hope for either of us?"

She shook her head. "I cannot say. You seem to have formed a more symbiotic relationship with your fragment. But that may change as it becomes stronger."

"My fragment... How did you find yours?" Kharnek asked. "Maybe there's a connection."

"Mine was housed in a crystal shard." Adjira raised one hand, palm up, and an image of a jagged, purple-hued gem appeared over it. "We found it during one of our trials. I did not realize its insidious influence until it was too late." Tears spilled down her cheeks, nearly invisible against the pallor of her skin. "I wish I had been stronger. You must be, or I fear all of Etherea will succumb to the Penumbra's hunger."

A loud *crack* split the silence following Adjira's statement. Fractures appeared in the barrier and with them came a thousand cloying whispers. The Sondrinel pressed her hands to her head and staggered back. "I can't hold it any longer."

Fragments of the barrier rained down on Kharnek as it began to collapse. The brittle pieces popped like soap bubbles when they struck him, their demise marked by flashes of white light. His eyes met Adjira's as the darkness surged in and enveloped them both. He reached out toward her, but she was engulfed by the black. Anger and hatred welled up within Kharnek, and he roared his defiance as his surroundings faded into nothingness.

CHAPTER 32

Wen darted overhead, ready to dive at a signal from Idrilia, but she could not see a safe opening. Orgar pinned the varg, his massive jaw around its neck, while Idrilia stabbed its skull between its ears. The creature's limbs spasmed, then it fell still. As slick blood covered its hilt, she left the dagger for now and charged toward Kalis.

Her legs felt as if she moved through mud. She glanced down, but nothing physically impeded her movements, but her progress was labored and suddenly she felt as if the weight of Evocus sat on her chest.

"Kalis," she gasped. Then, remembering his gift, she fumbled in her hip bag for the communication crystal. Unable to remove her gloves, she pressed the crystal to her temple.

Help, she thought, collapsing to her knees.

An immobilized Orgar whimpered near her while Wen dropped to the sand with a soft thud. Vayriel was somehow frozen in mid-air, having recovered from being thrown aside moments before. Idrilia watched as the Highblood's eyes closed and her lips puckered into a blowing shape. She exhaled, and a cloud of dust and detritus formed from her breath. It advanced on the remaining varg to obscure its vision. Several paces behind her, Kilahym fell to one knee, his face pale. Vayriel regarded him over her shoulder with wide eyes. Idrilia wondered what had happened but looked ahead again as the snarl of the approaching varg drew near.

With a quick upward pull, Kalis used his stone crystal to shape the ground again, impaling the varg high above on a mountainous spear. The Sondrinel twisted his upper body toward Idrilia with an expression of confusion and looked down at his unmoving feet.

Idrilia tilted her head to view the Sunscorned woman. One hand stretched out toward them as if gripping an invisible ball. The other hand sparked toward Kharnek with strings of light. Idrilia's eyes fluttered closed, but she fought to keep them open as her hand clutched her chest.

She missed what happened next in the battle, but the pressure released. Kalis and Vayriel fell to the ground as Idrilia gulped air. Grabbing her remaining dagger, she pushed up and whirled toward Wen. Her othwit appeared undamaged and shook her feathers out. Idrilia turned to the woman as Orgar bounded over to Vayriel.

Kharnek's opponent spun into a heel kick aimed at his abdomen, and, as he bent back to avoid it, she followed through with her other leg for a whirlwind kick. It landed, but Kharnek didn't budge.

"I'd know that move anywhere," Idrilia whispered. "Adjira?"

The woman flicked her dark eyes toward Idrilia. Kharnek attacked, blade aimed at her chest, but, with inhuman speed, she rotated out of the way, her hand poised to ram her crystal-tipped stave into him. But somehow Kharnek had anticipated the move.

She looked down at his blade protruding from between her breasts.

Adjira collapsed, sliding off of the dark blade into the dust. Kharnek tore her weapon from her hand and shuddered. He tossed the crystal, now emptied of the swirling black within, and its attached stave toward the nearest dead varg.

Idrilia dove forward. "Adjira!"

"It made me…it made me kill them," Adjira sobbed.

"Shh, shh. It's okay." Idrilia grabbed her hand. "What made you? What did you kill?"

"The Penumbra." Blood sputtered from her mouth. "Tell them…it wasn't me."

"Kalis! Vayriel!" Idrilia unwrapped her headscarf and pressed it into Adjira's wound as she called for help. "Hold on, guardian of light," she murmured softly to her fellow Sondrinel.

"I will try to slow the bleeding," Vayriel said, kneeling on the other side of Adjira. Closing her eyes, she placed a hand on the woman's forehead. Orgar sniffed Adjira's weapon before moving next to Vayriel.

Kalis rubbed the back of his neck. "Sorry, 'Dril, this is beyond me. I think we need the Healers Guild, you know…"

Idrilia signaled *hush* to him before locking her gaze on Adjira's blue eyes. "Vayriel is a skilled Highblood. You're going to be alright."

"I saw…every day I saw…what it did…what it will do. It destroys all."

"The Penumbra?" Idrilia prompted.

Adjira nodded then gasped, her body shuddering. Idrilia wondered if she should ask the Sondrinel to stop talking, but she needed to know more, in case…

"…feeds…life force…in him!" Adjira's eyes widened as she pointed.

Idrilia turned to look at Kharnek. He crossed his arms but said nothing.

"…my friends," Adjira sobbed, "I'm sorry."

Idrilia focused again on the Prioriate. Vayriel had opened her bag and withdrawn the sporestalk that Kilahym retrieved in Peatwick. She removed the cap and shook it over Adjira's face. Yellow spores cascaded down, and the woman's eyes closed.

"The bleeding has slowed, but her pain is great. This will help ease her suffering. There is no more that I can do for her."

Zinvar and Kilahym conversed in whispers as Vayriel rose with Orgar. Idrilia stayed by Adjira as the woman's breathing grew shallower. At some point, Kalis stepped away and retrieved her dagger from the varg carcass. Idrilia returned it to her hip as Adjira's breathing ceased.

"Is she…?" Kilahym's unfinished question hung in the air like a cloud.

"Axiom will want to know about this. About what was done to her for all these sidereals," Kalis commented as Idrilia rose.

Idrilia stared at the lifeless body, feeling like she was back at her grandmother's bedside, unable to feel her feet beneath her. She took a shuddering breath. "Let's see what more we can find out." Wen landed on her shoulder as she addressed everyone,, "Come if you want."

The group approached the site where Adjira had been living. Zinvar said he recognized one of the hanging pieces of fabric as an acolyte's robe, and Kilahym identified another as that of a Spectre. Idrilia tried to lose herself in logic, focusing on every piece of discovery like it was the most important in the realm.

Kilahym gestured to the large rib cage that framed Adjira's camp. "What was this creature?"

"Pre-Calamity historians hypothesize that many of the larger skeletons were herbivores, possibly used as pack animals, like we use camelids today," Kalis explained.

"You knew the woman who attacked us?" Zinvar asked Idrilia as he examined a propped staff.

Idrilia stared at the weapon. "Yes. I learned some of my fighting style from watching her. She was several classes ahead of me. And one of the few Sondrinel to change guilds. Adjira renounced violence in any form and became one of Axiom's foremost healers. It was controversial, but her prowess is why she was chosen for the Trials."

Kilahym inhaled audibly. "Then these weapons and robes…"

"Are the last Seekers," Kalis finished.

"What in the Grey Lady's sanguine slippers happened here?" Kilahym asked.

"What did she say—a penumbra made her kill them?" Vayriel added. "What is a penumbra?"

"I don't know," Idrilia responded.

"What is it?" Vayriel asked Kharnek.

"How should I know?" he replied gruffly.

"It is in you."

"You think that because a dying witch pointed a finger at me? You are even simpler than I guessed."

"Well, that is outright rude—" Kilahym came to Vayriel's defense.

"You moved like her," Vayriel persisted. "She was quick, but you matched her speed."

"Do you not draw on surrounding energy to enhance your battle prowess, like other mountain witches?"

"She might, but Komor doesn't," Idrilia challenged, stepping closer to Kharnek.

"And you used the life force to push me away," Vayriel affirmed.

"You are mistaken."

"Please…" Zinvar held up his hands. "Please. A woman—a former Seeker—has just died after assaulting us. Can we focus on that"—the priest gave Kharnek a scrutinizing look—"rather than seeding more mistrust?"

The warrior threw his hands up and stalked away. Idrilia made a motion of disgust behind his back.

Idrilia and Kalis examined the few possessions in Adjira's tent and the surrounding area. They agreed that Adjira, or the thing she had called the Penumbra, had killed the other five Seekers. She also wielded abilities never seen in Axiom or anywhere in Etherea that they could determine.

Except for Kharnek, Idrilia groused.

Unable to glean any more information from her dwelling, the Sondrinel returned to Adjira's still form and related their findings to the other Seekers. The pressure behind Idrilia's forehead abated somewhat when the others accepted her idea to return the body to Axiom. At least Adjira would not be forgotten, her fate unknown.

Idrilia felt the weight of responsibility settle upon her. She and Kalis now had two things to deliver to their home, and neither boded well.

CHAPTER 33

Light.

Too much light.

Zinvar averted his eyes from the barren landscape. Even in the shade beneath the rock overhangs at the edge of the dry riverbed, the brilliance proved near intolerable. He adjusted his eye covering once more, certain that this latest incremental change would provide the relief he sought.

Zinvar saw the torav an instant before it leaped toward Idrilia. The creature's tiny, sharp fangs dripped with a venom the priest knew to be lethal. Right before it landed on the Sondrinel, a familiar black blade tore through its body. Two cream-furred halves thumped to the ground behind Idrilia.

Startled, she whirled with a crystal in hand, ablaze with the flame of magic. Kharnek sheathed his sword.

"You might want to watch your back, Sondrinel."

The warrior stepped around Idrilia to continue toward his chosen patch of dry rock, where he and the priest would rest until the next cycle. A flicker of revulsion distorted her features. She disappeared into her and Kalis's tent in a huff.

Zinvar sought out friendlier territory and found Kilahym engaged in the process of setting up his and Vayriel's tent beneath the rock walls at the edge of Lake Stelwin. The beige contraption started as a square of fabric bound by twine. Once the twine was unwound, the tent sprang upward into a conical shape large enough to house two people and their belongings. Zinvar suspected that the tents, like the bags the Magister had gifted to the Seekers, were imbued with an enchantment of sorts. The spacious interior belied the humble exterior, as he discovered when he poked his head into Kilahym and Vayriel's newly erected temporary abode.

The Highblood pursed her lips at the sight of the priest and went about unpacking her belongings. Zinvar cocked his head.

"She grieves the loss of the wee desert beast," Kilahym explained. "And your tall friend's part in it has not endeared him any more to this one."

"Without his action, Idrilia might well be dead," the priest said defensively.

Vayriel twisted her head to regard him, her lavender gaze seemingly brimming with tears. "There is always another way. When we visit violence upon the creature-sons and -daughters, we invite it upon ourselves."

That cryptic remark haunted the priest as he ducked into his own shelter, which Kharnek had set up opposite the others.

"That was certainly a close call," Zinvar commented as he entered the canvas shelter. The warrior neglected to respond. "It's unusual for a torav to act in such an aggressive fashion. I wonder if there's a nest nearby."

"The Sondrinel likely set up their tent right on top of it."

"I doubt that. This is their home after all."

Kharnek snorted. "Yet they failed to consider all the members of our little caravan in their preparations for crossing this wasteland—their *home*."

"You mean Orgar? To be fair, they did eventually find a solution for his paws." The priest raised a finger. "And if they're so useless, why did you stop the torav?"

"What?" Kharnek ceased unbundling his bedroll and faced Zinvar.

"You hate the Sondrinel. You could have let the torav attack her."

"And drag her carcass all the way to Axiom? I think not."

Zinvar blinked, uncertain how to respond.

"Allowing the Sondrinel to be attacked would be counterproductive at this point," Kharnek elaborated. He opened his dark-green bedroll, which uncurled onto the floor of the tent with a gentle slap. "And should we encounter any more of her bewitched friends, the more blades at the ready, the better."

"I see." Zinvar stooped to open his own travel pack.

"Zinvar."

"Yes?" Zinvar about-faced to see a curious expression on the warrior's face.

If he did not know better, he would say that Kharnek almost looked…bashful.

"I have something for you. From the market in Ettrascus." Kharnek reached into a compartment of his belt. "It will help you with the dreams you told me about."

He extended his hand toward the priest. A small vial of dark-blue liquid glimmered there. Zinvar slowly reached out and plucked it from his outstretched palm.

"How so?" He eyed the liquid's unfathomable blue depths.

"Drink it before you sleep. You will dream, but you will have more control over what happens. At least, that is what I am told."

"So, I dream, but I stay aware?"

"Yes."

"I see." Zinvar tucked the vial into a pocket on the inside of his robes. "Thank you, Kharnek. You never cease to surprise me."

The warrior cocked his head, seemingly unsure how to interpret the remark. "Think nothing of it. I would not see you suffer more than what this world has already brought to you."

A speechless Zinvar could only nod. Before he had the chance to form words, Kharnek swept out of the tent, mumbling something about checking on their water supply.

Though Morakh's Shadow would have fallen by now in Komor, Zinvar tossed and turned, unable to sleep in the relentless heat and ambient light. He tossed aside the meager covering of his bedroll and sat up. His skin, clammy with sweat, detected a faint stirring of the air through the tent's entrance. The priest stood, careful not to disturb Kharnek, and pushed through the flap.

To his shock, instead of the piercing light of Sondrine's surface, he emerged into starlit darkness. The indigo sky overhead shaded into deep black as he craned his neck to look upward, and the stars burned brighter than he ever remembered.

"Beautiful, isn't it?"

Zinvar jumped. Beside him stood the woman from the tower. Instead of her gray uniform, this time she wore a simple white tunic and pants. She gazed up at the celestial display.

"This is how Sondrine once was, before what you call the Great Calamity. The sun rose and set, and the night crept in and away."

The priest did not understand the woman's talk of the sun rising and setting. Did she not know that only the moons did that?

"Who are you?" he asked, repeating his question from the last time he had seen her.

She smiled in response. "It is who you are that matters now. Your powers grow even if your understanding does not."

"You're right about that last part. And what do you mean? I don't have any powers."

Again, the woman smiled. "And yet you dream, do you not? Of things that seem impossible."

Zinvar's mouth dropped open. How could she possibly know about his dreams? Before he could get a word in, she spoke again.

"You have seen the destruction of another world." She raised her arm in a gesture that encompassed the encampment. "Tell me what you see here, priest of Komor."

Zinvar glanced at the bevy of tents and was about to reply that he saw nothing. Then a familiar azure glow caught his eye. He focused on the tent that housed the Sondrinel. To his astonishment, the blue haze formed the outline of a sleeping Idrilia and Kalis. Beyond them lay Kilahym and Vayriel's shelter. The pair from Heathström were surrounded by a soft pink nimbus.

Zinvar wheeled about and cried out. His body, still in the tent, evinced the same magical radiance as the Sondrinel. But Kharnek's form, in stark contrast to the rest, was blacker than the well of the sky outlined in deep purple.

"What is this? What is happening to me?" The priest held up his hands and stared at them as if they contained the answers he needed.

"Your eyes have finally opened. Now you can see the light in those around you"—the woman indicated the Sondrinel—"and also the absence of it." She pointed to Kharnek.

"You…you said before that there was something wrong with him. Was this what you meant? That he is dark inside where the others are not?"

The woman looked down at her hands. "Remember that the evil you see is not his own. Thrice now he has encountered fragments. The darkness within him is growing stronger. He must not give in. He will need your gift even more now. The strongest among us have suffered and been consumed by its promise of power."

Zinvar finally connected some pieces of her message. "Like Nerekesh? And Adjira!"

"The power they had was with but one fragment." Her voice began to fade, as if she were drifting away from Zinvar, and her form became luminous. The priest squinted in the sudden radiance. "All Etherea will tremble if the Penumbra rises."

Zinvar strained to hear her final words, which drifted at the edge of audibility. Above him the stars vanished, swallowed by the gaping void from his dreams.

Her whispered warning reached him:

"The Sleeper will awaken."

CHAPTER 34

Axiom's gates came into view in the distance. They were built into the canyon wall at a bend of the old riverbed that was the Leske Road. When they got closer, Idrilia hoped the sight would instill fear into the Komorese warrior. She glanced behind at his figure, his expression unreadable under his headscarf. If he noticed her scrutiny, he gave no indication.

Zinvar's solendrake stumbled when a rock shifted in the loose sand beneath it. Kharnek's head snapped toward the priest, his gaze fixed until the creature resumed its normal gait. This protective behavior suggested an ulterior motive to Idrilia, but she didn't care enough to analyze what that might be. Movement at her side caught her eye, and she turned forward again.

Quit, Kalis signaled, keeping his motions short and concealed.

Quit what? Idrilia signed back.

He's done nothing wrong.

Your memory is short.

And yours is too long.

Extending the little finger of her right hand, Idrilia made a flicking gesture from under her chin toward Kalis.

Was that necessary?

The rude expression complete, Idrilia huffed and turned her head away from Kalis. He should be her most stalwart supporter in expecting the worst from their Komorese companions, but instead Kalis seemed determined to occupy the middle ground. It was all so *obvious*; Kharnek's inhuman strength and speed, the rumors of invasion, and Adjira's accusation added up to one reality: a plot to subjugate all of Etherea. And she felt certain that Zinvar knew more than he was letting on. His quick defense of Kharnek when Adjira called out the warrior revealed that, whatever he might say outwardly, the priest remained loyal to his countryman. And then there was this mysterious Penumbra entity. Clearly, it was the key to Adjira and Kharnek's power, but it came at a terrible price. The body on the back of Kalis's solendrake testified to that. Could Kharnek even be considered human anymore?

Vayriel's positioned her mount near Idrilia's right side. "Thank you again for helping my life-friend," the Highblood said, glancing at the makeshift boots tied with twine around Orgar's feet. Orgar had been limping from the combination of heat and salt of the dried lake. Idrilia had improvised a solution for his red and irritated paws. "I apologize for reacting so openly. And that my unpreparedness caused you to sacrifice your sleeping mats."

"Though I wish her quick thinking didn't include us then having to sleep on bare rock." Kalis rubbed his back in mock pain.

Idrilia rolled her eyes. "We can get new ones once we reach the city, you know."

"Even so, I thank you. He is most important to me. He—the bond we share is difficult to explain if you have not felt it."

Idrilia's heart swelled. Vayriel had been near tears as she had examined the jeroti's paws. Her voice and actions, her expressions, had been full of emotion, and she had even surprised Idrilia with an embrace of thanks.

Idrilia glanced above, where Wen glided with wings outstretched. "I think I have at least some understanding. But if you have a story about the bond, maybe I can understand better. Not now, of course," she added hastily, trying to balance her want to know Vayriel better with the need to stay focused on the trials. "Think on it. I would be glad to hear it."

"Orgar the flying jeroti. That's a play in the making!"

Kilahym's animated voice came from where he rode behind. Idrilia chuckled at the bard's antics.

"With songs, of course. And it will be popular with the wee ones. A magical Highblood enchants her best friend to fly across the realms, visiting boys and girls who need a bit of cheer."

"That is not even close to the truth," Vayriel corrected, a hint of embarrassment in her voice.

"While flying, the jeroti comes too close to a whirlwind and is trapped inside. The Highblood is distraught and cries for help. And a Sondrinel—Sondrinella? You don't have gender-specific names, do you?—ahem, appears, riding a giant solendrake carrying a vine in its mouth as a rope to pull the jeroti to safety."

Idrilia could not contain her laughter. The proposed play could only be marginally inspired by the real event.

While the others continued their chatter, Kalis signaled that he was going to use the communication crystal. Idrilia's levity dissipated and she readied herself for what she hoped would be decisive action from the Council. In the tent the darkening before, they had decided Kalis should be the one to communicate their concerns about delivering the cube from Komor. They had debated sending Wen with a written message, but feared her absence would cause suspicion. Instead they decided to wait until the city gate was on the horizon, and the crystals were in communication range—which was now.

Idrilia made a fist and twitched her wrist. *Go ahead.*

Soon Axiom's entrance towered before them. Ornamented with columns and appearing from the outside to be two levels, the stone gate stretched from canyon floor to zenith. The bottommost level—made for the passage of those on foot—displayed stairs leading inside, while the architects had carved the top level into several watchtowers with window-like openings. Now that she had seen the Assemblage, Idrilia judged the structure in Waverling to be a fair representation of the original gate, with similar bas-reliefs decorating its surfaces.

Response? she signed to Kalis.

They heard. No new instructions.

Of course not. "Make peace with the guardians of Axiom!" one of the guards called out. "Who seeks entrance to the Steps of Light?"

Sentinels flanked four of the columns. The fifth guard, who spoke, stood at the top of the steps, centered before the doors. The guards were dressed similarly to Kalis and Idrilia, though they sported bright-orange sashes tied around their waists. A small dagger was tucked into the band of each. Every guard bore a stave latched to their back. A barrier of life-force energy shimmered like a blue mirage between the group and the Sentinels.

"We are the Truthseekers, stopping in Sondrine's capital to deliver a gift from Komor and the unfortunate news of Seeker Adjira." Wen preened a wing on Idrilia's shoulder as she announced the group.

"I know that voice."

Although he spoke quietly from behind one of the columns, Idrilia recognized this guard. Jerrod. She suppressed the urge to roll her eyes.

"Present your tokens," the first Sentinel demanded, beginning to descend the steps to the base level.

As if on cue, the four remaining guards widened their stance. The stomp of their boots echoed in unison as they flipped the side panels of their nuala robes behind the hilts of their blades—these were clearly not ornamental.

Locating the token in her side pouch, Idrilia held the crystal image of Kadaan at arm's length as Kalis did the same. Kilahym dropped his own identification in the sand and fumbled to retrieve it. He dusted the object off before presenting it.

The guard surveyed the group. Then she raised her right fist next to her ear, opened her hand and rotated it to face behind her. In unison, the four Sentinels drew their crystalline staves from their backs and approached the column nearest them. They inserted the thin ends like keys into recesses in the columns and gave the staves a sharp twist.

First, the spot directly in front of the lead guard faded from blue to clear, then it shimmered and receded from the edges of the carved rock. The azure wave coalesced into the shape of a figure with outstretched arms hovering in the air. Rays of light burst from her hands, blinding the Seekers, then vanished as swiftly as they had come. Any indication of the barrier disappeared with the light.

"Welcome to Axiom." The lead Sentinel indicated with an uplifted hand that the group was free to proceed up the stairs.

Idrilia and Kalis led the way, the camelid carrying the cube from Komor in tow, while the others filed two by two behind. They were nearly to the top before anyone spoke.

"Need any help with stabling your mounts, Idrilia?" Jerrod approached. Before she could respond, Kalis had maneuvered his solendrake between them.

"We've been here before, you know," he said icily.

Jerrod sidestepped Kalis. "How long are you here for? I'm off duty tomorrow and—"

"We aren't here very long," Kalis interrupted.

Idrilia shot him a reproving look before turning her attention to Jerrod.

"Not more than a day, surely. We have this *gift* from Komor to deliver, and." She glanced at Adjira's wrapped body, her stomach hardening. "And it will be good for the others to look around the city briefly before we head to Mount Hoestra. Get to know us, as is the purpose of the Trials."

Adjira deserved to be honored, not subjected to conniving questions from a sand writher.

"Is that your next Trial? Be safe up there. Wouldn't want your pretty skin to get frostbite."

Idrilia couldn't contain her eye roll. "Right. Because just my skin getting too cold is the worst thing that could happen."

"I'd keep you warm. Too bad I didn't get picked for the Trials."

"Who did you bribe to get this post?" Idrilia dismounted, stepping closer.

"Sorry?"

"I have to assume you slipped a favor to someone in Priorium to get you this prestigious temporary assignment while you finished your training."

"I earned this." Jerrod's voice dropped lower in tone. Idrilia could imagine his smile fading into a thin line behind his headscarf.

"Ah, yes, you must have *earned* it after I rescued your solendrake from a varg while you ran in the other direction."

"That's not how—"

"I don't have time for this. Step aside." Idrilia shouldered past him, leading her solendrake and camelid to the gate.

"At least I don't have to depend on my family name."

Idrilia paused, looking over her shoulder. "What's that supposed to mean?"

"Oh, come on." He spread his arms. "Everyone knows you and Kalis were only chosen because of your families' positions."

She spun around. "Right, because my family name is how I knocked you on your backside in our sparring final and took your weapon."

"I—I don't remember that." Jerrod glanced at the other guards, whose eyes peered at them from the slits in their headscarves.

Idrilia felt heat radiating through her body, though she stood in the shadow of the canyon wall. She took a deep breath and strode toward the gate once again. Unlike Jerrod, she'd earned this honor. He didn't know the battles she and Kalis had already participated in—and won—since they had left the city. He could kiss her basja-encrusted boots.

One of the guards tapped three times on the stone gate, then moved out of the way. Cracks appeared as the double doors slowly swung inward. Instead of using the person-sized door set into the rightmost rock slab, they would enter through the larger opening created by the two rock faces parting.

The guard who had tapped on the stone lowered her headscarf and joined Idrilia.

"He's even more insufferable than before," she whispered in a voice Idrilia had memorized. *Klaara.* "Though I'm surprised he hasn't heard of your unavailability. Congratulations on your upcoming union, by the way." Klaara nodded toward Kalis.

Idrilia nodded back though the words hit her as strongly as a blow from a solendrake tail. Klaara was *happy* for her. Her Klaara, quick of wit, who had shared sideways glances from the backs of their solendrakes and fierce expressions as they sparred, did not care.

"Uh, looks like you were right about your assignment," Idrilia offered, unable to meet Klaara's gaze.

"It's just a rotation for now. Testing out the sands. Good luck on the next trial!" Klaara elbowed Idrilia then turned back to her post.

Steeling herself against further thoughts of someone who might have been more than a friend, Idrilia led the group into the cavern home of the Sondrinel.

They were in a long, wide passage, and it wasn't until the stones clunked into place behind them, removing the outside light, that the crystal sconces on the walls were discernible. Kalis explained to the group that they would leave their mounts and pack animals in a paddock off a side passage, and that the heart of the city was much more open than these tunnels.

The Seekers were removing their head protection and unloading their animals when Kalis kicked a small stone Idrilia's way.

"That was brutal, you know."

"He deserved it," she responded, not looking up from her task.

"I wasn't implying he didn't."

Idrilia halted her motions. She turned a puzzled expression to Kalis and caught his eye as he winked. She grinned, then felt her cheeks grow warm. She turned back to her solendrake, loosening the final strap.

"Oh, good! Here you are." A young, clean-shaven man in a tan robe stood outside of the paddocks. The undecorated silver circlet atop his head let Idrilia know he was studying to be a Keeper.

"My name is Askel," he said. "The Council of Sondrine has requested your presence. I am to escort you and your, uh, delivery, as soon as you are able. Members from the Healers Guild will be here shortly to attend to the, um, deceased." He fidgeted with the hems of his sleeves, then hastily added, "I mean, just Kalis and Idrilia are requested. The rest of you can enjoy the city."

Vayriel stepped forward, spear in hand. "Where should we go?"

"Anywhere really," the envoy replied.

Idrilia smacked her palm against her forehead.

"Helpful as always, these Sondrinel." Idrilia caught her grin at Kharnek's comment before it grew.

"Go to the Hall of Remembrance first," Kalis offered. "It was built specifically for us Truthseekers should a Trial bring them into the city. We will pass it on the way to Concilius. Come with us and we can point the way."

Kalis tugged on the lead for the camelid burdened with the obsidian cube, and led them back to the main tunnel, the Keeper-in-training beside him.

"Any exciting places a bard should see, my good Sondrinel?" Kilahym asked. "A patron of the arts always seeks new distractions. And I'm not above settling into a shady hovel if it has enticing stories, if you know what I mean."

Idrilia frowned at him. "I'm not sure that I do. What are you implying?"

"Oh, nothing, nothing. I only meant I was open for any and all suggestions."

"If you have time, I'd suggest visiting Evocus and Priorium to start. The Hall of Remembrance is connected by a walkway from the east side of Evocus," Askel explained.

"Excuse me, I don't mean to interrupt," Zinvar began, "but without a point of reference, how will we know our cardinal directions?"

"Axiom has an orrery above the city, a representation of what you would see in the sky," Kalis explained. "Use it to guide your movements. And if you get lost, there are many Sentinels within who would be happy to point you in the right direction. Don't be afraid to ask." He clasped the priest's shoulder.

"I see. My thanks."

Idrilia explained how to recognize the central buildings and the significance of each. At the middle was Evocus with its many tiers. Connected to the right was Concilius, where the Council of Sondrine met. To the north towered Priorium. To the left of Evocus was Pedium. Idrilia's eyes lingered on the area where the graduation ceremony took place. Perhaps while they were here, she could find out what had delayed her acceptance into Axiom's military academy.

The tunnel opened into the central cavern, the ceiling soaring further than the eye could see. Idrilia inhaled the unique scents of the city she called home; the blending of the efforts of Axiom's guilds in sulfur, sweet bread, lichen, perfume, and rift-hot metal.

"There it is." Kalis pointed to Evocus. "Just follow the streets."

The group began to veer away from the Sondrinel, but Kilahym lingered.

"And this is where your Sondrine Edicts are etched in crystal, is it not? A towering five-sided obelisk, if I read correctly."

Kalis nodded. "Set in the place between the three buildings Idrilia was telling you about. Beneath the sun of the orrery. The original edicts were—"

"I know these! Read them in a fascinating historical, although rather dusty, tome at the Academy. Most bardic scholars affix themselves to the artistic literature, but there's music in history, you see. Protect history, obtain knowledge. Umm, er—five edicts, was it?"

"That's right. Each original edict and its longer definition are etched into a side of the obelisk."

"The tome made it sound like a most impressive sight. The Shrine of Laphrim is spectacular craftsmanship with crystal. But the words which your society is built upon, writ within the slippery surface...I'll tell the others we must go see your city central." Kilahym turned to join his fellow outsiders.

"Oh, and Kilahym?"

"Hmm?"

"Look closely at the streets, the columns, the carving of the houses into the rock—everything is etched and decorated. You might find the images interesting."

"Why thank you, good sir." The bard bowed with a flourish.

"Try not to get lost," Kalis laughed. "We'll see you soon."

He and Idrilia followed Askel. Once they were well out of earshot, their escort spoke again.

"The Council received your message and wishes to discuss the Komorese gift with you both immediately."

"Good. That was quicker than expected," Idrilia mused.

"They also need your reports on Adjira. Once they conclude their questioning, Kalis will be free to go. There's another matter they wish to go over with you, Idrilia, while you are here."

Idrilia felt her stomach tighten.

"Did they say what?"

"Something about reopening the case on the Komorese raider from last sidereal—the attack on your Pedium class. They have more questions."

Her heart raced. The nausea grew, and she thought she might be sick. This was why she hadn't been accepted into Priorium yet. Only nodding in reply, she tried to keep her face impassive as she looked from Askel to Kalis, hunting for any reaction.

They know. Oh, Kadaan, the Council knows.

Panic roared in her ears, blocking out any additional dialogue. She barely registered their approach to the building as her mind jumped from thoughts of how to slip away from the city and survive on her own—maybe she could live with the Highbloods, or join the Sunscorned—to the option of owning her choices and bravely telling the truth as her grandmother would have wanted her to.

She settled on her duty to protect Axiom against its enemy. She would address the cube and the strange black armor with the Council. What came after—she'd figure that out as it happened. For now, she stepped side by side with Kalis into the circular chamber, shoulders straight and chin high.

CHAPTER 35

The entrance to Concilius was as it had always been; Kalis had passed it every day of his childhood on the way to Pedium. The Sentinels posted outside the oval building in their ceremonial garb crossed their staves before the archway. As he approached, Kalis felt the tapered pillar's presence behind him, as if it draped the etched edicts all Sondrinel knew as a cloak over his shoulders.

Kalis removed the cube from the camelid, leaving it in the care of the vigilant guards. He and Idrilia followed Askel through the short arched tunnel and into the open chamber. All chatter ceased at their entrance.

Kalis wondered what Idrilia was thinking. He was afraid she might offend some of the Council with her open hostility toward the Komorese. Kalis considered what the Councilors would ask and what his responses might be until his mind was a cloud of what-ifs. He wanted to convey the qualms 'Dril and he had about the box he now carried and the attack they had faced in the desert upon departing Axiom so many weeks ago.

As the chamber opened, the walkway became a bridge, spanning a deep chasm between the tiered seating of those who wished to watch and the main pearly floor where the guild representatives awaited. The ceiling arched upward to half the height of Evocus. Sixteen of the seventeen Councilors' seats were filled, each nestled between carved columns. They were illuminated from behind by the colors from stained-glass apertures, each depicting a scene from their respective guild.

"Thank you, Askel. You may go."

The scrivener retreated from the room. A woman stood in the middle of the chamber, a jeweled circlet accenting her arched eyebrows. Parchments poked out of leather tubes at her waist.

"We have much to discuss," High Keeper Veloran began. "Twice you have sent us concerning news. Is that the cube from Komor?" She motioned to the obsidian item cradled by Kalis.

"May I, High Keeper?" He nodded toward the off-white floor.

"Please." She motioned toward the base of a large crystal next to her at the center of the half-circle formed by the Councilors. "You as well, Idrilia."

Together they climbed the remaining few steps and traversed the walkway approaching the blue-tinted crystal. It was as wide as Kalis's waist and reached the height of his chest. Its lower portion was ensconced in a bronze setting that hovered a foot above the polished, mirror-like floor. The crystal looked like an artisan had begun to carve a thick icicle, but changed her mind midway and instead hewed a desert blossom.

Kalis set the cube down gently. The clunk nevertheless echoed in the silent chamber. The Councilors sat motionless in their chairs, the weight of their scrutiny heavy on the Prioriate's mind.

"The Runner you sent from Heathström arrived early last week. The Council agrees that they would like to see the black armor you faced first."

Kalis saw Idrilia's face grow pale as she swept her gaze around the room. She hadn't practiced the communication crystal as much as he had wanted her to and focusing thoughts for all of the Council to witness had to feel daunting. With that in mind, he stepped forward.

"I will show the Council."

The High Keeper moved beside Idrilia, giving Kalis room to approach the crystal. He flashed a reassuring smile at Idrilia, then removed both gloves and placed his hands on the cool surface. Taking a deep breath, he relaxed his muscles and his mind as he exhaled, then closed his eyes. Behind the darkness of his lids, he recalled the memory of their battle with the two riders from Komor: their fireballs useless against the mysterious black armor, the death of their camelid, Idrilia's hand-to-hand struggle, the collapse of the cave wall.

Kalis opened his eyes but remained at the crystal.

"You attacked first." The statement came from a man sitting beneath the image of the Astronomy Guild.

"Of course! They were—"

The High Sentinel, leader of the Sentinel Guild, cut Idrilia's defense short. "They were clearly being stalked, and the riders were positioning for an attack."

"I've never seen armor such as that on any rider of Komor," stated a woman of the Delvers Guild.

"Can we say with absolute certainty that the assailants were Komorese? Is it not rumored that a former artificer joined the Sunscorned?"

Kalis missed which representative had posed the question, but the tone had an air of challenge.

"Who else rides a rift wyrm?" Idrilia's voice shook.

The High Keeper turned a calm gaze to her. "You are not on trial here," she rebuked gently. "If the Council has a specific question, they will ask you. This is the normal vetting process. I believe you know this." The High Keeper touched the central jewel on her forehead. "Are there any other questions for Kalis based on his memory deposit? No? Very well. Kalis, please show the Council your experiences with this cube."

Placing his hands on the slick crystal once more, Kalis closed his eyes again and focused on the two memories: the initial unveiling during the ceremony where the image of the Mahiratha had spoken through the unit, then the puzzling interaction with his ring and the strange symbols that emitted from it.

Opening his eyes again, Kalis removed his hands. He wiped his damp palms on the sides of his beige robe and backed away to stand next to his companion.

"Interesting that a realm that despises magic should seem to be in possession of it." The High Sentinel clearly had a similar impression to the Seekers' own. His words set off a flurry of debate between the guild representatives, and Kalis found it hard to keep up.

"Ah, but as history shows, things that are beyond our understanding hold a certain level of absurdity until they are studied and defined," the head of the Enumeration Guild observed.

"I volunteer the Artificers Guild to study the mechanism."

"I volunteer the metalworkers of the Delvers Guild as well."

The leader of the Eminents sat forward in her chair, the movement dislodging some of her elaborately plaited hair. "Should we not communicate with Komor first so that they know we received the item? Ignoring them seems ill-advised."

"And play right into their hands?" the High Sentinel scoffed. "Ignoring their past transgressions is ill-advised."

"Councilors, please," the High Keeper intervened. "It is clear we have varying opinions. There is much to be learned before any conclusions can be drawn."

Idrilia huffed beside Kalis, her frustration apparent. He squeezed her shoulder.

"Thank you for your caution in handling this matter, Kalis, Idrilia. Now, we wish to revisit the attack on Idrilia and Klaara's training class one sidereal ago, which may help the Council in these deliberations. Idrilia—" The High Keeper addressed the young Sondrinel. "Please show us those events."

"Just like the communication crystals," Kalis whispered as he clasped her hand again. "Think about what you want to show them."

"You don't need to stay for this," she murmured, sounding as if her mind was elsewhere.

"I will always stay, for you."

For once, Idrilia seemed grateful for his support, offering a gentle squeeze of his hand in response before she approached the center, her strides slower and less confident than usual. She reached out tentatively with one hand, finally making contact with the translucent material. Kalis realized that he had not replaced his gloves, so he did not have a receiving crystal to witness her memory.

The transfer complete, Idrilia turned, face pale and eyes lowered, and walked back to Kalis's side.

"That face—it was definitely Komorese."

"But he did not wear the black armor."

"Remember, though, this was a sidereal ago."

"This one rode a rift wyrm as well, like the ones our patrols have sighted recently."

The Council continued to converse among themselves, asking a few questions directly to Kalis and Idrilia concerning the interaction of life-force energy with the armor of the riders on the Leske Road. High Keeper Veloran acted in accordance with her role as facilitator, keeping the group on task and topic. A quarter of an hour passed before Kalis and Idrilia were engaged again.

"We can obviously agree on one thing," the High Keeper announced after several Councilors had posed resolutions. "This warrants further investigation as it is uncertain if the riders Idrilia and Kalis encountered were from Komor or if they were Sunscorned from the north in disguise. We have had a few recent incidents with the malcontents."

Idrilia tensed next to Kalis. He could almost hear her thoughts and shot her a look of warning.

The High Keeper continued. "The Council feels it would be unwise not to accept this gift from Komor. The evidence seen here today does not give a clear motive for any subterfuge, and it is not clear that these events are connected. The Council will reconvene to discuss further."

There it was. No action—yet. Kalis caught a glimpse of Idrilia's face and recognized the furrowed brow.

"The Council appreciates your time. I am sure you would like to return to your Trials. But before we adjourn, please share with us your confrontation with Adjira."

The Council allowed Idrilia and Kalis to relay the events via the crystal. Most of the Councilors' subsequent questions centered on Adjira's use of the life force and her final statements. If the Council knew more about the Penumbra, they did not state it.

"It is regrettable that this madness took hold of Adjira. So promising was her life. May she have found the path to the Rising open to her in her final moments. I will update her record in the Praeteritum and start the preparations for a service of remembrance," the High Keeper pronounced.

"The Delvers' Guild would like to send a team to the site to gather more information," said a woman seated before a window embellished with a depiction of the Steps of Light.

"Do we have three affirmations to the proposition?" High Keeper Veloran prompted. Multiple hands were raised. "The Council approves an exploratory venture by the Delvers Guild." She made note of the agreement on parchment pulled from a scroll at her hip. "Any other requests?"

"High Keeper, if we may," Kalis spoke up, "there is one more event that we think would be of interest to you."

With the High Keeper's approval, he and Idrilia related their experiences while traversing the storm wall.

"But you did not witness this yourself?" the High Sentinel asked.

"Only that the storm wall disappeared as the platform began its descent," Kalis answered.

The Sentinel frowned. "If the storm is no longer a barrier, ships from Komor could sail unimpeded."

"This could facilitate the trade they have just proposed," the leader of the Merchants Guild interjected.

"Or make it easier to invade our waters," the Sentinel countered.

"It seems we have another topic to discuss in great detail once more information is available," said the High Keeper. "The secundarium on this twenty-fourth day of Uma Vek is now concluded. We thank you for your attendance."

Veloran touched the jewels above her brow. The crystal beside her thrummed with a resonant sound that could be heard throughout the city, announcing the conclusion of the Council's special session of deliberations.

CHAPTER 36

Zinvar ran his hand over the cool stone of the painted mural. "A great light shone forth above them, and Kadaan beseeched her followers to remain ever vigilant, for one day, she would return to lead them out of the darkness that engulfs."

"Quite a tale to be telling." Kilahym clapped Zinvar on the back.

"Indeed, it is." Zinvar and Kilahym stood in the columned passageway that connected Evocus to the Hall of Remembrance, where they and the other Truthseekers were to stay while in Sondrine's capital city. The walls of the Hall and its auxiliary structures depicted various scenes from the history of Sondrine. Zinvar found himself drawn to this particular image.

"Do ye know the rest of the story?" Kilahym inquired, scratching his chin as he leaned closure to the pigments.

"I do. This mural tells the story of the Rising of Kadaan. According to Sondrinel legend, she was the first of their people to merge with the life force…what we call magic. What we see here is the moment of her transcendence, in less theatrical fashion than what we witnessed at Axiom's front door." Zinvar crouched to examine a set of glyphs nearer to the floor. "Here." He pointed. "This is the symbol of the artist."

Kilahym bent over and squinted at the ornate signature. "Not to be suspicious of your intentions, but why does a priest of Komor need to be knowing so much about the Sondrinel?"

"A fair question. Every member of the Priesthood can read the writings of the Sondrinel and is well-versed in their culture. In the past, that was driven by the necessity of understanding them as an adversary. To comprehend an enemy who is principally concerned with the pursuit of knowledge, you have to get inside their heads, determine their logic. Now, however, if Komor's offer of open trade is accepted, we can also begin an exchange of information that will benefit both our peoples."

Zinvar paused when the thoughtful look on Kilahym's face blossomed into a lopsided grin.

"You sound like a book yourself, Zin-Zinny but in the best way. They certainly picked the right man to change our minds about the flesh-eating, child-sacrificing, three-headed beasts of Komor." Zinvar made a face at the bard, who laughed and executed a short bow. "All in jest, my good sir," Kilahym assured him.

The duo began to walk toward the central rotunda of the Hall of Remembrance. Arched openings between the columns that supported the passageway offered views of the rest of the Esplanade, the district where Pedium and Priorium stood alongside Evocus. Beyond this central region, the city sprawled outward across a great plateau, which culminated in a steep drop-off into an underground lake. The lake, Zinvar had learned from Kalis, provided the city with a constant supply of fresh water.

Between the Esplanade and the main gate towered an enormous timepiece, large enough to see throughout Axiom. Above the timepiece, an ingenious mobile whirled in the air, suspended by magic. A blue crystal and two smaller orange shards orbited a huge pale yellow crystal that shone like the sun. Through some magical contrivance that Zinvar did not comprehend, the yellow crystal—the Star of Axiom, Idrilia called it—dimmed while the city slept, then surged back to full brightness while crowds bustled about its columned and arched walkways during the waking hours, known as a luminance. Despite its subterranean location, the soaring nature of the city's architecture eradicated any sense of enclosure that Zinvar had initially feared.

"I wonder what the Council wanted with Kalis and Idrilia? They've been gone for a while," the priest pondered aloud.

"Business about which the Sondrinel don't want sneaky Komorese to be hearing I'd wager. Speaking of which, where has your friend gone off to this time?"

"Kharnek? He's at the lake, replenishing our water."

"How alarmingly helpful of him—Vayriel!"

The bard skipped merrily toward his Highblood companion, who sat on the white marble steps leading into the Hall. Orgar lounged at her feet, his twin tails flicking up and down while Vayriel stroked the fur of his head. The jeroti raised his head for Kilahym to scratch beneath his muzzle. Zinvar halted at a respectful distance from the pair. He caught the last bit of Kilahym's excited chatter.

"—and then Kadaan rose into the light. Or something like that. He can explain." The bard looked at Zinvar expectantly.

Vayriel flicked her peach hair over her shoulder and regarded Zinvar with interest. "Kilahym says you know the stories of the Sondrinel. Is this true, servant of Morakh?"

The honorific startled Zinvar. "I—I have never been called that outside of my home," he stammered.

A small smile danced across Vayriel's face. "Your people are not the only ones who take an interest in the ways of their neighbors," she replied, her voice even.

"Fair enough. To answer your question, yes. We were examining a mural that depicted the Rising of Kadaan. She is to Sondrine what the Mother-of-All is to the Highbloods. In fact, there are many commonalities in your cultures' storytelling structures. You might find the images in the Hall interesting. The runes beneath each one explain what you are seeing."

Vayriel's confident expression faltered. Orgar whined. "I am certain I would find them beautiful. But I would learn little, since I am unable to translate these runes you speak of," she confessed. She glanced at her feet.

"You mean you can't read?" Kilahym's jaw slackened in shock.

Vayriel leaned on her knees and sighed. "Yes, Kilahym. That is what I mean."

"Not that that's a bad thing," he amended hastily. "In fact, most of my colleagues in Beechmarsh couldn't. It's quite commonplace among—well, it's not unusual."

"I would be happy to teach you," Zinvar offered. Kilahym and Vayriel turned in unison to stare at the priest. "I don't know how much time we'll have during the Trials," he cautioned, "but we could certainly get started."

"That is…very kind of you." Vayriel cocked her head inquisitively. "And what would you ask of me in return?"

"I would have you tell me more about the Sleeper."

A shadow fell over the Highblood's features at the mention of her people's nemesis. "That is a dark thing of which I do not enjoy speaking. But if those are your terms, I accept. With one condition: you must tell me why you seek this knowledge."

Zinvar bowed his head to avoid her penetrating gaze. "I have dreamed of this Sleeper. Well, not of him, precisely. I was warned about him." He went on to describe his surreal encounter with the mysterious woman near Lake Stelwin, omitting her warning about Kharnek. When he finished, Vayriel looked pensive, and Kilahym remained uncharacteristically silent.

"Have you had other dreams like this before?" Vayriel asked after a few moments of reflection.

"Yes, but only recently. And I keep having the same one over and over again, about—"

"You're an Occulum!" Kilahym blurted.

His proclamation puzzled Zinvar. "I'm a what?"

"An Occulum! You can dream the past, the present, and mayhap the future!"

Zinvar turned to Vayriel. "Do you have any idea what he's talking about?"

"I do. They are rare among my people but not unheard of. We call them the Eyes of the Daughter, for they are blessed with her sight. I believe that is what caused my vision when I drew on your life force as we escaped the storm wall creature-son." Vayriel hesitated before continuing. "There is a way to determine the truth of this if you are willing."

"At this point, I'll try anything."

She nodded and rummaged in one of the pouches that contained her assortment of herbs. "Go to Evocus when you can," she instructed while she searched. "Ask the Keepers there to take you to the Chamber of the Occulum and attempt to enter it. If you are successful then you will know who you truly are. So it has come to pass for those Highbloods who have journeyed here."

"You mean, they all went to this Chamber?" Zinvar queried.

Vayriel shrugged and at last found the object she sought. She withdrew it in her closed hand. "All the ones I know. It is said that the Eyes of the Daughter are always drawn to this place. There is something here that removes the veil of confusion from their minds." The Highblood extended her hand toward Zinvar. "Take this with you. When the time comes for you to enter the Chamber, consume it."

Zinvar approached Vayriel's proffered hand, which uncurled as he reached out. On her palm rested a small vial full of a familiar dark-blue liquid.

"Mo'fa says that it helps him achieve greater clarity in his visions. I believe it is called pressentia," Vayriel elaborated.

"I...am familiar with it. Though I did not know its name."

"Really? You know so much about so many things!" Kilahym chattered.

"The power of reading." Zinvar closed his fist around the vial. "And of people who care about you. Now, shall we begin our first lesson, my friends?"

"Yes!" the bard cheered, hauling Vayriel to her feet. He started to pull her down the passageway toward the same mural he and Zinvar had looked at earlier. "Did you hear that, Vayriel? He called us 'friend'! Do you think he meant it?"

"I think such terms are not lightly used, Kilahym," the Highblood answered with a lopsided grin, letting the bard drag her away. Orgar bounded after the twosome.

Neither of them saw Zinvar's thoughtful expression as he stared at the vial in his hand.

Later, once Zinvar had excused himself from Vayriel and Kilahym's company, he set out for the Chamber of the Occulum. He thought about inviting Kharnek to join him, but the warrior's aversion to anything related to magic stopped him from doing so. The gift of the pressentia stuck out as a rare exception to that, but Zinvar doubted that Kharnek grasped its connection to his latent abilities.

He arrived at Evocus. Sondrinel bustled about the main floor, hurrying to complete the endeavors of another moonrise. The multilayered tower housed the collected knowledge of Etherea's sunlit realm. Monuments to prominent Keepers punctuated the vast plaza of the ground level. Secluded alcoves for quiet contemplation lined the edges of the plaza, adjacent to crystal gardens tended by Keepers-in-training. *Scriveners*, Idrilia called them.

This was the true heart of Axiom, and the number of Sentinels posted as guards at every entrance testified to it. Zinvar noted the ornate azure armor they sported, with cerulean-crested helmets and flowing cloaks. As he crossed the polished tile floor composed of squares of white marble veined with gold, many curious glances were thrown his way. No one accosted him, though, until he reached the central shaft that enabled access to the upper levels of the tower.

"Halt." Two Sentinels flanked the entrance to the access shaft. They wielded crystal staves, crossed to bar Zinvar's path. "Entrance to the upper levels is restricted. State your business."

"I seek the Chamber of the Occulum, Guardians of the Light." Zinvar echoed the greeting he had heard Kalis and Idrilia use with other Sentinels.

"You may enter, Seeker, but please leave your staff with us. No weapons are permitted within."

Zinvar handed his staff to the Sondrinel who had addressed him.

"Thank you. You will find the Chamber on the sixth level. May Kadaan light your way."

The guards retracted their staves. Zinvar nodded politely and stepped into the shaft. On the opposite wall he saw eight yellow crystals arranged in a horizontal row. The one furthest to the left glowed warmly, while the other seven remained a dull amber. Zinvar approached the crystals and touched the sixth one, which illuminated while the first crystal winked out. The floor beneath him, in actuality a round platform, slid smoothly upward. Unlike the lift in the Assemblage, this one made no noise to indicate its rising.

The platform reached the sixth level and slowed to a stop. Zinvar exited the shaft and blinked while his eyes adjusted to the sudden darkness. This tier of Evocus did not enjoy the light of the Star like the lower levels. Crystals set into the floor and sconces on the walls lit the way through shelves of books that loomed in the dimness. As he began to question whether he had made a wise decision in coming alone, a tall Sondrinel woman in a light tan tunic appeared in his path. She wore the circlet set with a single white stone indicative of a trained Keeper.

"Greetings, priest of Komor. How may the Keepers serve you?"

"I seek the Chamber of the Occulum, Keeper of the Light."

"How interesting. Never before has one from Komor made such a request of us." The Keeper appraised Zinvar in silence. He found himself a bit unnerved by her scrutiny. "You must be one of the Truthseekers. Word had reached us that you arrived. I am surprised that you have time for pursuits outside of that undertaking."

"I am attempting to use my time wisely." Zinvar stressed the last word.

"Please understand I do not wish to discourage you. But many have come here, unencumbered by the burden of the Trials and left in failure. I would not see you shadowed by that as you continue your journey."

"I know that this is unprecedented. But I have reason to believe that the Chamber will show me…something I need to know. Something that may help me along the way," he persisted.

The Keeper considered this, and at last relented. "Very well. Please follow me."

She led the way to the other side of the access shaft, through the rows of bookshelves and busts of prominent figures, until they reached a hallway that curved out of sight. The Keeper motioned Zinvar to carry on.

"This passage will lead you to the Chamber. Should you require any further assistance, please do not hesitate to ask." She faded into the gloom.

Zinvar swallowed and regarded the hallway nervously. Faint whispers seemed to emanate from the empty passage, lingering at the edge of audibility.

He missed the familiar heft of his staff. Gathering his resolve, he took a deep breath and plunged into the corridor.

At the end of the hallway stood a door capped by a pointed arch. An elaborate eight-sided lock mechanism barred Zinvar's path, as did a curtain of magical energy that rippled with faint blue light over the door's surface. The priest pondered the barrier with a measure of frustration, until he thought of the vial Vayriel had bestowed upon him. Zinvar took it from his robes, the liquid within sparkling with an unusual luster.

His ruminations once again migrated toward Kharnek. Had the warrior known what he was giving Zinvar? Or was it an honest mistake? He resolved to ask Kharnek once he had completed this ordeal. Without further delay, he uncorked the vial and quaffed its contents.

A surge of tingling coruscated through the priest's limbs, as if a fire burned within him. The whispering he had detected before intensified, and he caught fragments of words.

Zinvar.

The sound of his name galvanized him into action. Without thinking, he thrust his hand forward at the wall of protective magic. His arm speared through, and he grasped the lock mechanism. The magical barrier retracted from the edges of the door, and the lock split into pieces beneath Zinvar's touch. The fragments began an orchestrated dance, clicking and spinning away to either side of the door, which parted at its center. Its dual segments swung inward to reveal a circular room.

A statue of Kadaan in the middle gazed directly at Zinvar. Like her other representations throughout Axiom, this one also lacked facial features, save eyes. But when the priest entered the room, what captured his attention was the imagery that burst into motion on the blank walls. Zinvar staggered in shock as he spun to take in the entirety of the Chamber, certain that his eyes deceived him.

On the stone, a familiar scene blossomed in cycloramic fashion: a besieged fortress between twin mountain peaks, the violet sky above the citadel torn by a black void. Zinvar's mind reeled. The force of recognition echoed within him until the reverberation threatened to drive him to his knees. Then he felt what he could only liken to the *snick* of a key inserting into a lock and opening it, and a flood of images invaded his mind. The torrent of dreams—memories, he realized—belonged to all the Occulum who came before him.

He saw flashes of cities engulfed in shadow, strange silver needles that swam between the stars, and creatures never seen on Etherea. Each recollection overwhelmed Zinvar with vivid detail but passed so quickly he knew he would not recall it. At last the flow ebbed until it settled on a memory that the priest had witnessed before in a mural. Now, he took part in it.

He knelt on the rocky surface of Sondrine before Kadaan, while a multitude of her followers observed. The touch of her hand on his shoulder left a lingering warmth.

"I gift you my sight that you may watch for the time of my return. You are the first, but many will follow." Kadaan's voice rang out to address the crowd. "Be ever vigilant, for the darkness that engulfs all still imperils our world."

Brilliant light followed her proclamation, a luminous burst that washed out even the sun. Zinvar looked up through the eyes of the first Occulum to gaze upon Kadaan one last time as she rose. He gasped, and his shock shattered the link to the past.

Zinvar tumbled to the floor of the Chamber. His body shook as he looked up at the statue of Kadaan above him. He could now easily add the face that Sondrine's artisans refrained from sculpting. The auburn hair, the gentle smile, and the gray eyes that regarded him with intensity and compassion were unmistakably those of the woman from his visions.

The priest rose shakily and bolted from the Chamber.

Run.

Zinvar stumbled out of the access shaft into the main plaza of Evocus. He gritted his teeth against the bursts of light and color that surged through his mind. The residual effects of the pressentia lingered, interfering with his perceptions.

"Are you alright?" one of the Sentinels guarding the shaft asked in concern.

"Yes, I'm fine, thank you," the priest mumbled. The Sentinel's ceremonial armor twisted around the edges into surreal patterns. Zinvar blinked, then resumed his flight toward the Hall of Remembrance.

The sound of his feet slapping against the marble floor echoed throughout the passage that bridged the Hall and Evocus. Before him, the floor appeared to shift so that it curved upward into infinity. Zinvar closed his eyes and plunged headlong down the corridor until he collided with what felt like a stone wall.

"Sorry, I'm sorry, oh—"

Zinvar looked up at Kharnek, whose brows arched. Realizing belatedly that he clung to the warrior to keep from falling, he released his grip and stepped back.

"You do not look well, priest."

"Master of the understatement," Zinvar groaned. A headache pounded against his temples, demanding to be released from the confines of his skull. He started to slump forward. Kharnek caught him before he fell.

"Zinvar? What is wrong?" .

Without forethought, Zinvar threw his arms around Kharnek, who stiffened at first, then slowly wrapped the priest in a gentle embrace.

"What's happening to me?" Zinvar pleaded. "I keep seeing things, things that have already happened."

"So it is true," Kharnek murmured. "You are an Occulum."

"Wait." Zinvar pulled back and glared at the warrior. "You *knew*?"

The other man averted his eyes. "The healer in Waverling told me."

"And when were you going to tell me?" Zinvar demanded.

Kharnek's cheeks reddened. "I had hoped it was not real. And I was afraid that you would be in trouble with the Priesthood if they found out."

"Because pretending problems don't exist always turns out well," Zinvar retorted.

"Would you have believed me if I had told you?"

"I...I don't know," he conceded, flexing his hands. "But you didn't give me the chance to. And that's what makes me sad. I thought—" Zinvar broke off, uncertain whether to continue.

"You thought what?"

"That we were closer than that."

"Ah." Kharnek lips flattened. The emptiness of the hall rushed into his silence and fed the anxiety that welled up in Zinvar. He started to turn away, but Kharnek's hand on his shoulder stopped him.

"Zinvar, please wait. I am sorry. I should have told you. You deserve to know the truth about yourself. I was just afraid—" Kharnek faltered. He swallowed, and then continued. "I was afraid that the Priesthood would take you away, and I would never see you again."

Releasing its grip on Zinvar's shoulder, Kharnek's hand shifted to his cheek. The callouses there tugged at Zinvar's skin, but he found the sensation oddly comforting. The fire kindled in him by anger drained away. "I never imagined that you would feel that way."

"There is much you do not know about how I feel, priest," Kharnek quietly replied. "I have not forgotten what you told me in Waverling. I give you my answer now." His intense gaze locked on Zinvar, who suddenly became aware of how close together they stood. A subtle incense-like scent lingered on Kharnek's leathers and aroused the priest's senses, as did the whisper of air passing through the passageway's open walls. "You are a better man than I will ever be, Zinvar. And while I do not deserve your interest—especially after this error in judgment—if you want me, I am yours."

The admission threatened to overwhelm Zinvar's reeling mind. His confusion must have translated into his expression, because Kharnek's face dropped.

"I am sorry; this was not the right time for this conversation."

A small voice in the back of Zinvar's head warned him that that was true, but he refused to let this moment pass. Gripping Kharnek by the waist, he drew their bodies together. "Be that as it may, I could use a pleasant distraction right about now."

Kharnek smiled down at him. "Does this mean I am forgiven?"

Zinvar feigned consideration, then laid his head against the warrior's chest. "Yes, apology accepted. Just...please don't keep things from me. If you're serious about giving 'us' a try, then we have to be honest with each other."

"I understand."

Kharnek's finger tipped Zinvar's chin upward until their eyes met. "Thank you, Zinvar." Then he kissed him, tentatively at first, until desire took hold and it became something more insistent. Zinvar tightened his grip on Kharnek's hips and enjoyed the answering rumble from within the warrior's chest. The length of Kharnek's sword had become trapped between them and the scabbard pressed against Zinvar's thigh, the feeling reminding him of—

"Oh, wyrmscales," Zinvar cursed, breaking the kiss.

"What is it?" Kharnek's dark-brown eyes blazed with concern.

"I left my staff with the Sentinels at Evocus. I should probably go get it."

"I will go with you." Kharnek grasped Zinvar's shoulder protectively. The priest shivered beneath his touch—the lingering effects of the pressentia amplified the heat of contact into fire.

"I would appreciate your company. I'm still a little rattled by what happened in the Chamber."

"Then I will stay with you as long as you need," Kharnek solemnly vowed. The warrior and the priest started down the passageway toward Evocus, their hands intertwined.

CHAPTER 37

Kilahym cleared his throat twice, adjusted the tautness of the dulcimer's strings, and proceeded to strum. He tapped his foot lightly and watched his left hand move over the strings. Twelve strums of arpeggiated chords by his count, and with a deep breath he began to sing, his tenor tones reverberating in the hallway.

"Rise, my dear lady
Rise, my dear friend.
The world has awakened
And you—still lie within."

The door opened wide enough for Vayriel to peek out. Her peach hair, parted on the side, flowed over her shoulders as she caught Kilahym's eye, then glanced up and down the hall. Her shoulders and arms were bare, save the silver ornament she wore on her upper arm..

"What are you doing?" she whispered. Kilahym continued to play his tune, freshly composed this Axiom's dawn when he could no longer sleep. The crystal sconces of the hallway pulsed in time with the music. Plucking additional chords, he continued into the next stanza:

"Why do you slumber
Why do you tarry
The world is awaiting
This stone sanctuary."

Vayriel glanced at her feet where Orgar now lay, head on his paws and sleepy cyan eyes gazing up at Kilahym from the crack in the door. The jeroti took a deep breath and huffed.

"Hush," she frowned, "the others still sleep."

"Ah, but you are awake, and that is what matters." Kilahym palmed the fretboard of his dulcimer, halting the vibrations and ending his tune.

"I was not before you became the singing mimic-wing," Vayriel grumbled.

"Oh, I apologize. I—I incorrectly assumed from our previous journeying that you were an early riser." The wall sconces ceased their flickering, several extinguishing completely.

"I might normally be. However, I did not sleep well. My head has pained me of late."

"Anything I can do?" Kilahym took a step forward, then immediately stepped back again. His doubt was put aside as she opened the door completely, her body still hidden behind it, and motioned for him to enter.

"Thank you, but no. I have a few herbs to try that Mo'mo sent with me."

She closed the door behind him. A crystal lamp near the bed filled the room with a faint illumination. Its presence brought images of the hours spent in the Bard Academy's archives, a single candle in hand as he perused the old stories and detailed descriptions of masques and the occasional accompanying drawing. He leaned his roseate dulcimer against the wall by the door and edged in further.

Vayriel was not using the bed—evident from the sheets bundled at its foot. Swiveling to face her, Kilahym became very aware that she was wrapped only in one of the sheets from chest to thighs, its teal color accenting her lavender eyes and skin like tall grass. Her feet were bare and as she walked to her pack the muscles in her calves were defined. As she knelt, Kilahym quickly focused on the opposite wall, his face heating.

"Erm, this is an, uh, interesting painting," he spluttered, looking at the hanging depiction of a funnel storm over a desert landscape, painted with delicate strokes.

"Is it?" Vayriel moved next to Kilahym. He kept his eyes on the painting. "A wind-swirl, like the one in Heathström," she commented. "Is this made by a different artist than the ones Zinvar showed us yesterday? The markings look different."

"Indeed, it is." Kilahym recognized the artist's name from many of the images that accompanied mythological texts at the Academy. "Did you say you've seen something like this in our realm?"

Vayriel nodded. "Yes. In the great plain beyond Skyveil that stretches north to the Jade Sea. Though the Everwind is unlike the scattered wind-swirls we saw on Sondrine's salt flats."

The bard nearly laughed. "I thought a whirlwind—wind-swirl, I like your Highblood term for the vortices—a whirlwind that large was nothing but a tall tale, pun intended. I stand corrected once again. The grand interplay of myth and magic is woven with threads of truth."

He stole a glance her way, admiring her elegant profile; the way her hair brushed her cheek in a nearly imperceptible wave before cascading over her muscular shoulder to rest on the thin fabric at her breast.

"But I babble. Ahem, well…" Kilahym approached the door. "If your headache is not too beauti—uh, painful, I'd be most honored if you would accompany me on a tour of Axiom."

"Should we not ready ourselves for leaving?"

"Bah, no one else is awake. We'll be back before they've had breakfast. Speaking of which, I've heard of a place we could try, the *Portly Pectully*."

Vayriel nodded. "The blood lily leaves have eased my pain. I would be happy to join you."

"Blood lily. Good choice. You would know best, of course." He laughed, scratching the back of his head.

"May Orgar come as well?"

Kilahym's gaze moved to where the jeroti sat, his tails twitching, his bright eyes locked on the bard. He forgot the Highblood's companion was in the room.

"Of course. Orgar is always welcome." He winked at the jeroti, who only blinked in return.

"What should I bring?"

"Just your body. That is, your person, yourself." By the burning of his cheeks, he imagined he turned a deep scarlet and retreated backward.

Vayriel tilted her head. He felt her lavender gaze assess him.

"Are you feeling well, Kilahym?"

"What? Yes, of course. Why do you ask?" The bard's back bumped against the door, his hand fumbling to locate the knob.

"Your face has been flushed since you entered. You might be developing an ailment. May I touch your forehead?" She held her palm out at head height and approached.

"Oh, no, no. Thank you. I'm well, quite well." Kilahym's hand found the knob and he twisted it, pulling the door so that it bumped the back of his shoe. "I'll meet you at the entrance then, shall I?" He bumbled through the small gap backward into the hallway, slowly closing the door on his forced grin. Vayriel's puzzled look was the last thing he saw.

"Grey Lady preserve me," he sighed, scratching the short hair around his mouth as he hastened down the Hall of Remembrance. "You are an idiot, Hymn. A blubbering imbecile. 'Bring your body, Vayriel.' Now you sound like a Komorese."

Not at all how he had planned the scene. He could almost hear Ansgar's laughter. The scoundrel would ruffle Kilahym's hair and gladly repeat the incident to everyone nearby who would listen. A troubadour Kilahym was not. He should have paid more attention to Ansgar's accounts of wooing.

Kilahym was still contemplating what had possessed him to compose such a dreadful serenade when he heard feet approaching. It was her and Orgar. Kilahym's heart leapt. She wore her usual Highblood attire, though her coat was missing and her spear was replaced with an instrument.

Kilahym smacked his forehead.

"I believe this is yours." Vayriel raised her eyebrows and handed him the instrument.

"Indeed. Who is the bard who leaves his instrument behind? One who is not worthy of such a title forsooth." Kilahym bowed low. "I pray, Highblood of the mountains, with a promise to the Grey Lady, that I shan't do it again. And prithee keep this most horrid secret of mine safe."

Vayriel laughed. The sound was like the tinkling of crystal chimes.

"If this is a terrible mistake, then you must have a most blameless existence. Mistakes help us learn. Do not be ashamed."

"That is true. Not the blameless part. I most certainly have my share of blunders and regrets." The bard raised a hand in remonstrance. "Don't move. I'll be quick."

Cradling his cherished dulcimer, Kilahym jogged to his room and deposited the instrument that had seen him through most of his career into his pack, slinging it over his shoulder. When he returned, Vayriel stood in the same location, and the exact posture, he had left her in.

"I didn't mean it literally. Come on, statue"— he poked her shoulder— "we have much to explore."

As they exited toward the heart of the city, the magical orrery above grew in brightness, signaling the start of the Lady's walk. Kilahym detected the scent of wet moss, like the forest near Beechmarsh, which he had first noticed upon stepping into Axiom the day prior. Recollections of his travels bubbled to the surface like the breath of a lake fish.

Vayriel's voice cut into his musings. "Do you think it is difficult for Idrilia and Kalis to be here? There is much unresolved between them."

Kilahym blinked several times. "Undoubtedly I have witnessed some discord, but I attributed it to the vagaries of our journey taking their toll. To what do you refer, your Highbloodedness?"

"Their impending life-union."

Kilahym halted. His jaw dropped open as he sidestepped around an ornate column that lined the side of the street.

"Surely you don't mean marriage—to each other? That look tells me you do. What—when—I don't even know where to start. How did you learn of this?"

"I heard it in Ettrascus when you were so fascinated by the woman with blood-hued nails and her music." Orgar passed between them, bumping the bard's leg. Vayriel followed, continuing toward the less grandiose buildings and some of the stairways to upper levels. "Are you promised to someone as well?"

Kilahym narrowly avoided a cart being pushed by a baker. "By the Lady's gray beard! A bard, promised? Few would choose such a wanderer's life. Not that I wouldn't be open to it, and bards really do make wonderful companions…but what about you?"

Vayriel shook her head.

"Someone in your coil you are interested in?" Kilahym leaned closer.

"Though my Mo'mo wishes it were different, no. I find I prefer Orgar's companionship on the mountain trails." She looked at him from the side of her eye. "And your friendship has been appreciated in these Trials."

Relief flooded through him, like the weight of a jeroti sitting on his chest had dissipated. He skipped a few steps.

"Though it might be because you remind me of something."

"Oh?"

"The way you trim your hair around your mouth is like a pawilo?"

"That's…is that really what you think I look like?" Kilahym caught Vayriel's grin before she turned her face away and laughed. "Alright, vexing Vayriel. You're in for it now. Be prepared. But after some breakfast. My stomach is beginning to feel like it is eating itself."

"That is the *last* time I trust Ansgar." Kilahym brushed the last bit of cream filling from his forehead as they stepped back onto the street. Vayriel scooped a small bit of icing from her cheek with her index finger and tasted it.

"I could not tell if they were enjoying themselves or if all of them were angry."

"'Inebriated' is a better description. I'm not sure if any of them had any idea what they were feeling. And it's barely after moonrise! I couldn't make out a single useful tale, what with all their slurring and belching. Really, I am sorry about that. I'd hoped it would have been more enjoyable."

"It was certainly entertaining." Vayriel reached over and brushed a gobbet of sticky pastry from his shoulder. "Where will we go next? I know that you sought inspiration for your stories."

"True, but I am not so selfish as to dominate the course of events. I want you to enjoy this adventure as much as I! First, I thought we could explore our musicality with unique Sondrinel instruments."

"I have only played instruments my coil makes. I would be interested to see these others."

A large smile stretched Kilahym's lips, and he clapped his hands together. "Then I know just the thing. Let us step forward before time runs away from us."

As he kept his eye out for where he really wanted to take her, he vowed to return once the Trials were over to give the city the time it deserved, taking in all the paintings, statues, and pottery. And an unstated hope that Vayriel and Orgar would come as well. The Highblood proved the best of companions, keeping him in line when he stepped too far while indulging his whims.

They ventured further around the city's perimeter, until they found themselves in the quiet avenues of a residential area on a wide promenade that overlooked the underground lake.

"Ooh, look at this." Kilahym pointed at a large crystal garden beyond some of the cantilevered homes. "I think I see crystal sculptures in there. Want to explore?"

Kilahym grinned at her back as she strolled onto a winding path; hopefully it felt a little like home to her.

Large formations like boulders and jagged clusters of varying heights lined the walkway. Benches dotted the path and sat before sculpted likenesses of prominent Sondrinel. Kilahym removed the dulcimer from his back and gestured for Vayriel to sit on the nearest bench.

"I should have asked much sooner. Would you like to learn how to play?"

"I would," she leaned forward. "But did you not wish to view instruments of Axiom?"

"In those I am not proficient. I would rather share the instrument which has resonated with my soul with you."

Vayriel nodded, lowering her eyes. Kilahym took the invitation and gently placed the dulcimer on her lap. Orgar lay on the stone beside her as Kilahym kneeled in front.

"The pair of strings here," he pointed to the ones closest to her body, "are the melody strings. By pressing into a fret, you change the pitch. Changing the pitch in a rhythm and strumming the strings like so"— he demonstrated— "you create a song. You try a note. Any note, it's very hard to make this instrument sound bad."

Vayriel chose the second fret from the top and gently pressed the double string. She ran her other hand's thumb across the base of the strings as Kilahym had done. A soft chord floated out of the wood.

"Now these," he pointed to a pair at the edge closest to him, "are drone strings. Typically, I tune one an octave lower. And when you strum across all the strings, you keep the drone strings the same note regardless. May I?"

At her nod he placed his hands over hers. A tremor cascaded up his arms and settled like a vandling flipping in his stomach. With one hand he moved hers up and down the melody strings slowly, pressing gently into the fret while he directed the other to strum with each new placement.

"Each new melody note interacts with the consistent drone," he explained as they strummed another chord. "Some notes harmonize beautifully, while others create tension."

Kilahym released Vayriel's hands, his heart beating faster. He watched Vayriel continue strumming, the unchanging bass note was like a wall the music leaned against. "The tension rises and falls with the notes of the melody."

Vayriel looked up and her last chord sang out. She met his gaze. "And the middle pair of strings?"

Kilahym stared into her eyes, the depths a pool of mystery. "Hmm? Oh, they can be used as more drone by selecting a complementary pitch, or more melody strings. You could use all of the strings as melody if you wanted. You have a lot of choices, and I do like to change it and try new styles."

Vayriel continued experimenting with the melody and drone combinations. Though she played no song the bard had ever heard, the music filled his soul from his head to his toes with invisible energy. He wanted to grasp Vayriel's hands and twirl her in a dance, throwing their heads back in giddy laughter.

She laid her hand on the strings, ceasing their vibrations, and raised her chin, a wide smile lifting her cheeks. Kilahym swallowed

"Thank you for sharing this with me," she said, as Orgar's rough tongue licked his cheek.

Kilahym wiped his cheek on his shoulder and patted Orgar's head then rose. He clasped the neck of his instrument as Vayriel cradled it out to him. "Thank you for trying. I think happiness can come from sharing what you love with the people who matter."

They stared at each other for several heartbeats. Kilahym cleared his throat and gestured to the crystal garden. "Shall we?"

The crystals shimmered in a variety of pastel hues. Kilahym likened it to walking within the bands of a rainbow, a thought he verbalized in the form of an impromptu poem.

Beneath the arc'ed colors formed
By skillful artist's hand
A bard and beauty sallied forth
To find the rainbow's end

"A rainbow is a color-arch," he clarified for Vayriel's benefit.

"I have seen them above the mountains. They are gates to the spirit-world for those whose time has come to return to the Mother-of-All's embrace."

The Highblood paused to kneel beside a low cluster of crystals, inspecting the area where they connected with the rock.

"Plants—I can hardly stop talking about them! Well, about anything, or so I've been told. But crystals! For those I will require the keen vision of thine Highblood eyes to differentiate their angular arrays."

"They still grow," she mused, a hint of surprise in her voice, "though they are hindered."

"What do you mean?"

"Do you see this?" She pointed to one of the vertical collections and the thin pole that stood on either side. "This type of formation would normally spread out along the ground. Instead, they are forcing it upward."

"Is that bad for the crystal?"

Vayriel stood, brushing her hair behind her shoulder. "It is best to let the crystal grow as it naturally would rather than have it be something it is not."

"My parents should have tended to crystals before having me," Kilahym grumbled, then waved Vayriel's questioning look away.

"Remember when we first met, and I promised to explain more about why the Highbloods set their village in a coil?"

He did remember. He opened his eyes in what he hoped was an eager expression as he nodded.

"The coil represents adaptability. It is the slow reveal of hidden things, the path of growth and learning all must take. We come back to the same point but with new knowledge having broadened the spiral." She made a swirl with her left index finger that slowly widened, the same way she had at the Moon's Quiver.

"The coil is the 'true path'?"

"Yes. The journey of life."

"And the 'true light'?"

"Understanding. Of yourself, the Mother-of-All, and her creation. You have found your path, and in doing so you are discovering the light. You seek to learn and share with others rather than focus on negativity. You walk the coil, and, with each pass, you are further from your starting point, but you have grown as the flowers and the trees do, with strength and wisdom."

Kilahym's eyes filled with moisture. How could she see all that? And through her comments, he saw himself for the first time, a mirror that showed him what he had always known to be true if he did not let the reflection become clouded by the doubt and fear instilled by his family. Vayriel, in a few short sentences, had broken those clouds apart.

Kilahym caught Vayriel's hand as it returned to her side.

"You are amazing, you know that?"

Clasping his fingers around hers, he directed her to the nearest statue. The statue's features reminded him of Idrilia's. Dropping Vayriel's hand, he scratched the stubble around his mouth.

"What does it say?" Vayriel pointed to the base, where a name was displayed on a plaque.

Feeling a wet scraping on his fingers, Kilahym pulled his hand up to his chest. "Orgar? My fingers are not food."

He made a face at the jeroti, who remained seated on his haunches with his head tilted, as if trying to understand the bard's words.

"Hmm, *In Remembrance of High Keeper Elsuota*," Kilahym read, chastising himself for forgetting Vayriel's admission of illiteracy. He vowed to do better. His thoughts strayed to debating which parchment he would use to compose her a poem once she could read. He was pondering the delivery method—*is "by bird" too forward?*—and almost missed the Highblood's next statement.

"She is beautiful." Vayriel's face tilted up toward the statue, the gentle curve of her jawline catching some of the dancing light from the crystal.

"Yes. Exquisite craftsmanship. Just like you."

Vayriel turned to face Kilahym.

"Not that you were crafted," the bard quickly corrected, waving his hands. His cheeks grew warm. "What I mean is, like her, you are beautiful. More beautiful, actually." He cringed at his words, but forged ahead. "You are music and magic and a cool breeze on a warm day. You're an old book and a new story at the same time."

"Kilahym—"

The bard carried on, lest he lose his nerve. "You make me nervous and giddy—I say silly things around you. You turn me into a bard who can't find the right words," he laughed. "You're like a new book I want to keep reading."

Feeling his stomach flip and flutter, Kilahym took a deep breath and swallowed. He reached out slowly with the goal of brushing Vayriel's cheek—

The sound of a squabble reached his ears and he faltered, eyes darting toward it. A tall block of crystals obscured the source of the sound from Kilahym's view. He focused on Vayriel, but his rhythm was broken. Orgar next to her panted, his mouth lolling open, revealing his pink tongue.

"I don't know if I'm making any sense. I don't even know what this is I'm feeling. But I want to keep feeling it. By the Lady, that sounds quite strange. But perhaps you understand." Feeling the awkwardness coming back, he looked away.

"Kilahym—"

He felt his stomach flip again, hoping for some sort of verbal confirmation that he was not insane, that she felt they had a connection as well. That he affected her the same way she did him. He searched her lavender eyes as she continued.

"—you honor me with your words, but I need—"

Shouting broke out from somewhere nearby. Vayriel and Kilahym jumped, twisting to look for the source of the commotion. Orgar whined and sniffed the air.

"That doesn't sound good," Kilahym observed. "We should go see what's happening. A bard and jeroti are ready to be of assistance, right, Orgar?" The jeroti pawed at one of his boots, and Kilahym looked back to Vayriel. "Does he usually do this?"

"Only to those he likes." A small smile graced her lips, then the Highblood moved in the direction of the noise.

"Oh, well, that is good. I suppose." Then he whispered, bending slightly in

Orgar's direction, "Quit that." But Orgar's head tilted up, and Kilahym barely pulled back in time to avoid the lapping tongue. "You're acting more peculiar than I feel." He reached out to pet the jeroti between his ears and was rewarded with the sand-like roughness again. "Alright. That's it. I'm not talking to you again until you pull yourself together."

From a short distance ahead a whistle sounded, and Orgar bounded after his life-friend, a bemused Kilahym following behind.

The scene Kilahym and Vayriel discovered at the other end of the crystal garden took him aback. Zinvar and Kharnek faced Kalis and Idrilia, a crystal formation with chamfered edges between them. Idrilia's face was red and Kharnek's hand lay on the pommel of his sword, which, for the moment, remained sheathed. Kilahym focused on the black scabbard, then glanced up at the warrior's face. It betrayed no emotion, but Kharnek's eyes were narrowed and did not leave the Sondrinel. The fur on Orgar's spine stood up, and the jeroti whined.

"Pardon the interruption," Kilahym began, "but what is going on?"

"Kalis and I caught these two sneaking around, up to no good, no doubt," Idrilia said harshly. She thrust an accusing finger out at the Komorese. "They should never have been allowed into the city."

Zinvar pointed his staff at his accuser. "As I told you, we were just exploring the city, as we were *invited* to do, I might add."

"Sure. And I'm Kadaan herself," Idrilia spat.

Kilahym looked at Vayriel, uncertain what to do. She watched the confrontation but did not move to intervene, so he elected to emulate her. Perhaps this moment was necessary to diffuse the tension that had built throughout the Trials.

"Your hostility is unfounded," Kharnek replied, "but regardless, your opinion does not matter. You are a wounded varg crying out for attention, desperate to claim something because you know that nothing, not even your future, belongs to you."

Ouch, Kilahym winced–the sentiment was one he'd oft received growing up—and out of the corner of his eye saw Vayriel do the same. They exchanged surprised looks as, simultaneously, they realized that they were sharing each other's emotions. Kilahym could sense Vayriel's concern, tempered by steady resolve, but there was no time to delve into their mutual revelation as the conflict between the other Seekers escalated.

Idrilia stalked around the crystal formation toward the warrior and priest. "You know nothing about me. You may have everyone else fooled, but I see through your deceit. I know that sea monster and the storm wall were Komor's doing. I know that there's something wrong about those cubes. And you're probably spending your time here looking for weaknesses in Axiom's defenses to exploit!"

"'Dril," Kalis cautioned.

She whirled on him, fury in her eyes. "Whose side are you on, anyway?"

"The losing one," Kharnek goaded, drawing Idrilia's focus back to him.

"Losing? I don't think so, *arslen*."

A flicker of imperceptible motion brought a crystal into Idrilia's right palm, which erupted into flame. Kharnek drew his sword in a blur. Idrilia's face twisted in fury when she saw the obsidian blade, and she unleashed the fireball on Kharnek.

"No!"

Kilahym gasped as Zinvar threw himself between the warrior and Idrilia. The magical blast caught him in the chest and sent him flying backward. He crashed to the ground in a heap.

Kharnek rushed to Zinvar's side to stand over him in a protective stance, sword extended toward Idrilia. "You will die for this, 'burnspawn," he snarled.

Idrilia hurled another fireball, which the warrior intercepted with his sword. The magic winked out when it struck the blade.

"Idrilia! Stop!" Kalis positioned himself between her and the Komorese.

"Get out of my way!" Idrilia attempted to shove past Kalis.

He stood firm and blocked her path. "What have you done, 'Dril? The Council will never let you become a Sentinel now!"

This statement seemed to penetrate the haze of rage surrounding the young woman, and she backed away with a dazed expression. Kilahym felt Vayriel's fingers slip into his and grip them tightly, her horror translated to him through their bond.

"I—I was only trying to protect Axiom," Idrilia stuttered. She whirled and ran out of the crystal garden, Kalis in pursuit.

Kilahym watched Kalis disappear around a large sculpture. Idrilia definitely broke the Trials' rule of respecting participants, one the Spectres made sure Kilahym understood given his realm's neutrality. But more importantly, Idrilia had violated the Waverling Accords by attacking an unarmed person.

Kharnek sheathed his sword and knelt next to Zinvar. "Zinvar, can you hear me?"

Turning back, Kilahym saw the warrior gingerly probing Zinvar's body. The priest groaned when Kharnek's fingers neared his rib cage. Kilahym and Vayriel rushed to the fallen Seeker.

"Can we help?"

Kharnek moved faster than Kilahym's eyes could follow to brandish his sword. A stunned Kilahym's eyes crossed as he stared at the blade so close to his face. His hands went up in surrender.

"Stand down, son of Komor," Vayriel commanded. "We mean you no harm."

Kharnek slowly lowered his sword.

"How badly is he wounded?" Vayriel approached Zinvar but stopped when Kharnek growled in warning. Orgar crouched, ready to spring at the warrior. "Please," Vayriel implored calmly, "allow me to help your friend."

"No one touches Zinvar but me," Kharnek ground out.

Zinvar moaned, and in a flash the warrior returned to him. Concern and anger etched his features.

"He needs a life-weaver," Vayriel persisted. "I do not have much experience with this type of wound. Allow us to send for one."

Kharnek finally nodded in response.

"Make haste, Kilahym. Seek out a life-weaver," the Highblood instructed him.

"I hate to be problematic, but I really don't know where to look—" Kilahym began.

"Go!" Kharnek roared.

Putting his hands up again, holding his breath, Kilahym pivoted and scurried away, Orgar's mournful howl following him across the streets of Axiom.

CHAPTER 38

A hush fell over Concilius as Kharnek strode onto the bridge between the entrance and the High Keeper's platform. Directly across from him, a stained-glass image of Kadaan's Rising kept watch over the room. Clad in the crimson leathers of the City Guard, his black cloak flowing behind him, the warrior knew he cut an impressive figure and held his posture military straight.

Idrilia stood beside the High Keeper, a sour expression on her face. Kharnek halted at the end of the bridge where it met the platform.

"The Council of Sondrine welcomes you, Kharnek, warrior of Komor," the High Keeper greeted him. He nodded curtly in response. "We have called this secundarium—a special session of the Council—to hear your testimony regarding the events that took place in upper Axiom earlier today, involving yourself, the priest Zinvar, and Idrilia of Sondrine."

"There is little to tell. The priest and I were exploring a crystal garden, which was certainly within our rights to do as guests in the city. We were approached in a hostile fashion by Idrilia of Sondrine. She accused us of crimes against Axiom and proceeded to attack us with fire. My companion, Zinvar, was injured in the attack and is still under the care of your healers."

From one of the arched openings that housed the seventeen Councilors, a female voice addressed Kharnek: "Were there any other witnesses to this?"

"Yes. Kalis of Sondrine, and the Truthseekers from Heathström. I believe that they have already testified accordingly, through...magical means."

"They have," High Keeper Veloran confirmed. "Does this then conclude your testimony?"

"It does."

"Very well. Idrilia, is there anything you would like to add to what you have already told the Council?"

Idrilia shook her head.

The High Keeper faced the rest of the Council. "Are there any other questions?"

"Just one." This from a male Councilor to Kharnek's left. "As a representative of Komor, you are entitled to request that our review be escalated into a formal inquiry. Do you wish to do so?"

"What is the difference?" Kharnek cast a sidelong glance at Idrilia, who blanched at the question.

"A review by the Council is strictly an internal affair," the High Keeper clarified, "whereas a formal inquiry would elevate this incident to become a matter of state. In that scenario, and given that a potential violation of the Waverling Accords is involved, the ramifications increase…precipitously." She rotated to face Kharnek, the hem of her tan robes brushing the stone floor. "As my colleague indicated, that option is available to you."

"I am no diplomat," Kharnek began, "and I am unfamiliar with your ways. What I know is that this attack violates the fundamental precepts of the Trials of the Innermost and the spirit of cooperation encouraged by those endeavors." He raised a hand to indicate Idrilia. "What she did could be considered an act of war."

This statement triggered a ripple of hushed murmurs. High Keeper Veloran raised her arms, and the susurrations faded.

"We will take that into consideration as we convene. For now, we ask that all those in attendance but the Councilors adjourn to the atrium."

Quiet conversations resumed while the various guilds filed out. Kharnek exited through the main entrance, while Idrilia was escorted through a doorway behind the Council platform. The warrior stopped to ask one of the guards how long the recess would last.

"Were you not provided with a sigil?"

Kharnek shook his head.

"Follow me, please."

The Sentinel led Kharnek to a bronze pedestal with a blue glass bowl atop it. Within the bowl lay several small tetrahedral crystals. The Sentinel plucked one out and offered it to Kharnek. He took it, and the crystal glowed a dull red.

"The color will change to blue when the Council is ready to reconvene. Its effective range is the entire city, so you are free to leave the Esplanade. The deliberation could be lengthy."

Kharnek inclined his head and marched out into the plaza in front of the Council building. He took up a post next to a crystal fountain, carved to resemble a Keeper. The representatives from the guilds were clumped together throughout the plaza. Many cast curious glances his way, but no one approached him.

Kharnek was used to feeling like an outsider, but he wished Zinvar were with him. The sight of the priest unconscious and singed had awakened a rage in him, but it differed from the elemental fury of the darkness he'd once known. This felt personal, like Idrilia's fireball had collided with his heart. Everything about the priest kindled a reaction within him that he could not entirely control. It seemed that Zinvar felt the same, but that would undoubtedly change were he to discover all that Kharnek withheld from him.

No more lies. A promise made to be broken. Already broken. Kharnek debated the wisdom of disclosing the truth about his purpose in the Trials and decided against it. Zinvar would discover that in time. He settled upon a conciliatory act: once the priest recovered, Kharnek would tell him about his own dark dreams. Perhaps Zinvar's powers as an Occulum could unveil the mystery of those and his strange abilities.

In his peripheral vision, Kharnek detected a figure approaching. He pivoted to face the individual, who stopped just out of arm's reach and dipped his head in respect.

"What do you want, Sondrinel?"

"To apologize on Idrilia's behalf, first of all." Kalis ran his hand through his cropped blue hair. "What she did—was inexcusable. But she's under a lot of stress and—she's never exactly been good at controlling her temper in those circumstances, you know?"

Kharnek glared at him. "What circumstances could possibly justify that?"

"She's…well, we—I mean, I…we're betrothed," Kalis blurted out. Kharnek stared while a stream of words bubbled from the Sondrinel. "But it was our families who decided that. And 'Dril is rightfully angry that they took that choice away from her. Being back in Axiom is a constant reminder of that. Anyway, she was already frustrated when she found you and Zinvar, and I guess that pushed her over the edge."

"Get to the point."

"The point is that I care about Idrilia, and I don't want to see her future ruined by this. So, I'm asking you, soldier to soldier, not to push for greater consequences than whatever the Council settles on." Kalis stopped and regarded him expectantly.

Kharnek stepped closer to Kalis, enough that his advantage in height became quite clear. "Let us get something straight, *soldier to soldier*," he sneered. "Were we not embroiled in this irritating political exercise known as the Trials, I would settle my grievance with your betrothed in a much more permanent fashion. And you could not stop me. But as it stands, I am forced to rely upon your Council to mete out the punishment she most assuredly deserves. So, tell me, why should I not ask for the worst possible outcome?"

Kalis remained undeterred by the warrior's proximity. "Call it a favor. One which I will repay."

"You already owe me her life once." Kharnek turned his back on the Sondrinel and walked away.

"Then do it for Zinvar."

Kalis's request brought Kharnek to an abrupt halt.

"You may not believe that it's possible for there to be peace among the realms, but he does. You would undo everything he has worked for just for revenge?"

No sooner had Kalis finished speaking than the sigil in Kharnek's fist gleamed bright blue, and the crowds in the plaza surged back toward the Council building. Kharnek shot one last look over his shoulder at the forlorn Sondrinel before stalking away.

"Our review of the incident concerning Idrilia of Sondrine is complete." The High Keeper gestured to acknowledge Kharnek and Idrilia, who stood in the same positions as before. "At this time, we will render our verdict. Councilors, if you please."

The men and women behind High Keeper Veloran rose in unison and approached the crystal in the platform's center.

"By the light of Kadaan, we seek the truth," she intoned.

"The truth awaits those who seek it," the Councilors answered and placed their hands upon the surface of the crystal. A warm glow suffused the chamber. After a moment, they stepped back to their seats.

The High Keeper touched the crystal, and a sound like the tolling of a bell echoed through Concilius. Her eyes shone with the same light the crystal manifested. Maintaining her connection with it, the High Keeper spoke.

"A verdict has been rendered. This is the judgment of the Council of Sondrine." Her voice sounded amplified, as though a thousand echoes of her words ricocheted off the chamber walls. "The actions of Idrilia of Sondrine were ill-considered and in violation of the statutes of the Trials of the Innermost. For this there is no excuse. Nevertheless, she shall remain a participant in the Trials, and she and the other participants will leave within the next twenty-four hours as planned."

Out of the corner of his eye, Kharnek saw Idrilia straighten.

"However," the High Keeper continued, "unless demanded by the direst of circumstances, she is not permitted the use of the life force for the remaining duration of the Trials. This will be enforced by a review of Kalis Vaktare's recollections upon the completion of the Trials. Furthermore, her crystals with destructive properties will be confiscated until such time as she is deemed responsible enough to have them returned to her care." Idrilia's face fell as the High Keeper addressed Kharnek directly. "Is this satisfactory to the representative from Komor?"

All eyes in the chamber turned to Kharnek. The room held its collective breath while he deliberated. Even Idrilia, brow furrowed, could not tear her gaze from the warrior.

"The verdict is satisfactory."

The astonished expression on Idrilia's face provoked a snort of amusement from Kharnek. Sighs of relief sounded from every corner of Concilius.

"Then the Council's decision is final," the High Keeper pronounced. She withdrew her hand from the crystal, and its aura faded. The Councilors rose and bowed, then vacated their placements. Kharnek interpreted this as a sign of dismissal and made to leave.

Halfway across the bridge, a familiar voice rang out.

"Kharnek!"

The warrior spotted Kalis in the lower ranks of the Sentinel Guild's seating. He looked up at Kharnek, a joyous light in his pale blue eyes. "Thank you."

Kharnek regarded him with contempt. "This is far from over, Sondrinel," he spat, and stormed out of the chamber

CHAPTER 39

"So that's why the Keepers come here, you know?"

"No, I did not know until you just told me."

"Right. But when you think about it, it makes perfect sense. Why keep potentially dangerous experiments in Axiom? Keepers' Rest was built after one such failed test leveled a building. I've heard so much about it, but to actually be going there…"

Kharnek clenched his jaw and fists as Kalis continued to elaborate on the history of their current destination. These sorts of anecdotes had followed the warrior for four cycles, all the way across the broad tan plain that stretched north from Axiom to the barren slopes of Mount Hoestra. The seemingly endless expanse was punctuated by clusters of dark-green vegetation and the slithering line of the Leske River.

Kharnek squinted into the brightness above and could just make out the snow line, where the dull brown of the mountainside faded to pure white. The air grew noticeably thinner and colder as they approached that boundary. He, Vayriel, Kalis, and Idrilia all seemed unaffected by the altitude, but Zinvar and Kilahym were visibly exerting themselves.

"This is…quite the hike," the priest panted, slightly downslope of Kharnek and Kalis. "Too bad we couldn't take the solendrakes."

"Their blood would freeze at this height," Kalis reminded him.

"As will mine if it keeps getting colder!" Kilahym exclaimed. The bard puffed his way up the mountain beside Kalis. They all trailed Vayriel and Idrilia, who led the group and conversed in hushed tones. Kalis's frequent glances at them told Kharnek where the Sondrinel's thoughts truly resided.

"They will have heavy cloaks at the shelter," Kalis said now, clapping the bard on the back. "And a roaring fire, my friend!"

"It will take quite a fire to warm these shivering bones, my good Prioriate."

Much to the warrior's relief, Kalis and Kilahym forged ahead on the climb. Kharnek hung back to check on Zinvar, who was leaning heavily on his staff.

"This is not what I had in mind when I imagined going up a mountain. It sounded much more grandiose and far less uncomfortable," the priest bemoaned.

"We have nearly reached the shelter. Then you will be able to rest."

"Thank Morakh for that. At least the view is spectacular." Zinvar indicated the plain below.

"It is nothing like the glory of Zel Morakh."

"No, it isn't," Zinvar agreed. He grinned at the warrior. "But I doubt you could persuade the others that frozen tundra and boiling lava is better than this."

Kharnek shoved him playfully in response but sobered when Zinvar winced.

"I am sorry. Are you still in pain?"

"It's more uncomfortable than anything. My robes absorbed most of the blast. And the salve the healers gave me has made the skin much less tender. I think it's more bruised from the impact than burned. Who knew that fireballs packed such a punch?"

Kharnek turned baleful eyes on Idrilia's figure further up the mountain. "She will pay for what she did to you," he vowed.

Zinvar placed a restraining hand on his forearm. "I'm sure she feels badly. She almost got kicked out of the Trials, and she can't use magic, which has to be hard. From what I understand, you're the only reason she didn't suffer worse."

"A decision I wish I could unmake."

Zinvar gave him a puzzled look. "I don't understand. If you're so angry with Idrilia, why spare her the worse punishment?"

"What punishment could be worse than being betrothed to her chattering companion?"

"He has been unusually talkative, hasn't he? Probably distracting himself from the fact that Idrilia has been avoiding him since we left Axiom." The priest waggled his staff at Kharnek. "Now, stop dodging the question. Why help Idrilia if you despise her so?"

"What I want is a secondary consideration to what is best for Komor. Relations with the Sondrinel are tenuous enough without adding a high-profile incident as a factor."

"I wasn't aware that you were concerned with relations with the Sondrinel at all." Zinvar's eyebrow arched. "Could it be that you've changed your mind about the diplomatic approach?"

"Would that please you?"

"Of course."

"Then let it be so." Kharnek resumed the upward trek.

"Wait!" Zinvar hurried after him. "Did you mean that?" The clatter of dislodged rocks trailed his pursuit. Kharnek increased his pace each time the priest drew near, leading him ever upward. They quickly overtook the rest of the group, who had halted at an outcropping dusted with snow. A round, domed structure nestled against the mountainside. Kharnek stopped next to Kilahym, a puffing Zinvar in tow.

A blue-robed Sondrinel man bustled out of the structure to meet the group. He smiled and bowed in greeting.

"Welcome to Keepers' Rest, Truthseekers. We are pleased that you have arrived safely. I am Jannu, the caretaker of this refuge. Please follow me and I will show you to your quarters."

The Keeper led the way into the structure, the interior of which was composed of three concentric rings. The outermost were rooms flooded with natural light and strewn with comfortable cushions. "These are for meditation or when the solace of solitude is required," Jannu explained.

The middle ring consisted of a passage that separated the outer ring from the innermost, which housed living quarters for visitors. "Ordinarily there would be other Keepers here or their students. But during the Trials, this place is reserved only for the Seekers," the caretaker explained. "Aside from myself, of course. I've been using the time alone to focus on my study of a fascinating crystal fragment that Idrilia herself recovered near Axiom. Quite unusual properties..."

Kharnek found the white-intensive color palette overbearing, but at least it was warm. Fires crackled in each room. The group disassembled, one by one, until only Kharnek and Zinvar remained with the Keeper. He brought them around the curved hall to the last open room, and motioned toward it.

"My apologies, honored guests, but there is only one room left," Jannu confessed. "If you would prefer to have separate chambers, I would be happy to furnish one of the quiet rooms."

"No need to go to that trouble," Zinvar said. "We can share a room. Right, Kharnek?"

Kharnek felt his pulse quicken. "Yes."

Jannu bowed and strode back down the hallway.

Once they were both inside the arched entrance, a silver barrier twinkled into existence. Kharnek gingerly prodded the magical obstruction. It yielded beneath his touch, and his hand passed through.

"Hopefully it isn't that easy to get in from the outside," Zinvar observed dryly.

Kharnek nodded in agreement, watching the priest discard his staff and satchel on the floor before turning back to the barrier. "I have seen such a contrivance before. It is solely for privacy."

"How fortunate for us that our hosts are unfailingly polite." The priest's voice came from much closer now. Kharnek twisted around to find Zinvar immediately behind him. "And that we yet have some time before the last part of this Trial begins."

Kharnek felt the flush of heat on his cheeks. "What do you mean?"

"I mean, it's time to reapply the healing salve. And you're going to help me."

Zinvar handed him a small container, then turned and began to disrobe. Looking over his shoulder, the priest smiled coyly.

"You can handle that, right?"

"Y-Yes. Yes, I can," Kharnek stammered.

"Good. I'd hate to think that Komor's finest would be stymied by a little medicine. Now, make sure you don't miss anywhere."

The warrior smiled back and gave him a playful kiss.

"I won't."

CHAPTER 40

Soft humming suffused the quiet room. A seed pod, like four paper pectully wings conjoined, hovered and swirled above Vayriel.

Breath of the mountain. In.

Breath of the mountain. Out.

Mother-of-All, I seek your guidance and your strength, this Daughter's Journey and always.

Orgar sat on his haunches opposite Vayriel. Though her eyes remained closed, she *felt* his presence within the life force. He strengthened her connection, and she could almost see the emotions of her nearby companions: light blue curiosity, red excitement, purple so dark it seemed black—black what?

Breath of the mountain. In.

Breath of the mountain. Out.

Was it the Penumbra that felt cold as a gulp of water from the mountain streams? There were times when Vayriel's connection to the Mother-of-All showed glimpses she was not yet strong enough to read. Like what she had felt from Adjira. Perhaps with time she would become a better wielder of the life force, just as they said her parents had been. Strong Watchers and very much in love. Vayriel had never felt a deeper love than with Orgar and her mother's parents. As she had asked Idrilia, wasn't that enough? Mo'mo did want her to find a life-mate. But Highbloods chose Highbloods.

She sighed.

Breath of the mountain. In.

Breath of the mountain. Out.

Mother-of-All, I do not know what my coil would say to this, and I ask for you to reveal the path which brings honor to my people. Guide my spirit, for it is drawn in one direction, and I am wary of choosing the wrong way.

The gentle tap of boots against stone penetrated her mental sanctuary. With a final slow exhalation, Vayriel let the seed drop into her lap.

"Oh, I'm sorry. I didn't mean to disturb you, you know."

"It is alright, Kalis." Vayriel opened her eyes to find the Sondrinel standing in the opening of the quiet room to which Jannu had led her.

"What's that?" He pointed to her lap, where tender green shoots had begun to peek out of the delicate shells.

"This is the young-root of a redbark tree. I will give this to Jannu for his kind attentiveness. Redbarks have many uses in the mountains."

"That is a wonderful gesture, Vayriel. Uh, what were you doing with it?"

"I used it to focus my connection to the Mother-of-All. While away from my...my home, I have found I am sometimes distracted. It can be harder for me to use the connection."

"I see. And this helps you, because it reminds you of home."

Vayriel sighed. "Normally, this is true."

"Keep trying. Priorates aren't trained in a day, you know." Kalis laughed. "I can't say that I've seen someone float a seed in the air before, so your connection can't be all that bad."

Vayriel uncrossed her legs, allowing Orgar to approach and nuzzle his soft fur against her cheek. Though Kalis's statement felt like an invitation, she hesitated in sharing more with him.

The coils knew that lowlanders and Highbloods should work together for the protection of the Mother's creation. But the coils also told tales of those who sought to use the Highbloods' connection to the life force for destruction, or who mistreated them because they did not understand the coils. This led to some coils forbidding outsiders. Though that weighed on her, Vayriel did not want to seem distrustful with her new companions.

"I sought answers that I did not receive. Yet..." She smiled. "I will continue to seek them."

"Well, I wish you the best in finding them, fellow Truthseeker. Sorry to interrupt. I was heading to find the others as Jannu wanted to see us soon. Are you coming?"

Vayriel nodded, rising. "Kalis, may I ask you a question?"

"Of course. What is it?"

"Your family—they approve of you becoming life-mates with Idrilia, yes?"

"Oh, yes! Very much so. They are the ones who arranged it, you know."

"Because you have known each other since you were young-ones."

"I guess that played into it some. But some betrothals happen without either party knowing each other."

"Do your people seek betrothals outside of your city?"

"Hmm, I wouldn't think so. It would go against our edicts, I think. 'Dril probably knows more of the nuances since her grandmother was a Keeper. Why do you ask?"

"I was…curious. This way?" Vayriel motioned toward the hallway leading to the outer edge of Keepers' Rest, her mind still racing.

She had not known Kilahym long, yet he had expressed feelings as if he were seeking a life-mate—in her. It was true that she enjoyed his company, and she knew that a friendship was growing between them. But could she trust him as she trusted Orgar? And then there were the coils…

Kalis opened the glass door. Bright light from the Watcher's rays sparked in Vayriel's vision, then cleared. Kilahym stood opposite Jannu with his back to her. She silently hoped that he would not bring up the topic here, for she did not yet know how to respond. *One must know their truth in order to tell it.*

Everyone but the two from Komor were present. Vayriel found herself standing next to Kilahym as Jannu continued answering a question posed by the bard.

"It's not really solitude as Keepers-in-training come here as well. More of…a break from Axiom life with a focus on training our minds for the Rising. And rejuvenating for our duties. The library has works of fiction from all over Etherea."

"I'll have to peruse that collection!"

The door once again opened. Kharnek and Zinvar eased up to the back of the group.

"And where have you two been?" Kilahym inquired with an amused expression, then dropped his voice. "Conducting a beastly ritual of darkness, no doubt. Oof!" He gasped as Vayriel jabbed him with her elbow.

"Jannu requires our attention," she scolded, a grin attempting to show and undermine her seriousness.

"Now that you are all here, I am pleased to announce that the next endeavor of the Trials of the Innermost is about to commence," Jannu began. "Your task is as follows: You are to collect the hide of a trägen and return it to me in this." The Keeper withdrew a round silver container from his robes that gleamed in the sunlight. "How you go about doing so is up to you."

Vayriel stiffened. She focused on breathing the mountain air through her nose, hopeful that she had misunderstood.

"That's…unexpectedly dangerous," Kilahym whispered.

"Be warned," Jannu continued, "the way is perilous. The path is full of crevasses that can swallow you whole. And trägen are not to be taken lightly."

"What is a trägen?" Zinvar asked behind her.

"Massive predators," Kharnek offered. "Claws and teeth as sharp as spears. They do not live in Komor but in the other realms even the vargs run away."

Vayriel blew a breath out in a cloud. "Trägen are enemies of the jeroti. Their white coats blend with the snow of the mountains, and they move with the speed of the wind. While vargs hunt for food or defend their territory trägen…" She shook her head. "They seek out battles, killing more than they could ever hope to eat. Some say they are tainted by the Sleeper. No Highblood has ever made one a life-friend." Gripping her spear tighter, she turned to Jannu. "But coil Watchers always find ways to divert their blood-red gaze from our Alusarean herds. You want us to kill a creature for no other purpose than this Trial?" She thought how she had enticed a trägen away from the alusarean of her coil, an act that had helped award her the position of Truthseeker of the Highbloods.

"How you obtain the hide is up to you. Also," Jannu wrung his hands, "there is another stipulation…You must complete the task within one day."

"What?" Idrilia blurted. "You can't be serious. Climb a giant mountain in knee-deep snow, defeat a trägen, and return within twenty-four hours?"

"We've trained for this," Kalis nodded. "The Council wouldn't give us something completely impossible. Maybe half impossible," he winked.

"With half of us untrained for anything in this task"—she glanced at Kilahym then Zinvar—"half impossible seems fully true."

"Orgar will be of great use as we navigate the mountain." Vayriel placed a hand on the jeroti's head.

"You may leave whenever you are ready. But I suggest that you hurry. The mountain climate is unpredictable, and the air feels stormy today." The Keeper looked up at the wisps of gray clouds that swirled about Mount Hoestra's peak, then passed the silver container to Kalis. "I also suggest that you make for the summit. The beasts shelter in caves near the mountain's peak."

Jannu bowed to the group, then departed.

"Now, no one get yourself gobbled up by a trägen." Kilahym beamed. "We still have a lot of Trials left. I feel a song forming."

Vayriel held a hand up. "Retrieve your things as quickly as you are able. We should heed Jannu's warning and set off before the breath of the mountain overtakes us."

Returning inside with the others, Vayriel plucked her bag from her room, already primed for a hasty departure as her Watcher training dictated.

Outside again, Vayriel's gaze traveled up the mountain slope to rest upon the jagged edge of the distant peak. With a silent prayer to the Mother-of-All to guide her steps, she pulled her hood up against the ominous chill. *I will not forsake my beliefs. I must find a way.*

The others joined her, and they began the long climb to where the trägen awaited, the warmth of Keepers' Rest fading into memory.

CHAPTER 41

The pervasive cold filled her nose and lungs, tingling as she took another breath. The crunch beneath her soft-soled boots was muffled to a squish in the wet snow, different from the deep layer that covered the upper slopes of her home. Using her spear for leverage, Vayriel traversed the incline effortlessly, gripping the wooden pole with gloved hands, the alusarean fur within providing warmth. She recognized the voice of the mountains, and, though the sounds were similar to her home, these whispers seemed distant and muffled, thin like the brush and trees at this elevation.

After some mumbled complaints from Kilahym and hushing of him from both Idrilia and Kharnek, the Seekers had settled into a quiet ascent. For a moment it felt like she was home with her fellow Watchers, trusting one another in their task. She wished the Seekers would trust one another. She looked over her shoulder again; Kilahym and Zinvar walked side by side the furthest away, while the rest of them dotted between the pair and where Vayriel scouted ahead.

They had to alter their climb, moving laterally for half an hour before ascending again, to avoid several crevasses that dropped in waterfalls of stone to depths impenetrable even by the Watcher's rays. Every minute, the wind steadily intensified.

After a while Kalis joined her. His headscarf hid his features beneath the beige hood of his long Ettrascan coat.

"See anything of interest?" He inclined his head toward their trajectory. "Or you, too, Orgar."

Vayriel glanced down at her four-legged friend. His nose exhaled a visible plume of heated air, and his white fur blended with the snow but for his vigilant gray ears, twitching as he listened to the Mother-of-All's creation.

She felt nothing concerning through their bond, but she took a deep breath, focusing on the spark of her being, feeling the energy within her chest. With a gentle push, she sent tendrils of power from her extremities. She waited for faint vibration, warnings that she received when an attack was imminent.

She shook her head. "Neither Orgar or myself have seen any signs. Look for five-clawed footprints trailing to a hidden cave."

"I trust your eyes more than mine here." Kalis gestured toward the white landscape. "You think we'll have to climb all the way to the summit?"

"It is likely." Warmth from her hood surrounded her ears, and the fur brushed her forehead as she lifted her head to eye the high, jagged rocks that peeked from beneath the distant snow, marking the final ascent to the Mother's fingertips.

She adjusted the notch of the snow-eyes on the bridge of her nose to better position the thin slits as she gazed at the sparsely blanketed outcroppings.

"Your eyewear is a bit like Zinvar's, you know, the way it ties behind your head," Kalis glanced behind. "I'm glad we all have our own solutions. Don't want any of us going blind."

Vayriel touched his shoulder, knowing he could not see her eyes. The Sondrinel had headscarves and Kharnek had goggles, while Vayriel wore an eye-covering carved from gray-bark that was smoothed into a shape resembling an oar.

"Yours remind me of Wen," Idrilia said behind her, "squinting when she's sleeping. It's cute."

The othwit soared above them, and despite the serenity of the landscape. Vayriel's thoughts kept straying to taking a creature's life just to obtain a trophy. It made her stomach roil. None of the others seemed troubled by it. But Vayriel could think of few ways to subdue a trägen without gravely injuring it. When the time came to act, would she be able to do what was necessary?

Vayriel tilted her head to the pale blue sky to confirm the Daughter's position, but her feet faltered. She could not see her, or the Watcher, through the haze of smoky white.

"The breath of the mountains. The Keeper is well attuned to the Mother's ways."

"Do you know what this is? Should we be worried?" Idrilia asked.

"We would do well to take cover. It is never certain if the breath will pass as a gentle exhale or as fierce as a varg's howl. You both have a tent, yes?"

"Yes, in my pack. Thank Kadaan I have never been in the mountains when a storm blew through."

"Thank the Mother, I have." Vayriel smiled, pleased with her imitation of a jest in the style Kilahym might use.

Idrilia ran down the slope, calling out to the others. "Vayriel thinks a storm is coming. Would you please act like a varg is at your heels?"

Vayriel's smile faded as the gusts increased and pellets of ice plummeted from the sky, drumming the hood of her coat and her shoulders like mischievous ratufa tossing nuts.

"It is already here." Vayriel raised her voice, "Quickly, we can use that boulder to block some of the wind."

The wind whipped with such fury that Vayriel had to lean on her spear to keep her balance on the slippery snow. She shivered, the cold finding gaps in her clothing to claw in its icy grip. Vayriel led the way to a slab of rock angled like the bough of a tree bent against a storm. She pulled the opening of her hood closer to her face against the volitant hail.

"Where do we go from here?" Kalis pressed his back against the rock next to Vayriel.

She squinted ahead, but all she saw was swirling white, as if the veil of the world had been lowered right on top of them. Peeking around the corner of the slab, she saw the same, and her heart felt like it had frozen over.

"Where are the others?" Her voice rose against the noise of the wind.

Kalis rotated to the side of the rock. "Idrilia!" he yelled, cupping his hands around his face.

But all Vayriel heard in response was more wind and ice.

"Orgar, see if you can find them. But stay with our footprints."

Vayriel focused on the bond between them as he lumbered away, nose touching the snow, anchoring herself for him to the invisible tether. She took several deep breaths, attempting to calm the storm within her, but she could not quiet it enough to hear the Mother's voice. If only she could sense her companions like she had at Keepers' Rest, she would feel comfort knowing they were alright.

Kalis leaned closer. "Should we go back for them?"

A tale from Mo'fa surfaced in Vayriel's mind about three coil Watchers caught in a storm. Two thought they could make it back to the coil and left the shelter of the fallen redbark tree they had lain beneath. They were found days later at the bottom of a ravine. She did not want the same fate for any of them. Her body stiffened, and she glanced around the edge of the rock. Even Orgar was lost in the white. She had to put her trust in their abilities.

She tightened the grip on her staff and turned back to Kalis. "I do not want us to lose our way…or fall into one of those crevasses we passed earlier."

"I understand your caution, but Idrilia—the others…"

"Where they are at this moment cannot be changed by either of us. And if we in turn are lost, we burden them to find us. If Orgar finds them, he will make them stay where they are. We should wait for the storm to pass."

"I'll follow your Highblood instincts. You're right, we could be heading in the wrong direction."

Kalis withdrew the tightly packed cloth of a tent and activated the mechanism that sprung the contraption open, just as it had its predecessor on the Leske Road weeks before. Vayriel's thoughts strayed to Orgar. For a moment, she thought she saw his form at the edge of visibility, where the fog swirled. But as the silhouette faded, she noticed horns on the top of its conical head. If it was a jeroti, it was not Orgar.

Kalis held open the tent for Vayrial to enter, then followed, fastening the flap behind them. The pattering sound continued, though the whooshing wind was muffled within the safety of the shelter.

The Sondrinel dropped his pack and knelt beside it as he pulled his scarf from his mouth. "What about some heat?" He reached inside his coat pocket and withdrew a red-tinted sphere. After shaking it, he placed it on the tent's floor. "Much better."

Vayriel's nod turned into a jolt as a thunderclap shook the canvas walls. "This tent may be insufficient," she said, removing her eye covering and scrutinizing the inner structure. The fabric was not made of alusarean skin like the dwellings of her coil but rather woven threads. What helped to keep dust storms out of the Sondrine tent would do well to keep out the snow, especially if it had been prepared with the right herbs to keep water from soaking it. But there were no herbs to protect against other dangers.

"I might have some stakes we could use to nail the cloth base to the ground. That might steady it from blowing over. Our weight might be enough, but I'd rather we not tumble around like a dry ball of scragweed in the desert."

"The ground is likely too frozen for stakes, but it is the spear-flash that concerns me."

"Spear-flash? Oh, lightning?"

She lifted her chin. "I can create a protective shield around us."

Vayriel focused on the outermost points of her body: the tips of her fingers inside her fur gloves and the pads of her feet where they pressed against the soles of her shoes. Then she tugged on each distinct point until she felt her core fill with radiating energy. She *pushed* it away from her, shaping it, and the familiar pale pink bubble filled the tent's interior.

"That's amazing!" Kalis's face lit with joy. "We have a crystal that does something similar. May I touch it?" He pointed to the edge of the bubble.

Vayriel nodded her head once.

Kalis reached tentatively toward the barrier. His hand bounced back gently as the tip of his finger connected with the translucent curve.

"Did it take you long to learn how to do this?"

Vayriel shook her head. "It was one of the first gifts from the Mother-of-All that I could summon. But I have been learning to improve it. Prior to the storm wall, I have only ever protected myself and Orgar at one time."

At mention of his name, Vayriel focused on his connection, feeling as if pulled in two directions between her tasks. Orgar's presence felt faint, and while her bubble flickered for a moment it held steady. He was further away than she would have thought. Had the others drifted so far away when the storm surprised them? She sent a question to him, hoping her energy was strong enough to convey her meaning. A few heartbeats passed, and she got the impression of safety but nothing more.

"I haven't yet mastered the protection crystal myself. Which I'm beginning to regret, given our circumstances. Oh, I almost forgot." He opened his pack and rummaged about. "The stakes."

Kalis stiffened.

"What is it?" Vayriel leaned forward, tilting her head.

"I forgot I still had this in here."

He withdrew his arm, his fingers cupped around a bronze item. Its sides curved gently against his palms, rising from a flat base. Kalis placed the object on the ground between them.

"I bought it in Ettrascus. For Idrilia. Have you heard from Orgar?"

"Yes, but let me try again. It was not more than a feeling of no danger."

Vayriel breathed deeply, stretching out from herself, trying to touch other foci of life-force energy. Her breath caught, then a slow smile formed. "Kilahym is there. And the others. Orgar will lead them back to Keepers' Rest for now."

"That's a relief. After the storm, we should keep going since we're limited on time. If the others catch up, great, but we can handle this."

Vayriel hesitated, then nodded. Already she felt a piece of herself missing as Orgar's energy faded from her detection. She dropped her hands to her lap, her eyes landing on the object from Kalis. To distract herself, Vayriel studied its jeweled ornamentation and intricate carvings. Filigreed edges artfully brought the creature to life from its eyes to its wings, and even the blue flower nestled between its talons.

"An othwit?"

Kalis shrugged, eyes downcast. "Open it."

Clutching the othwit's torso, Vayriel gripped the head near the painted beak, feeling a slight discomfort even though she knew this was not a living creature. She pulled upward. The hinge protested for a moment, then with a faint click, the catch released and the head tilted back to reveal metal discs and gears and a row of thin metal sticks. The gears began to turn, as did the largest disc, which Vayriel noticed was covered in a seemingly random pattern of tiny pins. The sticks tinkled against the pins, and music softly formed between them, the tune slow yet whimsical.

"It's a lullaby. One that Idrilia remembers her grandmother singing to her as a child."

"It is beautiful."

Kalis waved his hand then gently closed the othwit's head, silencing the melody. "I guess I won't be giving it to her now though. She wouldn't accept it. I should have given it to her on the boat."

"I could give your gift to her," Vayriel offered.

Kalis halted, his hand midway to his bag. "You'd do that?"

"I am your friend, Kalis, as well as a friend to Idrilia. She should be honored to receive such a gift. You have learned much of her spirit if you can choose something that will remind her of her joys and memories."

Kalis sighed. "I was thinking earlier that maybe if it was her choice, she'd love me, you know. If our marriage wasn't forced on her."

His smile, only half-developed, sent a wave of sadness through Vayriel's chest, and she had to refocus to strengthen the protective bubble before it faded.

"No matter. How she feels doesn't change how I feel about her. Thank you, Vayriel. I appreciate your offer. But I should give it to her myself. It's a whole new level of bravery." He laughed softly and returned the object to his bag.

Vayriel touched his shoulder. "Of your bravery, there is no doubt, Kalis of Sondrine. Now, let me secure our tent . We can rest while the storm passes."

Vayriel closed her eyes and searched through the lifeforce for the burrowing roots of mountain scragweed. She smiled and opened her eyes, coaxing the roots to push through the dense soil and wrap around the edges of the tent. Slowly, the fine threads thickened as they sewed themselves into the cloth. When finished, the roots looked like a circle of braided rope.

"I feel you are contributing far more than me already," Kalis said, gesturing to the roots. "Don't push yourself, you know. We will need all our strength for this Trial. Speaking of which…I couldn't help but notice your reaction to Jannu's description of our task. If you feel uncomfortable about anything, now is the time to say it."

Vayriel sighed and averted her eyes from Kalis's perceptive gaze.

"I do not wish to take life unnecessarily. It is contrary to all that I, and my people, hold sacred. If I had known—"

She broke off as a tide of emotions washed over her.

"I understand how difficult this must be for you. I guess this is why they call it the Trials of the Innermost, you know?" A wry grin twisted Kalis's face.

Vayriel could not help but acknowledge the truth in her companion's statement. The realization fortified her resolve to see this task through to its completion. She was a Highblood, but also a Truthseeker, and now she must reconcile those identities.

"You are right. When the time comes, I will be ready."

Vayriel lifted her eyes and met Kalis's gaze. He said nothing, pressing his lips together in a thin smile before setting about unrolling his sleeping mat.

It was not long before Kalis drifted off to sleep, but Vayriel stayed awake for a little longer, listening to the sounds of the mountain until she was certain it was safe to lower her shield. As she let the energy retreat back into her, she noticed she felt weaker from the exertion of maintaining the barrier than from the entire climb. Tired, she lowered her body to the cloth. As she closed her eyes, she imagined the familiar presence of Orgar's back warmly pressed against hers.

CHAPTER 42

Wind howled outside the walls of Keepers' Rest like a dirge. Kilahym removed his coat, plopping down next to Orgar as the jeroti watched snow whirl through the meditation room's window, ears flat against his head. Each puff of breath from the Orgar's nostrils left circles of condensation on the clear crystal as eyes were fixed upon the direction the Seekers had gone, and returned from. Well, almost all of them. The life force connection Kilahym felt with Vayriel at the storm wall hadn't returned, yet he felt wrenched in the same direction as Orgar.

Kilahym patted the jeroti's head. "All will be well, my four-legged friend."

Orgar nuzzled the bard's hand but never took his sight off the storm-shrouded mountain. Having ventured into the mountains only a few times, Kilahym had only ever seen a snowstorm as a cloud moving across the peaks. The Highbloods, however, lived among the slopes' various moods. Though he knew Vayriel would have well-learned skills to weather the weather, he couldn't help but worry at her and Kalis's plight. He needed a distraction. As did Orgar.

Kilahym patted Orgar between his ears. "Perhaps some music to pass the time and cheer up that sour mug?"

He retrieved his dulcimer from the pile of cushions where it rested. The meditation room offered many comfortable benches that sprouted from the floor like pale sporestalks, though he doubted any space was big enough for Kharnek and Idrilia to share.

"We could use a pleasant distraction," Zinvar said from where he lounged on the other side of the room. He and Kharnek occupied one of the broad seats.

"I was speaking of my friend Orgar, but your companion's face could use some joy now that you mention it," Kilahym needled. Kharnek's perpetually grim expression grew even more dour.

"Right you are." Zinvar rose from his place and crossed the chamber, his dull orange robes sweeping against the floor. The priest's garb reminded Kilahym of the long dresses his mother was fond of, the closest she got to a penchant for drama. Kilahym made room for Zinvar to sit next to him, sliding his journal—open to a drawing of a small prickly plant beneath a boulder—next to his thigh. The bard raised his chin to indicate Kharnek.

"What's eating at him? I bet you could cheer him up if you—"

"He's fine," Zinvar interrupted, before Kilahym could elaborate. Then he leaned in to whisper conspiratorially, "Actually, he's just in a foul mood because of being cooped up in here with Idrilia."

Kilahym hooted softly like an othwit. "Speaking o' her, where did our errant dilly-Drilly wander off to?

Zinvar gazed at the corner of the room Idrilia had vacated only moments ago. "I think she feels the same as Kharnek about being stuck in here together," he postulated. "And we're all worried about Vayriel and Kalis, never mind completing the trial on time."

"It is difficult to read another's heart, but in this I feel you are correct" Kilahym affirmed.

Speaking of hearts, Vayriel hadn't really responded to his confession in Axiom. He shrugged mentally—nothing he could do about it now, and either the Grey Lady or the Mother-of-All wanted them separated. What was the old phrase—distance makes love bloom? *Now, about that music.*

He hefted the dulcimer to cradle it across his body with the neck nearest his left shoulder and the base by his right hip. He strummed it tentatively, testing the tuning. The birds inlaid in the frets took flight beneath the thrumming strings. Zinvar seated himself on the low window ledge next to Orgar. Kilahym reached into his pocket and handed Zinvar the miniature instrument from Ansgard. He instructed the priest how to tap the silver surface in 6/8 time and wondered how a long press would alert his friend back in Waverling. He shrugged inwardly and began to play.

"On the side of the mountain
Our lady was born

A lovelier woman
Never was formed
Her lips like the moonrise
Her hair like a bloom
Eyes like the starlight
Skin soft and smooth
And she danced in the meadows
Through glen and through dale
She sang like the river flows
And she danced on the mountain
O'er hill and o'er dale
'Til the last light called her home."

Kilahym's voice lilted through the second and third verses before dropping in pitch to intone the final notes of the ballad. Zinvar applauded while the bard stood and executed a courtly bow before reseating himself.

"A lovely tune. Who or what is it about?" the priest inquired.

"At the Academy that little ditty was known as 'The Ballad of the Wistful Maiden.'"

"Time moves forward for this Trial, and we have to listen to this solendrake basja."

Kilahym and Zinvar looked over at the entrance to the meditation room. Idrilia loomed in it like a thundercloud, anger written across her face. She had shed her outer robes, leaving her daggers clearly visible. Kharnek's sword hand drifted toward his own sheathed weapon.

"Ah, the brooding one hath returned," Kilahym said. "With her lack of appreciation for the fine arts intact." He winked at Idrilia to soften the jab.

Zinvar nodded politely in Idrilia's direction.

"How long will we be stuck here?" She glanced at the large window. Either she did not see their gestures or pretended not to.

Kilahym shrugged, lowering his dulcimer to his lap. "Jannu said until the morning, but that remains to be seen."

"It's so cold. Kalis had a tent, so they should be fine…" Her voice trailed off as her eyes drifted to the floor. "I knew I should have brought one, too," she grumbled, snapping her head up. "We'll have to make up time when this storm eases up. I don't want us ending up like the fifth Truthseekers." She pointed a finger at Kilahym. "So no dawdling."

He clutched his chest in mock indignation, but Idrilia spun on her heels and left before Kilahym could respond.

"I do not dawdle," he said, leaning over to Zinvar.

The priest, who had been staring out the window, looked back at him. "You…become very focused at times. What did she mean by the fifth Truthseekers?"

Kilahym waved his hand as if swatting an insect from the Fens, "They never completed their Trials. Only group to fail halfway through. Well, outside of the missing previous Seekers, but we solved that particular mystery."

Zinvar seemed to mull over the information. The silence lingered like a snow cloud, the ambient wind gusts adding to the effect.

Kilahym cleared his throat. "How fares thee from yon lady's fireball?"

The Komorese grimaced.

"Ah, I'm sorry to bring it up, my friend."

"I just hate that it happened and now there is a rift among the Truthseekers. One that some of us"—Zinvar shot a glance at Kharnek—"seem unwilling to reconcile."

Kilahym cocked his head at the priest. "You would forgive her, even after she tried to light you afire?"

Zinvar nodded earnestly. "I'm forgiving by nature, and her ire technically was not aimed at me. But there's more at stake here than my feelings. The unthinking hatred that my people have for the Sondrinel, and that some of them have for us, will just continue if someone doesn't let the past stay there."

Kharnek snorted from across the room. "Fine words. We will see if you feel the same the next time your robes are charred and smoking."

"If they are, I'm sure it will be your fault, again," Zinvar shot back.

"I am not responsible for her lack of self-control."

"No, but let's not knowingly push for that result, shall we?"

"As you wish, priest."

Zinvar rolled his eyes and crossed his arms. He caught sight of the grin on Kilahym's face. "What has you smiling like a hungry varg?"

"Nothing." Kilahym's grin widened. "Well, I may be untrue. But it strikes my humble self that the two of you squabble as if you had been coupled for a great while."

The priest grabbed a pillow and hurled it at the bard. Kilahym deftly caught it, feigning hurt at the assault and tossing the gold-tasseled cushion back Zinvar's way. Zinvar aimed the pillow and lofted it again, but it was intercepted by a white blur. Orgar landed in a crouch, his tails wagging and his eyes darting back and forth, inviting the bard or priest to play. Kilahym whistled, and the jeroti bounded toward him.

"Someone is feeling better—oof!"

He collapsed beneath Orgar's weight, then wrestled the pillow free of the jeroti's maw and wriggled out from under him. Kilahym pitched the pillow at Kharnek, and it landed in his lap. Orgar streaked across the room, but skidded to a halt in front of the scowling warrior. Zinvar stifled a laugh at the jeroti's large-eyed gaze that implored this new participant to continue the game.

His amusement was cut short when the pillow crashed into his face, followed by Orgar. Kilahym rollicked with laughter as Zinvar attempted to dodge the jeroti's tongue in vain. The bard locked eyes with Kharnek, and a faint grin cracked through his resolute gaze. Kilahym returned the expression, then pounced on the squirming jeroti to help the hapless priest.

Wooden planks creaked beneath Kilahym's feet as he stepped onto the stage in the undercroft at the Bard Academy. A veritable forest had been shorn to create the expanse. The audience shifted to the edges of their seats, eager to hear the bard's latest composition.

Kilahym stopped at center stage. A number of tamed othwits peered at him from the rafters of the spacious chamber with curious speckled brown eyes. Their feathered heads swayed as Kilahym began to play. His song soared into the Academy above, giving pause to the hurried motions of Runners in their leather vests, bustling to deliver messages. The spellbound audience waited with bated breath as the music crescendoed and hung gloriously on a grand fermata, the pause before the song's inevitable conclusion—

Kilahym's joy deflated at the sound of his mother's voice. It punctured the melody with shrill, discordant tones.

"You'll never make it," she jeered.

Kilahym saw her now, perched in the rafters among the othwits. Her black dress hung like curtains over the timbers, reams of fabric that descended to shroud the stage. The audience murmured with disappointment. Then the dreaded sound: feet shuffling toward the exit while Kilahym strummed furiously, trying to recapture the stolen magic of his song. The strings of his dulcimer broke with a twang. Wooden splinters jabbed at his fingers.

Above it all, he still heard his cackling mother: "Utter embarrassment to the family name. Worthless child. Useless…"

Kilahym sat upright in his bed, the dream's spell broken.

"By the three-headed beast of Beechmarsh, what a dreadful vision," he announced to his empty room.

His back and forehead were beaded with sweat. He rolled off the sleep platform, carved out of the wall of the chamber like the other furnishings in Keepers' Rest. Soft gray light filtered through the privacy barrier, brightening the room just enough for Kilahym to find his sleeveless vest. He shrugged into it and slipped through the barrier into the darkened hallway outside, illuminated at its edges by smooth oval crystals set into the floor. The blue-white radiance soothed his troubled mind.

A dim recollection crept out of his subconscious to toy with his present thoughts. Mingled with his dream mother's banshee wail were the distinct tones of another voice and the howls of the wind. He moved further around the curve of the hallway toward the sound; these were the experimentation rooms, if he remembered Jannu's tour correctly. Odd that someone would be in there now, since the Keeper said those rooms were reserved for more…unstable research.

One of the doorway barriers glowed brightly, and, unable to contain his curiosity, Kilahym passed through the curtain of light.

Crystals in the floor joints cast a faint illumination on the room. A figure in Keeper robes sat hunched over a table, hands moving between beakers and tubes on stands. One flask sat over a blue flame, the liquid inside tinted with a whisp of black like ink for a quill, and graygrey steam wafted from the top.

"I didn't expect experiments while we were within these fair walls," Kilahym jested.

The figure spun around.

"Jannu! Didn't you say that's done here now since someone destroyed a guild hall in Axiom?" He wagged a finger at the Keeper.

"Kilahym," Jannu said slowly, then blinking, he sat up straight. "Axiom sent interesting samples. Your Sondrinel companions originally found them. Since you were to all be on the mountain"—he shrugged—"I couldn't stop once I started. Couldn't…stop…"

The man's eyes took on that far-away look whenever someone's mind wandered.

"Are you alright, Keeper?"

Jannu turned back to the table, stirring the inky water with a crystal pipe. "Yes, yes I am fine. Just busy."

Shrugging at the man's back, Kilahym stepped to the side to get a better view of what Jannu had on the table. His mind felt wide awake, a state that would be difficult to turn into slumber again. He resigned himself to no more rest. Maybe he'd step outside and check on the weather, waking the others if it seemed more favorable. He hoped the wind meant the storm was being pushed further away, allowing Vayriel and Kalis to move further toward their task.

From underneath a blue cloth on the table poked a purple shard, like a piece of ice chipped away from a larger chunk. It didn't look like any of the crystals Idrilia or Kalis used. Kilahym reached toward the cloth.

Jannu's hand clamped around his wrist. Kilahym yelped, pulling back but his arm wouldn't budge.

"Uh, Jannu?"

Jannu stood, gripped Kilahym by the front of his vest, and hoisted him off the ground like he weighed nothing. Slowly Jannu turned his gaze from the cloth and looked directly at Kilahym. The bard yelped again. The Keeper's eyes were a deep black that rippled like the waves of a storm-tossed sea. Kilahym pawed at Jannu's hands but nothing dislodged his grip.

Jannu glared at the bard. "You cannot stop me. This world belongs to the Penumbra."

Kilahym froze. "Last time I heard that name, people died. Well one person, but she'd already killed—"

"The whole. There are more. Here. Where are they?"

Before Kilahym could ask for clarification, he felt his life force begin to flow away from his body like beads of sweat on his skin. This was different from the feeling of Vayriel drawing from him within the sea creature. This felt cold. Draining. He reached for his neck, eyes widening when he remembered his ocarina was on the side table in his room. The only magic he ever had was tied to his music. He flailed his legs, panic churning his insides. He cringed when his feet hit Jannu's shins and the man did not react.

Then the Keeper threw his head back, his mouth open in the rictus of a silent scream. The crystals along the floor edge blazed with white light that forced Kilahym to shield his eyes.

"YOU WILL NOT HAVE ETHEREA," a female voice cried, seeming to come from within his mind.

Kilahym dropped to the floor as Jannu's grip released, and he covered his head. A tremendous crash resounded, followed by a profound silence.

The bard slowly lowered his trembling hands. The intense light was gone, and Jannu lay in a heap on the floor. Standing next to him was a figure in a long gray robe. He could still faintly see the wall through her. She turned her hooded head in his direction. She had gray eyes.

Kilahym dropped to his knees. "Grey Lady! I mean, Blessed Lady Laphrim."

"Please. I do not wish to be worshiped."

Glancing up, Kilahym saw her beckoning him to rise, though her form swayed for a moment like water rippling.

"The role you play cannot be overwritten, Kilahym. Vayriel will need your strength to complete her task. You must survive. All of you."

"What task? The trial?" Kilahym took one step forward. "Do you know if she's alright?"

She shook her head. "To stand against the Penumbra and save Etherea."

He scratched his chin. "Nothing like the weight of the world on our shoulders, hm?"

"You will be her conduit to greater power. But you must learn how to create it."

The thud of approaching boots reached him, and Kilahym turned around. Kharnek's towering figure emerged through the barrier. His eyes were as pitch-black as Jannu's had been. Kilahym took a step back as Kharnek's gaze passed around the room and landed on the Keeper's collapsed figure.

"What happened here?" The question rumbled deep in the warrior's chest.

"Why does everyone ask me what's going on when strange things happen? Like I would know? This is just like the storm beast all over again."

"Where is…" Kharnek blinked, and the darkness evaporated. The queasy feeling in the bard's stomach did not evaporate with it.

"You tell him," Kilahym turned toward the Grey Lady to find she was no longer there. Had she even been there at all? The bard scraped his hands through his hair.

"Did you see what happened here?" Kharnek demanded.

"Jannu was experimenting on something in those beakers, and then he started to babble. The way Adjira spoke before you… Anyway, some evil took hold of him. Strength like a warrior. I thought he was going to unalive me. Until the light came and…she was here. Did you see her?"

Kharnek shook his head. "Who?"

"The Grey Lady. She mentioned that blasted Penumbra again!"

"Here's where you disappeared to," Zinvar had stepped in just through the barrier. "I woke, and you weren't—Oh! What happened to Jannu?"

Kilahym sighed then repeated his story to Zinvar as Kharnek examined the Keeper's table. "I think it was the same woman you saw, Zinny. Though, I'm no Occulum. Penumbras and Sleepers—what does it all mean?"

"Her cryptic message is certainly consistent." Zinvar glanced at Kharnek. "We should probably summon Idrilia. We'll never hear the end of it if we don't include her in all of this." Zinvar motioned around the room.

"I will be the horn of bad news and wake up dilly-Drilly." Kilahym began to make his way back to the rooms. A half-composed motif of tri-tones and dissonance pulsed through his thoughts, which he began to whistle, the accompaniment to his mental replay of the events that just transpired. The whistle climbed the scale to a squeak when a large form moved in the shadows of the passageway ahead.

Kilahym relaxed when he discerned Orgar's familiar shape. "By the Lady, but you gave me a fright," he chastised. He reached out to stroke Orgar's ears and realized that the jeroti's fur stood on end. His cyan eyes stared intently in the direction Kilahym had come from.

The bard glanced back. Nothing was there. "We are all stricken with madness," he muttered to himself. "Come, friend Orgar. We have dreams to interrupt."

He started to move on, but Orgar blocked his way, nudging his leg.

"You want me to go back? Oh alright, I'll take you to Zinvar. You know, I'm starting to think you're replacing me with him as your second best friend. Stubbornest of all creatures, I name thee."

When they entered Jannu's research room, Kilahym saw that the Keeper had been sat up against the wall. Zinvar was talking quietly with him as Orgar lumbered over. The jeroti sniffed the Keeper, then sat next to Zinvar.

Kilahym shrugged at Kharnek. "Slight detour. I'll be back with Idrilia before you can say 'Penumbra.' On second thought, don't say that."

Shaking his head, Kilahym turned to exit the room, but light refracting caught his attention. He glanced at the table. The fragment had been removed from beneath the cloth and sat next to it. The purple hue within was gone.

CHAPTER 43

"As 'Dril would say, why take the safer, longer path when you can take the quicker one, you know?"

Kalis looked where Vayriel pointed: a narrow ledge that clung to the mountainside, its gradient twisting out of view as it hugged the peak. The ledge dropped into the largest crevasse they had encountered since leaving their tent.

"It *is* safer," she insisted. "We do not have the right tools to attempt a nearly vertical climb."

"But we could go around..." Kalis bent his neck painfully to stare at the sheer rock face dusted with fine snow. It shot above them like the canyon walls of the Leske Road. He noticed that he labored for a full breath.

"That would require returning to where we rested and searching again for alternate routes, which may not exist. It would take too much time."

While returning might reunite them with the others, they were running out of time to locate their quarry. Between the storm and their own exhaustion, they had set out at nearly Axiom dawn according to Kalis's timepiece.

"I'm used to Idrilia's impromptu decisions, but you have clearly thought this through. If you say we go this way, we go."

"Then I will lead. I have walked many such paths before. I will keep you safe."

"I trust you—friend."

Kalis's heart warmed at his choice of term. Something had changed since their separation from the others. He was glad to have the opportunity to learn more about the Highblood and regretted not spending more time with her previously. He could use her reserved confidence in his efforts to overcome Idrilia's stubbornness.

In front of him, Vayriel maneuvered deftly over several rock outcroppings, not unlike a jeroti, and approached the cliff. She shifted her stance so that her right foot was forward, toe pointing the length of the ledge, and swiveled her waist to bring her back nearly flush with the stone. Her left foot slid back. She clutched her spear close to her body in a double-handed grip, parallel to the ground. It reminded Kalis of the footing of a dance Kilahym had shown the Seekers upon reaching Keepers' Rest. Kalis had politely declined to join him.

Mimicking her approach, Kalis followed Vayriel while allowing space between them for any unforeseen stumbles. A strong wind gusted, though it did not carry the biting cold that had heralded the storm. Vayriel called out warnings and advice as they began the meandering ascent. Several tense minutes passed in silence.

"*Basja!*" Kalis's foot slipped, kicking a small stone into the abyss. He froze and stared into the depths, his heart pounding against his chest. Fear constricted his throat.

"Mind your footing," Vayriel called over her shoulder.

"Sorry. This is a little different than riding on the back of a solendrake. They stick to the walls for you, you know."

"If it is easier for you, you can wait behind, and I will continue alone."

"Of course not. We do this together." Kalis took a slow, deep breath and glanced over the ledge, not much wider than the length of his foot, once more. His eyes moved across the gap to linger on a shape which nearly blended with the snow-speckled rocks.

"Do jeroti live only in the mountains of Heathström?" Kalis asked as he began to shuffle behind Vayriel once again.

"Mostly, though Mo'fa has at least one tale of the jeroti living across the whole range. Why do you ask?"

"I thought maybe I saw one, but if I did it's gone now. I'm probably seeing things."

Vayriel halted a moment before stepping forward. "I do not feel Orgar, but to have a jeroti near, in vision or otherwise, is a good sign."

"I'll take your word for it." Kalis gritted his teeth as he navigated the treacherous path.

A short while later, Vayriel exclaimed that she could see the end, a bowl-shaped plateau that marked the final step to Mount Hoestra's cap. Though the ledge grew to the width of two arm spans, Kalis remained behind Vayriel until they reached smooth terrain twenty paces away.

The open area appeared ahead of Kalis as he rounded the rock face. The flat, snow-covered basin was speckled with stones but otherwise unmarked, and the escarpment surrounding them on three sides blocked the wind that had been their constant companion the last few hours.

"There it is. But I don't see any caves." Kalis removed his pack to stretch his arms and shoulders, tension releasing from balancing on the ledge. The final ridge wove against the pale sky like a string on the wind, encircling the back of the seemingly empty plateau.

"At times there are caves one can only see from above. We can climb there"—Vayriel indicated a small crag—"and use the rocks to pull ourselves onto the slope. Then we follow the ridge, like walking a frozen river."

They rested only for a few moments. Kalis felt his breathing return to an even pace, though still quicker than he was used to. They began to climb, Kalis using both arms to anchor his body, pushing and pulling where needed, as he maneuvered his feet from outcropping to outcropping to follow the Highblood. The stone projections rose like a disheveled stairway. He was thankful for all the hours spent training with the other Prioriates, which enabled him to keep pace with Vayriel.

Scrambling through the last snowbank, Kalis slung his leg onto the ridge and stood. His breath caught as he absorbed the view from Mount Hoestra for the first time. He had been so preoccupied with looking where he was going that he had missed the sweeping panorama.

"This is amazing. I can see the entire coastline. That way should be north, where the Reef of Pillars lies"—Kalis pointed to their left—"and back that way would be the Cliffs of Odium I told you about, you know." Rotating carefully, he motioned to the southeast. From this vantage point, all he could see was a flat landscape before him, as if, while he and Vayriel had been climbing, some magic had flattened all of Etherea save for the mountain range they stood upon.

Kalis marveled at the clouds below, like scraps of white cloth scattered across the desert sand. Beneath his feet, the width of the ridge was no wider than his stance before it dropped into a sheer slope. Kalis's eyes caught up with his mind. He flailed his arms, dropping to one knee and shoving a fist into the snow.

"Take my hand. We go together," Vayriel assured him, turning back with her free arm outstretched.

Kalis looked down the slope once more before placing his hand in hers.

Once again in single file, the pair proceeded with caution, following the narrow band to the point where the peak gathered its lines like a tetrahedron.

"There." The Highblood pointed with a gloved finger.

Kalis followed the trajectory and found himself looking at several entrances at the back of the basin. Their hungry mouths had been hidden behind boulders camouflaged by snow. Now he could see the dark splotches that foreshadowed greater depths.

"Vayriel," Kalis urged, "you should be the one to claim the hide. Without your guidance, in more ways than one, I would not have made it here." He withdrew the silver container from Jannu from within his coat and presented it to Vayriel. Its surface flashed in the sunlight rebounding from the snow.

"That is not necessary. You have been a partner in this journey."

"All the same, I'd like for you to have the honor." Kalis pushed his hand closer. "And I know 'Dril would want the same."

With a slight hesitation, Vayriel took the silver canister, and placed it in her bag. "Thank you, Kalis. Let us begin. I am anxious to find Orgar and the others. And I am sure you are eager to tell Idrilia of our success."

Kalis's face clouded. "Yes. We will see."

With the same carefulness, they advanced down the sloped ridge and descended the short rock face into the basin. Kalis led the way as they shuffled across the empty plateau.

They were halfway across the basin when they heard a low rumble that seemed to emanate from every side of the surrounding escarpment.

"An avalanche?" Kalis asked.

"No."

Vayriel's wary tone gave him pause. She spun the way they had arrived, spear brandished before her.

"Trägen."

Kalis's stomach knotted. He reached into his belt satchel, gripping a crystal as he pivoted the same direction as Vayriel.

A creature twice their height stood on its hind legs before them, its elongated muzzle open in a second roar. Kalis's head would fit easily into its gaping mouth, after being torn apart by its large front paws. Its exposed claws were the only dark part on its body beyond its ruby eyes.

The trägen lowered to all fours with a thud that echoed in the basin. Its wide head bobbed and swayed as it peered at Vayriel and Kalis with one eye then the other. Two thick horns arched out of the top of its head and curled down to its chin, while three thin, straight horns protruded from its forehead in a vertical row. Kalis gulped. Those horns and claws could easily shred them both.

Out of habit, Kalis crossed his arms over his chest and then dropped them to his sides, signaling a question to Vayriel. Remembering he was not with Idrilia, he repeated it verbally.

"Left or right?"

"I will take the right. Do not let it behind you."

The trägen lumbered forward; the muscles in its powerful shoulders rippling with each movement.

"Can you make that protective bubble again?" Kalis squeezed his crystal in a death grip, feeling the imminent heat of its contained energy.

"Yes, but that will limit our mobility. You must stay close to me."

"Do it."

Vayriel removed her eye covering and let it dangle around her neck. Her hood fell back, her peach hair stark against the white. She closed her eyes.

Before she could form the sphere, Kalis shook the crystal in his hand and launched it. The crystal exploded, fire erupting between the trägen's paws and up its chest. The creature roared louder than before, its chin tilting to the sky. Kalis saw that some of its long white coat was singed and blackened.

"Why did you do that?" Vayriel sounded alarmed.

"I wanted to scare it, make it stop advancing."

"A trägen cannot be scared. As long as it has breath left within it, it will come."

Kalis wagered she was correct. Although he had never faced a trägen, he'd heard the stories in Priorium of tenacious beasts who hunted for sport as well as sustenance.

As if the beast understood Vayriel's words, it began to lope faster. Kalis braced himself as her shield blossomed into existence around them. The creature thundered by, its black claws swiping at its prey. The Highblood and the Sondrinel flinched, but the assault bounced harmlessly off Vayriel's barrier. The beast roared in frustration and slid to a halt, spinning around too quickly for the duo to take advantage of its failed attack.

"It is too agile for this approach."

"I see that. How long can you maintain our protection?"

"I am uncertain. I was able to prolong its duration when I was reinforced with energy from Zinvar and Kilahym. But to draw from you now would weaken you, and we cannot risk that."

The trägen approached more slowly this time, stalking Kalis and Vayriel with the measured patience of an apex predator. Despite its bulk, the beast moved with a deadly grace. When it drew close enough, the trägen reared back on its hind legs and struck with its front paws. Blow after blow rained against Vayriel's projected defense. She staggered and her face turned pale, but the shield held. Kalis lifted his blade and slashed at the exposed undersides of the monster's paws.

Abandoning its ineffective attack, the creature shuffled backward once again on all four legs. Putting its nose to the ground, the trägen sniffed, inching forward. Kalis debated the next action he should take.

He feared the beast had found a weakness. If he waited, Vayriel's strength would be spent maintaining the shield, and when it failed, they would be overpowered.

Vayriel extended her spear, blunt end first, and thumped the bridge of the trägen's nose. It snapped at the pole, sharp fangs bared, but Vayriel recoiled the weapon back within the bubble. White paws swatted at the barrier, which held but contracted in size.

Kalis thought about what Idrilia would do and seized onto an offensive tactic.

He pulled an iridescent blue-green crystal from his belt and tossed it over the trägen's back, where it hovered and began to rotate. Faster and faster it spun, until thin lines of cerulean energy spidered forth. The air crackled and he saw the beast's fur stand on end. The bolts jumped and danced like whips of rope from the crystal to lash at the creature.

The trägen quavered beneath the onslaught of energy, similar to but less powerful than Adjira's attacks in the desert. The trägen stumbled backward. It shook its head and the glow in its ruby eyes diminished. The bolts flickered out as the crystal's rotation slowed, until it finally stopped turning and plunged to the ground.

Kalis readied another crystal.

"Kalis, no!" Vayriel cried, her face marked with concern. Her eyes were fixed on the creature, which had fallen over on its side. "Do not take its life!"

"It's either it or us."

The bubble around them vanished, either from Vayriel's worry or fatigue.

"No. There is always another way." The Highblood shook her head. "If we show mercy to the Mother's creations, they may show mercy to us."

"But…then how will we get the hide? You said you would be ready for this!" Kalis couldn't believe what he was hearing. The entire journey up the mountain would be for naught.

"I…had hoped we could disable it, enough to take only what we need but let it live."

"So, your people never kill anything?"

"I did not say that. We do when we must for survival." Her hand strayed to the hood of her coat. "I do not think this is such an occasion."

Kalis looked back to where the creature's stomach heaved in slow breaths, its enflamed eyes now shut. Maybe Vayriel was right. But he did not like the thought of leaving a vengeful creature behind them.

"We should be quick, then."

"I agree."

They had barely taken a few steps before the beast rolled onto its feet and charged.

Kalis froze. His weapon quivered in his hand, and he contemplated hurling it at where he believed the trägen's heart would be. But then he noticed that Vayriel's hands were cupped near her mouth, small roots poking out of her fingers. She dropped the seedling at her feet. A wave of dusty purple vines snaked across the snowy landscape, some thin, some as thick as two fingers. They grew ferociously toward the trägen, then sprang from the ground and enwrapped the beast, binding its limbs and body. They coiled and tightened as the trägen struggled to stand, only to be pulled down again. Small turquoise flowers with flowing red wisps at their centers bloomed along the vines.

The trägen roared, fighting furiously against its restraints. Its bellows of frustration were answered by a howl that carried across the plateau.

Kalis searched for the source, finding it atop the escarpment directly above them. The creature tilted its head back, issuing a long, modulating *ah-woo* sound.

"A jeroti. I wasn't imagining him after all."

"Her."

"What?"

"This jeroti is female." Vayriel pointed to her own head with two fingers, indicating the crystalline horns between the sky-blue-tipped ears of this jeroti.

Vayriel's eyes suddenly widened.

"Run!"

Kalis glanced toward the trägen. The flowers were wilting and the vines seemed to be freezing. He heard the dried plants crack and splinter as he raced through the snow after Vayriel. From the corner of his eye, Kalis saw the jeroti descending the sheer rock face in great bounds.

Abruptly, their enemy was before them. They skidded to a halt, placing their weapons between them and the attacker. A brown-and-cream blur collided with the trägen as the female jeroti came to the Seekers' aid. Claws Kalis had never seen used by Orgar extended and pierced the trägen's neck and chest.

"This way!" Vayriel rushed left, the direction the jeroti had leaped from.

Their ally landed with her forelegs bent low, neck arched, and fangs exposed in a snarl as her blue-tipped tails quivered high in the air. The trägen and jeroti circled one another as Kalis and Vayriel ran. They made their way toward the far wall. Kalis heard the clash of claws and teeth, but did not dare turn to see.

"We should gain the high ground!" he called as they ran. "Attack from above."

"We are as likely to fall. Distance will be our ally. Back to the way we entered!"

Glancing to make sure Kalis followed, Vayriel hastened to the edge. She slowed enough to scurry onto the slippery ledge that would lead them back.

Kalis hesitated when he heard a high-pitched yelp and turned back to the titanic struggle.

"Kalis, hurry!" Vayriel's voice sounded behind him. She was already several paces onto the outcropping.

The jeroti bled from many wounds as did the trägen, and the much larger beast raised its giant paw to strike again. Without thinking, Kalis launched a crystal that gathered snow from the ground beneath it as it flew, swirling and coalescing into a spear of ice that struck the haunches of the trägen. The jeroti used the distraction to sidestep out of harm's way and assail the trägen's side.

Kalis followed his companion. Once he stepped onto the ledge, she continued forward. They advanced as quickly as they dared. He moved slower than the Highblood as he concentrated on finding firm footing. They were quickly running out of wider ledge and would soon need to slow for the narrowing—a treacherous undertaking, even under the calmest of circumstances.

Then he felt a vibration beneath his feet. Claws scratched on the stone immediately behind him, and the trägen's triumphant roar echoed across the mountain.

Kalis looked back as the beast reared up, ready to deliver a death blow. Then it roared in agony as the jeroti struck it from behind. It crashed down on its front legs, its weight making the rock lurch and tremble under Kalis. He stumbled, and an overwhelming sickness filled his stomach.

Vayriel whipped around, her eyes wide, peach strands of hair trailing her in slow motion. Kalis reached for her as the ledge crumbled beneath him and the trägen. Her mouth opened.

Kalis cried out as he and the beast tumbled into the abyss.

CHAPTER 44

"Kalis!"

His name shrieked from her lips.

Vayriel watched his face fill with terror, and he slipped out of her reach, down into the depths of the chasm.

"No!"

The word was elongated, held in an anguished cry. She reached out, as if by making the motion she could stop time and save him. She tried to connect to the life force, to pull something from the Mother-of-All, but nothing happened. No familiar weight within her, no tingle at her fingertips. It was as if every sense had been cut away as Kalis vanished from her sight.

Vayriel inched closer to the edge, as close as she dared, and again tried to summon her energy. Anything to grab him. All she felt was emptiness.

Below there was naught but darkness that stared up at her in mocking silence. She could see nothing. A faint crash echoed from the depths, the crumbled ledge slamming into the ground.

"Kalis," she whispered, anguish twisting her lips and brow. She fell to her knees. "My friend. I have failed you."

Movement to her left pulled away her gaze. The female jeroti leaped over the void that had consumed Kalis, landing before Vayriel. She bent her head, touching her faceted horns to the ground. From her jaws dangled a torn-off piece of the trägen's pelt. Of the beast itself, there was no sign.

Vayriel sat back on her heels, reaching a tentative hand toward the jeroti to take the bloody fragment. The creature-daughter's pink tongue darted forward and licked Vayriel's palm. Though she wore gloves, Vayriel imagined the familiar sensation on her skin.

Her thoughts cleared marginally in the jeroti's presence, and after securing the hide in Jannu's vessel, Vayriel continued her search for Kalis. She lay flat in the snow and crawled forward until her head stuck over the edge, scouring the crevasse for a handhold he could have grabbed or a shelf he might have landed on. He could be injured and unable to signal for help.

Vayriel's heart sank. A sheer drop was all that met her eyes.

With limbs shaking, she pushed herself up from the cold ground and stood. Without her life-friend, and now without Kalis, a hollowness filled her chest. She was alone. The jeroti, licking her side, glanced up at the Highblood. She was injured, and blood marred her pale fur.

"Thank you for coming to our aid," Vayriel said softly, and reached for the satchel that contained the herbs and seeds from Mo'mo. Locating the dried sprig she needed—a cluster of white flowers with pink-orange centers—Vayriel used her mortar and pestle with a clump of mud to grind the farrow to a paste.

"I would like to heal you, if you will let me." She moved slowly toward the noble creature, relieved when the jeroti did not move.

Kneeling, Vayriel applied the pale orange paste gently to the gashes on the animal's side, then placed her hands above the injury. Closing her eyes, she reached for her inner spark. Her shoulders relaxed when she found it immediately. Similar to her method of creating a protective sphere, Vayriel *pushed* some of her gathered energy away from her, feeling it tingle through her arms and hands to her fingertips.

Her connection to the life force was open again, and as she linked to all of the Mother's creation, images and feelings swirled through her mind. As with Orgar, the female jeroti's presence enhanced her connection. She heard the breathing, the heartbeat, sensed the same basic manners of all creature-sons and creature-daughters and was reminded that she was never truly alone.

She saw the spirit of this jeroti and felt an untamable vitality, fierce and invulnerable. Vayriel gasped as she realized that this was the essence of *all* jeroti within the life force; they were all connected, sharing, guiding, teaching, and healing. With one paw, this jeroti touched the spirit-world while the rest of her body existed here. This must be how Orgar seemed to know so much, even before it happened, and how he enhanced Vayriel's own connection to the life force.

The healing began to sap what remained of her strength. She opened her eyes and withdrew her hands from the jeroti's side, the last image fading, a vision of a complete spirit: Highblood and jeroti intertwined. Though the injury persisted, the gashes were smaller and shallower than they had been, and the poultice covered the open skin. Vayriel was satisfied that she had at least expedited the healing process.

Taking her spear in hand, Vayriel stood and regarded the length of the ledge. Glancing behind her, she addressed the jeroti.

"Thank you, creature-daughter, for you have lessened my pain as well. I must continue my search for my friend. I would welcome your presence, if you choose to follow me."

Picking her footing carefully, Vayriel traversed the path she and Kalis had crossed together and returned to the more open terrain of the mountain's slope.

The cold wind lashed her face. She raised her hood and donned her snow-eyes to combat the harshness of the mountain once more.

A sense of comfort washed suddenly over Vayriel, and she looked up to find the horned jeroti before her, twin tails moving slowly up and down.

The pair circled the crevasse, the jeroti at Vayriel's side, looking for any means to enter it. If Vayriel had thought to find evidence that Kalis had somehow managed to arrest his fall, she found none from this side either. She walked the length of the chasm, the passage of time lost to her. With each minute that wandered by, the hope of finding him slipped further away.

Vayriel finally stopped, forced to admit that there was no way to follow Kalis's descent. And if she did not return evidence of their triumph in time, she would fail him again.

"I hope you found the true light, my friend. May the jeroti guide you to the spirit-world where I will see you again someday."

Vayriel should have stopped her long descent several hours ago, but still she walked. Quietly, she chanted a song accented by her footfalls, a lament for when one of the coil was taken back to the spirit-world. She sang but one stanza before a sob gripped her throat. Turning her head to the sky, Vayriel looked for the Watcher, and finding his rays, she cried out in sorrow and disbelief. An othwit alighted high on a nearby tree branch and hooted softly.

For much of the journey she had been alone, the female jeroti parting from her silently a short way down the slope. Though Vayriel knew that the Mother-of-All was around her, the appearance of a creature-daughter helped her overlook her cold-stiffened legs. She felt a flicker of recognition before another, stronger presence flooded her life force connection and she whimpered, body trembling.

A mass of white bounded toward her. Kilahym appeared from behind a snowbank knocked sideways by Orgar. Both rushed toward her, the others appearing quickly behind them.

"Hail, victorious Vayriel! I knew you two would be finished already. Jannu had quite the experience while you—where is Kalis?" Kilahym scanned the nearby area.

Meeting Orgar, Vayriel dropped her knees to the snow and wrapped her arms around her life-friend. She welcomed the subsequent warm embrace Kilahym threw around her shoulders as he knelt beside her. She breathed in the scent of parchment and ink that lingered on him, both companions a salve to her wounds.

"What is it? What's happened?" Kilahym whispered.

Looking up, Vayriel's eyes met Idrilia's. She stood, her leg pressed against Orgar's his side, and she rested her hand on his head, drawing strength from him.

She fought to keep her voice even. "Kalis—Kalis fell." The Highblood told the group, who now surrounded her in a half-circle, of the battle with the trägen. The mountain winds blew stronger.

"You could not retrieve him?" Kharnek's entrance to the conversation surprised Vayriel. She looked at him and shook her head slowly.

"I searched for many hours. I saw no way down."

"I don't believe it," Idrilia announced. "When he fell, did you see anything surround him? Was there a flash of light? Any sign that he used a crystal?"

"I know what I saw. He was there, then there was nothing."

"Show me where," Idrilia took a step up the slope. A spear-flash snaked across a far-off cloud.

"Should we complete the trial?" Zinvar suggested. "The time limit swiftly approaches."

A distant rumble murmured down the mountain. Vayriel thought she could feel it beneath her feet.

Idrilia whirled. "If the Trials matter more than one of our lives, then they can rot beneath the sands."

Zinvar opened his hands. "It just seems that Vayriel has done a thorough search."

Idrilia huffed. She took a step away, then paused as a pack of white toravs ran through the Seekers.

Kilahym yelped. "Well, this is unusual."

Vayriel gripped her spear tighter. "There is fear and…" She tilted her head, hearing the mountain tremble. "We must go. The creatures are anxious of a snow-slide. We must get to shelter."

"Wen sees something, but it isn't clear. She…she's flying back to us. Fine, we retreat. But we come back," Idrilia stalked passed Vayriel, trekking back through the snow.

The Seekers hurried down the mountain, looking without joy for the white dome and pillared portico of Keepers' Rest.

"Into these, place a memory of Kalis you treasure," Jannu explained, handing a crystal to each of them. The Keeper seemed fully recovered from whatever had happened, which Kilahym had been strangely reluctant to talk further about, and Jannu seemed not to recall anything more than a bump to the head. Vayriel and the remaining Seekers had coaxed from Idrilia the story of her and Kalis locating the Penumbra fragment as they had all reminisced about their time with their lost friend in preparation for this ceremony.

They gathered on the northern side of the building, overlooking a dry, orange-hued valley. Orgar lay at Vayriel's feet, a paw resting on her foot, while the others stood in a scattered pattern facing the Keeper. Vayriel looked at Idrilia, her face a mix of anger and sadness. Jannu had told them that the mountain pass Vayriel had descended would be blocked for at least a week while the slab of snow slowly dissipated in its slow, final spread. Recent storms and the collapse of the ledge Kalis had fallen from likely triggered the event. The route north to continue the Trials remained unimpeded, so reluctantly, Idrilia accepted there was nothing more she could do but press on.

Kharnek stepped forward, silently handing a crystal to Jannu. He stepped away without a word. Jannu lifted his hand. The crystal cradled in his palm stood on end and rose slowly. Though the sky was bright, the teardrop-shaped prism glimmered with an inner radiance as it continued to rise.

Vayriel watched it draw closer to the thin clouds and thought about the memory she wanted to send. Jannu said the sending of memories was a Sondrinel tradition; one that honored those who had left this world and returned to the life force. Many recollections clamored for her attention, but each had one thing in common: they showed Kalis's kindness. And the most precious memory of him, Vayriel found, was her last. Kalis sharing the musical othwit; Kalis making the tent warm; Kalis calling her "*friend.*"

Her memory ready, Vayriel closed her eyes and willed the thought to jump from her fingers into the crystal clutched between her hands. She relinquished the small prism to Jannu, and he lofted it behind Kharnek's.

Zinvar stepped forward and mumbled an apology, something about being unsure if he had used the crystal correctly. Again, the Keeper held his hand high and propelled the memory-laden object; it followed the same path as the others.

After Zinvar, Kilahym approached. "Kalis, son of Sondrine, warrior, Truthseeker, and friend. Know that despite our sadness, in spite of our loss, we will finish what we started—what you started with us. The greatest trial of all will be completing this journey without your presence."

He handed his crystal to Jannu, then cleared his throat.

"If it is acceptable, I would like to play a song." The bard withdrew the green ocarina from his neck. "Very tasteful, I assure you."

At Jannu's nod, Kilahym began to play. The airy, whistling tones broke the silence as he walked back to stand with the group. His music continued, a slow song that quavered with vibrato on the sustained notes. The melody reminded Vayriel of the first time he had played the instrument and how it had brought her memories of amber eyes above a fire.

Wordlessly, Idrilia presented her crystal to the Keeper and returned to her position on the far right of the group, where she stood apart. Kilahym's tune had no noticeable effect on her.

Whining softly at Vayriel's feet, Orgar pushed on his front paws and raised into a sitting position. To Jannu's right, the snow began to swirl. At first, Vayriel thought it was the wind, but the circulation was concentrated in one area. It grew into a whirling column as tall as Jannu, then sections moved independently of one another, some dropping low while others moved out and back in. It reminded Vayriel of the light painters at her Sending.

Kilahym's tune ended, and the snow drifted lazily to join the rest of the accumulated flakes on the ground. Zinvar quietly complimented Kilahym's song and excused himself. Jannu approached Idrilia; though his mouth moved, Vayriel could not hear the words. The Keeper turned away and walked toward his abode.

"I need to get my things, and my dulcimer," Kilahym whispered, stepping closer to Vayriel. "Do you want to come back inside?"

"Orgar and I will stay here," she replied softly, watching Idrilia.

"We shan't be very long. Come inside if you get cold. I'll make sure the others come this way before we start the journey north. And Vayriel?"

She pried her eyes away from the Sondrinel, turning to meet Kilahym's concerned gaze.

"It wasn't your fault. You know that, right? There was nothing you could have done."

She nodded, but she did not agree. She had replayed that awful moment over and over again in her mind as she had descended the mountain, seeing all the ways she could have used her connection to the Mother-of-All to save Kalis.

Her people taught that passing back into the spirit-world was a natural part of traversing the true path. But that passing was typically not sudden. While it held little comfort for what had already happened, Vayriel was reminded of a comment her Mo'mo had made to their Path-Shaper: *The path of the coil is shorter than your eyes tell you. Take care to do in this Daughter's Journey what you may not in the next.*

Vayriel watched Kilahym trudge away a few paces, as a weight like a fluttering vandling grew within her stomach.

"Kilahym?" she called after him.

He spun around immediately. "Yes?"

"I…thank you."

Kilahym bowed, then entered Keepers' Rest.

Vayriel looked back at Idrilia and watched the crystals fade into the clouds with her. They were tiny dots, small sparks of remembrance making their way to the spirit-world. Idrilia held her chin high as the last crystal faded from view.

A faint howl carried on the wind from somewhere high on the mountain— the long, mournful cry of a female jeroti. Orgar stretched his neck and pointed his nose to the sky, harmonizing with the agonizing lament

CHAPTER 45

A low growl rumbled in the silent cavern. Kalis scrambled away from the pile of stone that covered the fallen beast. He thought it was dead. Dislodged rock fragments clattered to the ground as the monster shifted and rose, its baleful red eyes scanning the gloom. It snarled when it spotted its prey cowering. Kalis stumbled to his feet and fled blindly from the subterranean chamber; the thud of his pursuer's footfalls shadowing his own as he dodged stalagmites and other stone projections. His breath came in quick pants as he lengthened his stride.

The right leg of Kalis's loose pants caught on a rock projection. It tore the fabric and left a gash on his calf. He yelped as he lost his balance and tumbled to the ground. The Sondrinel's head cracked against the stone and white spots burst across his vision, mingling with the milky glow of the sibilstones in the cavern ceiling. A triumphant roar spurred the young man back into motion. Too close. There was no time to flee, so…fight? *No*, he decided, *hide*. He made for a gap in the side of the main cavern, a narrow crevice that he doubted the monster could squeeze into. The scratch of claws against the sediment reached Kalis's ears as he wriggled through. Crouching down against the wall of the passage, he curled up into a ball, making as compact a silhouette as possible. He froze when the snuffling sounds of the beast filtered through the opening. It could smell the blood from his leg. Suddenly his concealment felt much less secure.

Something warm trickled onto his forehead. Was he bleeding? Gently, the Prioriate reached up and touched the sticky liquid. His finger came away covered in a substance so dark a purple it was almost black. Blood, but not his. Kalis slowly raised his eyes and found himself gazing at the underside of the creature's elongated jaw. Deep violet matted its white fur. Apparently, it did not survive the fall into the cavern unscathed. The beast sniffed, its powerful lungs seeming to draw in all the air in the confined space. Kalis trembled despite his best efforts to remain still. A cramp stabbed his left calf muscle, but he dared not extend his leg to relieve the tautness. Time slowed to a crawl as the creature withdrew its snout inch by inch.

Kalis slumped with a strong exhalation. He uncoiled his legs from their uncomfortable posture and prepared to stand. That was when the beast struck. Its bulk slammed against the rock walls. Long black claws swiped through the gap, rending the air as easily as they would human flesh. Its prey staggered back, narrowly avoiding the assault. The beleaguered Seeker retreated deeper into the passage, unsure how far back it might lead or if something worse awaited in its depths. His back crashed against a cool, smooth surface, and he spun around to face the glossy barrier. Despite its sheen, his visage did not reflect from the material; what little light there was in the crevice seemed drawn into its depths. The beast behind him must have sensed that he was moving beyond its grasp. It roared and attacked the walls with renewed vigor, and Kalis shoved against the impediment without thought, heart racing. To his shock, it yielded beneath his touch. A pale green luminescence radiated across the planes of the angular surface as he passed through it, and profound silence swallowed the monster's howls.

"Hello?" He posed the question to the perfectly opaque darkness he found himself in beyond the barrier.

Flickers of verdant light chased themselves around random angles, their edges visible only when illuminated. What was revealed suggested a chamber of unfamiliar geometry. As Kalis's eyes adjusted, he realized that the dancing points of light originated from a node in front of him. It rose from the floor to waist height, its contours strangely organic, like the "heart" of the sea creature that Kilahym often described. He crept toward it.

"Is anyone there?"

Again, silence met his inquiry. Whatever unexpected benevolence allowed him through the wall clearly didn't feel like talking. He drew nearer to the node, almost close enough to touch it.

Abruptly, the green light flared beneath the soles of Kalis's boots, then erupted across his body in a form-fitting latticework. He flinched at the radiance, which disappeared as quickly as it came. For a brief moment, he thought he glimpsed an outline of himself in the interminable darkness, rotating above the node as if it was being examined by an unknown entity. Then a single line shot away from Kalis's feet, jagging left then right across the floor to vanish behind an invisible corner. The glowing path pulsed when he took a tentative step forward.

Kalis followed the beacon for an indeterminable span of time and distance. The eerie flickers of viridian energy sparked at random across the featureless void of his surroundings. He couldn't imagine what would inhabit such a disorienting environment. Chitters and clicks emanated from unseen sources, setting his teeth on edge. His stomach growled, reminding him that it had been nearly a day since he last ate. The Sondrinel reached absently to his waist and cursed. His sword was there, but the supply bag was gone, likely buried in the pile of rocks back in the main cavern. No food, no water—the thought brought the dryness of his throat and cracked lips to the forefront of his consciousness. Perhaps once he got out of this place, whatever it was, he could find an underground stream and quench his thirst. Then he could survive long enough to find sustenance.

At length, Kalis's luminous guide brought him to a barrier much like the one he previously encountered. This time when he stepped through, his stomach lurched as if he missed the edge of the next step on a stairway. Then he felt solid ground beneath his feet, and light once again flooded his vision, but this was different: warm and amber. Kalis sank to his knees, a bubble of laughter escaping his throat.

Through some inexplicable power, the barrier brought him to a sea cave. Sunlight poured through the maw-like opening of the cave. A sea breeze whistled around the toothy stalactites that dangled from the upper edge, accompanied by the crash of waves. He breathed in the salty air, reveling in the rush of sensations.

Bursts of red and white exploded across his sight. Kalis grunted and pitched forward, catching himself before his face slammed into the rock. Combat instincts asserted themselves, and he rolled left. His assailant's weapon crashed against the ground where his head had been a moment ago. The young man sprang to his feet and drew his curved sword, shaking off the pain of the initial strike. He barely got his blade up in time to parry the next attack. The force of the blow shook Kalis's forearms, and his grip on the hilt faltered. He spun away, buying himself time to assess whom he faced.

His opponent wore the same loose, desert garb as Kalis, their features obscured by a similar brown headscarf and eye covering. When they swung their own weapon—a straightblade much longer and wider than the curved sword—the beige fabric pulled against huge muscles in their chest and biceps. If this continued as a contest of strength, Kalis was certain of the outcome, especially weakened as he was by fatigue. Instead of parrying the next swing, he batted it aside and danced away, moving closer to the edge of the sea cave. Then, he realized his mistake. As he drew nearer to the lip, mindful of his footing, he saw a drop of several hundred feet to the whitecaps below. Sheer cliff faces stretched out to either side, plummeting into the sea. He knew where he was now, for what good that did. Vayriel was right about the Cliffs of Odium having an ominous name.

"No escape for you, little Sentinel," the burly swordsman taunted. He spun the straightblade in a dramatic flourish as he approached.

"What do you want from me?"

"You should ask him." The attacker pointed behind Kalis with his sword. Twisting his head around, the Prioriate's eyes widened. A ship made of redbark wood, much like the trading vessels he saw in Ettra, hovered impossibly before the entrance of the cave. An imposing figure faced the opponents from the railing, strong arms crossed. He wore a crimson vest that left much of his tanned chest exposed and billowing white pants. Twin daggers dangled at his hips.

"Take him."

The command came in a rich baritone. Belatedly, Kalis understood the distraction as another blow fell and he crumpled to the cave floor.

CHAPTER 46

Basja, it was hot. It felt like fire crystals floated around her, radiating heat. Idrilia had never journeyed this far north, and though she had seen the expanse of desert barrens awaiting them from the ledge of Keepers' Rest, she was still disconcerted by the terrain. It was like crossing the salt flats of Eduma, but with jagged hills that gradually decreased in height the further the Truthseekers trudged from the Agermath Range, the foothills becoming plains. They were three days out from the outpost at Mount Hoestra, which left almost another two to reach the northern coastline, not including time to rest.

And the whispers followed her.

Through the eye slit of her orange headscarf, Idrilia glanced at the four followers a dozen paces back. They were slow, casual with their pace. She silently cursed her own suggestion to not retrieve the beasts of burden at the base of the mountain. Strategically, it was better to leave the sunlit creatures rather than take them through Heathström and into the darkness of Komor—where Jannu had directed them to go for their next Trial—but Idrilia missed the speed and ease afforded by the solendrakes and camelids.

"Yoohoo, dilly Drilly!" The bard's tenor voice lilted above the idle chitchat. "Would you mind slowing your admirable gait to accommodate those of us who are, uh, unused to your arid climate?"

The lone Sondrinel growled and shifted direction to avoid stepping on a low, pale green succulent—a rare sight on the northern branch of the Leske road.

Was Kalis lying broken at the bottom of a crevasse as he waited in agony for someone to come? Idrilia wondered again if they were too quick to assume the worst. All they had was the Highblood's word, and Idrilia needed proof. Kalis would have come back for her, she knew it.

Guilt broke through the anger, which had been her constant companion for hours, in a wave of nausea, but she pushed it away and gripped the hilt of her right dagger, driving the group toward the coast and away from the dwindling remains of the road. She knew their whispers contained judgment—of her leadership abilities without Kalis and her proficiency to lead them through the desert. She'd prove them wrong.

"Did she hear me?" Kilahym's voice continued, subdued. "Her strides are like a ratufa in pursuit of the last redbark nutlet before the finishing winds blow through and knock it from its perch."

"Let her be." Vayriel's voice joined the hush. "She would not leave us behind, and we are keeping close enough for signals."

"Do you know the wordless—voiceless—um, language of the Sentinels?"

"I do not. But my people listen to the silence of the fields and forests. It speaks without words and teaches us how to be at peace. I will know if Idrilia has something to convey to us."

"Ah, I see. Well, I just want our happy—not you, of course, stoic warrior, I would never call you *happy*—little group back together."

"I prefer she stay where she is," Kharnek intoned.

"She has been very focused since the memorial," Zinvar commented.

"Exactly!" Kilahym exclaimed, then lowered his voice again to a whisper. "Exactly. More so than usual, if I may be so bold."

"Kilahym," the Highblood cautioned.

"Hmm?"

"The loss of her friend affects us all, and we are all dealing with it differently. Give her time."

Time. No longer was it counting down to her betrothal. Time was hers again. Idrilia clenched her teeth, disappointed that her thoughts had taken this new direction.

"Well, whenever we find ourselves at the conclusion of this journey, I shall endeavor to immortalize these events in a grand play. The first act shall be entitled 'The Tragedy of Kalis the Brave,' the story of a young Sondrinel taken from his beloved too soon by a beast of the mountains. And the Council will declare a day of mourning each time it is performed."

Idrilia spun, her fighting robe whirling around her knees. "The Council is made of fools," she spat. But they couldn't know how ridiculous it was that the Council let this farce continue knowing what they did of Komor's current actions, punishing Idrilia instead of taking worthwhile steps.

"And you. You're supposed to be an expert of the mountains." Though she could not see the rest of her face, Idrilia recognized the wounded crease around Vayriel's eyes.

"That's hardly fair to Vayriel!"

Vayriel shook her head, "I lost my connection to the Mother-of-All, Kilahym. I was unable to save him."

Kilahym stopped, barring Vayriel's path with his hands splayed before him. The tail of Kilahym's kaleidoscopic scarf twitched slightly on a gentle but warm breeze. "It's still not your fault. Such events, moments, in the space of a heartbeat, should not be things attributed to within someone's control."

Idrilia pivoted north, turning her back to the pair. Kilahym's defense of Vayriel was becoming tiresome. Their voices faded as she placed distance between them.

She regretted the vehement words she hurled at the person who was the closest thing to a friend she had on this path of dust and dirt. It wasn't Vayriel's fault. But neither could Idrilia let go of the possibility that the Highblood might have left Kalis to die.

Looking above, she saw her othwit with wings spread wide, gliding with them. Idrilia whistled. Wen circled and dropped lower, a chittering call preluding her descent. Idrilia watched her glide to her outstretched forearm. The bird climbed to perch on her shoulder, the familiar action soothing Idrilia. She scratched the soft feathers of Wen's sternum and focused her eyes on the dry terrain. The group approached a cluster of scattered jeroti-sized boulders which lined the shallow trench—all that remained of the Leske river north of the mountains.

"Thank you for watching Orgar."

Idrilia stiffened at the familiar contralto voice. She chastised herself for letting the woman catch up during her introspection.

"I did very little."

"My friend. May I show you the moon?"

Idrilia frowned. "I assume you don't mean literally."

Vayriel shook the folds of her headscarf. "You offered to free me of my fears by showing me the moon. I want to offer the same to you."

"I don't have fears," Idrilia grumbled.

"Whether fear or grief I am uncertain. But you are troubled, my friend. You told me that fears can make us do things we otherwise would not." Idrilia flicked her eyes to the side, catching the outline of Vayriel's round face. Idrilia was surprised the woman remembered.

"We are concerned for you. I offered this to Kalis on the mountain before—before he returned to the spirit-world—if you wish to share that on which you dwell, I can listen."

"I don't even know where to begin. I have so much anger inside. It feels like at any moment it will explode from my chest. I haven't felt such rage since—" She debated if she should release the burden she had carried for two sidereals.

"I know. You told me on our ascent."

An invisible hand clutched Idrilia's breast, but relaxed when she realized the Highblood referred to their conversation about the basics of the encounter with the Komorese riders and Kalis's version.

"I feel relief too."

"You are relieved that you must no longer bind your spirit with Kalis's?"

"It sounds horrible to say out loud. And I'm sickened by that."

"It was something you did not want to do."

"It should have been me up there with him," Idrilia blurted, unable to stop her words. "I could have saved him. I don't know, maybe he's still alive. You never saw his body. I find it hard to believe that he would not have found a way to save himself from a simple fall when he's practically a Sentinel."

Vayriel stiffened beside her.

"I didn't mean… I don't think you are at fault, Vayriel."

"Yet you doubt me?" Idrilia slowed at the Highblood's serious tone.

"I doubt everything. That's what I do," she realized with her admission. She stopped walking near one of the larger rocks. "I don't doubt what you've told us. But until I see with my own eyes that Kalis no longer lives, there will be a part of me that labels him as missing, not dead."

"You believe only what you see." Her friend's statement held a tinge of disappointment, and the Sondrinel did not know how to respond.

"Should your hands be that pink?" Kilahym's voice broke through the silence.

Idrilia turned and saw him examining Zinvar's hands in his own, twisting them as if the angle of the sun was not right, though it blazed overhead.

"Let me see." Kharnek roughly positioned himself between Zinvar and the bard, breaking Kilahym's grasp. The bard mewled in protest.

"Where are your gloves?" Idrilia demanded. With exaggerated movement, she closed the gap between them.

"No one asked for your opinion, Sondrinel."

Idrilia kept her attention on the priest, the skin of his hands no longer sickly pale.

"I forgot to put them on."

"Fool. Do I need to tell you everything to do?"

"Enough!" Kharnek stepped forward menacingly, his voice rumbling within his chest, and shadowed Zinvar behind him. "He does not want your help. You almost killed him!"

Idrilia squared her shoulders and reached for her daggers, but a length of wood appeared before her. Vayriel held her spear in her left hand and placed her free hand to stay Idrilia's draw.

"Please—" the Highblood began. In her peripheral, Idrilia saw pebbles shift at the base of a nearby boulder, in an area none of them stood, and bit back a curse.

"This will have to wait," she spat. Holding Kharnek's dark stare with her own she flicked her eyes in the direction of the movement. He nodded in reply. Idrilia pushed the Highblood's spear lightly to the side.

"To me," Idrilia commanded, motioning Vayriel to stand at her shoulder. Kharnek pushed the bard and priest to either side of him. The group then tightened. Idrilia felt Kharnek standing nearly back-to-back with her. They faced a series of boulders that had been replaced by figures draped in loose cloth of desert hues. The figures drew their straightblades and encircled the Truthseekers.

CHAPTER 47

"What are ya lookin' at, ya filthy night crawler?"

The Sondrinel rogue kicked at Kharnek's right boot. He and the other captives slumped against the railing of the skykeel, the preposterous method of transport these bandits utilized. Redbark splinters stabbed at the warrior's hands where they were tied behind his back. He fervently hoped that these fools realized he had allowed himself to be captured.

"Bah, yer silence won't last when ya meet the Lord o' the Skies himself. He'll take yer pale skin and make a tablecloth out of it!"

"And you wonder why you were cast out of Axiom." Idrilia rolled her eyes from her position to Kharnek's left. An anxious Zinvar tensed between them.

"Ha! This one has spirit. Perhaps the Cloudsoarer will keep ya for himself." The man leered at Idrilia, his mirth fading as she skewered him with a glare that promised unending pain. Despite himself, Kharnek approved. The death of her betrothed unleashed something in the young woman, a ferocity like the fiery breath of an arach. He still despised her for what she did to Zinvar, but he also understood her driven nature.

"Where are you taking us?" This from the Highblood, who stood closer to the aft of the vessel. Vayriel was the only Truthseeker who was unbound, a bristling Orgar at her side. Their captors seemed reluctant to approach the jeroti, instead herding Vayriel and her protector onto the ship when they captured the group. Kharnek's face flushed at the memory. He and Idrilia had been a blur of coordinated attacks, precise and deadly, his own movements quickened with bursts of the Penumbra's strength. Even when more of the attackers burst from concealment, they were unable to penetrate the group's defense, especially when the agile jeroti entered the fray. Then the bard—Morakh curse his name—had walked right into the arms of one of their opponents. With a knife at Kilahym's throat, the group had no choice but to surrender.

"You'll see soon enough." A tall woman clad in a green version of Idrilia's fighting robes emerged from below deck. The crew of the skykeel moved out of her way as she approached the Seekers. She removed her headscarf, letting the wind ruffle her cropped blue hair. By the lines on her face, Kharnek judged her to be near her fiftieth epicycle. The woman stooped down in front of Idrilia and studied the Sondrinel's face.

"Well, well, a Volundar. I'd know those proud cheekbones anywhere. Tell me, is Elsuota just as insufferable now as when she was High Keeper?"

Idrilia's face resembled a thundercloud. Behind her back, Kharnek saw her hands ball into fists.

"My grandmother," she said through clenched teeth, "was twice the woman you could ever hope to be, Sunscorned."

"Was?" The woman's features fell then morphed back into a scowl. "Arrogance always was your family's particular strength." She straightened, and her demeanor shifted into that of someone accustomed to being obeyed. Kharnek knew the stance from officers in the Brotherhood. "Now listen to me, all of you," the woman addressed the group, "it is imperative that you cooperate from this point forward. I know who you are, Truthseekers, and you are far more valuable alive and intact. Axiom and Waverling will pay a handsome sum to see you returned safely. As for the pale ones among you, well, I'm sure Komor will light a torch in honor of your untimely demise."

The crew guffawed at the remark while Kharnek seethed. He felt the darkness within him rise, ready to snuff out these insignificant wretches who dared threaten him. The warrior forced down the urge. Now was not the time to unveil his power, not until—

The time of our ascent.

Kharnek shook his head. That thought was not his own; it belonged to the insurgent force within him. Ever since the altercation with Adjira, the warrior had battled a steady flow of insidious suggestions that crept out of his subconscious. His anger at the way it had endangered the Seekers at Keepers' Rest by possessing Jannu still burned hot enough to keep the Penumbra at bay. But the whispers kept crowding his mind, and he could not resist them forever.

Wisps of white cloud followed the skykeel as it spiraled down toward the sea. The waves curled in shades of emerald and topaz here on the northern coast, a striking contrast to the deep azure of the waters around Ettra. Columns of red-brown coral rose out of the breakers to heights that rivaled Zel Morakh's grandest structures. Each column was wider than six skykeels placed side by side.

"The Reef of Pillars," Zinvar whispered. He leaned in close to Kharnek. "They say it formed over a thousand epicycles."

The warrior nodded; his gaze focused on an opening near the bottom of one of the largest pillars that the skykeel swooped toward. As they drew closer, he discerned flocks of slicewings pinwheeling around the columns. The birds dove toward the waves in streaks of white and gray, their razor-sharp wingtips spearing into unsuspecting fish. Below the spectacle of their hunt, bright yellow and pink polyps wriggled at the column's base when exposed by wave troughs. The reef was a hub of life in an otherwise desolate land, making it an ideal choice for a bandit lair.

Kilahym gasped when the skykeel plunged into the opening in the coral, the tips of the masts clearing the brim by a finger's length. Of greater interest to Kharnek were the sentries concealed at the edges. They manned cylindrical devices that rotated to follow the vessel's trajectory, and he suspected these devices were capable of firing projectiles at intruders. His eyes were adjusting to the semi-darkness when red crystals flared to life on the skykeel's sides. The crimson light revealed a stone wall directly ahead of them. Idrilia and Kharnek were the only two Seekers who did not flinch when the skykeel shot upward before colliding with the wall, caught in a powerful updraft that lofted it toward the column's apex. The ship's ascent slowed as it cleared a wooden balcony that ringed the hollow interior of the column, caught by hooked grapples thrown by Sunscorned standing on the platform. They reeled the skykeel in until its edge bumped the planks.

"Alright you torav fodder, I want this ship scrubbed until I can serve dinner to the Cloudsoarer himself right off the deck!" The woman in green barked orders to her crew, who hurriedly set about accomplishing their tasks. She turned her attention to the Seekers. "As for this lot, they're coming with me."

"As you say, m'lady!" The Sunscorned who kicked Kharnek motioned to the others who stood guard, and they hauled the Seekers to their feet with the ropes that bound their hands. All except Vayriel, who was prodded forward by a duo wielding straightblades. Orgar growled at the men, and they wisely kept their distance. The tall woman led the guards and her captives around the balcony toward a set of stairs that spiraled up to yet another platform, this one a mere stone's throw from the ceiling. More red crystals flickered on the walls as the group veered to the right into a passage hewn into the coral. The sounds of a raucous celebration reached Kharnek's ears: boisterous laughter and the clink of glasses raised in toast.

They passed into a large hall illuminated by crystal-laden chandeliers that dangled from worn ropes. Tables that could seat ten men to a side lined the space on either side of the warrior. Sunscorned filled the room, drinking and tearing into plates of roast pectully and coral writher filets. The scents made Kharnek's mouth water. Cycle after cycle of travel rations made him forget that such indulgence existed.

"Go back to your hole, night crawler!"

A tankard's worth of brine beer splashed into Kharnek's face, prompting loud jeers and hoots of appreciation. Drops of the salty liquid trickled down his black leathers, leaving dark streaks in the dusty material. His rage boiled over, and it took all his strength to keep from breaking free of his restraints and tearing the offender's head from his shoulders. He noted Zinvar's worried glance and tempered the fire within. The woman in green seemed not to notice the insult, and the guards did nothing but push the Seekers toward a dais at the end of the hall. Set atop it was a gold-cushioned sofa, upon which lounged a handsome man in a sleeveless crimson vest and billowing white pants. A beautiful Ettrascan woman stood to his right, clad in similar garb made of shimmering gold thread. A muscular flame-haired man from southern Heathström knelt on his left. The man sported a golden loincloth around his waist and matching bands around his upper arms. The procession led by the woman in green halted at the foot of the dais, where she ordered the guards to throw down the pile of the Seekers' belongings.

"Welcome back to civilization, Lady Orym! I trust that your time in the sun did not addle your wits?" The gathered Sunscorned dutifully laughed at their leader's jest.

"Lord Molnkamp. I see that your fondness for...*playthings*...remains undiluted." The woman cast a dubious gaze upon the figures on either side of the sofa. Her superior sat upright and bent forward, fingers steepled in front of his intense brown eyes.

"Ever the voice of criticism, my dear, which makes you so infinitely useful if dreadfully dull. Alas! Greatness is rarely spared of flaws."

Kharnek found himself at once repulsed by and attracted to the carefree manner of this would-be ruler of rejects. Were they in Komor, he would have likely bought the man a few rounds of 'cano ale before sharing a meaningless if pleasant time beneath Morakh's Shadow. The man spoke again, interrupting his thoughts.

"Speaking of *playthings*, you really have outdone yourself this time, my lady of monochromatic dress." Lord Molnkamp rose and descended two short steps to the main floor, where he paced up and down the line of Seekers. His eyes skimmed over Vayriel, Orgar, and Kilahym in sequence before pausing on Kharnek. The warrior felt a familiar heat fluoresce within him beneath the Sunscorned leader's scrutiny. He quickly averted his gaze, but not before he caught a mischievous grin tugging at the corner of the man's mouth. Lord Molnkamp continued past Zinvar to Idrilia.

"My my, but you are lovely." He stroked his dark brown facial hair, trimmed to neatly encircle his mouth and chin before tracing his jawline.

"A Volundar, my lord," Lady Orym asserted. "One of Elsuota's grandchildren, almost grown up now."

"We all know you're getting up there in age my lady, no need to remind us," the Sunscorned leader replied dryly. He leaned in closer to Idrilia, who looked outright murderous. Molnkamp lowered his voice. "A High Keeper's granddaughter and a Truthseeker at that. You will command a high price indeed. Unless," he stepped back and bowed, "you would deign to join the ranks of the truly enlightened."

"I'd sooner kiss a varg."

Idrilia's flat rejection elicited chuckles among the gathered mercenaries. Lord Molnkamp's eyes hardened, and he marched back up to the dais, where he spread his arms and addressed the crowd.

"It seems our dear Truthseekers are not appreciative of the Cloudsoarer's generous hospitality." A chorus of boos resounded from the Sunscorned. Their leader motioned for silence. "Clearly they prefer to do things the hard way. Lady Orym, escort our guests…to the dungeons!"

The audience cheered as Lord Molnkamp took his seat, and the Seekers were ushered out of the hall, followed by hurled epithets. Kharnek felt the weight of those brown eyes upon him as he walked. Back out to the balcony they went, this time circling to a platform suspended from a system of ropes and pulleys. At Lady Orym's command, a team of Sunscorned lowered the platform, laden with the Seekers and their guards, down into the depths of the pillar. They sank into a gloom interrupted only by sporadic light from the ubiquitous red crystals.

Eventually, the platform stopped next to a much smaller balcony, barely suspended above a frenzied whirlpool that churned at the bottom of the coral formation. Through yet another passage they walked, the walls dripping with seawater. The discarded shells of tiny crustaceans crunched beneath Kharnek's boots. Lady Orym's guards pulled them into an oval chamber lined with six cells sealed by iron bars. Into one went Kharnek and Idrilia, while Kilahym and Zinvar were shoved into another. The guards pointed to a third cell and Vayriel and Orgar walked into it. They slammed the bars shut behind them.

"Perhaps a few days down here will teach you the wisdom of respecting others." Lady Orym moved to leave but paused at the entrance to the chamber. "Oh, and I almost forgot. When high tide comes in, you might have company."

She strode away, her green pants billowing behind her. The other Sunscorned filed out after the skykeel captain, leaving their prisoners with the echoes of waves that crashed beyond the passage. A pair of illumination crystals were ensconced in the wall by the exit, but their wan light barely reached the front of the cells.

"Well, this is a fine mess your sharp tongue has gotten us into." Kharnek crossed his arms and faced Idrilia. Her nostrils flared at the accusation. She pointed at Kilahym in the cell across from them.

"It's not my fault. If it wasn't for that half-wit getting caught by the Sunscorned we wouldn't be here! And need I remind you who saw them first?"

"Now, that's hardly fair—" Kilahym squeaked.

"Quiet!" Kharnek and Idrilia roared simultaneously, then glared at one another again.

"Who needs the Sunscorned to torture us when we have you two," the bard grumbled before slinking to the back of his confinement.

"Kilahym is right. Fighting among ourselves will only make our foes stronger."

"Ordinarily I would agree, Vayriel. But these are special circumstances," Idrilia replied, her hands instinctively reaching for her daggers that the Sunscorned took.

"Indeed they are. I have been waiting for such an opportunity. Now there's no one to stand between us." The menace in Kharnek's voice was clear, prompting the Sondrinel to drop into a fighting stance. He took a step closer, then a noise behind him made them both start. Someone—or something—else was in the cell with them.

CHAPTER 48

As Idrilia and Kharnek came nearly nose to nose, Vayriel took a step forward to the barred door, gripping the smooth metal with both hands.

The two fighters pivoted as the sound of a masculine groan entered their argument. At the same time, she noticed Orgar's tails rippling, and he cocked his head to the side.

Vayriel pushed onto her toes but could not see beyond Kharnek and Idrilia. "What do your senses tell you, life-friend?" she whispered. The Highblood was reminded of her companion fighting beside her, but this time excitement flowed from the jeroti rather than apprehension.

"Make peace with me." Although muted by the coral, Idrilia's strong voice accompanied her forward-weighted stance. Kharnek shifted to the side as a blue-haired figure crawled from the shadows at the back of their cell. The man's beige robes were tattered and dirty, and he had a crusted brown stain like dried mud on the leg of his pants. His face, shadowed with several days of inattention, came into view as the young man came into the light and rolled over onto his back.

"I could use some water, you know."

Orgar whined beside her and rapidly shifted his weight from paw to paw. Vayriel knew that hoarse voice.

Idrilia kicked the prone figure's boot none too gently. "How in the rising—what did you—why are you—*basja*," Idrilia cursed at last, ending her unfinished questions. "You have a lot to explain."

Proffering a leather gauntlet, Kharnek hoisted the recumbent figure to his feet, and the person ran a hand through his cropped hair. Idrilia made as if to step closer to him but took a step back, hands on her hips.

"I saw you fall." Vayriel gripped the bars tightly and her voice trembled. Her heart pounded, doubt and relief invading her senses like waves of distinct color layered in the clouds. She pressed her face against the small gap as if she could will herself closer to her friend whom she had thought lost. The young man stepped closer to the cell's door.

"Kali-kal! Oh, it is good to see you! Though you're a bit scruffier than I remember," Kilahym said from the third cell.

"I promised to keep you safe..." the Highblood's statement trailed off as she struggled to turn the thoughts that had plagued her since Kalis's apparent demise into words.

"Honored Highblood," Kalis nodded, a grin at the corner of his mouth.

The echo of emotions from Mount Hoestra gripped Vayriel's chest. Kalis took a breath to continue but Vayriel held up a hand.

"I have again seen your fall as many times as there are grains of sand in your desert. I was not strong enough in the life force to save you. But you would not have needed saving if I had let you take the trägen's life as you had wished."

Kalis shook his head. "No, you were right. The trägen deserved the same respect that we show each other. It, too, has a right to live."

Vayriel shook her head and lowered her eyes. "I have thought much on the values my people place on all life. But is the life of one creature-son more valuable than the life of a friend?" Tears rimmed Vayriel's lavender eyes as she returned her gaze to Kalis.

"Oh Vayriel," Kilahym intoned softly.

"If we killed every time we thought we *might* be in danger, what would we become? In our military training, we talk about a balance between thought and action, each situation needing consideration before execution—"

"*In the right hand knowledge,*" Idrilia quoted.

Kalis nodded. "You did exactly what Sentinels are taught to do. Don't second guess your principles just because a ledge broke, you know. Maybe if I hadn't stopped to help the jeroti, I would have been further along the path. We can't change what happened. I live. The trägen lived. There are always other choices. I learned that from you."

She nodded and glanced at Kilahym, recalling the fear she felt when the Sunscorned pressed a blade against his flesh and the defeat that weighted her movements knowing she did not possess the skills to save him. She vowed to become stronger so that would never happen again. Orgar nudged her knee with his snout, and Vayriel dropped her hand to stroke the fur between his ears.

"Well, I'm certainly ecstatic that you have returned. Though it means I'll have to edit my play with a new act, 'The Hero's Triumphant Return'."

"What?"

Vayriel watched as Idrilia shook her head and waved dismissively toward the forward cell. "The bard has been composing a tribute to you."

"*The bard* has a name," Kilahym groaned. "And why is this bard talking about himself in third person? Ack! I'm doing it again. Anyway, dilly-Drilly, now your betrothal can go on as planned. That is the most happiest of news!" Kilahym jumped and clicked his heels together as Idrilia crossed her arms. "What takes place in a Sondrinel wedding? Am I invited? I have just the song to play, which can fit into any part of the ceremony."

Composing her face into an expressionless mask, Vayriel's eyes could not help but stray toward Idrilia. Her friend's features could have been carved from stone. She extended her senses through the life force and was buffeted by waves of anger, confusion, and sadness.

Zinvar tapped the bard's shoulder. "I am sure there will be time to discuss this on the rest of our journey. I'm interested in how Kalis survived the fall."

"You said the trägen lived." Kharnek's flat remark entered the mix before Vayriel could say anything. She braced herself for a potential outburst about her recounting of Kalis's apparent demise.

Instead, Idrilia frowned at the warrior then addressed her fellow Sondrinel. "How did you get here *before* us?"

Kalis shifted his weight and winced, stumbling backward. He regained his footing before answering, "I think I really do need some water."

Stepping forward, Idrilia gripped his arm and directed him to the back wall. "You should sit." Idrilia pointed to his right leg and the gash in the cloth there. "And you're wounded. Trust these outlaws to defy even the most basic of protections outlined in the Waverling Accords."

"I'm alright, 'Dril. Just a little lightheaded. So many questions, you know. Where should I start?"

"The best place for any story is the beginning. Mayhaps we should let our Kal start there." Kilahym suggested.

"It is so good to see you all again." Kalis chuckled as he lowered his body and sat against the wall. Vayriel saw him favor his injured leg.

He detailed succinctly, a delivery very different than Kilahym's storytelling, how he had used a protection crystal to cushion his fall. Though it was successful, the protection was spent upon impact with an outcropping thirty feet above the ice crevasse's floor. The momentum toppled him over the ledge and he fell, knocking himself unconscious, though he did not know for how long. The shelf above created a cascade of rock and ice, many pieces landing on the trägen. Kalis continued his tale until he began to describe a barrier and a room with verdant light.

"Was it—" Idrilia made several quick motions with her hands.

"Maybe."

"Maybe what?" Kilahym threw a baffled expression at Zinvar before addressing Kalis. "I must have missed something in your, uh, breviloquence."

Kalis made a quick gesture.

"Fine," Idrilia acquiesced. When Kalis turned his head, she made a sweeping gesture beneath her chin with one hand's fourth finger.

Kalis described the dark, non-reflective geometric protrusion they had found while on their way to Waverling. "We can only speculate about its origins," he finished. Vayriel did not miss his pointed glance at Kharnek, who stiffened.

Zinvar coughed and drew everyone's attention. "That is unlike Komorese design. But the Priesthood has collected many artifacts similar in appearance to that which you describe. Their exact provenance remains unknown."

"Oh, really?" Kalis tilted his head. "I would like to hear more about that."

"As would I, but not right now. I want to hear the rest of your story first," Idrilia interjected.

"Fair enough. This wall, or whatever it was, had a non-reflective surface. When I was inside the chamber, I could make out sharp edges. It reminded me of the object, you know."

"And there was a green light, which led you out?" Idrilia clarified.

Kalis inclined his head. "Yes. This will sound odd, but it seemed almost...alive. The whole place did, for that matter. Like it was aware I was there."

"Like the creature-son in the sea," Vayriel murmured.

Kalis shrugged. "Maybe. Anyway, I stepped through another wall, or barrier, and found myself at the Cliffs of Odium."

"That journey should have taken you many days!" Idrilia exclaimed.

"I think maybe it's a new type of crystal that has much greater range than the spatial movement techniques I or the Sentinels have mastered. The Keepers Guild will want to study this."

"Do you realize he was at the bottom of the chasm you supposedly checked? I should have made us go back."

Vayriel's muscles tightened at Idrilia's remarks.

"Dril. Please. There's no way Vayriel could have found me."

"What do you mean there's no way?" Idrilia folded her arms. "She's one of the strongest life force users I've ever seen, and you're telling me she couldn't sense that you were alive?"

"I was unconscious. You know how difficult it is to detect someone in that state," Kalis retorted.

"You reached the cliffs, then what happened?" Zinvar interrupted before the argument spiraled out of control.

"Right. After that, I was ambushed by Sunscorned"—he reached a hand to the back of his head—"and was placed on a floating ship."

"How do you think it flies?" the priest asked.

"It has to be crystals."

"Using the same method of the lifts in Evocus," Idrilia put in, though she had not stopped glaring at Kalis and Vayriel alternately.

"But how did they get it?" Kalis countered.

Idrilia shrugged. "Stole it like they steal everything."

"From the Artificers Guild?"

"Maybe. But why didn't we hear of the theft?"

"This conversation is useless."

Idrilia whirled on Kharnek.

"Though a prison cell would suit you as a permanent home," Kharnek continued, "I suggest we turn our attention to more important matters."

"Escape!" Kilahym announced.

"Unless you can magic the prison bars away, our options are limited," Kharnek replied.

"Our options may not be that limited," Idrilia interjected, chin held high. The Sondrinel stepped to her cell's door and addressed Vayriel. "You wanted to be stronger in the life force. Now's your chance to test it."

"What are you proposing?" Kalis sounded intrigued.

"Wen. The Sunscorned took my communication crystal otherwise I'd try to see through her eyes. She's flying out there somewhere." Idrilla continued addressing Vayriel. "But you are somehow able to connect to the life force without a crystal. You've coaxed living things from seeds. You could ask Wen to help us scout."

"I see. Yes. I can try. Though my experience with creature-daughters is much less than it is with the root-born." Vayriel thought of the female jeroti, and the glimpse she had of the canine's view within the life force. She felt strength gather within her chest at the memory.

"I'm thinking the process would be the same as I use with a crystal. I'll walk you through what I do, and maybe it will help."

Vayriel felt this was partially said as an apology for the Sondrinel's remarks before. She knew Idrilia spoke only in anger, though the sting of the words remained. Her friend must know how guilty Vayriel felt after discovering Kalis alive.

Idrilia explained how she focused her thoughts on the othwit, the memories and emotions associated with their relationship, as a fixed point in the expanse of life-force energy. The crystal conduit would allow Idrilia to either send thoughts or see through Wen's eyes. The concept was very different from what Vayriel had been taught by her coil. Vayriel normally drew the life force into herself, and by doing so, she was part of the energy, able to shape it and use it and often interpret the variety within as emotions from its source.

Vayriel attempted to combine both approaches and felt the thoughts of many creature-sons and -daughters join her own. But it was like the shopping district in Waverling: loud voices, indecipherable from one another, coming and going in waves. This was not as easy as connecting to Orgar. "It'll take time," Idrilia encouraged after a deep sigh from Vayriel. "This is the first you've tried. Keep at it."

"I will keep trying."

"Do you hear that?" Kalis whispered. Vayriel froze and listened. Footsteps.

"Someone is coming."

The Truthseekers shifted into postures of docility. Vayriel sat next to Orgar and began to stroke his gray belly as he lay on his side. A familiar figure in green entered the room.

"Don't stop your chatter on my account," Orym said with a grin. Then when no one replied, she continued. "Very well. I only came to take a guest to dinner." She indicated Idrilia. "Lord Molnkamp's request."

CHAPTER 49

Rivulets of saltwater meandered down the walls of Kilahym's cell, exploring the contours of the red-brown coral. He imagined that the reef wept for the Seekers, shedding salty tears on their behalf. The phenomenon began only moments after the Sunscorned escorted Idrilia from the room.

"A bard among us, and the illustrious Cloudsoarer invites the least musical person in our party to dinner." Kilahym shot a glance at Kharnek. "Well, mayhap the *second* least musical."

"Undoubtedly, if he was familiar with your illustrious reputation, Lord Molnkamp would have begged you to play for him."

"But of course, my good priest! Does he not know—" The bard broke off his sentence to scowl at his cellmate. Zinvar slumped against the back of their confinement, knees hugged to his chest. Seawater left trails of darker orange in the rust-colored fabric of his robes as it dripped onto the priest's shoulders.

"Apologies, my friend. It was not intended as a slight."

Kilahym huffed. "Ah, but 'tis true what thou sayest. I am a player of little renown."

A shrug lifted the priest's shoulders. "Perhaps not after the Trials."

"After the Trials." Kilahym shook his head while stroking the brown scruff along his chin. "An unlikely future, given our current state of affairs. Though Vayriel may yet prove our salvation."

Across the chamber, the budding love interest in his tale sat cross-legged on the ground with her hands in her lap, eyes shut and twitching behind their lids. Her peach hair spilled out from the edges of her raised hood, which shielded her from the increasingly persistent streams of water entering the hollow. For more than an hour since the guards took Idrilia, Vayriel had remained in that position with no obvious success in her efforts to connect with Wen.

"I wonder what she is seeing," Kilahym mused. He toyed with the notion of attempting to connect with her through the life force but refrained out of fear of distracting her.

"Nothing." Vayriel exhaled and opened her eyes, regarding him with a forlorn expression. "Some glimpses, and for a moment I thought I felt the warmth of the sun on my—on Wen's wings, but the feeling was gone in an instant. I do not know the rhythm of this creature-daughter's heartbeat as I do Orgar's. Without Idrilia's memories to guide me, I fear that this will prove an impossible task."

"Don't be discouraged, Vayriel. If there's anyone who can do this, it's you." Zinvar pushed himself up from the floor with a rustle of fabric. He winced as the sleeves drooped against his sunburnt hands.

"Thank you. I will continue to try." The mountain-dweller closed her eyes once more. Kilahym clapped the priest on his back.

"That's more like the Zinny I know! You've been quieter than an alusarean with a mouthful of grass since we got here."

"I know. I'm sorry."

"If you care to share your woes, I would be delighted to be your audience. Granted I may someday turn them into a play. Consider yourself forewarned." Kilahym swept low in a bow fit for the Magister as Zinvar chuckled. The priest then gazed in the direction of Kharnek and Kalis's cell, the corners of his mouth downturned.

Zinvar's mouth drew a grim line. "It's him, of course. Each time I think that he's becoming a little less rigid in his hatred of everything that isn't Komorese, he quarrels with Idrilia. That, and I saw the way the Sunscorned leader looked at him...and he looked back. But I guess that's not fair. We haven't really defined much about our relationship."

"Ah. Jealousy is an ugly thing, my priestly friend, one that prompts the vilest of actions. Did I ever tell you the tale of the pyreflowers and the disgruntled lover? It's really—"

"Perhaps another time. I'm not in the mood for tales this cycle."

"Oh." Kilahym studied his companion's downcast expression before Zinvar shuffled to the back of their cell.

Kilahym put his hand in his pocket and started, withdrawing the object from Ansgar. He'd forgotten he had it. The troubadour's words came back to him: "*Squeeze this until a bell sound rings from it.*" Would Ansgar know where they were? Could he help them escape? It would be the material for an epic ballad but quite the fantasy. There was nothing Ansgar or a spy network could do for them.

The crestfallen bard began to hum a melody that Vayriel's coil played when he visited many synodies ago. He tapped an accompanying rhythm on the oblong like a haptic drum. The song told the story of a jeroti that taught the Highbloods how to see its shape in the sky-spirits' home, as well as those of the other creature-sons and -daughters. Their celestial outlines helped the mountain people find their way home and watched over them from where they shone in the sky. A chill coursed along Kilahym's spine as the song dipped into a haunting minor key, evocative of a Highblood lost beneath a clouded firmament. An image of Vayriel's lavender eyes glimmering above a fire floated into his mind, fixed upon him as he performed. He hummed louder, crescendoing to the song's climax when the jeroti appeared to guide the Mother-of-All's child.

"Kilahym?"

The Heathström native was so swept up in the tune that he didn't notice Zinvar's entreaty.

"Kilahym!"

Zinvar's exclamation snapped him out of his reverie. "What?"

His pallid companion pointed at the walls of the cell, where the water continued to trickle *upward*.

"By the Lady!" Kilahym swatted at a corona of droplets that had formed around his head. The scattered liquid floated idly through the air, unhindered by the laws of nature. Then the magic that suspended it dissipated. Kilahym spluttered as the collection of water crashed onto his face, much to Zinvar's amusement.

"How did you do that?"

"I didn't mean to!" The bard wiped his brow, flinging moisture off his skin. "Although, as you have witnessed before, sometimes when I play music, peculiar things happen."

"Peculiar indeed." Zinvar's eyebrow arched.

"I admit, it wasn't as useful this time as when I made the illusions…"

"I did it!" The exclamation drew curious stares from all the imprisoned Seekers. Vayriel rose to her feet, shoulders thrown back in triumph. When he met her gaze, Kilahym saw, or rather felt , impressions of the wind ruffling feathers, the sun above, and the waves below. The Highblood's eyes widened.

"You see it too," she murmured.

"I…we…we're both in Wen's head," the astonished bard pronounced.

"Fascinating. Now could we focus on doing something useful with that instead of ogling one another?" Kharnek glowered at the twosome.

A wide grin spread across Kalis's face as he ambled to the front of the cell he shared with the Komorese. "Well done, Vayriel! And Kilahym, it would seem."

The Highblood nodded. "Yes. His song helped me attune myself to Wen's music in the life force."

"And to him." Zinvar winked as Kilahym flushed a deep scarlet.

Vayriel quickly averted her gaze from Kilahym. "I…my people have created such…bonds among one another. It is a unity not too different from what is experienced with a life-friend. But, it is rare for this to happen with…with a lowlander."

Kilahym studied Vayriel's delivery. Was she nervous, ashamed? He had never heard her falter in speech like this before. Before he could reach a conclusion, his study was interrupted.

"Back to getting out of here," Kharnek growled.

The Highblood straightened, sweeping her hand around the prison. "Wen has seen the way. When we were first captured, she followed the skykeel in and flew to the top of the pillar. From there she has watched, and she has seen where they took our possessions."

"Now if we could just get to them…" Kalis mused, running his hand through his cerulean hair.

"I can get us out of the cells," Kharnek said.

Kilahym felt a dreadful stone form in his gut. He had a feeling he knew how the surly Truthseeker would go about accomplishing his stated goal.

"That's a bold assertion for a warrior with no weapon." Zinvar crossed his arms.

"Even without a sword, I could destroy these undisciplined wyrm-fodder. I can get us out of the cells when the guards return, if the Highblood can show us the way."

A chill shivered its way down Kilahym's spine. Phantom sensations of Jannu's fingers on his throat made him flinch. He averted his gaze from the warrior in favor of a friendlier countenance. Vayriel's eyes met his as they searched, and he instantly felt calmer.

"I can. Once we have our weapons, we must reach the top of the pillar," Vayriel replied to Kharnek, although she did not look away from Kilahym. "There is a bridge that connects this pillar to another, where the Sunscorned vessels are kept. With Wen's eyes to guide us, we should be able to avoid our captors."

Kilahym felt excitement charge the air in the prison like the aftereffect of a lightning strike. With a start, he realized that the feeling emanated from Vayriel, along with a sense of pride and satisfaction. Could she sense what he felt as well?

"Does anyone know how to fly a skykeel?"

The ensuing silence answered Kalis's question.

"Well, I guess we'll figure that out once we get there, you know?" he added with a nervous laugh.

"I should have stayed in Komor," Kharnek muttered.

"Yes, maybe you should have." The warrior blinked in surprise at Zinvar's comment. He opened his mouth to respond and was promptly doused by a flow of water that erupted from the coral above him. It trickled to a halt as quickly as it came, but spouts began to form in all corners of the chamber.

The increased gurgle of water across coral accompanied the sound of splashing footsteps. Kilahym gasped, and Orgar growled as two Sunscorned guards hauled an unconscious Idrilia into the room, the ends of her cerulean hair trailing through the layer of seawater that now covered the ground. One of the guards removed a key from within his robes and opened the door to an empty cell, where he and the other man unceremoniously deposited her limp form before locking it again.

"You piles of basja, what did you do to her?" Kalis snarled as he clutched the bars to his cell, his knuckles white. The two guards moved to stand a few paces in front of the angry Sondrinel.

"Shut yer mouth boy. What the Cloudsoarer wants, the Cloudsoarer gets, willing or not."

The Sunscorned laughed at their taunt. Kilahym's heart ached for Kalis. He would run through a field of pyreflowers to get to Vayriel if she were lying on the floor. Abruptly the guards flew forward and were pinned against the bars of

Kalis's cell. Kalis leaped back with a yelp, almost colliding with Kharnek. Kilahym squealed in terror when he saw the warrior's face. The Komorese's eyes were black as a starless night, while his gauntleted hands were clenched into fists at his sides.

"Take them out," the warrior commanded. His words slithered through the air, laden with reverberation as though many voices spoke. Kilahym cringed as memories of Jannu's possession at Keepers' Rest flooded in. Meanwhile, Kalis recovered from his initial shock and lashed out at the trapped guards. Two quick strikes knocked the Sunscorned to the ground in a heap, where they landed with a splash. The darkness faded from Kharnek's eyes as he stepped forward and reached through the bars to retrieve the incapacitated guards' keys.

"Time to go."

CHAPTER 50

Look away, Zinvar's subconscious urged. He focused with all his might on tearing his eyes from that awful darkness. It whispered to him. Promises of power beyond his wildest dreams tugged at his resolve.

"No," the priest murmured. He clapped one hand over his face and staggered back into the wall of the cell. The cool chill of water seeping through his robes blossomed against his scapulae. A squeal of terror reached his ears but he dared not look, for he was certain that if he did, the Penumbra would ensnare him. Then came the thud of blows landing on flesh, followed by silence.

"Time to go," Zinvar heard Kharnek say. His voice sounded normal. Slowly the priest lowered his hands and peered out of the cell. The warrior stood at the center of the prison with the guards' keys dangling from gauntleted fingers. He approached Kilahym and Zinvar's cell and unlocked it, pulling the barred door open with a clank. Kilahym wasted no time in scurrying out and enveloping Kalis in a hug. Zinvar trudged out, glancing quickly at Kharnek's eyes. They were their normal deep brown color. He sighed in relief.

"Are you alright?" The hand Kharnek placed on his shoulder induced a shudder down the priest's spine, and the touch was quickly withdrawn. "Are you in pain?"

"I'm fine." Zinvar pulled away, wrapping his robes tighter around his body. The warrior seemed confused by his reaction.

"We should probably let the others out, you know." Kalis extended his hand, and Kharnek tossed the keys to him. The Sondrinel freed Vayriel and Orgar before rushing to Idrilia's cell, where she lay unconscious. Opening the door, Kalis knelt by his betrothed, brushing aside a strand of cerulean hair that snaked across her forehead and emerald circlet. His other hand balled into a fist.

"They'll pay for this," he vowed.

"Vengeance later, escape now, methinks."

"For once, I agree with the bard." Kharnek glanced meaningfully at the passage that led to the rest of the Sunscorned base. Was it Zinvar's imagination, or did he hear shouts echoing from the entrance?

"What about Idrilia? I'm not leaving her here."

"Carrying her will slow us down. Leave her. Obviously, Molnkamp wants her alive, if only to ransom her." The warrior's statement shocked Zinvar. *How could Kharnek be so callous?*

"There is another way." Vayriel entered the conversation, her soothing tones bringing a stillness to the cell. The Highblood produced a glass orb filled with dull yellow powder. Removing the cork that stoppered the orb, Vayriel crouched next to Idrilia and held the container beneath her nostrils. The priest caught a whiff of something pungent, reminiscent of the sulfuric fumes that rose from the lava tunnels beneath Zel Morakh. Idrilia's eyelids twitched before gradually opening. She groaned and pushed herself up on her right elbow.

"What...in the name of Kadaan...is that *smell?*"

Zinvar stifled a laugh at the look of utter revulsion on the Sondrinel's face. She cast a glance around, assessing the open cell doors and noticing her tan tunic.

"Where is my nuala robe? And why am I over here?" Her eyes widened. "How did you all break free?"

"There will be time for questions later. Can you walk?" The vile look Idrilia shot at Kharnek answered his question. She rose to her feet, pushing away the hand Kalis offered to assist her.

"As much as I hate to admit it, the brute is right. We need to get moving."

"Yes, while we retain the nature of being unforeseen."

All eyes turned to Vayriel.

"I think what she means is the element of surprise," Kilahym clarified.

"Which we will definitely lose if we do not move *now*." Kharnek punctuated his phrase by a sweep of his black cloak as he stalked out of the cell. His boots sloshed into a layer of water several inches deep that had gathered in the sunken floor of the prison chamber's center. Zinvar watched a wave surge into the enclosure, carrying with it several round, green plants that floated on the surface of the water.

"I do believe that that's our cue to get out of here. The tide is a-rolling in!" Kilahym waded out of the cell after the warrior. The other Seekers followed, the priest casting a curious glance at the bobbing plants. There was a light green nub at the center, which shaded to deeper emerald tones near the edges of the circular top. He reached out for one. A pair of black eye slits opened at the sides of the "bud." Then the center split to reveal a mouth with twin, needle-like fangs. Zinvar yelped and pulled his hand back as the creature struck, barely avoiding the teeth glistening with venom.

"By the Lady's beard! Coral writhers! Never did I think to see the day when one of these beauties floated by," the bard exclaimed. "Might be best not to touch them."

"You don't say." Zinvar splashed away from the creature, which still had its beady eyes fixed on him. Its hungry stare reminded him of a rift wyrm.

"They masquerade as floating plants, to lure unsuspecting prey. Not that you're prey or unsuspecting," Kilahym hastily amended as he saw the priest's eyebrow arch. "You're a little on the big side for them...I mean, not that you're big, but—"

With a sigh, Zinvar strode out of the prison chamber, the babbling bard close behind and still attempting to apologize.

"This is what we seek."

Zinvar eyed Vayriel sidelong. Her forehead wrinkled in concentration.

"You're certain? I don't like standing out here in the open." Idrilia glanced about nervously, her hands instinctively reaching for her absent daggers.

"Yes," Vayriel nodded. "This is where our belongings are held, but I do not know how to enter."

Through her connection with Wen, the Highblood had led the group to a room sealed behind a rippling light blue wave of life-force energy. Thus far, the lower levels of the Sunscorned base appeared to be empty. Zinvar guessed Sunscorned did not often entertain prisoners, otherwise there would be more guards.

They ascended to the level where the skykeel initially docked. Across the wide expanse of the column's center were hollowed-out rooms that housed most of the Cloudsoarer's followers. Wen, from her perch at the top of the column, had watched the rogues coming and going from the chambers around the circular platform, taking equipment from the one they now stood before. Zinvar's attention fixed upon the octagonal lock at the door's center. There was something familiar about its design and what waited beyond it. A faint cold sensation made his hair stand on end.

"We could wait on the stairs for someone to open the door and catch them off-guard, you know."

Idrilia shook her head. "Assuming no one comes up the stairs while we're waiting. And that they haven't discovered that we are missing." She waved her hand in front of Zinvar's face, causing him to flinch. "Are you with us, priest?"

"Yes, sorry I—I think I might be able to open the door."

Hesitantly Zinvar reached out, his hand trembling as it neared the undulating barrier. He closed his eyes and thrust his arm forward. A tingling sensation danced across his skin, then Zinvar felt the cool stone of the lock beneath his hand. Abruptly, an image of Lord Molnkamp's face intruded into the priest's consciousness. The Cloudsoarer's knowing gaze and smirk grew closer and closer in Zinvar's perception, vanishing when the lock clicked beneath his touch. He opened his eyes and watched the device split apart, then the doors swung open, revealing four very surprised Sunscorned.

Kharnek, Idrilia, and Kalis leaped into motion, each disabling their chosen opponent in short order. A white blur collided with the fourth renegade, pinning him to the floor beneath its bulk. Vayriel calmly approached her life-friend. The jeroti growled as the man wriggled, straining to reach the straightblade that was knocked out of his hand when Orgar struck. A swift kick to his head ceased his struggling and prompted a raised eyebrow from Zinvar.

"I didn't know you had that in you, Vayriel," the priest remarked while he pushed the double doors shut. Vayriel stroked Orgar's head in praise for his actions.

The Highblood smiled at the Komorese. "There is much you do not know about me, friend Zinvar."

"And it would seem that there is much about our scholarly friend we do not know," Kilahym interjected. "Like how he is able to open magical locks."

"Yes, I'd like to know how you did that." Idrilia gave the priest an appraising look. He felt the uncomfortable weight of everyone's gazes upon him.

"I'm really not sure. But I saw a lock like this in the Chamber of the Occulum. And I was able to open it."

"Again, time for stories later. After we escape." The blunt words from Kharnek brought Zinvar out of the flow of memory. His warrior companion pointed at a large, redbark cabinet near the back of the oblong room. "Our weapons are in there."

Kalis cocked his head. "And how do you know that?"

The warrior offered no response, instead shouldering his way through the Sondrinel and heading toward the cabinet. When he reached it, he threw the doors open and withdrew his familiar obsidian blade, followed by the dagger Zinvar took from the Tower of Nerekesh. The rest of the Seekers crowded around and gathered their belongings, Vayriel hefting her spear, and Idrilia donning her nuala robe. Zinvar took his staff when Kharnek offered it and nodded his thanks. His fingers curled around the ebon wood, feeling the smooth, polished length.

"Is everyone ready?"

All the Seekers indicated yes to Idrilia's question.

"Are our eyes ready?"

"Yes. Wen has shown me the way to the skykeels," Vayriel affirmed.

Kalis shook his head. "Something none of us can fly, you know. Unless that's another hidden talent of yours, Zinvar."

"I'm afraid not."

"What of the Sunscorned?" Kharnek asked. Vayriel closed her eyes for a few heartbeats before responding.

"It would appear that the frivolity we witnessed upon our arrival has continued into the Daughter's hours."

Idrilia grunted. "Amateurs. You'd think criminals would have better security."

"Wen cannot get close enough without being seen to check for guards at the skykeel entrance and where the vessels are kept. We may face an unknown number of enemies," the Highblood added.

"That will not be a problem," Kharnek growled. He brandished his sword as he marched toward the doors, which opened as he pushed. Kharnek suddenly froze. Beyond him stood a lean Sunscorned man whose skin was much paler than the others Zinvar had seen. His white robes were splotched with green brine beer from the feast he must have just left. In an instant, Kharnek's blade was at the man's throat. The Sunscorned's green eyes bulged in fear, and he froze.

"Please, I meant no harm, I only came to—"

"Quiet, rogue. You and your master have much to answer for." Kalis plucked a crystal from within his robes and shook it gently, igniting a blaze within. The man continued to protest as the Sondrinel advanced. Zinvar frowned. His accent was familiar—almost as if…

"Wait!"

Kalis halted a few steps from the man, looking irritated. The priest approached carefully and drew back the man's right sleeve. On the Sunscorned's forearm coiled a distinctive tattoo of a serpentine creature with wings spread to either side. The body was rendered in black, but in contrast to Komorese tradition, the eyes were twin violet jewels. Zinvar gasped and lurched back.

"What is it?" Kharnek sounded concerned.

"Yes, tell me why I shouldn't set this man ablaze for his crimes," Kalis snarled.

"No! No, you can't do that."

"And why not?" Idrilia placed a hand on her right hip, her eyes narrowing dangerously.

"Because…he's my brother."

CHAPTER 51

"Spectres in paisley robes! You have a brother, Zinny?" Kilahym used both of his hands to scoop through his light brown tangles on the top of his head.

Kalis bounced his crystal hand in rhythm with his heartbeat as he watched Kharnek back his blade away from the Sunscorned's neck; he kept it lit within but did not set it aflame. He raised an eyebrow at Idrilia.

"I'm not surprised he didn't tell you," the newcomer began, flicking a wary eye at the obsidian blade where it hovered in front of his body.

"In." The warrior latched on to the robe's begrimed front and yanked the young man forward, deftly keeping his lengthy sword pointed at the same location as he shifted them both a stride into the room.

"You only know your own brother by his markings?" Idrilia challenged, as soon as the door closed again.

Zinvar opened his mouth but his brother's voice addressed the dispute. "Indeed. That happens when we have not seen each other in ten epicycles."

The priest frowned. "What are you doing here, Rinesh?"

"Looking for you, Zinvar."

Kalis was reminded how his own brother, Vari, took that familiar tone with him. "A Komorese held by the Sondrinel for ten years? I *must* hear this tale," Kilahym pronounced.

"Sunscorned," Kalis corrected. These bandits and raiders were lawless and far from members of Sondrine society.

Rinesh shook his head. "I am not a prisoner. The others were talking about the Cloudsoarer's latest find. My own brother, a Truthseeker. I could hardly believe it, but here you are."

"We should go," Kharnek stated.

"Although the way is empty now, it is unlikely to remain so." Vayriel gripped her spear with a softness Kalis recognized as her walking posture. Orgar, however, remained in a stance with hackles slightly raised and body crouched next to the Highblood.

"Always a truth-sayer, dear Vayriel. I shall have time later to learn these brothers' secrets. To the empty path!"

"He stays here," Idrilia pointed at Rinesh.

"We should incapacitate him like the others." Kharnek twisted his weapon in a backhanded grip and raised the pommel head-high.

"No please, Kharnek. We can take him with us." Zinvar placed his hands in front of his brother.

The warrior frowned. "Anyone other than an aerialist will slow us down."

Rinesh slowly raised his hand. "I am one. I steer the skykeels."

"Huzzah! What great fortune." Kilahym bounced in place.

Kalis again caught Idrilia's attention, and she rolled her eyes at the bard. "How convenient."

"First, Zinny can open the magical door, now his brother is a cloud-soarer himself."

"You opened the door?" Rinesh frowned. "Only Lord Molnkamp and the other outcast Occulum among us can do that."

"What is clear is that the Mother-of-All brought you to us to help us. But our journey is long, and you would not be returning soon," Vayriel said.

"It doesn't seem that I have a choice in the matter. There's another exit back there." He pointed to the far end of the chamber. "Just press the latch key, and we can climb the rope ladder to the docking level."

Kalis's initial thought was to disbelieve the Komorese, but he reminded himself this was Zinvar's brother. How would he want Vari to be treated were he here instead?

Kalis scratched his ear. "He's your brother, Zinvar. Should we trust him?"

"Yes," the priest said simply. "Please put away your weapons."

Kalis focused on the connection through his crystal, like a strap of leather tethering a camelid to a solendrake and turned a mental key. He felt the connection sever, or *lock* as the Master Sentinels explained. The glow of the red crystal vanished, and he returned it to his belt pouch. His hand, however, hovered near his side and his curved blade.

"We need to bind and gag him. We can't allow him to run or yell, lest he give away our location," Kalis said.

"Is that necessary?" Zinvar asked.

"It is." Kalis shifted his eyes from the priest. It was the right thing to do, but part of Kalis felt as if he were betraying Zinvar. The Komor emissary was, dare he say it, becoming a friend, and this younger boy was his brother. He could see the resemblance now—a similar nose and brow.

"If Zinvar trusts him, that is enough." Kharnek lowered his weapon and took a sidestep closer to Zinvar while staring at Kalis. Kalis let his eyebrows raise but decided to drop the matter.

"Well then, problem solved." Idrilia's voice sounded from behind Kharnek. Then her tone changed. "Idiot! Get back."

Kalis shifted to see Idrilia grabbing Zinvar and pulling him to the side of the room where Rinesh was now floating in a cream haze. A crystal on the floor sucked the mist-like cloud into itself, quickly condensing into the width of a string. Kalis's stomach tightened.

"What did you do to him?" The priest's voice sounded pained. The final particles vanished into the now cream-colored crystal.

"I diminished him," Idrilia explained. "He's safe, though we do need to hurry. Prolonged exposure can have…complications."

Kalis groaned. "The Sentinels *advise* against using it on humans, 'Dril."

"But it has been done before. It is done now. Let's go—before more surprises happen." Idrilia bent down and plucked the crystal from the rough floor.

She brushed past a rooted Vayriel toward the wall Rinesh had indicated. Kalis followed, feeling a sharp pain below his injured right knee as he stepped forward. He opened various containers, partially listening as the Komorese conversed. The need to hurry swirled within Kalis like a dust storm gaining speed. It was possible they had spent too much time already in this room.

As he rummaged, Kalis thought about what obstacles they might encounter, attempting to prepare himself for all outcomes. His mind felt slower as he grabbed an undamaged but lightly soiled replacement for his pants. As an afterthought, he grabbed two random headscarves and shoved them in his pack. His tongue felt like he'd licked the fabric, but he chose to ignore the parched feeling until they were safe.

"This must be the key he was talking about. It's ugly," Idrilia said from the back of the room. The others joined her. Molnkamp's face was embossed on a raised section of the wall the width of a palm. It was golden and had eight sides.

"He really is obsessed with himself," Kalis commented, scrutinizing the smiling face. Kalis felt his muscles quiver as his thoughts wavered to what Molnkamp might have done to Idrilia, the jeers from the guards reverberating in his skull.

"Should we go the direction the brother of Zinvar suggested?" Vayriel asked.

"It could be a trap," Idrilia said.

"I am more concerned that the way will not allow Orgar to follow. He can climb the redbarks of the mountains, but rope...I fear will leave his claws with no paw holds. I might be able to make him float, as I have done with smaller objects."

"Perhaps Kharnek can carry him! He's certainly burly enough, right, Zinvar?" Kilahym winked, crossing his arms below the loose strings of his dark shirt, and leaned against the wall.

"Hymn!" Idrilia reached out. Too late.

His shoulder pressed against the key.

"Whoops."

The wall rumbled quietly as it slid slowly to the side. Kalis dropped into a defensive stance, Idrilia, Vayriel, and Kharnek doing the same, as the opening revealed a dark recess made of the familiar coral. The small space was empty but for a rope ladder that dangled from above.

"You will be the death of us yet," Idrilia muttered, stepping into the passage.

"Dril, wait." She was already placing her boot into the first rung. "We need a plan."

"Climb, fight, escape. Anything I missed?" Kalis grinned at the memory her words hinted at.

The group reached the top. The entrance to the pillar's center illuminated the otherwise dark room. Kalis noted it housed rope and pulleys, tools of various sizes, and barrels, like a supply cache for maintenance.

Silently, Kalis signaled for the group to move away from the ledge. Vayriel stayed and closed her eyes. She breathed deeply and gripped her spear with both hands, bending her head to touch the green gems that dangled from the tip.

Orgar's head appeared near the lip then finished floating the remaining distance before inching toward Vayriel. As her eyes opened, Orgar's body touched the floor. He laid, chin on the surface with legs splayed, rotating his cyan eyes to his life-friend. A soft whine issued from the jeroti.

"Hush. You are safe," Vayriel whispered. "I promise I will not do that again unless it is completely necessary."

The jeroti whined again. Kalis chuckled quietly, moving away. Zinvar and Kilahym stood close to one another, whispering. Kharnek guarded the left side of the entrance while Idrilia flanked. She formed a circle with her fingers to signal all clear.

A thought sparked, and Kalis withdrew a red crystal. He activated it and dropped it from his hand, stepping back as he did so. The crystal erupted, orange and yellow flames engulfing the width of the rope rungs like wings of a falling bird, and set the fibers burning before it landed on the coral below.

"That was unexpected," Idrilia commented quietly.

"It will stop anyone from following."

"I agree. It's just…normally you ask instead of act."

Kalis shrugged. Idrilia's spontaneous nature had its uses, but he wasn't about to admit that; he'd never hear the end of it.

The group moved out onto the wooden platform that circled the hollowed-out pillar.

Fearful of echoes, they moved slowly, pausing before each opening while Kalis and Idrilia checked for Sunscorned. It was eerily quiet and empty as they followed Vayriel's directions, deciphered from Wen's view. Kalis found his mind continually strayed toward home. *Had Jannu sent word to the Keepers after the Sending of Memories?* Kalis imagined his mother's already thin lips pursed, eyes lowered as the High Keeper delivered the official record—a final entry in Kalis's life as recorded in the Vitaetum—for Leiria and Noval to sign. Lyna, biting her lower lip and refusing to cry; Vari taking her hand when no one was watching. Kalis's chest felt as if it would burst. He needed to send word as soon as he could to let them know he was alive.

The Truthseekers reached a spiral staircase.

They turned left toward a brilliant oval, but what lay beyond was obscured by the sunlight. Ghostly silhouettes danced in the opening. Kalis drew his sword as they approached and blocked an attacker's blade. As he suspected, the apparitions had been guards rushing from their posts.

"I knew it was too easy," Kilahym grumbled from behind.

At Kalis's left, he saw Idrilia engaged with another guard. Her daggers lashed out and neatly clipped the tendons in the Sunscorned's wrist. The guard dropped their weapon with a howl of pain, then fled.

Kalis dodged a thrust from his opponent and cleared his mind with a long breath, symbolically releasing tension in a concentrated flow of air. He heard the voices of his Priorium instructors telling him to open the connection of the life force through his blade and balance an inner calm. To use the weapon as he would a crystal.

The Sunscorned came at him again, straightblade gripped with both hands in an overhead chop. Kalis twisted his hands so that the blunt edge of his sword caught the impact, then with a small rotation of his body he allowed the metal of his opponent's to slide forward, scraping against the blade as it passed his right shoulder. The man, not much older than himself, was carried by his momentum, and Kalis instantly stepped forward, kicking the man in the gut. He grunted and stepped away from Kalis.

The Prioriate closed the gap. With narrowed eyes, the man executed a series of thrusts. Kalis parried each, batting them away like the small water bugs that skimmed over Axiom's underground lake. Suddenly the Sunscorned whipped the blade horizontal and low. Kalis attempted to dodge. The edge slashed his right leg, reopening the trägen wound.

He switched into an offensive stance as another jab was thrust at his chest. Instead of deflecting, Kalis jumped back and swung his curved sword down on the straightblade. As the two lengths of steel connected, pain shot through the Sondrinel's leg. With a yelp, Kalis staggered backward. The Sunscorned leaped into the opening in Kalis's guard and knocked the sword from his hand, leaving him open for a finishing blow. Kalis's eyes darted about in desperation, finally seizing upon the dagger secured at Kharnek's hip. He reached for it in the life force, and the weapon zipped through the air into his waiting grasp. A ringing sound emitted from the dagger as the Sunscorned's blade struck it and was narrowly deflected from Kalis's throat.

The unexpected parry threw the other man off balance. Kalis pivoted into him and lowered his shoulder, using his momentum to knock his foe to the ground. Then Kalis was on top of him before he could rise from his back, using his knees to pin the man's arms to his sides. The Sunscorned's eyes grew wide as the point of Kalis's weapon touched beneath his chin.

I can give you what you want, a voice said.

"What did you say?" Kalis growled. The Sunscorned's eyes widened again.

"N-nothing. I said nothing!"

You can make her want you, the voice offered.

Kalis looked toward Idrilia, but she was obscured by Kharnek's form. Then faint light from the purple gem in the dagger's hilt caught his eye.

Take me.

"Kalis," Vayriel's voice interrupted, low. "Remember what you said to me in the place of holding."

A feeling of warmth encompassed him, first from his shoulder then it spread across his skin and into his core. Kalis blinked, looking into the frightened face of the young Sunscorned man. Someone like himself who was only doing what he thought was best.

"What would we become?" he whispered, remembering his words to the Highblood. He withdrew the blade a few inches. Vayriel's comforting pat preceded her proffered hand. Accepting it, Kalis rose and turned away as a gurgling sound came from behind him. Kalis whipped around to see Kharnek withdrawing his ebony blade from the man's chest, a stunned Zinvar behind them.

"Why...why did you do that?" the priest demanded.

Kharnek would not meet the other Komorese's eyes, instead turning his cold gaze upon Kalis. "Never leave a fallen enemy behind you. It is the way of the battlefield."

The Sondrinel said nothing, knowing how close he had been to murdering the man in cold blood. Something had been influencing him, though, that Vayriel's touch dispelled.

"Your sword. And you will return the dagger."

Kalis's eyes flicked to the weapon again. Whatever allure it possessed was gone now, and he refocused his attention on Kharnek. He held the sword Kalis had lost, grip extended toward him. Wordlessly, he exchanged blades with the other man.

"I'm sure they heard our ruckus that time," Kilahym whispered.

"Let's go. I can see the bridge Wen showed Vayriel," Idrilia announced, then she stepped through the opening. Vayriel followed, once again offering her hand to Kalis.

He was thankful for the help as he stepped up and a sharp pain sheared through his calf. His leg buckled, but he managed to stay upright. Vayriel studied him intently.

"You are not yourself, friend Kalis. What troubles you?"

JONATHAN FULLER AND KRISTINA KELLY

Kalis thought of the voice. *What had that been?* He could be having symptoms of blood loss. He shook his head.

"Later. Let's get out of here."

Kalis jogged, wincing, through the opening and out into the brilliant light of Sondrine, onto a small platform. He hesitated, skidding to where his feet touched the edge of a hoop-shaped bridge. It spanned a gap nearly ten bounds of a solendrake and was wide enough for three to walk abreast. Planks laid in long strips, bent to form hoops and half hoops, made the floorboards and support structure.

"Like an enormous harp," Kilahym mused, stepping past Kalis to touch the dull green filaments, dragging his hand across them as he moved. The jeroti followed at his heels.

Kalis saw the high drop into the green of the Jade Sea through the sides of the bridge, which were lashed together with sea-vine cord. His stomach lurched, but he quickly mastered the sensation, as he had been trained. He stepped onto the planks, glancing back briefly to ensure that the others followed. The bridge quivered lightly with their steps, and they followed the path to a large opening at the next pillar.

"Predictable."

Ahead of him, Idrilia, Zinvar, and Kilahym froze. Lady Orym emerged from the opening of the pillar before them. In her hand she held an arm-length vaster, the short wooden pole glowing green. Sentries emerged from the darkness of the skykeel-sized opening and blocked the Truthseekers. They flanked her, three on each side, as she continued.

"When we found your cells empty, I knew you would make your way to our ships. Lucky for me you chose my lord's personal vessel. Now I have the pleasure of delivering you back to the Cloudsoarer myself. We can't be having you tell others where we are."

"Out of our way," Idrilia hissed, her daggers held ready.

"I'm afraid I must decline. Sunblessed!"

Kilahym took a step back and bumped into Orgar as the guards rushed forward to close the gap.

Suddenly Kharnek was where Zinvar had been, his dark sword still sheathed in the tight space of the bridge. The Komorese stepped forward, and quicker than Kalis's eyes could follow, he disarmed the sentry and snapped their neck.

Meanwhile, Idrilia sprung forward and slashed and kicked at two other guards.

Kalis used the newly vacated space to bypass Kilahym and move closer to the skirmish. He flipped a side pouch open and grabbed several crystals. A round one fell to the bridge with a thump; he knew without looking that it was a fire crystal. He hesitated, second-guessing his ability to control any of the destruction he could cause in the precarious position they were in.

"Now, now. I see you. You forget I know what those do." Orym's eyes locked on his. Between them, the two guards engaged with Idrilia dropped, one with Kharnek's aid. The remaining three sentries hesitated to take their place. The older woman sighed. "If you want something done right..."

Orym shifted her pole weapon over her shoulder and pivoted, throwing the rod end over end. As it rotated, it lost cohesion, and pieces of it flew off. Vayriel stepped forward just behind Idrilia. Her protective sphere shimmered around all of the Seekers. The poisoned fragments glowed green, spinning on their flat sides, then smacked the rose-hued barrier. The pieces dropped, clinking to the bridge floor.

"Interesting," Lady Orym muttered, then reached her hand out as if for the fallen pieces. They trembled then slid from all directions, sucked in by an invisible whirlpool, reconnecting and forming the vaster again. At the edge of Vayriel's shield, Kalis could see green smoke swirling within the crystal grip, then it flew back to its mistress's hand. "The coral writher's venom would have made this quicker. It would be much easier if we didn't need you *alive*. Take them."

At her command, the next wave of sentries stepped forward. Vayriel's shield vanished, and Kalis heard her breathing quicken. The Highblood whispered something to Idrilia, who nodded in return. Idrilia whistled, and a familiar figure burst out of the pillar with a screech.

The guards searched the sky for the source. Kalis used the distraction to switch out his chosen crystals for a pair he had never used outside of Priorium.

Orym signaled behind her. Sparks burst from the sides of the opening, and tiny black projectiles trailed the othwit's trajectory.

"Drop!" Idrilia shouted, without the whistle command.

Wen closed her wings and plummeted toward the sea. The rock-like shells flew past her as she unfurled her wings and soared under the bridge.

Molnkamp's second-in-command held her weapon before her. The vaster morphed into a curve, like a sickle blade of Heathström. But before Orym could use the new shape, Kalis acted.

Squeezing his hands, the warrior activated a cerulean crystal in each palm. He tossed one across the bridge to land behind Orym. Kalis focused on the remaining crystal in his right hand and felt a searing pain as if his body was both being ripped apart and condensed into his palm. The sunlight faded into a darkness impenetrable, and he lost all perception—the sense of his being, that he existed within the framework of biological mass, that there was anything but this emptiness—as surely as sounds and smells disappeared into a void. Kalis felt as disoriented as he had in the room of green light. When he had been alone.

But he wasn't anymore. The others waited, imperiled. Kalis focused on finding the pinprick of light he knew would be his exit from this place between physical and noncorporeal. The halfway point to the Rising.

Kalis reappeared behind Orym. He drew his sword and touched the blade to the front of her neck.

"Call them off," Kalis demanded, his face beside hers.

"Sunblessed," her shoulders sagged, "lower weapons and gather."

At her word, the sentries began to comply.

"Ouch!" Kilahym exclaimed, followed by a mournful, "Whoops."

Kalis darted his eyes to the bard. A ball of flame erupted as the spherical crystal Kalis dropped earlier plummeted from Kilahym's grip and sizzled out of existence into the Jade Sea.

"Hymn," Idrilia hissed between clenched teeth.

"Not as easy to use as they look, eh?" the bard asked sheepishly as he wiped the palms of his hands on his sides. "And they get hot fast. Nearly burnt my skin, then how would I ever pen poetry again?"

Vayriel placed a hand on the bard's shoulder, and Kalis returned his focus to his capture.

Orym grinned. "Your bard friend has a way of messing things up, doesn't he?"

"Hey—" Kilahym began.

"Look below. He has awakened the Stormbringer."

"It is trickery," Kharnek growled, "do not lower your guard. Finish her."

"Oh, I do not have a flair for the dramatic as my lord does. Have someone else look if you like. But I warn you, you need my help now. It is you who should lower your weapon. And come with me, before we are overtaken."

Kalis spun and saw an enormous mass rising out of the water. A puffed top, like a cloud of aquamarine, dripped with water that glistened and sparkled. Uncountable individual lengths of pulsing emerald and sapphire hung like matte cable from the ballooning lid. The creature continued to rise until the cables escaped the depth of the Jade Sea, lights dashing down its length to filamented ends.

The cables began to twist and squirm like coral writhers. Kalis realized this was exactly what they were. Each cable was a full-grown coral writher, much larger than the ones they had seen float into their prison. Their bud-like tops darted here and there, circling each other inside the collective shape. Each time a coral writher head touched the top, it sped the light trails across the surface into a frenzy. Occasionally, green lightning sparked in thin strings within the expanding cloud.

Where the organism had been, the water now looked more azure, like the coast of Ettra. The Jade Sea's color came from its inhabitants, Kalis realized: an amazing amount of coral writhers. The whole mass was at least as tall as the bridge. And it was floating toward them.

CHAPTER 52

"What was that move back there?" Idrilia asked as she assisted Kalis in securing Orym. They had tied knots in a headscarf to bind her hands and feet and were dragging her to her compatriots, whom Zinvar and Kilahym had bound and gagged.

"Not now," he said through clenched teeth, depositing Orym against the wall near the pillar's entrance.

Idrilia felt heat rising to her cheeks as she was reminded that he had kept knowledge from Priorium. The High Keeper had eluded to those abilities. But it was best to not let the others know details of the life force manipulation he had just accomplished. She glanced at Orym. Especially the deserter from Axiom, though a strange compassion swelled in Idrilia's chest for the woman.

Kalis limped over to Kharnek, his back to the others, and whispered. After a brief exchange, the Komorese left with quickened steps toward the embarkation ramp, weapon drawn while Kalis returned to her side. Idrilia watched, surprised at the initiative he continued to show since Zinvar's brother showed up.

Kaast! Rinesh.

Idrilia reached into her pouch and withdrew the crystal swirling with a cream color. She tossed it away from the others and watched as mist escaped, like a colored fragrance from one of her mother's scented oil vials, then formed the vague shape of and tightened into the taller brother's form.

"I promise I won't alert them I—" Rinesh continued his thought from before his encasement.

"Rinesh! I was afraid—" The sentence stalled on Zinvar's lips as his brother doubled over and retched.

"Oh, dear." Kilahym reached into his pockets and traveling sack as if to offer Rinesh something for his state, but the bard instead clasped his hands together before him in an odd greeting gesture. Idrilia barely stopped herself from shaking her head.

"My vision is impaired. How did I get here?"

"Well, you see, we—"

"No time," Idrilia interrupted Kilahym and grabbed Rinesh by his elbow, dragging him toward Kalis. "The blurry vision will pass. It's diminishing sickness. You said you can fly this thing?"

Rinesh nodded, then Idrilia called out to Kalis, who stood near the base of the ramp. "Here's our escape."

"What do you know about this creature?" Kalis asked, pointing back toward the opening.

The Komorese squinted along the indicated line.

"Orym called it a Stormbringer," Idrilia added.

"Oh. That's not good. I think...I think I'm going to be sick." Rinesh covered his mouth and heaved, as if he fought to hold back the inevitable. Idrilia felt her own stomach turn just watching him.

She addressed Vayriel, "Do you have any herbs that could help him?" The Highblood rummaged in her alusarean bag.

"Tell me about the Stormbringer." Kalis continued. "Is it a danger to us? Can we fly the skykeel while it is out there?"

"It would be very dangerous. The Cloudsoarer has instructed all aerialists to remain docked if a Stormbringer is roused. It directs bolts of energy at any objects that draw near. A defense mechanism. Like how a single coral writher strikes with venom when threatened. Only here, they've come together to protect their swarm."

"Thanks, Kilahym," Idrilia grumbled.

"Hmm? At your service, dilly-Drilly," Kilahym said.

She glared at him. "You woke the beast. What were you thinking?"

"He only wished to assist us," Vayriel defended. "What was done is done."

"Though—I *am* surprised that you were able to activate the crystal. You may have an aptitude for them."

Kilahym brightened. "Really? Umm, thank you?"

"Don't let it go to your head, bard," Idrilia muttered.

"Sondrinel. There she goes again!"

A grin tugged at the corner of Idrilia's mouth.

"Are we safe from the creature's energy within these—?" Vayriel gestured to the coral walls as she approached, handing a white sprig to Rinesh. "I feel life energy all around us."

Zinvar's brother began to chew on the brittle plant with a grimace. "Yes, we are safe. If the coral pillar is touched by the electricity, it is absorbed and initiates another growth of the lower levels. Above the water the polyps are mostly dormant or dead, but below the water they still live."

I don't think Vayriel can stretch her protective shield around the whole skykeel, but if we stay close together…" Idrilia gestured to the Highblood as her words trailed off.

"Yes, I can protect us if we remain together."

"Then we go now." Kalis motioned for Zinvar and Kilahym.

Idrilia placed fingers in her mouth and whistled loudly, the sound reverberating off of the concave interior of the pillar. A moment later, a happy hoot echoed softly, and Wen glided in to land on the tacked sails of the ship. Vayriel prodded Orgar, and the jeroti bounded up the embarkation ramp.

"I just need to activate the crystals at the wheel," Rinesh called over his shoulder as he jogged onto the deck. "If you and your companions can remove the anchors, we will float out."

"So the secret *is* crystals. Stolen technology," Kalis grumbled.

"No, Garron designed these ships," Idrilia said.

"Who?"

"The Cloudsoarer." She frowned as she answered, trying to recall how she obtained that information, including his name.

"Did he do something to you?" Kalis asked quietly, pausing to step closer. "I have this feeling that I'm not remembering everything from my…stay here."

"I—I don't really remember. Let's just get out of here." Idrilia grudgingly admitted to herself that she appreciated Kalis's concern, but, as usual, his timing could not be worse. She moved past him toward one of the anchors. The others followed, and between them, they released the skykeel from its tethers; it shifted like a solendrake freed from its stall. Rinesh showed Idrilia and Kalis the crystals embedded into the wheel, which he touched, explaining that the smaller crystals on the deck interacted with the larger crystals in the hold.

"You, with the instrument on his back."

"The name's Kilahym," the bard bowed deeply, nearly touching his nose to his knees, "though seeing as you are brother to my dear friend, you may call me Hymn."

"Hymn, go to the stern. There is a set of crystals in the railing. Press them in this order: yellow, peach, blue. Wait for my signal, then press the white rectangle."

"Peach, yellow, blue. Got it. I jest! Memorization is one of my bardic skills. Put your version of Komorese faith in me." Kilahym saluted, then ran as commanded.

"Zinvar, I need you and the others to ready the sails. Once we exit, I'll need them up and unfurled to steer. You might have to work in pairs at each mast."

"I'll join you," Idrilia told Vayriel. The pair, trailed by Orgar, strode to the main mast. Around the base of the wide column, they found several ropes and deliberated what Rinesh expected them to do. Idrilia tried to recall what the crews did on the boats between Ettra, hoping she retained some knowledge from her trips with her grandparents that could help them now.

"Where's Kharnek?" Kalis called, looking around.

"Below deck still, I would think." Idrilia rolled her eyes.

"Why did he leave us? When was this?"

Idrilia halted as she gripped her chosen camelid-colored rope.

"You sent him in ahead of us," Idrilia called over her shoulder, wondering why she had to remind him

"I—Did I? Why did I do that?"

"How should I know?" Then quietly to Vayriel, "What is the matter with him?" Idrilia could not think of a time where Kalis could not recall their actions that would satisfy Sentinel mission report requirements.

Vayriel froze for a moment before answering. "Kalis appears to be suffering from his injury. As soon as we are free from this situation, we should tend to his wounds. They are weakening his resistance against the darkness we saw in Adjira. It is still here among us."

Idrilia tilted her head. She watched Kalis hobble past them to meet Zinvar at the forward-most mast. Since a diminishing crystal had side effects, it was possible that the life force manipulation Kalis displayed had an equally unpleasant consequence on the body. Whatever it was, they just needed to finish escaping, and then they could help him.

Rinesh called for Zinvar to begin. Lights shone on the walls of the pillar, accompanied by a click and a hum, then the familiar sound of crashing waves returned. Small crystals illuminated the wall in a pale blue horizontal line, spaced evenly like a row of sand marbles in a game Idrilia played with Felune.

The skykeel seemed to freeze, no longer swaying in its suspension. Then with a slight jolt, the skykeel rotated until the bowsprit pointed toward the western-facing opening, like a hand on a timepiece ticking clockwise. To their left, the opening they had entered from showed an empty bridge. No Stormbringer.

Vayriel and Idrilia finished tugging, setting their sail in place high on the mast, as Kharnek appeared out of the door and climbed the few stairs from beneath the deck. He was not alone.

"Get yer hands off of us!"

"What'd'ya think yer doin'? We told ya before—"

"Silence," Kharnek growled, grasping two forms by the fabric near their necks and slinging them to the deck. His dark eyes surveyed the others.

"Brace yourselves," Rinesh warned. "Hymn, the last crystal."

The boat lurched. A *thoom*, like a metallic drum mixed with air over a large pipe, reverberated in the column.

Idrilia grabbed Vayriel's arm and with her other hand she gripped the mast. The skykeel burst through the opening into the full luminance of the sun, flying over the jade water. Idrilia stole a glance over her shoulder. Sunscorned stood at the first pillar's entrance, gesturing toward the vessel as it leisurely put distance between them. Idrilia smirked.

"Will you be in need of my arm much longer?"

Idrilia flinched, looking where she gripped the Highblood just below her triplicate silver armband. She loosened her fingers and mumbled an apology. Vayriel's large smile seemed to indicate that the Highblood found the encounter amusing. Idrilia edged closer to the port side, hiding her flushed cheeks.

The launching mechanisms had propelled them forward, Idrilia noted, but the sails were not yet filled to maintain or increase their escape velocity. If this had been a normal sea vessel, they would be idly drifting in the waters rather than skimming across them.

"Yer mad! No, no, no. Put me down. Arrrgh!"

Spinning toward the commotion, Idrilia saw a cloak fluttering as it as its Sunscorned owner was thrown over the side of the skykeel. The remaining Sunscorned held up his hands plaintively as he knelt on the deck. Idrilia bent over the side, catching the splash below.

Idrilia leaned an elbow on the railing. "Interesting method you have for dealing with our captives."

Kharnek's face was expressionless. "I did not ask for your opinion."

"Not that I disagree. I just think we should see if they have any valuable information first."

"They will only impede us, or attempt subversion."

"Or," Idrilia elongated the word, "they can tell us if we will be pursued. Or how they've kept these vessels unknown to the realms—we could use that."

"All of that is immaterial if we are dead or captured again," Kharnek fired back.

"What's our heading?" Rinesh asked before Idrilia could form a reply.

"Komor," Kalis answered, drawing closer to the wheel. "The next Trial will take place in the Fellwood."

"Into the hands of spirits," Rinesh muttered.

Before anyone could comment, a sound of successive *fwumps* filled the air. It almost sounded like Fey making fire explosion sounds with her mouth. Idrilia looked around for the source.

"I do believe our former hosts are attempting to prevent our unparalleled escape. They no longer care about using us to bargain with, apparently," Kilahym commented.

"They are not aiming for us," Vayriel said, her head tilted back.

Idrilia followed her line of sight. The writhing form of the Stormbringer had risen over the side of the skykeel behind Idrilia. It hovered like a misshapen creature—giant head and too many appendages. One of the individual writhers snapped forward. Idrilia jumped back from the edge. The creature latched its pointed teeth to the railing, sparks jumping from its twin fangs. More emerald writhers sprung from their complex weaving and darted from the mass toward the skykeel.

Idrilia drew her daggers as the creatures closest to her wriggled in an attempt to heave their long bodies over the side. With a backhanded swipe of her left hand, she sliced through the flat, plant-like head of one nearest her. Idrilia felt a jolt in her grip, which traveled painfully to her elbow, then the smooth quivering body of the coral writher fell away from the skykeel.

Shaking her arm as if to free it from the shock, Idrilia impaled the next writher between its beady eyes with her other hand. The same painful tingling traveled through her right arm. The ascending and descending tones of Wen's chitter preceded her swooping as the othwit dropped low and latched on to the length of another writher. Wen's talons tore the body from the skykeel; she, like other coastal othwits, was immune to the writhers' defense.

As Wen released the creature from her grip, Idrilia glanced at Vayriel. The Highblood spun her spear in quick, short movements, changing directions and alternating hands to whack each new writher with the blunt end, knocking them away from the ship. The young woman appeared unaffected by the energy that struck Idrilia. Orgar dashed from side to side, snapping his jaws at empty air as his life-friend knocked his catch away before it reached his maw. Vayriel's peach hair blew wildly with the wind and her movements. Idrilia moved closer, and the pair of women fought in tandem, each reflecting their own style and extended by their animal companions.

A coral writher floated between them, missing the railing in its undulating flight, the pulsing body oddly flat as it wiggled an *S*-shape through the air. Vayriel rotated to address the writher as Idrilia swiped down, severing the bud and frond from the filament tail. The Highblood's facial features dropped as she looked from the remains of the severed creature lying on the deck to Idrilia. Orgar turned his tails to face the Sondrinel before the Highblood, too, swiveled away, knocking another writher from the ship. A weight grew in Idrilia's chest at the afterimage of a disapproving Vayriel.

Idrilia debated how to proceed. More coral writhers launched themselves from the mass, yet the girth of the creature remained the same. It was hard to gauge how many individuals made up the twisting whole. Simply knocking them away did not guarantee their removal from this battle.

Resigned to avoid disappointing her friend, Idrilia batted the next writher that came close with the flat of her blade instead. Her target dropped, stunned, to the deck. Idrilia scowled at the result of her less than successful attempt at emulating the Highblood. Having them onboard was not part of the plan. As she debated the best way to get the now lightless carcass off of the ship and avoid its venomous bite were it to become alert, Orgar pounced, grabbing the writher mid-body in his mouth. He launched his white paws onto the railing, then with a shake of his head, tossed the creature overboard. Smiling, Idrilia stepped toward the jeroti and his life-friend.

"Look out!" Rinesh called.

The Stormbringer's cloud, now expanded beneath the pillowy top, sparked green lightning almost as fast as the lights dashing across the lengths of individual writhers. A green spark shot from the Stormbringer's aquamarine cloud. Vayriel's protection surrounded the two women just as quickly. The spark sizzled for a blink before ricocheting, following the length of the ship.

An agonizing howl broke the sounds of the Truthseekers' struggle. Idrilia swiveled to see lightning pulsing through the remaining Sunscorned's veins, glowing like Komorese tattoos all over his skin. The Sunscorned turned into a pile of sand; there was a hissing against the wood, and the man was gone.

Vayriel took a step forward, hand extended—the sphere of protection was gone. The anguish on Vayriel's face stopped any words Idrilia had in her throat. She had saved them only to reflect the killing bolt to another being. Idrilia could only imagine what the Highblood was feeling as Wen landed on Idrilia's shoulder, having hovered out of harm's way.

"By the lady! Eh, my warrior friends, mayhaps you have a plan to get us away from certain death—now, rather than, oh, when I'm a pile of unpleasantly gray ash!?"

"If we open the sails, we can grab the winds and move faster," Rinesh offered, pointing to the two masts with furled triangular sails.

Kalis nodded and set off toward them.

"Can't you life-force push them away?" Kilahym asked Kharnek, accentuating the question by flexing his arms awkwardly in front of him.

"Why are you addressing me, bard? I do not know—"

"The opposite of what you did to the guards," Kilahym interrupted Kharnek, the bard's words impossibly quicker than usual. "Push, not pull. It's rather simple. Grey Lady preserve us." His hand went to his forehead.

"You are mistaken. The Sunscorned—"

"Backside of a ratufa. We all saw what you did. I don't know how you did it, but those guards did not simply walk into your waiting arms to be kissed pleasantly by your pursed lips. You saw it, right?" Kilahym gestured wildly to the group.

Idrilia's head tilted. "Yes, it was like when we were fighting Adjira. And in the ruins by Peatwick."

"Vayriel, back us up here!"

"The guards snapped like a string on Kilahym's dulcimer to the door of the enclosure. Much like Kalis did on the bridge to appear suddenly behind our foes."

"Exactly, thank you, my dear."

"However, I do not think this is a use of the life force," Vayriel continued. "It is the power that Adjira warned us about."

"This conversation is a waste of time," Kharnek growled.

"You always say that. So, you aren't going to help?"

In response to Kilahym's question, Kharnek faced the looming Stormbringer. The bard ran his hand through his dark hair. "Well, who has the next scintillating notion as mine has been squashed?"

"Excuse me," Zinvar's voice addressed them tentatively. "Vayriel. Could you, uh, connect to the creature as you did with the othwit?"

Vayriel glanced at the remains of the Sunscorned. "I will try."

"We should still get these sails open. We'll never reach Komor without them—not that I'd be heartbroken over that." Rinesh asked for someone to climb each of the three masts, to which Zinvar and Kilahym volunteered, after getting hasty instructions from the aerialist. The others continued to dispatch the seemingly endless horde of writhers while Vayriel focused. Idrilia whistled, and Wen rejoined the scrimmage with her, wings folding and unfolding in a powerful wind dance. Like Orgar, she tossed any incapacitated ones overboard.

"There are too many!" Vayriel exclaimed after several more waves of attackers. She pinched the bridge of her nose, her other hand finding the top of Orgar's snout like a hand rest. "So many life thoughts. I cannot connect to them. As soon as I *feel* one, my mind slips to another."

"Try focusing on the whole. As if it is one creature," Idrilia suggested. "Zinvar's brother said the Stormbringer formed when many were in danger." The creature behaved like one unit, the individual bodies emulating a multitude of arms or legs. Vayriel agreed to try again, but moments later stumbled a step forward, leaning heavily on her spear.

"I am not…yet strong enough," she gasped, clutching a hand to her chest.

"Of course you are!" Kilahym encouraged, jumping down from the mast before Idrilia could console her. She shot a glare at the bard's back.

"You can do anything," Kilahym continued. "Bond with a beast lowlanders fear—no offense Orgar, the jeroti are rather misunderstood in popular culture—survive a trägen, grow flowers from the palm of your hand, communicate with wingy-ly creatures trained for battle." He nodded toward Wen. "You are quite the embodiment of bravery and perseverance. I wrote a poem about such a topic my first year at the bard academy. I think I remember how—"

"Kilahym." Idrilia rejected his not yet spoken request to recite the lyric.

"Oh, all right. Another time."

"I thank you, Kilahym, but the energy I have within is not enough to reach the Stormbringer. I—I *pushed* more of my life force than I should have tried. I felt it leave me, and my eyes went dark for a moment."

"Can you use me? I mean, can I help? Like before with Wen. Oh! You could draw from Zinvar and myself, like you did in the belly of the beast!"

Idrilia flicked her eyes between the two; she assumed Kilahym was referencing the creature within the storm wall. Whatever had happened with Wen must have been while she was unconscious.

"I have learned from my first effort. I will be careful to not draw too much energy from you," Vayriel agreed with a nod.

Kilahym smacked a stray writher away with his journal. "And hopefully you don't get visions of alien beings this time."

He stuffed his journal into his waistband and took Vayriel's hands in his. The Highblood trained her eyes on the Stormbringer, unblinking. She breathed deeply as Orgar placed a paw on each of their feet, completing a symbolic connection. Idrilia's eyes burned at the intimacy, watching Kilahym's brows soften as he focused on Vayriel.

Idrilia tore her gaze away, ready to strike down the nearest writher. But the creature began to undulate head over tail, making a circle in the air with its stringed ends inches before her nose. Writhers near Kharnek and Kalis mirrored the maneuver then returned to the Stormbringer whole. The creatures merged into the swirling, revolving form under the buoyant top. The Stormbringer whole floated back toward the coral pillars.

"Thank the lady!" Kilahym breathed.

Idrilia sheathed her weapons. "How did you do it?"

Vayriel's gaze lingered on the Stormbringer. "I sent them the feeling of home...I believe."

"Interesting," Kharnek said, putting his sword away as well.

"Amazing is more like it! You've saved us all with the promise of a soft bed and roasted pineberries."

Idrilia raised an eyebrow.

"What? I was using a metaphor. Anyways, well done, Vayriel!"

"Yes, great work!" Kalis chimed in, only to stumble in his step.

Vayriel dipped her head. "It is what the Mother-of-All would wish. We are alive, as are her writher daughters and sons. Kalis," she approached the Sondrinel, "let me tend to your wounds. You are not looking well, my friend."

As Vayriel took a pale Kalis by the arm, Idrilia walked to where Kharnek now stood at the rail of the ship.

"Nicely fought—for a Sondrinel," the warrior said without turning his head.

"You as well." Idrilia crossed her arms, watching the Stormbringer draw closer to the Sunscorned pillars.

"Your reluctance to kill is a weakness."

Idrilia huffed. "You don't know me. Besides, I think what Vayriel says has meaning."

"I will not hesitate to kill you when we fight."

"Humph. You haven't tried yet."

"When the time is right."

"Sure. I actually think you're beginning to like me."

"Never," Kharnek bit.

Idrilia walked away, the sound of explosions from distant Sunscorned weapons meeting her back as a grin tugged one side of her mouth.

CHAPTER 53

"Rinesh says about four days if the winds are strong." Kalis's voice broke the soft sound of the wind as he stepped beside Idrilia at the skykeel's prow. "And the Stormbringer should keep the Sunscorned occupied. We won't be followed, you know. At least not until luminance tomorrow."

Idrilia looked east from the back of the skykeel but said nothing. Kalis wondered what she was thinking.

He ventured again into the quiet. "That tyrant really did something to you, didn't he? You seem…different."

"I owe the style of my robe to him, actually," Idrilia spoke quickly.

Kalis leaned against the railing and stared at the sky. "How's that?"

"I believe he gave my grandmother one like it and it inspired similar designs."

"I don't see that pompous man giving anyone a gift."

Idrilia shrugged. "The memory is fuzzy, but I think it was an apology. Something to do with accidentally destroying…a building in Axiom many synodies ago. I remember hearing about it from my mother."

"A building in…wait, the Artificers Guild? You can't be serious." Kalis shook his head. "And yet…it seems like I recall him saying something about it, too. But how could I know that?"

'Dril regarded him, her brow creased by concern. "The timing would be right. I want to read through the Praeteritum volumes in Evocus to be certain." She tilted her head. "But, wait, how would you have known anything about it?"

Kalis shrugged. "After I was captured and before you and the others arrived, there's a gap in my memory. But it's not all gone."

"What do you mean?"

He faced her with his arms crossed over his chest. "It's...hard to explain. Random recollections come to mind now and then, but I can't place them in order of when they happened. But they all involve the Cloudsoarer. I think...I think that he asked me about Axiom."

Idrilia's face clouded. "I'm experiencing the same thing. He must have done something to us."

"It's only a rumor, but I've heard that the Sentinels found a way to use crystals to put prisoners in a trance-like state, one where they can't hide anything." Kalis clenched his jaw. "Or stop anything from being done to them."

Comprehension dawned on Idrilia's face. "Oh. You mean you think he might have...no. We would certainly remember that. And...I don't think he's like that."

Kalis's brows flew upward. "Not like that? What's that supposed to mean? He's a traitor to Axiom, 'Dril."

"It's not that simple," she huffed, placing her hands on her hips. "He used to be a well-respected scientist before that accident. And, if you think about it, he and the Sunscorned did nothing wrong except *think* differently than how the Edicts tell them to."

"I don't follow."

Idrilia rolled her eyes. "Someone didn't learn their history very well."

He spread his hands. "Care to enlighten me, then?"

She nodded and cleared her throat. "The Sunscorned are depicted as outcasts by the Council. And some of them are indeed involuntarily removed from Axiom because of their actions. Like blowing up buildings."

Kalis grinned. "I think you're reinforcing my point."

Idrilia tapped her foot impatiently. "I'm not finished. According to public records, most Sunscorned leave Axiom of their own volition."

The idea rocked Kalis. Why would anyone choose to leave?

"I know it's hard to imagine wanting to leave, but if everyone regarded you as a pariah for your choices, why would you stay?" A profound sadness colored her words. "I can't fully explain it, but I think that what Molnkamp wanted to know from us is whether things have changed. Whether we, as a society, had become more tolerant. And he found what he expected. We're no better than when he left. Still forcing people to follow a path they don't want to be on."

Every word she spoke pummeled his deepest convictions. He shook his head in frustration. "Where is this coming from? Did he mess with your mind, somehow?"

"I'm just thinking for myself," she shot back. "It might do you some good. If you weren't such a stickler for rules maybe you'd see why life is so unfair."

Kalis's eyes widened. "This is about us, isn't it? Our betrothal?"

She answered him with silence. Glancing around to make sure the other Truthseekers were occupied with tasks elsewhere on the skykeel, he lowered his voice. "Look, I know you resent me for what our families did, springing it on you—"

"You don't know anything about my feelings, Kalis Vaktare," she said coldly.

"Dril, be reasonable."

"*Reasonable?* What exactly is reasonable about forcing someone to spend their whole life with someone they didn't choose?" She broke off and stepped back, shaking her head. "I know you think the Sunscorned are bad, but I don't think so. I'm beginning to think it's the Council that got it all wrong. And my grandmother was trying to change all that."

Kalis raised his hands in protest. "A High Keeper wouldn't directly contradict the Edicts. Not even your grandmother, intrepid though she was."

"True. But the Council wants us to have one opinion of the Sunscorned because they are different. Because they challenge something about our society. But they have a freedom Axiom doesn't have. My grandmother wrote about it."

"Convenient that you remember this now," Kalis retorted. "Right after an enemy who would want you to feel sympathy for them used some unknown, mind-altering crystal on us."

His betrothed shrugged her shoulders. "It's not that. I haven't had a reason to engage in a philosophical debate on outcasting practices with you, or anyone, before." She huffed. "My parents think they are rightly exiled, basja of the realm and all that. What if it's just another outdated mindset?"

Kalis found himself struggling to control the emotions her words produced. What she was saying could be construed as treason. "Tell me what you remember, then."

"After…" Idrilia fought to keep her voice steady, "after my grandmother returned to the life force, I went to Evocus and read everything she ever wrote. I thought…I thought by reading her words I could hear her voice and that she would be with me still." She hid her face beneath her cerulean locks. "There was an entry she wrote about the Sunscorned. She ended it with something like, 'Instead of shunning the Sunscorned, we should seek to emulate them.' But more than that, she wrote about their initiative to *choose* what to do with their lives. You *know* my grandmother wanted me to choose my own guild."

Kalis took a moment to digest this information. "I know. And I...I'm trying, 'Dril, to understand. It's just hard to imagine life working like that."

She cocked her head. "Like what?"

"Like," he struggled to find the words, and the Penumbra's words returned to him unbidden, "Like you could have everything you ever wanted," he finished.

Idrilia's eyes brightened. "But don't you see? We *can*. We just have to stop listening to the people who tell us that we can't. No matter who they are."

"But...what if they don't mean well? We have no idea what the Cloudsoarer wants, much less—" he stopped, unsure whether to reveal what happened back at the Reef.

"Much less what?"

Kalis looked away into the endless blue of the sky beyond their vessel, its color marred only by the white wisps of clouds that scudded overhead. Their swirls reminded him of the eerie light that coiled within the gem in Kharnek's dagger.

"Kalis? What's wrong? Is it your leg still bothering you?"

A heavy sigh escaped him. "No, Vayriel's herbs took most of the pain away."

He felt her light touch on his arm, and his pulse quickened.

"Then what's going on? You're hiding something."

Kalis slumped. "I could never keep anything from you." He recounted the dagger's temptation to her, the words pouring out like a cup being emptied. He was afraid to meet Idrilia's gaze once he finished. Her hand, withdrawn midway through his tale, came to rest on the railing.

"So Vayriel was right," she murmured.

Kalis stiffened. "About what?"

"She thought that what claimed Adjira—the Penumbra—might still be around. And that your physical weakness made you vulnerable to it."

As the implications of her statement sank in, both Sondrinel lapsed into a speculative silence. The wind picked up, snatching at their robes like an errant child. Idrilia finally said what they were both thinking, "We need to be very careful."

Kalis eyed her sidelong. "Who are you, and what did you do with 'Dril?"

She glared at him, but there was no real anger behind it. "I know it's rare that I advocate for caution, but we've seen how dangerous Kharnek is."

He nodded. "That's true. Especially with those special powers he seems to have. Kilahym was right about that, you know."

"One of his rare accurate observations," she replied drily.

"Even so...it's possible the dagger might augment those abilities. If it's the Penumbra behind them."

Idrilia gawked at him. "If? Obviously, that's what's going on."

Kalis shook his head. "We can't prove that. And if we accused him again, he'd just blame it on our own prejudice against his people."

"I suppose you're right." A wry grin crossed her face. "Just this once."

They shared a soft chuckle. Kalis felt his heart lift at the sound of her laughter. Gently, he placed his hands on her shoulders and rotated her to face him. "Dril, about what you were saying earlier, I wanted to tell you—"

Kilahym's shout reached them both from the aft of the skykeel. "Yoo-hoo! Kali-Kal! Dilly-Drilly! Would you be so kind as to lend us your shipmanship?"

Grumbling, Idrilia broke away from Kalis, missing the disappointment that flashed across his face before he could stop it.

"Well, I guess we should see what trouble he's gotten us into now." She headed for the bard's location, then stopped. Twisting her neck, she eyed Kalis curiously. "What was it you wanted to tell me?"

He forced a smile. "We can talk about it later. Let's go help Hymn."

She grinned mischievously. "Race you to the back." Before he could reply, she took off, calling over her shoulder, "Last one there is solendrake droppings!"

Kalis heaved a sigh and ran after her.

CHAPTER 54

His brother was alive.

Now that the chaos of the Seekers' escape from the Sunscorned was a few hours behind him, the realization struck Zinvar with full force. He leaned heavily against the railing of the skykeel. The roughness of the wood biting against his palms reminded him that this moment was real. Peering at the wispy clouds and the sea far below, Zinvar lost himself in a recollection of the last time he saw Rinesh.

His brother's green eyes flashed with anger as he turned away, refusing to endorse Zinvar's decision to join the Priesthood. They were standing outside their family's home in one of the better neighborhoods of Zel Morakh.

"How can you do this? The Priesthood is the worst evil to ever befall Komor."

Confused by his brother's hostility, Zinvar tried to reason with him. "I know they've done as much harm as good. But that can only be changed from the inside, Rin. That's why I'm becoming an acolyte. To make things better."

Rinesh shook his head and laughed. "Better. Ever the idealist. One good person isn't going to change everything."

Zinvar bit his lip as moisture brimmed in his eyes. This unexpected rejection stung. "I don't understand. I thought you'd be happy for me."

"Happy?" Rinesh roared and whirled around. "While you've had your nose in those dusty tomes, I've been the one mother takes her problems out on. Do you see these bruises? They're from her." Rinesh thrust his forearm out, and Zinvar's eyes widened.

Mottled purple and blue blemishes dotted his sibling's skin, but that was not what captured his attention. Amid the bruises, a tattoo glowed with the redness of a fresh application. Rinesh hurriedly pulled back his arm.

Zinvar's voice was barely a whisper. "What...what have you done?"

"I found my own way out." Rinesh's hands balled into fists. "You've been too busy to notice, of course."

The harsh reply made him stiffen. "That's not true. I knew mother's illness had gotten worse. And that you hadn't been around as much. I thought you were just having a hard time handling everything. If I'd known she was hurting you—" He broke off, unable to finish. His chest heaved with suppressed emotion. "I'm so sorry, Rin." Zinvar tried to embrace him, but his brother stepped back.

"It's too late for that. Good luck, brother." Rinesh turned to leave.

"Wait!" Zinvar's voice stopped him. "Where will you go? If the Priesthood catches you, they...they'll have you executed." Rinesh looked over his shoulder and smiled wryly at him. "Try to stop them from doing that, will you?" Then he disappeared into Morakh's Shadow.

Zinvar's knuckles whitened as he gripped the railing. Many epicycles later, when his parents were killed, Rinesh was nowhere to be found. The anger Zinvar felt when his brother did not attend their parents' entombment ceremony had burned like a fire crystal. Then the resurgent Arakhist cult became too much of a threat for the Priesthood to ignore, and his anger was transformed into fear. A Time of Purification was declared. The Priesthood captured and executed the cult's leaders and drove their followers out of Zel Morakh. Zinvar had feared Rinesh lost—and with him the last of his family.

Now, here he was, alive and well, somehow having made his way from Komor to the northern reaches of Sondrine.

"What do you contemplate, priest?"

Kharnek.

Without intending to, Zinvar felt himself tense. He wondered if the warrior noticed. "The past," he answered.

The warrior's larger hand settled atop his. "I am here if you would like to talk about it."

Kharnek's touch kindled a whole other host of emotions, which overwhelmed Zinvar. A part of him did want to open up about the confusion triggered by his brother's sudden reappearance, but it was tempered by his disappointment in how Kharnek had behaved toward the Sondrinel during their escape. The latter sentiment festered like the poison from a coral writher's bite, and he chose to address it.

"I wish you would stop discounting everything Idrilia says."

Zinvar felt the other man's fingers tighten around his own.

Kharnek exhaled heavily. "I know, and I am sorry. It is hard to unlearn epicycles of hatred. But I will keep trying, for you."

"Thank you."

Zinvar looked up and found the warrior's eyes already on him. A tautness formed in his lower abdomen as he lost himself in their depths. Then a shadow marred the brown, as if Kharnek's pupils had leaked into his irises. The warrior abruptly turned away and released Zinvar's hand.

"Kharnek? What's wrong?"

"It is nothing," he answered too quickly. "I am just tired from the battle."

"I thought we were going to be honest with each other now." Zinvar rubbed the small of Kharnek's back. "Whatever's going on, you can talk to me about it."

The warrior continued to look away. "Thank you for your concern, but I am fine."

Zinvar stepped back and clenched his jaw. "Right. Whatever you say."

He collected his staff from where he had leaned it against the railing and walked away. He could feel Kharnek's eyes on him, and a flash of guilt made the priest falter in his stride. Gritting his teeth, Zinvar buried the feeling. He would not relent. If Kharnek really wanted to get to know him, he had to learn to open himself up—without Zinvar always doing so first.

Wind streaked across the skykeel's open deck as its sails snapped, Zinvar's dull orange robes fluttering to the same rhythm of gusts. He found himself drawn up the short flight of stairs to the raised aft deck, at the center of which Kilahym, Vayriel, and Orgar were seated.

"Zinny! We were beginning to wonder if you'd fallen into the sky," the bard said by way of greeting. He patted the wooden planks next to him. "Come, join our merry band!"

The jeroti's tails drummed happily against the deck as Zinvar sat cross-legged beside the bard, staff placed across his lap. Vayriel looked up from stroking Orgar's head. She smiled and nodded at the priest. He returned the Highblood's gesture, but the forced expression quickly faded.

"Where's your brother, Zin?" Kilahym asked, while scratching the stubble on his chin.

"He's down below. Said something about making sure that the power crystals were fully charged."

"Ha! Wouldn't that be a tragic irony? To escape the clutches of our fearsome captors, only to plunge to our deaths from on high. Speaking of which, what a stroke of good fortune that ol' Rinnet—"

"Rinesh," Zinvar corrected.

"—that Rinesk knows how to fly this contraption."

"Indeed. We are all most grateful for his assistance and pleased to see you reunited with him." Vayriel's assurance was accompanied by another nod. The priest found it hard to meet her perceptive eyes.

"I appreciate all of you trusting me enough to let him come with us," he said while looking at the deck, afraid of what their response might be.

"I don't think Dilly-Drilly and her resurrected partner-to-be are happy about it, but they'll come around."

"Ever the optimist, Kilahym," Zinvar replied drily. The bard beamed at the apparent praise. "But they still haven't come around to Kharnek, never mind another shadow-dweller."

Kilahym spread his hands. "Not to put too fine a point on it, but your *friend* isn't doing much to endear himself to them."

"He's trying—" Zinvar began then stopped, cheeks burning while Kilahym giggled. A smile tugged at the corner of Vayriel's lips, which she promptly hid by tilting her head so her face was covered with a wave of peach hair. "I mean, I suppose you're right. Even Rinesh seems to want nothing to do with him." The priest sighed. "I don't know why I still defend him."

"Perhaps because you want to—Ouch!" The bard recoiled from Orgar, who had nipped him lightly on an exposed upper arm. "Tempestuous creature," Kilahym grumbled, rubbing the offended skin. "What I wanted to say is that I think it's because you care for him in more than a friendly way."

"Yes, but sometimes he's a *monster*." The words tumbled unbidden from Zinvar. He buried his face in his hands, shocked at their import. Although his complicated feelings for Kharnek were strong, he had never admitted them aloud to anyone but the other Komorese.

A gentle touch on his knee prompted him to raise his head. It was Vayriel. Strands of her hair whipped across her face in the breeze. She scrutinized the priest intently, but there was empathy in her visage.

"I have only known you for a short time, friend Zinvar, but I know that when you speak, it is your truth." Vayriel looked down. "My people have always discouraged bonds between two men," she continued softly, "because they said the feelings were not real, that they were not right." The Highblood raised her head and set her jaw. "But I think it is my people who were not right. I see in your eyes, feel in your movements, and hear in your words the way you care about him. It is real. It is beautiful."

Zinvar felt tears burn his eyes. Her words buoyed his faltering spirit, but he hesitated to embrace the hope they offered.

"As usual, Vayriel is right. And besides, Kharnek isn't so bad."

The priest shot Kilahym a skeptical glance.

"Well, he is sometimes. But he definitely cares for you," the bard asserted. He clapped Zinvar's shoulder and leaned in to whisper in his ear, "And he *definitely* finds you attractive."

The Komorese felt fire on his cheeks and mocked throwing a punch at the other man as Kilahym snickered. Orgar raised his head from his paws and cocked his head, attention fixed on the two men.

"Sorry, Orgar, Kilahym is just being obtuse as usual," Zinvar apologized. He reached over and scratched the fur beneath Orgar's chin, prompting a burst of effulgent tail undulations.

"Obtuse! You wound me." The bard clutched his chest in mock pain. To his left, the Highblood stifled a laugh. A sense of longing came over the priest— if only he too could share something so carefree. But then would Kharnek be Kharnek without his perennial gravitas?

"Silliness aside, thank you both. I wish I could do something to repay your kindness."

Vayriel tapped her chin with her index finger. "I do seem to recall a discussion about learning to read."

The priest's eyes widened. He had forgotten his promise to teach her, made what seemed like an eternity ago in the Hall of Remembrance. "I am so sorry," Zinvar stammered, "with the Trials and everything going on there hasn't been time."

"There is no need to apologize. There was no opportunity until now, and besides, I have been learning to read in other ways. For instance, right now Kilahym is thinking about—" The Highblood broke off abruptly and swatted the bard's arm. "Beds? You may sleep like all of us at Daughter's rest. We are all tired, but Zinvar requires our focus."

"Speaking of which," Zinvar jumped in before the embarrassed bard could offer a rebuttal, "I also still want to know more about the Sleeper."

Just as before, when that name was mentioned, Vayriel's face clouded over.

"Yes, that was our agreement," she murmured. Straightening, she met Zinvar's gaze with resolve. "And I will honor it now." A whine issued from Orgar as he sensed his life-friend's unease. The Highblood reached out and stroked his head, quieting the restless jeroti. Her voice sounded remote as she began to speak.

"When second-son betrayed the Daughter, it was not only her light that was dimmed. The wickedness of his betrayal spilled into the creature-world, twisting and corrupting that which the Mother-of-All formed. First-son felt the creeping darkness, but the struggle with his brother robbed him of the strength to stop it. He begged the Mother to help him, but her grief was too strong. Though she mended the torn veil between the spirit and creature worlds, she could not undo all the damage caused by the Sleeper."

Vayriel waited as a low, mournful hoot emanated from Orgar.

"Over time," she continued, "the Highbloods were able to heal many of the creature-sons and -daughters, using our bond to restore the Watcher's light. But in some—like the vargs—the roots of darkness had grown too deep. With them, we cannot share the joy of life. They are cut off from us and will never bond as a life-friend with a Highblood."

"So are creatures like that thralls of the Sleeper?" Zinvar asked. He also used the interruption as an opportunity to sneak a glance at the deck below. There was no sign of Kalis, Idrilia, or Kharnek, much to his relief.

The Highblood's forehead wrinkled in concentration. "If I understand you correctly, no. They do not serve the Sleeper. They are only tainted by his wickedness."

"I see." The priest stared into the curtain of deep blue sky behind Vayriel before addressing her once more. "But what of the Sleeper himself? He's trapped forever, right?"

She shifted uncomfortably. Even Kilahym leaned forward from his relaxed pose, apparently just as intrigued by the question as Zinvar. With reluctance, the Highblood spoke at last.

"Many of the Daughter's Eyes—those who see as you do"—Vayriel inclined her head at the priest— "have warned us that should the Sleeper ever return, it would herald the end of our world. They speak of an unstoppable darkness that will sweep over all the Mother's creation."

"Sounds like Komor." Kilahym raised his hands in defense when Zinvar glared daggers at him. "No one appreciates a good joke anymore," he grumbled. The priest continued to scowl for a moment before motioning to the Highblood.

"Please continue, Vayriel."

She raised her eyebrows in response. "There is little more to tell. My people trust in the promise of the Mother-of-All. She will never allow such evil to be visited upon us again."

"But if it did happen?" Zinvar pressed.

"The Daughter's Eyes say that we will know if the Sleeper is about to wake because a man with his power will walk the realms—a man with shadows in his eyes."

A profound silence followed Vayriel's words.

"You don't think—" Kilahym began.

"No." The reply from Zinvar came too quickly. He knew where this was going.

"Zin, I know you care for him, but you saw it too…we all did, with Adjira and when we broke out of the Sunscorned prison."

He was right. Those pitch-black eyes haunted his dreams, but Zinvar could not bring himself to admit that. It felt like a betrayal.

"He isn't evil," the priest lamely insisted.

"I'm not saying he is! *You're* the one who called him a monster."

"Kilahym, please." Vayriel placed a hand before the bard to silence him. Her penetrating gaze unsettled Zinvar even further. "My friend, what have you seen? Of all of us, you alone have the ability to know the truth of this."

Zinvar felt an invisible hand squeeze his lungs. If he told them that he knew of the Penumbra lurking within Kharnek, they would use the information against him—and Morakh forbid that they tell the Sondrinel. But he counted the bard and the Highblood as friends. Looking up into their expectant faces, the priest made his decision.

"I've never had a vision about Kharnek and the Sleeper."

His heart pounded as the Highblood continued to watch him intently until she slowly nodded her head.

Kilahym, on the other hand, wore an expression of stunned disbelief. "Despite everything that's happened? The same fell force that lived in Adjira and overtook Jannu is in Kharnek. I think *he's* the Sleeper, and your feelings for him are getting in the way of you admitting that!"

Cold fear gripped Zinvar's heart as Vayriel and the bard stared at him. "That's ridiculous, Kilahym," he muttered, averting his eyes.

"It is not," Kilahym protested. "It's the only explanation that makes sense."

"Enough," Vayriel commanded. "If Zinvar says that we have nothing to fear from Kharnek, then that is all we need know. He is our friend, and we can trust him." The Highblood pulled her spear from the deck beside her and balanced it on her knees. "Let us say no more of this."

Kilahym's furrowed brow indicated that he very much wanted to say more, but for once the bard bit his tongue, a minor miracle for which Zinvar was exceedingly grateful. The priest forced a smile. "Well, I think it's time for me to make good on my end of our bargain." He uncrossed his legs and rose, feeling pinpricks of warmth as blood flowed back to his toes. "Fortunately, whoever this ship belonged to was something of a reader. Unfortunately, they also had a penchant for romance, so this may be an education in more than one sense."

Vayriel nodded at him. "I am certain that it will be fine."

"What of that tome you carry with you? The one that causes your brow to furrow like a field ready for planting?" Kilahym's inherent good cheer had apparently overcome his sullenness.

"The Word of Morakh? Aside from being dreadfully dull, Komorese script is completely different from the runes used in Sondrine and Heathström. I'll be right back. Watch my staff, please." The duo consented, and Zinvar headed for the cabin he shared with Rinesh, taking the steps down to the main deck slowly enough to detect a hushed conversation begin between Kilahym and Vayriel. He sighed and turned right at the foot of the stairs, then right again to enter the anteroom of the captain's cabin, a rectangular room with bookshelf-lined walls. The door to the cabin itself was shut. Zinvar ran his hand along the spines of the books, feeling the pebbly contours of the leather bindings made from alusarean hide. He inhaled, and the scent of the captive pages transported him to a simpler time, studying in the great library on Mora.

Zinvar began to examine the array of titles in earnest, settling on a novel with a pale green cover and a thin volume of poetry bound in violet. He was debating a third selection when the door to the captain's cabin behind him opened. The priest whirled and found himself facing his brother.

"Someone is a little on edge," Rinesh observed, closing the door behind him.

"Sorry. I—a lot has happened during the Trials already."

The ghost of a smile lifted the corners of Rinesh's mouth. Now that Zinvar had a chance to study his brother without the imminent threat of capture, he could look beyond the beige robes and arach tattoo to see the way epicycles in the desert had added lean muscle to his thin frame, lightened his dark brown hair, and tanned his pallid skin. A thin white scar jutted downward from his lower lip to the middle of his chin. This was not the angst-ridden boy Zinvar remembered—his sibling had become something altogether different, something that he would never fully understand.

"So I've gathered. Congratulations on becoming a Truthseeker."

Though Rinesh's compliment seemed sincere, Zinvar was hesitant to accept it. "Thank you," the priest said eventually, "although I never would have imagined it would bring me to you."

A harsh laugh burst from Rinesh. "I wish it hadn't. I worked very hard to stay as far away from my old life as possible. Never once did it cross my mind that the Cloudsoarer would drop you and that wyrmspawn you're traveling with into my lap."

"That 'wyrmspawn' defended bringing you with us," Zinvar replied hotly.

"Sure, after he nearly gutted me with that black sword of his."

Zinvar's lips flattened. "He's a warrior, and we were in the middle of enemy territory. What else would you expect him to do?"

"What else would I expect?" His brother barked out a low, guttural laugh. "I suppose I shouldn't expect anything else from a murderer."

The statement froze Zinvar in place. "What are you talking about?"

"You mean you don't know?" A faraway look stole over Rinesh's face. Then his brother's countenance hardened. "No, of course you wouldn't. He wouldn't tell you."

"Wouldn't tell me what?" Zinvar reeled with confusion.

"The truth about himself. Who he is, and what he's done." Rinesh stalked closer to the priest, wearing a grim expression. He stopped just outside of arm's reach.

"Stop being cryptic and just say it!" The outburst from Zinvar seemed to satisfy his sibling.

"I will. But first, I'm going to tell you a story, brother."

CHAPTER 55

The sky-spirits overhead shimmered like bonfires of hope for the lost souls of Etherea, their wisdom fixed points on an unreachable canvas. Vayriel raised her hand, delicately tracing the shape of the ratufa in lights where it floated high above, and laughed at the memory of Kilahym's face wrapped in a fluffy tail of the physical creature-son. The skykeel beneath her supine form creaked as if it glided through water and not air, but thus far she and Orgar were faring better than the last long boat ride.

For a moment, her thoughts changed to what the beings might be that were traveling between those lights. The darkening of the sky now afforded her better views of the sky-spirit clusters than she had ever seen from home, and the knowledge that the Truthseekers passing Skyveil and moving closer to Komor prodded her with a tender reminder that her Path-Shaper had sent her to bring healing to Etherea—yet another topic she had not yet discovered how to address.

"There you are." A form obscured some of the sky as she peered down at Vayriel.

The Highblood blinked, switching her focus from the stars to Idrilia. "Here I am."

"The others are debating whether or not you slept out here or rose before the rest of us."

"Which do you think is correct?"

Tapping her boot on the deck, Idrilia stroked her chin in feigned concentration. "I think both. You have the look of someone who has been contemplating for an hour at least."

Laughing, Vayriel pushed up on her elbows. "I have been thinking of many things this Daughter's rise." Her mind turned again to Kilahym as her stomach fluttered. "Did you have need of me?"

"Oh. I just wanted to check in with you. Make sure you're feeling all right after all of the life-force energy you used yesterday."

"You are kind to ask. Orgar and I"—Vayriel reached beside her to ruffle fur on the jeroti's head where he lay—"were able to recover much in our dreams. It was good to sleep outside once more."

Idrilia nodded, but her hands fiddled with the pockets at her hips, and she glanced behind her.

Vayriel tilted her head. "You have more to say. Please, sit with us."

With one last look over her shoulder, Idrilia sat down.

"I'm not good with apologies. So I'll just say it. I'm sorry. I'm sorry I dismissed your account of the sea creature. And that I doubted you about Kalis. No, please, let me finish. It is a fault of mine that I must see to believe, and I shouldn't place that burden of proof on you. I think that I…it's just something the Cloudsoarer said about his relationships that made me think…it made me think about the people I care for. How they make me…feel. And how I make them feel." Idrilia scanned Vayriel's face before continuing. "So just because you see things differently doesn't make it wrong. I see things differently than most of Axiom. And you've proven again and again that you hold knowledge in your left hand and combat in your right. I should trust you as I would any Sentinel."

Vayriel clasped Idrilia's hands and leaned closer. She saw the woman's eyes widen as Vayriel fixed her gaze on her companion.

"Does this mean that you believe me about the Penumbra as well?"

"That Kharnek's insides are as dark as his actions? Wholeheartedly. Actually, that's what sparked me babbling like Kilahym. Kalis and I were talking about the Penumbra." She continued, explaining the Sondrinel's recent revelations. "And I wondered, could the Sleeper and the Penumbra be the same thing?"

Vayriel released Idrilia's hands to lean back, catching a frown on her face as the Highblood gazed at the Daughter's glow. "For that to be true, the Sleeper would already be awake."

"And you say darkness will spread all over Etherea. The end of our world."

"It does not feel like the end of things." Vayriel did not know why, but she knew that she would feel it. There was too much life all around for the Sleeper to have woken.

"No, it doesn't. Regardless, I'm keeping an eye on him." Idrilia glanced over her shoulder again, but if she was looking for Kharnek, he was not there. "When I can."

The faint hoot of coastal othwits tickled the silence. Wen replied, and a brief othwit conversation sang across the clouds. Vayriel welcomed the familiar warmth—the vocalizations of the cliff dwelling birds drove away the chill left by thoughts of the Sleeper. Vayriel looked at Idrilia, finding the woman watching at her.

Idrilia cleared her throat. "Well, the Sleeper just needs to stay asleep, so we can finish our Trials."

Vayriel nodded, though her inner eye turned to a memory of her mother's parents—their reminder that just as true-names held power, knowing what was to come could cause someone to take different steps along the path. Or try to stop those steps from coming to pass. To stay on the true path, she could not rely solely on herself. It was time to enlist another ally.

"Among the Daughter's Eyes, there are a few who have seen another vision. It is a tale known only to those the Path-Shaper chooses." She hesitated, uncertain if she should be sharing this, but Idrilia's earnest expression restored her confidence. Clearing her throat, she continued, "My mo'fa has seen this vision. There is a woman said to be a bridge between the spirit-world and the creature-world. When the Sleeper rises from his slumber, and with the help of the Watcher, she will find the light—the true light that all Highbloods seek in walking the coil. The light of the Mother-of-All. And with this light she will vanquish the awakened darkness and the Sleeper."

"You know I'm not a believer in prophecies, but I like the ending to this one a lot more. Why haven't you told the others?"

Vayriel took a deep breath. "It is a great responsibility and burden. If one person can stop the Sleeper's destruction, it is a secret which should be protected as the path-shapers have done."

"I get that, but we're your friends. We're in this together."

The Highblood nodded, accepting Idrilia's warm hands clasping the top of hers. It gave her the confidence to continue. "My mother's parents believe I am the one."

Idrilia's brows inclined. "'The one'?"

"They believe that I am the one in the vision."

"What? How?"

"The Highblood woman of the visions wears a silver armlet like the one I wear."

"Where did you get it? There have to be others like it."

Vayriel shook her head. " My mother found it in the crystal caves. No other Highblood has one like it. But this is just one future possibility. The other…"

"Is that Etherea is forever in darkness."

The two women were silent, each caught in her own thoughts. Kilahym's laugh carried across the length of the ship. It seemed the others were all venturing out on deck again.

"Idrilia?"

"Hmm?" The warrioress's face brightened.

"What will you do about your betrothal?" Vayriel hoped the Sondrinel's wisdom would be the final confirmation of her own feelings.

Idrilia looked to the stars. "Kalis and I have been remembering things from our interviews with the Cloudsoarer. I…I think if I wanted to, I'd have a place with the Sunscorned. Little pieces of memories keep coming back of that missing conversation with Molnkamp, but I have a clear impression that they'd take me and all of my counter-Axiom opinions. I tried to talk to Kalis again about living a life we choose—I choose—but I don't think he really gets it. If Axiom won't let me deny this marriage, maybe I'd leave for good this time."

"Would you not miss your family?" Vayriel pressed. Thinking of permanent separation from her mother's parents filled her with sadness.

"Of course. And Kalis. But an unhappy life isn't much of a life, is it? Wouldn't it be better to find a place that accepts me as I want to be?"

Vayriel thought about her own coil. Though not as reserved as some of the others, would they accept her bonding with an outsider, contrary to custom? "Axiom would benefit more from your influence than from your absence. You could help your sisters follow your path."

"I had thought to take them with me if I left. They could be anything they wanted, without judgment, with the Sunscorned." She rubbed her brow. "But that's worst-case scenario."

"The life of our previous captors is not a gentle ride on a water-glider."

Idrilia laughed. "No, I guess they aren't the most civilized. Anyway, I don't like pondering what-ifs. I'll address it then if it comes to that."

"I fear that I may anger my coil as well."

"What? Why's that?"

"I have become connected to a lowlander in a way that…just is not done. But I do not want to deny that connection any longer."

Idrilia's eyebrows lifted. "Really?"

"To deny my feelings would be to deny that the Watcher is always in the sky."

"Then, it's romantic?"

Vayriel averted her eyes. "I believe so. My heart flutters like a pectully, and my stomach leaps like a jeroti."

"Oh, Vayriel. You don't know how long I've wanted to tell you that—"

A shout caught Vayriel's concentration, and she saw Kilahym vying for Orgar's attention. Her stomach flipped, and Orgar rose, his tails flicking.

"But I do not know if I am ready to make it known on the east wind," she said quietly. "I should attend to my supplies," she mumbled and jogged past a bemused Kilahym, who was promptly tackled by an ecstatic Orgar. Vayriel disappeared down the stairs to the decks below.

CHAPTER 56

Wind whipped across Kharnek's cheeks. He knew it would turn them the same color as that of Zinvar's sunburned hands, which had faded from angry scarlet to pale pink during the last cycle. Those hands were clenched into fists.

"Why didn't you tell me?"

Kharnek's pulse raced as he considered the priest's question. Far below the skykeel, the ocean curled in gentle waves. The evanescent sunlight sparkled on the foamy crests, but in the distance the sky darkened into the shadow of Komor's eternal night. Two cycles had come and gone since the Truthseekers had escaped the Sunscorned lair, two cycles of watching Kalis stumble around after Idrilia like a young sikari chasing its mother while the bard and the mountain witch cavorted with her pet—and two cycles of silence from Zinvar, unbroken until now.

"There was no reason to," the warrior answered. He tore his gaze from the looming shadow and faced his accuser. "And if not for your brother, you would never have known."

"You're so predictable. Secrets upon secrets. Is that always how it's going to be between us?"

The question shook Kharnek. He knew that eventually his past would catch up to him, but he had not expected it to happen so quickly.

"What exactly has Rinesh told you?"

"How the warriors have been slaughtering dissidents like him for epicycles. And not just their leaders, but all of their followers. Even the women and children—" Zinvar stopped, overcome by horror and anger.

Kharnek chose his words carefully. "The Arakhists knew what would happen when they broke away from the rest of Komor. And your brother knew what he was getting into when he joined them. He and the others like him are creating an internal division that we cannot allow, not when the rest of Etherea already despises us."

"So, for the good of the many, you persecute and destroy the few?" The priest crossed his arms, then a strange expression stole over his face. "It's no secret that my ideas are unpopular with some of the more traditional elements of the Priesthood, but here I am, a Truthseeker and ambassador of peace. Unless that's another lie."

Kharnek pivoted, attempting to maintain his composure. Behind him, Orgar leaped onto a surprised Kilahym and pinned him to the deck of the skykeel, licking the hapless bard's face while he squirmed. The warrior felt a pang of envy at the carefree display. They did not know the struggle of having a duty to fulfill that superseded personal feelings. And there was no doubt in his mind that he felt something for this naïve, irresistible priest. Zinvar mistook his silence for an answer. "I suppose you do exactly what they tell you to do. Never questioning whether it was right." A trace of sadness colored the words.

"No," Kharnek said quickly, his heart in his throat, "I would not want it to come to that." He inhaled deeply to calm his racing pulse. "You are thinking about this in terms of right and wrong, when it is not that simple."

"It is for you, because you're just 'following orders.'"

"The Priesthood's orders!" Kharnek bellowed, spinning to face Zinvar. "Did you not stop to consider who tells the Brotherhood what to do? Whose dictums demand the destruction of all who oppose the will of Morakh?"

Zinvar shrank back from the outburst. "I—I didn't—"

"No, of course not, because you have not heard the screams of those you killed when you try to sleep. You have not watched the life leave someone's eyes, have not heard them *beg* for mercy that you cannot grant, because somewhere a *priest* thought it was necessary that they die." The warrior broke off, his body trembling with suppressed ire.

"Your eyes, Kharnek," Zinvar said softly.

Without looking, he knew that they had turned black. Kharnek cursed and closed them, trying to rein in his rampant emotions. He felt Zinvar's hand close gently around his upper arm.

"It's back, isn't it? The Penumbra?"

Kharnek looked up sharply. He saw a glimmer of fear in the priest's eyes— they were the same color as the sea below—as well as compassion.

"How can you know that?" the warrior whispered.

"I've dreamed of it, or seen it, I don't really know the difference…ever since that night at the Tower of Nerekesh. There was a woman who warned me that there was darkness in you and one day it would return." Zinvar seemed to weigh his next words. "And she said it would destroy us all," he finished.

It was as if a death knell resounded in Kharnek's head at the priest's revelation.

"So, it does not matter that I resist. Eventually it will overcome me."

"We don't know that," Zinvar protested. "It was only a dream, and—"

"It was more than a dream, and you know it. Such is the nature of what the Occulum see."

"Perhaps, but that doesn't mean we just give up and let the Penumbra win!"

"We? This is my fight, priest. And I have already lost."

Zinvar started to interrupt, but Kharnek pulled his arm away. "You should stay away from me. If I cannot defeat this enemy, at least I can keep you safe from it. From *me*." He stormed off, attracting a concerned look from the Highblood. Kharnek descended the sixteen steps into the crew compartment of the skykeel, passing Idrilia and Kalis's cabin on the way to his own. From the sound of it, the two Sondrinel were engaged in relatively amiable conversation .

Their voices tapered off as he rounded the corner that led to his cabin, but instead of continuing forward, he found himself turning around and going down the other branch of the corridor. A crystal lantern flickered near the passageway's end, casting eerie shadows upon a door crossed by bands of cast iron. As Kharnek drew nearer, the light guttered and died, plunging him into darkness.

He waited, feeling the skykeel rock, hearing its hull creak as air currents pushed against it. Rinesh told the Seekers that the skykeels were built to withstand the worst storms. Kharnek hoped so, especially if Rinesh's tales of a massive cyclone occupying the plains north of the Agermath Range in Heathström proved true. He tore his mind away from Zinvar's recalcitrant brother. That one was trouble, but he would try to be civil for the priest's sake.

The Whole.

Kharnek shook his head. Not the whispers. Not again. They seemed to emanate from behind the door. Despite his instincts screaming for him not to, the warrior reached for the handle and found it unlocked. He pushed the door open and beheld a room crowded with treasures. Kharnek stepped inside, careful not to tread upon the piles of gem-encrusted circlets that spilled forth from chests laden with luxurious robes. The garments were trimmed in trägen fur and what looked suspiciously like the snowy-white of jeroti pelts. Wealth such as this could only come from pillaging merchant vessels. Kharnek felt his disgust for the Sunscorned increase as he surveyed the lavish heap, but his attention was quickly commandeered by a macabre sight.

In the far left corner of the room, a skeleton slumped against the wall. An unraveling blue coat bunched about its shoulders, and the hilt of a golden cutlass protruded from its ribcage. Kharnek approached the gruesome trophy cautiously, wondering what possessed the Sunscorned to keep such a thing. As he drew nearer, the thin rays of sunlight that crept through the treasure room's shuttered portholes struck an object clasped in the dead man's hands. The glinting surface revealed a crystal cylinder filled with black sand.

Kharnek frowned. He had only seen sand like that on the Isle of Mora. The dark sediment hid the blood of hundreds of the Brotherhood's recruits who proved a little too slow to raise their guard in sparring sessions or incurred the wrath of a superior. Moving closer, the warrior noted the interlocked, toothed gears that shoveled sand from one half of the crystal enclosure to the next. The mechanism was definitely of Komorese design. Where did the Sunscorned—?

We know you.

You belong to us.

A platinum greave crunched beneath Kharnek's heel as he lurched back, overcome by the cacophony in his head. The sound of the Penumbra speaking was like thousands of glass windows shattering while a multitude of voices screamed. He clasped his hands over his ears in a vain attempt to silence the noise. The sand in the transparent cylinder writhed and twisted within its confines, and to his horror Kharnek found himself reaching for it. He fought the compulsion, tendons standing out in his neck as he strained.

The Whole.

We are a part.

We will be complete.

The warrior gritted his teeth and arched his back in an effort to pull his trembling fingers away from the swirling sand.

We are you.

With a gasp, Kharnek felt the Penumbra's grip on him strengthen and his hand darted forward, passing through the crystal as smoothly as a ship parting the fog. Tendrils of sand snaked around the warrior's forearm, then thrust upward to plunge into his open mouth and eyes as he screamed in horror. Images of rectilinear shadows upon darker shadows overtook Kharnek's mind before he crumpled to the floor.

Footsteps in the corridor. Someone was coming.

Up!

The Penumbra forced its unwilling host's body to its feet. Distantly, it heard the warrior screaming in the corner of his mind that could not be fully subsumed. This one was strong, and like every other being on this accursed planet, the light remained inside him, too powerful to be extinguished…for now. And she *continued to interfere, the captain of the humans. The ignorant fools actually venerated her. Nevertheless, she was a potent enemy, one who could not be defeated until the Whole was restored. Then this world, this entire universe of light, would be darkened forever.*

There would be resistance, as there had been when the Penumbra first entered this universe. Energy. So much energy to consume in this new home—fresh, strong energies—and the Penumbra hungered to satiate its unfulfilled need. For it had consumed most of the energy from its home. It was starving.

The beings here ripped the Penumbra into their universe—an experiment gone wrong but a blessing for the Penumbra. Despite their mistake, that race had succeeded in sealing the breach between universes, stranding the Penumbra here. But they lost everything in the effort to stop the horror they let in.

The Penumbra was disoriented then and surprised that the Xendra would fight against the inevitable. But it would not make the same mistakes now that it had time to understand this universe and its energy vessels. It had left that initial world in darkness and turned toward the brightness of Etherea, devouring worlds to sustain it during its journey. It did not understand the waves of energy that swam about Etherea's core until it enslaved a human thrall. The Penumbra and its servant had nearly been destroyed by the one called Kadaan.

But with each fragment recovered, the Penumbra grew stronger. With each recovered piece came memories and knowledge from the humans. With each splinter of the Whole, more abilities manifested in familiar intensity. It would not be long before it could consume worlds again.

The host body staggered, forcing the fragments of the Whole to gather their strength. They stabilized the warrior's motions as a lean young man in loose-fitting beige robes appeared at the entrance to the room. The Penumbra rifled through Kharnek's memories until it matched the narrow face with the proper name.

"What happened? Are you alright?" the man—a Sondrinel—demanded.

"I…am."

A skeptical look crossed the young man's face as he crossed his arms.

"Are you sure? You don't look so good, you know. Paler than usual, even."

Kharnek smiled. "Yes, Kalis. Everything is just fine."

CHAPTER 57

The heat was getting to her, and the discomfort of sand in every crevice beneath her robe was as irritating as having to write reports for the guild after every expedition. Which she dreaded yet again after finding nothing but stairs to nowhere. If the people of Sondrine had lived here before the great calamity, all evidence had been erased. What did she expect to find in the deep crevasses of Lake Stelwin? Still, the landscape of Sondrine was far preferable to the confines of Axiom, forced to interact with all of those people. Fahana gathered her tool bag and wrapped the climbing rope around her foot and leg. Using the sliding hand grip, she began the slow ascent, pulling herself foot by foot up the length of rope.

She reached the lip and pulled herself over the edge into the full sunlight. The tent was just as she'd left it several paces away. She felt the robe clinging to her damply. Fahana had worked up quite a sweat on the ascent. With any luck, she'd be out of those clothes in moments. Perhaps with Lolin, her aid. She'd been drawn to him inexplicably these past two days, but out of professionalism she'd tried to ignore the attraction. No longer. She pushed open the flap of the tent.

There he was, sitting at the desk with his back to her. His strong, tan shoulders glistening with beads of sweat, his shirt discarded on the floor. Fahana approached softly, removing her headscarf and dropping it behind her. She stopped behind him, then reached out to stroke the muscles of his upper arms.

"Fahana?" he asked, turning toward her, confusion on his face.

"Shhh," she soothed, caressing his cheek with one hand as she released the ties of her robe with her other. She dropped the garment to the floor. Lolin's eyes grew wide. Fahana licked her lips as she watched him survey her every curve.

"Well, that took an unexpected turn," Kilahym muttered and *thwumped* the halves together, the bound parchment a mallet striking a muted drum. With his thumb, he traced the gold lettering on the maroon cover, the title script extending to the edges in a spiraling vine with leaves that looped back to the center in intricate designs.

"What are you reading?"

Vayriel's resonating voice broke through the bard's mind fog, a lasting effect from the realm created by words, and he glanced up from his musing. She sat at a long table in the ship's mess hall alone. In his stupor, the bibliophile had left the library in the captain's quarters, descended into the heart of the ship, and meandered past the rooms of his companions to wind up in the eating area. Kilahym, delighted to find his wandering steps while reading had steered him here, made a quick bow to the poised lady.

"I thought it was going to be either a rousing adventure novel, the sort where the hero or heroine discovers a mysterious ruin full of treasure, or—completely at the other end of the literary spectrum—a scholarly explanation of Axiom. It was neither."

Vayriel stifled a giggle. "May I see?" she asked, pausing her sorting of the herbs spread out before her like pieces of a puzzle. Her alusarean bag lay open and empty to the left of the assortment.

"Certainly. But I don't think you'll enjoy the material."

"I will determine that." She smiled, the small tug that pinched her cheeks and drew back her lips in radiance. The bard felt his heart leap, and he could not deny her any more than he could stop the way she made him feel, nor would he want to.

Kilahym deposited the volume into her outstretched hand, a palm both delicate and seasoned, as her arm stretched across the wooden table. She traced the shapes on the cover with her fingertips as she squinted in concentration, accenting the unique shape of her lavender eyes. First, her lips moved silently, then she slowly sounded out the title.

"The Flame of the Stone Hunter?"

"You're such a quick study! Verily, Vayriel, any other student would take many lunations to reach such a budding proficiency. Zinvar will be excited at your progress."

"Mo'mo says that my mother could learn any task with ease." She shrugged. "And that my blood carries some of her skill."

"Don't diminish your own efforts. I know you've been practicing. So, by this title, what do you think the book is about?"

"One who searches for fire crystals," Vayriel stated matter-of-factly.

"See? It got you, too! Apparently the 'stone hunter' has a double meaning. She, the main character, is an archeologist, but she is also rather stoic and off-putting. There's the 'stone' part. Think if our dilly-Drilly and Kharnek had a daughter what that young lady's disposition might be."

Vayriel's eyebrows shot up. "Oh."

"Indeed. Ghastly. And the flame, well, I believe it is not fire but the heart's desire"—he winked—"if you know what I mean."

"Life-friends?"

"What? Ha! No, no. Umm, amorous longing, the search for evening companionship, the pleasure in the arms of another?" Kilahym felt his cheeks grow warm. Vayriel, however, looked at him with her head tilted. He cleared his throat. "Where is dear Orgar?"

Vayriel straightened her posture and appeared to look through him. Kilahym was about to wave his hand before her unblinking gaze when she fluttered her eyes and fixed them on his own.

"He chases Wen. The two have been playing on the deck for some time."

"I wish I could do that. Listen in on them at will. Whatever I have is sporadic at best. At worst, it's positively dangerous—the fiasco with the Stormbringer, water drops and flickering lights which seem innocuous now but"—he shrugged—"maybe not next time. And I need to be your 'conduit of power,' not a conjurer of laughs at birthing day celebrations."

"You must keep practicing. The images you created during our first trial and at Kalis's memory ceremony—"

"False ceremony, I suppose."

"They are as skillfully crafted as those by the light weavers of my coil."

"You really think so?"

Vayriel nodded.

"Woohoo!" Kilahym leaped with joy, then leaned against the table.

"You connected with me in a way I did not think possible. You have already shown you can do this thing She asks of you. Do not sweep your abilities under an alusarean. I am certain you are capable of even more."

Images raced through his head, many of them involving him center stage flinging bolts of lightning from his palms at creatures bent on harming them. "Do I need to borrow a crystal from Kalis?"

"Do you believe that a crystal is required to connect as I do to the Mother-of-All?"

"I—well—is that a trick question? Clearly, you are able to connect without one. And I have on occasion, obviously. But Kalis and Idrilia…they have a different sort of magic."

"What is different about it?"

"Well…yours is more of the healing, protective type. And theirs is…"

"Destructive."

"You could say that."

"It is true that we each focus on our affinities, but we are all capable of harnessing each of the Mother's gifts. For the benefit of the Mother's creature-sons and -daughters. Or choose the least harmful path if that is not possible. Not until now have I directly been told to destroy."

"So you *can* do what they do with fire crystals?"

Vayriel sighed and touched a petite pouch among the scattered sundry. Flames flickered to life around her wrist and danced down her fingers, catching the contents on fire as the blaze vanished from her hand. The air filled with a sweet floral scent.

"Oh wow! And your skin remains unblemished. Fascinating! But I didn't mean for you to ruin your supply of…."

The tightly coiled leaves within the netted bag unfurled, switching from a blackened tint to bright orange tops. From within the twisted petals, deep purple soot puffed from the centers. The sight reminded him of a cone-shaped plant he'd read about in his favorite field guide, its seed pods only released by fire.

"At times the eye is deceived. Only through fire will the ash-bane release its medicine and its young-root for the next planting."

Vayriel gently opened the drawstrings of the pouch and plucked a seed, no wider than the white of her nail, from the center of one of the dried flowers.

"By the Great Lady's eyelash. Life born of fire. Much of the poetry I've read on the subject of fire often ends in tears…or rage…or just something about Komor. What about the sneeze leftovers? This…" Kilahym wiggled his finger, indicating a thick powder that coated the inside of the bag.

"For treating bites from the tiniest of the creature-sons and -daughters."

"There certainly were many of those in the desert—luckily, I was more often repulsed by their quadrillion tiny legs than bitten by their hidden fangs. Partially owing to our Sondrinel counterparts making sure we had the correct outerwear. But I digress." The bard flung a leg over the bench to sit perpendicular to the Highblood. Vayriel grinned.

"Do you always share all the thoughts within you?"

"Oh, certainly not. One must maintain the air of mystery as a bard. Keeps the audience ever at the edge of their seats wondering just what I might be up to next. A bard must preserve some secrets, especially when this bard wants to keep a certain Highblood interested so she does not grow bored." He winked. When no reply was forthcoming, Kilahym heaved a sigh. "Alas, I fear my overtures have found no soil to take root within the garden of your heart."

Vayriel looked away as a flush colored her cheeks.

"It's all right," the bard continued, "I am accustomed to the sting of unrequited affection. If my words do displease, then they shall never again depart the gates of my lips."

She shook her head, peach tresses tumbling over her shoulders. "I did not say that. But I cannot say more than what is within me to say."

Her response unleashed a torrent of disappointment in Kilahym. He bit his lip and struggled to keep from showing it, but he could detect the sadness in his voice when he finally spoke. "I see. I am sorry to have made you uncomfortable. It won't happen again."

He made to rise from the table, but Vayriel swiveled, heaving one of her legs over the bench to face him directly, and clasped his hand between hers.

His heart skipped a beat, and he froze, afraid any movement would break the physical connection.

"You misunderstand." Her voice was soft but firm. "You are kind and thoughtful, and you open your heart freely to everyone you encounter. These are all qualities I desire in a life-mate—I just never thought I would find them in a lowlander."

Kilahym's mouth formed an 'O' shape. He sat down quickly. "I didn't think about that. Is it forbidden for Highbloods and, uh, people like me to be together?"

"No." Vayriel released his hand and sat back. "But I do not think it has often occurred. And many of the coils do not approve of such bonds. If I am to one day be a leader of my people, I must not think only of myself." She crossed her arms and met his gaze fully. "Do not take my silence on this subject as rejection. It is just too soon for me to speak as surely as you do."

Kilahym exhaled, unaware until then that he had been holding his breath. All hope was not lost, then. "Fair enough. Although, I hope you realize that I really just wanted us to be more than friends, not yet, ah, life partners, as reaching that stage does take some time, yes?"

Vayriel frowned. "You mean you do not want to spend your entire life with me?"

The bard's eyebrows flew upward. "Ah, well, I—yes, but—" Then he saw the mischievous grin tugging at the corner of her mouth. "Oh, but you jest with me. Well played, m'lady, well played."

She laughed, and it was like the sound of a babbling brook in a sunlit forest. "I understand your meaning, Kilahym. Now come, let us return to your instruction."

"Aye! Help me help you."

"If we can recreate the connection we had at the reef—"

"You know, I didn't feel drained at all that time. Not like in the sea creature's innards."

"And it remained when I touched the Stormbringer's mind, though less strong."

"Then maybe I could enhance you, instead of merely being a vessel from which you drink."

Vayriel nodded. "If I did not have to worry about draining your energy, I could…I do not know, but I am excited about the possibilities."

She grinned and Kilahym beamed back at her. "Right. Recreate. I was humming…"

Kilahym breathed deeply and began to hum the tune from the pillars. He found his mind still raced, and he closed his eyes lest he stare intently at Vayriel. How would he connect to her? Starting by visualizing her, he wondered what she was thinking. His feeling for her welled up inside of him until he thought his chest would burst.

"You feel anything?" he asked, peering from one eye.

"Not yet."

"Me neither." Though truthfully he felt everything except what he needed.

At her prompting, Kilahym tried again and focused on the movement of air from the cabin to his nose and lungs. He thought about a connection where their minds crossed like paths in the forest, sharing steps but for a few strides before veering off on their own course. He focused on other times where his music had been involved and tried to recreate the same mental and emotional frame of mind. He felt his emotions jostle like gentle waves in the ocean and then intensify at times like a growing storm. As the bard jumped from memory to memory, like they were stepping stones across a stream, his foot found a slippery surface, and he fell. The water here was cold and black, and he floundered like a child who had not yet learned to swim.

Then there was a presence, which approached slowly as if from a great distance. It took the form of pastel light, a pyre flower pulsing weakly in the gloom. It grew closer until the light touched him, and he felt a warmth cascade over him. *Vayriel.* Could she see these memories? He hastily ripped his mind from the shadowed thoughts, images of his mother and father, and churned the seabed into a murky cloud that obscured the view. He opened his eyes.

"We were connected," Vayriel said breathlessly. "For a moment I felt your…emotions as if they were mine. What is this pain you hide so that no one will find it?"

Vayriel's gaze penetrated him as she placed her hand over his heart. It beat ferociously in his chest, and he was sure she could feel the drumming.

Kilahym flicked his eyes to her hand. "It's nothing."

Her face hardened. "It is not nothing."

Kilahym made a noise with his lips. "I have a lot of unpleasant childhood memories. I'd prefer to forget them."

"There is a story of a man who builds his home under a great redbark tree. One day, the man notices the tree has holes in the trunk. But he does nothing, the bark-borers will not bother him. Then one day the tree turns brown and the leaves sprout no more. But the man does nothing; he did not need the leaves anyway. Soon the heavy branches crack the trunk, but he does nothing. For the branches are not near his dwelling. But then a wind comes and tears the branches down and crushes him inside. These memories you have are like the tree. You must not be the man who does nothing."

"Oh, I've done something. I left my home as soon as I could, and I'm not going back."

"But these memories go with you. Those you did not leave behind. Tell me what they are, Kilahym. Let me see you."

Kilahym took her hand in his, resting their hands between them on the wooden bench. She did not withdraw.

"I would not deny any request thou makest of me. How could I? I teased earlier that I must keep secrets, but secrets turn stone to dust." He breathed deeply. "Here it goes. My father was, is, a timid man. I didn't realize how timid until I was probably ten. By then I'd already started to be his defender, but I didn't know I was doing it until others my age began to laugh at him. Imagine this scene." Kilahym released Vayriel's hand and began to gesture as if opening a curtain. "A boy is at the stalls in the bazaar of Beechmarsh. Many shoppers of all ages are bustling with baskets. There's a line for the fruit stall, and the boy fiddles anxiously with his hands. He's next in line. He has to ask for something for his mother. The woman behind the stand is grumpy and short with all the people before him. Now it's the boy's turn. She rolls her eyes as he fumbles his words, and he finally just points to what he wants. She needs to know how many. Three, he says, one for each of them. She doesn't hear him. He has to speak up. The line grumbles behind him. The boy hands over his coins and grabs the bag. Back by his mother's side, she complains that he didn't get enough. The boy must go back. The boy is scared of the fruit cart woman. Isn't three enough? His mother's face turns red, and her voice rises as she tells him, where everyone in the town can hear, that he will never amount to anything."

Vayriel regarded him knowingly. "This happened more than once."

"All the time. Nothing I nor my father did was ever right. My mother had to correct whatever we had done wrong and tell us off as she did so.

"Even when I made my first tunic, it wasn't good enough for Mother. Father hadn't criticized it, and I'd made it in his own shop, by the Lady! But as I stood there, berated by her unrealistic expectations, my father stood by silently." Kilahym scoffed, and his lip curled in disdain. "Why would he defend me when he would not defend himself? Other shop owners gossiped about my parents' relationship. He never confronted them. Out-of-towners tried to take advantage of him, and he just gave in to their demands.

"And when I wanted to partake in certain activities, like music, he deferred his decisions to my mother. They were always 'wastes of time' to her, and I carried on with my apprenticeship with Father as a tailor."

Kilahym shook his head. "Do not pity me. Despite her bite, I was never beaten, though I was spanked a few times. Those few times instilled a fear within me such that I always tried to please my mother, always thought about how she would react. I didn't want to disappoint her. And I didn't want to disappoint my father. My father showed me care and love despite his flaws. Every decision was reached after great consideration, and the choices I made were made as if they both stood near me."

His Highblood friend squinted. "Do you make decisions that way still?"

Kilahym's shoulders drooped. "I certainly hope not. I like to believe I make careful decisions as needed but for my own benefit."

"There is a hesitation, though, at times."

He looked up. "What do you mean? I speak what I think, often to disastrous results or embarrassment."

"For things that are important to you, I think you deliberate more than you admit." Vayriel removed her hand from the bench and gestured. "Remember the Trials Ceremony? You paced the room excessively."

"I just wanted it to be my best performance yet. Three realms were watching. I wanted everyone to see I was not a failure."

She pointed at him. "Hear your phrasing? I know that you have confidence, yet there is a piece of you that is afraid to make mistakes. You hid away this part of you from the rest of us so well. Perhaps distracting us with your humor. But I have felt it. It is like a wall between you and the life force. To connect with the Mother-of-All, those barriers must be removed."

Kilahym scratched his head. "How do you propose I do that? Apparently, my childhood is not as behind me as I thought. Fantastic. Remind me to burn that poetry journal Ansgar gave me. So much for writing things down as a form of catharsis."

"That was a kind gesture of your friend. It must have had some impact, as you are here today as a tall tree and not a bending sapling."

He cocked his head. "Umm, thanks?"

"You must confront the reason for the walls."

"Oh no, no, no, no." The bard waved his hands in protest. "You aren't going to convince me to...to..."

"Return to your family."

"That."

Vayriel seemed to consider this as she looked out the mess hall's lone porthole. Through it, Kilahym could glimpse a few wisps of clouds that broke the darkened mass of the sky. He wondered how much of Heathström was left to traverse.

At length, she turned back to him. "When a difficult event comes to pass, a Highblood's coil provides strength. I can be your coil."

His breath caught. "Does that mean...you'd go with me?"

She nodded, a closed-mouth smile on her lips.

"Even though my mother might suck all of your happiness into her dark pit of a heart?" he asked incredulously.

Vayriel raised her eyebrows and pursed her lips, a twinkle of playfulness in her lavender eyes. "If she tries, then I will tell her that a terrible Highblood curse will follow her for all her days if she is unkind to you and me. Ratufas will gnaw her toes in her sleep, and pectullies will sting her when she leaves her house."

Kilahym whistled. "Remind me not to make you unhappy. But, she *is* still my mother, so maybe leave out the pectullies."

"There is no Highblood curse, Kilahym."

"Truly? I am aghast and elated at the same time. But Vayriel—and I mean this from the very bottom of my verbose being—thank you. I cannot tell you how much it means to me that you would offer that."

Vayriel nodded. "I would do the same for any of my friends, Kilahym. However, *this* I do only for someone I care for...as perhaps more than a friend."

She leaned forward and placed her hands on either side of Kilahym's cheeks as she drew her face close. She tilted his head down and pressed her lips against each of his eyelids.

Kilahym's eyes widened. "That's...unconventional."

Vayriel drew back and blinked. "Is this not how affection is shown among the lowlanders?

"Technically, you could say yes. But here, let me show you the way I learned."

Steadying his quaking muscles, Kilahym took one of her hands in his. He scooted until their knees touched. With his free hand, he brushed her wavy locks over her shoulder, gently caressing her hair as his hand moved to the base of her head. With a gentle motion, he drew their faces together, pressing his lips to hers.

The door to the mess hall popped open.

Kilahym jumped, breaking the kiss.

"Vayriel, Kalis just..." The Sondrinel's eyes flicked between them, then settled on Vayriel. "I'm not interrupting, am I?"

"Understatement of the last hundred synodies, 'Dril," Kilahym grumbled.

"When you aren't busy," she replied icily, "Kalis wants to speak with you."

"Both of us?" Kilahym asked.

"Yes."

A long pause ensued following Idrilia's reply, during which the Sondrinel glared daggers at them both.

Vayriel broke the silence. "Idrilia, we were just—"

"Save it for someone who cares," the other woman snarled.

"I am sorry, Idrilia," the Highblood pleaded, "Please—"

The door slammed behind her.

"—stay."

CHAPTER 58

"Are you certain you didn't imagine it? You haven't felt yourself lately." Idrilia made a quick gesture to indicate her statement meant the missing memories from the Reef, a phenomenon she still hadn't fully recovered from.

"No, I'm sure of what I saw. He turned around and…his smile was unnatural, you know. And his eyes…" The pair exchanged a nod toward one another. *The Penumbra.* Idrilia saw the shifting of soft peach in her periphery but made sure to keep her focus off of the Highblood. Every time she saw her standing next to Kilahym, her veins boiled. It was best to not look at them at all.

They congregated in a lower storage room; a tight space for five people even without the littered supplies. Crystal lanterns, small replicas of those from the ship's hull, cast a pale blue glow across their faces from where they hung in the corners of the room. She remembered thinking, as they fled onto the skykeel, that the half dozen orbs hanging from corroded iron links looked like the crystal in Concilius if time had aged it.

"Perhaps we should ask Zinvar? He does know him best. Speaking of the priest, where is Zinny?" Kilahym commented.

Idrilia focused on Rinesh, who stood across from her. "His feelings have compromised his judgment." Like those ridiculous novels in Ettra's market where the Heathström characters spend the entire plot batting their eyelashes at one another. Moronic.

"He wasn't informed of our meeting," Kalis clarified.

"Oooo, clandestine."

Idrilia rolled her eyes at the bard's excitement. With a quick gesture, she signaled the equivalent of *He's ridiculous* to Kalis, who only shrugged.

"Zinvar will be upset, but it cannot be helped," Rinesh joined. "I have already told him of the danger a Guardsman poses, unaware that he has feelings for him. Leave it to my brother." He shook his head. "Despite my predisposition to not trust any of you—let alone this Kharnek—I truly did see him behaving oddly before this meeting."

"I think we all have," Kilahym muttered.

"What did you see?" Idrilia prompted.

"I was checking on the power crystals below deck. Even if it means being stuck with all of you, I'd rather not fall out of the sky," the Komorese said drily. He gestured to the walls of the room. "I'd noticed there was a power drop earlier and wanted to inspect them, since I'm not sure they were fully charged before we left. While I was investigating one, Kharnek appeared beside me. Scared me like something out of the Fellwood."

"Pause a moment. Do you mean to tell me the location of Trial number three is a scary, creepy sort of wood with ghastly creatures?"

Vayriel elbowed the bard, eliciting a sound of protest from him as she motioned for Rinesh to continue.

"As he stood there, the crystal I was inspecting lost more power. At the time, I didn't think much of it—just thought that since the crystals were already having trouble, it was another instance. It flickered back to life once he walked away." Rinesh folded his arms across his chest. "It's probably just a coincidence."

"Maybe," Kalis asserted. "A situation could be harmless, but assuming it is not without proper evidence can lead to disaster."

"A lack of understanding, too, can lead to disaster."

Idrilia smiled despite herself. "Well said, Vayriel."

"Wise words, indeed" Kilahym added. "Many a fear comes from that which we do not understand."

"I wouldn't say that Vayriel is fearful of anything," Idrilia challenged.

"I wasn't implying that, dilly-Drilly. I was just—"

"No, you're just repeating what we've already said."

"Well if you'd let me finish, I would clarify my compliment," he placed a hand on Vayriel's forearm, "and give Vayriel better praise in poetry."

Idrilia pivoted toward Kalis and placed her hand on his shoulder. "I think we should return to the task at hand." She winked and fixed her companion with her gaze.

"Uh," Kalis raised his brow but continued, "well, Rinesh you have unique ties to Zinvar and a better understanding of Komorese than I do. What do you think our actions should be?"

The other man spread his hands. "You seem awfully eager to have the help of someone who you know very little about. And I'm still not sure that the Cloudsoarer won't have my head removed for my part in your escape. It might be in my best interest to do nothing."

Kilahym's eyes widened. "But...you said you would help us!"

"And that you wouldn't mind leaving," Kalis put in.

"While your friend's blade was waiting to gut me," Rinesh said tartly. "Hard to say anything else under those circumstances."

A hush fell over the group as they considered his words, punctuated by creaks from the skykeel's hull. Idrilia met Rinesh's gaze before he quickly broke it off, and in that moment, she glimpsed the fear of betrayal lurking beneath his outward hostility. That was a feeling she could understand—whatever trauma was in Zinvar's brother's past, it cast a deep shadow.

She cleared her throat. "You're right. We put you in an untenable position, and now here we are asking for more from you without offering anything in return. So, let's change that." She stepped toward him. "Kharnek is a potential threat to us all. Help us, and we'll do our best to protect you. And, once we reach Komor, you can take the skykeel and go."

"Dril!" Kalis's voice was fraught with tension. "That would leave us alone in unfamiliar, unfriendly territory."

She waved a hand to forestall any further objections. "Which we already were going to be. And it's not like we could fly the skykeel on our own, anyway."

Kilahym snorted. "She's got you there, Kali-Kal."

Ignoring the bard, Idrilia stepped forward and thrust her hand out toward Rinesh. "Do we have a deal?"

He eyed her warily. "Do I have a choice?"

She chose her reply carefully. "If you say no, then it would be in all of our best interests to part ways immediately. Fly us to the nearest port, and we'll take our own paths. Right, everyone?" Idrilia stifled Kalis's imminent protest with a stern glare. Sweeping her gaze around to Vayriel and Kilahym, she waited until they nodded their consent before looking back at Zinvar's sibling.

Rinesh gave her an appraising look, then hesitantly shook her hand. "I'm probably going to regret this," he muttered. "Alright, if I'm to help you, I need to hear more about what's happened with Kharnek."

Vayriel spoke first. Idrilia's gaze moved at the sound of the Highblood's voice before she realized it. The woman's lavender eyes caught her own. Idrilia felt her breath catch, then she snapped her eyes away. She found herself staring at a discarded crate in the corner. "Idrilia and I have spoken some," the Highblood said slowly, "and as I've told her, I still feel the presence of the Penumbra here. As to its motives, or Kharnek's, and whether they are one, I cannot say. I would like for us all to trust one another and be as a coil. But...I feel that some caution now is needed."

"I know I will appear as but an amateur dramatist by bringing this up again, but...Kharnek. Guards. Whoosh!" Kilahym made an animated gesture, folding his arms to his chest. "He made the Sunscorned take flight with nary a touch upon their corporeal selves! Last I brought it up, Kharnek dismissed it as if I had imagined it. But that's not the first time we've beheld such an extraordinary display of unnatural abilities."

"You're talking about Adjira," Idrilia said flatly.

Kilahym nodded excitedly. "And his frightful speed when evading the fire-spitter."

"It was awfully similar, you know," Kalis mused, his brow furrowed. "Adjira could move objects without touching them. And seemed able to enhance her own strength and speed."

Vayriel shuddered. "And the way it felt through the life force was the same. Like the sun had become cold and dark. It was almost as if the life force was— gone."

Idrilia and Kalis exchanged looks. They had seen the life force seemingly vanish before.

"Uh, 'Dril," Kalis's tone sounded hesitant, "what about what you saw in Axiom?"

She exchanged a quick set of signals with her companion to confirm his intent. Their correspondence lasted only seconds. Telling the others made sense. *I'll do it*, she signaled.

"I have reason to believe the blade Kharnek carries can negate the life force," Idrilia announced.

Vayriel recovered from her shock and responded with questions first. Idrilia found herself drawn to focus on the Highblood in spite of her previous determination to not look her way. She explained how her fire crystal had seemed to be absorbed by the warrior's blade and summarized how Kalis and she had seen a similar material before the Trials.

"Arsanth," Rinesh murmured. The group turned in unison to regard him.

"Pardon?" Kilahym questioned.

"I think Kharnek's sword is made of arsanth. It's a metal that was once harvested in northern Komor, in the region now known as the Fellwood. Legend holds that the champions of Morakh used arsanth blades to destroy the arakh riders who made their home in the nearby forest. I know the story well because I was once an Arakhist."

The bard scratched his chin. "What's that, Rin?"

"The short version? A religious order dedicated to the adult form of rift wyrms." He pushed the sleeve of his tunic up to reveal the tattoo that originally identified him to Zinvar.

"Those statues from the Etherea Assemblage?" Kalis asked. Moving to get a better look at the inking, Idrilia drew close to Kalis so that their arms touched. He glanced at her as Rinesh continued, but she flicked her gaze to the pair by the door. To her disappointment, they focused solely on Rinesh.

"The same. Arsanth was mined for a short time before the settlement and mining operation was destroyed. Everyone assumed it was the Arakhists, and as retaliation, those who rode the arakhs were slain. Normal weaponry has little to no effect on the scales of the fireborn creatures, but the priesthood found arsanth blades could negate whatever power protected the wyrms. I didn't know they were still in use until I saw Kharnek's."

Idrilia's eyes found Kalis's face. "So, why does he have one?"

"If it does negate the life force as you say, perhaps that is what I am sensing in Kharnek. Not the Penumbra as we feared," Vayriel offered.

Idrilia scoffed. "Don't be ridiculous. A sword wouldn't endow him with the abilities we've seen." The Highblood's expression dropped, and Idrilia's heart fell with it.

"Vayriel has a point. I suggest that we remain observant and notify this group of any new developments. We know our concerns and can stay vigilant, trust one another, and protect each other," Kalis advised, a statement often spoken—with some variation—by those of the Sentinel Guild. "I trust that we are capable of relaying a message to one another discreetly and without needing to immediately form a council."

"If we notice something which needs to be discussed, we can arrange to meet again." Rinesh nodded.

"Then it is decided," Vayriel stated.

The group dispersed from the storage room. "I really want to investigate this treasure Kalis saw," Kilahym said quietly to Vayriel.

"It would be wise for both of us to practice our connection to the Mother-of-All."

"Oh, alright. But above this dreary ship-innards—I need some sea air to tousle my hair."

Idrilia heard Vayriel's hearty laugh ahead in the corridor. Rinesh followed, and Idrilia took a step behind him.

"Dril, will you stay a moment?"

She stopped. Beyond relaxing with Wen or reading the Cloud Soarer's library, Idrilia couldn't think of anything she was needed for. Vayriel was too busy with the bard. She watched the door close behind them, a pang of longing gripping her throat, before turning to face Kalis.

"What's wrong, 'Dril?"

"Nothing. Why?"

"You were…unusually reserved with your opinions. And if I'm not mistaken, you agreed with me more than you ever do."

She wanted to correct him, but he was right. To her annoyance, he had always been able to understand her moods—mostly. She huffed.

"Those two," she gestured to the door. "Gallivanting around when we have the Trials to complete. You'd think they could wait to indulge themselves until after our tasks are finished. Especially now that we have a threat in our own group. Our focus should be on that."

"You would rob them of their happiness? Ask them to ignore their feelings for each other?"

"Not their happiness. But if they would kindly ignore their *feelings* until our Trials are over."

Kalis chuckled, to which Idrilia responded by placing her hands on her hips. Making light of her ire was not what she wanted from him.

"When someone feels that connection, that they've found a person they can't imagine being without, you can no more stop the sun from blazing in Sondrine than you can stop yourself from feeling that way. I would know."

Idrilia tensed.

"I didn't mean to say that to make you uncomfortable. Hymn and Vay, they have this friendship that is growing beyond."

"But she's supposed to be my friend, too." Idrilia dropped her gaze to the floor, feeling as if she had become the age of Fey, a child whimpering to get her way.

"Hopefully I'm still your friend." Out of the silence, a gentle tinkling cascaded into a familiar, soothing tune.

Idrilia raised her eyebrows. "That's—"

Kalis nodded, opening his palm to reveal a music box nestled within it. *"Luctus Iuvante.* I wouldn't presume to know how you feel, but I think there's more going on in that amazingly active mind of yours than I ever have the right to know. So I wanted to give you this."

Kalis closed the music box, revealing the bronze face of an othwit. Idrilia took the gift from him and studied life-like details in filigree and sparkling jewels. She felt comfort wash over her as she tilted the head back again, and the music started where it left off. She could almost hear her grandmother singing along.

"I've held on to it since Ettra. The right time never seemed to come, you know. And then somehow when I lost my other pack to the Trägen, I still managed to keep this. At first I thought it was a sign that you, in a way, were with me. But now it's more symbolic of me releasing you—to you."

Idrilia closed the top of the owl, the memories of her grandmother receding with it, and refocused on his blue eyes. What was he saying?

"I know freedom is important to you. The ability to make your own, educated choices. And I'm sorry it took me this long to realize that our betrothal took that away. Before I fell at Mount Hoestra, I spoke with Vayriel. Things I wanted to say to you, but you had always pushed me away before I could. She didn't say much," he laughed, "but somehow she got me to think about this— like one of Master Lioni's philosophy prompts. They say that a betrothal grows into love. I wanted that to be true. But at what cost? The announcement of our betrothal was the happiest moment for me. But you changed. At every turn I met your ire. Your frustration and your anger stayed with me even while I hobbled away from the trägen. As I sat in that Sunscorned cell alone, I kept seeing your look of betrayal when we met your parents—when I didn't stand up for you...for what you wanted."

Idrilia's mind whirled like a tempest. So many hours spent angry at Kalis, angry at their situation and the traditions which put them there. Although she had already decided not to partake in the betrothal, if Kalis was agreeing with her...

"I miss how things were before all of this, you know? But more than that, I want you to be...you. The person I love. Your strength of mind and will, unhindered by whatever intangible binds our betrothal has placed on you. I would see you responsible for every choice, every word written in the Vitaetum under Idrilia Volundar. And even if I don't spend the rest of my days as your spouse, I would want to spend the rest of my days as your friend. If you would honor me with such a designation."

Idrilia felt as if a solendrake lifted from her shoulders. She clutched the bejeweled othwit, tears forming as she opened her mouth to reply.

The door behind her burst open.

"Something's the matter with Orgar!" Kilahym said with labored breaths, one hand on his chest.

Idrilia sniffed, pushing back the emotions. "And Vayriel?" She asked, her mind clearing.

"She is attending to him now."

Kalis and Idrilia quickly followed the bard above deck. During their clandestine meeting, the skykeel had moved further toward the distant blackness that marked the sunless landscape of Komor until it engulfed all in shadow. Idrilia glanced to the east. Beneath purple and pink clouds gleamed the faintest sliver of pale yellow on the horizon.

Her soaring spirit descended as they approached the fallen jeroti. Orgar lay on his side on the red-brown deck, looking more gray than white. Four paws stretched out in linear pairs as he arched his neck, the tip of his snout pointed toward Vayriel. The Highblood knelt in front of him, one palm placed between his ears.

"What's wrong with him?" Idrilia asked.

"I do not know. His spirit is so weak that I cannot hear him." Her voice broke.

Idrilia stiffened, flipping her communication crystal out of her side bag, and focused on Wen. The othwit, perched on the main mast—her favorite look-out point—felt the same as always. The Sondrinel relaxed her shoulders. Whatever plagued the jeroti had not found her flying companion.

"Oh, I do not feel well." Vayriel placed her free hand to her own forehead, still maintaining contact with her life-friend. The scene made Idrilia think of the Highblood's account of Mount Hoestra and how she had helped heal the female jeroti. Idrilia wondered if Vayriel had used too much of her energy as she had done at least twice so far. Did the Highblood never think of herself before she helped others? A wave of guilt passed over Idrilia.

Kilahym knelt beside Vayriel, his face etched with concern. "What can I do?"

Vayriel sat unblinking, as if she did not hear the bard. He swiveled, casting his anxious gaze at Kalis and Idrilia.

"We were at the front of the skykeel when Vayriel reacted as if she'd been stabbed in the chest. She immediately sprinted to Orgar. We found him here. I didn't see what happened before and immediately ran to find you two. What can we do?"

"Can't you help him, Vayriel?" Idrilia intertwined her fingers. "Through your bond?"

The Highblood shook her head. "I don't know." A whistle broke through the sound of the wind and snapping of the sails. Rinesh waved to them, and after glancing around the deck, he stepped away from the helm.

"This may sound like I'm looking for ways to blame him, but just before the creature fell, Zinvar was petting him. Kharnek came over, and it looked like your jeroti companion did not like him at all—ears back, tails limp. Zinvar and Kharnek went below deck, and next I looked over, the canine was like this."

Vayriel grabbed Kilahym's arm and spoke in hushed tones. "Kharnek is no longer."

"What do you mean?" Kilahym patted her vise-like grip on his forearm.

The Highblood blinked rapidly before turning toward the bard. "The light of his spirit has been engulfed by darkness, a void. Orgar felt this from Kharnek. It is one that is many. It is the Penumbra." Vayriel shuddered.

"Are you certain?" Kilahym asked.

She nodded. "Orgar shared his memory-image with me. His life force was pulled from him, like the crystals Rinesh uses on the skykeel. What did you call it, a power drop? Orgar feels like I do if I have used too much of my own life-force energy. I felt this through our bond."

"We need to act. Now," Idrilia said sternly.

"Whatever is going on could have us at a disadvantage, you know. If Kharnek, or whoever he is, can impact our crystals…"

"We might not be able to use them. And we can't let him near Vayriel."

"She's our only other fighter, but you're right. We can't risk having her lying on the deck as well."

"If I may interject. Knowledge is quite a powerful weapon as well. Wit and whimsy triumphs when all else fails, so the saying goes. Though I really think wit should be the first weapon one goes to. *In the right hand knowledge*, yes?"

"Left hand. What do you propose?" Kalis brought the bard back on track.

"The Tale of Pyreflowers and Loved Twice Scorned."

"What are you babbling about?" Idrilia tried to look down on the bard, but as he was only a few inches shorter now that he stood, she instead narrowed her eyes dangerously.

"One of these days I'll get to tell you all the full story. But to execute this symbolic plan, we are going to need the help of our Zinvar."

CHAPTER 59

The flash of Idrilia's stunning crystal tore through the meager covering of Zinvar's headscarf. Its brilliance was a hungry varg, biting ferociously at his light-sensitive eyes. Even with his foreknowledge of what to expect, this was far worse than he anticipated. He felt a brief pang of sympathy for the now unconscious Kharnek. The warrior's muscular form lay sprawled across the deck of the cabin he and the priest shared, where Zinvar lured him so the Sondrinel could spring their trap.

"I hope he'll forgive me for this," Zinvar wished aloud as he unwrapped his scarf.

Idrilia's brows shot up. "Forgive you? If he has any decency, he should thank you. And all of us, for not doing the smart thing and just throwing him off the ship."

"You have a way with words, Dilly-Drilly," Kilahym chimed in from where he and Vayriel had appeared at the cabin's entrance. "A way that oft reminds me of the manner in which a hammer bludgeons the unsuspecting nail."

"Well, then, you'd best beware," Idrilia retorted, mimicking the bard's flowery speech, "lest you become the unsuspecting nail."

The quasi-hostile banter baffled the priest, but his thoughts quickly returned to his felled companion. He had been reluctant to participate in the others' plan to incapacitate Kharnek, but he ultimately caved to their logic—the warrior was too dangerous to confront directly. And Zinvar knew that they were not wrong to accuse Kharnek of harboring something deadly.

"I have seen the darkness within him," Vayriel had proclaimed, "and Orgar's senses do not lie. It is—powerful. We glimpsed only a fraction of this in the battle against Adjira and in moments since then."

"More importantly, it is an immediate threat to us all. You saw how it affected the jeroti. He's still hiding down in the hold. Imagine if that spread to the rest of us," Kalis posited.

Zinvar sensed that he would not dissuade his companions, but he had successfully lobbied for an attempt to free the warrior from the Penumbra's influence. Nevertheless, the sense that he had irrevocably betrayed Kharnek's trust persisted.

"Are we all going to stand here staring, or will one of you help me restrain him?" Idrilia demanded, cutting off the priest's reverie.

"I doubt it would matter, you know?"

"Kalis is correct, but it is better to take the enemy's weapon before he finds it." Vayriel looked directly at Idrilia and Kalis. "We should also remove his sword. It could interfere with what we now attempt."

Zinvar cocked his head. "How so?"

The Highblood shared Rinesh's explanation of arsanth while the Sondrinel set about tying Kharnek's wrists and ankles, using rope scavenged from the hold. Zinvar winced as Idrilia cinched the knots far tighter than they needed to be. Kalis took the warrior's sword and placed it out of reach. Now that he was aware of its unique properties, Zinvar was troubled by the possible reasons for Kharnek to possess it.

Kilahym interrupted his thoughts. "Where is your brother, Zinny?"

"He's monitoring the crystals that power the ship," the priest answered, "just in case. We know that whatever has possessed Kharnek affects the life force in a negative fashion. If its influence expanded to that area of the skykeel, well…"

The bard nodded. "Ah, yes, that would be undesirable." His voice dropped lower so that only Zinvar could hear. "I have not told this tale, for I feel it is yours to relate. But I think you have known the truth about Kharnek and the Penumbra for some time."

Zinvar's stomach dropped to his feet. "You're right, of course."

"What are you two whispering about?" The suspicion in Idrilia's glare skewered Zinvar's guilty conscience. It kindled a resolve that, over the course of the Trials, had slowly gained momentum, like a stone rolling down a hill. All eyes swung to Zinvar as he stepped into the center of the room, directly beside Kharnek's still form.

"A secret, but it will be secret no more." The priest regarded the other Seekers one at a time, gauging their reactions. Kilahym smiled in encouragement when Zinvar looked his way.

"This thing that has taken control of Kharnek...the Penumbra...I knew it was there and that this would happen. In a manner of speaking," he added hastily as Idrilia's eyes widened. "I have seen it in dreams or visions, whatever they are."

"When you say it is known to you, what do you mean?" Kalis asked, his brow furrowed.

"I have seen it within Kharnek. More than once." Zinvar went on to explain each of his visions regarding the Penumbra. "I'm sorry I didn't say anything until now," he offered to the ensuing silence, "but I didn't...I wanted to believe that Kharnek was stronger than the evil within him. And I still don't entirely understand what the Penumbra is, much less how to deal with it."

As the priest was finishing his statement, Idrilia's head was already shaking in disbelief. "I cannot believe this. We suspected, but you *knew*. All this time you endangered us all, for the sake of...what, exactly? Protecting your romantic fling? What a reckless, foolish thing to do."

"You're one to talk," Zinvar replied sharply.

Before Idrilia could respond, Kalis stepped between her and the priest. "What I can't believe is you two. We have enough problems without returning to bickering amongst ourselves."

"Yes. Kalis speaks truly. Disunity at this time is as dangerous as the Penumbra. Only together can we hope to truly vanquish this foe."

"Thank you, Vayriel. Now, I think we can all agree that it was wrong of Zinvar to withhold this information," Kalis began, to which Idrilia nodded vigorously, "but I think we can all understand why he would do so. Especially given the unusual circumstances of how he obtained it."

"That's still no excuse for endangering us all."

"No, it isn't," Zinvar agreed, noting Idrilia's surprise, "which is why I can only apologize for my poor judgment." The priest longed for the comfort of his staff, stowed away under his bunk for the moment. Revealing what he knew had placed him in a precarious spot with the others—this would be his first test of the bonds of friendship among the Seekers.

"Which takes a courage of its own." Scratching the half-formed beard on his chin, Kilahym came to Zinvar's defense. "And Zinny is not the sole keeper of secrets among us; that much is clear."

"That is true," Vayriel agreed, "I have only told some of you about my true purpose in being here."

Zinvar's brows shot up. "You're the last person I would have suspected of having an ulterior motive."

A flush colored the Highblood's cheeks. "It has been my own uncertainty that has stood in the way of saying more. Much like what you described about revealing what you have seen."

"Entirely understandable," Kilahym commented, patting her on the shoulder.

Zinvar watched Idrilia shift her hands from her hips to cross over her chest. "Go ahead, Vayriel. If this is what I think it is, you have nothing to fear from telling us."

The Highblood nodded slowly, then related the prophecy given to her before the Trials. "My people believe me to be the one foretold who will stop the Sleeper."

As she spoke, Zinvar's mind drifted to the moments before he tumbled into the canal in Waverling. There had been a woman wielding tremendous power, and with her in the heart of the inferno was someone else. Someone, his instincts told him, close to her. *Could it be?*

"That's quite the burden to carry," Kalis said. The Sondrinel rubbed the back of his neck. "What you are saying aligns with certain...signs that the Occulum, not just Zinvar, have seen of late. The Council warned us about an unknown threat before the opening ceremony, but it didn't make sense at the time."

The priest cocked his head. "That provides context for something I saw around the same time." His eyes sought Vayriel's and locked with them. "I believe your people may be correct. And that Kilahym may have a part to play as well."

"*Me?*" The bard placed a hand on his heart.

Zinvar inclined his head. "Yes. Call it Occulum intuition."

After a long pause, Kalis ventured into the silence that followed, "We've made a lot of progress in learning to trust each other and work together. Let's not forfeit that now. We're supposed to be better than that, you know?" Gesturing to the group, the Sondrinel continued, "Yes, we are from different realms, each with its own reasons for wanting us to be here. But we don't have to let those old divisions dictate our future." Kalis looked admiringly at his companion, a spark of pride glimmering in his eyes. "If there's anything 'Dril has taught me, it's that we are free to choose who we are and what we will become." He spoke to the others. " So, no more secrets." Kalis stared directly at Zinvar, and he bowed his head in assent. "And let's try to not assume the worst about each other," he finished, swiveling back to Idrilia.

She crossed her arms but offered a tight-lipped nod. For their part, Vayriel and Kilahym smiled and agreed.

"Well spoken, my friend. And they said I was diplomatic," Zinvar joked.

Kalis shrugged. "Almost dying has a way of changing your perspective." A bright grin spread across his face. "And I think I have an idea about how to solve our Penumbra problem."

"For what it's worth, I don't think this is a good idea."

"We know, 'Dril, but the majority ruled in favor of this."

"The majority can shove a pile of crystals up their—"

"'Dril!"

The Seekers were arrayed in the same semicircle around Kharnek as when he fell, with the Sondrinel to Zinvar's left, and Vayriel and Kilahym to his right. Despite finding himself on the opposite side of the argument from her, the priest could not fault Idrilia for her sourness. Kalis's plan to use one of the Sondrinel communication crystals as a bridge between Kharnek's mind and the priest's was fraught with risk.

"Only the best healers in Axiom attempt this and only with the severest of cases," the Prioriate explained, "because the crystals really aren't designed for this purpose."

"They're meant to relay thoughts between conscious minds, not serve as windows into anyone else's," Zinvar guessed.

"Exactly. It requires incredible concentration to force one's entire consciousness through the crystal and into a closed mind. Useful for disorders of thought, but"—Kalis shrugged—"this is something else entirely."

The other risk, Zinvar knew, was that in the effort to reach Kharnek his own consciousness might become untethered from his body. If that happened, he would either be trapped in the warrior's mind with a hostile force or lost in the crystal—perhaps permanently. His corporeal form would slowly wither and die, at which point his consciousness—what Vayriel called his true self—would also diminish into the life force.

"You are certain that you do not wish for me to undertake this challenge in your stead?" The Highblood's sincere offer warmed Zinvar's heart. Perhaps he underestimated his new friends' capacities to forgive.

"Thank you, but I'm sure. Kharnek knows me the best so his mind should be more receptive to my presence. And if I fail and he wakes up, you're the strongest in the life force among us, which makes you our best defense against the Penumbra."

Vayriel's lips parted to speak, then she bowed her head in acceptance. Gathering his robes, Zinvar knelt on the deck beside the immobile warrior. The wooden planks bit at his kneecaps, but he felt nothing—his focus lay entirely upon Kharnek.

"I'm ready." Zinvar grasped one of his companion's hands—they were cold as the howling wind atop Mount Hoestra.

Kalis nodded, and with a clever flourish, he released his communication crystal from its gauntlet housing. Delicately, he handed the orb to the priest, who clutched it tightly between his pale fingers. Closing his eyes, Zinvar imagined his thoughts streaming through the device toward Kharnek, like a torrent of volition. A strange sensation—like the tug of a small child on her mother's hand—signaled the intervention of the crystal. *Just as Kalis described,* Zinvar mused.

No sooner had the thought formed than a torrent of the priest's own memories inundated him. The softness of his mother's cheek pressed against his forehead as she cradled him dissolved into the sound of a young man sobbing—and Zinvar recognized the mournful cries as his own from the darkening when he learned of Myal's murder.

"Zinvar!"

The shout cut through the onslaught of recollection, providing Zinvar the brief respite he needed to regain control of his faculties. He dropped the communication crystal. The moment the object left his hand, the flood of memories ceased, leaving merciful silence in their wake. As the priest's senses returned to him, he realized that sweat beaded his brow and every extremity was afflicted by tremors.

"Zinvar! Can you hear me?" Kalis's face swam into view, the Sondrinel's aquiline features blurred as if underwater.

"Yes." The Komorese grimaced as a muscle in his jaw spasmed. Apparently, his whole body tensed during the attempt, a reality his aching shoulders soon affirmed.

"I was afraid of this." Kalis knelt on the deck beside him, one hand supporting the priest's back and the other offering a cup of water, which Zinvar gratefully took. The cool liquid splashed against the back of his dry throat, driving off the mental fog.

"This is the echo you were talking about?"

"Yes. The defenses around Kharnek's mind must be too strong. They deflected your thoughts back at you, and for a moment, you saw into your own mind."

"I felt it," Vayriel spoke, her face pallid and etched with concern. "There was pain, loss...something terrible happened."

Zinvar coughed then drew in a deep breath. "Something worse may happen if I don't succeed."

"You can't possibly be thinking of trying again," Idrilia said, clasping her forehead.

"What choice do I have?" Throwing back the rest of the water, Zinvar reached into his robes and withdrew a glimmering vial. The blue substance within the glass tube seemed to hold a light of its own. Before any of the Seekers could react, the priest unstoppered the vial and quaffed its contents. He heard a cry of dismay from Kalis as he snatched the fallen crystal from the floorboards, then the cabin around him faded into flickers of memories not his own. The familiar pull of the past latched on, threatening to drag the priest into yet another reminiscence.

No, Zinvar thought, *I want to go this way.*

The tension yielded to his will, and he found himself standing outside the flow of history, an onlooker to its currents. Faces and landscapes flashed by, but he remained still, surrounded by curtains of indigo mist. Beyond the torrent appeared a point of ruby light. The light drew nearer and nearer to the priest until he was engulfed by its radiance.

When at last the brilliance receded, Zinvar found himself within an enormous, faceted space. Crystalline towers rose about him, stretching upward to disappear into swirls of roseate clouds pinpricked by dots of scarlet luminescence. He could not see a ceiling beyond the firmament. When he looked down, the floor beneath appeared to be made of panes of translucent pink crystal, through which he espied seemingly infinite depths. Tearing his gaze away from the vertiginous sight, Zinvar peered into the distance. Angular lines of darker magenta suggested massive walls that defined the space, though they were so far off that he suspected walking for days would bring him no closer.

Despite the overwhelming scale of the communication crystal's interior, Zinvar was undaunted. Its geometries felt familiar. He suspected that he was not the first Occulum to venture here, for he could vaguely discern the outlines of dozens of faded azure footprints on the floor—paths that would lead him to any number of undiscovered truths about his forerunners.

But this was not his destination, the priest reminded himself. Marshaling his thoughts, Zinvar focused on Kharnek, and the crystal obliged. Though he did not move, his surroundings began to hurtle past so quickly they blurred into pinkish mist. Far ahead, but drawing closer, shades of red and orange spilled into view, like the flow from a volcanic eruption. The mist cleared, and Zinvar found himself astride a narrow basalt bridge. Across it stood a formidable gate, sheathed in iron and flanked by dark spires that arrowed upward, their tips struck by bolts of lightning that speared down from colossal storm clouds. Fragments of a familiar crumbling citadel rotated amidst the thunderheads, the alien facets of their architecture a stark contrast to the Komorese style of the gate. The gate itself was set into the side of a cliff, which plunged down into the abyss that the bridge spanned. A ribbon of molten orange glowed far below.

Zinvar inhaled deeply before starting the perilous crossing. Gusts of wind from the tempest overhead snatched at his robes, threatening his balance. Small pebbles of volcanic rock whipped through the air, slicing his bare skin. One sheared a hot line across his cheek, leaving crimson agony in its wake. As the priest lowered his head and pushed onward, he felt his connection to the communication crystal becoming ever more tenuous, like a bowstring drawn too tightly. The storm's fury swelled with each step until Zinvar despaired of ever making it across. Then the wind ceased to howl. No more gritty missiles bit at his flesh. He looked up, and he was at the gate.

Though weary, the priest's voice was strong when he called out, "Let me in!"

A deep groan resounded from the structure, but the gates did not move.

"Kharnek!" Zinvar called, eliciting another creak from the doors. Still, they did not open. Squaring his shoulders, the priest stood upright and extended a hand, palm outward, toward the monolith.

"Let. Me. *In*."

A tremendous shudder ran through the entirety of the gate and shook the cliff beneath it, nearly knocking Zinvar from his feet. Then a tiny crack of orange light appeared between the two halves of the mighty doors. Soundlessly they swung away from him, revealing a gray, storm-tossed sea beyond. Through the crashing waves capped by spume, he could faintly see a path of stepping stones that reached toward the horizon. His journey was not over, then, but he was closer—somewhere in that chaos was Kharnek, and he would find him and bring him back. He set his jaw and marched through the gate, into the jaws of the waiting maelstrom.

CHAPTER 60

The woman's features dissolved into nothingness as darkness engulfed her. She stretched out a hand toward Kharnek, fingers pointed in accusation.

"May you burn for all eternity in the fire beyond Morakh's shadow," Myal pronounced, offering a final curse before the creeping darkness overtook her completely. Then, a falling sensation made the warrior's stomach lurch as he fell into oblivion with his victim.

No one heard Kharnek's scream as he awakened from the dream. Ever since the Penumbra had taken control of his body, he had relived the memory of Zinvar's mother's murder and others like it over and over. The cycle of horror, guilt, and self-loathing eroded his resolve until all that remained of the proud warrior was a small bubble of consciousness, like the one Adjira had created. To Kharnek, the fragment of himself appeared like a deserted isle, a golden circle set in a field of turquoise. Sunlight streamed down upon the burning sand though it did not harm his skin like the harsh brilliance of Sondrine. This was made even more miraculous by his nakedness—he had been stripped of all dignity. Ominous storm clouds that marked the Penumbra's advance upon his redoubt swirled on the horizon. With the passing of each cycle, those clouds drew ever nearer. When they arrived, Kharnek knew he would cease to exist.

At first, he dared to believe he might break the Penumbra's control. When it violated him aboard the skykeel, its hold on his body was not absolute, and the Komorese's resistance yielded what he hoped were obvious interruptions of normal movements. For a short time, Kharnek also saw what the Penumbra was doing with its borrowed flesh between forced recollections—and he felt it grow stronger when it absorbed the life force from the ship's power crystals. Shortly thereafter, all sensory input was blocked. That was when the assault of memories began in earnest.

Despite years of military conditioning against every conceivable method of torture, nothing could have prepared Kharnek for the Penumbra's ability to manipulate and use his own past against him. It knew him, had known him since childhood when it found its unwilling host, and now it pressed that advantage. Once again, the warrior scoured the barren sand for something with which to end his own life, if such a thing was possible in this place. His hand closed upon a sharp fragment of rock. Before he could wield his newfound tool against himself, another memory obscured his senses.

He was young, a boy of no more than five epicycles—far too young to be wandering the outskirts of Zel Morakh alone. Clad in filthy gray rags, Kharnek stole between the slender stalks of rift wort plants, their tips laden with bulbs full of purple juice. This field was ripe for harvest, and ordinarily he would have stripped the bulbs from the plants to exchange them for food, but this time he was after something far more valuable. It was whispered that crystals had been discovered in the caverns beneath the city. Komorese were forbidden to possess such objects as they were considered to be totems of sacrilege. Even so, wealthy citizens with a taste for the taboo would risk the Priesthood's wrath and hand over a lot of muura for a crystal. Kharnek licked his lips, imagining how much food he could buy. Enough to last for an epicycle, at least— perhaps longer, if he rationed it.

At the edge of the field, the boy found what he sought: a crack in the ground, the air above it roiling from dissipating heat. Squeezing his way between the lips of the narrow opening, Kharnek slowly wriggled his way down the sloped passage within the crevasse. At length, it deposited him into a much larger space. The cavern was dark except for the thin trickle of moonlight that filtered through the passage Kharnek just exited. Tearing off a strip of his garment, the young Komorese wrapped it around a cluster of rift wort stalks he took from the field and broke the juice bulbs, drenching the cloth with purple liquid. From what remained of his clothes, the boy withdrew a thin, cylindrical device fashioned by one of the revered timepiece craftsmen of Zel Morakh. The wealthy priest he took it from no doubt missed it, but it would serve a far greater purpose for Kharnek—it would light the way to his salvation from a life on the streets.

If it worked.

Clicking the wheel, he smiled as a flame spouted from the cylinder's end. The fire sprang hungrily to the doused cloth on Kharnek's makeshift torch. Rift wort juice burned brightly and slowly, the perfect fuel for what could be a long hunt in the dark. Making his way down the lava tube, Kharnek carefully watched for the telltale glitter of crystal formations. The tunnel, carved by nature's wandering hand, ascended, descended, and curved at random. Between the

*geographic changes and the oppressive heat, the journey was grueling. Yet with the tireless energy
of a child, the boy pressed on, sweat dripping from his unruly mass of hair.*

*After many hours of fruitless searching, Kharnek rounded a corner and found himself
facing a branch in the tunnel. Holding his torch up to the left corridor, he was greeted by the
same impermeable blackness through which he already passed. When he raised the flaming
brand to the right, however, its radiance glinted off something further down the tunnel.
Excitement spurred the boy's fatigued legs into rapid motion. Kharnek ran toward the reflected
light, and in his haste, he neglected the black void in the rocky floor into which he pitched
headlong.*

*Morakh was with him, for the drop was only a few wyrm-lengths. Even so, he crashed
painfully onto the basalt below. The impact freed the torch from his grip to careen into the
darkness. It vanished into the oblivion of a nearby rift in the ground, and Kharnek lay
motionless for a moment, stunned by the fall. When his eyes adjusted to the absence of the
torchlight, the Komorese became aware of a faint amethyst-hued glow. Sitting up, he stared in
wonder at its source.*

*At the center of this miniature cave within a cave stood a stone pillar, atop which rested
a purple crystal the size of Kharnek's fist. The light suffusing the chamber came from within its
faceted depths. There was a strange rippling quality to the crystal's luminosity, as if it were
submerged. Kharnek rose to his feet and crept nearer to the pillar. When he was close enough to
reach out and touch the crystal, he discerned strands of black squirming within the violet glow
like tide writhers in the ocean.*

Light.

*Kharnek jumped and spun about. There was no one in the cave with him. So where did
the utterance come from?*

Too much light.

*This time he whirled to squint suspiciously at the crystal. Surely it could not talk. And
yet, this was unlike any formation he had ever seen. It would fetch a priestly ransom in the
underrift market.*

*Kharnek laid both hands on the crystal, prepared to grapple with the stone for its release.
As soon as his fingers made contact with its angular surface, he felt a coldness steal over them,
then creep up his arms until his whole body felt as if it were plunged into the frigid waters of Zel
Morakh's harbor. The black strands within the crystal suddenly twisted through its surface and
began to coil up the boy's forearms. He shrieked in terror and tried to withdraw his hands, but
an unseen force held them in place. As the darkness reached Kharnek's head, the amethyst light
flared, and he collapsed to the ground.*

The warrior gasped and fell to his knees on the sand. Fractured shells bit at
his skin, but it was nothing compared with the panic that gnawed at his mind.
This was the worst attack yet. The wind picked up, and the waves cast themselves

with reckless abandon against the shore. He closed his eyes. It would all be over soon.

"So that's how it all began."

The warrior did not move. He knew that voice, but its owner could not possibly be here. This was another trick of his nemesis. Then he felt a hand on his shoulder, warm against his bare skin. Kharnek looked up, prepared to defend himself from another onslaught, but his gaze met with a familiar face.

"Zinvar?"

When the priest smiled, the warrior thought it was the most beautiful thing he had ever witnessed. He exploded up from the sand and wrapped Zinvar in a trägen embrace, lifting him from the ground in his exuberance. The horror of his imprisonment faded, replaced by a sense of comfort that Kharnek never knew he would feel. Then his combat instincts reasserted themselves, and he set the priest down at arm's length.

"Are you real? Or is this some new form of torture?"

Zinvar smiled. "I'm as real as one can be inside someone else's mind."

If this was a simulacrum created by the Penumbra, it certainly knew Zinvar's sense of humor. Kharnek let himself relax fractionally.

"But how can this be?"

"That's a very interesting story I'll tell you after we've gotten you out of here," the priest answered. His features became downcast. "This place—I can only imagine what you've endured. Reliving the worst of your memories."

"You saw them?" The warrior's heart raced as he thought of Myal.

"Not exactly. The closer I got to you, the clearer they became, but it was more feelings than actual images. But now that I'm here with you"—the green in Zinvar's eyes suddenly changed to a glimmering cerulean as he spread his arms— "I could see everything. Know every moment, every thought." For a long moment, during which Kharnek's heart drummed in his ears, the priest remained frozen in that position. Then the blue receded, and Zinvar dropped his hands to his sides.

"But that wouldn't be right. Secrets are meant to be told, not taken."

"Some secrets are kept hidden for a reason," Kharnek bit out. The harshness in his own words surprised him. Zinvar shook his head sadly.

"You're losing yourself to the Penumbra right now because of keeping secrets."

A loud crack made both men jump. They studied the sky over the sea, where a jagged line of perfect darkness rent the wall of thunderheads. The blackness seeped out of the rift and stole the color and then all form from the distant waves. Kharnek felt a profound despair grip his heart—Zinvar was too late. His defenses were finally overwhelmed.

Another memory burst into the warrior's mind, this time on the Isle of Mora, when the Priesthood first discovered his abilities gifted by the Penumbra.

"Show us," the trio of enrobed men demanded. Kharnek did not move, remaining tight-lipped with all the stubbornness a thirteen-year-old boy could muster. Even when the training sergeant's whip left angry welts on his back, he did not cry out. Nor did he give these bloodthirsty men what they desired.

"You dare defy a priest of Morakh?" the sergeant bellowed. "You'll learn respect one way or another. Bring him in!"

To Kharnek's dismay, two soldiers dragged his sparring partner Ylnat into the room and began to pummel him ferociously. The warrior moved to intervene, but the sergeant stepped between him and Ylnat with sword in hand. A roiling fury built within Kharnek at the injustice, at the way the man sneered, and he could no longer hold back the darkness...

When it was over, the sergeant and both of the soldiers lay unmoving on the floor, their throats slashed. The priest at the trio's center offered a cold smile to Kharnek before turning to leave the room. His companions followed, leaving the young man alone with the dead.

"NO."

The scene dissolved, replaced by Zinvar's anxious face.

"I'm sorry, it happened too quickly for me to stop it. But I can hold them back, at least for a little while."

Kharnek blinked. "You can stop the memories?"

The priest nodded. "I don't think the Penumbra has ever encountered an Occulum. And—I can't fully explain it, but it seems that all the Occulum, past and present, are connected. I know what they experienced. It's like they're guiding me."

Kharnek pushed aside his shock to grapple with the reality of the Penumbra's approach. "Then you need to let them help you get out of here. Now."

"I'm not going any—"

"Zinvar, for once listen to me!" The warrior gripped the priest's upper arms and looked him in the eye. "You cannot stop this. You have to go."

"I can't."

"What?"

"I said I can't." Zinvar met his gaze steadily. "The way I came is gone."

Whether it was the priest's doing or not, Kharnek suddenly had a vision of his lover's journey across the stormy sea. Each stone sank behind him as he advanced, taking with it any hope of returning, but he never looked back.

"Zinvar," the warrior's voice broke, "I do not deserve what you have done. I deserve my fate." Kharnek pointed to the darkening sky that was closing in on the beach. "I deserve that and everything it has done to me."

Zinvar shook his head. "No, you don't. The Penumbra killed those men, not you. It used you."

"Because I allowed it to do so. I relished the power it gave me even when it brought about the deaths of innocent people. What Rinesh told you is only the beginning of what I have done." Kharnek shivered as the wind grew frigid. The sea was now gray, and the waves near the shore began to freeze at mid-crest.

Zinvar's voice broke when he responded. "Do you think I don't know that?"

Kharnek's heart plummeted.

"Do you think I don't feel the walls you've built to keep yourself safe? That I don't notice when you steer the conversation away from your past? I barely know who you are—and sometimes I wonder if I've fallen for a monster."

The words ripped away the warrior's self-destructive shield. He felt the hurt in Zinvar's confession and saw the fear in his eyes. To be so vulnerable—it took a strength which Kharnek knew he did not possess. But he could learn.

"No more lies."

It was only a whisper, but the effect on the scenery was profound. The frozen waves surged back into motion, and some of their original hue was restored.

"No more lies," Kharnek said again, louder this time. The entire island rumbled. Rocks scattered across the sand thrummed and rose off the beach, hovering in the air. The crack in the sky vanished, and the storm began to diminish in potency. Drawing Zinvar close to him, the warrior pressed his lips against the priest's.

A moment that felt like an eternity passed before Zinvar pulled away and met Kharnek's gaze with eyes brimming with moisture. "No more lies," he affirmed, then kissed the warrior deeply. Kharnek surrendered to the flood of emotions the act unleashed and clung to Zinvar with all his might.

Sunlight pierced the clouds and spilled over the island, brightening until the sand and the sea vanished into blinding white. When the effulgence waned, Kharnek found himself lying on his back on the floor of the skykeel cabin he shared with the priest. Zinvar knelt beside him. When their eyes met, Kharnek smiled—and it was truly him.

CHAPTER 61

Kalis leaned on the railing, watching the hanging crystalline lanterns cast a golden glow around the skykeel's hull as if it were surrounded by a floating ring of bioluminescence. Rinesh had brought additional crystal lamps from the hold and attached them to the masts to assist those foreign to Komor. These Concilius-style orbs hung from polished iron links, unlike the weathered chains outside of the ship, having experienced less of the salty sea air. The light helped, but Kalis's desert eyes still found it difficult to adjust.

He saw neither cloud nor coast ahead, only blackness. He half expected to see the lava trenches withering across the frozen landscape. But basalt outcroppings and a single, barren forest were the prominent features of northern Komor. Nearer to the Agermath Range glowed red-orange striations of the volcanic rifts. He knew of the terrain based on Itineratum records, their details preserved from a not-so-far-removed time when war was a constant companion of Sondrine. Current border scouts brought more updated details, but their maps were limited.

Silence interspersed with the creak of wood or the snap of a sail pervaded the skykeel's top deck. Kharnek stood in what Kalis assumed was a Komorese military rest at the bow of their vessel. Alone. Kalis knew Idrilia didn't trust that the warrior was now free of the Penumbra, but Orgar and Vayriel no longer felt the negative presence.

Kalis thought through the recent events as he leisurely paced the length of the ship, making sure he'd covered as many possible as he could, but Kalis's thoughts continued to divert to Idrilia. He still loved her. That hadn't changed. He would just love her as he had before—no joyful marriage ceremony. He couldn't be sure, but Idrilia seemed less abrasive, less like she avoided his presence since their conversation. Only time would tell.

In the history of Axiom, Kalis wondered if there had been any other betrothed who refused. There had to be a way to allow them both to continue their separate lives. The Council wouldn't force them against their wills, surely. That seemed decidedly un-Sondrine. And Kalis knew he didn't want to be coupled with anyone else as a replacement.

A scuffling to his right broke his line of thought. Zinvar, clothed in his priestly raiment, made his way from the cabin stairs carrying his pack and staff to stand by the warrior. He couldn't hear what words they exchanged, and out of respect, he altered his patrolling path to stay on the back half of the ship.

Kalis suspected more transpired in the communication crystal incident than had been stated. Something more personal than the rest of the Seekers needed to know. There had been a change between the two, a gentleness between them that hadn't been there before.

"The Penumbra is no longer a concern," Zinvar had told everyone.

Kalis was skeptical, but even more shocking had been Kharnek's apology to the group.

"I apologize for putting you all at risk," the warrior had said, "I carried this burden for so long that I did not think it could be shared with anyone. But Zinvar has shown me there is a better way."

Kharnek had then shared the story of how he became the Penumbra's host. Despite his disinclination to trust the other man, Kalis found himself capable of sympathy for his plight. To be gripped by that horror from such a young age...well, it was little wonder that Kharnek kept everyone at arm's length.

Kilahym's voice intruded upon his ruminations. "Felt a little tingling in my abdomen. Though, that could be the ration I ate earlier. Sondrinel might travel with it, but I don't think I can develop a taste for gritty bars. But I do think I almost had it that time!"

"Keep practicing," Kalis heard Vayriel answer. "It will take many passings of the Daughter for your abilities to surpass those of the young-ones."

"Was that a jab, vexing Vayriel?"

The pair exited the lower cabins merrily, followed by a sour-faced Idrilia. Kalis caught her eye, and she came to stand next to him. She wore her usual gradient blue Nuala robe and her hair tied out of her way. In addition to donning her gloves, she wrapped the orange headscarf around her neck against the cold. Kalis plucked a crystal from his hip, shaking it to activate the warmth.

"Thanks," Idrilia mumbled, taking the crystal from his proffered hand.

"Ready to leave this enchanted vessel?" Kalis asked as he took his bag from Idrilia.

Her eyes narrowed as she shifted her own pack on her shoulder. "You know very well this is—"

"I'm joking, 'Dril." Kalis smiled, elbowing her.

"Just don't go joining a traveling show with your jokes. They'll send you home immediately."

Kalis saw her lips tug in a grin as she turned away from him. He felt his heart soar but quickly reminded himself that this behavior was common between them. At least it had been prior to the betrothal. Kalis was glad to have that friendship back. Though he fought it, an emptiness crawled into his heart where once was joy for marrying Idrilia.

The Seekers gathered near where Rinesh steered the skykeel.

"You can be an instigator of change," Zinvar pleaded. "Others must have a similar story of persecution. Together, you can inform all of Zel Morakh."

Rinesh snorted. "You think that will matter? The Mahiratha will squash anyone who supports us like fekwa beneath their boots. Claim I spew heretical lies to undermine and corrupt Morakhism."

"I will stand by you. As a priest they—"

"Oh, Zinvar," Rinesh laughed bitterly. "I appreciate your attempt, albeit naïve, to reconcile. But I have long counted myself free of Komor. I may look Komorese, but I will not be a part of that society any longer."

The priest sighed, and his shoulders slumped. "Then where will you go now?"

"Back to the Reef."

"And when that whim no longer interests you?"

"You do not know me, brother," Rinesh growled.

Zinvar's eyes flashed. "Because you will not let me! Even before our parents' passing, you jumped from intrigue to intrigue, and that trend continues. Only this time you left no indication as to where I could find you. For *epicycles*. You are my *brother*."

Kalis glanced at the others, the same mix of confusion and discomfort he felt on their faces.

Rinesh shook his head sadly. "Family cannot always come first. I'm sorry, but it's for the best that we once again go our separate ways."

Rinesh touched lighted crystals set around the wheel. The air across Kalis's eyes lessened, and for a moment, the wood beneath his feet dropped lower. Rinesh indicated that the cliff came into view, though Kalis could not see further than the rails of the ship into the deep darkness. Overhead, thousands of white stars dotted the sky above the sails. The Seekers moved to the middle of the rail and the disembarkation area. Rinesh would steer them to the cliff on his own to Kilahym's disappointment. The crystals set into the back railing were only for docking and launching from the pillars.

"There it is!" Zinvar called out, pointing to something perpendicular to the ship that Kalis could not see.

"How far?"

"I would say two boat lengths."

"I'll bring us closer."

As Rinesh worked, the lanterns hanging from the ship's sides cast their light on a structure protruding from the depths. A cloud shifted, and the northern moon's light revealed a rock arch extending from the natural coast like a bridge into the water. Kilahym excitedly declaimed a string of poetic descriptions as his first reaction to such a sight. As he stared, Kalis thought it looked more like a long leg bent, ready to spring, than a bridge.

"I would like to make a proposal." Zinvar paused, giving enough time for the group to look his way. "Just as Kalis and Idrilia led us through Sondrine, I believe it would be prudent to allow Kharnek and myself to lead you in Komor. We are familiar with the terrain and dangers, and our eyes are more accustomed to the darkness."

"A logical proposition. But may I inquire as to what dangers we may face?" the bard asked. Zinvar turned to the warrior, who answered.

"This far north and above the rifts, the largest foe is the cold," Kharnek fixed a pointed gaze on Kilahym, and the bard tightened the drawstrings of his long-sleeved shirt at his sternum, "followed by the land itself. The rocky landscape can be as treacherous as climbing the mountains. The frozen soil is slick, as are the lichen-covered rocks. Mind your footing that you do not trip."

"By leading, we can point out those areas and help avoid any injury. If you agree."

"That is a generous and wise offer, Zinvar. The Daughter's light will help guide us, and I can help as well." The Highblood stamped the butt of her spear lightly before her on the deck. With her left hand, she cupped the tip, as if whispering into the multi-faceted crystal. Suddenly, light escaped from the gaps between her gloved fingers. She withdrew her hand, revealing the full crystal which radiated a pink as bright as three lanterns. She moved the pole to her left side, a trail of light lingering like mist before dissipating.

"We won't be completely blind," Idrilia replied, reaching into her hip bag.

"We can illuminate our path, somewhat," Kalis echoed Idrilia's movements and retrieved his illumination crystal. In tandem, they activated their crystals and tossed them above their heads. He smiled at her, the expression quickly fading as he remembered she was forbidden from using the life force.

"Don't say it," Idrilia breathed. "Not tripping and falling to my death in the sea qualifies as 'extreme circumstance.'"

Kalis shrugged, knowing the point could not be argued with her, though he feared the consequences that awaited her from the Council when they returned.

"I should be able to protect our group from anything we encounter," Kharnek continued. "But in the event we encounter a threat, I will alert everyone quickly."

"I'm sure we will notice without you pointing it out to us." Idrilia's retort held more of the teasing tone Kalis was familiar with.

Kalis cleared his throat. "I think we can all agree having you both as our guides and eyes ahead is beneficial." Kalis nodded to the warrior, who nodded in return. "And to help make this journey more comfortable for everyone…" Kalis withdrew several fire crystals, activated them, and began handing them out.

"What's this?" Zinvar asked as Kalis gave a warm crystal to him.

"It will keep a small radius around you warm, for a time. We—I'll," he corrected himself, "have to recharge it once it cools, so just let me know, you know?"

The priest nodded his assent. Vayriel and Kilahym gratefully accepted the crystals, but Kharnek shook his head, saying his leathers offered ample protection from the elements. Kalis suspected that the refusal had more to do with the crystal's nature than anything else.

The vessel descended, the rocky arch seeming to rise to meet them. An unseen mechanism clicked, then the ramp extended, sounding like soft drums until it dropped on the outcropping. Rinesh tossed a rope to the far side of the fixture, tying it off to a notch on the railing.

"Since we don't have the offsetting crystals from the docking pillars, the skykeel will sway marginally on the anchor. It is best to move across the ramp at a steady pace."

"Thank you, Rinesh. You have aided us more than could have been expected. I will tell Axiom of your actions."

"You don't have to do that. I'm not sure I want them to know of me." Rinesh laughed.

"Either way, it was a pleasure to meet you. Although our time was too brief, you know." Kalis clasped the young man's hand. He regretted not learning more about him on their journey. Rinesh brought out a longing in Kalis to see his own brother, to reconcile their relationship.

"By the Grey Lady, would that we had met under different circumstances." Kilahym grasped Rinesh on the shoulders with both hands. Then, as if on impulse, he pulled him into an embrace. The expression of shock on the aerialist's face made all but Kharnek laugh.

"It was a pleasure to meet you, Hymn."

"Are you certain I can't take just a *tiny,* insignificant, 'ittle piece of the treasure with me?" Kilahym asked, releasing Rinesh.

"I'm afraid not. The Cloudsoarer would notice. And if I have any hope in not being demoted to cleaning the latrines, I better bring back his ship *and* all of its treasure."

Kilahym slumped his shoulders and stepped away, kicking something on the deck Kalis did not see.

"I do not have many friends in my coil, but I count you among them." Orgar's tails undulated next to his life-friend as he pressed his muzzle against the side of Rinesh's leg. "Be safe, Rinesh of the Sunscorned. May you walk the true path and see the true light." Vayriel clasped her hands before her and bowed her head.

Then it was time for the brothers to say farewell. They exchanged a brief embrace, speaking in hushed tones so Kalis could not overhear what was said. But when Zinvar walked away from Rinesh, there was no missing the hurt in his expression. Idrilia whistled, her othwit promptly bursting from hiding behind some sails, but instead of landing on her shoulder as usual, Wen alighted on Orgar between his shoulder blades.

"Betrayer," she snarled, but her tone held no true malice.

Their goodbyes given, the Truthseekers began to leave the vessel. When Kharnek and Zinvar reached the sea arch, Orgar crept across, his tails horizontal to balance his movements and his ears flat against his head. Vayriel followed behind him, her left hand in mid-raise as if ready to catch him with the life force. Once Kilahym reached the other side with a joyous whoop, Idrilia and Kalis crossed the divide.

The wind snagged at the tails of his robe and rippled the loose cloth of his pants. He became aware of how cold the air was, realizing the airship must have had a mechanism to diminish the wind. He repositioned his headscarf, as he had done on Mount Hoestra to not block the sun but the cold from his face, as the wind sheared through the crystal's sphere of generated heat. He shuddered, remembering his fall and escape from the trägen. His hand reached out to grab Idrilia's, then made a fist, the blue leather tightening over his knuckles. She cast a concerned look behind her, and taking a deep breath, he moved forward without comment, their lights hovering in tandem.

Safely together again, the Seekers waved to Rinesh, then carefully picked their path over the basalt to step on the cliff and advanced further inland. Kalis's shoulders relaxed. It was good to be on solid ground again.

Kharnek gestured into the darkness. "We will move east from here and somewhat south."

"You've been there before?" Zinvar asked.

"I have."

Kalis noticed a small crease in the warrior's brow. Something unseen passed between Zinvar and the warrior.

As promised, Kharnek and Zinvar led. Kalis expected Idrilia to move forward into a more scout-like position, but she surprised him by remaining at his side. Dare he hope her feelings would become more like his? To distract himself from impossible thoughts, he imagined how they would look from above on the skykeel—dots of light moving slowly across the landscape.

CHAPTER 62

From the moment they started the two-cycle journey toward the Fellwood, Zinvar had yet to hear Kilahym fall silent. He listened now as the bard quoted an unknown text to Vayriel.

"All the creeping things keep their heads low, lest the frigid gale tear them away; the lichens shed their pallid glow, upon this barren, forlorn gray," Kilahym recited.

"Forlorn gray what?" Vayriel asked.

"Ah, my dear Highblood, that is the beautiful mystery of poetry, you may ascribe whatever meaning finds import in your most inward self."

Zinvar imagined that Kilahym winked at Vayriel, and the ensuing smile brought warmth to his heart. However, it did nothing to thaw out his frozen limbs. The oppressive cold slinked beneath his robes into every crevice of his body, biting at his exposed skin. Even the stars seemed like chips of ice glinting in the great emptiness betwixt them.

Kharnek seemed preoccupied with leading the way, and the Sondrinel remained several paces behind, so Zinvar drifted toward the duo from Heathström. "I'm glad to see that my homeland is found deserving of verse."

"Ah, Zinny! So kind of you to join us. I trust that all is well at the forefront of our gaggle of travelers?"

He offered the other Seeker a thin smile. "All is well. Kharnek says we are less than a cycle away from the Fellwood."

"The name of our destination bespeaks an ill omen," Vayriel commented.

"It is somewhat less than confidence-inspiring." Kilahym stooped to examine the ground. "Ooo, look, another of those creatures with the appendages—ow!" Kilahym shot a hurt glance at Orgar, whose undulating tails had whacked him across the face. Zinvar covered his mouth to hide his chuckling.

"We have enough to consider without stopping to examine every creature-son and -daughter that crosses our path, Kilahym." Despite Vayriel's stern tone, merriment shone in the Highblood's lavender gaze.

"You sound like Kalis," Kilahym needled.

She laughed. "I am like the mimic-wings, who echo the songs we sing to them."

"There are certainly worse traits you could be learning. Like natural distrust," Zinvar added darkly. He watched Kilahym and Vayriel exchange looks.

"Were we mistaken to think that all is well with you and Kharnek?" Vayriel asked.

"Oh, it's not Kharnek I'm talking about." The priest waved his staff in the direction of the two Sondrinel, who walked between him and Kharnek at the front. "They don't realize it, but their 'private' conversations via communication crystal have been completely accessible to me ever since—well, since we saved Kharnek from the Penumbra. And they still have doubts."

"You mean you can hear their thoughts?" Kilahym's eyes widened.

"Not all the time. Only when they're using the crystals."

Kilahym cocked his head. "How does that work?"

Zinvar shrugged in response to the bard's question.

"There is much about the Daughter's Eyes that remains unknown, even among the coils. However," Vayriel elaborated, "I suspect that some of their abilities are deliberately concealed, both as an advantage and to avoid reprisals."

A bitter laugh escaped Zinvar. "Yes, if I've learned anything about people, it's that they fear the unknown. Perhaps I shouldn't have said anything."

"No, you shouldn't be afraid to explore your full potential, Zin," Kilahym countered. "Although, I don't think eavesdropping on our Sondrinel friends will do anything to endear you to them."

"You're right of course." He sighed. "I just wish they could see Kharnek the way I do."

"That will take time, my goodly priest." Kilahym clapped the Komorese on the back. "Fortunately for you, we are all stuck together for at least several more weeks."

In his peripheral vision, Zinvar saw Vayriel straighten. "There is light in the distance."

The two men looked at her, then scanned the blank tundra ahead. Scant moonlight limned the boulders and broken rock smattered across the landscape for as far as Zinvar could survey. Patches of sickly green lichen disrupted the monotonous view, but aside from that, he could detect no change on the horizon.

"My light-starved eyes do not see what you do, my dear," Kilahym replied.

"I cannot see it either, but Orgar can. His sight is far better than our own."

"It must be, because even with me being used to the darkness, I can't see what you're talking about," Zinvar interjected. "But it has to be the Fellwood."

"Is the forest ablaze?" Kilahym wondered aloud.

The priest grinned. "No, but it has a light of its own. You'll see."

Kilahym gestured dramatically. "What a strange new world we find ourselves in, where the forests are illuminated while the sky is not."

A loud *crunch* from beneath the bard's foot disrupted his discourse. The horrendous smell that followed assaulted Zinvar's nostrils and left his head reeling. Next to him and Kilahym, Vayriel pinched her nose in disgust while Orgar whined.

"By the Lady!" the bard exclaimed, "What grotesquerie have I summoned from the ground?"

"That was a fekwa," Zinvar answered between coughs, "a six-legged creature that emits a noxious odor when crushed. We would do well to move away from here, in case there is a nest."

The Komorese led them away from the creature's squashed remains, and step-by-step, the reek dissipated. Even so, Zinvar suspected they would be smelling fekwa for a while. Orgar as well, if the way he pawed at his snout was any indication. Several scrapes of his soles against the rocky terrain helped dispel the yellow-green ichor that clung to his sole and the pervasive odor.

"Is the Fellwood home to these creature-sons as well?" Vayriel asked the priest, scrunching her nose.

Zinvar shook his head. "No, fekwa colonies prefer open spaces, where they have fewer natural predators. The Fellwood holds horrors of its own."

"You must explicate that a little further, Zinny."

For a long moment Zinvar said nothing, uncertain whether to reveal yet another bleak moment from Komor's past. Especially given its connection to his brother's order. The preternatural silence of Komor crept in—the susurration of the wind in his ears mourned the absence of sunlight.

Remembering his promise to the other Seekers, Zinvar took a deep breath before speaking. "The Fellwood is the site of a tragedy, and for many epicycles, it has been considered a cursed place because of what happened there. I am surprised that we are being asked to enter it."

Vayriel waved a gloved hand. "Why is that?"

"Because many who go into the Fellwood do not return," he answered. "It is, supposedly, haunted by the spirits of those who were slain there."

"Well, what an entangled plot this has become." Waggling his eyebrows dramatically, Kilahym leaned toward Vayriel. "And if it's like most forests, things could get thorny."

Zinvar saw her lips curve upward in token recognition of the attempt to lighten the mood.

"The coils speak of such places, but only to frighten children into obedience. At least, that is what Mo'mo did when I was young."

"But you told me that there are places where the veil between us and the spirit world is thin," Kilahym said to Vayriel. She nodded.

"Yes, but outside of Zinvar's visions, I have never heard of someone who has entered the spirit-world interacting with the physical-realm again. But the Mother-of-All communicates with us in many ways."

Zinvar waved his staff to indicate the distant forest. "I suspect that the Priesthood may have greatly exaggerated the rumors of hauntings in the Fellwood, but the danger is real. When I was studying on Mora—"

"The dark island?" Kilahym blurted, his interruption earning him a warning tap from Vayriel's spear. Zinvar noticed and smiled faintly.

"I've never heard it called that, but yes, it's an island off the coast of Komor, very near to Zel Morakh. Anyway, the Priesthood dispatches acolytes—those who are studying to become priests—on 'paths of discovery,' which are basically tasks that the Mahir don't want to waste their time on or risk their own safety doing. Like the Trials but without a higher purpose."

"I mean no offense, friend Zinvar, but your people do not seem very kind."

The priest bowed his head. "None taken, Vayriel. Their ways—*our* ways undoubtedly seem rather barbaric to you. But you must understand, Komor's history is riddled with unrest. When the Priesthood united the disparate city-states beneath its mantle, there was resistance, and they imposed some rather draconian rules to ensure their power remained intact. Nowhere is that more evident than in the way they treat their own people." Zinvar shifted his shoulders beneath his robe. "But I digress. One of the groups of acolytes was sent to the

Fellwood, including Avir, a—close friend of mine. He, and the rest, never came back, and the Mahir never said what happened. When I questioned one of my instructors, it earned me seven cycles of scrubbing the temple floors."

"But someone must have *some* idea of what happened," Kilahym protested.

"Only the rumors that pervaded the acolyte dormitories, which ranged from spectral monsters to a portal to the Everburn."

"Such pleasant people, your Priesthood," the bard commented wryly.

"I haven't even told you about the human sacrifices yet."

A guffaw burst from Kilahym's lips, which quickly faded as he saw the serious look on the priest's face.

"Oh, you did not jest?"

"No." Zinvar shook his head, but he could not contain the smile that spread across his lips.

Kilahym pointed at him. "Ah ha! I knew it. Your larks are improving, my friend."

Zinvar returned the bard's smile. "We should all try to hold on to our sense of humor over the next couple of cycles. Komor can be a difficult place, even for those who know it well. Speaking of which, I should check in with Kharnek." He waved farewell and strode into the gloom ahead, giving the Sondrinel a wide berth as he made his way forward. It was a risk, revealing what he had to Vayriel and Kilahym, but they had proven themselves trustworthy. And Zinvar needed confidantes outside of Kharnek. He and the warrior had become closer since their victory over the Penumbra, but the Guardsman still struggled with empathy towards their fellow Truthseekers. Especially Idrilia.

Zinvar hurried to catch up with Kharnek's longer strides. Once he was abreast of the warrior, he reached out and squeezed the other man's bicep. "Thank you for being our guide. When I said 'we' would lead the way, I really was volunteering you."

"How could I refuse?" Kharnek smiled down at him. "You did just save my life."

"Very true." Zinvar clasped the warrior's hand in his as they walked, enjoying the comforting strength of Kharnek's calloused grip. "Speaking of which, I need to catch you up on a few things that happened while you were…"

"Not myself."

"That's a good way to put it." Zinvar went on to relate Vayriel's revelation of the Highblood prophecy and his suspicions about how it connected to his vision in Waverling. The information was absorbed in silence by Kharnek, who, as usual, displayed no reaction to what he was being told, at least not that Zinvar could discern. "I don't fully understand why I believe Vayriel," he finished, "but something about it just feels...right. True."

The warrior tilted his head to one side. "Then it likely is."

Somewhere in the cold expanse around them, a tundrat loosed its chirring mating call. Zinvar moved closer to Kharnek so their arms brushed.

"Had we not defeated the Penumbra, I would have feared that I was the threat Vayriel described," his lover pronounced. "So, who or what is this 'Sleeper'?"

"I don't know." Though he did not verbalize it, the same thought had occurred to Zinvar. "They have yet to be revealed. But it's hard to imagine something worse than the Penumbra."

"Whatever it is, we will face it together," Kharnek declared, making Zinvar smile.

"Yes, we will," he affirmed. He hesitated a moment before continuing. "There's something else I wanted to talk to you about. Well, ask of you, if I may."

"Of course. Anything."

Zinvar kept his expression neutral. "I'd like you to try to forgive Idrilia."

Kharnek's fingers clenched around Zinvar's hand, then relaxed. "In many ways, that is a far larger demand," he rumbled.

"I know. But I wouldn't ask if it wasn't important to me. To all of us," Zinvar amended. "We're so close to being truly united as a group. I feel that if we—if you—can show forgiveness to her, that will break down the final barriers between us."

Zinvar felt Kharnek's gaze upon him. "I understand your reasoning. But I find it odd that you ask me this now when you are obviously unhappy with the Sondrinel."

The priest twisted his head to regard his lover. "How do you know that?"

Kharnek's shoulders lifted slightly. "You keep looking back at them with concern written all over your face. A blank scroll, you are not. I am trained to pay attention to these things."

"Well, you have me there." Zinvar smiled ruefully. "I'm a little hurt that, after all that has happened, Idrilia and Kalis still don't trust us. And I'm trying to remain objective, but sometimes it's difficult when it feels like I'm the only one putting in that effort."

"I see." Kharnek was silent for several footsteps, then he squeezed Zinvar's hand. "Then for you, I will let the past be the past. You were the one harmed by Idrilia. If you can forgive her, so can I."

A bright glow of happiness fluoresced in Zinvar's innermost self. He had expected this conversation to go poorly, but Kharnek once again pleasantly surprised him. "Thank you," he murmured, and he lifted the warrior's hand to press a gentle kiss to it.

"As I said, anything for you." Kharnek stroked Zinvar's wrist with his thumb. "Now, there is something I would ask of you."

"What's that?"

"Although the Penumbra is gone, there are things it left behind. Memories that are not my own," Kharnek explained. "You seemed able to manipulate them to a degree. I would like you to try to expunge them."

Zinvar's brows flew upward. "You mean...remove them entirely?"

The warrior nodded. "I want all traces of its stain gone."

"That's understandable." Zinvar gripped his staff tightly as he considered the request. "I want to help, of course, but I barely know how to control any of my abilities as an Occulum, let alone with the kind of precision you're talking about."

"I know. But I have faith in you. And I would like you to try."

The priest met Kharnek's gaze. Moonlight made the warrior's deep brown eyes glimmer like the waters of Zel Morakh's harbor. They were beautiful to him. Zinvar never wanted to see their light fade into the Penumbra's shadow again. "All right," he agreed, "I'll try."

Kharnek's shoulders dropped, and he grinned broadly. "Thank you. You have no idea how much that means to me."

Zinvar flashed a wicked smile. "Why don't you show me how much later, once we're settled in?"

The Guardsman winked. "It would be my pleasure."

CHAPTER 63

"Basja it's cold." He *felt* Idrilia's exclamation in his mind, breaking the silence for him alone. They had long since ceased their mental discussion concerning Kharnek and the Penumbra. Everyone showed signs of fatigue, evident by their subdued conversations.

"You can fix that, you know," Kalis thought back.

"Me? I thought you were overseeing my life force ban?"

"I won't tell." Despite his joking inflection, he meant it. He would sacrifice his own place in Axiom to see her reach her goals, even if that meant lying to the Council. He hoped there was a way to share only parts of memories into the Concilius crystal when they asked for proof of her compliance. Just as he chose now to not relay his revelation to Idrilia through the communication crystal.

The pair reactivated their fire crystals. He relished the feeling of warmth washing over his body and stiff fingers.

"The clarity of your thoughts has improved," Kalis attempted.

"Thank Wen for that. I've been practicing with her since she's been in this free-flying mood. The mind of an othwit seems to be not that different from yours."

"I'm not sure if that's an insult or—"

"Simply a statement. I mean only that we can keep talking, and Kilahym won't chastise us for using our hand signals."

"Is it so bad to include him?"

"When he annoys me, it is. And he's currently annoying me."

"Why?"

"You know."

"He is a friend to you, just as Vayriel is."

Idrilia's thoughts ceased. Kalis glanced at his friend and saw her drop a crystal into a pouch on her belt. He grimaced. That did not end how he wanted. Kalis was enjoying their renewed friendship and searched his mind for a topic that would engage Idrilia again. His eyes caught the bard, under Vayriel's guidance, lifting several pebbles in the air with invisible hands.

"I've been meaning to ask you what you think of Kilahym's abilities. He seems to be progressing."

The pebbles hovered over Vayriel then dropped. Kilahym gestured frantically in apology as the Highblood quickly brushed the debris from her hair.

Idrilia snorted. "If you call that ability."

"I just mean that neither he nor Vayriel directly use crystals, you know."

"Actually, yes. I have given that some thought but…"

Kalis nodded, understanding. "It contradicts our training."

"All our lives we've been taught that crystals are paramount to Sondrine's use of the life force and a key component to the Rising. What if…what if it's all wrong? Ugh, I hate even saying that."

"But that's what being a Truthseeker is, you know? We're supposed to share, learn from each other, challenge thoughts."

Idrilia laughed. "I just didn't think we'd be challenging our own."

Kalis nodded again. Every Axiom guild used crystals somehow, as the practice was supposed to help them get better at using the symbolic doorway the crystals created to the life force. If that wasn't accurate…

"Do you think Adjira was able to Rise?" Idrilia asked quietly.

He hesitated, remembering the High Keeper's words. "Keeper Veloran didn't sound confident, but Adjira was strong in the life force. She may have already had experience with transport crystals, too, which would have helped point her to the end goal."

"I think I'm just in time for a new tale. What, pray tell, are transport crystals?" Kilahym asked cheerily.

The bard, Vayriel, and Orgar had dropped back to rejoin the Sondrinel.

"Is this what you used to defeat Orym?" Vayriel inquired.

Kalis nodded. "Transport crystals are in some ways like what you've already seen 'Dril do with a diminishing crystal. With a diminishing crystal, the essence of a thing is condensed into life-force energy and stored for a time within the crystal vessel. With a transport crystal, you condense yourself into that essence and use the pair of crystals like a road within the life force. The result being instant travel and further practice for the Rising."

"That makes sense," Idrilia cut in. "You would just need to then push yourself to break from the singular road and out of the crystal into the greater stream of the life force. Why don't they teach this to everyone? Wouldn't everyone have a much better chance at the Rising if they did?"

Kalis shrugged. "I think it has to do with the natural progression of how those on the path to Priorium are taught. A diminishing crystal should be perfected before a transport one is attempted. A second transport crystal should be used and mastered before attempting to travel to another person's location, which is difficult to do with any accuracy. Everyone's ability to progress from one skill to the next is different."

"Seems a might bit elitist to me, if you don't mind me saying," Kilahym said, scratching his chin.

"I don't disagree now that we are really thinking about it. As I said to Idrilia, that is what the Trials are supposed to do—make us challenge our thoughts."

"It is good to reflect on what is supposed to be truth and what *is* truth, though having one's closely-held beliefs challenged can be as unsettling as a ratufa in your bedroll."

Idrilia laughed, in spite of her earlier mood.

Kilahym cleared his throat. "If I might impose another question on you. This merging with the life force, the Rising, is it just the great life after death?"

"It is more than that. A higher level of existence by which we transcend a physical body to become part of the life force and have access to the collective knowledge held within that stream. We keep our awareness of self, but such distinctions become trivial."

"Highbloods believe that when our spirit returns to the life force, it maintains its uniqueness as well. The Mother-of-All cares for each of us in the spirit-world as if her own sons and-daughters. I hope to see my parents when it is my time, though due to how they…how they died, it could be that they are sky-spirits."

Idrilia shifted uneasily beside Kalis but made no comment before Vayriel asked her own question.

"What happens if someone is unable to Rise?"

Kalis opened his mouth to answer, but Idrilia waved him off. "I'll take this one. The Healers Guild actually visits everyone who is near death—whether simply from old age or due to an illness, like my grandmother. They use a similar technique to what Zinvar used to enter Kharnek's mind with the communication crystal. Only, they use it to show the person advanced crystal techniques. It is everyone's choice whether to seek the Rising, and some do not try. But if a person is unable to try, such as a sudden death, Sondrinel believe that their life-force energy simply becomes part of the life force."

"I see." The bard nodded thoughtfully.

"Do you believe in the Grey Lady, Kilahym?" Kalis asked, turning the conversation.

The question seemed to surprise the bard as his brows shot up, but he took it in stride.

"Aye, as much as any other dweller of Heathström." Kalis sensed the evasion in the answer.

"Then you believe, as the Spectres do, that if you die having been a faithful follower of her tenets, you will join the Grey Lady in paradise?"

Silence followed, except for the sound of the group's boots crunching on the ground. When Kilahym did speak, it was in an uncharacteristically halting manner.

"Once I would have said yes. But Vayriel, the things she has shown me about the life force—I no longer know what to believe." The bard paused as Vayriel took his hand. After a moment he looked at Kalis. "Why do you ask?"

"Ever since the trägen and my fall, I've often thought about what happens after we die. My people have the Rising. And then there's the Grey Lady's paradise, the Highbloods have their spirit-world,...and Komor probably believes in something similar. Don't you ever wonder if perhaps they're all the same thing?"

Kilahym's eyes widened. "But how could they be?"

The Sondrinel lifted his shoulders in an expressive shrug, catching Idrilia's gaping mouth out of his peripheral. "I just see many similar elements between the religions of Etherea, and two things they all have in common."

"What's that?" Idrilia challenged.

"One," Kalis lifted a finger, "is their expression of our most fervent hope: that there is something more beyond this physical existence."

"My, what deep thoughts you have, my friend." Kilahym laughed at a higher pitch than usual, and Kalis wondered if the conversation made him uncomfortable. If so, his fellow Seeker's curiosity outweighed his trepidation, for the bard asked, "And the second?"

"They all create conflict and division between us."

"But we are here to work together, are we not?" Vayriel interjected.

"That we are." Kalis smiled. "And I think this conversation shows we are doing just that."

Kharnek's voice broke into the conversation, "We are close."

"What do you see?" Kalis called ahead.

"Look for the repeating light just left of center."

Kalis strained against the bleak darkness ahead, and after squinting, he could see a faint pulsing light on the horizon.

"What is that?" Idrilia questioned.

"Guards are signaling their position. We are expected."

"Fantastic! A welcoming party!" Kilahym cried expectantly.

Kharnek sneered. "Do not get your hopes up, bard."

"Alrighty, warrior. Do you mind if I call you 'warrior'? Seeing as you and Idrilia have chosen to call me by a label lately, I am only too happy to return the favor. Oh, ghastly! That sounded far less jesting and much more brooding than I would have liked. Dual-wielder! You are tainting my creativity!"

Kalis choked back a laugh. The Seekers quickened their steps.

As they drew closer, looming shadows painted the emptiness. The Fellwood was as tall as the forests east of Waverling that he and Idrilia had passed through to complete their first trial. Distinct lines of yellow and orange formed the light pulse. Two guards in sleek leather armor, similar to Kharnek's, stood next to a waist-high stalk as wide as their chests with a magenta cap like an umbrella. By tapping the top, they created light currents from the fleshy underside.

Kilahym looked around curiously. "Where are the trees for this, eh, forest, Zinny?"

"These are them. The sarkumak."

Vayriel frowned. "This is not a wood."

"I agree. This is a gross mislabeling. Why, it would be like me calling my dulcimer an ocarina."

"We greet you in the name of Morakh and his servant the Mahiratha, Truthseekers."

Kharnek raised his left fist to his forehead in response to the soldiers' welcome salute. It took Kalis a moment to realize the glowing violet orbs about five feet in the air behind the guards were eyes. The crystalline scales of the rift wyrms made them nearly undetected as they reflected their surroundings. But now that he knew they were there, Kalis could see they were secured to the thick sarkumak stalks.

"You should be dead." The Komorese looked at Kalis, the statement carrying an undertone most unpleasant. "The Magister informed the Mahiratha at Zel Morakh that you perished."

Kalis groaned. The Magister would have got the news from Axiom, which meant his family thought him dead.

"Surprise! He's alive. It's an interesting story, however. On a blustery day on the Cliffs of Odium, Kal-"

"This changes our orders. Guardsman Kharnek, as the ranking soldier, we request that you provide a report to Captain Ahlet." The guard motioned to the base of the sarkumak. A communication cube identical to the gifts from Komor during the Trials ceremony lay on the ground.

"*There are more of them!*" Idrilia shouted in her thoughts.

"*So it seems. But does that really surprise you?*"

"*Not in the least.*"

"I assume the news of Kalis's death originated with Sondrine?" Kharnek asked.

"It did."

"Then let us first see what Axiom's reaction is. Kalis, contact your Council."

Despite the command, Kalis felt overjoyed at the chance to let his family know he was alive. A look passed between the two guards.

"Guardsman, I do not need to remind you that this is Komor's property." The soldier's voice sounded strained.

"That is a most obvious assessment. Why do you think I would want the Sondrinel to speak with his people?" Kharnek was responded to with silence. "When an error is identified, it must be corrected. The source of the misinformation is Axiom."

"And you want to embarrass the Council by having *him* deliver the message." Kalis noted how the pronoun carried disdain.

"Precisely. And as all three realms are working together for the Trial, it is likely that Axiom will want to speak with Waverling before advising Komor of any adjustments to the upcoming Trial. Zel Morakh has told you the Trial details?"

"Yes, Guardsman. It is as you say. The return of this Sondrinel may change the instructions."

Turning to face him, Kharnek's face contained an expression Kalis thought seemed apologetic. Perhaps the warrior's talk was devised to allow Kalis to contact home. If so, Kalis wanted to thank him.

Kharnek accompanied the others into the forest to set up camp, which left the guards and Kalis at the cube. Kalis and Idrilia continued to mentally discuss, often projecting their thoughts at the same time which made the conversation seem almost instantaneous. The guards presented Kalis with a key, then retreated only five or six paces away. By the time Kalis approached Komor's cube, he and Idrilia had formed a plan.

The familiar labyrinthine geometric designs covered the large surface. Kalis flipped the six-sided key over in his hands, a slight tremor from his elbow to his fingertips as he mentally formed what he would say. Possible questions and answers swirled in his head like a cyclone until he suddenly thrust his hand to the recess at the top and clicked the key flush. Immediately, orange light filled the lines on the cube like the water in the floor of the Etherea Assemblage. As instructed by the guards, Kalis waited for the lights to steady, then he simultaneously tapped three of the symbols surrounding the opening where he placed the key, the haptic interaction eliciting a slight vibration beneath his ungloved hand. He felt his ring burn and stepped back from the device, putting a stride between him and the cube. The ring remained warm but not unbearably so as faint light broke the darkness.

As wide and as tall as his arm spanned a blurry image displayed above the cube. It hovered like a window without support. Growing clearer, it revealed alternating chairs between columns that sat empty, stained glass depicting the guilds above each.

"Make peace with me," he said gently, unsure how best to garner the attention of anyone nearby in Concilius and to keep his voice low from observation.

"Who's there? Oh, this thing's powered on." A familiar figure in a tan robe, his head minutely accented by a plain circlet, turned an invisible corner and displayed before him. "Kalis? You can't—you're—this must be—"

"Askel! It is good to see you. Is the High Keeper near? Or any of the Council?"

"A forum just adjourned. They might still be in crystal range."

The Keeper-in-training rummaged in his pockets and produced a communication crystal. Kalis glanced over his shoulder confirming, to his chagrin, that the two Komorese were still present.

"The High Keeper will be here soon."

High Keeper Veloran entered the visual shortly after, along with the High Sentinel.

"By the Rising—forgive me, Askel, for not believing you." The High Keeper appeared calm, though her eyes conveyed more emotion. "Go. Leiria has a class she is instructing at Pedium. Bring her here to see her son."

"These last several days have been hard for your family." While the High Sentinel representative spoke, Keeper Veloran flashed a set of quick hand signals.

Are you alone?

No. Two enemies behind, Kalis signaled back.

Keeper Veloran used a more complex set of hand signals which he recognized, though it took him fractionally longer to comprehend. The Sentinels taught a simplified argot that focused on words and phrases beneficial to their skill set as warriors and patrollers.

Kalis followed her instructions and depressed the top of the key. It sank further into the recess before popping halfway out, its sides gleaming with inscribed symbols. He touched one that vaguely resembled the Sondrinel script for "quiet," and all ambient noise ceased to reach him. The eerie silence unnerved Kalis, but a quick glance back at the guards showed that they did not realize anything had changed.

He addressed the High Keeper. "Everything just got quiet. Really quiet."

Her shoulders relaxed. "It appears to have worked." Seeing his confusion, she continued, "One of our researchers identified the symbols on the cube as a match to certain pre-Calamity texts stored in Evocus. Our translation efforts are ongoing, but we have learned a great deal since you were here. Including how to trigger a 'privacy mode,' as you have just done. We may speak freely while this is enabled."

Kalis's eyes widened. "That's incredible. So, the cubes predate Sondrine?"

"They are older than all the realms," the High Sentinel affirmed, "and they are capable of far more than communication."

It occurred to Kalis that Peatwick's Prophet might be another relic from the same era. There were similarities in how it and the cubes displayed information.

"While our knowledge grows rapidly," the Sentinel leader continued, "we may have made a grave tactical mistake in allowing this device into Axiom. Already, there are signs that Komor moves against the other realms."

The Truthseeker could not help but look back at the Komorese soldiers. Would they dare attempt treachery in the middle of the Trials?

"Kalis," Keeper Veloran spoke, returning his attention to her, "I am sorry to burden you with this information, but your safety, and that of your friends, may depend on it. We have lost all contact with the Magister—it is likely that Waverling is now under Komor's control. The rest of Heathström appears to be safe, but do not go back to the capital after your next trial. Return here under whatever pretense necessary."

Grim thoughts coursed through his mind. "I understand, High Keeper." His brow creased. "And it's even more important that you hear what I have learned since my, well, untimely demise."

She nodded. "Jannu brought the news himself immediately after the others left Keepers' Rest. What happened after the Highblood saw you fall?"

Kalis summarized the events from the trägen battle to the present, frequently interrupted by the High Sentinel. He was careful to avoid any mention of the Sunscorned's location—although protecting it went against everything he was taught, Idrilia's observations had struck a chord with him. *And besides*, he thought, *if war with Komor is coming, we may need their help.*

Keeper Veloran and the High Sentinel exchanged a concerned expression as Kalis explained the events of the Penumbra and Zinvar's journey into the communication crystal.

"So Kharnek has life force-canceling abilities," Keeper Veloran mused. "Similar to the strange powers that Adjira manifested."

"Had," Kalis clarified, "Zinvar appears to have removed the Penumbra's influence. Vayriel can no longer detect its presence in him."

Keeper Veloran tilted her head. "That is fascinating. The Highbloods have always been a mystery to us, but their prowess with the life force cannot be denied."

The High Sentinel's brow furrowed with concern. "Gone or not, the implications of Kharnek's abilities are staggering. They would render our primary advantage over Komor's numbers useless. We must ensure that this...Penumbra does not return."

Veloran nodded. "The Delvers Guild's efforts are ongoing—"

"They've learned nothing," the High Sentinel interrupted her, an annoyed look etched into his patrician features. "Those bumbling fools and their expedition are a waste of time. We should be strengthening our defenses, not digging in the sand." He looked back at Kalis. "And finding our enemy's weaknesses. Prioriate, think hard. Is there anything else you can tell us about the Penumbra that could help us defeat it?"

"There are fragments," Kalis explained. "Kharnek found one in the tower near the border between Komor and Heathström and another in the, ah, vessel we stole during our escape. Each time he came in contact with one, it was absorbed and made the Penumbra in him stronger.

"We must find and eliminate these," Keeper Veloran replied.

"That will take time." The High Sentinel shook his head sadly. "Time that we may not have. If we can even destroy these fragments."

"About that," Kalis said hesitantly, "Zinvar may be able to help. He has been...seeing things."

"I am reluctant to trust anyone from Komor right now," the High Sentinel said, "but perhaps we can learn from his success against this threat. Tell us what you know."

Kalis felt relieved. He would finally get to put his conjectures before people who could critically analyze them. "Zinvar has had visions of a woman who brought warnings of the Penumbra. She has never revealed her identity, but she seems to understand it and have some power over it. She was able to stop it from taking complete control of Kharnek when he found the fragment in the tower."

The High Sentinel regarded him incredulously. "You expect me to believe that these...premonitions have strategic importance?"

Kalis's spirits fell, but Keeper Veloran gestured excitedly.

"Don't dismiss this in haste, Leto. I think that what the priest is seeing is a vision of Kadaan." She spread her hands. "My research into the Occulum has led me to believe that they all share the same first vision of her. And, it is possible for her to still communicate with them. Kadaan is trying to help us."

"That's absurd," the High Sentinel retorted. "You sound like Elsuota." He and the High Keeper engaged in a furious debate about Kadaan, one Kalis sensed had begun a long time ago. Their discourse was interrupted by a woman's voice, firm and commanding, outside of the square of the visual. Kalis's heart leaped.

"Mother! I'm here!"

"Kalis!" A lean figure stepped in front of the others, elbowing them out of the way.

He grinned. Though her eyes were red-rimmed, she looked the same as when he last saw her: blue hair pulled halfway up out of her face.

Her voice shook with emotion. "I never questioned the Keepers. Maybe I should have, but surviving that fall was improbable. Were you injured? Oh, I have so many questions; I don't know where to start."

"We will fill you in later, Leiria." Kalis caught the quick signal from the High Sentinel warning his mother that they were being watched. "Kalis has reached Komor for the next trial."

Leiria squared her shoulders. "Of course he has. I'm so proud of you, my son. If only this technology allowed me to step through to touch you."

"I promise I'm real," Kalis laughed. "Is father coming? Or Vari and Lyna?"

His mother's face fell. "Your brother and sister are in class. I sent Askel to tell them, then ran straight here. Your father is on patrol. I'm sorry they aren't all here with me."

"That's alright, mother. Maybe Vari and Lyna will be here soon. If not, please tell them I send my love. Make them hug you for me. I'm so sorry I worried you all."

She flapped her hands in protest. "You have nothing to apologize for." The High Sentinel gestured, and his mother nodded. "I'll tell your brother and sister as you asked. I love you. Stay safe."

Keeper Veloran placed a hand on Leiria's shoulder and smiled. "We are overjoyed that your son is alive, but we should let him get back to the Komor Trial. In the left hand knowledge, Kalis."

"And in the right, combat," the High Sentinel growled.

Kalis inclined his head as the image of Concilius collapsed on itself, like a waterfall suddenly blocked, and fell into the cube. Sounds from his immediate environs rushed in like a flock of slicewings; the harsh laughter of the guards as they made some joke about "lightspawn,"; the chirring of insects hidden in the Fellwood. Kalis's mind raced, repeating the words of the High Keeper. Idrilia would want to know this new theory about Kadaan. But there was one more action he had to take while the chance presented itself.

Kalis stepped to the cube, slowly surveying the area. Under cover of him removing the key, Kalis removed his ring, now growing intensely warm.

A screech and an angry chitter broke the silence. Kalis rotated on his heels to see one of the guards attempting to grab tawny wings.

"It is that lightspawn's pest! It took my timepiece."

"*Everburn.* The rift wyrms are loose."

"I will chase the bird. You retrieve the 'wyrms."

The guards split up, one racing through the stalks of the Fellwood following Wen's path, the other sprinting in the direction the wyrms dashed.

Kalis smiled, imagining the moment Idrilia cut through the reins, and turned back to the apparatus. Just as he did on the boat, Kalis held his ring close to the cube. He jumped as the compartment popped open, even though he suspected that it would. With a final glance around the area, Kalis crouched and deposited his ring into the familiar recess.

Lights raced on the surface within the labyrinthine grooves, no longer the steady fluorescence from before. Once again symbols appeared above the glossy black box in fiery hues and scrolled to vanish into nothingness several feet in the air. Unabated by his surprise this time, he could focus on more detailed observation. Some of the fast-moving glyphs reappeared from the cube's top in the same column, more or less, of movement.

Kalis took a deep breath. With his right hand, he tapped a random combination of locations near the edges of the key. Nothing happened. The symbols continued to scroll. He tried again and again, pressing various edges simultaneously. When nothing happened Kalis grumbled and stood up, watching the scrolling symbols.

He focused on the repetitions, counting the seconds before he saw a symbol reappear in the same column, noting if and where the same shape materialized in another column. Selecting a glyph shaped like an orb, Kalis reached out hesitantly to poke the air as it appeared in five different columns, his ungloved fingers dotting the image like music notes in wide intervals on a staff.

The symbols stopped.

In their place appeared an image like a ring tapering to near points at the end. The large symbol faded into a new image—a spherical shape on a dimmed background. Dark and light patches of blue, green, and tan filled the sphere. Nodes similar to the glyphs he'd touched earlier seemed to be stamped at random around and on the globe itself, and some of them glowed.

Kalis jabbed his index finger into the middle of the display. In response, the shape unfurled and flattened into a rectangle, hanging in the air like a tapestry. Lines writhed around the edges, and additional forms dotted the view. Three of the widely spaced nodes made a diagonal line across the image. As he stared, he began to see other features of the realms.

Yes, if he looked at the right portion of the display, two large ellipses were arranged in a position like Lake Eduma and Lake Stelwin. Kalis's eyes followed the diagonal line to the far left where it branched north and south. The landscape, if it were indeed a map of Etherea, seemed desolate but for scratched lines. Were these the rifts of Komor? At the bottom left, near a small island, one of the nodes glowed purple. Zel Morakh? Kalis touched the lighted glyph.

Dashes overlaid the image—Kalis counted twenty-two. They began to flash.

"Enter your access code."

Kalis jumped at the voice transmitting from the communication device. He couldn't place the accent, though it reminded him a bit of Vayriel—straightforward with minor inflection.

"Request for ICON full observation mode declining in five seconds. Enter your access code to enable."

Kalis waved his hands through the image as if he could scatter the particles like dust.

"Unauthorized system access detected. Security drone dispatched to this location."

The map turned bright red and blurred amid a shrill tone. Kalis snatched the ring from the device and everything ceased.

Tugging his gloves back on, he hid the family ring on his right hand beneath the leather. As soon as the crystal embedded touched the skin of the back of his hand, he sent a thought to Idrilia.

Did you hear that?

Hear what?

Like a whistle. Or a bell.

No.

Good. Something interesting just happened. And the Council had intriguing news as well. I'll tell you on my way. Oh, that was a great diversion, you know.

I do.

CHAPTER 64

The sarkumak forest stood as tall as redbark trees, some reaching higher to the sky-spirits than any Vayriel had ever seen, their trunks a mix of membrane and wrapped vines. Thin fronds from blue-gray ferns branched from scattered boulders, a remnant of the landscape they had crossed to get here. No ratufas with bushy tails scampering through foliage. She missed the mountains and her coil, but mostly her family. Pleading to the Daughter above to keep her family safe, the moon's familiar light reflected on moving clouds like sky streams. Just as Zinvar said they would, the top caps of the sarkumaks moved; bent slightly off-center now, they highlighted that it was mid-hours and followed the orb's path toward the day's eventual end.

Vayriel sat cross-legged beside the fire she had assembled. After parting with Kalis, Kharnek led them here, near a small fissure expelling warmth, along with a thin rope of steam writhing upward. The Truthseeker's found coil now sat some distance from the opening. She breathed deeply, crinkling her nose. Not far enough to escape the smell—like compost and rotten pectully eggs.

Kilahym sat nearby, strumming softly on his dulcimer. He had scribbled ferociously in his notebook after arriving at this resting point. Vayriel smiled at the memory of walking across Komor, Kilahym stopping at each new plant in wonder like a young-one, then trying to draw without stumbling as he followed the others.

She shifted slowly, releasing herself from the sleeping Orgar; short yips and grunts told her he dreamed. She crawled over to the bard, pushing aside a few bell-shaped cups of moonvine that lined the ground; they were a purple as dark as the sky. Kilahym smiled through his humming, finishing his melodic line, as she crossed her legs in front of him. Thin stalks with small fronds grew behind him, accenting his head as if he had tail feathers.

"Thine eyes are reflections of memories yet made," Kilahym spoke softly as the last notes hung in the air. Vayriel felt her chest flutter as he stared into her eyes. "Orbs that demand truth. That control chaos. Pray, do not blink for I fear the spell will be broken. And I want to be held in your power."

"Only you control you, Kilahym. I have no power over you."

"Ah, but you do. Oh, please don't frown. It's a welcomed power."

Vayriel relaxed her expression but felt a lingering churning in her stomach. She shook her head. "I would not knowingly use my life force to control any creature-son or -daughter. I would influence but not control."

"I did not mean to suggest…in hindsight my poetic selection was probably poor. You're right. I *choose* to be affected by you. I just like how you make me feel, even though that often helps me create mishaps as much as masterpieces."

"I like what you call mishaps. They are all a part of how you walk your true path. And…I like how you make me feel, too."

Kilahym blushed. "Well, then. If you like it, I shan't always strive for perfection. I hear such efforts often end with gray hairs and a round belly and little satisfaction anyway. May the Grey Lady aid me in my efforts and keep my bardic figure in pristine condition for as long as possible. But enough of me. What thoughts were you sending into the great sky?"

"I was thinking of our purpose. And how different this forest is from home."

"Ah, yes. This forest—if we can even call it that—certainly is unique. I never imagined that the sporestalks I've eaten with many a meal had older, larger brothers. Do you think they know?" he whispered conspiratorially. "To think, I might be eaten by them as revenge for my misguided culinary choices."

Vayriel laughed. "I do not think they would want to eat you."

"Pray tell why? Am I not appetizing in appearance?"

"As appetizing as a trägen berry, but it is what is inside. With all of the words and music you keep within you, I am certain you would taste like parchment."

Kilahym bleated, and the pair laughed deeply.

Kilahym gestured toward Idrilia as she walked past. "Is it just me, or has Idrilia been avoiding me? More than usual, I mean. Our lady Sondrinel always has a general air of unapproachability about her."

The giddiness inside Vayriel transformed into a weight within her stomach. "I am afraid she is avoiding me. Recall how she left like the wind when we were…showing affection—"

"—mmm, kissing," Kilahym said with a mischievous smile.

Vayriel dropped her hand on his knee. "—do not distract me. What I mean to say is, I had told her I was not yet decided on how I felt about you, but then later she saw us kissing. I am afraid she must think I am full of half-truths."

Kilahym patted the Highblood's hand. "No, no. She can't fault you for revealing your truths to whomever and whenever you please. Oh! Oh…" He drew out the last sound. "I should have seen it earlier. *The Tale of Crystaleen and Jova.*"

"This is another Heathström tale?"

Kilahym beamed. "A favorite troubadour tale of Ansgar's, full of lovers' woes. Crystaleen and Jova were both in love with Thelonius. Daily they tried to impress Thelonius, each attempting to outdo the other. Eventually, they dueled, and when Crystaleen won, she took Jova by the hand instead of killing her, and they married."

"I do not see the connection to Idrilia."

"I'm Jova, she's Crystaleen, and you're Thelonius!"

Vayriel pulled back from Kilahym. "You and Idrilia will be married?"

"What? No, I mean that both of us are competing for your attention."

"But you said that Crystaleen and Jova loved Thelonius."

"Precisely!"

"You must be mistaken," Vayriel let her eyes drift to where Idrilia stood with her back to them. "For Highbloods, it is rare for two women to share that kind of bond."

"I'd wager it is just as unique in Sondrine as well, given the whole betrothal for bloodlines stratagem." He shrugged. "But it wouldn't be the first time I misread someone's romantic inkling. You could always ask her."

"I do want to make sure that she is not angry with me."

Kilahym pressed gently against the crook of her arm, his voice was soft. "How are you feeling about the whole saving the world thing?"

For the first time in many Daughter's journeys, Vayriel felt the old tug that she was not quite adequate. She was but a shadow in her parents' footsteps. No, those were thoughts of a young-one who didn't yet understand her place within the Coil. She knew who she was. She knew the stones of her path and the voice of the mountain. But were the stones her Path-Shaper said to follow the correct ones? Idrilia's path was laid out by her family and her city's rules, but she was challenging them, forging her own way. *What if the true path is not a coil? What if it is a tree with many branches, and each is a choice, yet they all reach the sky at the end?* Vayriel almost smiled in spite of her conflicting thoughts. Perhaps at last she was not thinking what the coil would do, but what Vayriel would do, as her friend had challenged. After all, the Mother-of-All had appeared to Kilahym, but her voice remained silent to Vayriel on the subject.

She squeezed her shoulder with the opposite arm. "If it is to come to pass, worrying will not change it. But I do wonder how I can best prepare. I do not feel strong enough yet to defeat such an enemy on my own."

"You won't be alone." Kilahym brushed her cheek. "I'll be with you. And you have my permission to use as much of my life-force energy as you need. I'm sure the others would say so as well."

"I appreciate your offer, but I fear that will not be enough to defeat the Sleeper. Even if he is not as large as the moon, our ancestors viewed him as powerful enough to rule the southern sky." Vayriel took a deep breath. "I must strengthen my connection to the Mother-of-All. As must you." She accented the last word by tapping the bard on his nose.

"Yes, yes, alright," he laughed. "But…how do you think the sun—your Watcher—will provide you assistance? Has he ever directly interacted with any in the coils before?"

"Not that I know of," Vayriel exhaled.

"I'm sorry. I don't mean to burden you with figuring things out now. We'll figure them out together. Maybe we can shoot some pyreflowers at him. Like a big 'Hey look at us! We need your assistance!" Kilahym waved his arms to emphasize.

Vayriel laughed then kissed his cheek. "You have a way of making light in the darkness."

The bard's face softened. "You're really worried about this, aren't you?"

The Highblood's shoulders slumped. "My Path-Shaper sent me in hopes that I could spark a mending of the discord between Etherean people. Yet, still Kharnek and Idrilia are like trägen and jeroti. If I cannot help us become a coil, how can I save the world from darkness?"

"'Tis true. We are the great microcosm of the entire social and political conflicts of Etherea. Humankind at its best and its worst. But"—this time Kilahym tapped Vayriel on the nose—"do not underestimate yourself. You've directly faced the Penumbra, communicated with two monstrous creatures, and battled back many more. I can go on if you wish."

"It is not the same. You speak of what any coil Watcher would do."

"Not to dismiss the great talents of Highblood warriors, but I have not heard tales of them subduing a Stormbringer with merely a suggestion of warm beds."

Vayriel blushed. "No, there are no Stormbringers in the mountains."

Kilahym held up a hand in a flourish. "Beyond that, Kalis and Zinvar are— dare I say it—*friends*. That wasn't always so. More progress has been made than you think."

"But is it enough?"

"When the blood lily grows, it does not sprout from seed to blossom in one day. It takes time. And what we have growing here is hope. Hope that after these many years of the Trials of the Innermost, we will have a new song to sing. One that is sung from the highest, brightest point, to the deepest, darkest chasm."

Vayriel's chest swelled. Through a tendril in the life force, she felt Kilahym's sincerity. She didn't know when she had focused on his energy, but she felt that she could even see a trace of pale red in the air around him.

"I am glad that you believe in a future that sees us all united."

Kilahym placed his hands over hers. "I am glad that you are here to make those blood lilies grow."

Blood lilies under a tree. Vayriel breathed in sharply. "I do remember you. Your eyes have always been familiar to me, but my memory did not preserve a face." But that face came back like light paintings suspended before her.

"Are you referring to my trip to your coil? Please say you are."

She leaned closer. "After the tales had ended that moonset around the fire, I found you studying a patch of blood lilies. You tried to eat one." She laughed.

"But you stopped me. Telling me that I should save the crimson blossom until I needed it most."

"And you put it in your pocket."

He squeezed her hand. "Then you promptly made a new stem grow and bloom to restore the one I'd plucked. When you placed your hands on the ground I thought, rather stupidly, that I could help and put my hands on top of yours."

"It was a nice gesture. It told me you cared for the forest. But…after that, I do not remember."

"That's because you fell asleep!"

"I did not!" Vayriel laughed.

"You did! We chatted for a long time, but then I looked up, and you were laying on Orgar sound asleep. Oh, I'm so glad you remembered."

"It was something about how you placed your hands on mine just now. And how you spoke about blood lilies. Of all of the Mother-of-All's flowers, this must be why I have always loved them."

"And you're the reason behind why I'm fascinated with flora…and own every *Silverman and Sörsen* guide."

Throwing her arms around him, Vayriel gave Kilahym a short kiss on his lips then pulled back to see his eyes wide.

"Did I do that correctly?"

"No, no—no, I mean yes! I just wasn't expecting it. I liked it." He smiled.

Her heart fluttered as she felt Kilahym's hands on her hips. Orgar's snout bumped under her arm, breaking their connection. Ruffling his fur, Vayriel's gaze traveled over Orgar's head.

"I will be back, and you must tell me more of what we spoke of so long ago," Vayriel said standing. "I will remember, I just need to be reminded." She lifted her fur-lined hood, planting her feet in steps unlikely to disturb the soil, as if stepping out from the shadows to approach a predator.

Coming up beside Idrilia, Vayriel steeled herself and spoke. "What do you study in the distance?"

"I'm just watching the area," Idrilia responded shortly.

Vayriel stepped beside her. Her cheeks tingled in the fire's absence, and puffs of condensed air floated from Idrilia's open mouth.

"I can feel that you are upset with me. Will you tell me what I have done?"

Idrilia groaned. "I think I'm more upset with myself. For thinking that you…look, just forget about it."

"What were you thinking?" Vayriel pressed, wondering if what Kilahym had said before was true.

"I—I need time to figure out what I'm really feeling. I'm a mix of emotions." She glanced over her shoulder. "Kalis basically said we didn't have to go through with the betrothal. While that's a relief…"

"You are uncertain how your people will take the news."

"That, and now I'm free to feel however I want. There was someone I was close to in Pedium. Do I go back and see if she has feelings for me? Do I see if I feel differently for Kalis now that I'm not forced to marry him? Do I act on what I'm feeling right this moment?"

Vayriel stiffened as Idrilia rotated and fixed her with an intense stare. Several breaths passed before the Sondrinel blinked and turned back to the sarkumak forest.

"I have *feelings* for you, Vayriel. I thought I could rationalize myself out of them, but it's not working. I thought if I could ignore you and Kilahym's *relationship* that the initial jealousy I felt would turn out to be nothing. Well, it's turned out to be something."

"I am honored that you feel this way, Idrilia. With my people, it is rare, but a high honor to share feelings with another woman. It is the ultimate reflection of the love that the Mother-of-All has for her creature-sons and -daughters. Unfortunately, I have never felt that way for another woman. I am sorry."

"So am I," Idrilia said softly, turning her back on the Highblood.

"Why are you sorry? You should not apologize for how you feel."

"Whenever I—the last time I felt this way, it didn't go well either."

"What happened?"

"She got abducted by Komorese raiders. Lost her memory."

Vayriel's brow lifted. "The person is Klaara."

"And then I was going to tell her when we were at the gates but she—" Idrilia straightened, tilting her head slightly. "Excuse me. I must find Wen."

Vayriel froze. She watched as her friend disappeared behind clusters of thick stalks of the sarkumak, her stomach twisting. She moved into a familiar position like guarding the perimeter of her coil as Vayriel wondered what Idrilia had meant to say.

CHAPTER 65

He ran, but the shadow was faster. An unstoppable wave of darkness swallowed the tunnels of Xiel Metris behind him. In the winding corridors of the subterranean metropolis, the Xendra mounted their final defense against the onslaught with beams of pure energy—they slowed the tide but could not stop it. Through the telepathy that united their race, he knew the same scenario was playing out across the planet. The mountain fortress at Telech Tal had been sundered. The Singing Sea, its waves laced with thrumming crystals, was emptied. All that remained was this city.

Shame filled Hueteotl for his part in bringing this doom upon his people. It was his team who pushed too far and opened the door to the apocalypse in their relentless pursuit of greater power. They found it—but it also found them. The screams of Xendra pulled into the shadow reverberated in his mind, and finally, he could no longer run. Collapsing to the ground, Hueteotl turned and faced his end.

"Shek!"

Kharnek swore as the forced recollection came to an abrupt end. Instinct drove him to his feet, where he crouched into a fighting stance with weapon in hand. The warrior bore a sharp dagger, with a glimmering purple jewel set in its hilt. Torchlight filtered through the slight gap in the opening to his shelter, animating the gem's facets in an unsettling, familiar way—though since the episode on the skykeel, they no longer writhed with the Penumbra's contained energy. Kharnek hurriedly returned the dagger to its sheath. It was the only thing he wore besides his gray training shorts.

A wide-eyed Zinvar stared up at him, sitting cross-legged on the bedroll they now, on occasion, shared. This was their first attempt at letting the priest try to exorcize the fragmented memories the Penumbra left in its wake. His burgeoning powers as an Occulum seemed apt for the task, but it was a process of trial and error. And unfortunately, it seemed Kharnek would have to relive every horror before the grafted memories could be erased completely. Sweat beaded on his forehead, a testament to the strain he had endured in the last few hours.

"I think that's enough for one cycle," Zinvar suggested.

"Yes. We should rest. The trial will be exacting."

"Any thoughts on what it may be?" The priest extended his legs and curled up next to Kharnek as the warrior settled in beside him.

"If I knew, it would not be a trial."

Despite advocating rest, sleep eluded the warrior. While he appreciated Zinvar's efforts on his behalf, the inherent risk was enormous. If the priest stumbled on the wrong memory—forgiveness had its limits.

Moving with the silent grace of a trained soldier, Kharnek rose—careful not to disturb the sleeping man—and slipped through the fabric flaps at the entrance to their shelter. The chill of Komor's surface clawed at his bare flesh. Kharnek welcomed the discomfort. The embrace of misery was among the first things members of the Brotherhood learned—painfully and quickly. It made them stronger, and right now, it was the stimulus he needed to dispel his lingering fear. The Penumbra was defeated—yet it still haunted his mind. And Kharnek could not elude the gnawing suspicion that these recollections were harbingers of a potential future.

The soft crunch of booted feet on basalt reached Kharnek. He stepped into the shadow at the edge of his shelter, hoping to avoid the attention of the Komorese guards he expected. A cloaked figure rounded the fading embers at the heart of the Seekers' encampment. The warrior tensed until a familiar pair of white tails blurred passed him into the darkness. Quickening her pace, the figure—whom Kharnek now recognized as Vayriel—tilted her spear forward and took off in pursuit of the jeroti. She ran by close enough that he could have touched her, but she seemed not to sense his presence. Despite his burgeoning curiosity, Kharnek could not leave. The other Komorese were already suspicious of his accommodating attitude toward the foreigners. Whatever the Highblood found in Morakh's Shadow, she was on her own to face it.

"My lord?"

Kharnek whirled to find two guards behind him. They both looked terrified and ready to run at a moment's notice. "Yes?" he growled.

"We're sorry to disturb your rest," the guard on the left began, "but your superiors request an update on your mission."

"Fine. Hold on."

A few minutes later, Kharnek emerged from the shelter in his full armor. He hoped he had not woken Zinvar. Glaring at the two men, he motioned toward their camp. "Lead on, then."

They practically fled toward the safety of the other guards. The warrior sighed and followed after them. It seemed his reputation preceded him. Which could be problematic, now that his Penumbra-given abilities were gone. At least, he thought they were. Zinvar's probing of his memories had made something recoil into the furthest recesses of his mind. Whether that was just the secrets Kharnek was hiding from the priest or another menace, he could not tell.

He marched into the camp, aware of the sidelong glances and hushed whispers from the other soldiers as he made his way to the command tent. Two guards waved him in. Pushing aside the canvas flaps, Kharnek entered to see that the communication cube was already active. Captain Ahlet and one of the Mahir were conversing with the leader of the Komorese contingent in the Fellwood. A thin scarlet strip on the left epaulet of the man's armor denoted the rank of lieutenant. There was something familiar about his broad-shouldered stance...

Kharnek entered the cube's field of view and saluted to catch his superior's attention. He returned the gesture and made to dismiss the other soldier.

"Thank you, Lieutenant. Leave us until the Guardsman summons you."

When the lieutenant pivoted, his eyes met Kharnek's and widened in terror. The warrior offered him a thin smile. "Congratulations on your promotion, Valin."

Valin scuttled off without a word in reply.

"Thank you for coming, Guardsman Kharnek." The captain motioned to the warrior's surroundings. "I did not want to interrupt the Trials, but much has changed since we last spoke."

The Mahir cackled. "Interrupt the Trials? That is the whole point, Captain."

Ahlet shot the priest an irritated look and continued, "Thanks to the intelligence you provided about the anti-Spectre movement in Waverling, the city is now ours. We have removed the Magister and installed her former handmaiden's daughter as the witches' new leader. Her first action will be to announce an expanded trade agreement with Komor, the terms of which will permit us to freely move military assets across Heathström."

"We anticipate resistance from the populace when this announcement is made," the Mahir added, folding his arms. "That is when we will move our forces into the city under the pretense of helping the Spectres maintain order." The priest flashed an evil grin, just visible on his enshrouded face. "And it will all be perfectly legal."

Kharnek maintained his outward composure, but the news rocked him. None of this was supposed to happen until after the Trials. He cleared his throat. "What of the Sondrinel? They will not take this news lightly."

"They already know." Captain Ahlet frowned. "Somehow, they were able to listen in on our communications. ICON has since revised the cubes' encryption protocols, but it was too late to prevent them from learning about our plans for Waverling. Our sources indicate that Sondrine will recall its representatives from the Trials within the next few cycles. When that happens, you are to go to the garrison at Zel Gorragkh and await further orders."

"What of Zinvar?" The warrior held his breath while he awaited the reply.

Ahlet cocked his head. "That is the priest who accompanied you, yes?"

"He is not to return to Zel Morakh," the Mahir interrupted, his words laced with venom. "That fool and his blasphemous ideology must be silenced."

"Although it pains me to admit it, the servant of Morakh is right." The captain regarded Kharnek with a grim expression. "If Zinvar indicates that he plans to return here, you must stop him from doing so. At any cost."

A chill coursed down the warrior's spine, quickly sublimated by hot anger. The Mahir had taken advantage of Zinvar's naivete, as they did of so many. He felt his old hatred of the Priesthood swell, threatening to boil over.

"You seem troubled by this directive," the Mahir slyly observed. "Perhaps we should entrust the blasphemer's fate to someone else."

"No." Kharnek's response came sharp as a whip crack. Inwardly chastising himself for the uncontrolled reaction, he took a deep breath before continuing. "I will see to it."

A moment of silence, then the Mahir nodded. "Very well."

Captain Ahlet offered Kharnek a nod. "I have the utmost confidence in your abilities, Guardsman."

"Speaking of which," the cowled priest said, "we have heard rumors that you have been less than circumspect with the use of your Morakh-given gifts."

Kharnek stiffened and clamped down on his desire to lash out at the man's image. "I have done only what was necessary, servant of Morakh."

"I hope that is true, for your sake. He who dwells in the shadow does not look kindly upon those who abuse his grace."

The Mahir then vanished without another word. With a sigh and heave of his shoulders, Captain Ahlet regarded Kharnek with an appraising stare. "It is as he says, Guardsman. I cannot protect you if your actions put our realm at risk. Whatever the coming cycles bring, do not jeopardize your mission or the Mahir's faith in you. The Brotherhood can ill afford to lose our greatest advantage over the lightspawn."

"I understand."

Ahlet saluted. "May Morakh's shadow cover you."

The cube emitted a soft whirring sound as the image of Kharnek's superior disappeared. Rage balled the warrior's hands into fists that shook with the force of his emotions. Once again, the Priesthood had brought him to the precipice of destroying everything good in his life. And he only had at most a cycle or two to make an impossible choice. For all his training and strength, Kharnek felt powerless, an unmanned vessel tossed by the waves of outside forces.

He roared and flipped the table the cube rested on. It crashed to the floor amid a heap of maps and empty cups. The commotion drew Valin back inside the tent.

"What's going on?"

The sight of the other man opened a black well within Kharnek that he drank from deeply. Power surged through his limbs and lashed outward, hurling Valin back through the opening of the tent. The seething warrior stalked outside and waved off the guards coming to investigate the disturbance. Locating the site where Valin landed among a pile of supplies, he approached the cowering lieutenant.

"No one is to disturb me before moonrise. Is that understood?"

Valin stared at him, mute with fear.

"IS THAT UNDERSTOOD?!" Kharnek bellowed. The lieutenant cowered before his wrath but managed a barely audible affirmation. Satisfied, the warrior headed back to the Truthseekers' campsite, relinquishing the dark energy coursing through him before he entered his and Zinvar's shelter. Shame and worry flooded in its wake, and he carried their twin burdens into a restless sleep.

CHAPTER 66

Warmth passed over her cheek like an exfoliating balm. Vayriel roused, grasping her spear beside her. Blinking quickly, she cleared the haze of dreams and saw Kilahym breathing deeply, still asleep, an arm's length away. He had done well with his life force practice, though his focus had wavered. Vayriel decided to end their session when he doused the communal fire with the contents of Kharnek's cup, much to the warrior's frustration.

Why was she awake? Vayriel felt eyes on her and noticed Orgar. He sat on his haunches at her side, his gaze intense and unblinking. She could feel his breath through her hair over her ear. He bent his head and nudged her face with his cold nose.

"What is it, life-friend?" she whispered, brushing her hand over his muzzle and up between his raised ears.

Orgar whined, and turning his body around, he exited the tent.

Checking that Kilahym had not awakened, Vayriel took her spear and followed the jeroti, pausing to grab her cloak despite her haste. Since leaving Waverling she always slept with her fur-lined boots on, a Watcher routine. With spear and coat placed nearby at sleep, she could be ready to defend the coil within a breath.

Vayriel stepped out of the tent into darkness. Faint purple light hovered in the distance like a footpath into the forest. Ahead stood her Orgar where the embers of their fire scarcely glowed. Orgar bent his head behind him, and she focused on his piercing aqua eyes—the only easily visible part of his body.

Returning his attention toward the forest, he bolted forward, paws padding softly on the permafrost. Behind him trailed a translucent rose-hued ribbon. Was he following the purple light—or was the light a shape?

Orgar! she shouted within the life force, her heart pushing the feeling of the thought toward him as he bolted. Vayriel dashed after the jeroti, jumping over the remains of the fire. A memory flashed from Waverling, Vayriel chasing her life-friend over the canals. Here in Komor, the moon had begun to rise, though she took little notice of the additional light it offered—the sky was a blanket of stars draped over the forest.

Like the lost spirits in the Highblood origin of stars tale she told the Truthseekers last Daughter's rest, she now raced in a niche between the physical- and spirit-world.

She passed the last shelter of their encampment. A familiar brooding presence stood there just beyond her vision, but the life force said there was no danger. She could see Orgar's tails flash in the moonlight, and the thin dusty pink wisp trailed behind him. Various sizes of sarkumak pulsed with color in the distance, a background to the shades produced when she pushed the caps at her knees to the side. She danced around smaller ground plants in her pursuit, some of them faintly glowing in midnight palette, primarily to preserve their life— though she also wished to avoid the stench of a smashed fekwa. The cold air tinged her eyes, forming droplets in their upturned corners. She moved fast enough that the air flipped her loose peach waves behind her.

Then Orgar stopped.

Before him, nose-to-nose, sat a double-horned jeroti. Her figure glowed in soft transparency. Orgar lowered his muzzle a fraction. The female rose, turned, and ambled in the same direction Vayriel and Orgar had been following. This female reminded Vayriel of the jeroti on Mount Hoestra. Orgar glanced at Vayriel and waited for her to approach. Side by side, the pair followed the larger canine.

They stayed several paces behind her, so when the creature veered behind a large boulder, her body, then tails, disappeared from sight. The Heathström pair cautiously followed, rounding the rock in time to see the jeroti sit, chest puffed and chin tilted high. A gloved hand moved slowly to rest between the crystalline horns. A Highblood. At least, her attire bespoke the familiar themes. She gripped a staff with a crystal light-holder at its end like the implements used by Path-Shapers. Like the Path-Shapers, the woman wore her auburn hair braided, the length in front of her right shoulder, and alusarean fur adorned her hood on the outside. But her eyes set her apart. No Highblood had gray eyes.

"Mother-of-All," Vayriel whispered.

"I am known by many names. Some would call me the Grey Lady. Those who have the sight in the east would call me Kadaan." Her voice broke the darkness, firm and warm.

"I have been praying for your guidance on questions that lay on my heart. Have you come to answer them?"

The woman shook her head. "I cannot answer everything, but I can tell you what I can. I have come because you can hear the cry of the crystals, the plea they send out to end the creature-daughters' suffering from the Penumbra. Just as I did. I arrived here long ago from the place of the sky-spirits with Second-Son and the Sleeper. We were not united then, just as you stand divided now. Had we been, the outcome might have been different. Remind the others that you must work together."

Vayriel's mind raced. "Where was the Daughter?"

The woman hesitated. "My dear friend came with us but was torn from the creature-world by the Sleeper. She tried to warn me that he had succumbed to the Penumbra before he slew her."

Vayriel tilted her head to gaze at the sky. Bright dots of light shown above. She knew the Highblood story well, that those whose life was ripped from them, like her parents and the others who died at the crystal caverns that day, became sky-spirits. Yet, after the memory ceremony for Kalis, she had begun to wonder if the memory crystals created the speckled display, like luminous paint on the sky, instead. And then there were the sleeping beings who sailed among the lights towards Etherea.

"I have seen into the place the sky-spirits dwell. There are others who feel very much *alive*," Vayriel proceeded to tell the Mother-of-All of the vision she saw while in the creature in the storm wall. "Who are they?"

The woman lifted her chin, too, to gaze above. "It is possible they are of the ones who created the calamity. Their kind was here before I arrived, though we did not know it."

Vayriel felt her heart sink. "Then we have yet another enemy who seeks to destroy all life."

The Mother-of-All's face softened as she fixed her gray eyes on Vayriel. "I do not think that they meant to cause us harm deliberately. Did you sense malice in the sea creature?"

"It felt more like a tool waiting for hands to use it than a threat," Vayriel suggested.

"Do not fear them, but do not count on them for aid. Their lights were almost extinguished before by the Penumbra."

Vayriel brightened. "Zinvar has defeated it within Kharnek. We only need to find the remaining pieces."

The light on the woman's staff flickered as if blown by the wind, and the jeroti at her feet pawed the ground. "The darkness is only sleeping within him. Which is why I have come to you. I have sent my warnings through Zinvar, but the Penumbra fragments continue to be reclaimed. You cannot let the Sleeper awaken. And the Penumbra inside Kharnek must be destroyed, or the Sleeper will grow even stronger. Strong enough to open a path for the pieces to rejoin the whole. If he succeeds, then they can end all life in this galaxy."

For a moment, her appearance changed. Instead of Highblood raiment, she was clothed in slender long sleeves and pants the same hue as her eyes, then her coat and over-pants returned. "I cannot remain unseen for long. The Daughter's Eyes remain vigilant. I must go. I cannot let my presence trigger more rash actions as it did among the lowlanders. Find the fragments and destroy them. But if the Sleeper awakens, use your ICON. It can guide you when I cannot."

The woman clasped the upper left of her arm.

Vayriel mirrored the movement, feeling the familiar presence of her silver armband beneath the leather of her coat. "How do I use it?"

"It will react to the presence of other devices like it. When that happens, the artificial creature-sons ICON has released into your bloodstream will help show you the way. Even now, they guard against illness and prolong your lifespan."

Vayriel struggled to grasp this reply. Orgar whined as both images of the jeroti and the woman began to fade.

"Wait! How do I reach the Watcher and find the true light? How do I defeat the Sleeper?"

The Mother-of-All answered as her voice began to fade. "I see many threads. Too many. They are shifting. I do not know which will come to pass. But you are not alone in this journey. Find help from the ones who walk beside you, and seek my footprints."

The figures disappeared. Orgar sniffed the air and ground where they had stood before returning to Vayriel. The Highblood's mind raced. She inspected her surroundings, aware now that she was far from the encampment. The path back was unclear, but she thought she could orientate herself by the stars. She could not fathom what the Mother-of-All had meant at the end. One thing she was sure of—Vayriel would not sleep any more this Daughter's rest.

CHAPTER 67

A pall hung over the gathered Seekers, as palpable as the mist that shrouded the sarkumak this cycle—or so it seemed to Kilahym. They were gathered at the edge of the Fellwood, facing a semicircle of Komorese soldiers. Downcast expressions littered the group. Even Vayriel's irrepressible strength, the sparkle that always lit her lavender gaze, was dimmed. And from the way her eyes darted about, the bard deemed her distracted as well, which unsettled him.

"Truthseekers!" one of the Komorese bellowed, "Your task today is a simple one. Even the children among you will be able to manage it."

Out of the corner of his eye, Kilahym saw Idrilia bristle. Kalis frowned and squeezed his left fist. The bard wondered what words passed between them. No doubt they would displease Zinvar, if he was listening in. From the sour expression on the priest's face, he was.

The guard continued his explanation. "You are to journey into the heart of the Fellwood. Each of you must bring back two cuttings of bloodletter's knife, a rare plant that is sacred to the Priesthood of Morakh." From a pouch at his waist, the soldier produced a vine-like plant. Its leaves were narrow viridian spikes with crimson-tinged edges that seemed to glow in the moonlight. Kilahym emitted a soft "oo" at the sight. He had read about this variety of heartvine. It grew in dark places where only the moon's light reached and, when ingested, inflicted paralysis. Having now seen it firsthand, he understood how the plant got its macabre name.

"Be warned, the greatest perils in the Fellwood are not physical. This cursed land will show you the faces of those long dead and whisper promises in their voices. If you heed nothing else, remember this: Do not listen to them. Otherwise, you will become yet another victim of the Fellwood's snare." The Komorese surveyed the group from left to right until each nodded to indicate their understanding. "There is one other stipulation," he continued. "The Mahiratha has decreed that you are to undertake this Trial in pairs. You are free to choose with whom you journey. If there are any questions—you should have paid better attention."

That was apparently all the guidance the Seekers would receive, because the soldiers formed up and headed back to their encampment. Kilahym scrutinized their helms as they marched past: twin flanges that traced the jawline, rising to a peak at the center of the forehead where a broken circle emblem was emblazoned. Though he could not explain why, he found them deeply unsettling.

At Vayriel's side, Orgar emitted a low growl until the last of the Komorese disappeared among the sarkumak.

The ensuing silence as the Truthseekers regarded one another felt cold and heavy to Kilahym. He cleared his throat and drew everyone's attention. "I say, that was quite the introduction to this, ah, next Trial. Anyone else not in a rush to traipse about this haunted copse of tree poseurs?"

Idrilia tossed her hair and glared at Zinvar and Kharnek. "Your people's hospitality is every bit as brutal as the landscape."

"At least they haven't thrown fire at you," Zinvar retorted.

"Not yet."

Kalis placed a warning hand on Idrilia's shoulder. "Fighting amongst ourselves is not going to get us anywhere with this Trial."

"You're one to talk. We all know where your loyalties truly lie, *Sondrinel*." Without another word, Zinvar whirled and marched into the Fellwood, leaving several raised eyebrows in his wake.

Kilahym recovered from his shock at their friend's uncharacteristic behavior. "What's gotten into Zinny? Now he sounds like you, Kharnek—er, no offense."

"None taken," the warrior ground out. Kharnek peered into the forest, concern etched across his visage. "I'll go after him. The rest of you can decide how you want to split up in the meantime."

It might have been his imagination, but Kilahym thought Vayriel sounded tense when she replied, "We will do as you say. May you walk the true path."

Kharnek returned Vayriel's nod before stalking into the Fellwood.

Kilahym watched the warrior's broad shoulders disappear into the forest. Before he could so much as offer the briefest poetic commentary on what just took place, Kalis approached and claimed him as his companion for the Trial. The taller man then dragged him by the arm toward the sarkumak, despite Kilahym's protests.

"Keep quiet!" the Sondrinel hissed in his ear. "This is for their own good."

The Heathström native's mouth formed an 'o' shape. Taking one last glance back at his dear Vayriel, he observed a calm acceptance on her features—and perhaps a glimmer of joy in her lavender orbs? Idrilia's face resembled the storm wall the Seekers passed through so long ago. Thoughts of a sweeping tale of a goddess of winds and surges coalesced in Kilahym's mind, but his inspiration vanished with his awareness of the forest around him…glowing. Coils of violet light traced the irregularities of the ground in a radiant tapestry. Moonvine, Zinvar had called it, its beauty revealed beneath the light of its namesake. The sarkumak emitted their own faint luminance, tinged pale green, while their smaller cousins clustered about their base in tiny explosions of pink. Kalis loosed a low whistle.

"Well, well, not so barren after all," the Sondrinel mused.

"Indeed not! Such a beauteous display! Oh, I do hope Vayriel also casts her gaze upon these wonders."

"Assuming she and Idrilia haven't resorted to murder to overcome the awkwardness between them, I would guess so," Kalis drily replied. He finally released his grip on Kilahym's arm.

"You don't really think it would come to that, do you?"

"Of course not. I was only joking. 'Dril has a temper, but she isn't a killer."

Kilahym bobbed his head vigorously, as if agreeing could make it so. "There has indeed been some, ahem, tension between the two of them. It has been a cause of great concern and puzzlement to Vayriel." Cocking his head, the bard peered curiously at Kalis. "Have you spoken of this with your betrothed?"

"Not at length. But for your own good, I wouldn't ever refer to 'Dril as my 'betrothed' when she's around. For one thing, it isn't applicable any longer, and even if it were, I doubt she'd appreciate the notion of belonging to anyone."

"Alas! I fear my intention in using such a term has been misconstrued. I meant no—wait, isn't applicable?" Kilahym's eyes widened. "You mean…?"

"Yes," Kalis answered. He resumed his forward plunge into the depths of the Fellwood, and the bard hurried to keep up with the taller man's long strides. The effort brought welcome warmth to his chilled extremities. Even with the spare cloak he'd borrowed from Vayriel, he still felt the cold touch of Komor's eternal shadow.

"Alas, what cruel fate! That young love should suffer so early an unexpected demise."

A frown creased the Sondrinel's forehead. "I wouldn't call it dead just yet."

"Ah! Hope does always blossom like the moonvine beneath the silvered light. Even so, you have my most sorrowful of condolences."

"Thank you." Kalis seemed to withdraw to a place far within his own mind as he and the bard continued their journey into the Fellwood. The landscape undulated slightly, like one of the rugs in Kilahym's old home in Beechmarsh that would never lie flat. Such disruptions in Isle's mandated order of things brought out the worst of his mother's tyranny. His father would slovenly smooth the wrinkles, knowing that they would never disappear, each time she complained.

These accursed coverings will be my end, Firran. Can you imagine my delicate form, sprawled out in agony because someone *lacked the initiative to keep our house in order? Must I do all the thinking?" she exclaimed, hand thrown against her forehead in dramatic repose.*

"Quite right, quite right, my beautiful twillily," Firran muttered.

"I am beautiful, aren't I?" Isle cooed.

"Yes, you are lovelier than the light of a thousand moons."

The recollection churned Kilahym's stomach. Having witnessed the quiet strength with which Vayriel carried herself, and Idrilia's overt assertiveness, he could not imagine capitulating to someone else's every whim in such a spineless fashion. Exposure to their way of thinking had already changed him—and he had no doubt it was for the better. With any luck, he could carry this newfound knowledge of his true self back to Beechmarsh, and forge a better relationship with his family...and Vayriel, the Lady willing.

As if reading Kilahym's thoughts, Kalis spoke up, "You and Vayriel seem to have grown quite close."

"Yes, yes we have. It was a most fortuitous twist of fate that brought us together in these Trials we now undertake."

"Indeed." The Sondrinel nodded. "And where do you think fate will take both of you once the Trials are over?"

"Were it my decision, it would take us somewhere together. I can only hope that she is of the same opinion."

"I have no doubt that she is. Although," Kalis smirked, "I wouldn't trust my judgment regarding relationships at the moment."

Kilahym had no ready response to that and chose to drop the subject. The sound of their footsteps was muffled by a carpet of creeping flora as they entered a particularly dense section of the forest, where the sarkumak stalks crowded close to one another. To Kilahym, it looked as if they were huddling together to escape the cold. He and Kalis were forced to sidle between the tall fungi, close enough that the bard noticed the peculiar odor of their flesh—it reminded him of roasted pectully, if the meat were rolled in dirt. The dish was a delicacy in Beechmarsh, and for all her foibles, Isle was a fabulous cook. It was one of the only things Kilahym missed about her.

"How is your life force training proceeding?" Kalis asked.

"I am learning to wield it as assuredly as you and Dilly-Drilly."

"Oh?" Kalis's brow arched. "Perhaps a demonstration, then?"

"Well, I don't know that I have anything useful in my repertoire for our current situation. Conjuring a map is alas beyond my capabilities. But—" He reached over his shoulder, and finding the wood neck of his dulcimer, he withdrew the instrument with a triumphant whistle.

Kilahym lowered himself to his knees then rested the length on his thighs to tune the melody strings down in pitch.

"What are you—?" Kalis started but Kilahym shushed him.

Strumming a few notes to test, the bard nodded, feeling the notes from the instrument's drone strings combine together with the melody to create the melancholic atmosphere he wanted. Some called the tone of the tuning sad, but Kilahym found it peaceful.

He closed his eyes and focused on the music, like a small stream flowing to meet a river: the life force. He knew he was listening to energy around him when it felt like popping out of a closed box into an amphitheater that could seat thousands. Kilahym set his dulcimer aside and gently touched a coil of vine before him, attempting to emulate Vayriel's movements he had seen so many times.

"Move," the bard breathed, pushing the thought into the life force at the same time.

The moonvine responded, shrinking away from his hand, the motion repeated on shoots further down the vine's lengths, creating a foot-wide path free of the fauna.

Kilahym brushed imaginary dirt from his hands and stood. "See? Not completely useless. Now I can walk and not get tangled in these blasted things every step."

Kalis's eyes widened.

"Speechless, I see. I, too, am a little surprised at myself, but Vayriel is a good teacher and—"

"Kilahym, look," Kalis said urgently, pointing at the musician's feet.

Glancing down, Kilahym groaned. "I knew it was too good to be true."

The moonvine was twisting around his ankles, lashing them together as it grew up his leg. He struggled against it in vain before he remembered he had started this and could maybe stop it the same way. Mentally, he reached for the tendril of the life force he'd happily drifted on moments before but couldn't find it. Thankfully, the growth stopped at his hips. Kilahym pulled at the glowing cords, filling the quiet with grunts of effort. He glanced up to see Kalis's face plastered with mirth.

"Would you like some assistance?"

The bard sighed. "If you would be so kind."

Taking his sword, Kalis cut him loose. His companion didn't say more about it, but Kilahym felt the Sondrinel's silent laughter as they continued through the tightly packed sarkumaks on their previous course.

The two men exited the claustrophobic grove and found themselves in a clearing that eschewed illumination of any sort. Even the moonlight appeared to skitter away from the gloom, chasing itself back into the firmament. Withdrawing a crystal from his front pouch, Kalis filled it with life-force energy. The charged crystal threw silver-white radiance before the Seekers, revealing swirls of black fog that clung to the ground. Kilahym looked down to witness his legs disappearing into the calf-high layer of concealment.

"That's a rather disconcerting view," Kalis observed.

"A master of understatement, as usual." The bard could not help lifting his leg to assure himself that the attached foot remained so.

"Maybe with more light..."

The crystal shone forth brighter and pierced the fog with its luminosity.

"Bravo, Kalis! That seems to be doing the trick." Bending over, Kilahym peered at the revealed terrain. Clusters of viridian leaves limned in deep red formed a spiky blanket across the clearing. "And you have inadvertently uncovered that which we seek."

"Good. Let's grab that plant and get out of here. This place—it reminds me of the Penumbra."

Using Kalis's sword, the bard quickly obtained the requisite samples of bloodletter's knife, and the duo exited the clearing in haste. Behind them, the fog reclaimed the clearing, swallowing all traces of disturbance.

"I hope we can find our way back now." A shiver coursed down Kilahym's spine at the thought of remaining lost in the Fellwood.

"Not to worry. Idrilia has been using Wen to keep an eye on her position and ours. If we continue southeast, we'll be fine."

"Thank the Lady we have you two. Without Zinvar and Kharnek, you're our only hope of getting out of this accursed forest."

Kalis frowned. "Speaking of them, what's gotten into Zinvar? He's been such a strong proponent of cooperation between the realms, but that scene at the camp seemed a bit...hypocritical, you know."

"I wouldn't hold it against him. Zinny has been through a lot of late. He probably just needs a hug," Kilahym said cheerfully. A violent sneeze cut short his good humor, followed by several more. "Goodness me," he exclaimed, wiping his nose, "there must be something in the air here. There is, after all, a fungus among us."

Kalis peered curiously at the bard. "What do you mean?"

"Is it not common knowledge that fungi reproduce through spores? By your face, I see it is not." Kilahym waved at the sarkumak. "They are, no doubt, floating about us, perhaps even gathering in merry bands in our nose hairs, if the currents of the air see fit to whisk them there."

"I see." The other man frowned. "There aren't any side effects, are there?"

The bard shrugged. "Aside from my expectorations? Not really. Although, certain fungi, when consumed, do produce a certain dream-like state. Some people even claim to unlock the key to others' minds when in this induced trance. Rather like what Zinvar can do now."

Kalis came to an abrupt halt. "What?"

A sense that he had inadvertently let a wild beast loose from its burlap sack stole over Kilahym. He desperately tried to backpedal. "Ah, well, I referred to Zinvar's journey into Kharnek's mind, naturally."

Skepticism dripped from Kalis's words. "Is that so?"

Kilahym heaved a sigh and averted his eyes from the Sondrinel's piercing gaze, torn between telling the truth and respecting a friend's privacy. Then he thought about what happened the last time he kept Zinvar's secret. This, like the Penumbra, affected the entire group. It should be in the open. He looked up and met Kalis's eyes. "No, it's not. Zinvar has...indicated, to Vayriel and me, that he can hear what is being said when you converse via crystal."

Kalis paled and shrank back. "That...that can't be."

"It does seem to hail from the realm of absurdity," Kilahym agreed, "but Zinvar alluded to overhearing some rather uncharitable thoughts from you and Idrilia during our journey to this faux forest. Is, ahem, is that true?"

The Prioriate looked miserable when he answered. "Yes."

Kilahym clapped his hands. "Well then! There you have it." He stepped closer and clapped Kalis on the back. "If it's any consolation, he can't listen all the time. Only when you use your fancy crystals."

"That doesn't make me feel better, Hymn."

The duo resumed their walk in silence, interrupted only by the occasional chirring of hidden insects and birds. Kilahym hoped that his accidental revelation would not create yet another rift between the seekers. Every time they started to bond as a group, something would happen to open old wounds. He despaired that, at the end of the Trials, they would find that completing the tasks was all for naught if they did not learn to look beyond each other's differences.

"Did Zinvar say anything else? About what he overheard?" Kalis asked.

Kilahym shrugged. "That was all. But he did seem hurt by it."

"Then perhaps he shouldn't be eavesdropping on private conversations," Kalis replied testily.

"I don't disagree. But, given the opportunity, would you not do the same?"

"Perhaps you're right. Hold!" The Sondrinel abruptly raised a clenched fist.

"Hold what?"

"Hold still!" Kalis whispered. His eyes were fixed straight ahead. Following his gaze, Kilahym beheld a peculiar sight. A gleaming white figure strode through the Fellwood in the distance—quite literally through it, as it passed through the sarkumak without impediment. The silhouette suggested a tall, lean man to Kilahym. With a start, he realized that it was moving toward him and Kalis.

"What do we do?"

"I...I don't know." Kalis's gaze met his companion's, and the discomfiture Kilahym saw there nearly made him take off running. "I've never seen anything like this before."

"Do you think this is one of the mind-tricks the soldiers were talking about?"

The mention of the Komorese's warning seemed to refocus the distraught Sondrinel. "Yes, it has to be. Let's see if we can circle around it."

Kalis led the bard in a sweeping arc that took them to the figure's left. Still it drew nearer, changing direction and pace to match their movement. Whispers chased the edge of perception, taunting Kilahym with undeciphered words—and then a name emerged from the susurrations quite clearly.

Kalis.

The bard and Sondrinel froze.

"What *is* this?" Kilahym whispered in horror. The glowing figure was nearly upon them, and its features began to resolve into gray contours upon gleaming white. Skeletal cheekbones followed by eye sockets emerged to frame an aquiline face. Although the bard could not place it, something about the bone structure was very familiar to him. Then he glanced at Kalis and realization dawned: it was taking the appearance of a Sondrinel. And from the slack-jawed expression his friend bore, Kilahym guessed that it was someone Kalis knew.

In a burst of motion, the figure shot toward the two men. Shielding his face, Kilahym instinctively ducked as a burst of white light from Kalis's hand clawed at the darkness of the Fellwood, forcing it to retreat in a single moment of pure radiance. Then the light vanished as quickly as it came. Lowering his arms, the bard cracked an eye open. The figure was gone.

"Are you okay?" Despite the phenomenon they had just witnessed, Kalis sounded calm. His military training at work, Kilahym supposed.

"Limbs, head, striking good looks, and undeniable charm all accounted for." Straightening to his full height—which still only put him at shoulder level to Kalis—the bard surveyed the forest, which had once again descended into gloom. "What *was* that?"

"I don't know, but we need to get out of here before it returns." A tremulous note crept into the Prioriate's voice.

"You don't think it will, do you?" The thought chilled Kilahym in a way even the Komorese climate could not

"We're not going to wait to find out."

Kalis hastily led the bard away from the site of the figure's disappearance, no longer bothering to minimize the sound created by his steps.

Before he could stop himself, Kilahym blurted out his suspicion: "You know who that was, don't you?"

Without missing a stride, Kalis nodded. "I knew them, yes. But that can't have been who I think it was."

"Why is that?"

Turning his head to regard Kilahym, the Prioriate stared through him and at a far-off place as he answered.

"Because she's dead."

CHAPTER 68

"While this time of quiet allows me to listen to the new creature-sons and -daughters of Komor, what is the source of your silence?"

Idrilia's heart skipped, but she continued hiking, knocking a mid-sized sarkumak cap out of her way. It glowed blue at the touch. *Basja stinking basja Trial. Gathering a plant. Just like Komor to waste our time. And ghost stories, as if that would scare me into failure.* Her light crystal floated at her knees, highlighting the ground cover in silver-white.

"I just have a lot on my mind," Idrilia finally grumbled, her breath making moist puffs in front of her.

Kalis, if you can hear me, I'm going to kick your arse to the moon. Him picking the bard over her. He knew what happened the last time they got separated. Idrilia glanced at the Highblood. No, that wasn't what was bothering her. *I don't have time to focus on my feelings in the middle of a Trial.* She wanted to think, just her, Wen, and her grandmother's lullaby. Idrilia's hand reflexively went to the side bag that held her othwit music box, and a rush of emotions hammered against her resolve. She mentally cursed him again for also stirring her emotions for him with his kindness.

"Are you upset with me?" Vayriel questioned.

"I'm just frustrated at the world right now, Vayriel. And I wish I hadn't told you my feelings, alright? Look, let's just focus on our task."

Intending to keep her whirling storm of thoughts inside rather than exploding at her friend, Idrilia refocused her attention to search for dangers, as well as the required plant. Several moments passed in silence.

"I have been thinking. Why did you not choose to follow your grandmother's path instead of the warrior's path?"

"It fits me," Idrilia said defensively. "And it was *suggested*. Why?"

"You challenged my beliefs and asked me to think beyond what my coil has taught me. Something you do very well. You told me you enjoy the histories and knowledge guarded in Evocus. That you wanted to contribute like your grandmother did in adding to those volumes. Topics that…how did you put it?"

"Topics less…socially explored."

"I am trying to understand why one path spoke more to you than the other."

Idrilia smacked a stalk out of her way. "Pedium educates the young with the ultimate goal of finding their aptitude. When you come from a family of Sentinels, it's hard not to have such an aptitude. And there are very few who choose something other than what the instructors recommend."

"But Adjira did?"

A grin tugged at Idrilia's mouth. Vayriel noticed many things others seemed to miss. Idrilia found Vayriel's confidence and her level of knowledge—although sometimes naïve—attractive.

"She was skilled in several areas recognized by the guilds. I know one other person like that— Klaara's father. He switched guilds as well."

"Could you switch? If you wanted to?"

"I don't know if they'd let me. And then there's my family…" She trailed off, her mind drifting to one more thing that, if found out, could prevent her autonomy.

Movement on the ground pulled Idrilia from her thoughts. A multi-legged *thing* spindled out from a hole at the base of a sarkumak. The fekwa clicked its front legs like pinchers, latching on to scrub, ripping it out. Before it could eat the morsel, from the shadows a torav-like creature sprung and devoured the fekwa. The stench in corporeal form oozed down the torav's throat. It should have expelled the foulness before it could be poisoned, but it chose to swallow. How often she had done the same.

Idrilia shivered. She hid the truth from everyone, and it ate at her like sand in the boot, creating a blister. Wasn't it time she told someone? Away from those who, if they knew, would reassign her to the Quorum—the guild of misfits—or exile her.

"Do you remember the story Kalis told, of me rescuing Klaara on Lake Eduma?"

"Yes. From the Komorese attack."

"That's…not how it happened." She stroked Wen's chest. "There were two Komorese in those Kadaan-awful eye goggles, not one like everyone thinks. The second Komorese arslen waited at the bottom. When Klaara landed, the protection of the crystal I had tossed broke, and he was on her immediately. If only I had Wen that day. Klaara fought him with her scimitar as I forced my solendrake to race down the canyon wall. She was on the ground when I arrived, taking blows to her face. She wasn't fighting back anymore." Idrilia steadied the quivering in her voice. "The arslen kept beating her, yelling something about her being a blasphemer of Minothrall, or whatever they call their deity."

Idrilia scoffed. She knew the name but could not bring herself to honor them with accuracy. Her stomach twisted as she dredged to mind the Komorese telling Klaara her place was behind a man, not as his equal. That Sondrinel deserved to be sent to the Everburn for allowing women to think they could be remotely as intelligent as men. Each point he made was accented by a punch or a kick. In her memory, she saw herself launch from her solendrake before the reptile's last leap, with the tails of her fighting robe rippling at her calves.

"Will you tell me what happened next?" Vayriel asked softly. The coil Watcher maneuvered around a clump of scragweed, her arm brushing against Idrilia's. She felt her heart rate increase with the brief touch.

"I tackled him, then rolled back—to put myself between him and Klaara. He cursed me with whatever foul language the dark-spawn use. Before he attacked, he promised me he would end me; he'd cut the useless parts from my body. And then find my family. That he would make fine companions for his friends of any sisters I had. He said he was entitled to some reward. That maybe he'd take his reward from me first, then have Klaara later."

Idrilia felt nauseous. She wanted to envision a door slamming down in her mind like she always did to block out the real memory. Instead, she wedged a rock in the opening and let the darkness emerge like the shadows that surrounded the nearby Komor forest.

Klaara falling back, headscarf askew, her cuts caked with dust. The feeling that Idrilia's heart was being pulled out of her chest, that her head would explode with rage if she did not act.

"I couldn't—wouldn't allow him to touch her anymore. I had drawn my daggers while he spoke and launched while he still taunted me. We fought for some time. And I finally subdued him."

Twists and kicks, blade against blade while the intensity of the sun shone, unmoving like a moment frozen in time. Sweat trickling down her back and stinging her eyes. An opening she pounced upon with eagerness, somersaulting to hit him with the full force of her legs' momentum, knocking him to the ground. He moved to his knees, but Idrilia struck his temple with the pommel of a dagger, knocking the goggles askew. He caught himself before faceplanting in the dust.

"You do not have the courage to do what any Komor child could do," he sneered.

Idrilia clenched her teeth as she flipped her dagger to a reverse grip.

"Broken lenses," Idrilia whispered. The image that always haunted her.

"What does that mean?" Vayriel's voice echoed the thoughtful pinch of her brow.

"I killed him."

Vayriel stopped, her voice pitching higher. "You killed him?"

"Yes. And he couldn't hurt me or Klaara anymore," Idrilia defended.

Orgar whined at Vayriel's side. "Kalis does not know the truth. Did Klaara keep your secret?"

"I would not make her lie for me, if that's what you are insinuating."

"I did not mean—"

Idrilia waved her hand. "Klaara suffered great injuries. That was the longest hour I'd ever experienced, waiting for the rest to arrive." Idrilia swallowed, trying to control the flood of emotions. "She didn't remember much, which worked in my favor. I…feared the consequences of my actions. Being barred from applying for Priorium, disappointing my father, being forced into the Quorum. The Waverling Accords state that unless in self-defense or an accident, we don't take lives." Despite the gravity of it all, one thought had weighed the heaviest: what her grandmother would think.

"How would they know?"

Crunch of bone. Pool of blood.

"I drove my dagger into his skull. Then I covered it up. I cleaned Klaara's face up as much as I could and moved her into what little shade the crevasse offered. Every time I looked at her …" Idrilia groaned. "I diminished the rider and his blood. It took me several tries as I'd never done blood. I examined the other rider and found him dead, his neck snapped from the fall. It would look like an accident."

Vayriel gazed into the darkness, her hand resting on Orgar. "The version of the story Kalis told us."

Idrilia nodded. "I said that we fought before he grabbed her, which was the reason for her bruises and cuts. And the body showed evidence that he'd fallen to his death."

"I do not agree with your means, Idrilia. But I can understand your protective instinct. It is a good instinct to have. I, too, have seen what Komor's worst can do. But the few rotting berries do not represent the whole vine, as we have seen with Zinvar. There is often another way. Could you have used the diminishing crystal or slowed his movements with cold?"

Idrilia glowered. "Of course, there's always another way. But you weren't there! You didn't have to make the decisions I did. Maybe Zinvar isn't like the others, but this Komorese was vile. If there's one, there are others. And I will always be on my guard against them."

Vayriel chewed her top lip. "Then you have no remorse for your actions?"

"I don't know!" she shouted, throwing her arms out wide. "I protected Klaara the best way I knew how. But I've had to keep the truth from everyone. From my best friends."

She hated herself for that. Her legs nearly gave out in Concilius when the Council asked her to show them the attack. Kalis had been tender, encouraging, though her real hesitation was whether she could hide parts of her memory, not if she had the ability to use the crystal.

"I believe that you care deeply for many, but your actions that day were extreme. Your vigilance to protect those you care about are similar to my own, however—" Vayriel's eyes shifted focus to look beyond Idrilia.

Idrilia raised her eyebrows, "What is it?"

Vayriel pointed to where their light ceased to penetrate the darkness. "I thought I saw the Mother-of-All again, just there."

Turning, she caught a glimpse of a shape darting behind a large sarkumak where her friend indicated. If it *had* been there, it was more mist than physical form, like the effect of a diminishing crystal.

Idrilia halted, touching Vayriel's shoulder. "Did you say *again?* When did you see her?"

"While you and the others slept last Daughter's Set. She came to offer guidance on our true path. She says that she is your Kadaan. And the lowlanders' Grey Lady. She is all three that we revere."

"And you are just now sharing this?" Idrilia frowned. As they spoke, their breaths briefly mixed in a cloud between them.

"I did not know how to reveal what I had learned in the presence of Zinvar and Kharnek, but now I do not think that it matters. She was here to give me a warning."

The Highblood recounted her experience, and as she spoke, the recent conversation Kalis had with the High Keeper aligned with what the mysterious woman had told Vayriel. She tried to reach Kalis through the communication crystals to alert him of the danger Kharnek could still pose, but her mental shouts were met with silence; she must be too far from him.

"I am saddened that Kharnek is not fully free of the Penumbra. And for Zinvar, as he believes he defeated the darkness," Vayriel finished.

"Prior to the Trials, I wouldn't have even considered acting on the words of an apparition. But there have been many things which have challenged what I, what Axiom, understands of the life force. And of the Occulum, for that matter," Idrilia hesitated, debating her next words even though she herself had demanded all of the Truthseekers keep no further secrets, especially about the Penumbra. "The Council believes that finding and destroying the Penumbra fragments should be a priority as well."

"Then we should find the others immediately and forgo the Trials." Vayriel motioned to the forest with her spear. "The greater survival of the world depends on us."

Idrilia held up a hand. "I don't think we should reveal our hand just yet. Don't you think it's a convenient coincidence that this woman shows up each time before all sorts of solendrake basja hits the table? I'm not doubting what you saw, but not everyone is benevolent. And this could be a trick of the Penumbra, trying to get us to quit the Trials or some other action that serves its purpose. Like having us accuse Kharnek with his soldier brothers nearby, and then Komor has an excuse to detain us."

Vayriel's lips pressed together thoughtfully before she spoke. "I did not feel the emptiness as I have before with the Penumbra's presence. But I understand your caution. I would not wish our action to prompt these things you fear." Then she nodded as if answering an inner question. "Let us complete our task first, then together we can figure out how to tell the others. I think the bloodletter's knife might grow better near the heat vents. I suggest we head to that steam plume."

Vayriel pointed to where a tendril of fog cascaded above the forest tops into the light of the moon. Like Idrilia's emotions, the cloud was tight as it slowly released into an infinite space. They crunched over the permafrost as Idrilia reflected. She felt unresolved with her feelings for Vayriel and at having revealed her deepest secret, but that paled in comparison with the growing dread she felt about Kharnek. He was a tangle of sand writhers that needed to be expelled from the group. And she might be the only one willing to do what must be done next.

CHAPTER 69

Anger and frustration made Zinvar's temples throb as he advanced deeper into the Fellwood. He knew Kharnek would follow him, so his plunge into the forest's depths came at a frenetic pace. The risk of getting lost was subsumed by the surge of antipathy he felt toward the Sondrinel Seekers, which had prompted his sudden departure. Zinvar knew from his eavesdropping that they still suspected Kharnek of harboring a great menace. Even Kalis, who he considered the more reasonable of the two, could not hide his wariness. But what bothered him just as much, if he was honest with himself, was that their suspicion struck a chord with his own fears. While rummaging through Kharnek's mind, Zinvar had come across places that were inaccessible even to his Occulum powers. Despite his promise, Kharnek still kept secrets from him. And, as the events of the Trials had proven, those secrets could be deadly.

These thoughts dogged the priest as he rushed further into the Fellwood's depths. The sarkumak grew dense in this section of the forest. What little moonlight found its way through the canopy evanesced in the eerie glow of bioluminescent flora. Like most of Komor, the terrain beneath the carpet of vines was rocky and undulating, making for slow progress.

When Zinvar finally emerged into a clearing in the forest, the moon floated midway through its arc across the sky. Here, its luminance dusted an array of abandoned machinery scattered throughout the glade. A boom with claws dangling from its end—the priest guessed it to be a type of crane—lay half-buried in the wreckage of a large conveyor. Buckets full of glittering black material lay spilled on the ground—the oily reflection of light on its surfaces reminded Zinvar of the Komorese soldiers' armor.

The scene resembled Rinesh's story about the Arakhist movement's defeat. This had to be the mine, Zinvar realized, as he wandered around the site. Charred bits of metal attested to the heat of the fires that burned the mining equipment, and even the priest had to admit it looked like the destruction caused by an arakh's flaming breath. The bits of discarded ore were unmarred. Zinvar picked one up, marveling at its lightness. If this was arsanth, he better understood why it was so sought after.

Zinvar replaced the ore and moved to continue his exploration of the ruins. He slipped on loose gravel and his next footstep found empty space. Arms wheeling, Zinvar lurched back and narrowly avoided falling down the gaping entrance to the mine itself. His heart pounded as dislodged bits of dirt plummeted into the abyss. The jagged hole in the clearing's center was large enough to swallow an entire skykeel. Peering into the mine shaft's depths yielded naught but infinite blackness to Zinvar's scrutiny—until something glinted in the depths below. He dropped to his knees and cautiously leaned forward, but the darkness refused to give up its secret.

A wild idea took shape in Zinvar's mind. Leaping to his feet, the priest scanned the broken machines until he found a length of metal cable, severed from the conveyor by an unknown force. He secured one end to the conveyor and backed up to the hole, testing the security of his makeshift apparatus with firm tugs. The cable held, even when he drew it tight and leaned back so it supported all his weight. Dropping his staff, Zinvar slowly lowered himself over the edge and began his descent toward the mysterious gleam below. The roughly-hewn walls offered many footholds, but the greater danger proved to be the priest's own nerves. Many times, the cable slipped in his sweaty palms and Zinvar's stomach lurched with each almost-fall. He had no idea how deep the mine shaft was, but he doubted he would survive an unrestrained trip to the bottom. Forcing such thoughts away, he continued toward the reflected light until he found himself just above it. The priest's forehead bore the sheen of perspiration, and his muscles burned. To his relief, a natural outcropping in the rock wall jutted out just beneath his destination. Lowering himself onto the ledge, he kept one hand on the cable, and with the other he wiped away the sweat that stung his eyes.

His blurred vision cleared, and Zinvar found himself staring at a rectangular crystal embedded in basalt. Disappointment flooded the priest. He risked death for nothing but this? In frustration, he reached for the crystal and tore at it, expecting it to be lodged too firmly to move—but to his shock, it emerged smoothly from the rock. Zinvar stared at the six-inch-long object clutched in his hand. There was nothing remarkable about it at first examination, but the longer he looked, the more he suspected that this was no ordinary creation of geology. He tucked the crystal into his robes and began the arduous climb back up.

Half an hour later, the exhausted priest crawled over the edge of the hole. His robes were an even darker orange from the sweat soaked into them, and his arms trembled from exertion. For a long moment, Zinvar simply lay on the ground, luxuriating in the relief of having survived the ascent. Then curiosity reasserted itself. He sat up and withdrew the crystal, cradling it in his palms. This time, he glimpsed a faint swirl of violet light within its facets. A chill ran down his spine as a sinuous whisper reached into him.

Light...too much light.

"What are you?" Zinvar whispered, but he already knew.

Alone...scattered. We were scattered...

"Scattered by what?"

By her...

"Who?"

Captain...the Captain. Kadaan. She made the Whole...many.

"What do you mean?"

She could not destroy us, so she scattered us. Fragments, across this world.

The longer the crystal spoke to him, the more coherent its words became, as if drawing strength from Zinvar. He could feel the cold tendrils of its presence infiltrating his mind, searching for a chink in his mental armor.

"You are the Penumbra."

You have known us before.

"Yes. You took Kharnek from me. But you lost."

No. Before...

A memory rose unbidden into Zinvar's consciousness. The mine disappeared, and the basalt walls of a Komorese dwelling rose around him, lit by flickering torchlight. He stood at the center of a hallway. From the shadows at its end, a woman brandishing a dagger emerged and rushed toward him. Long brown hair streamed behind her as she ran, fury etched into her visage. As she drew nearer, the priest recognized her wide green eyes, so like his own. Myal prepared to plunge the dagger into his chest, but a black miasma roiled outward from Zinvar's hands, consuming his mother in a flash. The priest tried to cry out, but he had no power over this recollection. He fell to his knees as footsteps approached from behind. Twisting his head toward their coming, he caught his reflection in an obsidian mirror. Kharnek's face looked back at him. Zinvar reeled as the moonlit mine returned and the crystal blazed amethyst in his hands.

You see...we knew you all this time. Better than you knew the one you love.

A sound like glass shattering assailed his senses—the Penumbra laughing.

"You know nothing," the priest said through clenched teeth as he rose from the ground. He could feel the fragment's full strength now, trying to claim him as its host. It shrieked as Zinvar lashed out with a wave of pure volition, of the will to not be controlled, and the crystal exploded. The force of its destruction caused the priest to stumble back toward the mine shaft. Arms wheeling, Zinvar screamed as he pitched over the edge. His fall was arrested by a strong arm that encircled the priest's waist, unceremoniously hauling him out of the chasm. Zinvar's eyes—squeezed shut as a last defense against the inevitable—popped open, and he looked up into the face of his savior.

Kharnek.

CHAPTER 70

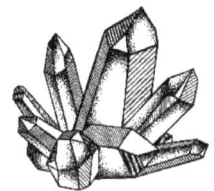

The Fellwood.

Kalis reflected on the name. A fell place indeed, where growing things crept from frozen soil, fed by the warmth of volcanic activity. Fire beneath ice. An apt metaphor for his former betrothed's attitude toward him, if he was honest.

"I am worried about Zinvar," Kilahym spoke up, interrupting Kalis's reflection. The bard crossed his arms and rubbed his hands up and down them. "And about freezing to death."

"Better frozen than dinner for a hungry ghost."

"Maybe he prefers his food that way." Kilahym shuddered. "Frozen dinners, can you imagine such a chilling thing?"

"I prefer not to."

"How do you know it is, er, appears in the likeness of someone you knew? The face of it was like someone had smeared wet paint with their hand on a canvas."

"Not for me." Kalis glanced at the bard. "The features were clear."

Kilahym tapped his lips. "Hm…"

"I think I know that look." Kalis elbowed Kilahym. "What are you writing in your head?"

"More like rewriting a flora book I'm expecting needs a new edition. This is completely conjecture but since the sporestalks of Heathström can cause hallucinations when eaten…"

"You mentioned that. What about it?"

"Despite their truculent demeanor, those soldiers did warn us about seeing things. I think the sarkumak are to blame. But, perhaps because I have eaten some of their cousins, I have a bit of a resistance. You are affected more acutely than me?"

"Are you asking if I am?"

Kilahym snorted. "I'm hoping your logical mind finds my creativity to be accurate in this case."

Kalis shrugged. "We do not have anything like the sarkumak in Sondrine, so I think you have a valid point."

"Whew!"

"Look." Kalis pointed. "I see a fire."

The bard squinted at a wavering point of light in the distance. Although still a fair walk away, the sight lifted Kalis's spirit. The nightmare of the Fellwood was almost over.

When they eventually walked into the clearing that served as their campsite and presented the soldiers with their prize, the men waved them away.

"Go back to your tents and await further instructions," the tallest Komorese barked. An air of agitation pervaded the campsite. Kalis noted the furtive whispers passed between the Komorese giving orders and his secondaries, the way the men clutched the pommels of their swords. This was a unit preparing for action, or he was not a Prioriate. Kalis motioned for Kilahym to wait and approached the apparent leader.

"Excuse me. Is something going on?"

"Nothing you need concern yourself with, Sondrinel," the man sneered.

"For some reason, I doubt that. It looks like you're about to leave, even though the rest of us aren't back, you know?"

The soldier shot him a withering glare, but Kalis refused to be cowed. He rooted himself in front of the Komorese, arms crossed in a decidedly Idrilia-like fashion. When the man started to walk away, he followed.

"Ignoring me is not going to make me go away, you know."

No response was forthcoming, so Kalis jogged ahead of the soldier and blocked his path. To the Prioriate's surprise, Kilahym appeared at his side.

"Or me."

The soldier cast his eyes skyward. "Morakh help me." Then he thrust a gauntleted finger at the Seekers. "You want to know what's happening? Go to the node and ask your people."

Kalis blinked.

"The node?" Kilahym wondered aloud.

"Yes, the node. The cube? Like the ones given to Sondrine and Heathström?"

"Oh." Kalis nodded understanding. The soldier walked away, muttering something about "ignorant fools" under his breath. Were there Volundar blood running through his veins, Kalis might not have let the slight go.

"By the Lady, what a strange day this has been, and it seems to be destined for even stranger things," Kilahym opined. The bard's well of optimism seemed to be running dry if the fading light in his amber eyes was an accurate measure.

As they made their way to the cube, Kalis felt pressure mount behind his forehead. He knew this tension—Sentinels called it battle precognition, a subtle warning from the body to be ready for the unforeseen. Most scholars attributed its origins to the warrior's connection to the life force, but Kalis suspected this was an atavistic physical response ingrained in all humans.

Kalis activated the cube. This time when the image flourished into life above the device, the entire Council appeared. They must have been in session, and their grave faces made Kalis's heart sink. From her place at the semicircle's center, High Keeper Veloran spoke.

"Kalis, we are relieved to see you well. And your fellow Seeker." She nodded at Kilahym, the jewel on her forehead glinting. The bard offered a short bow in response.

Kalis felt the phantom pressure on his ears that was the surrounding ambient noise vanishing; Kilahym poked a finger into his own ear.

"There, I have secured this connection. We did not expect to hear from you so soon. Or that the Komorese would allow you to contact us. Have you completed the Fellwood's trial already?"

Kalis nodded. "It is good to see you as well, High Keeper. Kilahym and I have successfully completed the trial, and we await the return of the other Seekers from the forest. However, the guards stationed here are behaving…oddly. They will not tell us what is going on. "

"Unfortunately, I bear the burden of telling you that the Trials are now over," Veloran continued solemnly, "and that you all must return to your homes as quickly as possible. We have learned that the Magister is dead—"

"By the Lady," Kilahym breathed, stiffening next to the Sondrinel.

"—and Waverling is destabilizing. A coup attempt by rogue elements within the Spectres has created total anarchy in the city. We suspect Komorese involvement as the cube within Waverling has been unreachable since the twenty-first of this month. Our border patrols also report refugees from the conflict moving eastward toward Sondrine. The first may reach Axiom before Est Vek ends, if they move quickly."

"That's practically now. Laphrim protect them," Kilahym muttered as he bent his chin to his chest. "Will I even have a home to return to?"

Leaning forward slightly, Veloran favored the bard with a kind smile. "There is still much for us to confirm. Electing to continue the Trials in the wake of Kalis's apparent death was one of the hardest decisions this Council has ever made. We thought it best for all Etherea to honor the intent of the Trials and continue even in the face of dire adversity." The High Keeper sat back in her chair, and her features grew stern. "But not all the realms sought to emulate our example. For that reason, we are withdrawing from the Trials, and Heathström is following suit."

Given the current state of affairs, Kalis suspected that this was a softened version of the truth. If Komor had created the chaos in Heathström, they would take advantage of it and eliminate the one real impediment between them and their sworn enemy in Sondrine. The shadow of war once again darkened Etherea's future.

Before either Seeker could pose more questions to the High Keeper, a brilliant streak of pink light arrowed into the sky over the Fellwood. The light climbed to a height that made Kalis crane his neck to follow it and hung suspended in the air before bursting into dozens of lines. Delicate traceries remained in the Sondrinel's eyes, reminding him of a certain Highblood's fireside display.

"It is Vayriel." Kilahym squinted at the distance. "She calls for help."

"How do you know?" Kalis questioned.

The bard pointed, "It looks like Highblood light weaving, if crossed with a pyreflower. She has a history with those. Actually, it is the shape of a blood lily. It has become, somewhat, I think, a symbol of our connection. Hers and mine, I mean."

"But how do you know she needs help?"

"I feel it." He clutched his chest in emphasis. "Through the life force. Our connection has become stronger ever since...well, recently."

Directing his attention back to the cube, Kalis addressed the High Keeper. "I am sorry Keeper Veloran, but our companions require assistance."

"Do not apologize. Go, help your fellow Seekers. In your actions, the spirit of the Trials of the Innermost lives on." The High Keeper motioned, and the image of the Council vanished. Kalis stared into the Fellwood. He had never tried using a person instead of a crystal as his endpoint for moving through the life force, but it should be possible.

He looked over his shoulder at the bard. "Wait here."

Before Kilahym could react, the Sondrinel closed his hands around two crystals and vanished into the space between the physical world and the non-corporeal realm of the life force. He reappeared next to a young sarkumak, feeling lightheaded. Looking over the cap, he saw an astonished Highblood staring at him two solendrake-bounds away. She was englobed by a familiar tacky substance. The tip of her spear protruded from the pallid sphere, as did the twitching end of Orgar's right tail.

"Kalis! How did you come to be here?"

"I used the life force to travel here when we saw your signal. Like back at the Sunscorned base. Anyway, what happened?" Casting his eyes about, Kalis hesitantly asked as he approached, "And where is Idrilia?"

"I am fine, but I fear for Idrilia. Please, can you release us from this prison?"

With a nod, Kalis reached into the life force and ordered the protection crystal to melt away. The jeroti shook himself fervently. Kalis knew that the protection spheres left no residue, but the sensation of being inside one was unpleasantly wet.

"Thank you." Vayriel flicked her peach hair over her shoulder and placed a protective hand atop Orgar's head. "I feared we would be too far for anyone to help."

"Idrilia did this."

A moment's pause, then the Highblood nodded. "Yes, but it is not what you believe. We encountered one of the apparitions the men of Komor warned us about. It took the form of someone very dear to Idrilia. I tried to stop her from following it, but—"

Kalis was already shaking his head. "'Dril wouldn't listen."

"No. She trapped Orgar and me and fled, chasing the apparition. It was only moments ago. We may yet be able to stop her, if we work together."

"Do you know where she is?"

"Yes." Vayriel closed her eyes. "Wen is with her. They have not gone far; they are northwest of us."

"That's all I need." Kalis readied himself to walk between worlds again and braced for the inevitable muscle weakness that would come from a second transport in quick succession. "You said the apparition took the form of someone dear to Idrilia?"

The Highblood indicated her assent.

"Who was it?" Kalis felt his pulse racing, knowing even as he awaited the reply.

"It was a whisper, so I am uncertain if I heard correctly," Vayriel cautioned.

"Who was it?" the Sondrinel repeated, sweat gathering on his palms.

"She called her 'Grandmother.'"

CHAPTER 71

She dodged a decurrent sarkumak, then ducked under the umbonated top of the next, its under-ridges outlined in faint blue. She attempted to run on the unfamiliar terrain, but could move no faster than a jog—though her heart raced as if she ran sprints in the courtyard of Pedium. Her ears strained to make out words in the cacophony of whispers that surrounded her in an otherwise soundless cloud of thick fog. Each footfall she made was a hammer, her passage stirring the clouds of particles that threatened to fill her lungs with each deep breath. The figure drew no closer, yet it did not leave her behind. *She* did not leave her behind.

Idrilia had to know. *Was this even possible?*

Skidding to a halt, Idrilia glanced wildly in all directions, searching for the now-vanished white glow among the floating particles. Was this how fog always behaved? Wen settled on her shoulder, brushing her feathered wings against Idrilia's face as if brushing away the fog.

"Stop that," she whispered, eyes darting across the darkness.

To the southwest and deeper into the Fellwood, the glow appeared, again in the shape of a woman.

"What did you say Kadaan looked like when you saw her?"

Idriiiilia., the whispers sang.

"I mean the Mother-of-All…Vayriel?" The Sondrinel whirled around to no one. She took a step back the way she had come, a shadow of a memory surfacing of Vayriel and Orgar surrounded by... The apparition moved, catching her attention. Then it stopped as if waiting for her.

Though the details were hazy, Idrilia knew Vayriel had Orgar, which allowed her to make a quick decision to pursue the luminescence instead. Her mind felt two steps behind her actions, and she took a deep breath to clear the feeling of rocks weighted on her chest, this feeling of urgency, as best she could. She proceeded more cautiously, watching the shadows for a Komorese trap.

The form led her to the largest sarkumak she had yet seen. It—she— stopped and gestured for Idrilia to come closer. Idrilia hesitated, studying the visual.

Though she held the shape of a woman, Idrilia saw large roots branching behind her translucent form. The luminous image held details of a physique congruous with the shadow of bone beneath. The representation was both magnificent and terrifying. The woman wore a robe tied by layers of belts hanging at varying angles. Parchments poked out of tube-like pouches, and a notebook was stuck to her hip. Oval ornamentation bubbled along the hems of her robe sleeves and fabric edges. The shape matched her circlet, a double teardrop shape hanging against her forehead.

Idrilia touched her own forehead, an exact copy resting there. In spite of the disconcerting view of the underlying bone, Idrilia knew the place of every wrinkle on her aquiline face.

"Grandmother?" Idrilia's voice croaked.

In response, the image of grandmother Elsuota parted her lips. She gestured with one hand to the sky and with the other to her side.

"I—I can't hear you, grandmother." Idrilia shook her head quickly. "I have so many questions. I've missed you so much!" Her voice broke, and she squeezed her eyes shut, trying to push the tears back before they could form.

"Your memory guides me. I try to remember everything you said, do as you did. I need your guidance. I...want to know that I haven't disappointed you." She paused, feeling her chest shake and her eyes burn. "I see now that—Sondrine needs to change. You were so brave. You wrote about it when others wouldn't. I read everything when you...died."

The former High Keeper seemed to float backward, away from her granddaughter, arms still gesturing in a frozen pose. It reminded Idrilia of depictions of Sondrinel Rising.

Her heart skipped and she took a step closer, not wanting any more space between them. "But how are you here? Do we retain some physical form when we rise?" She groaned. "I still can't hear you. Can you signal to me instead?"

Elsuota's arms lowered to her side, then her hands moved in an awkward jumble of words only partially recognizable. Idrilia picked out a few words like "life force," "secret", "rising", and "help you."

"The life force and the Rising? I've been doubting if we know as much as we think we do. And here you are." Idrilia gave a short laugh.

A sizzle and a faint pop broke the silence.

"'Dril!" A voice called. "Stay away from it. It's not what you think!"

Kalis had materialized to her left, just at the edge of the large sarkumak. He looked pale, probably from the energy expenditure of his life force travel method.

"It's her; I know it is," Idrilia called, turning her head.

He started walking toward her, hands splayed to his sides. "Please, come away from that thing."

She frowned. "*Thing?* This is High Keeper Elsuota. Show some respect."

"It looks like her, but it's not. Kilahym and I saw her in the forest before we found Vayriel."

"And why did Vayriel leave me? To be with Hymn, I suppose."

"What? You encased her in a protection crystal."

"I would remember that, Kalis." Idrilia crossed her arms over her chest.

"But you did. You imprisoned her and Orgar. Vayriel tried to help you. She must have sensed something, you know. To keep you from following this, this vision. It's a defense mechanism of the sarkumak. Kilahym says their spores could alter our perceptions—make us see things that are not there. The Komorese soldiers weren't trying to simply scare us into failing our task."

"Stop trying to confuse me." Idrilia shook her head, trying to make sense of why Kalis would be saying such things. Her head felt clouded again. She closed her eyes and inhaled, focusing on her breathing to slow her racing pulse. The exercise dispelled the fog enveloping her mind. She could feel the lingering effects of its influence, but it seemed her awareness of it lessened its power over her. Blinking, she looked first at Kalis, then for the apparition. It was gone.

Kalis must have detected the sorrow in her face, for he stepped closer and gently took her hands, squeezing them. "I'm so sorry, 'Dril."

A single tear coursed down her cheek. "I'm the one who should be sorry. I was so eager to see my grandmother again that I let this illusion deceive me. And Vayriel and Orgar...how will they ever trust me now?"

Kalis gently squeezed her shoulder. "It wasn't your fault. You and I seem to be affected more strongly by the Fellwood than they are. Kilahym said something about him and Vayriel possibly having some resistance. It affects us all, only at different intensities."

"Really?" Idrilia freed her hands to wipe at her face, then scowled at the surrounding forest. "What an awful place. Let's just finish this trial so we can get out of here."

"Your departure is not permitted."

The voice came from behind Idrilia. She whirled and drew her daggers, noting in her peripheral vision that Kalis had moved to flank her. They faced the speaker, a figure roughly Kalis's height wearing the rust-colored robes of the Komorese Priesthood. The figure had raised its hood, shrouding its face in darkness save for its eyes, which glowed amber.

"Who are you?" Idrilia challenged.

The figure tilted its head to study her. "You do not carry the command access object. Do not interfere. Use of lethal force has been authorized."

Kalis brandished his sword. "From your appearance, I gather you are here on the Priesthood's behalf. A servant of Morakh."

"No." The figure spread its hands. "I am ICON. The Priesthood of Komor serves *me*. Morakh is an illusion that comforts humans and ensures their compliance."

Idrilia stared. None of this made any sense. She glanced at Kalis, and he seemed just as perplexed.

ICON pointed at Kalis. "Give me your command access object, and your life will be spared."

"What are you talking about?" Idrilia demanded.

"I think it wants my ring," Kalis said slowly. He looked over at her. "Because of how it interacts with the communication cubes."

"Oh." Idrilia watched the figure, but it had no visible reaction to Kalis's statement. "But why?"

"That is none of your concern." ICON tensed, and the amber of its eyes flared. "Give me the ring. You have five seconds to comply."

Idrilia saw Kalis's hand signal from the corner of her eye. They would take this enemy together, like they were trained. She circled around ICON to flank it, putting enough distance between her and Kalis that they could not be attacked simultaneously. Her heart beat a furious tempo. If this being was powerful enough to control Komor, it was not to be underestimated.

ICON sighed. "Humans. You came all this way to a new world, and still, you learned nothing."

When ICON moved, it was so fast that Idrilia could barely track it. It lunged toward Kalis and unleashed a flurry of punches he just managed to parry. He launched a counterattack that caught his assailant's forearm. To Idrilia's astonishment, his sword sliced through the fabric of the robe only to ricochet from ICON's limb with no visible effect. The skin underneath ICON's robe was a strange pearlescent hue that gleamed in the sarkumak's light.

Idrilia moved in, wary of ICON's speed. There was little doubt in her mind that her daggers would be equally ineffective, but she could distract it from Kalis and give him time to improvise. She lashed out with her left-hand dagger. In the blink of an eye, ICON whirled and deflected it, then stepped inside her open guard, striking her stomach with an open palm. The force of the blow drove the wind from her lungs. She staggered backward, barely managing to raise her daggers and catch the kick that followed.

"Dril! Go right!"

She heeded Kalis's direction and dove away from ICON. A crystal struck ICON in the chest and exploded, hurling their attacker into a sarkumak trunk. Smoke rose from ICON's robes, but it appeared otherwise unharmed as it rose from the ground. Idrilia exchanged a panicked look with Kalis.

"What is this thing? None of our attacks are working."

He nodded. "This foe is beyond us. We have to run."

The Sondrinel spun to flee, but ICON was faster. Idrilia pitched forward and skidded across the ground as it struck her between her shoulder blades. She winced as rocks tore at her face. Turning her slide into a somersault, she rolled to her feet and spun.

Kalis looked back at her. His mouth was open, but no words emerged. ICON's hand protruded from his chest, dripping with blood. A shriek escaped Idrilia as the hand was withdrawn, and Kalis slumped to lie at ICON's feet. The entity appeared to examine its crimson-stained hand before returning its attention to her.

"It is over. Go, and you may live."

Idrilia replaced her daggers in their sheaths and withdrew two crystals. If Vayriel could use the life force without crystals, maybe her training shards were enough...but if they failed, she was doomed. "It's not over yet. Not as long as I'm still alive."

ICON cocked its head. "You cannot harm me. If you fight, you will die."

She shook the crystals, which flared with life-force energy. Fighting back tears, she met ICON's amber gaze. "Then I will rise. Sondrinel do not fear death." Closing her eyes, she fought down her simmering rage and the agony of loss. Idrilia focused, opening herself to the life force more than she had ever done before. It flowed through her like a river of light, pouring into the waiting vessels of the crystals. Then, she felt the warmth of a familiar presence in the current.

I am with you, granddaughter. This is not your time.

Idrilia's eyes flew open. With a shout, she brought the crystals together in front of her and unleashed their gathered power. A spear of searing white stabbed outward and tore through Kalis's murderer. As the light from the blast faded, Idrilia blinked away green and purple dots and gasped. Her attack had left a gaping hole with glowing edges in ICON's torso. Flickers of light and sparks flashed from inside it.

ICON looked down at the damage, then back up at her. "I have underestimated you. I will not make the same mistake again." It toppled backward and was still. Idrilia drew her daggers and approached with slow, precise steps. Idrilia's muscles tensed. ICON's eyes still shone with their faint amber luminescence, though it began to flicker and fade as she watched.

"Though you destroy this body, I will remain. I am eternal. I am ICON."

The light disappeared, and ICON fell silent. Idrilia waited a few breathless moments to make sure it would not rise again before rushing to Kalis's side.

"No, no, no, no, no, no, no!"

She dropped to her knees next to his still form. His eyes remained open, staring into the blackness of Komor. She gripped his wrist, searching for a pulse.

"Hang on, Kalis. Don't you die on me. Not after I—" She couldn't put words to the confusing feelings she had for him.

"You stupid, brave fool," she whispered. "You shouldn't have followed me." Her voice rose with every word. "I didn't ask you to save me!"

Her stomach lurched. She looked at her hands resting in her lap. Those hands had failed to save him.

Floods of memories with Kalis assaulted her fortitude. Childhood games. The othwit music box. Now that she had been free to choose who, and if, she would marry, would she have chosen Kalis? She would never find out.

A primal yell erupted from her lips, and she rose, grabbing crystals from her pouch and hurling them. Tears streaked her cheeks, and she let them flow, hot and wet, until the dismal landscape of Komor sucked the life from them, crusting them to her skin. Each of her crystals exploded, shooting giant blades of flames that burnt the sarkumak in a semi-circle around the scene.

"Idrilia?"

She spun to the sound of the voice, brow so furrowed she only saw through slits the figure of Vayriel and Kilahym.

"What in the Lady's name happened here?"

Idrilia let the remaining crystals in her hand tumble to the ground as she took a jerky step toward the Highblood.

"You must heal him! Maybe it's not too late!" Her voice sounded hysterical and pleading to her ears.

"Kalis is injured!" Vayriel charged forward with Orgar.

Idrilia wrung her hands as Vayriel placed her hands on Kalis's chest and forehead, careful to avoid the ragged hole from ICON's deadly touch. The crystal tip of her spear, tossed to the side of his body, glowed brightly. Vayriel breathed deeply as several beats thudded against Idrilia's chest. The Highblood's shoulders slumped, and she shook her head, returning her hands to her lap.

"I am sorry, Idrilia," she said softly, "Kalis has returned to the Mother-of-All's embrace."

Idrilia's shoulders slumped. "This is all my fault."

Kilahym gave her a confused look. "What? How?"

"If only I'd been stronger." She shook her head. "It doesn't matter now."

Kneeling beside him, Idrilia placed her hand on Kalis's and squeezed.

She slid Kalis's ring from his finger, spinning the family heirloom slowly between her fingers. *If Komor wants this, they will have to chase me to the moon and back.* She dropped it into her crystal bag, then began repositioning his body.

"What are you doing?"

"I have to take him back."

"Carry him?"

"Yes, Kilahym. This is my burden."

Orgar howled. Vayriel placed a protective hand on the jeroti's head, her eyes studying Idrilia. "Please, let us help. He was also our friend."

"Thank you, but no. I have to do this. For him." Idrilia brushed her face with her arm, eyes stinging. She stood Kalis up as best as she could, hoisting him beneath his arms. She squatted, then gritted her teeth as she slung his arm over his shoulder and stood, trying to balance him on her back. Once she felt stable, she turned to find Vayriel and Kilahym examining ICON's body. Orgar's hair stood on end, and he growled at the corpse.

"What...*is* that?" the bard asked.

"I don't know. It killed Kalis." A lump formed in Idrilia's throat, preventing her from saying more.

The Highblood placed a comforting hand on her upper arm. "We should go. It may not have been alone."

"No, I—" Idrilia swallowed. "I think it was. But it was connected to Komor. The Trials are no longer safe for us."

CHAPTER 72

Staring up into Kharnek's eyes was like peering into an arakh's maw. An eternal flame burned behind the dark brown irises, its heat threatened by black swirls of self-doubt and internal conflict. These were the eyes of Zinvar's lover. The eyes of a murderer.

Instinctively, the priest shoved against the warrior's chest, but he could never break the hold of those strong arms. Kharnek got the message and spun to release him safely away from the mine pit.

"What in the 'burn is going on with you?"

Zinvar wrapped his arms tightly around himself and said nothing. Nausea roiled his stomach, and his heart raced. This was all too much at once—to find his mother's killer, to find he loved him, and the shadow of the Penumbra loomed over it all. He considered running, but in his heart, he knew he could never outrun or hide from this.

"It's you. It was always you," he murmured. The words unlocked a torrent of feelings, and hot tears spilled onto Zinvar's cheeks. Anger burned through the sadness, and the priest looked up at Kharnek with a varg's feral snarl. "And you *knew*."

"What are you talking about?" Kharnek protested, his gaze flitting from side to side.

"You know exactly what I'm talking about, you spawn of a stunted wyrm. But in case you've forgotten, let me *show* you."

Without any of the gentle finesse of his earlier attempts, Zinvar thrust the memory of his mother's death into Kharnek's consciousness, forcing out all other thoughts until the warrior was forced to relive every moment in excruciating clarity. The priest relished each flicker of pain Kharnek felt, the way his mind squirmed within Zinvar's grasp. This was the secret that ate at the warrior's core, that undermined his attempts at transparency, that fed the defeated, but very much alive, Penumbra in the recesses of his psyche.

Sweat started to roll down Kharnek's pale forehead as he trembled in Zinvar's mental hold. When the priest finally released the warrior, he collapsed to his knees, all his mighty strength devoured by the forced recollection.

"I could make you relive that forever, you know." Zinvar's threat was as cold as permafrost.

"How...how did you find out?"

A bitter laugh escaped the priest. "An accident. The Penumbra remembers all that you did while you were in its grasp."

"Then you know that I was not myself when your mother died."

Rage hotter than the magma that coursed beneath Zel Morakh flowed through Zinvar's veins. His hands balled into fists.

"Is that how you've justified it to yourself for all these epicycles? By blaming it all on something else?"

Kharnek rose to his feet, but his eyes remained fixed on the ground. "That is unfair. You have seen what the Penumbra does without the consent of its host. This is an emotional reaction caused by shock. I have seen it many times in battle."

"More excuses," the priest snarled, "and I'm not talking about what the Penumbra did. It's what you did *after* that proves how much of a coward you really are."

"I did what I had to do to survive!" The pleading note in Kharnek's voice was new, but incapable of dousing the fire in Zinvar. He took a step toward the priest, who immediately pulled back. "You do not understand—"

"I understand all too well. I've been inside your head, you idiot." Zinvar jabbed a finger at the warrior. "You murdered my mother and father and let the Priesthood call them heretics to hide what you did. And then you kept it from me. So much for no more secrets."

"Zinvar—"

"No! Don't say a word. I don't want to hear any more lies."

Silence fell. The moon overhead began its slow arc down to the horizon and beckoned to Morakh's Shadow. When Kharnek finally looked up to meet Zinvar's gaze, the priest felt the unspoken apology emanating from his lover. It almost broke his resolve.

"Sorry isn't good enough," he said softly, "not this time."

Kharnek's shoulders drooped. "This is why I did not tell you. Because I knew I would lose you."

So much sadness was conveyed through those words that Zinvar had to resist the urge to enfold the warrior in a comforting embrace. His anger, fueled by the pain of betrayal, burned like the stars overhead. The dichotomy of emotions made his head swim. Love and hate fought for dominance in his heart, waging their war with memories of tender kisses and promises unfulfilled.

Kharnek moved to within arm's reach and spread his hands in supplication, dropping to his knees before the priest. Zinvar took a step back.

"I cannot change what I have done. I cannot erase the pain of your loss or the hurt I have inflicted by hiding the truth from you. And I cannot possibly ask you to forgive me." Kharnek paused, the search for words evident from his expression.

"And I will not. Not ever."

The Guardsman flinched, visibly stung by the assertion. Nevertheless, he forged on, "I cannot promise I will never hurt you again either. But I cannot let you go. I love you, nekhi."

A shudder ran through Zinvar. "Nekhi" meant destined. It was a Komorese word for a person who caused irrevocable change to another's life—and without their influence, the changed one would not have grown to become better. It was possible to encounter multiple nekhi throughout one's lifetime, and their appearance might only be momentary. But Zinvar knew Kharnek used the word in its romantic sense: two beings, entangled forever by fate, and without each other, destined to suffer.

"That is what you are to me. That is why I would sooner throw myself upon my own blade than try to forget how I feel."

Zinvar's focus sharpened. "To forget how you feel," he whispered. An idea blossomed in the recesses of his mind. It grew into a poisonous flower, the wicked edges of its petals gleaming with malice as he examined them. All it would take was one whiff of its heady perfume...

The priest smiled down at the kneeling warrior.

"You should not have told me that."

Confusion etched itself across Kharnek's brow. "Why not?"

Zinvar stepped back, putting more distance between them. "You are right; we are nekhi. But it is you who has changed me. Without you, I would not have the strength to do this." Before Kharnek could respond, Zinvar breathed deeply of the dark flower's fragrance and turned his power on himself. Shadows crept across his vision. Just before the priest lost consciousness, he felt the warmth of tears sliding down his cheeks. He touched his face in wonder before collapsing to the ground.

Zinvar opened his eyes; it was nearly moonset. A headache threatened to split his skull in two. He sat up and groaned, pressing his hands to his temples. The pressure helped alleviate the pain, and he began to take in his surroundings. A clearing, filled with wrecked, ancient machinery, and to his left—

"What in the—who in the 'burn are you?" The priest shot to his feet. A tall, dangerous-looking man crouched only a few feet away from him. Zinvar's head whipped back and forth. "And where am I?"

"You do not know?"

The man's deep voice made Zinvar's skin tingle. He was attractive, and likely a warrior, if the sword dangling from his waist and his muscular build were any indication.

"No, I...have no idea how I got here."

A strange expression flickered across the warrior's face. It almost looked like he was in pain. "And you do not know who I am?"

Puzzled by the question, Zinvar cocked his head. "I'm sorry, but no." Casting a glance to his left, the priest at last spotted something familiar. He retrieved his staff from the ground with a sense of relief. For some reason, he was having trouble ordering his thoughts—they were a nest of coral writhers coiling in his head. Judging the stranger to be no immediate threat, Zinvar approached him.

"I am Zinvar. I am a Truthseeker participating in the Trials of the Innermost. Do you have any knowledge of my companions?"

For a long moment, the man just stared at the priest. His intense scrutiny unsettled Zinvar, and he could not meet the brown-eyed gaze for long.

"You truly do not know who I am?" the warrior whispered.

"No. Should I?"

"It is no matter. Your friends are nearby. I can take you to them." He rose and walked toward the forest. Zinvar hurried to keep pace with the man's long strides, noting the black leather boots and matching armor—undoubtedly of Komorese design. The priest looked over his shoulder at the pit at the clearing's center and shuddered. Something about it disturbed him to his core, though he did not know why. He shrugged off the sensation and refocused on the warrior.

"Thank you for your help."

No response.

"If you are to be my guide, may I know your name?" Zinvar ventured. The man stopped, and the priest nearly collided with his broad back. Turning his head to regard Zinvar, the warrior quietly answered.

"My name is Kharnek."

The warrior quickly resumed their journey, but as he looked away, Zinvar thought he caught a glint of moisture in Kharnek's eye.

CHAPTER 73

Invisible hands gripped Idrilia's temples and forehead, pushing on the back of her eyes. The weight of her grief manifested in tangible form as her shoulders burned and her legs gave out.

Declining more offers of assistance from Vayriel and Kilahym, she withdrew three trapezoidal crystals with shaking hands. She knocked them together, the crystals emitting a soft humming in response, and placed them on Kalis's body. Like the platforms in Evocus, he slowly rose a foot above the permafrost on an invisible gurney, and with his headscarf lashed to his boot, Idrilia directed him around sarkumak the remaining short distance to the campsite.

The sight of their shared tent sent her muscles into contractions as if she fought to keep them attached to her bones. She collapsed next to her friend's body and let hot tears pour into her hands and his scarf as she positioned her back to the others. She didn't want to see them, nor did she want them to see her. She knew she was a failure. Idrilia kept seeing the moment of his death, searching for the actions she *should* have taken. This feeling of helplessness was too familiar.

As hard as she tried, she could not push back the memories of her grandmother, so raw from being exhumed in the Fellwood. How Idrilia had sat at her bedside, holding her hand in those final days. Idrilia had wished to hear her grandmother's voice, to know that she was proud of her. Just as Idrilia wished she could have told Kalis how much she valued his friendship.

"Not to add despair to our grief," Kilahym broke through Idrilia's mind cloud as he approached the embers of the campfire, "but the Trials are off."

Vayriel's boot nudged the soot-blemished pile, and quill-thin lines of smoke wafted into the air. "I know that Kalis…that his return to the Mother-of-All is difficult for us all, but we must continue. We have much to discuss, but we should not give up now."

"No, no—that's not what I meant. For the first time in—huh—I don't know how long, I meant exactly what I said. No frills. No seasoning. They've canceled the Trials. If the Trials were a tundrat, Sondrine has bopped it on the head with a staff. Finished. Book closed. Last note of the ballad. Final stanza in our epic poem."

Vayriel frowned. "How do you know this?"

"Blast! My apologies. In the, uh, commotion and aftermath I did not have a chance to tell you. Kalis spoke through the box, er, cube with his homeland."

Idrilia wiped her eyes with her orange headscarf and pivoted just enough to see the Heathström pair. Kilahym hurriedly explained the exchange between Kalis and Keeper Veloran.

Vayriel studied the fire as she coaxed it to life. "The Magister was a strong leader. Her people must mourn her loss."

"I will never forget seeing you and Orgar riding in the Magister's gondola like long-time friends."

Vayriel took a deep breath. "They intend for us to return to our homes?"

"Aye. And in our actions, 'the Trials of the Innermost live on.' I wonder if there was more meaning behind that statement. Maybe we are supposed to continue the Trials in spite of it all! But…if Komor isn't expecting us, mayhaps they would try to slay us on site. That would be dreadful!"

"Or send another one of those…*things* after us," Idrilia growled, joining the conversation.

The bard leaned forward. "What do you think it was?"

"I don't know. But I have questions for the two Komorese who are conveniently missing." Idrilia clenched her teeth against an inner conflict that rose; Kalis had wanted her to trust them, Zinvar at least. "If this thing was to be believed, it said it controlled Komor's religious leaders. What kind of basja is that?"

"You don't really believe that Kharnek and Zinny had anything to do with Kalis's…Kalis's…" The bard glanced at Vayriel, as if asking for assistance in forming the sentence, but the Highblood had laid down, her eyes directed to the star-filled sky.

"His murder," Idrilia bit. Her anger felt like a favorite blanket, and she clutched it closer. "This thing came for him. It didn't seem the least bit interested that I was there. If another shows up and we are still here, Kalis has died for nothing. We should go. Besides, Vayriel and I think the Penumbra is back."

Idrilia flicked her eyes to the Highblood, but she remained silent. A familiar semi-circle of haze hung in the air over where she lay.

"You're doing it again," Kilahym whispered out of the corner of his mouth.

Vayriel blinked quickly and pushed up on her elbows; at the same time, the pale pink glow of protection dissolved.

"What are you thinking of, music of my heart?" Kilahym asked softly.

"The spirit-world. And whether Kalis found his way or became a sky-spirit."

"Like your parents?" Kilahym asked.

She nodded.

"Kalis is—was—strong of mind and of physical strength. If anyone could navigate the life force like a ship captain, it was he."

Idrilia bit back what she wanted to say. Kalis had been her friend longer than any of them. She deserved to grieve too, but there were more pressing matters.

"Vayriel," Idrilia prompted. "I was just starting to tell Kilahym what your vision said about the Penumbra. Would you fill him in?"

The Highblood nodded and explained what the Mother-of-All had told her, as well as what she and Idrilia had discussed already.

"But Idrilia was not sure that this vision could be trusted," she concluded.

Kilahym tapped his chin thoughtfully. "This 'wood is extraordinarily odd. Zinvar seemed incredibly angry when he left—I have never seen him that way. And you, Idrilia, acted…er, well, different as well. These spores seem rather potent. I'm solidifying my conjecture to Kalis—I think Vayriel and myself have a resistance of sorts as sporestalks of Heathström, though much smaller, may be of the same genus. She has but a slight headache, and I've only a case of the itchy nostrils."

Idrilia frowned, but the bard continued before she could comment.

"Though we did see things as you did," he amended. "But the point. I forgot to get to it, I see. Ahem, that is to say I believe what Vayriel saw was not a hallucination. And based on my limited exposure, this doesn't feel like it has the flare of the Penumbra about it. It's always 'too much light' and 'let me be whole.' But what do we do now? And why didn't Kharnek's brothers-in-arms come back? They tell us the Trials are over and just leave us in the middle of a forest. Beechmarsh isn't the liveliest of towns, but at least the Moon's Quiver offers suggestions for entertainment nearby. Komorese apparently let you muddle about in the dark."

"Maybe they thought ICON would destroy us all," Idrilia suggested.

"That's an unpleasant thought. If they planned to kill us, wouldn't they have done it and not waited for the creepy robe fellow?"

As much as she hated it, the bard had a point.

"Did you say ICON?" Vayriel asked, grasping her left arm. "The Mother-of-All called my armband by that name."

"Are you certain?" Idrilia asked.

"She said, if the Sleeper wakens, that my ICON would help me."

Idrilia scoffed, then seeing Vayriel's hurt expression, she pinched the bridge of her nose. "I don't have enough information, but that just seems unlikely."

"Dilly-Drilly has a point. One ICON looks human but was sent to kill Kalis, whereas your ICON is, at least on the surface, ornamental. A classic case of 'things aren't always what they seem,' I would wager."

"I do not know how it is supposed to help me," Vayriel said to Idrilia defensively, "but she said that it would. The Mother-of-All's designs are never fully revealed, otherwise our search for the true path would not be a journey of discovery and growth."

"Ah, here you all are. It is good to see you, my friends." A gentle voice interrupted any further conjectures.

It made Idrilia sick, how pleasant Zinvar could be.

"Where have you been, Zin-zinny?" Kilahym asked, springing to his feet as the priest and warrior moved from the forest and into the camp. A firmness etched Kharnek's face as if he were made of stone.

"This soldier located me some distance from the camp. I do not know how I ended up there, but I am grateful for the random encounter, as he offered to lead me back to you."

Raising her eyebrows, Idrilia exchanged a glance with Vayriel.

"A good jest, my friend. As if you could convince us that you and this handsome muscle were not in love. Ha! But the jest is rather ill-timed, I'm sorry to inform you."

Zinvar's eyes widened. "Love?"

"Granted, you don't bat your eyes at one another, nevertheless I *assumed*— I mean, you two do—that is to say you're.." Kilahym awkwardly moved his hands as if shaping a ball, then with a sigh, he interlocked his fingers. "You at least care for one another!"

"I've only just met Kharnek within the forest."

"Vayriel, am I losing my mind?"

Kharnek sighed. "I will spare you any additional wasted time with this ineffective exchange. Zinvar's memory is altered. He appears to remember nothing of me, but he remembers the rest of you."

Idrilia shot up, drawing her daggers. "Then he won't care if I slit your throat now and be done with it."

"Whoa, whoa, whoa," Kilahym protested, but the Highblood had already placed herself between the two other warriors of the group. Idrilia paused her approach.

"Explain about Zinvar." Vayriel jabbed her chin at the warrior, angling her walking spear toward him.

"I found him. He no longer knows me. This is all I can tell you."

"All that you know, or all that you are willing to share?" Idrilia challenged, pushing up against Vayriel's outstretched arm.

Kharnek's eyes narrowed. "I had thought we had moved past your petty threats, Sondrinel. I will not make the mistake again of showing you any compassion."

"As usual, attempting to distract from yourself with bravado. We know about ICON. I destroyed it. When will they send another for the rest of us?"

The warrior tilted his head. "I think you have been in the forest too long."

Idrilia growled, pushing past Vayriel.

"Wait, wait!" Kilahym pleaded. "Zinvar, this thing, this ICON said it was from the Priesthood. I mean, it claimed that it controlled the Priesthood. That Morakh is an illusion shown to its followers. It came for Kalis. Do you know if any of this is true?"

Zinvar looked at each face of the Seekers, his own expression plastered with confusion. "I have no idea what you are talking about. What has happened? Where is Kalis?"

"See, my blue-haired friend? They know nothing."

"How convenient that Zinvar has just lost some of his memories, too," she sneered but did not advance.

The need to strike out boiled inside her like the lava in the nearby rifts, and Idrilia fought to keep it within her trenches so that it did not burn her friends. As if sensing her inner battle, both Orgar and Vayriel moved toward her; the Highblood placed a comforting hand on her shoulder and motioned for her to sit next to the jeroti. The gesture sent a breath of cool air through her veins, and Idrilia knew she needed to take a step back and think. Her battle-readiness leaving her as she crouched next to Orgar, Idrilia once again felt the nausea seep back into the pit of her stomach.

She missed the connecting dialogue but heard Kilahym finish telling the Komorese of Kalis and that the Trials were canceled.

"Then I will rejoin the Brotherhood." Kharnek bent to retrieve his bag.

"What about the rest of us?" Kilahym asked.

"It is of no interest to me." The Komorese warrior stepped between Kilahym and Vayriel.

"Where's he going?" Kilahym whispered. The three Seekers watched as Kharnek trudged to the southern edge of their camp. There he paused.

"Leave Komor quickly, and find somewhere safe," he delivered ominously. Then he turned and made direct eye contact with each of them. "And please...take Zinvar. He is better off with all of you." Before any of them could reply, Kharnek disappeared into the darkness between the thick sarkumak trunks.

"Well. What a pile of ratufa poop this day had turned out to be. Kalis dead, Zinvar's memory bungled, and Kharnek abandons us."

"Kilahym, please," Vayriel chastised, touching Zinvar's shoulder. "How do you feel, Zinvar?"

"Other than confused, a little like I just woke up from a deep dream, but that is all. And I expect it will pass."

"You really don't remember Kharnek? You weren't just *pretending*, so that you could wound him in a quarrel?" Kilahym diverted.

"It is only now that I'm led to believe that I *should* know him."

"Pyreflowers ignite! What else don't you remember?"

"I—I don't know. You will have to let me know if I…misremember anything else."

"Come." Vayriel motioned for the group to rejoin Idrilia. She sat staring at Kalis's body, and the others followed her gaze. Orgar inched forward and laid his muzzle on Kalis's chest. She knew she should follow Kharnek and see where he was slinking off to like a wounded varg, but her body wouldn't move.

"Should we bury him?" Zinvar asked after the ensuing silence.

"No." Idrilia's voice sounded raw to herself. "We don't bury our dead."

Flames flickered in Vayriel's lavender eyes as Idrilia tossed another of Kalis's crystals vehemently onto the pyre. Idrilia felt her cheeks flush from the heat emanating from the pile of sarkumak stalks beneath Kalis's remains; with the emotional balance of her counterpart now gone, heat grew again within her. Her eyes burned, but she did not know if that was the result of the smoke or the tears which had so easily flowed during the Highblood's eulogy.

"I…I have neither the eloquence of Kilahym nor you. Would you speak?" Idrilia had asked Vayriel concerning the funeral—something Zinvar had proposed. Instead of another memory ceremony, Idrilia acceded; though she would rather not agree with the priest, she also wanted a vocal memorial so she wasn't alone in her own head. The Komorese, Zinvar explained, laid their dead in tombs. But as the Sondrinel clarified to the others, the heat and desert landscape of Axiom affected burials poorly, and thus they practiced elimination of the physical body.

"The sorrow which we feel," Vayriel had told the seekers, sharing Highblood wisdom, *"is for our own loss. We are not sorry that a son or daughter has returned to the Mother-of-All. We are saddened by the absence that journey has created in our own hearts. We return his body to you, Mother-of-All, in the tradition of Axiom, and ask you to bring his spirit to your side. Kalis would make a great guide for the spirit-world."*

Then lyrical notes soared from Kilahym's ocarina like mournful hoots of othwits.

Idrilia hugged herself tightly. Orange and blue flames hid what was left of Kalis, but she stared as if she could will him to rise out of the flames, to walk to her and embrace her again as friend.

"What do we do now?" Kilahym's murmur broke the silence that followed the dirge of his ocarina.

"What do you want to do, Kilahym?" Vayriel asked in return, leaning her head on Orgar. "When the Trials ended, I was to bring knowledge back to my people. But something is not right in this world. I have seen that although Heathström started the Trials of the Innermost for this purpose, the realms are no closer to a united Etherea. And I would see that wound healed. But first I…I want to seek out the Penumbra pieces as the Mother-of-All instructed."

"If only she had told you where they were or how to go about accomplishing this task. Regardless, what I don't want to do is give up. This whole business of ending the Trials feels like just that."

"I wish that I had the experience that Mo'mo does. She would know what to do."

While a part of her wanted to comfort Vayriel, tell her that she was undervaluing her own experiences, Idrilia's mind remained bent to one purpose; it wore a gulley in her mind like years of sand blown over stone. She glared as Kilahym addressed the focus of her thoughts.

"Well, we have Zinny! He defeated some of the Penumbra before. Though, I suppose that was only temporary. But ne'er you worry, my friend." Kilahym patted Zinvar's shoulder. "You are but still learning your Occulum-ness."

Zinvar shoulders slumped. "And I'm afraid that I may have to relearn much of it. I don't have any memory of defeating a penumbra."

"Komor must pay for what they have done today," Idrilia declared, her voice low.

The priest locked eyes with her, and he took a step forward. "I don't know what I have to do to prove to you that I had no knowledge of this ICON. Kalis was my friend, too, Idrilia. I feel his death as acutely as if he were my brother."

She scoffed and quickly returned her attention to the fire. "I will follow Kharnek and learn the truth. You all can do as you please."

Kilahym waved his arm wide. "You can't be serious! If they want you, us, dead, then going into the heart of their realm alone is a really, really bad idea. Think what you will of Kharnek, but I think something of him is surviving the Penumbra. His warning was, in his own style, for our safety. We can live to fight another day—together."

"This is exactly what I am talking about." Vayriel's voice was firm. "We are all descended from the same calamity. We are all sons and daughters of the Mother-of-All. Despite our differences, there is a greater challenge ahead of us. Let us be the first participants to truly succeed in uniting. I will face the prophecy on my own if I must, but I am stronger with you, Idrilia. With all of my friends. Will you lay down your anger and help me?"

Fresh tears welled up in the Sondrinel's eyes. Like running off to chase the vision of her grandmother, Idrilia knew that she was once again being selfish. Stomping around the lava fields of Komor would not bring him back. And Vayriel needed her.

Idrilia took a deep breath. "I'll need to tell the Vaktares about Kalis at some point. But you have my blades at your side for now, Vayriel. Where do we begin?"

Kilahym clapped his hands. "This is so exciting. It's like the quests of the old songs. Zinny, are you coming too?"

"It seems I may no longer be welcomed in my homeland. The warriors have not returned for me, and this Kharnek left me. Without the Trials, it will be difficult to influence the cooperation of nations, but if there is a greater goal, then I will help how I can. If only I could remember—" Zinvar paused as Orgar growled. Head lowered, long fangs bared, the jeroti held his tails stiff behind him while his chest rumbled threateningly. The sound of crunches on the permafrost registered faintly in Idrilia's hearing.

"Something approaches," Vayriel whispered, sliding her left hand down her spear and tilting the crystal point before her.

Idrilia drew her daggers as a figure burst through a clump of young sarkumak as tall as the figure's long brown jacket. A violet feather stuck out of his hat.

"Ansgar?" Kilahym shouted incredulously.

"Varg!" Ansgar waved his hands as if shooing Kilahym.

"How rude. I've certainly been called worse but—"

"No, behind me!"

The strange man leaped forward and dashed behind the four Truthseekers. Kilahym peered over his shoulder. "What are you doing? Are you hiding?"

Vayriel urged miniature sporestalks to grow, rapidly expanding into a sarkumak barrier where the man had come from. But nothing followed.

"We are safe," Vayriel announced.

"For now," Idrilia muttered, her thoughts turning toward ICON.

"I do not think there is a varg. Orgar and I do not detect one." The sarkumak shrank back into the ground with her pronouncement.

Ansgar hmphed quizzically.

"You're hallucinating," Kilahym offered while waggling his eyebrows. "It happened to all of us. You see, the spores—"

Ansgar sauntered forward. "Ah, now I understand. So, we meet again, bright eyes." He winked at Vayriel. "Loved seeing that magic thing you do in action."

Ansgar tilted his hat by the brim as Kilahym coughed. The bard stepped next to Vayriel with his arms crossed. Idrilia shook her head. Of all of the places for Kilahym to meet an old friend.

Kilahym cleared his throat. "Ansgar, how are you even here?"

"Ah, yes. After seeing you on the stage— I did come to your little ceremony—I, well it's a long story. Do you two have a *thing?*" he asked, pointing between Vayriel and the bard. "Because I'm definitely getting a vibe here."

With hands on hips, Kilahym tapped his foot impatiently. "Tell the long story, if you please."

"Always easy to read. Very well then." Ansgar tipped his hat back into place. "I never was as good as Kilahym in telling ballads. My skill is more in making love…" Though he looked around, Idrilia wasn't sure who he was addressing before his eyes locked on Kilahym, and Ansgar continued "…shine through verse. The great Spectres decided they were no longer amused by my presence and politely suggested that I find a new home."

Kilahym rolled his eyes. "Ugh. I knew it. They finally kicked you out. What did you do this time?"

"Let's just say I ran a discount Runner's office."

"Discount? Their prices aren't that high to begin with. How did you make a profit?"

Ansgar grinned. "Well…there weren't any Runners. I made up the replies."

"Grey Lady, preserve you," Kilahym grasped his forehead.

"It certainly tasked the creative ink in my quill. Do you know how much drivel people send to one another?"

"I don't want to know." The bard shook his head. "But why did they send you all the way to Komor? That's a bit extreme to banish you from Heathström altogether."

"They only tossed me out of the capitol. I was going to sneak back in, disguised as a trägen pelt—"

Kilahym hid his eyes beneath his hand. "I'm not even going to ask."

"—but the city went on lock-down. No one in or out. Rumor in the trading caravans, stuck outside the gate, was that a group of rebels were attempting to overthrow the Spectres. What with their oppression of the male population, I can't say they didn't have it coming. We heard all manner of commotion, even saw a few explosions. Anyway, there's a saying that I've always lived by: *When danger is a comin', you best get to runnin'.* And that's what I did."

"But why here?" Zinvar inquired.

"I heard there was treasure," Ansgar shrugged. "There are treasures of many varieties if one but looks." His wandering gaze landed on Zinvar. "The ink lines on your face really accentuate your cheekbones in a most flattering manner, but I'm sure you've been told that before. How rude of me, I didn't catch your name?"

"Ansgar, stay on topic," Kilahym rescued a bemused Zinvar. "What treasures specifically?"

"Some old, abandoned mine, which might hold bodies of hundreds of Komorese. I figured either I'd get rich or find material for more stories. A troubadour's gotta make a living one way or another." He winked again, this time at Zinvar.

"How do you know that there is a mine here?" Zinvar asked.

Ansgar shrugged. "I know people."

Sheathing her daggers at last, Idrilia decided that Ansgar was perhaps worse than Kilahym in his ability to annoy her but was not a threat. "What *people?* The events at Waverling just happened, and there's no way you walked here in that space of time."

"Oh, just people in taverns. You know how they talk."

"No. I don't." Idrilia crossed her arms and inclined her chin. "It's a little convenient that you show up precisely where we are. Don't you think?"

Ansgar laughed, but it sounded forced. "What are you Truthseekers doing here, anyway? Is this one of the Trials?"

"That is also a long story," Vayriel intoned.

Kilahym waved his arms wildly. "Stop trying to change the topic. Answer Idrilia, please. I urge you to be truthful or, or, or Orgar will know and bite your leg off."

In response, the jeroti peeled back his lips to reveal his fangs with a soft growl.

"Oh all right, but they won't like it. It's the knowledge-for-purchase people I told you about, Hymn."

Idrilia bent forward. "A *spy* network?"

"Harmless, really. I honestly don't know more than that. Except they told me not to go back to the city because, you know, *chaos.* Oh all right! By the Lady's unmentionables, stop giving me that look, Hymn. I used a magical transport that's placed outside of Waverling for use by the network."

Idrilia's brows shot up. "What kind of transport?"

"I don't know, I'm a man, remember? I stepped on it and instantly was outside of the Fellwood."

That sounded like what Kalis had experienced after his fall with the trägen. Kalis had said he'd instantly been transported from the odd cave to the Cliffs of Odium. But why would something like that lead to Komor? Idrilia filed the thought away, not wanting to give Ansgar any more information to sell to his contacts.

Kilahym proceeded to explain the cancellation of the Trials and Kalis's death to his friend. "But why did you come *here*, right where we are?"

Ansgar huffed, his shoulders sagging. "I was told to intercept you to get the latest since no updates are coming from the Magisterium on your progress. Here I am." He laughed nervously with a shrug. "Here," he pulled out a familiar metal object, "I was going to sell this to Komor too, but I feel a bit ashamed. I want you to have it. Two for your collection."

Kilahym took the offered rounded rectangle as Idrilia stepped to get a closer look.

"That's mine. Well, I found it. When Kalis and I encountered that weird varg pack."

"Ah, the vomiting varg."

Idrilia ignored the bard. "I wondered where that shopkeeper was going to sell it."

And why did he know you would want it? She eyed Ansgar but kept her thoughts to herself.

"You can have it, Dilly-Drilly. And we can play duets together."

Rolling her eyes, she placed the object in the pouch with Kalis's ring. "While this has been amusing…Vayriel, we all agreed to help you. Where should we go?"

"Maybe Vayriel's grandfather can tell me what happened to my memory. Would your people be open to us visiting?" Zinvar asked. "I feel that I could be much more helpful to our situation if I could recover at least my knowledge of defeating—"

Idrilia's muscles tensed, and she shot him a warning glare.

"—destroying artifacts," he amended.

"We could take shelter in Skyveil. My coil is open to visitors and would be safe. Mo'mo and Mo'fa can help guide us in how to help Zinvar. And perhaps the Daughter's Eyes have had more visions that would point us in the next steps we should take."

"It's the start of a plan, at least," Idrilia conceded.

"Then it's settled! Together, we can do great things. You can come with us, if you'd like," Kilahym said, turning to Ansgar.

"I must decline," the troubadour said as he removed his hat and placed it over his heart once more. "Fortune and glory await, little Hymn. Though, maybe not in there." He thumbed over his shoulder, indicating deeper into the Fellwood.

The remaining Truthseekers packed their possessions, and as Kilahym turned to bid his Bard Academy friend farewell, Idrilia caught a glimpse of his purple feather fading into the forest. Kilahym mumbled an insult, and the group headed east.

Idrilia glanced at the smoldering pyre once more and saw a figure of fog fade into nothing. She blinked, uncertain to trust what she saw as a lump formed in her throat. A Sondrinel friend waving goodbye.

PRONUNCIATION

Of historical interest is the seemingly random method by which the locations in Etherea were named. However, taking into consideration that three separate cultures (each with at least one subculture) exist in Etherea, it is easy to recognize the origin of the influence of each label. As has been written by High Keepers before me, those names that match our shared language, rather than showing clear influence from Komor, Sondrine, or Heathström, appear to be concentrated in the north. As for pronunciation, each realm has a slight variation from the others, often creating confusion (and in some cases arguments) over which dialect is accurate.

-     *Taken from Praeteritum, Vol. 3*

People ◯ | Places * | Creatures (

Adjira	add-JEER-uh	◯
Aluan	ah-loo-AWN	◯
Alusarean	al-loo-SAR-re-in	(
Arakh	air-ACK	(
Camelid	Kam-UH-lid	(
Concilius	con-SIL-ee-us (*sil* rhymes with *bill*)	*
Eduma	eh-DOO-muh	*
Elsuota	EL-sue-OH-tuh	◯
Eranth	err-RAHNTH	◯
Evocus	ee-VOH-cuss	*
Falsten	FALL-stinn	◯
Felune	FEY-loon	◯
Gamin	GAM-inn (*gam* rhymes with *lamb*)	*
Heathström	HEETH-strum	*
Hedek	heh-DECK	◯
Hoestra	HER-struh	*

Idrilia	eye-DRILL-ee-uh	O
Ifen	EYE-fin	O
Ilya	ILL-ya	O
Jehana	ya-HAN-uh	O
jeroti	ya-ROE-tee	(
Jerrod	ger-ROAD	O
Kadaan	kuh-DAWN	O
Kalis	KAL-iss (*kal* rhymes with *pal*)	O
Kharnek	KAR-neck	O
Kerru	KERE-roo (*kere* rhymes with *here*)	O
Kilahym	KILL-uh-HIME (*hime* rhymes with *time*)	O
Komor	koh-MORE	*
Laphrim	LAUGH-rim	O
Leiria	Lay-EAR-ee-uh	O
Leske	LESS-kuh	*
Lyna	LIE-nuh	O
Mahir	mah-HERE	O
Mahiratha	mah-here-ATH-ah	O
Motesh	mow-TEHSH	O
Morakh	MORE-ack	O
Myal	MY-all	O
Natak	nuh-TACK	O
Nera	NEAR-uh	O
Noval	NO-vall (*vall* rhymes with *ball*)	O
Nuala	new-ALL-uh	O

Orimere	OR-eh-meer	*
Pawilo	puh-WEE-low	(
Pectully	PICK-tool-ee	(
Pedium	PEH-dee-um	*
Priorium	pry-OR-ee-um	*
Proja	PRO-sia (rhymes with *ambrosia*)	*
Ratufa	Ruh-TOO-fuh	(
Saita	SIGH-ee-tuh	◯
Solendrake	SOH-lin-drake	(
Sondrine	SONN-drin (*drin* rhymes with *chin*)	*
Trägen	TRAY-geyn	(
Torav	tore-AVE (*ave* rhymes with *have*)	(
Tundrat	tuhn-drat	(
Vandling	VAND-ling	(
Vari	VAR-ree	◯
Varg	Vahrg	(
Vayriel	VAE-ree-ell	◯
Vaktare	vac-TAR-ay	◯
Volundar	VOLE-un-dar (*dar* rhymes with *star*)	◯
Zel Gorragkh	Zehl GORE-agk (*Zehl* rhymes with *bell*)	*
Zel Morakh	Zehl MORE-ack	*
Zinvar	ZINN-varr	◯

MARKING TIME

While all realms mark the progress of time with the same duration quantification by means of the Komor-crafted timepieces, our words for those durations are not always the same. It is not uncommon to hear at least Sondrine and Heathström idioms used in daily exchanges at the Ettrascan markets. (For a more in-depth review of differences in dialect, see the sections on Linguistics beginning with Pronunciation on page 74.)

- *Taken from Praeteritum, Vol. 3*

Komor

Night / Sleeping hours - *Morakh's Shadow*

Daylight / Waking hours - *Morakh's Light*

Full 25-hour day - *cycle*

Tomorrow - *next cycle*

Today - *this cycle*

Morning - *moonrise*

Midday / noon - *pinnacle moon*

Midnight - *fell moon*

Week - *cyclad*

Month - *four cyclads*

Year - *epicycle*

Century - *hundred epicycles*

Heathström

Night / Sleeping hours - *moonrest*

Daylight / Waking hours - *Lady's walk*

Full 25-hour day - *day*

Tomorrow - *tomorrow*

Today - *today*

Morning - *moonrise*

Midday / noon - *midmoon*

Midnight - *moondark*

Week - *week*

Month - *lunation*

Year - *synody*

Century - *hundred synodies*

Highbloods

Night / Sleeping hours - *Daughter's rest*

Daylight / Waking hours - *Daughter's hours*

Full 25-hour day - *day*
Tomorrow - *tomorrow*
Today - *today*
Morning - *Daughter's rise*
Midday / noon - *mid-hours*
Midnight - *mid-rest*
Week - *week*
Month - *step*
Year - *Daughter's Journey / Journey of the Daughter*
Century - *Hundred Journeys of the Daughter*

Sondrine
Night / Sleeping hours - *darkening*
Daylight / Waking hours - *luminance*
Full 24-hour day - *day*
Tomorrow - *tomorrow*
Today - *today*
Morning - *dawn*
Midday / noon - *midluminance*
Midnight - *middark*
Week - *week*
Month - *month*
Year - *sidereal*
Century - *centenary revolution*

Note: Due to the use of Komor timepieces, each area marks the passage of hours, minutes, and seconds the same.

ACKNOWLEDGEMENTS

Kristina W Kelly

So many people weave in and out of my own writing journey it is hard to capture them all. You all are so appreciated. To the best writing partner I could ask for, I write words in the sky for you, Jonathan. Your own writing style taught me to be a better writer and your enthusiasm and support made it possible to create this novel. You are always there to inspire me, motivate me, or calm my inner Idrilia. There's no better feeling than waiting for you to read and comment on our next chapters. To my husband, Scott, who listened to my woes and elations of various plots, characters, and rewrites—thank you for believing in me and watching the children during writing time. To our publisher, thank you for stepping into the world of Etherea and finding it worthy of sharing with the real world. To my parents, who gave me bookshelves of stories to explore and a typewriter in my room, thank you for encouraging my love of stories. To my friends who continued to show excitement and interest in TOTI, your steady interest helped amplify the creative symphony. Brian H., Danielle B., Robin Y., JWU. To my college professor of Native American Storytelling, your encouragement to become a storyteller is always with me. To our editor, Samantha, you made our bag of magic crystals shine. Thank you for polishing every word so that TOTI glows.

Jonathan Fuller

It is a truth universally acknowledged that in every writer's origin story is a pivotal teacher. Or, in my case, teachers. Thank you Pauline, Kurtz, Maggie, Daniels, Nanci, Slagle, and Becky Fields for stoking the flames of creativity and teaching me the art of critical reading. I'm forever grateful to you all. To Matt and Philip, thank you for your unwavering support and friendship. A very special thanks to Elizabeth and the team at Hansen House for giving this story a home and making this author's dream of being published come true. Adan, Jose, Kaley, Kandlyn, Tog and Thomas, and everyone I call chosen family, thank you for encouraging and inspiring me throughout this grand adventure. Life wouldn't be the same without all of you. Mom and Dad, you instilled a love of learning and reading in me from an early age that culminated in the writing of this book. My writing journey truly began there, and you were the catalyst for it. Finally, I must offer my thanks to my incredible friend and writing partner. Kristina, you've been a stalwart companion for many years and through a number of significant life changes. Our friendship has been a beacon amid stormy seas and continues to grow and evolve in wonderful ways. It's been a joy and privilege to embark on our coauthoring endeavor and there aren't words enough to express the pride I feel in what we've created together. None of it would have been possible without your skill as a writer, your tech genius, your ability to pick up new skills and concepts incredibly fast, and your keen emotional awareness. Thank you for always being there as my friend, confidant, collaborator, and source of inspiration. Wherever life takes us next, I know one thing: I can't wait to see how this turns out.

ABOUT THE AUTHORS

Kristina W Kelly

Since childhood, writing stories on her mother's typewriter or trying to catalog her own books like a library, Kristina has been in love with storytelling. Her undergraduate pursuits focused on Psychology, Music, and Computer Science. With trumpet as her main instrument and a connection to nature, Kristina often works music and vivid landscapes into her writings. She loves going on new adventures in the great wide somewhere (sometimes just by picking up a new book). Kristina writes science fiction, fantasy (often combining the two), short stories, novels, novellas, and poetry. Some of her short stories received honorable mentions from the Writers of the Future contest, including Silver Honorable mention. Her poetry appears in several places including publications from the Poetry Society of Indiana. She dabbles in other instruments, plays videogames, and tends to her flower garden and two children where she resides in Indiana with her husband.

Website: www.kristinaseyes.com

Twitter & Instagram @kristinawkelly

Jonathan Fuller

Jonathan grew up amid the sprawling corn and soybean fields of rural Indiana. Raised in areligious household, he was drawn to reading and writing as a medium to explore there conciliation of traditional values with sexuality. After completing a degree in English, he migrated to the West Coast before moving to his current home in Austin, Texas. He spent several years in the automotive industry before transitioning into his present role in higher education. When not writing, he's likely playing flag football or spending time with his chosen family.

Twitter: @diary_of_j

Milton Keynes UK
Ingram Content Group UK Ltd.
UKHW011300221123
433051UK00008B/393